"Tell me, Captain [...] wn yourself to be resou[...] six distinct escapes that [...] ver camp you were in, it [...]

"Six? I think that's probably right, sir."

"So you can break out ... How do you think you would be at breaking in?"

Kostyshakov unfolded his arms in a painful attempt to sit more upright. "Sir, I ..."

"I have a proposition for you, young man. How do you feel about your royal family," Hoffmann asked, "or, rather, your *former* royal family?"

"While I breathe," Daniil replied, and they do, they remain my royal family."

"The Bolsheviks cannot possibly let the tsar and his family live," Hoffman said bluntly. "At some point in time, the decision will be made—it is part of the inescapable logic of revolution—that they must die before they can become so much as figureheads for the enemies of the revolution."

"I don't believe it," Kostyshakov replied. "Even the Bolsheviks—"

"Don't delude yourself, Captain Kostyshakov; the tsar and his family are as good as dead."

Daniil grew very silent then, staying that way for what seemed a long time. When he finally spoke, it was to say, "You didn't come here to tell me all this just to torture me, General Hoffmann. What is it that you want?"

"Put simply, it is this: I want you to select a few dozen trustworthy officers and noncoms, then that ... committee to select several hundred others, of all ranks. And then the lot of you are going to go and save your royal family."

THE ROMANOV RESCUE

Turning Point, 1918

TOM KRATMAN
JUSTIN WATSON
KACEY EZELL

BAEN

THE ROMANOV RESCUE

Copyright © 2021 by Tom Kratman, Kacey Ezell, Justin Watson, and Monalisa Foster

A Baen Books Original

Baen Publishing Enterprises
P.O. Box 1403
Riverdale, NY 10471
www.baen.com

ISBN: 978-1-9821-9226-6

Cover art Dominic Harman
Photos courtesy of Tom Kratman
Maps by Randy Asplund

First printing, November 2021
First mass market printing, November 2022

Distributed by Simon & Schuster
1230 Avenue of the Americas
New York, NY 10020

Library of Congress Control Number: 2021037713

Printed in the United States of America

10 9 8 7 6 5 4 3 2 1

For: OTMAA

CONTENTS

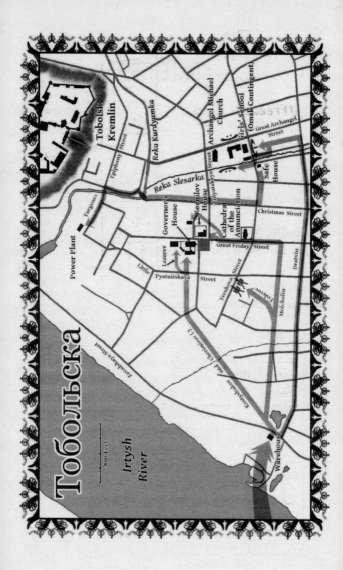

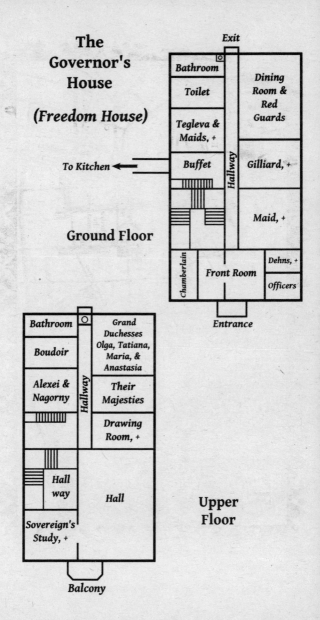

The
Governor's
House

(Freedom House)

Ground Floor

Exit

| Bathroom |
| Toilet |
| Tegleva & Maids, + |
| Buffet |

To Kitchen ←——

Dining Room & Red Guards

Hallway

Gilliard, +

Maid, +

Chamberlain

Front Room

Dehns, +

Officers

Entrance

Upper Floor

| Bathroom |
| Boudoir |
| Alexei & Nagorny |

Hallway

Grand Duchesses Olga, Tatiana, Maria, & Anastasia

Their Majesties

Drawing Room, +

Hall way

Hall

Sovereign's Study, +

Balcony

THE ROMANOV RESCUE

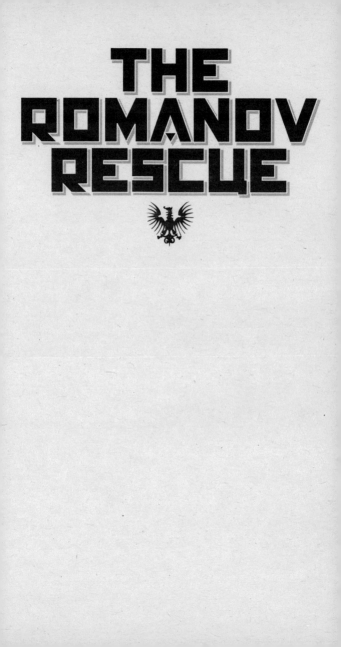

PART I

Chapter One

Fort IX, Ingolstadt

Fort IX, Ingolstadt, Bavaria

Guards Captain Daniil Edvardovich Kostyshakov, late of His Imperial Majesty's Kexholm Guards Regiment, shivered uncontrollably in a slight depression on Fort IX's forward glacis. It was a fine thing that the depression was slight, because Kostyshakov, himself, was fairly short.

And this is one of those rare occasions when I wish I were shorter still.

The walls of the cells were wet and slimy, with mold growing in the corners. As with many places where large numbers of men are held against their will, the place had an aura of misery and despair about it, greater than the mold and the slime, alone, could account for.

Fort IX was the prison camp for the hardest of cases, the worst of the repeat escapees. As such, since determination and courage know no nationality, it was at the moment, or had been in recent memory, stuffed with Brits and French, Russians and Italians, the odd Belgian from time to time, and whosoever else had found themselves the unwilling guests of the Kaiser and had tried repeatedly to remedy that situation.

Sitting south of the city of Ingolstadt, and just about five hundred meters southwest of the small town of Oberstimm, Fort IX, a polygonal fort, was an old outwork of the defenses of the town, which were also, in practice, the defenses of the Bavarian capital of Munich. It was built of a mix of concrete and granite, with no small amount of wood and iron where called for, the whole overladen with about ten meters of damp earth and surrounded by a massive, water-filled moat to the south, east, and west, and a much narrower one to the north.

It wasn't the sort of place anyone would want to spend the holidays. That said, if it was hell for a Briton or Frenchman or Russian, in 1917, it had been *home* to generations of German soldiers in the decades before that.

The cells for the prisoners were tunnel-shaped, with curved roofs, and measuring about twenty-six feet by fifteen. The tunnel shape, an almost perfect half circle, made it impossible for anyone of normal height to stand upright except toward the center where the roof was highest. The normal complement of a room was six officers, and normally it would contain six beds, a table, plus a few chairs. Sometimes numbers within a cell fluctuated. In these cases, the guards were careful to remove the wooden beds, or any chairs excess to need. Failure to do so was a guarantee of the excess furniture being turned into firewood to warm the otherwise damp and miserable cells.

Because Fort IX had not been designed as a prison, but as a defense, the cells were connected, each to the two to either side of it, by narrow passageways. These the guards had long since boarded up. The board barriers had, too, long since been compromised by the prisoners, with enough boards being made detachable to allow a man to squeeze through, and the job being done precisely enough to allow the boards to be replaced again, quickly, with nothing seeming amiss.

The German guard known to the prisoners as "Blue Boy" quickly counted heads in Room Forty-three. He knew all the prisoners' faces by sight, in the open air, but in the dim light available at night in the prison cell, the best he could do was by size and shape.

"Blue Boy" called off the names of this cell, "Le Long?" "Here." "La Croix?" "Here." "De Robierre?" "Here." "Moretti?" "Here." "De Gaulle?" "Here." "Desseaux?" "Here."

Then "Blue Boy" reported to his chief, whom the prisoners referred to as "Abel," "All present, *Herr Feldwebel.*"

The cell was then locked and the two Germans moved on to the next.

The prisoners had had much time to practice for this. It never took less than six seconds for the Germans to get to the next cell, and never longer than eight.

Thus, in order of event:

Second one: Le Long ripped the coats hanging in front of the wooden block to the passageway and moved them to one of the beds.

Seconds two, three, and four, De Robiere, with an expertise born of much rehearsal, pulled off the cut-out section of the wooden barrier. Moretti, who trended rather short, used the first four seconds to position himself while pulling on a dark green coat—it was originally in what was called "horizon blue," but had been dyed—the next two seconds to launch himself through the gap revealed by the removal of the boards, and the last to get in position with the occupants of the other room, Room Forty-four. There were five men in the room, and six beds. Moretti made the sixth. He just stood to as the door opened.

Again "Blue Boy" made his roll call. "Lustianseff?"

"Here," answered Lustianseff.

"Kotcheskoff?"

"Here," answered Kotcheskoff.

"Kostyshakov?"

"Here," answered Moretti . . .

"All present, *Herr Feldwebel.*"

Before crawling out into the glacis, Daniil had waited in a basket full of dirty clothes, sitting in one corner of the fort's eastern half, waiting to be taken to laundry. It was fortunate he was short, there, too, as, in the first place, the basket *was* already pretty full, and in the second, six or more hours in a not very large basket can give terrible cramps to the legs.

Indeed, it had been both a blessing and a horrible agony to finally emerge from the basket, with agonizing shooting pains overwhelming his legs as feeling returned to them.

From the basket, once Daniil was able to move his legs without wanting to scream, he'd moved to and then crawled up a ramp and then, after waiting for a sentry to pass, into the battlements atop the fort. Daniil had begun his mental count, once the guard passed, *one . . . two . . . three . . . four. . . .* Then he crossed and waited in the lee of the battlements for the guard to return and move off again. *Five . . . six . . . forty-two . . . seventy-five . . . ninety . . .*

At least, though, it had been tolerably warm there in the basket, thought Kostyshakov, with another spasm of shivering. *I wish the moon would hurry up and go down, though I'd settle for a large bank of thick clouds.*

Daniil didn't have a huge amount in the way of escape equipment and supplies. He mentally inventoried his small stash. *I've about three days' worth of food, most of it anywhere from a little past to well past its prime. Along with the food there is a quantity of pepper. Since home has apparently collapsed, well, thank God for the generosity and largesse of the British and French prisoners, who have little enough of their own at the moment. But however little they've had, they've been generous, even so.* He felt for the compass one of the British prisoners had managed to make him. *Yes, it's a crude compass, but crude is better than nothing.*

All the prisoners shared any information they had—thin though it was—about the surrounding area; he also had a crude map derived from that limited information, plus a more general one of the way to Switzerland.

His coat had been modified by one of the French officers—he'd had a background in fashion—for rapid transformation into a German officer's heavy wool coat. To his boots were glued pieces of cloth, to deaden the sound of walking. He likewise had a hat that might not pass close and careful scrutiny, as well as good, lined gloves of his own. He'd taken a double sewn blanket, light-colored, washed out gray on one side, green on the other. The blanket was now slung across his chest and over his shoulder. With two sides, it was for two purposes.

A knife, fork, metal cup, and wire cutters fashioned by hand from a nicked pair of pliers completed his assembly, though he had one other item on his person. This was a billfold, which contained, besides some money, a folded postcard of two tall and elegantly dressed, to say nothing of quite beautiful, young women. He'd have given up his food before giving up the postcard; food just fed the body; the image of one of the young women fed his soul.

Though Daniil might have mourned his scant assets, he had this much going for him, *Who travels light, travels fast.*

The on-duty sentry passed, none too quietly, walking the rampart surmounting the fort's earthwork. At the same time clouds, thick and pregnant with snow, closed in over the fort, barring the moon, and dropping everything into something approaching pitch blackness.

If I don't get moving soon, I won't have to be caught; the Germans will simply come out in the morning and pry me off the dirt, then use me as an ice supplement to preserve food in their mess.

He had the sentry's timing down already. Once the man had passed Daniil slithered down the glacis, finally settling into the slight depression he'd found by earlier study, while planning his break.

And now we wait for the guard to make his rounds again.

There was wire at the base of the glacis. With the next passing of the guard, Daniil low crawled to it, snakelike. Then he took the blanket and, putting the dark side out, covered himself with it. The sharpened pliers came out next. He selected a place as near the upright pole as possible, gripped just past that with his glove, put the snippers around the wire and squeezed. It made a noise but, *Much quieter than I feared. We didn't have to cut much wire in the east, but the British and French told me how it was done.*

It took several more cuts, two of them much delayed by the return of the sentry, before Daniil had cleared a path through. It must be understood, too, that the barbed wire of the Great War was not much like cattle fencing. It was stouter, the barbs were longer, there were a lot more of them, and hence they were much closer together. More than once Daniil had to bite back a curse as the prongs pierced his skin.

Mentally crossing himself, he pulled the blanket in closer to his body—*No time to roll it properly*—then finished passing through the wire. The moat was right there, on the other side.

Daniil hesitated at the moat, afraid of what could happen when he crossed it. *If they'd let some children skate or play on the ice I'd have more confidence in this . . . ah, but stop sniveling, you chose this way because the Germans don't look as carefully here, probably figuring no one is dumb enough to try.*

Slowly and carefully, he reversed the blanket. Now the light gray—interestingly enough, *ice* gray—side was up. Covering himself with this, he eased himself out onto the ice. *Since I can't be sure how strong it is, I must spread my weight out. Helps that I'm not very big, too. And, fortunately, I've lost a bit of weight here. The Germans are usually better with prisoners than that, nutrition-wise, too. Things must be hard if they're feeding us as poorly as they are. Indeed, I think they've lost more weight than I have.*

The ice was smooth as glass, as he'd expected. Now his mess knife and fork came to the fore. Taking one piece in each hand, he used them to dig ever so slightly into the ice, creating a grip, the sound mostly muffled by the blanket. He was a little surprised that he picked up a degree of speed; the more he travelled the faster he went.

Braking is going to be . . . uh, oh.

Unable to slow down on the nearly frictionless ice, Daniil crossed his arms overhead and waited for the worst.

The blanket helped again, here, deadening the sound of his arms smashing against the opposite bank, itself frozen as hard as any ice.

Didn't do much to soften the pain, but I'm not complaining.

And, finally, here I am, at the far side of the moat, and pretty much out of the guard's area of responsibility.

Speaking of which . . . Still keeping the gray side up, and putting his knife and fork away, he rolled over onto his back and looked. *Yes, there the old Hun is, marching to and fro and with no clue I'm gone.*

Daniil moved as the clouds covered the moon, in little fits and starts. Finally, with the moon down at six minutes after five, he felt he could move with a little less care and a lot more speed. He headed to the southwest, skirting the towns of Baar-Ebenhausen, Reichertshofen, and Langenbruech. He lost some time by doffing trousers, stockings, and boots, trying to disguise his scent in the Paar River. He also left a goodly sprinkling of his little store of pepper to upset the inevitable dogs. By the time he'd done all that, he thought he could see the first faint glimmer of morning, off in the east. Spying some haystacks, he ran to one of them. Then, after excavating an area for himself, he fed himself feet first into the hole he'd created, pulling the rest of the hay carefully in after himself.

And now we wait for night, for the search to reach this area and hopefully pass me by. Assuming, of course . . .

There are some problems that can certainly be foreseen but still not be provided against. One of these, in Daniil's case, was morning roll call, conducted in the bailey of Fort IX. There'd be no dim light, here and now, to mask Moretti's impersonation, no shadows to blend and mask faces. There'd be no hasty passageway to allow a prisoner to move from one place to another. Instead, there was:

"De Gaulle?"

"Here," answered the tall, ungainly, big-nosed French officer.

"De Robiere?"

"Here," said De Robiere.

"Desseaux?"

"Here," agreed Desseaux, adding, "Unfortunately."

"Kotcheskoff?"

"Here," answered Kotcheskoff.

"Kostyshakov?"

"Here," answered Moretti, still wearing his assumed coat.

"La Croix?"

"Here."

"Le Long?"

"Here."

"Lustianseff?"

"Here," answered Lustianseff.

"Moretti?"

"Here," answered Moretti.

"Blue Boy" looked up and glanced quickly at the spot from which he thought he'd heard two answers.

"Kostyshakov?" he repeated.

"Here," answered Moretti, slouching low so as not be seen and with an attempt at a more convincing Russian accent.

"Moretti?" called "Blue Boy."

"Here," answered Moretti.

"*Herr Feldwebel!*"

German soldiers with bayonetted rifles, most of the

soldiers older and some sporting limps and scars, walked around the hayfield stuffing their bayonets into the loosely piled, beehive shaped, haystacks.

"Come out! Come out, Captain Kostyshakov!" shouted the leader of the Germans, the small and rather intelligent noncom whom the prisoners called "Abel."

"We know you're somewhere in this area! Why don't you save us all some trouble and just give yourself up? You've made a fine attempt; there no shame in failure when the odds are stacked so badly against you."

Meanwhile, Kostyshakov thought, *You're bluffing, Hun. If you knew I was here you'd just drag me out.*

But the Germans, in their methodical way, kept prodding the haystacks. Perhaps inevitably, one bayonet thrust took Daniil in the backside, digging into flesh about half an inch deep. He managed to stifle his own scream. This wasn't quite enough.

The searcher, keyed perhaps by a degree of resistance not normally to be expected in a haystack, noticed an area of blood on the end of his bayonet. Drawing the rifle back and examining the point of that bayonet, he was quite sure it hadn't been there before. "*Herr Feldwebel!*"

Shit.

Northern Gate, Citadel of Brest-Litovsk, Belarus

He had the face of a butcher, that man, an impression only strengthened by the six-foot, four-inch, and very heavyset, frame above which that face rested. Mind, if he had the face of a butcher it was also the face of a highly astute, well-cultured, and remarkably intelligent butcher.

He was fat, to some considerable extent, but the fat didn't extend to his brain.

Butcher-faced, he may have been. Fat? Yes, that too. but Major General Max Hoffmann was not a butcher of men or, at least, not of his own men. Aged forty-eight now, and having served his country, in peace and in war, for thirty years, Hoffmann stood at the pinnacle of his profession. A mere major general? At the pinnacle of the warrior's profession?

Even so; Hoffmann was the chief of staff—a position very unlike that of the chief of staff of any other army of that day or any other—of Ober Ost, the German high command in the east. Moreover, not only did the German Army follow the orders and plans he crafted, so did both the Austro-Hungarian and the Bulgarian armies. This was because, under the system prevailing in the German Army at the time, the chief of staff was the brains of an army. A man with character could command—and Hoffmann was most fortunate in that his nominal chief, Prince Leopold of Bavaria, *could* command—but thinking deep, hard, and above all, *well* was a different matter entirely.

An evening walk was normal enough, when time permitted. Tonight, though, upset and annoyed with the Bolsheviks, Hoffmann felt the urge for a longer walk.

"I think, Brinkmann," said Hoffmann to the major—also of the general staff—accompanying him on his walk, "that I could not have taken another minute of that Bolshevik peasant eating with his fingers and using his fork as a toothpick . . . or, come to think of it, another second of that murderous Bitsenko bitch regaling Prince Leopold about her murder of Sakharov."

The other man, Brinkmann, pulled cold air through his nostrils, contenting himself with, "Indeed, and I don't mind you inviting me, sir; Admiral Altfater, with whom I was sitting in the anteroom, is a fine gentlemen, but everything he says about the disintegration of the Russian Imperial Army is depressing. It could have been us. If we're not both careful and lucky, it could *still* be us."

"I know, Friedrich; I've spoken to Altfater myself. It's depressing because, as you say, there but for the grace of God, go we. It's a damned thin line we hold, and that across a long border, between our people and the Reds."

Stepping through the brick gate of the town's citadel—which was also the site of the peace negotiations with the Bolsheviks now ruling Russia—Hoffmann led the major into the town or, rather, what remained of it after the Russian Army, in its retreat, burnt it to prevent its use by the German Army. Beside him, Brinkmann's cane echoed louder than his footsteps.

A more sensitive man might have bemoaned the destruction of the town and the hardship inflicted on its people. Hoffmann, however astute, was not sensitive.

Even so, the town was starting to come back to life a bit, too, as some of its former citizens returned to recreate their old homes and businesses. There hadn't been a huge improvement yet, even so.

"We're being foolish, Brinkmann," said Max, "and in more ways than one. We shouldn't be making peace with the Bolsheviks; we should be marching on Moscow to restore some kind of civilized government."

"It wasn't so long ago," Brinkmann reminded him, "that you were all in favor of letting the Bolsheviks rule

Russia . . . and ruin it, that Germany needed a break from the Russian threat. What's changed?"

Hoffmann didn't answer immediately but continued walking, in silence. Finally, turning right to take up Masharova Prospect, he answered, "I didn't know everything then that I know now. I didn't know about the terrorism, the murders, the oppression and persecution of faith. I'm not ashamed; who could have predicted such a thing from a people as faithful to God as the Russians? Primitive in many ways they may be, but faithful they have always been, too."

They reached a point where, normally, Hoffmann would have turned around. This night, however, he could not. Snowflakes began to fall as the pair continued plodding to the east.

"You served there, didn't you?" asked Brinkmann. "In Russia? Before the war?"

"Yes, for a while, six months, to learn the language, and then, too, I was for a number of years, five, actually, in the Russian Department of the General Staff."

"Ah, that would explain your faculty with the language then."

"That, yes, but . . . did you hear something?" Hoffman rotated his head in the direction from which the sound— an odd and strange sound—had come.

"No," the major shook his head; "I was listening to you."

"There it is again." The cry was faint, but it sounded liked, *"Nie, nie, nie; Adpusci mianie!"*

"Now *that*," said Brinkmann, "I heard. A woman, I think. Or a girl. She seems upset."

Keeping his head and eyes fixed on the direction from which the woman's—or girl's—cry had come, without another word, Hoffmann undid the retaining strap of the holster on his belt. Without any particular notion of what his chief had in mind, Brinkmann followed suit. It wasn't necessary for Hoffmann to say, "Follow me." He led off and Brinkmann followed as surely as a rainbow follows the rainstorm.

The sounds—the *cries*—ended. Even so, Hoffmann followed the heading he had set for himself. The pair crossed a space distinguished only by charred timbers before coming to a cobblestone road.

"There will be four of them," Hoffmann whispered. "Well, at least four."

"Four of what?" asked Brinkmann. To that Hoffmann didn't give an answer. There was no need to because shortly they came to a waist-high stone wall, against which also lay four rifles, outlined in the quarter moon's worth of light. They both could see someone holding down a woman's arms with one hand, and another covering her mouth, another two forcing her legs apart, and a fourth holding something in front of his crotch, dropping to his knees between the spreading legs.

I suppose it's only logical, thought Brinkmann; *there has to be four for efficiency's sake. This is something I'd just as soon not have known.*

Hoffmann, for all his undoubted military skills, was considered to be one of the worst horsemen and—literally and absolutely—the worst fencer in the entire German Army. There was nothing wrong, however, with his hand-eye coordination when a pistol was involved. *Besides, at this range I can hardly miss.*

The pistol barked.

So much for Herr Schwanz-im-Hand.

The second shot released the woman's—or girl's—hands and mouth, allowing her to release an instant ear-splitting shriek. If the shooting upset her at all it was tolerably hard to tell.

Brinkmann, having transferred his cane to his left hand, took aim. His shot then did for the right leg holder, as Hoffmann finished off the left.

Hoffmann then, and much to the horror of both the major and the woman, walked forward and proceeded to put another bullet into the brain of each of the assailants. After that he bent to offer the woman a hand up. The act of lifting also allowed her dress to fall back into place.

Only then did he realize that the "woman" *was* actually quite a young girl, perhaps fourteen years old or, if she'd been well fed recently, maybe even thirteen.

"*Dziakuj*," said the girl, leaning against the mountain in the form of a man. "*Dziakuj*," she repeated, throwing her arms around him. Hoffmann let her stand like that for a few minutes. *The poor thing is shaking so badly. Don't think I blame her.*

"I recognize at least one of these," Brinkmann said, using his cane to ease himself down to one knee. He twisted by the chin the bloody, shattered, brain-leaking head of one of the corpses. "I've seen him standing guard on one of the Bolshevik diplomat's huts."

Hoffmann holstered his pistol, then put hands on both the girl's shoulders and eased her gently away. He had his first real view of her face. *Pretty thing,* he thought. *Or she'll grow up pretty, anyway. If she grows up.*

"Do you speak Russian?" he asked the girl. "German?"

"*Leetle* Russian," she answered. "*Leetle*. Speak Belarus better."

"Who were these?"

"*Dunno*. Me walk home from Papa's store. Grab me. Next, you see what they do. Try do."

"Did they speak Russian, at least?"

"Not to me. Not understand they speak, anyway."

"Okay, girl. What is your name?"

"Maryja," she answered. "Maryja Pieliski, sir."

"Are you all right, Maryja?" Hoffmann asked. "Will you be fine going home now?"

"Yes. Think so, sir. You save me before they . . ."

She doesn't need to describe this, or think about it, Hoffmann thought. "Okay. Go home then and tell nobody what happened here. Bad for all of us if you do."

"I go. I say nothing." Before she turned though, she threw her arms, at least as far as they'd go, once more around Hoffmann's more than ample waist and repeated, "Thank you. Thank you! *Thank you!*"

As she scampered off, footsteps clattering on cobblestones, Brinkmann searched through the pockets of the corpse he'd been inspecting. "Here's the . . . well . . . paybook, I suppose, for this one."

Hoffmann took the proffered booklet and thumbed it open. "It's written *in* Russian," he said, "but it *says* he's a Latvian."

"Makes sense; they're the most reliable troops the Reds have."

"Animals," Hoffmann pronounced. "Just animals. And we've turned them into our neighbors for the foreseeable future."

"It reminds me of when we took Riga, last September," Hoffmann continued. He led off once again, rescued girl and Bolshevik corpses for the nonce forgotten. "There, the Russian Army had so badly disintegrated into a rabble that none of the people felt safe until we drove them out."

"Well . . . Russians, after all," Brinkmann said.

Hoffmann stopped for a moment, somewhat incredulous. "What, you think Russians are invariably rabble? It is not so, Brinkmann; I assure you it is not so. Whether with Suvarov in Italy, or at Eylau under Bennigsen, at Poltava facing the Swedes or Borodino versus Napoleon, the Russian soldier has always been well disciplined. I saw him fighting the Japanese around Port Arthur. The Russian soldier is docile, quiet, and unassuming; he is also innately brave. It's not him, not the Russian soldier; it's the Bolsheviks who have ruined him, at least for the nonce."

"The Cossacks?" Brinkmann countered. In many circles, the Germans not least, the Cossacks had a reputation for pillage and rapine, along with the other usual battlefield atrocities.

"Different role, different culture," Hoffmann explained.

Brinkmann accepted this without demur, though he retained his private doubts. "They'll be trying to infect us, too, with their propaganda."

"They already are," Hoffmann said. "I refused them their demand to be allowed to send it to our soldiers. They've officially accepted my refusal for now . . . but in the long run? We have to do something about them."

"What can we do?" asked Brinkmann. "I note that our

own newspapers, and the Austrians', too, are in high dudgeon over your refusal to let the Reds spread their propaganda."

"Indeed," said Hoffmann. "One would almost wonder whose side the papers are on, except we've known for years they're on the enemy's side. On the plus side, the British, French, and American papers are largely on ours. Seems a universal problem.

"As to what we can do ... maybe nothing," Hoffmann admitted. "But I am recalled to see Ludendorff in Berlin in about two weeks' time. I'm going to try to make them see reason."

He said the next sentence without conviction. "Someone *has* to see reason ..."

Later that evening, in his quarters, under a dim lamp, Max Hoffmann put his own reason to work, sketching out a possibility with a few branches and arrows, with the overall grand object of getting rid of the Bolsheviks.

But how? But how? We can't do the work for any number of reasons, and even if we did, we'd get no thanks from it and do no good, even if we succeeded. But maybe ...

At one point Hoffmann shouted out to his aide, "Find me the report from Jambol, Bulgaria ... no, I don't remember the date, only that it was marked 'Naval' and was a little over a month ago."

Berlin, Germany

Hoffmann entered Ludendorff's office fully intending to brief him on a particular idea he had. Faced with the quartermaster general's cold anger over a certain diplomatic faux pas, however, that ambition quickly died.

"How could you let such a note pass, Hoffmann?" Ludendorff demanded angrily. "You should have stopped it before the Russians were misled and then stomped off in a huff. You *speak* Russian, for God's sake; you should have made sure there were no such misunderstandings. Moreover, why didn't you inform me of its contents?"

With someone of Ludendorff's sheer force of character, coupled to the sudden and unexpected absence of the warmth and cordiality that had existed between them even since before the war, Hoffmann was almost flabbergasted. He kept his cool enough to explain that he had assumed, and had every right and reason to assume, that Ludendorff had been fully briefed by the Foreign Office.

"Moreover, the problem was not one of translation but of sheer understanding. The Russians had simply blithely assumed that no forcible annexations meant no self-determination, even though self-determination was one of *their* principles, when they entered into the negotiations. How is one to prevent *that*? Didn't you all, after all, discuss this at the meeting on the eighteenth?"

"We did not," Ludendorff admitted. "As to whether you were justified in assuming so . . . well . . . I supposed so. My apologies then. I am under a good deal of strain of late."

"I understand," Hoffmann said.

"So lay out for me, then, both the status of the negotiations and of the front. You may consider this a dress rehearsal, because His Majesty wishes you to come to the Bellevue Palace for lunch, where he is certain to want the very same things."

Bellevue Palace, Berlin

Hoffmann had stepped out into the cold air. He was aware that the deeper problem in Russia, and his possible solution, had not been discussed with Ludendorff.

And how could they have been, given how angry he was? Add to that his dominance and inquisitiveness over the dress rehearsal. And then there was the lack of time, given where I have to be and when.

About ready to turn around and return to brief Ludendorff, Hoffmann realized there was a car waiting for him outside the *Generalstabs Gebaeude*. A one-armed captain of the guards—there were a great many one-armed captains floating around Germany by this point in the war—guided him to it, while the driver held the door for him. Berlin traffic was not notably heavy at any but the worst of times. Now, at this stage of the war, civilian ownership of motor vehicles had declined by over eighty percent. Oh, there were still some private cars, but most had been pressed into military service. This car, a Daimler Mercedes, took Hoffmann swiftly—albeit coldly, given the open top—south through empty streets to the equally bare Zeltenallee, thence westward to deposit him at the Palace.

Kaiser Wilhelm already knew that watching Hoffmann eat his way through an entire lunch was not something for the faint of heart. He consoled himself at the carnage with the thought, *Perhaps he eats enough for four, but he thinks enough for four thousand. He's a bargain.*

Meanwhile, between chomps, Hoffmann thought upon his kaiser. *I must be careful here. What was it Bismarck said of him, before he was dismissed? Oh, yes, he wants every day to be his birthday. He is unsure of himself and arrogant at the same time. Intelligent, but without much in the way of self-discipline to make use of that intelligence. He craves the new and detests monotony. Well . . . perhaps I'll have something new for him, since I couldn't mention it to Ludendorff.*

Hoffmann, still seated at the table and without recourse to notes or maps, gave the kaiser the same information he had given Ludendorff, right up until Wilhelm asked his opinion on what was coming to be called "The Polish Question." His concern was where the new border was to be drawn in the east, and the presumptive expense of the new German-sponsored state of Poland, which was to be ripped from the hands of the Russians.

Hoffmann demurred, or tried to, knowing that Ludendorff and Hindenburg, both, had fanciful notions of new divisions and corps of Poles, marching to shore up the western front at the stamp of a teutonic foot. He also knew, *Ludendorff has forbidden us telling the kaiser anything without his approval. That was half of what this morning's dress rehearsal was about.*

The kaiser, in any case, was having none of it. "When your supreme war chief demands your opinions on any subject, it is your duty to communicate them to him quite irrespective of their coinciding with the opinions of the General Headquarters or not."

I see no end of trouble for me from this. Nonetheless, he is right; it is my duty.

"There's another matter I'd like to discuss, too, but to answer your question, I think we'd be fools, Majesty, to take any more of Poland and of Poles than we absolutely had to. We've had substantial numbers of them since your multi-great grand uncle partitioned Poland, one hundred and forty-five years ago. They've never really become reconciled to it.

"Yes, fine, we could use two strips, one to shield the Silesian coalfields and another on the Malwa Heights; one hundred thousand Poles, no more. Let the rest *be* Poles, allies if at all possible, but happy to be themselves and not *ersatz*, pseudo, and deeply unhappy Germans."

Hoffmann didn't know if the kaiser spoke truth when he said, "I've been thinking along the same lines, frankly; we don't need them; we can't use them; so why should we want them?"

"And what was that other matter?" the kaiser asked.

"It has to do with your cousins, in Russia."

"What about them?" the kaiser asked. Wilhelm retained a good deal of annoyance toward both his cousin, Nicky, and Nicky's wife's beautiful sister, Ella, who had flat refused Wilhelm's proposal of marriage decades before.

"You know they're going to be killed, of course, Your Majesty. That's the logic of revolution. All of them: your cousin, his wife, their beautiful daughters, and their only son."

"I've tried not to think about it," the kaiser admitted.

"We can't avoid thinking about it any longer, Your Majesty," Hoffmann insisted.

"What can we do, then?"

Hoffmann smiled, his eyes wandering to the Christmas tree standing in one corner. "Oh, I have a couple of ideas on the subject . . ."

Interlude

Tatiana: Our Romanov Christmas, 1917

It's hard to believe that it's already Christmas. It has been both too short and too long, almost like we've gotten lost in time and are still trying to figure out where we are.

The road ahead of us is unclear, like riding through a snowstorm in the sledge on a moonless night. All we can see is a small circle of light from the lamp. It surrounds us, a pool of flickering safety. That's what they told us back in July. That moving us to Tobolsk was for our own safety—the provisional government protecting us from the Bolsheviks.

But I fear that it is just an illusion, very much like that flickering light and the way it's being cut through every second of every day by hard, cold, snow. It looks beautiful—benign even—but it can kill you. The snow can be harsh, cutting. Deadly.

Ever since we set foot in this house on the twenty-sixth of August, I have been filled with dread. No matter how much I push it down, it resurfaces.

It's not just the changes. They put the retainers and servants across the street in the house of a rich merchant, a Mr. Kornilov. I wonder if they asked. I worry that they just showed up at the door one day and said, "We're the masters of this house now, move out." Or was Mr. Kornilov honored to host our entourage, to have us as his neighbors? If so, I'd like to thank him. I'd like to reassure him that he'll be compensated. That we didn't just take. But I cannot. So I add this embarrassment to the ever-growing list of things I cannot control, that I have no say in, that I bury alive.

It's not my place, after all. Papa is no longer tsar which means I'm not a grand-duchess. I'm just a girl. It's something I've wished for, and now that I have it, I realize that it's not the milk and honey I expected it to be. Before, I had status but no responsibility, no power. Now, I feel as if responsibility—for things I've not done, did not know of, had no say in—hangs above me like the blade of a guillotine. I still don't have power and now I don't even have status. Except maybe that of a pawn, and everyone knows what happens to those.

Our knights remain with us: Monsieur Pierre Gilliard, our French tutor; General Tatichtchev and Prince Dolgorukov, my father's aides; Drs. Botkin and Derevenko; Countess Hendrikova. And of course, our guard. They are soldiers from the former First and Fourth rifle regiments and have been with us for years. They were with us at Tsarskoe Selo, under the command of a Colonel Kobylinsky, who has been very nice to us.

I spoke to the men of our guard. They were, as they had always been, men with whom we shared a common past. We talked about their families, their villages. They spoke of the battles they had seen during the Great War. They still called my brother "The Heir." I knew that he held a special place in their hearts because they would find ways to entertain and distract him.

They even welcomed us in the guard house and invited us to play draughts with them.

But this is not Tsarskoe Selo. We can no longer walk out in the open. Instead we must be satisfied with a very small kitchen garden. It is not just the lack of space that is so stifling. It is being under observation. Soldiers from the Second Rifle Regiment look down upon us from their barracks.

We've been on display our whole lives, but that was different. That was when we left the much-cherished isolation of our home. If we had any illusions about being captives, they are now all gone, at least for me. I feel fate tightening its grip on us in so many ways.

It started, not with the size of the house or the yard. Those were just physical manifestations of something far more sinister.

It started in September with Commissar Pankratov and his deputy, a narrow, stubborn, and cruel man named Nikolsky. Commissar Pankratov is a man of gentle character. He is well-informed and has made a good impression on my father. He has been kind to us children.

Mr. Nikolsky however, scares me. He delights in tormenting us, in inventing fresh annoyances that he trots out anew each day. He ordered Colonel Kobylinsky to take our photographs and had numbered identity cards made for us. We must carry them, as if we were inmates in some vast prison, as if our guard haven't been with us for years.

It's a bit of revenge, you see. And although I didn't see

it at first, it became more obvious as time passed. On November 15th the provisional government was overthrown. It was one of many events that disappointed my father.

He had abdicated to save Russia. But instead, he'd made way for Lenin and his acolytes to destroy the army and corrupt the country. I knew that that decision would haunt him forever not just because he failed to save Russia, but because it had also harmed his people and his country.

As the weeks passed, what little news we've gotten has worsened. We told ourselves that we didn't have the entire picture, so things weren't as bad as they appeared. We knew that we didn't have enough information to predict the consequences of what was going on in the world. That puddle of light that surrounded and defined our existence wobbled and shrank and cast false shadows as the storm intensified, as the flakes of snow turned to barbs of ice, as the temperature dropped and the sun hid like it was never going to rise over us again.

And behind that intensifying storm was our kind Commissar Pankratov. One wouldn't have expected kindness to come from someone who was an acolyte of the Bolsheviks. But he had good intentions: intentions that blinded him to what he was doing.

In my heart I know he did not do it to harm us. I can't imagine that the thought would have occurred to him. He was an enlightened man. He thought that introducing the soldiers to liberal doctrines would make them good citizens and patriots in a post-imperial Russia. He planted those seeds of thought in their minds with all the right intentions. But a thought-seed's success depends on the type of soil in which it is planted. And when it was planted in the men of the Second Regiment, the one unit of the guard that were not "our guard" but our guards, that seed bore ill fruit.

Commissar Pankratov's liberal ideas and good intentions infected these men—like so many others throughout Russia—with Bolshevism. They formed a Soldiers' Committee whose decisions overrode those of Colonel Kobylinsky. It was at that moment that they ceased to be a military unit and became petty tyrants. We were the unfortunate recipients of their tyrannies. It must've been intoxicating to them, to have such power for the first time in their lives. It was then that I learned—through the pain they brought to my mother—that the tyranny of the many is no different than the tyranny of the few. It is the same tyranny that these men supposedly detested.

I couldn't believe that Colonel Kobylinsky allowed it. It wasn't until later that I understood why. These kinds of committees, known as soviets, were cropping up all over the country. Peasant soviets. Factory soviets. Village soviets.

It was in this environment that we, nevertheless, worked on making the most of our lives. We had always been, very much, about our family. We continued going to services, rising very early to walk surrounded by soldiers to the dimly lit church across the street. Alone, we prayed.

We continued our lessons, sometimes in the large hall, sometimes in my room or Alexei's. We girls took turns taking care of Mama, who was often unwell. We organized games and amusements. The cold forced us together in the drawing room, taking turns on the sofa, for we weren't given enough wood to heat the entire house. The dogs begged for our laps and we were grateful for their warmth and companionship.

When Mama was well she did needlework or played with us. This family peace, this being out of the public eye, something that we had once craved for so earnestly, became bittersweet and soured as our isolation continued.

We spent long months knitting woolen waistcoats for our entourage. I'll never forget Monsieur Gilliard with his piercing eyes and stiff wing collars, his distinctive twirled moustache and goatee, as I handed him his waistcoat on Christmas Eve. I'll never forget how my hands trembled with foreboding. I took that foreboding and hid it, not wishing to spoil the evening.

Chapter Two

L59

Jambol, Bulgaria

They always seem so big at first, thought Mueller. *I remember, too, when I was terrified at the though of taking off in one of these.*

The idle thought made *Funktelegraphie-Gast*—basically, "Signaler" or "Signalman"—Wilhelm Mueller smile as he stood with the rest of the crew and watched their zeppelin, the L59, emerge from her hangar in all her gorgeous, lumbering majesty. Like the rest of the men around him, Wilhelm wasn't new to the harrowing, thrilling world of zeppelin aviation, so he knew very well that while L59 might seem incredibly vast as one stood on the ground and watched her fill the sky overhead, quarters inside the military airship gondola would be cramped at best. He and his fellow crewmen were close, but they were about to get a lot closer over the next few days.

Wilhelm's best friend on the crew, machinist Gustav Proll, jostled Wilhelm from behind, recalling him from his woolgathering.

"She's out," Gustav said, nodding his head toward the zeppelin. Wilhelm glanced up again to see that the dirigible had, indeed, slowed to a stop outside her hangar, and the tow team was busy tying down her mooring ropes. "Time to go."

Wilhelm nodded and clapped Gustav on the shoulder as the two of them started across the wet grass of the launch field. Storms yesterday and the day before had delayed this moment, but the clear cerulean expanse above them meant the wait was finally over. The mission would launch today. Here and there, members of the Bulgarian ground crew called wishes for good fortune in accented German. Wilhelm and the other men accepted these as their due, sometimes nodding in thanks as they climbed up and into the various crew compartments.

The familiar miasma of engine exhaust reached out and wrapped around Wilhelm as he pulled himself up into the forward control compartment. He felt Gustav tap him on the calf in farewell as the machinist remained below and walked aft toward the hellish external compartments where the L59's monstrous engines smoked and screamed and propelled them through the sky.

Not for the first time, Wilhelm thanked his lucky stars that he'd been trained as a wireless operator, and therefore got to spend most of his time in the forward control compartment. They could still smell the engine fumes, but it was nothing like the noisy, vibrating, hellish environment of the engine compartments.

On the other hand, being up front was no picnic either. Between unexpected turbulence, freezing temperatures, and unpredictable weather at altitude, no one on the crew of a zeppelin had an easy time of it. It was a mark of a man's toughness—both physical and mental—to be selected for airborne service. They were an elite group, hand-picked for this important mission, and justifiably proud.

In Wilhelm's mind, and he knew likewise in the minds of his crewmates, flying was worth every hardship. To soar high above land and sea, to look down upon cities and mountains and oceans alike was an experience like no other, and Wilhelm was willing to face a thousand hardships for the opportunity to do it again and again. Nothing compared to flight. Nothing ever would.

Kapitaenleutnant Ludwig Bockholt, L59's skipper, stood with legs splayed wide as his eyes scanned the horizon out the forward window. The deck of the gondola swayed and bumped, but unless they encountered heavy turbulence, it was nothing compared to the motion of a surface vessel. Still, old habits died hard. Plus, he was the captain of an Imperial Navy airship. It was fitting that he stand like one.

On his left, the ship's wireless set let out an audible squeal and a crackle loud enough that the young petty officer sitting at the station flinched and ripped the headphones from his ears. Ludwig raised an eyebrow and looked in his direction.

"Everything all right, Mueller?"

"Aye, sir," Mueller said, having the grace to look a bit

shamefaced as he replaced his headphones. "Just a static burst. It's possible we've a storm ahead."

"Why do you say that?" Ludwig asked, his tone mild. He noticed that his second in command and his chief enlisted man both turned to observe the conversation between their captain and the wireless operator.

"Well, sir, it was that static burst," Mueller said, squaring his shoulders as he, too, noticed the additional scrutiny. "Procedure is that we bring in the wireless antenna during storms, lest we attract a lightning strike due to the ionization along the metal antenna that ignites the hydrogen in the bag."

Ludwig nodded. This was common knowledge among airship crews, and one of the reasons they tended to give storms a wide berth when able.

"The thing is, even when we're well outside of range of a lightning strike, the massive ionization of the storm can still cause smaller static discharges. The antenna will pick these up, and the wireless set will emit a crackle or a squeal, as you just heard."

"I see," Ludwig said, then turned to look again out the forward window. They had just crossed the last of brown hills and tall cliffs of the Turkish coastline, and the wine-dark Mediterranean stretched ahead, glinting in the afternoon sun. Up until now, the sky above shone clear and blue, no sign of a cloud in sight.

Yet.

Ludwig raised his binocular glasses and peered at the horizon. Sure enough, a dark, ominous smear hung low over the barely visible Cretan coastline.

"It seems your reasoning is sound, Mr. Mueller,"

Ludwig said, lowering the glasses. "There does appear to be some convective activity over Crete. We shall have to circumvent it if we can. We may not have the fuel to go far."

Ludwig turned and bestowed a small smile upon the young wireless operator. "I appreciate your timely warning, Mueller," he said. "Well done."

The younger man smiled for just a moment before his military bearing snapped back into place and he nodded. "Aye, sir," he said. "Thank you." As Mueller turned back to his wireless set, Ludwig watched as his chief enlisted man, Engelke, nodded as well, acknowledging the scene.

Not that Ludwig was particularly surprised by Mueller's intense competence. Indeed, *all* of his men were excruciatingly good at their jobs, especially considering that the merest bit of the technology they used was cutting edge. Transitioning from the surface navy to the air service was highly competitive, and only the best of the best joined the elite airship crews. He rather expected his men to perform in such an admirable manner.

Still, Ludwig thought as he raised his binoculars once again, it was important to acknowledge excellence, especially in front of his peers. The man would perform all the better for it. And heaven knew they needed nothing less than consistent excellence on this particular mission!

"Operation China Show," as it was called, was by far the most ambitious undertaking by a military zeppelin crew in all of history. Whenever he thought of the sheer audacity of the plan, Ludwig couldn't decide whether he should feel more pride or fear about what they were attempting to do. Since he was a military man, and no stranger to action, he usually defaulted to pride . . . but the fear was always there, too.

They would fly for four days south across the African desert to deliver fifteen tons of badly needed weapons and supplies to General von Lettow-Vorbeck and his *Schutztruppe*. For nearly three years, the aptly named "Lion of Africa" had kept three hundred thousand British, Belgian, and Portuguese troops occupied down there, where they could do no harm to the German Imperial troops hammering it out on the Western Front. General von Lettow-Vorbeck had never lost a battle, and his mastery of lightning raids and guerrilla tactics made him a constant thorn in the side of the Entente colonial forces.

But none of that could continue without supplies. And with the British Navy prowling the Mediterranean as they did, a surface-based mission would be little more than a suicide run. But while the British claimed the sea, Germany led the world in the air.

And he, Ludwig Bockholt, was in command of this most audacious aerial resupply mission. It all had to be conducted with the utmost secrecy, of course. For while German fighters, at least for now, were far superior to anything owned by Britain or France, an enemy plane could still shoot down the slower zeppelins. Indeed, the differing speeds between lighter-than-air and heavier-than-air craft meant that an escort of fighters was completely impractical for this trip, even if there were places for them to stop and refuel along the route.

Which there weren't.

But the sky was large, and Ludwig had never been a man short of nerve. So he and his elite, dauntless crew would trust in skill, secrecy, and luck to complete this resupply run, saving the Lion of Africa, and making history in the process.

When he lowered the binoculars again, Ludwig couldn't hold back a smile.

"Bring the antenna in now, Mueller."

"Aye, sir," Wilhelm said, keeping the relief out of his tone. After the heady experience of having the captain praise him in his work, he'd returned to his task of monitoring the wireless communications with renewed vigor. But the static and squealing had only increased over time. While they drew ever closer to the island of Crete, the ship herself started to buck up and down as the air turned more and more turbulent from the storm's outflow. As the bucking continued, Wilhelm's knuckles turned white from his death grip on his console. He tried hard not to think about the fact that if the turbulence got bad enough, the ship could actually break apart in midair.

Sometimes, such knowledge wasn't necessarily helpful.

Wilhelm removed his headset and pulled his heavy leather gloves on over the lighter woolen ones he used while operating the wireless. His tasks required a good deal of manual dexterity, and the larger gloves made him fumble-fingered on the set's dials. He pulled his flying helmet down tighter over his ears and stepped back onto the narrow catwalk that formed the deck of the gondola. Then he turned sideways and eased his way between the rudder and elevator operators, careful not to jostle either man as they struggled to keep the ship flying through the unpredictable air in a controlled, coordinated manner.

The deck heaved underneath him, and Wilhelm reached out a hand to steady himself on the bulkhead as he stepped carefully out onto the catwalk that connected the two compartments. It was unusual for a zeppelin to have such a feature, but L59 was a bit of a one-off. The catwalk was little more than a horizontal ladder cage that contained the captain's command communication tubes and the electrical and hydraulic lines required to operate the elevators and rudder.

Wilhelm drew in a deep breath and pulled his scarf up over his nose and face, then unclipped the safety tether they all wore attached to their specially designed belts and fastened it to the rail of the catwalk. He slowly stepped out into the howling, whipping wind and began to pull himself rung over rung back to the aft compartment, the engine compartment. As he drew closer, the noise and stench of L59's five engines began to hammer into his skull, and he spared a moment of pity for Gustav and his other friends consigned to this hell for the four days of the journey.

"Wilhelm!"

Gustav's shout barely cut through the din, but Wilhelm recognized his friend's squat frame, even though he wore the usual layers of uniform, warm coveralls, and protective overcoat. Gustav pushed past his fellow machinists and raised his goggles up on his forehead to grin at Wilhelm as he pulled himself in through the hatch and swung down to his feet.

"What're you doing back here, then?" he asked, his

eyes crinkling up on the corners. "You getting good power for the wireless? Our engines are purring like kittens back here, though the air does feel a little bumpy."

"We're circumnavigating a storm over Crete," Wilhelm said, leaning forward to shout the words into Gustav's ear as he unclipped his safety tether and returned it to his belt. "I'm to pull in the antenna."

"Right," Gustav said. He pulled his goggles back down over his eyes, and turned his body aft, waving for Wilhelm to follow. The gesture was unnecessary, as Wilhelm knew very well where the antenna winch was located, but he followed his friend out of courtesy. This was, after all, the engine compartment, and therefore Gustav's domain.

He nodded at the other men peering at various dials and indicators as he squeezed past them, careful not to touch any part of the huge engine that rumbled and smoked in the center of the gondola compartment. That engine, and four more like it, provided the thrust required to move and steer L59 along her course. On the far side of the engine, Wilhelm could see the empty machine gun mounts that normally held their defensive weaponry, just in case any enemy fighters showed up to play. For this mission, however, every kilogram counted, and so they'd left the guns behind and trusted to stealth and secrecy. Wilhelm hoped it would be enough.

"Here, let me get out of your way, so you can get to the winch," Gustav said, pressing his body to the bulkhead once they'd made their way past the bulk of the engine. Wilhelm nodded and squeezed his friend's arm, then eased by him in the narrow space and pulled the hand crank out of its stowage cradle.

The deck bucked upward again, and then back down, causing Wilhelm to stumble against the bulkhead. He caught himself with one hand on the stowage cradle and kept his feet splayed wide as he shoved the male end of the crank into the female receptacle on the winch. Then he took a deep breath of the stinking engine compartment air and began cranking.

It didn't take long for his back and shoulders to burn with the effort. The zeppelin's wireless antenna wasn't as long as the antenna used on some of the surface fleet vessels, but it was long enough. Wilhelm fought to keep his breathing steady as his legs and back and arms worked the crank around and around, reeling in the delicate-seeming steel cable even as the rising wind whipped it to and fro.

Finally, just when Wilhelm was fearing he'd have to ask for help, the winch *clanked* loud enough to be heard over the engine's thrum, and the safety bolt fell into place on the antenna spool. Wilhelm closed his eyes and breathed a prayer of thanks as the deck shuddered and lurched with more turbulence.

With shaking arms, he detached the crank and returned it to the stowage cradle, then wiped his sweating brow and pulled his own overcoat closer around his throat. Up here, in the chill of altitude, sweat could be deadly. He straightened his aching back and turned around to see that Gustav had gone back to work on the engine itself. He was tuning it to withstand the unpredictable air from the storm, no doubt.

Wilhelm didn't interrupt him, just squeezed on past as he made his way back forward to the command compartment. With the antenna retracted, they would be unable to receive any signals, but he wasn't going to be accused of abandoning his watch. Besides, as soon as they had gotten safely around the storm, the captain would order the antenna extended again, and Wilhelm would need to be there to hear it.

"How far off course have we come?" Ludwig asked. He didn't turn his head, trusting that his navigator was ready with the answer. Sure enough, the man spoke up almost immediately.

"Nearly a hundred miles, Captain," the navigator said. "Most of it due to the turbulence. But I've calculated an intercept course that will make up the distance and still see us overhead the African coast by dawn."

"Excellent," Ludwig said. "Give your new course to the helm. Well done, gentlemen," he went on, allowing himself a small smile. "I believe we're out of the storm entirely. Very good work by all concerned."

He could feel his men stand a little straighter at this praise, and he felt a surge of warmth in return. As a young officer, he'd had the occasion to observe two different ship's captains and their various command styles. The first, *Kapitaen* Leitzke, had been a staunch traditionalist. He remained consistently aloof and cold with his men, and even, to an extent, with his officers. He'd been a successful commander, in that they'd completed their missions to a satisfactory level (all training missions, at that time, before the war). But there'd been no brilliance on that ship, no fire in any of the men. Leitzke's addresses had lacked sincerity and passion, and so they'd remained merely "good enough," and Ludwig had never been satisfied with that.

The other captain he'd served under, Captain Oursler, had carried a reputation as a bit of a wildcard. Unlike Leitzke, Oursler spoke with the crew as a whole on a regular basis. He took watches for himself. He spent an inordinate amount of time with his officers, constantly coaching and developing them, giving them opportunities to learn. He worked extensively with his senior enlisted men as well and entrusted them with much of the responsibility for the discipline of the crew.

The result was like night and day to Ludwig's first posting. Captain Oursler's ship consistently outperformed the others in her group. Every man on that ship, Ludwig included, had felt a personal investment and pride in her mission. It had been a heady experience, and a valuable lesson in leadership that Ludwig took with him to the skies. He believed in praising his men in public and with very few exceptions, reprimanding them in private. The result was a tight-knit, highly competent group that functioned like a dream. He knew he couldn't take credit for all of their excellence—after all, only the best were chosen to be here—but he felt very strongly that his leadership style worked well, enabling them to complete the most difficult of missions.

God willing, that would include this one.

He raised his binocular glasses again and looked out at the glimmering sea spread before him. Africa waited just beyond that horizon. Africa . . . and destiny.

Wilhelm made a face as he lifted the mug and downed

the last of the bitter, strong *ersatz* coffee in it. It was hot, but he didn't mind. They'd overflown the coast near dawn, and as the sun burned its way up the sky, the heated gas lifted the zeppelin higher and higher. Wilhelm felt the beginnings of his usual altitude-headache knotting between his brows, compounding the fatigue that came from over twenty-four hours on duty at this point. Fortunately, the coffee tended to help both conditions. As did the sugar in the chocolate, and the bread and sausage they ate for rations.

He took another bite of his chocolate, a tiny one. He needed the sustenance, but he did *not* need the shame of losing his stomach on the command deck. It was better to eat slowly and steadily, he'd learned. Especially as the day wore on and they rode the great heated columns of air deeper into the punishing blue sky. Even as he had the thought, the deck fell beneath his feet, and then bumped up hard enough to buckle his knees and send his stomach roiling. Wilhelm gripped the edge of his wireless console and focused on breathing steady, calming breaths.

"Bit of rough air, sir."

Wilhelm recognized the voice as that of the zeppelin's elevator operator. He was the chief *Obermaschinisten-maat* on board, and as such, was the most senior enlisted man.

"Indeed," the captain said, "and it's likely to continue for some time as we cross this desert—"

Another violent bout of turbulence rocked them, different from the last. Instead of being tossed up or down, Wilhelm was thrown sideways, towards the nose of the zeppelin. He reached out, hands scrabbling at the edge of his console, the cold metal biting into the wool-wrapped flesh of his hands as he fought to stay upright. Just as suddenly, he felt himself rock back aft, and *then* the deck bucked up beneath him in the usual fashion of heavy turbulence.

It felt almost as if they'd hit something solid, but they were thousands of feet in the air!

"All stations, report!" The captain's voice cracked through the control compartment like a whip, and Wilhelm felt, more than heard, it echoing down the communication tube to the aft engine compartments.

"Rudders all clear, sir!"

"Elevator clear, sir!"

Wilhelm shook his head, forced his thoughts to coalesce and stared at his wireless console.

His lifeless wireless console.

He depressed the test tone switch.

Nothing.

"*Scheisse,*" Wilhelm muttered under his breath. "Captain, the wireless has failed!"

"Message from the engine compartment, sir!" A white-faced man burst out as he looked up from the communications tube. "The forward engine has seized up!"

Wilhelm swore again and hung on grimly as another burst of turbulence rocked them to and fro, rattling their teeth. Without the thrust from that engine, their forward speed would be greatly diminished, leaving them even more vulnerable to the British fighters that they knew were stationed in the Sudan below. But even worse than that . . .

"Sir," he found himself saying, before he'd even realized he meant to speak. "The forward engine powers our wireless. Without it, we're deaf and blind. If I go aft, while I can't do anything about the engine, I may be able to rig an auxiliary power supply for the wireless from one of the other engines."

"Go, Mueller," the captain said, his tone firm, but calm. "And have the machinists report back on what they can do to get the engine started again."

"Aye, sir," Wilhelm said, and turned to follow the breathless messenger back aft to the engine compartment.

As soon as they arrived, Wilhelm recognized his own exhaustion and strain reflected in the drawn faces of the machinists frantically working on the seized forward engine. Only one remained apart, and he slumped tiredly behind the empty defensive machine gun mounts and wearily scanned the surrounding sky.

Wilhelm looked around and finally found Gustav crouched near the deck, peering up at the underside of the engine and uttering a low, steady stream of invective.

"Gustav," Wilhelm said, his voice pitched low. When his friend didn't respond, Wilhelm reached out and shook his shoulder. "Gustav!"

"Wilhelm!" Gustav said, shaking his head and straightening quickly. "You really are here. I thought it was just another vision."

"Vision?"

"From the fumes. On long flights, sometimes we get them. What are you doing back here? It's not a good time."

"The wireless gets its power from the seized engine,"

Wilhelm said. "I'm going to try to see if I can reroute it somehow. And the captain wants a report on how quickly you'll be able to bring this one back into operation."

Gustav shook his head, his already grim expression darkening.

"Not going to happen soon," he said. "The reduction gear housing is cracked. She needs to be completely torn down and rebuilt, and I don't have the materials or space to do that here."

Wilhelm swallowed hard at the bitter edge of despair in his friend's voice. He clapped Gustav on the shoulder.

"No matter," he said. "We've got four more, yeah? But that makes it all the more important that I get some power to the wireless, otherwise, we're blind and deaf over enemy territory."

"Right," Gustav said, straightening. "I might be able to help you there. Your wireless is powered off of this dynamo, here." He pointed to an incomprehensible lump of metal sprouting wires in several directions, mounted on the external case of the engine housing. "None of the other engines have one quite as large, but there *is* a smaller, emergency dynamo on the next engine aft."

"How much smaller?" Wilhelm asked.

"You're looking at about half power."

Wilhelm grimaced. "That will power the receiver, at least," he said. "Though we won't be able to transmit. Still, better than nothing. Show me this emergency dynamo, my friend. Let's get our eyes and ears back up."

Wilhelm and Gustav worked as quickly as they could manage. To Wilhelm, it felt as if his mind surged ahead at a feverish pace, leaving his body behind. Before long, his fingers began to lose dexterity, and he struggled to focus and force his exhausted body to obey and finish the delicate task. He could easily see how Gustav and the others complained of "visions" in this place. Between crushing fatigue, the grinding noise, and the ever present stench, he thought he might just go mad.

"There," Gustav said, finally. "That ought to do it."

"God willing," Wilhelm said. "I'll head forward and check."

"Be careful on that catwalk, Wilhelm," Gustav said. "And use your safety strap. We'll be watching if you need an assist."

"I don't know how you stand it back here, my friend," Wilhelm said, shaking his aching head.

"It's what we do," Gustav gave him a grim smile and patted him on the shoulder. "Now go. And call back through the tube if it's not working. You're too tired and addled to make *two* trips down the catwalk now."

"The 'tube,' as you call it, isn't mine to use, Gustav. You know that. I'll do as the captain orders." Wilhelm rolled his shoulders and settled his leather belt on his hips, bracing himself for the harrowing crawl back to the forward compartment.

"Well said, Wilhelm," Gustav said. "Fair enough." He clapped Wilhelm on the shoulder once more and accompanied him back as far as the useless hulk of the seized engine, then lifted his hand to wave farewell as Wilhelm squeezed once more through the bodies of the other machinists hard at work trying to find a solution that just wasn't there.

Once more, Wilhelm hooked his safety tether onto the

catwalk and ventured out into the naked sky. Though the whipping air took his breath away, it *did* help ease the fume-caused headache that had been pounding through his skull. He tried to breathe slowly through the fabric swathing his mouth and nose, as he pulled himself on burning, shaky muscles hand-over-hand to the safety of the forward compartment.

Hands gripped him by the shoulders and pulled him forward. Warmth wrapped around him as the sudden cessation of the punishing wind cut off. Other hands peeled his frozen scarf from his face.

"Wilhelm?"

"Sir," Wilhelm gasped. "My . . . apologies. I think . . . the wireless . . ."

The navigator who'd caught and assisted him helped him further, pulling him up to stand. Wilhelm found that he couldn't uncurl his frozen fingers enough to unclip his safety tether, so the officer did it for him, and then handed him a mug.

"Careful," the navigator cautioned. "It's barely warm, but you could still scald yourself. What about the wireless?"

Wilhelm took a sip of the coffee, which felt deliciously warm, and drew in a deep breath.

"Yes, sir. I think I was able to restore power to the receiver, at least. The machinists say that the forward engine is a complete loss, however. There's no way to fix her in the air."

"Damn," the navigator said. "I'll tell the captain. You go check on your wireless set."

"Yes, sir," Wilhelm said again. He nodded respectfully

and made his way carefully back to his own crew station, cradling the mug of coffee and fervently wishing that he never again had to make that trip during this mission.

Ludwig clapped his exhausted navigator on the shoulder.

"I have the ship, Heinrich," he said softly. "Why don't you step around to the officers' berth and get some rest."

"Aye, sir," *Leutnant zur See* Maas said, fatigue and gratitude threading through his tone. It was near midnight, and the command deck was quiet. Most of the men had also been dismissed back to their crowded common berth compartment to get what rest they could. As the captain, Ludwig had the luxury of a tiny closet all to himself, and he'd taken himself there shortly after sundown for his own rest. Experience had taught him that he couldn't care for his crew if he didn't also take care of himself. So once dusk had found them high overhead of the Nile and following its course south, he'd left the ship in the capable hands of his officer for a few hours.

"Looks like it's you and me, Wilhelm," Ludwig said to the young wireless operator sitting at his console.

"Aye, sir," the young man said, coming smartly to his feet. Ludwig waved him back down to a seat. There wasn't a need to be quite so formal during the middle watch, not with nothing going on. And though the man looked worlds better than he had after his harrowing heroics that afternoon, his face still shone pinched and pale in the dimly lit compartment.

"Did you get some rest, Wilhelm?" Ludwig asked. "Stay seated, for God's sake."

"Aye, sir," Wilhelm said. "I did. The *Obermaschinisten-maat* ordered me into the berths and told me not to come out for a solid four hours. He kept a careful log of any transmissions, sir, I checked."

"I would expect nothing less," Ludwig said, hiding a smile. The young man looked both terrified and gratified to be having this late night conversation. Funny as it might seem to him, he could understand, given the differences in their respective ranks and stations. He nodded at the man, then lifted his binoculars to look out the front windows, thus releasing Wilhelm from any further discussion.

It was a beautiful, clear night. Stars studded the sky like a spray of chipped ice on midnight blue satin. The moon, just barely past half, rode high, spilling stolen light on the desert terrain below. Up ahead, the Nile shone, a close, silver ribbon twisting through the hills as it pointed their way south.

It was closer than it ought to be, actually.

Ludwig lowered the binoculars and frowned, then turned to try to focus on the dimly lit altimeter. He squinted his eyes, bending toward the instrument panel. He was barely able to make out the numbers painted on the dial.

Two-thousand, nine hundred feet?

That couldn't be right. He reached out and tapped the gauge. Sometimes, the needles could get stuck . . .

"Captain, a message."

Ludwig straightened and turned back to Wilhelm at the wireless console. The young man held out a pair of headphones, and he wasted no time in putting them on.

Ludwig could read Morse as well as any signaler. He translated in his own mind as the message repeated. "*. . . Break off operation. Return. Enemy has seized greater part of Makonde Highlands, already holds Kitangari. Portuguese are attacking remainder of Protectorate Forces from south.*"

"Wilhelm," Ludwig said quietly, his voice calm, even as the bottom dropped out of his stomach. "This is genuine?"

"I authenticated the code, sir," Wilhelm said, sounding as sick as Ludwig felt. "It's genuine."

"Very well," Ludwig said. He took a deep breath and stepped over to the message tube. He didn't think Wilhelm or any of the other men on the night watch could see, but perhaps he could be forgiven as his hand trembled just a little when he pulled the speaking cone to his face.

"Crew, this is the Captain," he said, hearing his own voice echo into the tube. "We have been recalled by the High Command. Prepare to come about."

A chorus of disbelief and outrage rose from both the officers' compartment and the crew berths that lay on the other side of the bulkhead from the command cabin. Heinrich, his navigator and second-in-command, charged up onto the command deck with his coat undone and his hair all askew from sleep.

"Sir, you can't be serious!" Heinrich said, and the men piling in after him raised their voices in agreement. "We've come so far! Been through so much! This message can't be genuine! Von Lettow-Vorbeck is lost without these supplies!"

"*Leutnant* Maas, you forget yourself," Ludwig said coldly to Heinrich.

"Sir, you know I'd never disrespect you, but consider! A recall now? This makes no sense! It must be the British—"

"*Leutnant*!" Ludwig thundered, just as the zeppelin lurched and tilted. He'd ordered her elevator set to fly with their nose up at four degrees above the horizon throughout the night. A tell-tale shudder reverberated through the floor, and Ludwig spun, throwing himself toward the instrument panel.

"Nose down!" he yelled, as his eyes locked onto the altimeter. The needle began to spin, slowly at first, and then accelerating as they fell through the skies. "Nose down, full power from all remaining engines! We've stalled in the cold night air!"

The deep thrumming that always existed in the background picked up in pitch as someone—maybe even the unfortunate Heinrich—picked up the command tube and relayed his order to the engine room. The captain heard men grunting and swearing behind him as they fought with the elevator controls to try to bring the behemoth's nose down in order to get her flying again.

Slowly, their pitch attitude changed.

Too slowly. The altimeter needle continued to spin. Two-thousand feet. One thousand nine hundred ninety feet....

"We're too heavy! Engelke, get some of the men and head back to the cargo compartment. Jettison the heaviest cargo—ammunition, the machine guns—and about half of our own ballast. We can pick up more if we need it once we're once again in friendly skies."

"Captain, the supplies—"

Ludwig whirled around and stabbed a finger at Heinrich Maas, his eyes angry and hot.

"Enough!" he spat. "Engelke, take *Leutnant* Maas with you and if he does not help jettison the cargo *as ordered*, then jettison him as well! This is not a game, gentlemen! We are a warship at war and *we have our orders!*"

Shocked silence reverberated through the compartment, broken only by the engine's scream. Ludwig looked into his navigator's wide eyes and let the man see his steely determination. Maas looked away, and Ludwig glanced at the airship's senior noncom.

"Aye, sir," his senior enlisted man said, swallowing hard and nodding.

"Go," Ludwig said, keeping his tone low and hard as iron. In the back of his mind, he began to consider how he'd paint this incident in such a way as to save his young, momentarily foolish, officer. Perhaps he could blame it on fumes, or lack of sleep, or a legitimate suspicion of enemy action. He'd think of something. Maas was a good sort, and he'd never caused problems before.

The men scurried away to do his bidding and Ludwig turned back around to look out at the desert floor that stretched impossibly far in the moonlit night.

They saved her, but barely. Wilhelm didn't know how close they'd come to crashing in that frigid night, but he'd seen the altimeter reach as low as one-thousand five hundred feet, and suspected they'd gotten even closer than that. But the captain's order to jettison cargo and ballast had stabilized the ship and gotten her flying again.

He wished he felt relieved.

The truth was, the journey thus far had been hellish. Easily the most difficult mission of his life, and he knew he was not alone in that. Reports from the engine compartment spoke of increasing hallucinations and men passing out from the severe pains in their heads. It only got worse once they'd come about, as well. Men could push through a lot of pain in pursuit of glory. It was much harder once defeat was assured.

By the time the sun rose to warm the air and expand the gasses in the bag again, they had established a course back to the north, across the enemy territory through which they'd just come. Tension ran high throughout the crew, sure that the damned British fighters would be on them at any moment.

The day wore on and on. Wilhelm refused to leave his station again, straining his ears for any transmission, any break in static, anything that might give them warning as to the presence of enemy fighters.

But nothing came. The static stayed steady, and through the grace of God alone, nightfall saw them crossing the Egyptian coast and soaring out over the Mediterranean once again.

Ludwig felt like weeping.

He could do no such thing, of course. Not in front of his men, ever, but certainly not now, at the end of a grueling mission that had ended in ignominious failure. It didn't help that he ached with a fatigue that burned through his muscles and pulled at the edges of his mind, making it nearly impossible to focus. Still, his men no doubt felt worse than he, and so he summoned every bit of will he had to keep his spine straight, his chin lifted.

Remember, he whispered to himself. *Remember who you are.*

Ahead, the wide landing meadow at Jambol beckoned just below the horizon. He could imagine the scramble of the ground crews as they watched his ship's unscheduled approach. Though they flew at nearly one hundred kilometers an hour, it seemed impossibly far away; and their pace seemed an impossibly slow crawl. Normally, at the end of a mission, the men would be all smiles and jokes at this point, with hearts light and merry at the prospect of a few weeks at home.

Not so today.

He listened as his noncoms and officers—including poor Heinrich, who had not said another word out of line since Ludwig had threatened his life—performed their landing routines. He gave the appropriate commands at the appropriate times, and L59, battered and bruised from her marathon journey, finally settled softly to the ground once more.

Ludwig lowered his head, closed his eyes, and lifted his thoughts in a very heartfelt prayer of thanksgiving, for his life, for the lives of his men, and for the safety of this truly magnificent ship.

Remorse rippled through him. She deserved better.

They all did.

"Captain?"

Ludwig looked up to see Heinrich, his face pale, his hands shaking as he held out the ship's official diary.

Ludwig took the book, which was open and ready for him to record their landing entry and mission summary data.

"Captain, I am so sorry—"

Ludwig lifted a hand. Shook his head.

"You forgot your place for a moment, Heinrich. That is all. It will not happen again," Ludwig said, his voice hard, but not unkind.

"N-no, sir," Heinrich said. "It will not."

Ludwig nodded. "The summary data, then, if you please, *Leutnant*?"

Maas blinked rapidly, inhaling through his nose as if gathering his composure, and then nodded crisply. "Yes, sir. On her latest mission, codenamed China Show, Imperial Navy Zeppelin L59 flew a total of 6,800 kilometers in 95 hours. Due to a recall from the high command, her mission was aborted, and this flight was conducted without pause or refuel, making it the longest flight by a military aircraft in history."

Ludwig froze, looked up from his record of this summary.

"You're sure, Heinrich?" he asked.

Heinrich gave him a tremulous smile. "I am, sir. They taught us that in university. The pre-war record is significantly shorter, and none of our other missions have been so ambitious."

"And the enemy doesn't fly long-range zeppelins," Ludwig finished, speaking half to himself.

"No, sir, they do not."

A slow smile spread across Ludwig's face as he bent to finish his sentence. He signed off the log, signaling the end of the mission, and closed it with a flourish, then shared his smile with Heinrich.

"Thank you, *Leutnant*," he said, formally, "for that data. And for making our mission less of a failure."

"Sir?" Heinrich said, confusion furrowing his brow.

"We did our job, but we were recalled through no fault of our own. The men are demoralized by that, as you, yourself, are well aware. But now, with this information . . . well. You've given us something to celebrate! Come with me, my boy. You can help me tell the crew. If we can do this, we can do anything!"

Interlude

Tatiana: Many Summers

It was not our fault that the guards turned on us.

Today we celebrated the birth of our Lord. We were grateful to be together under the small dome of Tobolsk's church, kneeling before the altar. Most of the soldiers of the Second remained in the narthex but one, then a second, followed us cautiously into the nave. I could feel the weight of their gazes on my back as we took our places, Mama and Papa and Alexei in front, we girls behind.

I couldn't shake the weight of their sight from my shoulders. It made me shudder, not from the cold that had followed us in, but from the scowls on their faces, the way they looked at the saints painted on the walls.

Looking away, I sought the friendlier faces of the choir standing at our left and our right. I recognized among them some of the people that had crossed themselves as we had passed them in the street.

Father Vasiliev entered through the Beautiful Gate and took his place, his voice rising above us as he led the service, but the words were lost to me. I wanted, more than anything, to lose myself in the imagery of the icons, in the vibrant colors of their robes, the gilded halos, the looks on the faces of the saints painted on the wall before us. I wanted the comfort that the images of our Lord and His blessed mother could bring. Unlike the sternness of John the Baptist and the Archangels Michael and Gabriel, she had a gentle look on her face.

I don't know how long I stared at her and only her, but my vision swam. I blinked away the tears and an icon I had never seen before appeared. Seven figures, a mother and father, with a son between them, and two daughters on either side. They were painted like the saints, in rich robes, the children's hands folded together as if in prayer, the mother and father holding admonishing palms outward in front of them. I blinked again and again, hoping the image would go away, but it stayed with me, becoming clearer with every heartbeat.

Mama, Papa, and Alexei. We girls. All of us as we are now, not grown, not old. Martyrs.

I shook my head and looked down at the floor. I didn't dare look back up as my skin shivered around me, crawling underneath my clothes. I thought then that I would crumple and fall and I think I would have had Father Vasiliev not raised his voice.

"A prosperous and peaceful life," he was saying, "health and salvation and good haste in all things, Lord grant your servant, the Sovereign Emperor Nikolai Aleksandrovich, and save him for many and good summers!"

The choir sang in response. "Many, many, many summers! Many, many, many summers!"

Would we see another summer?

"God save him!" they continued.

Yes, God, save my father.

"Grant him, Lord! Many, many, many summers!"

With each word goosebumps rose on the back of my neck, my arms. I was shaking and didn't know why.

The fall of heavy boots thundered by, cutting through the voices, carrying two of the soviet soldiers toward the deacon. He stepped back, into the icon-covered wall, his eyes wide.

"Take it back," one of the soldiers said.

Papa pulled me off the kneeler and pushed me towards Mama and my sisters. He placed himself between his family and the other soldiers who had come bursting in. The choir had backed away as well, casting aside their books, taking refuge through the gates.

"No. I can't," Father Vasiliev said, shaking his head. "I won't." He cast his gaze towards Papa as if seeking direction and then deciding a moment later that it didn't matter. He refused to revoke the prayer, even when they threatened to kill him.

After their treatment of Colonel Kobylinsky I thought they could commit no greater act of insolence. I was wrong. I understood the concept of mutiny. But this. This was something else. It wasn't just that they were drunk on power over men. They were drunk on power over God.

That night, still shaking with the fresh memory of it, I prayed. I prayed for Russia. I prayed for us. I prayed for the deacon. And I prayed for the men who believed so fervently that the deacon's words had so much power that they must be retracted and at the same time believed they could command God. I prayed for their souls and a return to their sanity. I refused to believe that it was anything but that.

So naïve was I.

Chapter Three

Major Brinkmann, Left,
and Major General Hoffmann, Right

En Route to Fort IX, Ingolstadt, Bavaria

Max had tried, he really *had*, to get word to Ludendorff before the latter walked into an ambush at the Privy Council meeting that had shortly followed his own lunch with the kaiser. He'd failed, and now both Ludendorff and Hindenburg were threatening to resign if the kaiser didn't knuckle under and back off of his doubts on the Polish Question. Worse, they were demanding that Wilhelm relieve Max as Chief of Staff at Ober Ost, which would be potentially devastating to German fortunes in the east.

Great men can also be very small sometimes, Hoffmann thought, as he headed south to Ingolstadt. *On the other hand, clever ones, like myself, can be very naïve.*

I wonder why I haven't been stopped from beginning with my little scheme. I suppose . . . no, I am almost certain . . . the kaiser is simply keeping quiet so as not to provoke another row in Berlin. That said, it's at least possible he's trying to maintain a small measure of self-respect over the true ruler of Germany having become the quartermaster general, whom the kaiser dare not overrule.

Oh, well, on the plus side he's at least stood up for me; here I remain at Ober Ost. I am not an especially humble man, and I know I am not, but it's not arrogance to know that here I am irreplaceable.

Max walked through the northern gate of the fort, over which proclaimed the year "1870."

Odd timing, Hoffmann thought; *they built a huge and hugely expensive set of forts precisely when Germany unified to the point where invading it had become very difficult. Oh, well; Bavarians.*

No guard searched *him*, of course.

The commandant of the fort, Hoffmann decided, was not so much incompetent as excitable and lacking in self-discipline. He was also rather fawning, which made him both distasteful and cooperative, extremely so in both cases.

"We don't have as many Russians as we used to, *Herr General*," the commandant explained. "We used to be mostly Russian, but they've been getting moved out for a while now."

"Moved to where?" *Shit.*

"Different camps, sir," the commandant answered. "No particular pattern, but most went to Zittau. Where they may have been sent from there, I have no clue of."

"Well, what *do* you have here?" Hoffmann demanded.

"Two partial cells of Russians, mixed in with British and French, only," the commandant replied, "six men, of whom one is on a charge, and in solitary confinement for two months, for attempted escape."

"Indeed? How far did he get?"

"Farther than most," the commandant admitted, then beamed, "but we still caught him within ten kilometers of the fort. He—Captain Kostyshakov—is the senior Russian prisoner at the moment."

Kostyshakov attempted to rise to attention when Hoffmann and the commandant entered the cell where he was recovering from the bayonet wound to his posterior. It should have been healed, but infection had set in, an infection his body was only slowly coming to grips with, with the aid of the German medical staff. He couldn't quite make it, though he didn't give up on the attempt.

Hoffmann noticed a particular postcard on a small

table facing the bed. *Interesting,* he thought, *the subjects of that photo.* Under the postcard was a series of journals, most of which appeared to be German military. *Also interesting, and commendably optimistic, that's he's keeping up with modern doctrine.*

"You can leave now," Hoffmann told the commandant. "My business with the Russian doesn't concern you."

"Yes, sir. Of course, sir. If you need anything . . ."

"I'm sure we shall be fine."

"Yes, sir."

"Oh, and give me the *Captain's* file before you leave."

Once the door to the cell had shut, Hoffmann made a patting motion, urging Kostyshakov to lie back down on his bed and relax. This was something less than ideal, as his new wound insisted he lie on his stomach. Stubborn to a fault, as his file said he was, Kostyshakov lay on his back, infection, stitches, pus, and blood be damned.

Hoffmann took a seat that groaned under his weight. Satisfied it would hold him, at least for a while, he opened up the file. He began to read it through, quickly but carefully. Occasionally, the German would *tsk* or *hmmm* or chuckle. Once he muttered, "Clever." At several points, he read aloud, for effect.

". . . mmm . . . A less than model prisoner . . . numerous escape attempts. Tsk . . . scorning our lavish welcome. Captured, July fifteenth, 1916, near the village of Trysten . . . Battle of the Stokhid . . . acting commander of a Guards battalion as a senior captain . . . hmmm. . . . Guards captain and lieutenant colonel are the same . . . both K7, if I recall correctly . . . before that . . . company command, Second Company, Kexholm Guards regiment . . . machine gun detachment commander before that...wounded at Tannenburg...joined Guards 1910...1906 graduate of Pavlov Military Academy... First Cadet Corps before that... Order of Saint Anne, 4th Class... Stalislaw, Third Class... Saint Vladimir... Saint George..."

Two or three times—Kostyshakov lost count—the German stopped reading and looked at the curved ceiling contemplatively. Finally, reaching the end of the file, he closed it and turned his attention back to the Russian.

That study went on a long, intense, and uncomfortable time, before Kostyshakov lost his patience and asked, "Is there something I can do for you, General? And how do you—how does that file—know these things?"

Good, thought Hoffmann, *he is patient but not too patient. Also not dull-witted.*

"Ah, my apologies, Captain," said the German in flawless Russian. "I'm Major General Max Hoffmann. You have, perhaps, heard of me."

"Chief of Staff, Ober Ost?" Kostyshakov asked, a little incredulously. He knew the German staff system reasonably well.

"That would be me, yes. As to your file; I suspect it was captured in the same battle you were in, or shortly thereafter, and made part of your file for our purposes. It's in Russian, which I doubt anyone—well, anyone German—before me has thought to read. If they had, you would have been in this place a lot sooner, long before so many escape attempts."

"Well, now I really *am* intrigued," Kostyshakov said. "This is a signal honor, sir. But, more to the point, to what do I *owe* this signal honor?"

Again, Hoffmann reverted to quiet study, not answering the question.

For his part, sensing a sort of mental game in progress, Daniil simply folded his arms and proceeded to stare back.

And very quick on the uptake, too. I think I can make use of this young man.

"Tell me, Captain," Hoffmann said, "you have shown yourself resourceful at breaking out of places; six distinct escapes that got you outside the walls of whatever camp you were in, if I didn't lose count."

"Six? I think that's probably right, sir."

"So you can break out . . . how do you think you would be at breaking in?"

Kostyshakov unfolded his arms in a painful attempt to sit more upright. "Sir, I . . ."

"I have a proposition for you, young man. But first, tell me what you know of circumstances in Russia."

"Not that much, sir. I know the tsar abdicated, and that Kerensky has formed a government."

Something about the tone in Daniil's voice when he said, "Kerensky," prompted Hoffmann to ask if he knew him.

"We've never met, sir, no, but I know *of* him. I've read some of his work, notably his exposure and treatment of the Lena Massacre was important. But . . . although Russia needs to modernize and even liberalize, I don't think Kerensky is the man to do it."

"Why not?"

"His heart's in the right place, but he's far too left wing, and even too innocent, for the job."

"I see," said Hoffmann. "Well, you will be pleased to note that Kerensky is no longer in charge of the Provisional Government. His place has been taken by Vladimir Ilyich Lenin . . ."

"The *Bolshevik*?" Daniil asked, distress in his voice. "The Bolsheviks are in charge of Russia?" He let his compact torso fall back upon his medical cot, then covered his face in the crook of one arm. "I should have known, except that here part of my sentence was to be deprived of Red Cross parcels and newspapers."

"It gets worse," Hoffmann said.

"How can it be worse? How can it possibly be worse than that godless Bolshevik, Lenin, ruling Russia?"

"Russia's dropped out of the war."

"Still not as bad as *Tsar Lenin*," Daniil said. "For he'll be the tsar, even if he scorns the title."

Hoffmann continued, trying to shake the Russian, "The imperial army has mostly disintegrated."

"Of *course*, it did," Kostyshakov agreed. "How could it *not* with the Bolsheviks at the helm?"

"Germany is stripping away, which is to say guaranteeing the independence of, Finland, Poland, Estonia, Latvia, Lithuania. That's about one third of the Empire's population, just under ninety percent of its coal, perhaps half of Russia's industrial base, and about a quarter of the rail system.

"It didn't have to be," Hoffmann continued, not necessarily with perfect honesty. "With the tsar or even with Kerensky we could have made a far more generous peace. But with the Bolsheviks in charge? Germany has to secure itself against them."

"No doubt," Daniil replied. *And I even do understand it, at least to some degree.*

"So how do you feel about your royal family," Hoffmann asked, "or, rather, your *former* royal family?"

"While I breathe," Daniil replied, "and they do, they remain my royal family and . . ."

"Yes?" Max prodded.

"Nothing, sir. Nothing important."

Hoffmann stood, again causing the chair to groan in relief, and took the two steps to the night table next to Kostyshakov's bed. He picked up the postcard, saying, "Beautiful girls. German girls, really, for the most part, which is a good deal of why I'm here to see you. I've never met either one, though I saw them from a distance once when they were little above babies."

Kostyshakov's eyes took on a sort of dreamy look, as if they were piercing the veil of time to look back. "I was wounded again," he said, distantly, "in nineteen fifteen. It was a fairly heavy dose of shrapnel. It looked touch and go for a while. I was evacuated to a hospital at Tsarskoe Selo to recover. My nurse was . . . the one on the right, Tatiana Romanova. Wonderful, wonderful girl. The other, Olga, is sweet but not strong. Tatiana is *strong*.

"Beyond my station, of course; even leaving aside that I am a probably a little too old for her; my family wasn't ennobled until my grandfather was awarded the Order of Saint George, Fourth Class, for fighting on the frontier."

"Yes, and I'm not even a 'von,' " Max said. "It doesn't matter. The point is, you feel you do have obligations both to the tsar and the royal family, professionally and morally, and to this girl, personally?"

"Yes. And as for the girl, still, a man can dream."

"That may prove unfortunate and your dream a nightmare," Hoffmann said. "The Bolsheviks cannot possibly let the tsar and his family live. At some point in time, the decision will be made—it is part of the inescapable logic of revolution—that they must die before they can become so much as figureheads for the enemies of the revolution."

"I don't believe it," Kostyshakov replied. "Even the Bolsheviks—"

"Are you at all familiar with the French Revolution?" Hoffmann interrupted. "Does the name Marie Antoinette not ring a bell? The Princess de Lamballe? How many hundreds, how many *thousands*, of others?

"Don't delude yourself, Captain Kostyshakov; the tsar and his family are as good as dead."

Daniil grew very silent then, staying that way for what seemed a long time. When he finally spoke, it was to say, "You didn't come here to tell me all this just to torture me, General Hoffmann. What is it that you want?"

"I mentioned—well, suggested, at least—a proposition, I think," Hoffmann said. "Put simply, it is this: I want you to select a few dozen trustworthy officers and noncoms, then that . . . committee to select several hundred others, of all ranks. And then the lot of you are going to go and save your royal family."

Kostyshakov looked stunned. He barely managed to croak out, "We're going to—"

"It has to be you, you see," Max interrupted, "you Russians that do it. Any German attempt to save them, barring some support not arising to direct combat, would simply contaminate them and take away what little legitimacy remains to the Romanovs."

"But how do we . . . ?"

"I'm not sure. I have a rudimentary sketch of a plan, no more than that. The short version is that you will select your force. Meanwhile, a small team of yours, quartermaster types, will be given free reign over captured stocks from your own army and the western allies, and perhaps some of Germany's arms, if they're ubiquitous enough or unknown enough. Another small team— with carrier pigeons, I think, if we can find some champions with the necessary range—will set out early, perhaps on horseback, to determine exactly where the tsar's family is being held. This is a one-time possibility; we cannot launch our effort without that knowledge.

"While the arms are being collected, and the patrol is out hunting, you will organize and train your force."

"How . . . mmm . . . how *big* a force are we talking about?" Daniil asked.

Hoffmann didn't need to consult any notes. "Call it 'six hundred' of which you can take perhaps five hundred with you, if my understanding of some things is accurate. Nice round numbers, no? They're not absolutely fixed, either."

"There's no way for me to sneak 'several hundred' men through the lines, through a country that is rapidly disintegrating, into close proximity to the tsar, without being seen and thus triggering the murders you suggest are inevitable anyway. It just cannot be done."

"Oh, certainly not," Hoffmann agreed. There was a heavy admixture of good-natured laughter in his next words. "That's why you're not going to march across country, except for that forward patrol. Oh, no, my fine Russian *Guards Captain*; you and your men are going to go to your target in the *highest* style you can imagine.

"We'll discuss that, however, later. First we have to get you out of here."

Since Kostyshakov continued to sit, unmoving, Hoffmann asked, querulously, "What? You have another objection?"

"Yes, General; how in the name of God do you propose that one of my men is going to be allowed to ransack *your* dumps of captured arms, ammunition, and other supplies and equipment?"

"Don't be a fool, Kostyshakov, or, at least, give *me* credit for not being one. I'm going to assign to you my own Major Brinkmann, a genuinely brilliant general staff officer, and he'll have a small staff to assist, as well as a company of our own plus one of locals to guard your camp. The staff will include a paymaster to continue payment of camp currency. Best I can do, there. Well . . . and we can arrange better food, at least as good as our own frontline fighters get, and a commissary with a few luxuries."

"There is still one objection, General Hoffmann, a final one, security. One word of this leaking out and . . ."

"Ah, that quintessential Russian paranoia. No, not just one word, Kostyshakov. It would take, it almost always takes, a pattern of facts that fit together to lead to a conclusion. We cannot hide your existence completely, so we'll put out two mutually contradictory stories. One is that, since Russia is out of the war, we're recruiting volunteers—mercenaries, in effect—for the western front. The other will be that we need a police force for the portion of Poland we will surely, and against my *very* strong advice, steal.

"We're also going to vociferously deny any such scheme as Polish police and western front trench fodder, which should go a long way toward confirming in people's minds that both are absolutely true. Add to that that you're going someplace fairly desolate and rather miserable for your training, the kind of place no one is likely to stumble upon inadvertently. And, except for things like rifle ranges and rehearsal areas—and those can be explained away, if necessary, as being for the guards—there won't be anything to raise suspicion."

Hoffmann took off his pince-nez glasses, to clean. "There is one matter; I'll need your parole, yours, and the paroles of those officers and men whom you recruit, that for as long as we're engaged in this enterprise you will not try to escape and will prevent any one of the men from escaping."

"Done," Kostyshakov said, without a moment's hesitation. There was no hesitation in the first place, because there had already been an agreement between Germany and Imperial Russia to allow officers to give their parole, their word, which agreement and word allowed them to leave the confines of their prison camps and stroll around a bit. There was no hesitation in the second place, because, "I will do anything, put up with anything, endure anything, to be the hand that frees my tsar and his family from the Reds."

"Good," Hoffmann nodded. "Now come on; I need to browbeat the commandant to get you out of here and put you together with Brinkmann to get this circus on the road.

"By the way, how's your German?"

Now it was Kostyshakov's turn to laugh. He answered in perfect Bavarian-accented German, "I learned it in high school. I have since had a year and a half to perfect it, here, and good reason to do so."

"Excellent," said Hoffmann. "And we'll have to get you outfitted with a proper—Russian—uniform. Speaking of which, where are your medals?"

"I left them with one of the French officers, sir, a Captain de Gaulle. He was captured at Verdun. Were it possible—yes, I know it's not—I'd put him in the battalion and take him along."

"Well—can you walk? With difficulty? Good. Let's go get your medals and anything else you've left behind."

Hoffmann and Kostyshakov found the tall, lanky Frenchman sitting at a table, reading a hand-written manuscript and making notes from it. He looked up at the disturbance and, in one great motion stood, picked up Daniil, and twirled him about the cell like a child.

"Put me *down*, Charles, you bloody great frog!"

"Daniil, I'd heard—we'd all heard—that you had been wounded and captured. It's good to see you, my old friend, back on your feet."

"I can't stay, Charles; I have to go with this gentleman."

De Gaulle studied the German, briefly, then pronounced, "General Hoffmann; sir, I am honored."

"Captain de Gaulle, is it?"

The French officer preened that so important a

German knew his name. Kostyshakov thought, *Now that was a generous and decent thing to do, making an obscure foreign captain feel important.*

"Yes, sir."

"What are you reading, de Gaulle?" asked Max, pointing at the neat pile of paper on the table.

"Not so much reading, sir, as re-reading. They're the notes for one of the Russians who used to be here, one Mikhail Tukhachevsky. I promised to safeguard it and return it to him after the war."

"Why didn't he . . ." Hoffmann began to ask, before dawning realization hit. "He escaped, didn't he?"

"Yes, sir," De Gaulle replied. "I still don't know how he managed it."

"Ah, Tukhachevsky," Daniil mused; "he's an interesting mix of brilliance and madness, fair mindedness and fanaticism, all tied up in a neat little bundle wrapped with infinite personal ambition. A hell of an officer, in many ways. I'm going home, soon, Charles; I can see it to him if you wish and sooner than you are likely to."

"Would you? I'd feel terrible to die in this miserable place"—de Gaulle let his eyes roam over the damp walls for a bit—"with my promise unfulfilled."

"You'll be wanting your medals, too, I suppose, and your other personal things?"

"Please."

"I'll get them, along with a satchel for Tukhachevsky's manuscript."

Asked Hoffmann, "So what, my good Captains, is Tukhachevsky's vision?"

"He sees a maelstrom," said de Gaulle, "with columns

of armored cavalry ignoring their flanks, their own rear, everything, to get at and destroy the enemy's rear . . . or at least to force them to keep displacing."

"Do you agree?"

"Not really," Kostyshakov answered. "He's never read your Clausewitz, so never grasped the idea of the culminating point. Unlike the cavalry of Tukhachevky's vision, cavalry reliant on its sabers and able to feed its horses off the land, modern mechanized cavalry, as Tukhachevsky sees it, needs a mass of everything from ammunition to spare parts to fuel to replacement personnel if they're to keep going. That's the part he refuses to see. You can take some risks with your flanks, yes, but you ignore your enemy, and his independent will, at your peril."

"So where do you see the future heading?"

"From what I've read in your journals, *Herr General*, I see the future being the infantry squad or platoon, built around the light machine gun, supported by masses of artillery with which it maintains continuous contact, via radio, with tanks leading, and led by a man full of willpower and determination."

"Hmmm . . . interesting," said Hoffmann.

It's almost worth it, thought Daniil, as he passed out of the camp under the glaring eyes of Abel and Blue Boy, *to have taken a stab to the buttocks to see the faces of those two as I leave, accompanied by one of their generals, with my medals on my chest. Almost worth it . . .*

Zittau POW Camp, Zittau, Germany

The walls of the office were painted revolutionary red.

From them hung banners proclaiming, "Death to the Tsar," "Long live the rule of the Soviets," "Lenin, Lead us into the Future," and "Down with the Opiate of the Masses."

Kostyshakov, now *sans* medals, likewise epaulettes, who had come up with the slogans and arranged for the room to be painted red, sat at a long table, flanked by six other pro-Tsarist officers and a like number of noncommissioned officers he'd hand selected and personally interviewed the day before. There were a few others, but they were off with Brinkmann and his assistants rounding up materiel.

The day promised to be a long and exhausting one. The Soviet, for thus they chose to call themselves for the nonce, had to interview, after all, some sixty-seven noncommissioned and enlisted candidates, today, and more in a different camp, on the morrow. These had been chosen by the commandant of the camp, working with one of Brinkmann's underlings.

"Bring in the first one," Kostyshakov ordered. Immediately the German *Unteroffizier* at the door called out, "Dragomirov; report to the Committee."

From left to right, as they faced, the officers of the board consisted of Lieutenant Boris Baluyev, sporting a remarkably fierce moustache, Lieutenant Georgy Lesh, Captain Mikhail Basanets, Captain Daniil Kostyshakov, Captain Ivan Dratvin, Captain Pyotr Cherimisov, and Lieutenant Vilho Collan, a monarchist Finn, and thoroughly pale and blond as Finns are wont to be. Each man wore a clean Russian uniform with no rank insignia and no indicator of regiment, though all but the Finnish officer had come from the Guards. Only one had been known to Kostyshakov from his own regiment: Basanets. But Basanets had known Collan and Dratvin, Collan had known and vouched for Cherimisov, while Dratvin stood for Baluyev and Lesh. After personal interviews with Daniil, they'd been accepted, "with reservations."

To the right of the Finn were one sergeant and two *Zauryad-Praporshchiki*, those being Sergeants Major Nenonen, another Finn, much taller than Collan but otherwise much alike, and Sergeant Major Pavel Blagov, who was missing a piece of his right ear, plus *Podpraporshchik* Mayevsky, wearing a piratical eyepatch. To the left of Lieutenant Baluyev sat *Podpraporshchik* Gorbachyov, as well as Sergeants Berens and Kaledin. The latter was a Don Cossack, dark of hair and eye, answering to "Filip," and the only Cossack present on the board.

None of them wore any rank. They all looked terribly serious, too, enough so to make Dragomirov pause and stutter in his reporting. And then there were the slogans on the banners hung on the walls. Dragomirov almost missed that there was a chair awaiting him.

Well, what the fuck do I care about the tsar, after all? Dragomirov asked himself. *If it gets me out of here, I'll kiss Lenin's figurative ass.*

The interviewee saluted more or less properly, which the others ignored, announcing, "*Mladshy unter-ofitser* Dragomirov, reporting as ordered." *Mladshy unter-ofitser* was a rank somewhere in the range of corporal or junior sergeant.

Kostyshakov said, "Saluting is a relic of the oppressive past, Comrade. We don't indulge in it." He then ordered Dragomirov to take the chair to his own right.

"Tell us, Comrade," Daniil began, "How do you feel about the glorious workers', soldiers', and peasants' revolution now underway in the Motherland?"

"I'm all for it, Comrade," Dragomirov answered. "Down with the blood-sucking tsar and all his evil brood."

Kostyshakov pursed his lips and gave a serious and approving nod. Then he turned his head to his left, asking, "Comrade Basanets?"

Captain Mikhail Mikhailovich Basanets, easily the tallest man on the board, with dirty-blond hair and bright blue eyes, said, "Who was the greatest enemy of the people in your village, Comrade?"

That was a toughie for Dragomirov, since it was *his* family that owned most of the land and most exploited the peasants. But, needs must and all.

"My father, the swine. He squeezes the peasants like they were sponges!"

Basanets twisted his head to the left even as he nodded in approval. "Very good, Comrade. I have no other questions, Commissar Kostyshakov."

Daniil looked to his right, inviting Captain Ivan Mikhailovich Dratvin to speak.

"Tell me, Comrade," asked Dratvin, short, and dark, and built like a fireplug, "who here in the camp is most likely to support the revolution, and who remains a puppet of the tsar? Think hard, now, for this is important."

After Dragomirov had given a dozen names of people he considered reliable to the revolution, and a couple who he claimed were "Tsarist hyenas," Kostyshakov let two more of the board question him, which questioning went to his military record. Then he said, "I think we've all heard enough," and asked for a consensus. Everyone on the board gave a literal thumbs up.

"Very good, Comrade Dragomirov," Kostyshakov said. "It will be some time before all is in readiness—peace is being negotiated between the Germans and ourselves, even as we speak—so keep your health, don't try to escape and risk being killed, and wait for the call to come to the defense of the revolution. Why, in a gesture of internationalist good spirits, the Germans are even segregating the Tsarists, the better to keep them from hindering the revolution."

Pointing to the door on the left, Kostyshakov said, "Please go through that door and wait until our business is finished here. Don't wander; there is a German guard and, to me, he looked a little trigger happy."

After Dragomirov had left, Kostyshakov called for the next interviewee. The German at the door bellowed out, "Mokrenko? Rostislav Alexandrovich Mokrenko, report! *Podkhorunzhy* Rostislav Alexandrovich Mokrenko, report!"

Mokrenko entered, then stopped short as he took in the red walls and redder slogans. Drawing himself to his full height of five feet, eleven inches, Mokrenko cast a disgusted eye in the direction of Kaledin and spat, then demanded, "What is this shit?" he asked. "I'll have nothing to do with it!"

Kostyshakov pointed to the other door and said, "Get out, then, Tsarist swine, and wait."

"He *was* one of the ones mentioned by Dragomirov as being an incorrigible Tsarist," said Sergeant Berens, after the door had slammed behind Mokrenko. Berens was the one who had been detailed to act as secretary.

"I wish they would all be as easy as these two but, of course, they won't."

"I know Mokrenko," said Kaledin, wearing the good-natured grin that rarely left his face. "Good man. I can hardly wait until we tell him the truth."

"He looks rather thin," said Basanets, himself half emaciated.

"We'll put some meat on their bones with a better diet and some exercise," Kostyshakov answered.

Corporal Vasenkov, young, slender, and prematurely balding, was by no means an idiot. He knew one of the officers of the supposed Soviet, Captain Cherimisov, and knew beyond a shadow of a doubt that there was no possible universe in which the captain could ever be anything but a fanatical Tsarist.

As he walked to report to the "Soviet," Vasenkov also thought, *And Cherimisov is also not sneaky enough to infiltrate anything like this supposed "soviet." That means this is all bullshit; they're looking only to separate out revolutionaries from reactionaries. So where would a good communist like myself belong? In with the reactionaries, to sabotage them. Therefore:*

"Corporal Vasenkov reports, Sir. But save your breath; I want nothing to do with you stinking communist scum."

It was a weary group of Russians, Cossacks, and Finns who finally repaired themselves to the quarters the Germans had set aside for them. Of the sixty-seven interviews they'd conducted they'd had to reject forty-six. The twenty-one they'd accepted—Mokrenko plus all those sent after him through the door on the right—had identified between them another forty-one reliable enlisted men, and all of those were, even now, on their way to a tented holding camp before being moved, en masse, to their penultimate destination, a camp—code named "Budapest"—being put together in the hills about seven miles west-northwest of Jambol, Bulgaria.

And, thought Kostyshakov, with something analogous to weary despair, *we've still got to hit the camps at Doeberitz, Skalmierschustz, Stalkovo, Hammerstein, Muenster, Tuchel, Koenigstein, and Czersk. There's no way to do this with one board. I'm going to have to split the board into three and trust Basanets, Cherimisov, and Dratvin. They can hit three each over the next four or five days. But I've got to get to Camp Budapest and come up with a table of organization and a doctrine. I can only hope that my quartermaster and his German escort are taking everything that isn't nailed down.*

Railroad, between Ingolstadt and Munich

In a happier time, in a higher-class carriage, it would have been called "The Orient Express." As it was, it was just another second-class carriage on overworked rail lines. Brinkmann, having left Kostyshakov's rat-faced quartermaster, Romeyko, in the care of an experienced *Feldwebel* of supply, along with half a dozen armed guards and a corporal to oversee them, was travelling with Kostyshakov to Camp Budapest. It was about a sixty-hour journey, normally, but closer to seventy-two or even ninety-six, now, what with the exigencies of war. The steady clacking of the wheels might have put either man to sleep, but they had both resisted that siren's call, so far.

Kostyshakov noticed that Brinkmann had a cane trapped between one leg and the wall of the carriage they rode in. He considered asking about it, but some people were sensitive to reminders that they'd lost something with their wounds, so Daniil decided to let it be.

While fighting off that call to sleep, Daniil still closed his eyes, tightly, picturing a group of soldiers bursting in with single shot, bolt action rifles, bayonets fixed, having their one shot at something—*Ah, but it's probably too dark even to tell*—and then going forward with cold steel, even while the enemy shot down their prisoners whom they knew the positions of better than did the rescuers.

All right, we need a way to both temporarily blind the guards, while not blinding ourselves, then a way to light up the scene for ourselves, after they're blinded.

"It's never been done before, you know," Brinkmann said to Kostyshakov. "Everyone by now knows how to go into a tight space and kill everything that moves, but I can't recall any serious instance where anyone went into a tight space and tried to avoid killing the bulk of the people that were in there, unarmed, while killing a few of those who were armed."

"I know," Daniil agreed, looking up from a notepad on which he'd been scribbling intermittently but furiously. "And I'm trying to puzzle through it from the perspective of organization, doctrine, training to execute the doctrine, weapons, communications . . .

"And I don't really know what I'm doing, just as you suggest.

"I don't even know how I'm getting there."

"All will be made clear soon," Brinkmann assured him. "Why don't you tell me what you've got? I may be of use."

Kostyshakov agreed, "Indeed, why not?"

With a sigh, he began to lay out what he'd figured out of the problem, so far. "In the first place, while they could be on a boat, or a train, or a tent, or in a series of caves, the odds are overwhelming that, when we find them, they will be in a guarded building."

The German nodded sagely. "Correct, so far, I think. A guarded building—or maybe a compound—would be the way I would bet it."

Daniil continued, "Okay . . . good . . . the building, it will be either lit or it will be dark. If at all possible, we'd probably prefer it to be dark, or, at least, we would if we could see and the guards could not.

"I think I have a way to do that. We can use photographer's flash powder and replace most of the explosive in hand grenades with it. Might even want to use our army's tear gas grenades, as being better for dispensing powder. We'll know the grenades are going to go off—at least after it's announced, we will—and can shield our eyes. That however . . ."

"Still leaves the problem," Brinkmann said, "of how you see to shoot after the flash is gone. Even if you've flash-blinded their eyes, you are just as blind as they are. I may have a way."

"Really?"

"Yes. We make a kind of electric torch—it's a flattened cylinder with a dynamo in it—that you wear on your chest. It has a ring on a chain that you pull and get, oh, maybe five seconds of fair directional light. Five seconds in combat is a long time."

"Can we . . . ?"

"I'll wire my *Feldwebel* escorting your Captain Romeyko to lay in a supply. But how many do you need?"

Kostyshakov considered a number, cut that in half, and then cut it in half again and yet again. "Sixty? Eighty? I wouldn't refuse two or three times that number."

"Sixty should be possible," Brinkmann agreed. "Maybe more but with the war on . . ."

"And the grenades and flash powder?"

Brinkmann waved his hand dismissively. "Oh, those are *easy*."

"Wonderful. But then we have the problem of getting through doors. Some, of course, can be broken down by main effort, but some are going to be stout enough that a steel lock is weaker."

"I cannot help you there," the German replied. "I have no idea how to do it myself. Explosives?"

Daniil frowned, then said, "Would be fine except for the possibility of the odd tsar, grand duchess, or crown prince on the other side." He didn't mention the tsarina because in both his opinion and the opinion of most Russians, putting her on the other side of an explosion could only be to the good. *Okay, that was both unkind and unfair. Based on what I saw of her at the hospital, she's mostly just out of place and shy.*

"I can see that," agreed Brinkmann. "And even if you had trained lockpicks, it would be very slow."

"Too slow. And then we have the problem," Kostyshakov

continued, "of needing more and handier firepower in very close quarters."

"Shotguns to simply blow locks apart and . . . well, I make no promise that I can get any, let alone many, but we have a new machine gun . . . a machine pistol, really . . . that's very nice. It's *not* light, mind you, and the range is quite limited, but it is handy and is excellent for taking someone down in a hurry at close range."

"Limited range, for our purposes, would be fine," Kostyshakov said.

"I'll tell my man escorting Captain Romeyko about those then, too; that, and to order some."

"There's one other thing," Kostyshakov asked, "Do we know for a certainty where the royal family is being held?"

"They were moved," Brinkmann said, "from Tsarskoe Selo to possibly Tobolsk, arriving sometime in August of last year. The last we've heard, they're still there. But we have also heard of other Romanovs being held in Yekaterinburg. It is possible that they've been moved. It is possible they will be moved.

"Have you thought about organization?" Brinkmann asked.

"Yes," Kostyshakov nodded, "at least tentatively. Wherever they are, there's going to have to be a super elite force to go in and rescue them. I am thinking somewhere between seventy and ninety men. Wherever that is, the odds are good there will be a substantial guard force or relief force nearby. For that I am thinking two companies, but heavily reinforced with all the firepower we can come up with. Any force needs an organization for support, both combat and more mundane matters like medical, mess, and transport."

"Can you do all that with the limits General Hoffmann set you?"

"I think so. I *hope* so, anyway."

Citadel, Warsaw, Poland

Somewhat unsurprisingly, Warsaw's central location not only meant it was a key rail center, it also meant it was the location for one of the German Army's salvage companies,[1] of which there were thirty-nine, that took enemy equipment, secured it, repaired it, organized it, and re-issued it when called to do so.

Those supplies and equipment could be anything from medical supplies to mess kits, artillery to rifles and machine guns, uniforms to *Gulaschkanonen*, to whatever the mind can imagine an army using. Some of it could even be one's own equipment, captured by an enemy and then recaptured by one's own forces. The Germans, being both tidy by nature and also having to fight most of the civilized world on a relative shoestring, were more thorough about combing a battlefield for *Beute*, loot, than most.

This particular dump was staggeringly large.

---

[1] We're guessing here. There were, in fact, thirty-nine salvage companies that operated along the main lines of communication of the German Army, east and west. Where they were at any given time is a mystery. Warsaw seems a likely spot for some kind of huge dump of captured materiel, following the Gorlice-Tarnow Offensive in 1915. Nor is it likely that the Polish Legion would have used any of the Russian uniforms; theirs seem to have been closely based on German, with the addition of red piping to the collars and pockets, for example.

"Rifles, seven hundred," said Captain Romeyko, Kostyshakov's ugly quartermaster. He was accompanied by a tall German noncom, *Feldwebel* Weber, dark blond, mustached, and slightly stooped.

"What kind?" asked the supply clerk through Weber. "We've got thousands of standard rifles, plus some of our own sniper rifles, plus a modest number of shorter carbines in your caliber."

"Four sniper," Romeyko replied. "Are those Model 1907s over there? Yes? I'll take twenty. Can we have those over and above the seven hundred? I'd hate to run short, you know?"

"No problem," Weber said.

"Water-cooled machine guns, six. Uniforms, large, three hundred and eighty. Also four hundred and eighty, each, uniforms medium and small. Rank insignia; I'll write down a list. One thousand, four hundred blankets. Packs and load carrying equipment, ammo pouches and canteens, seven hundred sets. Hats, oh, seventy-five each of every size, up to nine hundred. Gloves, same. Boots . . . boots are harder to guess at . . . let's say, one hundred and eighty pair each, from sizes thirty-eight through forty-two. Woolen footwraps . . . one thousand, four hundred pair."

The *Feldwebel* translated, got an answer from the clerk behind the counter, laughed, and conveyed the answer to Romeyko.

"'Rifles are easy,' he says, though he may have to send to the depot at Kuestrin for that many. Machine guns have been mostly taken already; he has four of your own Model 1910. Ammunition is plentiful, too. The uniforms and hats are easy. Insignia and field gear are easy. He says you can have a hundred times that many if you want them. But German soldiers like your boots for the winter, and your gloves as well. Same for your blankets. Also, we use the same general kind of footwraps, when we can't get socks."

"But *Feldwebel* Weber..."

"Don't worry, sir," said Weber. "We can get all those from German stocks. May not be what you want. May not be the highest quality, not what you might have expected of us three or four years ago, but they'll do."

The clerk at the counter said something else which definitely piqued Weber's attention. The *Feldwebel* said something to the clerk, which sent the latter scampering off into one of the back bins.

He came back bearing something that nearly made Romeyko's beady eyes water.

"A Lewis gun? Here? My God..."

"He tells me," said Weber, "that he's got twenty-seven of them. He thinks they all work. But they're in your caliber and not worth converting to ours, while supplying your ammunition to them would be such a confusing pain that nobody wants them. With as many magazines as... no, 'four hundred and eighty-one magazines,' he says."

"If I can have them, I'll take them all. And, shall we say, two million rounds of ammunition."

"He says the ammo is no problem, either," Weber said, "though he doesn't have that much here. Three or four million rounds if you want it. But we might have a problem shipping it."

"How about two thousand hand grenades? And, yes, four million rounds would be very nice."

"He says he has that some of your kind of grenade, but if you want our kind . . ."

"Both? Both would be good. As many of both?"

"We can get ours, yes."

"Cots? Mattresses?"

Weber asked. "No," he translated, "but I am sure we can find some straw ticks, lumber, and nails."

"Well . . . at least the tents should be set up by then," said Romeyko. "Pistols?"

Weber checked. "Yes, he has a great many of your pistols. 'All you could possibly want,' he says. But he adds, 'But why would you want them?' "

"Because it's on my list," Romeyko replied. "Strikes me as a pretty good reason."

"No reason is good enough to saddle your men with Nagant 1895s," Weber countered. "Let me check something."

A fairly lengthy bout of German followed, which Romeyko could not follow. When it was done, the *Feldwebel* said to the Russian, "He's got a fairly esoteric collection of pistols, ranging from the Nagant, to some almost fifty-year-old American Smith and Wesson single action revolvers, to some Lugers captured from us and then recaptured by us, to a couple of dozen Mauser C96s, unfortunately not in nine millimeter, to . . . well, the most interesting are the American ones, the newer kind. In eleven and a half millimeter? Real manstoppers."

Romeyko interrupted, "How many of the Amerikanski ones does he have?"

"A hundred and forty-seven," the German answered. "Ammunition can be gotten for them, too. They're still here, he says, because, again, the ammunition is non-standard now."

"How about a round hundred and twenty of those? With maybe five hundred rounds each? A thousand would be better."

"He says he can do that . . . and that you might as well take all the ammunition he has, about eighty thousand rounds."

"Great! Compasses?"

"Would those wrist-mounted jobbies work?"

"Adrianovs? Splendidly."

"He says he has about fifty of those."

Interlude

Tatiana: Cutting Firewood

Colonel Kobylinsky's kindness manifested in the strangest of ways. Papa had been increasingly anxious, being locked up in the house, while having nothing to do. Alexei was well, too, and whenever he could manage it he took advantage of doing as much as he could.

He did this despite knowing that a slip, a fall, a cut, would result in weeks of pain. Mama and Papa not only allowed it, but encouraged it, because they knew he could not live his life otherwise. But I feared that their decision to give Alexei this freedom had come too late because here in Tobolsk, there were fewer opportunities for him to do all the boyish things he'd not been allowed to do all his life.

That's why, when beech trunks arrived, Papa asked for saws and axes to cut the wood down to size and Colonel Kobylinsky agreed.

I pulled on my coat, hat, and gloves, and followed them into the side yard, eager for some fresh air and sunshine.

Flexing muscles that had once been too weak to lift him off his pillow, Alexei worked the saws and axes with Papa, cutting the trunks down to size for use in the kitchen and the stoves. Even with four of us girls huddled together, our bedroom was an ice-house.

The scent of sawdust mixed in with the crisp, cold air. As the pieces fell off the sawhorse I picked them up and stacked them and kept thinking how nice it would be to have the rooms warm once again.

Papa and Alexei's cheeks were red from the cold and the effort, but they both had smiles on their faces.

Back and forth the saw went, singing its way into the wood, accompanied by labored breaths. Joy, our little liver-colored spaniel, ran about sniffing and barking. Her long, silky ears almost touched the ground as her nose worked.

Meanwhile, Ortipo, our French bulldog, was running back and forth, playing fetch with a couple of the guards. They had found an old lawn tennis ball—a ratty thing with a wool cloth covering the rubber—and used it to entice Ortipo into playing.

He was such a mischievous little thing, with his too-big ears that stood up atop his head like antennae, that one could not help but love him.

The soldiers would fake throwing the ball and he'd scold them, stocky body jumping up and down like he had springs in those little legs. The soldiers would laugh, then throw the ball, and Ortipo would be off like a shot.

He'd pick up the ball, strut it back, and exchange it for a pat on the head and then wait expectantly, tiny little tail vibrating with anticipation, until it was thrown again.

As Papa placed a fresh log on the saw horse, Alexei wiped his nose and said, "I miss Vanka."

Of all of us, I knew that Alexei missed Vanka—his donkey—the most. The former circus donkey loved pulling the sledge and doing tricks. He was also an expert pickpocket. No matter how hard anyone tried to hide treats, Vanka would figure out how to get them out, usually to much giggling and wonder.

Back at Tsarskoe Selo the soldiers had first shot Alexei's pet goat. Then the deer and swans. That's why I dared not think of what had happened to our pets. We dared not ask. Instead, we locked the memory of them in our hearts, for that's all we could do.

That's all that was left to us. And enjoying the ones that were still with us.

I noticed an oddity among the soldiers who guard us. Mama and Papa seemed completely oblivious to it, but Olga and I, the "big pair," have always been too close for me to have missed it. There's a new soldier among our guards—I didn't quite catch the name, Dostov-something or other—and my dear sister, Olga, is decidedly *interested*. Indeed, watching them dance around each other, it was all I could do not to laugh, they're *both* so obviously *interested*.

I can understand it, I think. He may be from a peasant background, and I'm not even sure he's literate, or much so. He's a big one, too, this Dostov-person, from his height to his corded muscles to the gleam of latent ferocity in his eyes. There's still no doubt; looking at him you know that *here* is a *man*, one who can protect what is his. And, God knows, we all need a protector now, and Olga more than the rest of us.

Chapter Four

Governor's House, Tobolsk, Russia

Tobolsk, Russia

Chekov's old rank meant nothing now. As newer men in the First Rifles, Chekov and Dostovalov drew night guard shifts first, so Chekov woke early in the evening of his sixth day at Tobolsk, swung his legs off the wooden board that served as his bed and stood, stretching with a mighty groan. His back creaked as much as the wood planks beneath his feet. The barracks room was quiet, a handful of other night-shift soldiers comatose among the rows of wooden bunks. The rest of the night shift was probably still in town getting drunk and making mayhem. He saw Dostovalov's bunk empty—easily distinguished by the fact that it was the only one properly made.

Must have woken early. Hopefully I can catch up to him in the canteen.

Chekov pulled his pants on quickly then jammed his arms through his shirt sleeves and started buttoning up. His big friend had been making cow eyes at the oldest Romanov girl, Olga, the one with the lovely round face, ever since they'd first seen one another in the hallway. The girl had a melancholic air to her when she spoke but always seemed to brighten around Dostovalov, and she took frequent occasions to step outside for chats with him. Chekov had forged a wordless alliance with the second Romanov daughter, Tatiana, to keep an eye on the deposed grand duchess and impulsive veteran soldier. Still, he didn't want to leave Dostovalov alone in the mansion for long; the man was really quite good at talking young women into very bad ideas.

On that dark thought, Chekov jerked close the knot on his bootlaces, slung his rifle over his shoulder, then pushed through the barracks door. He marched rapidly to the canteen. It was a short walk. The door of the canteen creaked open to reveal a couple of dozen brown-uniformed guards already at the dinner meal. The room was dominated by three long picnic tables with a griddle and pot against the far wall.

A bar of soap sat, seemingly untouched, at a sink near the entryway. Chekov frowned as he turned on the faucet and began to rigorously wash his hands, as had been his custom ever since he was a small boy under the watchful eye of his father, a surgeon. The water was pleasantly cool and Chekov kept his hands under the spray for half a minute. Having completed his exorcism of microbes,

Chekov twisted the knobs on the faucet to full off, waved his hands dry as there was no towel, and proceeded to the buffet line to retrieve his food.

A chubby, disinterested looking cook piled eggs and *kolbasa* on his plate and there was a pot of thick black tea next to the griddle from which Chekov poured a mug. Settling down at the far end of one of the tables, Chekov started to inhale his meal as rapidly as safety and a modicum of manners permitted. The manners were not for his fellows, most of whom ate like pigs, but simply more ingrained habits of childhood.

"Hey, Chekov."

A rough voice drew Chekov's eyes up from his meal. A tall, broad man, as big as Dostovalov, approached. His brown-yellow eyes held none of Dostovalov's warmth though as he sat down, uninvited, across from Chekov. The man had black hair with a pronounced widow's peak over his hatchet nose, and crooked, yellowed teeth were visible in the middle of his bristly black beard. Chekov had seen the man around, he was with another company in the First Rifles, but they hadn't been introduced.

"Yes, how can I help you, Comrade . . . ?" Chekov kept his voice level.

"Yermilov," he said. "Washed your hands like you were getting ready to take tea with the tsar over there. Thought you were a hardened war hero, not some bourgeois fop."

Hygiene is counterrevolutionary now?

"All the war heroes are dead," Chekov said, in between bites. "I'm a survivor, and I have the habits of a survivor."

"Oh, daintily washing your hands is what survivors do?" Yermilov said.

"Indeed," Chekov said, he set his fork down and gave Yermilov a steady, unimpressed look. "I lost boys to German shells, bullets, mines, gas, but unlike other units, none of my men died shitting their brains out. Know why? Because we washed our fucking hands as best we could before we ate."

"That why the Imperialists gave you their shiny medals? Your table manners?" Yermilov said.

Chekov snorted and picked up his fork again.

"Leading men in war isn't just about the shooting and screaming," Chekov said. "It's about the little shit you do in between to keep the men alive and able to fight. Then again, I expect you wouldn't know anything about that, would you, Yermilov?"

The big man's nostrils flared and color tinged his cheeks.

"That's right, I was never cannon fodder in the tsar's useless war," Yermilov said. "From what I hear, though, all the 'little shit' didn't actually keep your men alive after all, did it?"

Chekov's hand clenched painfully on the handle of his dinner knife. For a second, Chekov imagined Yermilov grasping at its hilt with sticky, red-coated fingers as he died, yellow-brown eyes wide, gasping for air around the dull blade planted in his throat. He was sorely tempted to make the image a reality.

The conversation around them stopped, a couple dozen brown-uniformed men stared, waiting to see how the new man would react. Forcing a deep breath in through his nostrils, Chekov banished the gratifying vision of murder and calmly sawed off another piece of *kolbasa*.

"So it would seem," Chekov said. "Do you have a point, Comrade Yermilov?"

Chekov maintained his level, unfazed stare as he chewed another bite of sausage and egg.

"Just this, Chekov," Yermilov said. "Don't think you're better than the rest of us because you managed to kiss enough ass to get both the tsar's flunkies and the Provisional Government to think you're some big hero."

"Right," Chekov nodded. "Well, I don't know that I'm better than any of these lads," Chekov gestured with his chin to encompass the room, "And I'm definitely not better than anyone because I'm a war hero. But I'm better than you, you personally, Yermilov, because you're a pathetic *mudak* with a chip on his shoulder and you waste better men's time with your bullshit because you *know* that's what you are."

Yermilov put a boot on the bench, making to leap across the table, but Chekov's reflexes were viper-quick. As far as his nervous system was concerned, he was still on the front, ready to kill Germans. Chekov's left hand shot out and grabbed a healthy clump of Yermilov's coarse black hair. Using the man's own inertia against him, Chekov slammed his head down into the table with a mighty *crack*.

When his head came back up, blood poured from Yermilov's over-prominent nose, while his eyes were unfocused. Chekov, hand still entwined in Yermilov's hair, pulled his opponent off balance and forward, then twisted, so he sprawled across the table on his back, sending Chekov's dinner flying across the floor. He pressed his dinner knife, point first, into Yermilov's throat hard enough to draw a bead of blood. Looking up he saw three men closing in from another table.

"That's far enough," Chekov said, his voice eerily calm. He twisted the dinner knife just a little so the bead became a trickling line. Yermilov's three would-be rescuers stopped. Chekov took a good look, memorizing their faces. Then he looked down into Yermilov's piss-shit eyes, which were now wide with fear.

"I want you all to hear this," Chekov said, looking up again, voice echoing throughout the now silent mess hall. "I'm not a hero. I'm not the tsar, or the Party, or the father who knew the postman was humping your mothers. I'm just a man who has seen too much shit and wants to be left alone. Tell your friends.

"Wanna prove your manhood? Take it to the whores down at the brothel. They'll at least pretend to be impressed for a couple more rubles or a dozen eggs. Wave it at me and I'll chop it off and feed it to you."

Chekov looked down at Yermilov.

"And as for you, Yermilov," he said in a lower voice. "I'm not interested in boxing with you. You give me any more shit, I'll slaughter you and your friends over there like pigs. Understand?"

Yermilov's jaw worked silently for a second, but he didn't have enough fight in him to mouth off to a man with a knife at his throat.

"*Da*," he said.

Chekov applied a fraction of an ounce of pressure to the blade, just to see Yermilov's eyes widen in terror again. Point sufficiently made, he withdrew the knife and released the man's hair, then shoved him from the table to the floor. Setting the knife back on the table, Chekov retrieved his rifle and slung it. Without another glance at Yermilov or his friends, but with his right hand clenched on the contraband pistol in his jacket pocket, Chekov walked with an intentionally casual gait, first to clean the tip of the knife and then back to the food line.

"I'm sorry," he said mildly to the cook. "There was an accident and my food spilled. Could I get another plate?"

"Anything you want, Comrade," the chubby cook said, hastily ladling out another helping of *kasha*, some *kolbasa*, another slab of bread, a dollop of butter, and some *salo*.

His appetite was gone, chased away by the adrenaline dump, but Chekov knew he would be hungry later if he didn't eat now. So he secured his second plate, returned to his spot at the end of the third table, and resumed eating, more slowly this time. Yermilov, helped by his cronies, made his way out of the canteen. All their eyes were firmly fixed on the floor as they went.

The previous guard shift was already off duty by the time Chekov reached Freedom House. And, of course, Dostovalov stood at the back entrance, his tall, wide frame dwarfing Olga's slender figure. Dostovalov laughed at something the girl was saying and the smile on Olga's face would've lit up Petrograd. Chekov picked up the pace, gravel crunching under his boots as he stomped up to the back door.

Well, at least he doesn't have his paws on her.

". . . it's true," Olga said, continuing their conversation as Chekov drew near. "Whenever Alexei was upset with Mama and Papa he used to pack up his toys and 'move' into my room and declare me his mother."

"A handful, your little brother," Dostovalov said.

"Yes, but you must understand he's been denied so much because of his condition," Olga said, earnestly.

"Indeed," Chekov said, slicing coldly through their conversation. "A terrible condition. A peasant boy with hemophilia would almost certainly have died by now."

Olga's pretty face fell, Dostovalov's darkened.

"That was unkind, Sergei Arkadyevich," Dostovalov rumbled.

Chekov sighed.

He's right, it's wrong to flog a young girl with things that aren't remotely her fault just because of her parents.

"It *was* unkind," Chekov said, kicking the toe of his boot against the Freedom House's stone steps. "I apologize, miss."

Dostovalov glared at Chekov, clearly wanting him to offer a more elaborate apology, but Olga seemed mollified.

"It's quite all right," Olga said. "I know we've lived a relatively comfortable life; at least up until now. It's thoughtless of me to complain when so many have suffered as much or worse."

Oh, sure, make me feel like more of an ass by being gracious.

"Not in the least," Dostovalov said, quickly. "Right, Sergei?"

"Quite right, indeed," Chekov said with a small nod. "Your family has quite enough to be getting on with."

Olga smiled again, though not without a hint of reserve.

"Anyway, Tatiana will be done helping Mama settle in for the night soon," Olga said, with a regretful look at

Dostovalov. "I should probably go back inside so she doesn't fret when she gets back to our room."

"Good night, Olga Nikolaevna," Dostovalov said.

Olga smiled demurely.

"Good night . . . *Antosenka*. I'll see you tomorrow."

Chekov waited until the door shut behind the girl before he rounded on his friend with an incredulous look.

"'*Antosenka*'?" Chekov said. "Since when are you *Antosenka*?"

Dostovalov grinned and shrugged.

"Just because she's the tsar's daughter doesn't mean she can't flirt a little," Dostovalov said. "Not everyone wants to be an ascetic like you."

"Just keep your hands off of her, all right?" Chekov said. "In the current climate fraternizing with the tsar's daughter could get you shot by either side."

"You think the monarchists can pull it together long enough to be the 'other side'?" Dostovalov said.

"I don't know. Maybe," Chekov said. Both men were wise enough not to ask aloud the open question of what side they would be on should a force of Tsarist Loyalists come knocking on the Tobolsk Governor's Mansion's front gate. "General Dutov and his Cossacks keep making noise."

Besides, we both know we're on the side least likely to get us killed—whichever that ends up being.

"In the meantime we've got plenty of problems already," Chekov said. "No trying to sleep with the tsar's daughter."

Chekov related to his friend Yermilov's challenge, his own answer to it. Dostovalov chuckled and shook his head once Chekov was done speaking.

"What's so funny?" Chekov said, rubbing his hands together for warmth.

"You are," Dostovalov said. "You're mad at me for flirting when you nearly murdered another soldier twenty minutes ago. Yes, word travels that fast around here. My friend, I don't know how you form your priorities, but you may need to reexamine what worries you and what doesn't."

"No one is going to shoot me for beating up a bully in the mess," Chekov said.

"Except maybe the bully and his friends," Dostovalov said. "New order, new rules; sometimes it seems like no rules."

"Only one rule," Chekov said. "It's just us, Anton. We gotta live. If others want to help, great, and we'll help them if we can, but at the end of the day it's you and me."

Dostovalov's cheerful face grew somber as he considered Chekov's words; after a moment he nodded.

"*Da*, you and me, Comrade."

Every third night they were off and, since their sleep cycle was well and truly screwed in any event, Chekov and Dostovalov usually stayed out late enjoying the limited pleasures of Tobolsk. As soldiers in the employ of the Provisional Government, they were able to get food and liquor in exchange for their paper currency without having to barter.

Their fourth night off, they had dinner in a small restaurant, really a couple of block tables in the parlor of the butcher's house. Rationing precluded the existence of normal restaurants. The cozy wood-floored room was sparsely furnished and lit by two flickering oil lamps. The food was good. God alone knew where the butcher was getting the meat and produce to make decent meals.

As far as Tobolsk's night life went, Chekov thought the butcher's little eatery about the best option available. Every other place was crammed with Red Guards or recently discharged soldiers or prison guards from the local penitentiary, all throwing their weight around, waiting for an excuse to brawl.

There were a couple of local brothels, but Chekov didn't have much interest. He wasn't, despite his friend's jests, saving himself for marriage. He'd paid a whore for her services once but found the process awkward and sad and had a hard time even finishing. It had contented him from that point forward to handle pent-up sexual frustration himself, in private.

Chekov noticed, though, that Dostovalov appeared to have lost his usually healthy appetite for whoring. His big friend only snorted when Chekov asked him about his apparent lack of interest.

"Have you seen the poor creatures working in the brothel here?" He said, then held up a hand in negation of his own questions. "No, of course you haven't, you're still vying for sainthood. Well, trust me, there's nothing there you want to stick your prick in."

Chekov eyed his friend suspiciously.

"Since when is there *anything* you don't want to stick your prick in?"

Dostovalov shrugged eloquently and continued to shovel thick orange *solyanka* soup into his mouth.

"You're not avoiding the local talent because you're pining over the grand duchess, are you?" Chekov said.

"Well, technically, she's not a grand duchess anymore," Dostovalov said, leaning back in his chair and wiping his mouth with the back of his hand. "But I don't pine for anyone."

"Good to hear," Chekov said before taking another spoonful from his bowl. "We have enough problems."

"Right," Dostovalov said. "What *are* we going to do with this mess?"

Chekov chewed up and swallowed a spoonful of pickle, sausage, and broth, then glanced around the room. The butcher and his wife busied themselves in the kitchen shifting iron pans around their wood-burning stove, well out of earshot. No other patrons filled the tables this late.

"It looks like the civil war is inevitable," Chekov said. "In which case, we don't have a lot of great options. I suppose we could desert."

"Yaroslavl is a long way from here," Dostovalov said. "And my hometown is even farther."

"Right," Chekov said. "They probably check the trains at every stop for deserters and travelling cross country in winter is a good way to freeze to death."

"We could steal horses," Dostovalov said.

"There are no civilian horses around here; they've already been eaten or requisitioned," Chekov said, shaking his head. "Or they're hidden. If we steal army horses, that just gives them more incentive to hunt us down. And let's say we get away, I know you're a rustic outdoorsman but I'm not at all confident about living off the land for more than a week or two, how about you?"

"I was a farmer, Sergei, not a woodsman," Dostovalov said. "There's plenty of wild game, but precious little shelter. Anytime we come into town looking for a place to sleep we'll be in danger of getting pressed into one army or the other."

"Or shot as deserters," Chekov agreed. "We stay here for now, I think. At least we've got food and a warm place to sleep. We can always run later if we have to."

"What about your friends from the mess hall?" Dostovalov said just before finishing off the last of his soup.

"Yermilov and his cronies haven't given me any more shit," Chekov said. "If they do, we can always arrange an accident."

Dostovalov grunted his agreement, leaned back in his chair and held up two fingers to the butcher, indicating he should bring two servings of the local *samogon*, home distilled liquor that was far less legal and far more available than proper vodka. The chubby man hustled over to their table with a jug and two wooden mugs.

"Here you are, Comrades," he said.

The home-distilled hooch gave off a pungent, burning odor as the butcher filled their mugs.

"Phew," Chekov said, rearing back. "Are you selling us the lamp oil, Grandfather?"

"Now, lads," the butcher protested, "This is the best *samogon* you're going to find in Tobolsk!"

Dostovalov grabbed his mug and knocked back a large swig. A grimace contorted his features as his throat worked. He coughed violently and slapped his hand on the table once the liquor was down.

"Jesus, what did you ferment to make this? Your knickers?" Dostovalov said in a husky voice.

Chekov laughed, and the butcher's brow furrowed with offense.

"Relax, Grandfather, just a jest," Dostovalov said after he finished coughing. He laid several more rubles on the table. "In fact, leave the bottle. It'll do just fine."

The butcher snatched up the rubles, appearing mollified, and left them to their drinking.

"It doesn't taste as bad as it smells," Dostovalov said.

"That's a low bar," Chekov said as he brought the mug to his lips and sipped at the liquor. After the fire of grain alcohol subsided, Chekov thought he could detect a bit of the wheat. He exhaled loudly and swallowed.

"Well," he said, choking a bit. "It's not the worst rotgut I've tasted, but it isn't exactly the *pevach* either."

Dostovalov's answer was interrupted by the door to the butcher's house swinging open with a *bang* against the opposite wall. A cold gust caused the flame of the wood burning stove to flicker, and chilled Chekov's skin, despite the warmth of the fire and the liquor in his belly. The three men who entered with the wind chilled him more.

Ensign Matveev led the trio into the dining room. He glared as he stepped inside, eyes glittering over his snow-coated beard. Chekov doubted the head of the Soldiers' Soviet was here looking for hooch and some hot soup. Worse, Yermilov's ugly, snaggletoothed face appeared in the doorway behind Matveev, followed by one of his cohorts from the dust-up in the mess hall. Yermilov grinned maliciously at Chekov as he stepped inside.

"Good evening, Comrade Ensign," Dostovalov said.

Matveev nodded at Dostovalov and Chekov, then turned back to Yermilov.

"All right, Yermilov," he said, deep voice dark with annoyance. "I am here, at one in the god-damned morning. What's the misconduct I'm supposed to witness?"

"Comrade Ensign, take a sniff at their drinks," Yermilov said, pointing like a schoolyard tattletale. "That isn't tea, it's *samogon*. Chekov and Dostovalov are trafficking with *kontrabandisty*."

The butcher sucked in a sharp breath at the accusation of bootlegging. With food critically low across the country, the Bolsheviks had declared it illegal for anyone to distill wheat, or any other foodstuff, into the high-proof liquor. Depending on Matveev's mood, the butcher and his wife could be fined, or they could be executed, Chekov thought furiously.

How the hell did Yermilov know we came here?

"It's not theirs, Comrade Commissar," Chekov blurted.

"It isn't?" Matveev said, raising a thick black eyebrow.

"No, Comrade," Chekov said, shaking his head. "In point of fact, we actually have had that bottle since Pskov."

The butcher exhaled and his posture relaxed fractionally.

"It's true, Comrade Ensign," Dostovalov said. "We picked it up on our way back from the Front and have been waiting for a night off to celebrate. Smell it like Yermilov said and I think you'll agree it's Ukrainian; no Russian would brew such foul cow piss."

Dostovalov held the bottle out to Matveev. The ensign took the bottle and sniffed from the neck. Grimacing, he recoiled from the booze.

"You're right, that smells like a Ukrainian whorehouse

on Monday morning," he said. "Well, lads, you know you're not supposed to be drinking contraband liquor, so I'm afraid I'll have to tell Colonel Kobylinsky to take your next two free nights."

Chekov maintained a firm, deadpan expression. Yermilov's face fell at Matveev's leniency.

"Comrade Ensign," he protested. "This is a serious breach of discipline, surely—"

"Yermilov, if I flogged every man who got into some illicit liquor, I couldn't muster a squad to guard Citizen Romanov," Matveev said. "And if you ever wake me up in the middle of the night for something this frivolous again, I'll have *you* flogged. Get out of my sight."

Chekov did allow himself a small smirk over Matveev's shoulder at Yermilov. The ugly bully and his lackey departed, their shoulders hunched against the freezing winds outside.

Matveev sighed, then turned his attention to the butcher.

"Citizen, I am not a man of mysticism but reason," Matveev said. "Nevertheless, I prophecy that the Tobolsk Soviet will send inspectors tomorrow afternoon to ensure there isn't any hoarding or illegal distilling happening on these premises. I trust they will find nothing, *da?*"

"Of course, Comrade Ensign," said the butcher. "Thank you!"

"No thanks necessary," Matveev said. "It is supposed to be the *people's* revolution, after all," he added in an undertone.

"As for you two," Matveev said. "I'd watch myself if I were you. Personally, I wouldn't piss on Yermilov's face if his nose was on fire, and neither will Kobylinsky, but if he gets those assholes from the Soviet involved, you could find yourself subject to discipline anyway."

Chekov nodded grimly.

"We'll keep that in mind, thank you, Comrade Ensign."

Dostovalov washed as best he could without inducing hypothermia in the freezing barracks bathroom. Fall had brought yet another revolution and a steep decline in temperature. Of the two, Dostovalov was far more concerned with the cold weather in Tobolsk than he was with the Bolsheviks in Moscow.

He parted his hair carefully then dragged a cold razor across his cheeks, chin, jawline, and neck, paring his facial hair down to just his thick, black moustache. Hygiene complete, he dressed in uniform and overcoat rapidly, grabbed his rifle, and hurried out into the frigid night air.

Tonight Chekov was out with some of the other lads, attempting to make some more friends to counterbalance Yermilov and his thugs. Personally, Dostovalov thought they should just proceed with Yermilov's *accident*. Chekov argued, probably correctly, that Yermilov's untimely death occurring so soon after he informed on them would certainly rouse suspicion.

That's why he's the thinker, and I'm the doer, speaking of which—

Dostovalov hopped a waist high picket fence—such a pedestrian barrier to the residence of what used to be the imperial family—and made his way through the snow to the back door of the governor's mansion. Two uniformed men stood, shivering, on either side of the door. Dostovalov raised his right hand in greeting.

"Dostovalov, right on time!" the young man on the right said. This was Virhkov. The other guard, another youngster named Blokhin merely nodded his greeting.

"Virhkov, shhh," Dostovalov said. "Wouldn't want to wake Citizen Romanov or his family, would we?"

"No, I suppose not," Virhkov said. "Thanks again for covering our shift."

"Don't mention it," Dostovalov said, then, acting on impulse, he peeled a few rubles out of his pocket and handed a couple each to Blokhin and Vhirhkov. "In fact, buy a round for the lads on me, eh?"

Their young, unlined faces lit up.

"You're a real pal, thanks," Blokhin said. Virhkov nodded rapidly behind him.

"Off with you, youngsters," Dostovalov said, grinning. "Go have fun."

The two youngsters trudged off through the snow. With the proper guards relieved, Dostovalov settled in for another sort of vigil. He leaned against the wall, a dreamy smile curving his lips. He imagined Olga, lithe of limb and slender of figure, wrapping herself in her thick coat even now, perhaps tiptoeing her way out of the bedroom she shared with her three sisters. Was she as excited to see him as he was to see her?

What has gotten into me? Sergei was right, I am pining.

The back door creaked open and Olga, bundled in a thick black fur coat, stepped out onto the back patio of the mansion. She smiled at him, blue eyes sparkling like sapphires in the moonlight. Dostovalov inhaled deeply.

"Good evening, Olga," he said.

"Good morning, you mean, *Antosenka*," she said, her smile turning impish. "It's almost two, I thought you'd found better company."

Dostovalov chuckled and shook his head.

"I can think of no better company in all the Russias," Dostovalov said.

"I bet you tell all the girls that," Olga said, shivering against the cold night air.

"Perhaps," Dostovalov said. "But I've rarely meant it before."

Olga slapped his arm and laughed merrily.

"'Rarely,'" she quoted. "You *are* an impudent scoundrel. I've known men like you."

"Forgive me, Your Highness," Dostovalov said. "But I don't think you've *known* a man like me in your life."

Olga blushed, but then her face fell.

"Please don't call me that," she said. "They hauled away Bishop Germogen just for praying for my father as 'the Emperor.' I don't want you in trouble."

"It's two in the morning," Dostovalov said. "I doubt there's anyone around to hear us, but I take your point."

"Please do," she said. "Say, do you have a smoke? It's freezing out here and I could use one for my nerves."

Dostovalov obligingly tapped out a cigarette and lit it for her. Olga took a long drag off of it and sighed. Dostovalov nodded in approval; the girl hadn't flinched at the ration-card quality tobacco.

"You're wrong, you know," she said.

Dostovalov's eyebrows shot up, and he tilted his head at her.

"Not about *that*. No, I mean I've been around soldiers—and not just the officers. Tatiana and I worked in a hospital for the wounded. That's where I picked up this habit."

Olga gestured with her cigarette, then took another large puff.

"I know," Dostovalov said. "They made sure we knew about you and the empress tending the wounded."

"It wasn't just photographs for propaganda, you know," Olga said. "We assisted in procedures, helped save some lives, even. And we would sit and talk with the boys while we sewed or knitted blankets. Brave, wonderful boys, most of them. Mother, Tatiana, and I were exhausted all the time, but we were happy. What we did mattered. One of my favorites, Mitya, had a big black mustache like yours. Though of course his manners were so very refined."

Olga softened the last with a gently mocking tone and a smile.

"An officer, I presume?" Dostovalov said, frowning.

"Yes, an officer," Olga said. "Don't be jealous, *Antosenka*. Once he was recovered, he went back to the front. I was very sad when he left. Then the February Revolution, and the October. I don't even know if he's alive still."

Olga was quiet for several seconds, her gaze far off, her expression unfathomable.

"I know the war was terrible," Olga said. "I saw the men maimed by it. But I think what's coming is so much worse. I'm afraid. For my family, yes, but for all Russia as well."

Dostovalov gently grasped Olga's shoulder through the

thick fur and drew her close. She stiffened at his daring, but then relaxed, leaning into him, and accepting the comfort he offered.

"I think they'll let you leave eventually," Dostovalov said. "The communists don't want to anger Britain or the rest of Europe at this point, not while they're so fragile."

"They also don't want the monarchists to have figureheads to rally around," she said. "No, they're not letting us leave Russia alive."

Dostovalov squeezed Olga tighter, her body warm against him even through his coarse uniform and her furs. There, in the bitter cold of the Siberian winter, her fragility was a tangible thing, the fear coiled inside her warring with the nobility and dignity expected of her. Even with the Romanov Dynasty thrown from the halls of power into captivity, Olga and her family carried themselves upright and proud—but not with the idiotic, inbred arrogance he'd seen from so many of his officers in the Army.

Never as politically aware as his friend, Chekov, Dostovalov had simply viewed the nobility and royalty as something that, much like bad weather or pestilence, God meant to be endured. They were inflicted upon the common man to build character in the here and now and make the fruits of the hereafter all the sweeter in comparison. He neither loved nor hated the imperial family as he neither loved nor hated a snowstorm—the existence of both were mere facts of life, no sense staying mad about them. He expected the communists would be no better, and thus was unperturbed that they seemed to be fucking everything up.

The Romanovs as people, though, were nothing like

what he'd expected. The former emperor was unpretentious, quiet, polite, and practically radiated integrity. His love for his children shone in every word and deed, and their adoration of him was just as obvious. After three weeks observing them around Freedom House, Dostovalov allowed himself the uncharacteristically philosophical observation that maybe they'd simply been too good a sort of people to rule Russia effectively. Except perhaps the empress, she seemed like a bit of a reclusive loon, but even she had been polite and cordial in her own clenched-jaw fashion.

And amidst them all, Olga shone brightest to the war-hardened Dostovalov. He admired her tenderness with her ailing little brother, her unabashed affection for her sisters, especially Tatiana, and the way she struggled valiantly against her own melancholy to find the joy in even simple, day to day chores. The tendrils of their shared doom seemed to grasp her more tightly than they did the serious and practical Tatiana, the affable Maria, or the incorrigible Anastasia, but still Olga shone in defiance of her blackest thoughts and feelings.

She was, he thought, *simply magnificent.*

I've enjoyed so many women in my short life, why, oh, God, would You decree I must love a deposed princess?

"Whatever happens," Dostovalov said. "I'll defend you."

"And how many girls have you told that?" Olga said, drawing away enough to search his expression.

"One," Dostovalov said. "I've promised one young woman in my entire life that I would defend her no matter what came."

Olga's eyes widened, and she took a deep breath, then exhaled slowly, creating a small cloud of smoke between them. She shifted, not out of his arms, but to face him. She tilted her head back and closed her eyes, her lips parted invitingly. Dostovalov leaned in and kissed her.

Her arms encircled his neck and she pressed herself into him with abandon. For several glorious seconds, there was no war, no impending catastrophe, even the freezing indifference of Siberia seemed to abate. When their lips parted, Dostovalov took a deep shuddering breath, Olga's eyes shone as she smiled up at him.

"You should come inside, *Antosenka*," she said. "We'll catch our death out here."

"Guards are not supposed to enter the mansion," Dostovalov said.

"Unless invited to do so," Olga said. "I'm inviting you for the reason that you will protect us more ably inside with some hot tea inside you. If anyone asks, of course."

Olga opened the door quietly and pulled Dostovalov along with her into the Freedom House.

Rubbing his hands for warmth, Yermilov grinned crookedly as the back door of the Freedom House swung shut. Two weeks of skulking paid off—the giant oaf really was fucking one of the Romanov girls. The oldest one, the prettiest one. Some of the men talked about the second daughter, Tatiana, but Yermilov had always thought that bitch too skinny, too German-looking with her thin face and cold gray eyes. Olga looked like a Russian girl.

Yermilov had allowed room for little else in his thoughts but revenge on that bastard Chekov for the humiliation he'd inflicted in the canteen. Sadly, after the slip up with the bootlegger, Chekov had proven too clever by half. He did his duties, he ate, he drank, a lot, but never to the point of stupefaction, he slept, he rose and repeated. He and Dostovalov socialized with others from their detachment in the First Rifles, Tsarist bootlickers, the lot of them. The Romanov girls flirted with them like whores, and they curried favor with the former emperor as if he were still in charge of the country. Pathetic.

In any event, Chekov had been too smart to slip up, but his big friend was clearly nowhere near so cautious. Dostovalov was thinking with his cock, and that was going to be the death of them both. And Nikolashka's little whore daughter might get more than she was bargaining for while he was at it.

Interlude

Tatiana: Tobolsk

Monsieur Gilliard and Papa spent the last few days building a snow mountain. They hauled water by bucket. It was so cold that the ice formed in the bucket as they moved it between the tap and the hill.

But it was a welcome distraction and we were all looking forward to tobogganing.

Unfortunately, Monsieur Gilliard fell and twisted his ankle and wasn't able to enjoy the hill he'd helped build.

We girls ended up covered in bruises, all from sliding down the hill, but we didn't care. What were a few bruises to us? We were out in the sunshine, laughing, our hearts beating in our chests, our breaths puffing small clouds in front of our faces. We were alive and, more than that, for a little while we were *living*.

It wasn't long, however, until Siberia's famous winter finally hit us. The crisp, sunny days turned dark and cold. Wind rattled the windows and the rafters, an unwelcome stranger pushing its way in until the glass was thick with ice.

We spent what seemed like endless days inside, wrapped in the thickest knitted cardigans. Despite wearing our felt boots and our heaviest coats, we were cold as we huddled in the corridor to keep warm.

Sometimes Papa read to us, but today it was too dark and his voice was giving out from a cold. We dozed as we sat up against the wall. Mama, sitting in her wheeled chair next to Papa, had her head propped up against his shoulder, her eyes closed, breathing evenly. A warm blanket lay across her lap. Usually she preferred to sew or write, but the cold made her fingers too stiff.

Sleep was beckoning to me too, but a creaking sound pulled me out. Olga was gone.

I pushed up and quietly made my way downstairs and up the long passageway to the kitchen, the only other room that was warm enough.

Olga was sitting at the table, head in her hands. She'd taken off her woolen cap, and her blond hair, still short like all of ours from our bout of measles, lay plastered to her scalp. It seemed duller somehow and I didn't think it was the gray light falling through the shutters' narrow slits.

As I crossed to the table, I stepped on a cockroach. They were everywhere, the filthy things. It was a good thing that Mama didn't come in here often.

I slid into the chair next to Olga and placed my arm around her.

She'd never taken much interest in her looks or been bothered by how she appeared to others, but now I saw something else—a haunted look that didn't come from her ill health. It was the look of someone who, having loved and lost, had resigned herself to that loss.

"Are you all right?" I asked.

She nodded and returned her gaze to her gloved hands.

"Missing Mitya?" I prompted. Dmitry Shakh-Bagov had been Olga's favorite at the hospital where we had worked as Red Cross nurses. A Georgian adjutant in the Life Grenadiers of the Erevan Regiment, he had been the latest in a series of crushes.

Like all the others, he wasn't an appropriate prospect for a grand duchess, no matter how much Olga wanted him. She hadn't mentioned him in months and I thought she'd gotten over him, but as I looked into her eyes I realized two things. The first was that she hadn't, though she may have been in the process of replacing him in her affections. The second was that she was in mourning. For him. For herself. For what it all meant.

I put my arm around her, and drew her closer. It wasn't just the uncertainty that we were facing. It was the realization that things were getting worse and worse. I no longer believed that we would be allowed to peacefully retire to a private life, whether here in Russia or elsewhere. And I could see now that neither did Olga.

"We have to put on brave faces," I whispered into her ear. "For Mama and Papa."

She swallowed and nodded. Tears pooled at the corners of her eyes and the ghost of a smile settled onto her face like the mask that it was.

Did mine look as ill-fitting?

Chapter Five

German Military Locomotive, 1918

Kermen, Bulgaria

The sun was still down and the moon not yet up as the locomotive screeched to a halt in a cloud of steam. From inside the cloud—it and the station illuminated by the electric lights of the station—came the shrill cry of the whistle, the shriek of brakes, and the nails-on-a-blackboard sound of steel tires trying to grip steel rails. The whistle, contrary to many suppositions, was not always to warn pedestrians ahead, but also to tell the other locomotive that a stop was coming, so they could brake as well.

Behind the locomotive rode the tender, a coal and water car to feed the locomotive, while behind it stretched a dozen troop cars, two of what Daniil took to be mess cars, from the smoking funnels atop them, another three troop cars that he supposed were for the German guards, and nine more mixed freight and flatcars, presumably holding the equipment, ammunition, and perhaps some of the food.

Yes, food, he was certain, *based on the sound of mooing cows from near the rear of the train.* Daniil stood up from the large trunk on which he'd been sitting while awaiting the arrival of his new command.

The last three troop cars opened first, with about eighty uniformed and armed Germans emerging.

That's less than they carry and less than Brinkmann told me were on the guard detail. Presumably the others got off on the far side to ensure nobody escapes. He glanced down at the trunk.

Most of the Germans spread out, forming a thin double line of skirmishers, encompassing the entire train station and loading platform, and facing in both directions. A handful of Huns, officers and senior noncoms, proceeded to unlock and push aside the sliding doors, allowing crowds of Russians to emerge, squinting against the light.

So thin they are, the enlisted men, thought Daniil. *Their uniforms barely fit. The Germans must have fed the officers better than the rank and file, it seems, even in Fort IX. How's that going to play out with rations that are less than great even for front line combatants?*

From each carload, one or two officers plus one or two senior noncoms came to Captain Kostyshakov for instructions. Romeyko, having arrived the previous day with an even larger load, was not among them, but was puttering with something else on the platform.

"The camp's about four *versts*[2] northeast of here," Daniil told them. "It's mostly uphill. Job one is to load the equipment and supplies on the wagons. Whatever doesn't fit the wagons goes on our backs.

"Job two is to make sure no one runs. For that . . ."

Daniil turned and opened the trunk, revealing a goodly number of pistols, plenty of spare magazines, holsters, plus several thousand rounds of strangely labeled ammunition.

"Romeyko, when I've finished, issue each company first sergeant and above one pistol, three magazines, and enough ammunition to fill them, plus one round."

"Gentlemen, if someone tries to desert—note I said 'desert,' not 'escape'—it will be on us to shoot them, if necessary. Better that than be seen as being mere stool pigeons for the guards.

"Once you have your arms, take charge of the men and get those wagons filled. They're not marked by company; Romeyko will sort all that out when we get to camp.

"Job three . . . Basanets?" Daniil had to strain his neck to look the tall captain serving as his executive officer in the face.

"Sir?"

"Job three is for you, Mikhail Mikhailovich, to take a detail through every car occupied by our men and make

---

2 A Russian unit of distance close to, but just slightly longer than, a kilometer. Four *versts* would be about two and a half miles, or an hour's easy walk, on flat and level ground, for a man in good shape, bearing a heavy pack.

sure they are completely devoid of any hint of who we are, what we are, where we came from, and where we're going. No graffiti. No notes stuck in cracks. Nothing left behind. And get some of the shit from the cars carrying the cattle and spread it around."

"Yes, sir," Basanets agreed.

"Job four is marching to the camp. I want us to be out of here before sunrise—before the first hint of sunrise—with everyone accounted for and nobody in the town the slightest bit wiser about who we are.

"Questions?"

Seeing there were none, Daniil said, "Go, then. Draw your pistols."

The officers and noncoms saluted, turned about smartly, and began to crowd around Romeyko.

"What *are* these?" Basanets asked. "I've never seen..."

"Amerikanski M1911s," Romeyko answered. "Big bruisers, eleven and a half millimeter. The tsar bought something like fifty thousand of them. Some thousands ended up captured by the Huns. I talked a supply sergeant in their army out of one hundred and twenty, with magazines, plus another two hundred and forty magazines, and holsters and ammunition pouches for the lot. And a lot of ammunition. It didn't take a lot of effort; he was just as happy to be rid of them. They've got slots on the holsters we can fit our belts through.

"You may as well go first, Mikhail. Pick one. Don't forget your magazines and holsters."

Basanets reached down and grabbed as he was told.

"Read off to me the serial number, please?" Romeyko asked.

"C49715."

"Very good, thanks," said Romeyko, jotting the number down in a ledger himself. Ordinarily, this would be a job for a Russian *podpraporschik,* a noncom, or even one of the rank-and-file clerks. As it was, everyone was too busy so Romeyko took weapons issue upon himself. It had, too, the advantage of putting him near the horse drawn wagons to make sure they were fully loaded.

"Next! State your name; take your pistol, your holster, your magazines, and your ammunition. Don't be greedy, twenty-two rounds *only.*"

"Dratvin, Ivan . . . C84386. But I don't even know how to load this thing, let alone use it."

"Right . . . five-minute class after we finish issuing."

The sun was just peeking over the horizon when the column set out. It might have begun to move sooner, but two of the men, thinking they might escape and perhaps get home a bit sooner, attempted to hide above the train's axles and had to be flushed out at bayonet point. These now marched awkwardly, looped rope running from one neck to the other, gagged, with their hands tied behind their backs, stumbling, too, from the rope that kept their feet to no more than a two-foot, eight-inch step. A senior noncom, *Zauryad-Praporshchiki*—or Sergeant Major— Blagov walked behind them with a sharp stick, prodding them to keep up and kicking them when they fell, then lifting them by their hair.

Almost none of them knew just why they were here, where they were going, nor to do just what. Neither had the locked cattle cars they'd been brought in given them any degree of confidence about their individual or collective futures. They didn't even know where they were, not even to the level of what country.

Daniil turned around, walking backwards to watch the column ambling along behind him.

The officers and noncoms we've armed already walk straighter. But the mass of them? They walk like sheep, listless, stupid, unknowing, and uncaring. Of course they do; they're still weak from the camps while a few days' decent—well, half decent—food on the train wasn't enough to restore them.

And they are demoralized, still, Kostyshakov thought. *Can't blame them; they don't really know anything. Probably worried about the future. So . . . in a little bit . . .*

Halfway to camp, when the column was out of sight and out of earshot of the town, Kostyshakov, marching at the front, veered off the frozen dirt road and led the column into a half circle, in open field, just off the road.

When they were halted there, in that half circle, Daniil put up both hands, palms facing himself, and made come hither motions with his fingers, directing the men to break ranks and crowd in around him. The German guards gave each other questioning looks but didn't interfere.

Once the soldiers were clustered around, the nearest perhaps a dozen feet away, Daniil ordered, "Front ranks . . . sit!"

That made it possible for the men to both hear and see him better, as well as for Daniil to see them better. He waited then a few moments more for the two in fetters to make it to the rear of the assembly.

"Guardsmen," he began, "it is time now, now that we're

out of sight from prying eyes and out of hearing for eager ears, to tell you *why;* that, and what's coming over the next few months.

"We are, in the first place, going to a camp that has been set up for us by the Germans, with whom—and I cannot emphasize this enough—we are no longer at war. They're going to be guarding us, still, but that's to keep word of what we're engaged in from getting out.

"It's not a bad place, I understand, that camp; tents, yes, but they have wooden floors, warm liners, and there are stoves for each with an adequate supply of coal. In this camp—it is called 'Camp Budapest,' and no, we are nowhere near Budapest—we reform as a composite Guards battalion. This battalion will eventually consist of two rifle companies, Second and Third, plus the First Company, consisting of the Headquarters and Staff platoon, which will include a small intelligence section, plus all supply and support, plus various heavy weapons. Oh, and a small strategic reconnaissance section. There will also be a short company's worth of replacements. Finally, the smallest company, Grenadier, will be specially armed, equipped, and trained to take the lead in accomplishing our mission.

"No, before you ask, we will be paying zero attention to your previous regimental affiliations. Note, too, that though we are all from elite regiments, and our own battalion is elite, among us Grenadier Company will take a large share of the very best and will have rank to award commensurate with that.

"No, also before you ask, except for the support specialists in First Company, I don't know who will be in which company. We are going to spend about three weeks, possibly four or even as many as five, if we must, identifying a certain type of man for Grenadier Company.

"Grenadier Company will not even form until we have identified the people who will fill it. All of us, until then, will be in First, Second, or Third.

"You will be well fed; much better fed than the poor bastards left behind in the prisoner of war camps. Indeed, as you may have noticed on the train, we are now on the German feeding scale for their own combatant personnel. Yes, I understand the train food may have been a little rough and ready; it was still better than the previous camps'. You will also be paid, and at a better rate than you were getting in camp, too. Some alcohol will be available for purchase, but it will be rationed. We have no room for drunkards."

And my, didn't that *perk them up?*

"Security, however, means no women. No, not even whores."

That got a groan, but it was mostly joking. Nobody really expected field brothels in the Russian army.

"If you can't fuck the calories off," Daniil continued, "you can reasonably expect to burn off all that extra food through training and working. Now . . . questions?"

One man, seated on the ground, raised his hand.

"Yes?"

The man who had raised his hand stood to attention. "Umm . . . beggin' yer pardon, sir, Corporal Panfil, Leonid."

"Yes, Panfil?"

"To do exactly *what*, sir?"

Daniil laughed, lightly. *Nice when you can predict question one so completely.* He raised his voice to carry.

"Hmmm, didn't I tell you all? I guess I didn't. We're going to go save the tsar and his family."

Rostislav Mokrenko, Cossack by birth, cavalryman by trade, and prisoner of war until quite recently, still shook his head ruefully at how completely he'd been suckered by the red walls and redder banners of the interview room at Zittau.

I should have known, he thought, *when I saw Kaledin sitting there that that was no assembly of Reds. He's more of a Tsarist than I am. Hell, he's more of a Tsarist than the tsar is . . . or was.*

Glancing to his right, Mokrenko said to Kaledin, "You dirty bastard; you could have told me sooner."

"Couldn't, Rosti. Couldn't take any risks with anyone spilling their guts. C'mon; you're an old soldier; you *know* that, even without being told."

"I suppose," the other Cossack conceded. "And, what the hell; we get back into action."

Head up, as the heads of the rest were also proudly up now, Mokrenko whistled the first nine notes of the hit song of a few years prior, *"Farewell of Slavianka,"* the notes usually accompanied by, *"Vstan zva Veru, Russkaya Zemlya."* Arise for the faith, O Russian Land.

From where Mokrenko marched, side by side with Kaledin, the tune was picked up and the words added by each marching soldier, many perhaps thinking of his own farewell from his woman, years before:

"The moment of parting has come to us,
    As you look to my eyes with alarm . . ."

✣ ✣ ✣

Marching a dozen ranks back from Mokrenko and Kaledin, Vasenkov thought, *Of course you sing, you reactionary swine. And I'll sing with you, since I must.*

Camp Budapest

The singing hadn't lasted the full distance. Even with a modest pace and no equipment to lug by hand—the wagons had, in fact, proved adequate to the need—the men were worn out by the time they reached the camp's gates.

They passed through the gates, now guarded by German soldiers who, now seen in daylight, looked a bit long in the tooth, between several ranks of tents, and onto a bare parade field, unadorned by anything like a reviewing stand.

I'd like to blame it, thought Daniil, *on not feeding them breakfast at the station, but that's not it. They're just in wretched shape. Speaking of which, I wonder what . . .*

"Basanets?"

"Yes, sir?" the captain asked, from on high.

"Take charge here for a bit. Divide them into their three companies, then turn matters over to Sergeant Major Blagov to see them through the mess and equipment issue. I want to go see what's being served."

"Yes, sir," answered Basanets, accompanying it with a thin sketch of a salute.

The mess was one of the few solid buildings constructed so far, the others being the guards' mess, the officers' mess, the armory *cum* supply office, and the headquarters, plus a few officer's shacks. Most officers, like the ranks, would bed down in tents, on straw. Even the sparse hospital, to be under a civilian MD, Dr. Gazenko, was only five tents separated from the main area and from each other. And one of those tents was to serve as an examination room, while another was for billets for medical personnel.

The messes were not large enough to actually seat anyone; for that there were tents and wooden tables and benches. There might be buildings to eat in, eventually. Even where buildings stood already, though, the wood was cheap stuff, roughly sawn, and crudely assembled.

Just before entering the mess kitchen, Daniil passed by an enormous pile of mess kits and a crate of eating utensils, tied into sets, overseen by one of Romeyko's few clerks. The kits were Russian models: copper. Their general form was like the Germans', kidney shaped when looked at from above, but the dimensions were rather different. Water was steaming in a large kettle slung over a wood fire, for the troops to sterilize them before use. A few crude brushes hung from a rack next to the kettle.

The clerk stood and saluted, which salute Kostyshakov returned, saying, "At ease, soldier. Hand me one of those, would you?"

"Yes, sir." The clerk reached down and grabbed one kit at random. Opening it, Daniil found it was perfectly clean.

"Are they all this clean?" he asked.

"Yes, sir; very thorough people, don't you know, the Germans; that, and sanitary. Well, I suppose they have to be, packed in like they are. But apparently all the battlefield leavings they salvage they also clean and maintain."

"How many do we have of the kits?"

"On the theory that some would be defective—none of them are—Captain Romeyko got seven hundred and fifty. We have a good many extras."

Hmmmm, thought Kostyshakov, *that's a lot of pretty high-quality copper we can trade, if anyone has something to trade for it.*

Daniil passed the mess kit back. "I'll draw mine with the rest of the officers, after the men are fed."

He stopped then to examine the lay of the kitchen. The door was just a space covered by a piece of canvas. The exterior walls were mud-chinked. There was some kind of oiled paper over the windows, impossible to see through but admitting a degree of light. An overhead covering, held up by four-by-fours and extending perhaps twenty-five feet from the door, provided a modicum of shelter for some of the troops. Gravel lay over the dirt, in near enough to the exact dimensions of the overhead shelter.

Of course, that's not about troop comfort; that's about keeping the ground dry—or drier—to reduce dragging mud into the mess.

Stopping at the door and pulling the canvas aside, Daniil felt the wood framing the door. It was overlapping rough-sawn pine with the bark still on. *Some class of wood, at least, is still plentiful. Speaking of which . . .* Daniil walked into the kitchen, hot and steaming after the cold morning air.

Pointing at the grayish brown half loaves on display, Daniil asked of the elderly German noncom responsible for both kitchens, "What's in the bread, *Feldwebel . . . ?*"

He noticed the chief cook wore an Iron Cross, First Class, on his apron. This was not common.

"*Feldwebel* Taenzler, Herr *Oberstleutnant* . . ." the head chef hesitated.

"It can't be worse than what's fed at the prison camps, Taenzler."

"It varies with what's available," the German admitted, "and, yes, better than what's served in the camps, from what I hear." Picking up a half a loaf, the German continued, "These loaves have *some* wheat, a lot of rye, some lentils, some maize, a good deal of potato flour, and . . ."

"And a bit of sawdust?" Daniil prodded.

"Not sawdust exactly, that's only for bread for prisoners of war, and that only if we're desperate, but wheat and rye *bran*, yes. Under ten percent by weight, but yes, sir, bran. I won't say that some bakers, unscrupulous or desperate, take your pick, don't sometimes resort to 'tree flour'—or even worse things—but the army? No."

Well, I'm glad of that.

"Is that what's authorized for a combatant ration?" Daniil asked.

"Yes, sir."

"Okay, what else have we got?"

"Officially? Officially, Sir, the men get about five or six ounces of meat a day, but officially Germany is winning the war, too. It's very difficult, I find, to reconcile those two bits of information.

"Unofficially, a lot of the meat will be 'war sausage,' which we call a 'mouthful of sawdust'; no, there's no sawdust in that, either. It's mostly vegetable in origin, flavored with some blood, some meat scraps, some offal, some fat. It's not sawdust, but it *feels* like it is. I counsel against enquiring too deeply as to where the fat came from; suffice to say that at least it isn't human. Oh, and water, too, of course, lots of water.

"We might get fish, occasionally. It's likely to be past its prime. Some of the meat, too, will be horse . . . but you don't get much meat from a horse anymore, what with overworking and underfeeding.

"Frankly, we get what we can at the front and those behind get less. But, then, too, it could be worse; we could still be trying to keep body and soul together with rutabagas, and not enough of those. And cattle starving because people were eating the rutabagas that the cattle usually ate.

"We'll have some potatoes," the chief cook continued, "some vegetables—I have my men scrounging for nettles for soup—occasional cheese—no, it isn't *good* cheese— some peas, some beans. Every man's supposed to get an egg a day but two a week is a surfeit of riches; one is more likely and not *every* week. Most of the time there will be a kind of fake egg made of potato or maize, some coloring, and maybe some additives that don't bear thinking about. Butter is . . . well . . . it's curdled milk, some sugar, and also some food coloring. Sometimes we get *Schmaltz*, which has the great virtue of, at least, being mostly real. Today, we have enough *Schmaltz*. Coffee . . . we have enough *ersatz* . . ."

"Roasted acorns, beechnuts, and chicory? I've had that; we all have," Daniil said.

"That, yes. It's not good, especially, but it *is* a little

better than nothing. And on a cold winter's night . . . not much sugar for it, mind, and rarely any milk."

"And this," Daniil asked, "is what you're feeding your own men?"

"When we can get it," the cook answered. "Sometimes we can't. Mind, there *is* a better ration, but it's usually only fed for a few days, maximum a week, before an offensive. It's close to real food. But talk about mixed feelings . . ."

Note to self, talk to Brinkmann about getting on that superior ration scheme.

Daniil sniffed. "Stew?"

"Yes, sir, stew. I thought about porridge for breakfast but not only didn't I have any real milk, I figured something a little heartier might be more to taste after the camps. Besides, we were able to scrounge some mushrooms to eke out the little bit of meat for today."

"How did you end up running a mess?" Daniil asked, pointing at the Iron Cross.

The cook grabbed a long ladle and tapped his left leg with it, producing a hollow, wooden sound. "Verdun," he answered, in full and complete explanation.

Daniil shook his head; he'd heard about the battle in great detail from de Gaulle; there were no words for someone who had gone through that particular hell on Earth. Finally, he said, "While you don't actually work for me, do let me know if there's anything I can do to help with your operation here. We'll do our best."

As I am pretty sure you will, old soldier.

"There is one thing, *Herr Oberst*? I could use at least one Russian cook to advise me on Russian recipes."

"Now *that*, *Feldwebel* Taenzler, is an excellent idea. Indeed, we have some cooks, six or seven. Let me arrange to send them to you, some or all. Do you have anyone who can speak Russian?"

"Polish? *I* can at least get by in Polish."

"We might have a Pole."

While the men were drawing food, to be followed by individual equipment, less small arms, in one part of the camp, in another the remarkably unlovely Captain Romeyko and his assistants were laying out unit equipment packages on the still grass but soon to become dirt street in front of the quartermaster's shop. This consisted of nine Lewis guns, in 7.62x54R, each, for Second and Third Companies, plus two 37mm light infantry cannon, French captures, two Russian Maxim heavy machine guns in the same caliber as the Lewis guns, for First Company, as well as two 13.2mm antitank rifles the Germans had been willing to part with.

Still more sat in the quartermaster shop, unneeded as of yet; more Lewis guns, extra 37mm jobs, a couple of the extra heavy machine guns, plus four sniper rifles the Huns had also been willing to pass over.

"Ammunition for all this?" Kostyshakov asked Romeyko.

"It's not infinite," Romeyko replied, "but it's surprisingly generous. The Huns may not be able to produce enough food, but they seem to be able to produce more than enough ammunition.

"Of course, since what they're giving us was mostly captured from us in the first place—well, us, the British, and the French—'generosity' may not be the precise word."

"What have we got?" Kostyshakov asked. "Roughly, I mean; I don't need to know down to the round."

Romeyko pointed to a large angular, tarp-covered pile outside the camp, saying, "About a million, three hundred thousand rounds of our own rifle and machine gun ammunition. More should be coming. There's also four thousand rounds of the German stuff, for the sniper rifles they gave me."

"How many of those?"

"Four, but I figured we'll wear out two in training and want to take two with us."

"Okay," Daniil agreed. "Go on."

"We've got a bit over eleven hundred rounds of the 37mm. I could have gotten more but some looked a little iffy...well, no, worse than a little iffy. Again, I'd say 'generous' except that it's captured French stuff and not compatible with their own 37mm infantry guns."

"Horses and mules?" Daniil asked.

"'Tomorrow,' the Huns say, but I am cautioned not to expect too much."

"How about grenades?"

"Hand grenades? Just over twenty-one hundred of theirs and a like number of our own. There's also a drum of the photographer's flash powder you wanted. That's got to be enough, based on comparative sizes, for a few hundred grenades, at least."

"Shotguns?" Daniil asked.

"Two, no spares, few hundred rounds of birdshot. Apparently, the Huns don't issue them to their army, nor generally capture any. The two I was able to get were taken from civilians in the occupied zones."

"The machine pistols?"

"Not yet," Romeyko said. "My German counterpart has a request in, but it hasn't been filled."

"We really need those," Kostyshakov said. "I don't even want to *think* about trying this with just rifles."

"Well, we've got the pistols," the quartermaster pointed out.

"Think you can get another few hundred thousand rounds of the Amerikanski ammunition to practice with?"

Romeyko shook his head, doubtfully. "Maybe, but they probably wouldn't have let me have the pistols at all if they'd had enough ammunition to justify issuing them to their own."

"Nag about those machine pistols, then; we have to have them."

"Yes, sir."

"How about the dynamo lights?"

"Those, at least," Romeyko said, "the Germans have come through with."

"How many?"

"Sixty-two, but three of them don't work. And we don't have anyone with a clue to how to fix them."

"Have we asked . . ."

"Yes, sir; the Huns don't know either."

Something about the two rows of nine Lewis guns each bothered Kostyshakov, but he couldn't put his finger on just what it was. He stared at them a long time, thinking hard. It mattered. He knew it mattered but . . .

"Crap," he said aloud. Then he told Romeyko, "We're

going to be pulling the Fourth Company's personnel out of Second and Third. That means one of two things, either Second and Third will get shorted one of their Lewis guns, or Fourth Company will have to train people—and it won't have the time for this, starting so late—on light machine guns they know little or nothing about."

"Put out two more, one for each rifle company?" Romeyko asked.

"Yes, and quickly."

Mokrenko, Kaledin, and Panfil signed for and took their mess kits, mugs, and eating utensils from Romeyko's clerk, opened the mess kits and examined them, then dipped them in the hot water by their wire bales. They swished their utensils around in the water, poured the water out into the kettle, then got in line under the overhang. Ahead of them the canvas "door" barely ever closed, and never fully.

The mess line ran almost the full length of the kitchen, with only a two-foot gap to allow passage between the cooking area and the space where the men to be fed passed.

First up, Mokrenko saw, was an enormous pile of bread. *Three pound loaves*, he guessed, *one half per man*. He followed the men ahead of him by sticking his half loaf under his left arm.

Next came a thick stew, ladled into the lower half of his mess tin by an indifferent cook. What it was thickened with, he couldn't tell. Neither, looking down into his steaming mess tin, could he see any meat in it, though he thought it would at least have some much-missed fat.

There wasn't any butter for the bread, but as each man got to that point in the line, a German cook took his mess kit and knifed onto it a few tablespoons of what looked to be some kind of fat.

Kaledin sniffed at it, warily. "Smells like ... chicken ... maybe."

Seeing the doubtful look on the Russian's face, the German cook dishing out the *Schmaltz* beckoned for him to stand closer. The cook then broke off a piece from the bread under Kaledin's arm. On this he spread a little of the *Schmaltz* before offering the piece back to the Russian.

Doubtfully, Kaledin took the proffered bread and popped it into his mouth. "It's not bad, actually, though we'll probably have to find happiness elsewhere. I'd prefer salo." That latter was basically pork fat, cooked or raw, sliced or diced, and something of a delicacy to the Russian palate.

"What is it, though?" Panfil asked.

"Chicken fat, I think, purified or rendered. Strong tasting, but one can certainly eat it."

"We're all skin and bones," Mokrenko said. "Anything to put on a little meat and fat would be to the good."

"Yes, but eat slowly," Kaledin counseled, "if you don't want to lose everything you'll have eaten."

Unsurprisingly, nary a scrap or crumb of the food was wasted. Men used to long semi-starvation will rarely turn up their noses at the unfamiliar. Outside each mess tent were three more kettles of water, two to wash and rinse out the mess kits, in succession, and one boiling kettle to sterilize them.

Sergeant Major Blagov stood there, a glaring, fearsome presence, inspecting at random to make sure the men cleaned their kits before leaving the area.

"From here, go to the area by the main gate," Blagov bellowed. "One of the personnel clerks will give you your company area. Go there and wait. From there your companies will take you to equipment issue."

Kaledin was sent to Strategic Recon, First Company, while Panfil went to the infantry gun section, and Mokrenko likewise to the strategic reconnaissance section of the same company. The clerk also told them where their company billets stood and directed them to report to the company sergeant major, forthwith.

While every man selected by the committees could read and write, few of them had watches. The company first sergeant for First Company, Mayevsky, fiercely mustached, with a patch over one eye, directed them to go to different tents, make themselves at home as best they could, telling them to assemble at noon to go draw personal equipment and uniforms.

At noon First Company formed ranks, in a single mass of just under two hundred and four men, plus the two sergeants major and First Sergeant Mayevsky standing outside the formation. At the latter's command the company faced right and marched to the issue area.

The issue area consisted of about twenty wagons, for the nonce without horses, lined up in two rows of ten, fairly widely spaced. From the first wagon, each man was handed a knapsack—a rather crude, khaki-colored canvas thing with no frame, uncushioned straps, and a simple tie at the top to close it—plus a smaller cloth bag of similar color.

"As you get your equipment, either put it on or stuff it in those," a quartermaster noncom advised.

The second wagon was piled high with hundreds of *furazhka*, the visored, peaked caps worn almost universally by the Imperial Army, and *papakhas*, which were pile winter caps, plus "Adrians," steel helmets of a French design.

Mokrenko and Panfil expected to be given any old hat, with instructions to trade it off or make it fit for himself. Instead, the clerk looked them over, went to one part of the wagon behind him, and then another, returning with two *furazhka* that actually fit fairly well. The pile caps he passed over were big, but that was to be expected and preferred. A French-manufactured helmet followed.

"You'll have to remove the French insignia yourselves," the clerk said. "No, we don't have Imperial insignia for the helmets. Supposedly someone is soon going to be working on it."

The third wagon was fronted by a pile of shirts and tunics. "Find two shirts that fit," said the man on that station. "Big is all right; make sure they're not too small. The tunics are probably going to be a little big, anyway, given how much weight you've lost."

And so it went, through trousers, two each—"No belts for your trousers; no suspenders, either. Take a piece of rope and a bit of wood and make your own!"—through boots, "*sapogi*" in Russian, two pairs of foot wrapping, called "*portyanki*," and a heavy overcoat of a better manufacture than the Imperial Army had seen since 1915 or so.

Each man got an adjustable leather belt with shoulder

straps and cartridges boxes for it, plus a shovel to hang from it. A Zelinski model gas mask was hung over one shoulder and a bread bag, a kind of a loose purse for men, over the other. Into the knapsack also went a pair of decent lined leather mittens. One canteen was given to each man, as was a small pot for boiling water and a bayonet without scabbard. Tent section, rope, poles, and pegs all went into the knapsack as did a small notebook, towel, toiletry bag, tin of fat for waterproofing boots, boot brush, and a little uniform repair kit with needle, thread, buttons, plus this, that, and whatnot. Three wool blankets—none of them of the best by this stage of the war—plus a ground cloth completed the ensemble.

Interlude

Tatiana: Old Flames

Before the revolution—rather, the revolutions—the three of us, Mama, my sister Olga, and I, worked in a military hospital. Olga, as it turned out, just couldn't deal with the suffering, the stress, or the sheer physical work involved. I think she might have been able to take on any two of those; all three, together, were just too much for her. She was put to work handling administrative and clerical matters, which suited her a good deal better than changing bandages and emptying bedpans . . . or holding the hands of the dying.

Me, I just wanted to help. No . . . no, that's not quite right, nor quite honest; I wanted to feel, by helping, and for the first time in my life, like an active, useful human being. They still tried to shield me from it, of course, and it took a good deal to convince everyone that I was serious about taking on duties at least as onerous as anyone else had.

I flirted with most of the patients, at least a little. Why? Why, because I thought morale was critical to healing, and it wouldn't hurt their morale any for me to flirt with them.

One was more than flirting, however. There was an officer of the Guards—everyone knew who he was so I won't mention the name—already well decorated for bravery and advanced beyond what his years would suggest. He was fairly short, not much taller than I was, a little dark, and with maybe some Tatar in his ancestry. It was his grandfather, I think, who had been the first one ennobled in his ancestry, so marriage was out of the question.

Still, a girl could dream, couldn't she? Me, I dreamt of a happy life, somewhere in the country, with cows and chickens and a brood of children, his children and mine, and hopefully none of them bleeders like my poor, dear, utterly frustrated brother.

Maybe if we could both have run off to America . . .

Chapter Six

One of Sergeant Kaledin's "Patients"

Camp Budapest, Bulgaria

They had Russian machine guns, rifles, and uniforms, Amerikanski pistols and light machine guns, and French light cannon.

It wasn't even twenty-one hundred hours and already the waxing crescent of the setting moon hung low in the west. There were no electric lights, and it was far too dark to risk the small parts of the various special weapons by detailed familiarization of the troops with them at night. There was a surplus of talent as far as the heavy machine guns went. The same could not be said for either the Lewis guns or the 37mm infantry cannon. Still, time was short and what there was of it *had* to be used,

The only man in the battalion who knew anything about the Lewis guns was Sergeant Major Nenonen, and *nobody* knew anything about the 37mm jobs.

Fortunately, Corporal Panfil could read French, while the Germans had thoughtfully provided a French manual with the guns. Right now, Panfil, with a gun next to his pallet, the wheels and caisson having been left outside, pored over that manual by the light of a flickering candle, his officer, Lieutenant Federov, looking from over his shoulder and trying to puzzle through the instructions, too, while *Feldfebel* Yahonov and Sergeant Oblonsky manipulated the gun by the instructions given.

"So what happens if you miss?" Yahonov asked.

"It gives...mmm...two methods. The simpler one says..."—Panfil scanned over the text of the pertinent section, then translated the gist of it—"to keep your hands away from the traversing and elevating mechanisms—in other words, leave the gun alone—and then move the deflection and elevation knobs to put the telescopic sight on the explosion," he patiently explained. "Then, without touching the sight's controls, to use the elevation and traversing wheels to get your sight picture back on the target."

"Deflection?"

"Right and left, but reversed."

"Let me think about that for a bit," Yahonov said,

working out the process in his mind. "Ooooh, I see; what's happening there is that it turns into an instant bore sighting or zero, while adjusting for atmosphere, wind, and weather, yes?"

"Must be," Panfil agreed.

Daniil had just finished explaining what he suspected would be needed for a landing area. Lieutenant Turgenev, a former Guards Cavalry officer, detailed to intelligence, and currently leading a small detachment of mixed cavalry and Cossacks, furiously copied down nearly every word.

"All that comes," Kostyshakov said, "from a couple of articles I read while at Fort IX. After I meet with the captain of the airship I might have better guidance. Also, it ought to be within one to two days' march from wherever you find the Romanovs. Now come back tomorrow, noontime, with a tentative plan," Daniil added.

"You're too generous with time, sir," the lieutenant said sardonically.

Daniil made a dismissive get-thee-forth gesture with his hand and fingers. "There *isn't* a lot of time, Turgenev, and less for you than for us. So quit wasting what we have and get to work."

"Yes, sir. Sorry, sir."

The young horse soldier turned intelligence officer let himself out of the crude wooden shack.

As with Panfil's tent, a candle, too, burned in Kostyshakov's lone hut. Like Panfil's, lacking fat, the candle's light was poor. *The war's made everything decrepit and decayed*, he thought. *I think, unless we're both very lucky and fight very hard, that someday people* will look at this war the way we see the war between the Spartans and the Athenians; the great calamity that ruined our civilization beyond redemption.

Still, so far, so good, Daniil also thought. *We've got arms and equipment, ammunition, men, food... even horses and mules are supposedly coming in the morning. We've got an organization—that went better than expected, probably in good part because of Sergeant Major Blagov—and a plan of sorts for changing it to what we really need, when we really need it.*

But I wish I had some better idea of how to train for this, some better idea of who to select for the Grenadier Company than "he who does good." We've got almost no facilities. The men are in rotten shape but they're still going to have to build what we need.

Which is what, exactly? Well... we need a range for the machine guns and cannon. The same range will also do for the snipers, once we select them. Doesn't need to be much, about a tenth of a verst by a verst and a half will do. Hmmm... maybe we can dig positions and run wire out for field telephones, then put men in strong trench positions to raise and lower targets, as we tell them to via the field phones. I wonder if Romeyko has phones and wire stashed away with his horde. If not, I wonder if he can get some.

Yes, if he can, that should be good for the Maxims, the Lewis guns, and the snipers. I think maybe we just put out a bunch of targets for the 37mm cannon, and have no men downrange when we use those. So... okay, different days for automatic and cannon fire... different days for the snipers, too, I suppose.

Then we need a range for the grenades. We have enough to expend two or even three for every rifleman, convert a couple of hundred to flash powder, and still have enough explosive ones for the mission. Hmmm . . . maybe have each man throw one a few dozen times before they pull the ignition cord. Will they stand up to that much abuse? Better ask the Germans how they do it. Wooden mockups, maybe? Hmmm . . . wooden mockups with a lead core?

We're going to need a good rifle range, call it six tenths of a verst by . . . oh . . . a tenth or a twentieth, maybe. But how do we set up targets and give feedback?

Daniil spared a glance at the rough lumber of his shack and thought, *No way we'll get enough finely cut lumber for the usual frames. Maybe we can use smaller targets, and have men hold them up on rough poles, bringing the poles down to mark the targets. T-poles, I think.*

"Targets? Targets?" he wondered aloud. "Can we get targets from the Germans?"

We'll have to dig in the men down range a good eight or ten feet. Those wretched little shovels won't do. Ask the Germans—I am growing so tired of that phrase—for real picks and shovels, a hundred or so, each.

Ah, but then finally, we're going to need a place to train for and rehearse the actual mission which is a rescue. And that . . . I am not sure. Maybe the sergeant major will have some idea.

Camp Budapest

"Maybe we could dig a house—a complex building, or the spacing of one—down into the ground," said Blagov, scratching at his half right ear, to Kostyshakov. "You know, open top so we can see and evaluate the men going through the drill. We could even close it off, sometimes, for them to practice it in the dark with just those cylindric li— Dear God! What are *those?*"

Blagov pointed at his first glimpse of the miserable collection of mule- and horseflesh shambling though the gate of the camp.

"Damn . . . just damn," Daniil shook his head in despair.

There were only eight horses and two dozen mules, which was substantially less than Kostyshakov had asked for. Far worse than the numbers, though, was that these animals looked more than half-starved, with ribs showing more or less plainly, backbone sticking up like an irregular rail, hips outlined, and the withers very sloped.

"I think they call them 'horses' and 'mules,' Sergeant Major," Daniil said. "Though I am not sure why."

"How important are they to the mission?"

Kostyshakov thought for a bit. "Well, a half dozen or so of the horses are very important, and become so soon. There's some time for the rest to heal up . . . if they can heal."

"Kaledin," was Blagov's instant judgment. "He's another Cossack, probably could ride before he could walk. I doubt we have a better candidate for getting them back in some kind of shape. If they *can* be brought back to some kind of shape."

"Okay, so assign him to the quartermaster and—"

"He's already assigned," Blagov interrupted, "to the reconnaissance team heading into the interior to pin down and report on the royal family. And those have to leave within, as you said, sir, about a week."

"Well, I'm supposed to meet with Turgenev at noon, Sergeant Major. Could you send someone to advise him to bring the entire detachment? Thank you."

"Effective immediately, Lieutenant, Sergeant Kaledin is detailed to the quartermaster to try to get those horses and mules into shape."

"Bu'... bu'... bu'?"

"No arguments. Kaledin, go now. Some of those animals look to be about to keel over. The sooner you start getting them in shape the more likely some of them will survive."

"Are they that bad, sir?" Kaledin asked, dark eyes going sad.

"Words fail," Kostyshakov said.

"I see, sir. Yes, sir, I'm on my way."

After the sergeant had departed, Kostyshakov demanded, "What's your plan, Turgenev?"

"Step one, sir," the lieutenant said, "is that someone is going to have to give me a great deal of money, and probably a mix of it. If we each had a string of the best horses in the world, the distance is on the order of four thousand *versts*. That's four months of travel..."

"You don't have four months."

"Yes, sir, I know. So we're going to have to rely mainly on less secure, certainly less secret, but faster means. That means we walk to Kermen with everything we can carry and maybe grub a lift for the rest of the baggage from Taenzler. From there we take a train to as near to Burgos, that Black Sea port, as we can get. Now Burgos, what with the war, isn't too bloody likely to have continuing ferry service to, say, Rostov-on-Don. There will probably be smugglers galore, though, who would risk it."

Kostyshakov nodded, "They're likely as not to be pirates, too. That means you go armed, but also with arms that can be hidden, knives and pistols, both. And *that* means practice." He turned his attention to the five men remaining after Kaledin's departure. "Any of you familiar with pistols?"

"Familiar, sir, but that's all, all for any of us except the lieutenant," answered the next senior man, Mokrenko.

"The men know their way around a lance or a carbine a lot better than they do a pistol," added Turgenev.

"Right . . . add to your plan one day of pistol familiarization. Maybe two."

"Yes, sir," said Turgenev, continuing then with, "From Rostov-on-Don we try to take a riverboat if we can, or charter one, if we can't, or buy decent horses if we can't do either. The rail may be running, too, though I have my doubts. If none of those are possible, then there's no way to complete our mission in time."

Wordlessly, Daniil just nodded his understanding. *One of those*, he silently agreed, *ought be available.*

"I think we'll be able to go mostly by river, though, and am planning on it. We follow the Don as far as possible to get as near as we can to Tsaritsyn. At that point, we likely *must* buy horses to get to the Volga. That's the area where the Reds' control is limited, which must mean intermittent rail connections, at best.

"That means, once again, we'll need money, though we'll probably have to sell the horses for anything we can get at Tsaritsyn.

"We can follow the Volga to Samara, and then take a train to Yekaterinburg and then onward to Tyumen. From there, once again, we must buy horses to get to Tobolsk. Yes, we could try to catch the river boat to Tobolsk, but it would be better to arrive as unseen as possible. For that matter," the lieutenant paused to scratch his head, "even if we could go by river, we can't count on that river not being totally frozen . . . so . . . horses."

"The Germans tell me," Daniil said, "that they believe the family is in Tobolsk. But I figure we can only be sure that the royal family will be in one of those two places, Yekaterinburg or Tobolsk. Timeline? And add a couple of days at Yekaterinburg to see if they're there or coming there."

Turgenev consulted his notebook, making a couple of quick corrections. "Here to Kermen, about one day. Kermen to Burgos, maybe two. Burgos to Rostov-on-Don . . . I'm a cynic and a skeptic; five, minimum. If we can get a steamboat up the Don, three days, plus three to buy new horses and ride to Tsaritsyn. If not, probably nineteen. Then five days by boat to Samara. Rail to Yekaterinburg, logic says one but cynicism tells me two. Then three days in Yekaterinburg. Then to Tyumen, call it one day. Buy horses and race to Tobolsk, maybe six.

"That's thirty-one days to Tobolsk, if we're lucky. Fifty, if we are not.

"As to how we're to tell you where they are, I have no clue. I asked around to see if anyone knew anything about carrier pigeons. Turns out Lieutenant Antopov, in Second Company, used to race them. He says they're good, the best of them, for maybe two thousand *versts*. This is twice that. We need something else. I asked the signal officer, Lieutenant Dragonov. No, sir, radio won't work. Oh, we could, maybe, if we used a rail line to act as an antenna, send a message out. Maybe even receive one. But, in the first place, they're too big to carry, while in the second place, if the Reds or the anarchists see us with a radio they'll just stand us against a wall and shoot us."

"I agree," Daniil said. "What's your monetary breakdown?"

"Six men for two months, at twenty rubles a day, seven thousand three hundred, call it. That's not generous, by the way; we'll not be staying in fine hotels nor eating in expensive restaurants.

"Train and boat passage . . . I think we'd be making no mistake if we budgeted two thousand per man. Horses? Two horses per man, plus saddlery, if we can get a boat to Komovka on the Don, but four per man if we cannot. Four per man from Tyumen to Tobolsk, plus saddlery. I confess, I have no idea whatsoever what a horse may cost back home now, in paper rubles, let alone forty-eight of them, plus the saddlery. I think we'll be in the one thousand to fifteen hundred range if we can get gold rubles. That would be fifty to seventy-five thousand rubles, most of it in gold. But then there'll be the tips and bribes. Some we'll get back when we sell them and some of them, at least, should still be alive at the end of the mission for sale . . . unless the Bolsheviks notice them and confiscate them."

"We'll not count on the Bolsheviks' appreciation for the sanctity of private property," Daniil said. "I'll ask the Germans for a round hundred thousand rubles. They'll probably want receipts when this is all over, as well as receipts for what you got when you sold them. Thorough people, the Germans."

"Yes . . . well, sir, I'll try. But any receipts that tend to show how far we've travelled are also a death sentence if the Bolsheviks catch us, or even notice us enough for a search."

"No receipts," Kostyshakov said, instantly.

"But we're still stuck with how to even let you know once we've found the tsar and his family."

"Let's go find Major Brinkmann."

Brinkmann tapped his cane as if impatient. After several taps, he reluctantly said, "There . . . is a . . . way, but . . . come with me."

A bare ten minutes later in his own quarters, he explained. "We maintain a small office in neutral Sweden, in Stockholm. It's in the guise of a trading firm. Send them a telegram; they'll forward it to us. Well . . . they will after they're told that certain telegrams from Russia are to come to our office. But you're going to need a code book, a set of prearranged terms, that are neither obvious nor suspicious. Best, I think, if it's simple enough to be memorized, though that's asking for a lot. And your signal to the Stockholm office . . . maybe a particular trading firm, yourselves. Furs?"

"Furs make sense," Kostyshakov agreed. "So the Pan-Siberian Import-Export Company?"

"Works for me," said Lieutenant Turgenev.

Horse Paddock, Camp Budapest

Never going to work, thought Kaledin, gazing upon the

sorry spectacle of equines listlessly munching on thin, frozen grass. Some lacked even the energy for that, but just stood there, blankly.

The Cossack sergeant wasn't alone; one of the cooks, Private Meisner, not needed by the German mess section, accompanied him. This was a private who was, at least, used to horses since mess trailers—*Gulaschkanonen*, in German—all used horses to get around.

These poor beasties, about half of them already have two hooves in the grave . . . or the sausage factory, as the case may be. Triage? Look for the ones who have a chance and slaughter the rest to feed the troops? I don't see a better way but . . . I love horses and have a soft spot for mules. I don't have it in my heart to kill them until there's no choice left.

I'll do my best and let God decide for me.

Now, for step one, let's look them over closely. I count . . . one, two, five, eleven, twenty . . . .thirty-one? There were supposed to be thirty-two, eight horses and twenty-four mules . . . I count . . . seven horses only.

Kaledin walked to his right around the clump of equines and forest of legs. He was less than a quarter of the way around it when he spotted the bay lying on one side. He didn't want to spook the animals by running, but picked up his pace until he was close enough to see that the supine horse wasn't even breathing.

The sergeant stopped and crossed himself, Orthodox fashion, up, down, then right to left. Then he walked over to the horse and took one knee, reaching out to stroke its now cold forehead.

"Poor thing," he muttered, "poor abused thing."

Kaledin felt a tear forming and dashed it away. In truth, he liked horses a lot *better* than he liked most people.

I'll have someone come for you in a bit, old friend. I am sorry, but I cannot guarantee you will not end up in a pot or as sausage. Yes, as a matter fact we are that hard up at the moment. Yes, I know it is also somewhat risky.

"Meisner?"

"Yes, Sergeant?"

"Go to the mess, ask what they want to do with the dead horse. If nothing, notify the quartermaster to send someone to take it away and bury it."

"Yes, Sergeant."

Kaledin then stood, pulled a small notebook and pencil from a pocket, and went to the first horse to be examined. *Chestnut gelding,* he wrote, *about sixteen hands high. Shod. Poorly. Probably Oldenburger. Neck, discernible. Withers, faintly discernible. Spine, can't see individual vertebrae. Tailhead, prominent, hip rounded, discernible. Ribs, prominent. Shoulder, discernible. Prognosis, fairly poor but possible.*

From that one he studied another horse, also a likely Oldenberger, and then three mules in succession. Doing the entire herd took almost until sundown. Before that, Meisner had returned, as well as a group from one of the rifle companies to drag the dead horse away.

"They need food," Kaledin told the boy. "They need it desperately, but they're too far gone down the road to starvation to eat much at any one time. Overfeeding will kill them as surely as no food would." He pointed, "You see that chestnut one? We'll start with him. Get him a mix of lucerne and hay, then add to it about a little bit of oats, just a few ounces, a handful or so. Put it in a feed bag and hang it for the poor thing..."

"How much, Sergeant?"

"About two *funt*, no more, in total. We'll refill when they've had a chance to digest fully. It's going to be nearly an all day, all night job for us, boy, for at least the next two weeks. For the mules make it about a fifth less. And when we're finished, we go collect blankets from the quartermaster."

The men digging the horse's grave weren't the only ones digging. The entire Second Company, for now armed with nothing but their miserable little entrenching tools, worried at the ground at one end of a hollow field. About six hundred meters distant, the bulk of Third Company pounded in numbered stakes with rocks, dug individual pits, and filled some sandbags, three or four for each pit.

Sergeant Major Blagov and two of the company first sergeants paced the line, encouraging the men and occasionally enlightening them with a firm boot. From a deep and long draw, a few hundred meters to the east, came the sound of steady firing as a team of long service noncoms confirmed or fixed the zeroes of all the rifles; that, or rejected them as unserviceable.

It was slow work, digging, what with the ground being so frozen. At least, though, it was warm work; the frozen-breath pine trees sprouting from each man's face every few seconds told of a bitter temperature, indeed.

Meanwhile, in a small copse of woods to the north, everyone from First Company not otherwise engaged chopped at trees to bring down some lumber. There were no decent saws yet, so, again, the entrenching tools had to do. There were also no horses available, as all but three of the ones who had pulled the wagons from the train station had been returned, the three being two for Romeyko's operations and one horse and one wagon, assigned to the mess. When they did manage to fell a tree, the heavy machine gun section became the beasts of burden and hauled the trunk to the wood-splitting area near the target line where the light cannon section split them into useful poles.

"They're coming; they're coming!" Romeyko had promised.

Going to take days, thought Sergeant Major Blagov. *Fucking days. And we would be done by noon tomorrow if we had the proper tools!*

Brest-Litovsk

Hoffmann looked over the telegram sent to him by Brinkmann.

One hundred thousand rubles in gold, they want? Ten thousand ten ruble coins? Almost ninety kilograms of gold? I don't think so. I could give them twice as much, three times as much, in captured Russian Imperial currency. We've captured pay chests enough to cover that much. But the coins, the actual article? In that quantity? Not a chance.

For one thing, that much in coinage would raise suspicions and attract attentions I do not want or need. I am still on Ludendorff's and Hindenburg's persona non grata list. They'd object to anything I do now, out of sheer spite. Thank God the kaiser hasn't told them anything about our little project.

He summoned an aide. "Telegram Major Brinkmann, at Camp Budapest, *'Ober Ost* will provide six thousand rubles in coin. The rest must be paper currency. I can increase the currency, even substantially, if needed and wanted.'"

Camp Budapest

Five Russians showed up at *Feldwebel* Taenzler's kitchen. None of them was a Pole. Taenzler knew, distantly, that a lot of Russian ranks had been taken from German practice. *Job one, find out who's senior.*

"*Feldwebel?*" Taenzler asked, looking from Russian to Russian. "*Feldwebel?*" The Russian pronunciation was close enough. "*Wachtmeister?*" This also produced no response.

"*Unteroffizier?*"

One Russian raised his hand, answering, "Ilyin, *Mladshy Unter-ofitzer.*"

"Close enough," said Taenzler. "Ilyin Mladshy," the German said, gently, thinking the latter was the surname, "let me show you our kitchen . . ."

The sergeant major still had all three existing companies out digging, less three men armed with bayoneted rifles who wandered the camp as guards, and the two would-be deserters from a couple of days prior who were living in an open pit they'd had to dig themselves, said pit covered with a lattice of tied logs.

The guards were only there to prevent pilfering. The exterior of the camp was guarded by Germans manning machine guns in towers, while the labor parties and the range area had a double ring of armed Germans and, outside of that, armed Bulgarians to keep the prying eyes of the local populace away.

Those two detainees were also on bread and water. A couple of the worst blankets had been tossed to them, as daily were tossed their pound and a half of bread, no *Schmaltz*, and a canteen of water.

The three companies were out, but the sergeant major remained behind for the nonce. Right now he stood over the two in the hole and asked, genially, with a brilliant smile, "How's the food down there, boys?"

"Oh, it's a feast, Sergeant Major, a veritable feast."

The voice had an accent, enough so that Blagov asked for names.

"Kowalski, Sergeant Major," answered one.

"Chmura," said the other.

"Poles, then?"

"Yes, we're Polish," said Chmura.

"Not especially common in a Guards regiment," Blagov observed, fingering his half-missing ear. "What twists of fate brought you to the Guards, and what depths of idiocy caused to you try to desert? You're lucky we didn't just shoot you, you know."

"We weren't trying to desert, Sergeant Major," answered Kowalski. "We thought we were escaping."

"That doesn't make sense."

"Sorry to disagree, Sergeant Major, but, yes, it does. When we ducked under the train we'd just come out of rail accommodations for prisoners. The only armed men we saw were Germans. As far as we knew we were still prisoners and had a duty to try to escape."

"Didn't your officers and noncoms tell you not to?"

"The world is full of collaborators, Sergeant Major," said Chmura, "and has no dearth of traitors."

Well, that much is true, thought Blagov, thinking back to Dragomirov and any number of other rejects. *And, then, too, we hadn't given anyone but the officers and senior noncoms—and not all of those—any idea of what was going on. Maybe that was a mistake.*

"I don't trust you two; let's be clear on that," said Blagov. "Even so, I'm going to give you a chance to prove me and the commander wrong."

A single sharp whistle from the sergeant major brought the three camp guards at a run. "Lift the cage off them," Blagov said.

"You're not making a mistake, Sergeant Major," said Kowalski.

Under the circumstances, it wouldn't do to leave two people living under a cloud but sharing a common language and culture together.

"Either of you speak any German?" asked Blagov.

Only Chmura raised a hand. "Mine's fair, Sergeant Major. Never as good as my Russian, though."

Why didn't I already know this? Blagov asked himself. *If the commander needs to know something about the men of the battalion it is my duty to have the answer right there.*

That was a case of the sergeant major being too hard on himself; this unit had just come into being, so *of course* he didn't know every man.

"Go report to the mess. Look for Junior Sergeant Ilyin. You, Kowalski, come with me."

Without another word, Blagov set off briskly for the front gate, on his way to the range area. He suddenly stopped. *Shit, neither of them have drawn any uniforms or equipment.*

"Halt!" Blagov barked. "Instead, come with me. We'll set you up with the quartermasters before you go to work. And get those blankets you've been using."

"Hoffmann says paper, with a little gold, not all gold," Brinkmann informed Kostyshakov and Turgenev, north of the camp, not far from where the battalion dug and cut, making their known distance range. "Six thousand rubles in gold coin. I complained but, from the wording, I think he's going to be inflexible on this, and probably doesn't really have any choice."

"How much paper, Major?" Turgenev asked.

"Now that's interesting; he's willing to go much higher on the paper to make up for the loss of gold. We might be able to double the request, or even more."

"If serious inflation kicks off, where horses are concerned, we might not be able to carry enough paper. If it doesn't, we might have too much."

"Where did it come from?" Kostyshakov asked of Brinkmann.

"Probably captured pay chests. It'll be good, honest paper, at least, not counterfeit."

"Double it?" Kostyshakov asked Turgenev. "A mix of high, medium, and low value notes?"

"Do we have any choice?"

"No," said both Kostyshakov and Brinkmann simultaneously.

"Then I guess it will have to be." The junior officer grew contemplative for a moment, then observed, "Maybe we'd be well advised to rob a bank."

"Better to rob a Bulgarian bank," said the German, "before you leave Burgos. You would not, after all, want the Russian police and the Reds to take special notice of your presence in Russia."

"Maybe," agreed Turgenev. "But make our getaway on what, those old nags your army sent us?"

Another horse had died in the night, quite despite the careful feeding and quite despite the blankets Kaledin and Meisner draped over them.

On the plus side, the food had given each of the equines something to crap out, which also gave Kaledin the chance to inspect the droppings for worms.

Nothing, which is good, but in a week or ten days, if we can put a little meat on their bones, I think a modest solution of turpentine in their water would be to the good, in case they've got a residual infection of the evil little bastards.

"Hey, Meisner?"

"Yes, Sergeant."

"Trot over to the quartermaster's office and ask for some turpentine, a *vedro* of it. Tell them it isn't immediate, but in a week would be good."

Quartermaster's Office, Camp Budapest

Frustrating, thought Captain Romeyko, *purely frustrating. Hmmm... well maybe not all that pure, since there's an element of humiliation to the matter, as well.*

A whitewashed board was affixed to one wall on Romeyko's small office. The board was divided into three sections with two hand-drawn charcoal lines. The left side was labeled "ROUTINE," and the other "SPECIAL." In between was lettered "TRANSPORTATION."

Under ROUTINE were such matters as "Daily ration draw," and "Ammunition type and issue." On the right, under "SPECIAL," were written "Machine Pistols," "Pioneer tools," "Horse blankets," "Blacksmith," "Money," "Field telephones," "wire," and about two dozen other items that had, so far, proven beyond Romeyko's ability to fix or acquire. A couple of items were crossed out, including "Saddlery," "Radio," and "Carrier Pigeon." One big glaring need was "Map of Rodina." As it turned out, Brinkmann had to send to the General Staff office, in Berlin, to get a usable scale map of western Russia, up to and including Tobolsk. Even Ober Ost's only went as far as the general line of the Volga.

Very few of the items on this list had an expected arrival date.

Somewhere, mused Romeyko, *somewhere, possibly in Warsaw, there is a repository of captured maps where, if they looked, the Huns would find maps of Russia going all the way to Vladivostok. No doubt it is all well filed and documented, but we—in our miserable state—just don't know who to ask.*

In the middle column, conversely, there was almost nothing written, just the daily, "Wagons to draw rations for seven hundred"—*okay, OKAY; so Taenzler is drawing some extra and I'm helping? So sue us!*—"from the railhead."

Even as he thought it, from outside came the creak of wagon wheels, leaving the camp on their way to the railhead.

Interlude

Tatiana: Mock Battle

I followed the clanking sounds down the hall to discover Alexei and Kolya in mock battle. They had taken some branches from the wood pile and fashioned them into daggers and guns. They were well armed, with extra branches tucked into the belts of their coats and one in each hand.

I was so thrilled to see them happy and playing, to see Alexei up and about, that I didn't tell them to take their noise and chaos back outside.

Kolya was Andrey Derevenko's, the doctor's, son. Boys being what they are, Alexei behaved for Derevenko, Nagorny, his sailor-guard, and Papa whereas he ignored Mama, Olga, and me.

Taller than Alexei, Kolya had been my brother's playmate and best friend for years. He was as loyal a friend as Alexei could ask for.

Kolya thrust the bent stick in his right hand forward, aiming for Alexei's belly. Alexei jumped out of reach just in time and hit the wall with his back. I winced, but they continued their back and forth, along with accompanying grunts and yelps.

Joy and Anastasia's Cavalier, Jimmy, bounced happily

around them, their silky hair still damp with melting snow.

Alexei got the upper hand and drove Kolya into the salon. Kolya staggered backward, lost his footing, and landed on his back. He rolled away just in time to avoid being poked with the sharp end of a branch but Alexei pointed the bent stick serving as a gun at him and made shooting sounds.

"You're dead," Alexei said triumphantly as the two spaniels swarmed Kolya and smothered him with kisses.

Kolya's giggling only encouraged the dogs, as if they wanted more of that happy, tinkling sound.

"Tatiannnaaaa..."

We all turned towards the source of the sound. From underneath a pile of too-big clothes, Maria rose to glare at us, her hands on her plump hips. Anastasia was likewise decked out in one of Papa's shirts and hats. His wide, leather belt looped around her waist.

"We're rehearsing," Anastasia piped in.

Ah, the play. My sisters were putting on another play.

"French or English?" I asked.

Kolya pushed himself up from the floor and straightened his coat.

"English, of course," Maria said. "It's our room for ten more minutes."

Alexei and Kolya shrugged. They resumed their battle over the girls' protests and eventually yielded the room back to them when the shrieking got too loud.

That image of Alexei standing over Kolya with his mock-gun stayed with me the rest of the day. It morphed from a boy at play to a man at war, a man that I feared we would never see. Either a fall or a cut would get him. And no matter how much he played at being a real boy, he wasn't and could never be.

His world was so unfair, so foul, so unkind. It denied this brave, bright boy even the simplest pleasures by making the hemophilia hang over everything he did, no matter how small, how normal.

My brother deserved better. I had seen him put on a brave front so many times. How, for Mama's sake, he'd let Rasputin pray over him. Yet there had been a keen intellect in Alexei's feverish eyes. One that told me that he wasn't taken in by the *starets,* one that told me that even in the throes of pain and fever, he still cared about Mama enough to pretend.

One that told me that my brother, whatever his faults, would have made a great tsar.

Chapter Seven

Feldwebel Taenzler and his *Gulaschkanone*

Range A (Rifle), Near Camp Budapest

First and Third Companies were still hard at work putting in a range for the heavy and light machine guns, as well as the 37mm cannon. Their little spades could be heard, faintly, *chink-chink-chinking* away, from off in the distance.

Today was expected to be a great day. Today was Number Two Company's first day on the rifle range.

There were firing points numbered One through Forty, running left to right. From the deep trench and berm, in and behind which the target handlers sheltered, toward the camp, there were roughly one- by two-meter raised dirt beds, at one hundred and fifty, three hundred, four hundred and fifty, and six hundred *arshini*[3] from the target line. At seven hundred and fifty *arshini*, instead of raised beds, the battalion had dug down to create positions for firing in a standing supported mode.

As with most rifles of the era, the Model 1891 was capable of engaging mass targets—columns of men moving in the open, for example—at greater than five hundred meters. Indeed, the sights of the models scrounged by Romeyko were marked for as far away as thirty-two hundred *arshini*, or roughly two thousand, two hundred meters.

Again, though, that was for mass targets, not individual ones. More practically, in the hands of a reasonably well-trained soldier, effective engagement of a man-sized target at five hundred meters was probably worth the effort . . . if the target were standing still and approximately upright. Engagement of a moving target was, for any rifleman, *extremely* problematic and kinetic success in such engagement largely a matter of luck.

Though every man in the battalion was literate and numerate, mistakes still happened with this kind of thing. Thus, rather than putting up just numbers at the target line, successive relays of men had tramped down the grass in straight lines to mark each firing lane.

Even so, thought Sergeant Major Blagov, *some idiot is*

---

[3] The *arshin* was an archaic Russian unit of measure, set by Tsar Peter the Great at exactly twenty-eight English inches.

going to fire at his neighbor's target. Always happens. I suppose it always will.

The weather was actually not bad, for Russians, hovering at about forty-three degrees Fahrenheit, or about six degrees Celsius. For someone from, say, Saint Peterburg, this was equal to a balmy early April morn.

The field telephones and communications wire hadn't yet shown up; they probably never would. Still, the noncoms had worked out a system of whistle, trumpet, and visual signals. Following the somewhat superfluous command of, "Set your sights for lowest possible range," superfluous because, below thirteen hundred *arshini*, there was no setting, a whistle blast caused forty men in the long, deep shelter of the trench and the berm to raise forty targets on high.

The next command, by voice, came from the firing line. "Load one clip of five rounds!"

That was easy enough; all the ammunition broken down, so far, came in five round clips. These the troops inserted into a slot above the magazine and, with a single push, forced all five rounds down. The clips were then tossed, with bolts slammed and twisted home to chamber the first round.

There was no need to order the men to take the weapons off safe; their rifles hadn't been on safe to begin with. Indeed, the Model 1891 could not be loaded with the weapon on safe.

"Commence firing!"

Camp Budapest

"'The market here in fill-in-the-space is good' will

mean all the Romanovs are in one place, whichever one we put in. But what if they've been split up?" asked Lieutenant Turgenev. "How do we account for that?"

"Maybe value and sex," suggested Mokrenko. "We use the most valuable, the sable, as a stand in for the tsar. After that, the fox for the tsarina. After that, the blue fox for the grand duchesses and the polar fox for the tsarevich."

"I'm not sure that's the actual relative value," said Turgenev.

"Maybe better if it isn't," Mokrenko admitted. "But there's a problem; nobody is going to go to the expense of sending a wire to Sweden for one polar fox. It's inherently suspicious.

"So maybe," he continued, "we just add zeroes to the actual number, as many as we need to be something besides suspicious. So . . . one hundred is just one. Four hundred blue fox are just the four grand duchesses. So are four thousand, if we find the market is big enough to justify that.

"That works. Write that down, Goat."

"Yes, sir," answered Corporal Koslov, whose surname, in fact, meant goat.

"We need codes for places, too," said Turgenev. "One for each stop on our itinerary. And then a way to designate different places."

"Yes," Mokrenko agreed. "We might, after all, find that they've been sent somewhere completely different than we expect."

"North and south from a known point?" Turgenev suggested. "Also east and west? How about by money? North is rubles; south is kopeks. What for east and west, though?"

That took some thought. Finally Koslov suggested,

"America is east; England is west. Murmansk is north. Odessa is south. We make it a two sentence effort—no, three—for each part of the direction. The first establishes a known point, whichever it is. The second, couched as being a place to send furs to, establishes a direction. The third the distance from that point in that direction. Then we do it again for the other cardinal direction."

"Seems complex," Turgenev said.

"Yes, sir, but we're running out of time. We still have to familiarize on the pistols. We still have to get the money. And we still have to leave soon if we're to get there on time. Besides, at least that way doesn't obviously look like a coded message, which anything that gave coordinates would, and which anything that used an offset to give coordinates also would."

"Directions and money it is. But let's make it rubles and kopeks for each part, with rubles being ten *versts* and kopeks being one."

Mokrenko nodded sagely. "I think that works, but we're going to have to be very careful to make our figures nonsuspicious."

"Yes, we are," Turgenev agreed. "Now let's start working on enemy situation."

"Invert numbers," said Mokrenko. "One hundred and twenty-three would mean three hundred and twenty-one, for example. At least that keeps us, well, usually, from sending a suspiciously accurate number. And, if they're the same, one hundred and thirty-one Red Guards, for example, we don't have to be that accurate; we call it two thirty-one, which means one hundred and thirty two, and is close enough to the truth."

"Okay . . . I can see that, Sergeant. Then . . . squirrel for red soldiers . . . mmm . . . martens for machine guns . . . rabbits for cannon . . . excellent condition is excellent troops . . . not of the best is rabble . . . more coming is more coming."

"Let me try something," said Goat. "So we see two hundred and five Red Guards around the tsar and his family, who are all together. The guards have eighteen machine guns. There are no cannon. Five hundred more Red Guards are coming in a week or ten days."

"The message, then, would read: 'The market here is good STOP I was able to pick up five hundred and two squirrel pelts STOP only eighty-one martens available from my dealer STOP no rabbit fur and no word of any coming STOP supposed to be one hundred and five more rabbit available in a week or ten days STOP quality of what we have is not of the best STOP shall I wait . . .' meaning, 'the Romanovs are here, guarded by two hundred and five guards now. They are all rabble. They have eighteen machine guns, no artillery and none coming, five hundred and one, which is close enough, more Red Guards supposedly en route and expected in a week or ten days.'"

Turgenev stroked his chin. "That 'shall I wait?' It reminds me that we need to be able to receive a message, too, once we're in one place to stay. Hmmm . . . my stomach is rumbling. Let's go eat lunch; we can work as we eat."

Range A (Rifle), Near Camp Budapest

Feldwebel Taenzler cracked the whip above the horses,

being most careful not to hit them. These beasts were in much better shape than the poor miserable things turned over to the Russian battalion, about a quarter of which, at this point, had died, though the rest were on their way to recovery.

Taenzler had given some thought to the notion of butchering the dead horses and mules but, given that they hadn't *necessarily* died of starvation, he'd recommended against that and the Russian commander had listened to him.

The pair gave a little forward lurch, setting both the limber and the *Gulaschkanone* into forward motion.

Fired by wood, the *Gulaschkanone* was a modern marvel. The *Kanone* part of the name came from the smokepipe mounted to one corner. The *Gulasch?* Well, that was a simple one pot meat dish that the device could make in its large central pot, as it could make any kind of stew, in sufficient quantity for about a company. The marvelous part included that the thing could do so while on the move, plus that it had a means of spreading the heat evenly across the surface of the main cooker. This was a double boiler of sorts between the cooking pot and the firebox, containing glycerin. It also had a tub to heat tea or coffee, as well as a kind of griddle.

What it could not do was provide much in the way of variety, stew or pasta or boiled vegetables were pretty much it, and only one of those at a feeding.

It would have been woefully overtasked for feeding a small battalion, as it was now, but then Taenzler still had the kitchen at the camp, plus plenty of cooks now, what with the additional Russians. He planned on feeding the crew working on range building, then going back to refill the stew pot, to bring hot stew to the men using the rifle range. He'd been around the German Army long enough to know who could drop what they were doing to come and eat, and whom he would have to wait upon as they finished absolutely necessary tasks to a schedule. The firers fit into the last category, the range builders into the former.

The Pole, Chmura, recently assigned to the kitchen, had proven a big help. At his translation of Ilyin's suggestion, Taenzler and the cooks had begun scraping the *Schmaltz* directly into the daily stew, where, by dipping, the Russians ate it with considerably more relish than they had when it was spread on bread.

Though it's perhaps just as well that they don't know that the fat comes from crushed and processed Maybugs. I wish I hadn't made the mistake of asking, myself.

The newly building range wasn't far. It seemed like mere minutes before Taenzler found himself pulling on the horses' reins to bring the *Gulaschkanone* to a stop at a likely spot. Chmura stood and, in Russian, called for the men to drop their shovels, collect their mess tins, and line up for lunch.

They didn't need to be told twice.

"You know," said Corporal Goat, on the road to the mess tent, "we might be being *too* paranoid here. All businesses have secrets they don't want to share. Maybe we'd look more suspicious, not less, if we didn't put in something that actually looked like a secret we were trying to keep from competitors."

"Maybe put in a substitution code, you think?" asked the lieutenant. "Use it for something . . ."

Turgenev stopped progress, as did the other two, at the edge of a company street. It was stop or risk being run over by sixteen men, racing along in two groups, each group hauling a 37mm infantry gun on wheels, plus a small ammunition caisson ahead of the gun. Turgenev recognized Lieutenant Federov running along ahead of the first gun, while a *Feldfebel* he didn't know paced the second. The three stopped to watch the drill.

"I know nothing about artillery," Turgenev said, "but I've always found the drill involved to be a fascinating dance."

First, Federov stopped, made a show of looking through the binoculars hanging from his neck, then thrust out one arm in a different direction from the one they'd been racing toward. Swerving to avoid hitting the lieutenant, the four men pulling the caisson made a tight circle to the left, stopped the caisson, let the pole drop, opened the ammunition chest and extracted four containers of ammunition, each holding sixteen rounds of ammunition and weighing, per container, about fifteen kilograms.

The men hauling the gun stopped it before running their lieutenant over, then lowered the trails to the ground. One of the three then pulled the pin that retained the front leg of a tripod, knocked that leg down into position, then replaced the pin. This locked the leg in place while turning the gun's carriage almost into a tripod. He then pulled another pin, thus detaching the gun's soon to be tripod from the axle.

The other two members of the gun crew joined to lift

the gun slightly off the axle. The first man then rolled axle and wheels out of the way, to the left.

They then lowered the entire gun assembly to the ground. With the pull of another pin, the gun and recoil cylinder were detached from the pintle. The squad leader helped one of the men get the eighty-eight pound tube and cylinder assembly onto his shoulder. The tripod and pintle assembly took a bit of effort as well, but was longer, better balanced, and inherently more stable. The remaining crewman was able to walk it up to the vertical position, then bend, put his shoulder into it, and stand upright on his own.

At that point, the second gun had come up abreast of the first and begun its dance, just slightly behind in time.

Turgenev heard Federov shout, "Follow me." At that point, the gun crew trotted off, hauling gun and ammunition by main force, until the view of them was lost to the intervening tentage. The drill was fast enough that the second gun crew began trotting off about the time the first crew disappeared.

"Getting there," said Mokrenko, "aren't they?"

"Yes," said Turgenev, "but for them as for us, time is a limited resource. Let's go . . . and about that substitution code; are businesses that unsophisticated? A mere substitution code when actual, by God, *money* is on the line."

"I confess, I don't know," Mokrenko replied.

"No clue," added Goat.

"Let's presume they're not," said Turgenev. "What else might be available to us?"

"Books," said Goat, who was no dummy.

"Books?"

"Sure, sir; we get two copies of the same book, two *exact* copies. Any word we want is going to be found by a combination of a page number, a line number, and a word on the line number. Inefficient? I'm sure. But probably pretty secure."

"What book?"

"Oh, I don't know. Maybe *War and Peace*?" Goat offered.

Mokrenko shook his head. "Sure has enough words . . . but we're Russian, for God's sake. Maybe some book less obvious? Something that *isn't* by Tolstoy or Dostoevsky?"

"Lermontov?" suggested the lieutenant.

Goat offered, "Or maybe Chernychevsky?"

"Maybe better, because more obscure," Turgenev said.

"You know," said Mokrenko, "We might be well advised to find a telegraph station away from wherever we may find the royal family, and as far from their guards as possible."

"Point," agreed Turgenev.

"May not be possible," said Corporal Koslov. "And there's no train station or even a near passing line in Tobolsk, if they're still there."

"There will be a telegraph station in Tobolsk," Turgenev said. "They'd never have brought the royal family there without a way to give the order to kill them in a hurry."

"Also, 'point,' " conceded Goat. "But if so, sir, there's still not going to be another station in easy distance. What? Tyumen? Could we even get back to Tyumen in time to give the word."

"No," Turgenev said. "Well . . . six days? Maybe we could."

"I wonder if we could get a man attached to us who

knows telegraphy and a portable set for him that we could to tap into the wires?"

"Army math," Turgenev reminded. "If you must have one of something to end with you must start with more than one."

"Maybe so," Mokrenko said, "but, under the circumstances, we'll be lucky to get even one."

Those words brought them to the mess where the lieutenant said, "No more talking until we've got our food and are on our way."

"A minute and thirty-two seconds," announced Federov to both gun crews, together, seated in a semicircle on the ground between the pair of cannon. "A minute and thirty-two seconds from me designating a stopping point to both guns, side by side, ready to fire. You know, that's not bad. I think maybe we're ready for the real ammunition."

"We're ready, sir," said the *Feldfebel*, "but the range is not. What we can do, though, is put the guns up, draw our rifles, and go knock off the requirement to qualify on the M1891s. That would be a good use of our time."

Federov considered that for perhaps as much as three seconds, then said, "Let me know, *Feldfebel*, when everything is secured and we're ready to march to the range."

Machine Gun and Cannon Range (Under Construction)

The men building the range were still eating when Kostyshakov suddenly appeared on the dirt road.

Both First and Third were commanded by senior lieutenants, Boris Baluyev for First and Georgy Lesh for Third. They ran up and reported to Kostyshakov as soon as they spied him.

Lesh spoke first. "Any word on the pioneer tools, sir? This would go so much faster if we had them. And we've still got to do the deep digging for the building clearing."

"We need more lumber, too, sir," added Baluyev, blowing aside facial hair as he spoke. "Trying to do this with entrenching tools is, well . . ." Baluyev took off his mittens to show blistered, bleeding hands. "See, sir? And the men? They're in worse shape than we are. We've *got* to get those pioneer tools."

"I know. Romeyko's at wit's end. The Germans are trying but nobody seems to have anything to spare. What they had to spare seems to have gone west with the divisions being shifted to face the French and British and, now, the Americans."

Lesh scowled. "Hell, sir, we could *make* our own wooden handles if they'd just get us the metal parts!"

"Yes, sure. But we don't have those either. Now quit complaining and show me what you have managed to do here."

"Georgy has something special to show you, sir," said Baluyev. "While he's setting that up, I can walk you around."

"Fine;" said Daniil, "go get your demonstration set up, Lesh."

"Yes, sir." With a hasty salute, Lesh trotted off.

Baluyev led Daniil to the firing line. The first thing

Kostyshakov noticed was a set of large screens, at either end.

"What are those for?" he asked.

"The infantry guns, sir. Their tactics involve leaving their ammunition wagon, along with the mule or horse if they have one, in safe defilade. They manhandle the guns forward. But we don't have anywhere with a suitable hill, nor any particularly good means of raising a hill. So we put these up to give a simulation of defilade. It's not perfect because the guns can't go over them but have to go around. But then, they're *supposed* to go around.

"The heavy machine guns will do something similar. And we have two so both can be on the range at one time, or, when we don't need both, either one has a choice of where to go. Or they can split sections."

"Good thinking in general, though I'll ask the Germans if there's a place we can use that has actual hills or ridges, too."

"I think Lieutenant Federov would appreciate that, sir.

"Now between the two screens, we've put in spots for five Lewis guns at a time." Baluyev pointed down range, saying, "Note here, sir, that we haven't put in anything for the Lewis guns to shoot at that's closer than seven hundred and fifty *arshins*. For that they may as well use the rifle range, no?"

Kostyshakov considered that, then gestured a general agreement.

"What are you using for targets here?"

"You can't generally see them, sir, because they're camouflaged, but we have forty-five deep pits we're digging. Men sheltering in those will raise targets on whistle command. Scoring, since those will be machine guns being scored, will be from the firing point rather than the target. That's for the Lewis guns and the Maxims when shooting targets at range. We're also building frames to put basic machine gun targets on, but I'm having trouble figuring out what to do about our traversing and elevating mechanisms, and our usual targets being in Russian, and the only ones available, the Germans' targets, being in metric."

"If you had heavy duty paper and paint or ink," Kostyshakov asked, "oh, and rulers, I suppose, could you make our kind of targets from scratch?"

"Probably, sir, though we'd have to test them with our guns, too, to make sure they're right."

"I'll see if we can squeeze that material out of the Germans."

"That would be great, sir, and . . . I think . . . Lesh is ready to show you something."

"Lead on."

The trail blazed by Baluyev led first to the center of the range, and then half a mile downrange to near where most of the troops dug. Daniil saw nothing of any particular interest, even when they reached where Lesh stood, beaming. In the course of it, they passed four enlisted men, just waiting.

"You had something to show me, Lieutenant?"

"Yes, sir. But you're almost standing on it."

Daniil looked down and saw a neat board, about one *arshin* on a side, or perhaps slightly less. A wheel was attached to the center of the board, via a vertical spike. The heads of four more spikes had been driven through the board, holding it firmly to the ground. Rope—roughly half inch stuff—led off in both directions from the wheel, which seemed to have a cavity around the rim in which that small bit of the rope lay hidden.

"It came from one of the manuals we got from the Germans, the one for the 37mm cannon, sir."

Beginning to lose patience now, Daniil exclaimed, "*What* came?"

"Oh, sorry, sir; moving targets for the machine guns and the light cannon."

"I really don't . . ."

"Watch me, sir." With that, Lesh ran about one hundred meters toward the far firing line, to where the four previously idle troops waited. Bending, he and the men picked up the free end of the rope and began to walk to the south.

"Look over there, sir," said Baluyev, pointing to a clump of bushes from behind which slid a small sled, moving at the same pace as Lesh and his detail of rope haulers. Suddenly the sled picked up speed as the haulers started to run.

"It's just going to lock up on the . . ." Daniil shut up as the sled suddenly changed direction, still moving forward at a man's running speed.

"How . . . ?"

"There's a knot in the rope, sir. It doesn't fit the cavity around the wheel so the rope jumps out of it, then pulls the sled in the direction of the next wheel, which can be just about anywhere."

"Fucking fascinating," Daniil said, wonder in his voice. "I've never seen . . ."

"Neither had we, sir. Neither had Federov. But as soon as he saw it he also saw the potential and brought it to us."

"Bloody marvelous. It's *impossible*—well, it's *been* impossible—to have moving targets before, at least as far as I've ever heard, but this . . . Oh, this is going to be so much fun!"

"Yes, sir."

"How much did you have to do with this, Baluyev?"

"Less than half, sir."

"Okay. How good are you with explosives?"

"Better than some, less good than others, sir."

"Well. I have this project for you."

Quartermaster's Shop, Camp Budapest

Romeyko, the battalion quartermaster, looked over the task board on the wall. It was better prioritized now, to be sure, but it was also substantially more full. *For every problem we solve, two more arise,* Romeyko mentally groaned. *And some of the problems are starting to appear unsolvable.*

Looking over the task board, Romeyko saw:

Machine Pistols
Pioneer tools
Nails
Map of *Rodina*
Canvas or heavy paper
Paint or ink
Straight edges, drawing
Horse blankets
Portable telegraph set

Money
Nine *Kindjal*
Nine *Shashka*
Lamb *papaha*
Blacksmith
Wrist watches, or at least some kind of watches, for 150
Field telephones
Communications wire
Cavity wheels
Nine hundred *arshini* of good rope
Spikes, heavy, sixty
Boards, one *arshin* square
Sheet tin
Civilian clothing and shoes, Russian
Binoculars
Lathe to turn dummy grenades
Lead ingots
Explosives, bulk

He didn't bother to look past those, but estimated: *And still two dozen important items after that. Different important items, yes, to some extent, but the number never shrinks.*

He was also starting to feel the pinch of transportation, what with the need to haul ammunition to the rifle range—*and more ranges, soon enough, as well as more and heavier ammunition*—to having to feed the troops at several different locations, locations too far away from camp for them to walk back for lunch and dinner. The need to draw from the railhead hadn't changed, but the need to disperse to where things would be used, while still drawing in firewood, too, since the coal was proving insufficient to the need, meant his three wagons still on loan were not enough.

Thank God for Taenzler.

Feldwebel Weber, who spent about half his time inside the wire, working with Romeyko, and half, outside, fighting with the system to try to get Romeyko the material the Russians needed, asked, "Something bothering you, *Herr Hauptmann*?"

Romeyko just pointed silently in the direction on which his eyes were already fixed.

"Well," said Weber, "I have one good thing to report. One company set of pioneer tools has been found in the salvage depot at Kuestrin, along with a couple of dozen spares of various types. Also the other seven hundred thousand rounds of M1891 and belted Maxim ammunition has been secured. Should be here in about ten days, eight if we're lucky."

"Machine pistols?" Romeyko asked, hopes suddenly buoyed up by the news.

"They remain a problem," answered Weber. "Major Brinkmann, bearing a requisition from Hoffmann, himself, has gone to Baden to try to get a portion of the first batch coming off the assembly line."

Camp Budapest

There was a kind of constrained parade field in the center of the camp, surrounded on three sides by the off-white tents of the three companies, with a mix of tents, wooden buildings, and a dirt road, leading to the main gate, on the fourth side. In the middle of that field, under the supervision of Sergeant Major Nenonen, thirty men—thirty often cursing men, ten minimalist gun crews—went through the arcane but necessary ritual of disassembling and reassembling the frustratingly complex light machine guns.

Nenonen was the only man of the battalion with previous training on the Lewis, that having been a lengthy and difficult course run the prior year, not too far behind the then front. Nenonen was a veteran of the Finland Guard Regiment of the Imperial Guard.

"Step one," Nenonen shouted, "is to remove the magazine. That's that round thing on top for you, Private Durak. We do this by sticking a finger into the hole—you know how to stick a finger in a hole, don't you, Corporal Blyad?—and push that little button, then lift."

The troops tittered; neither man was actually addressed by his proper surname, but each had picked up a not necessarily complimentary nickname from his comrades, basically "dummy" and "fuck," the latter for a corporal too much given to bragging about his amorous conquests.

"Now set the magazines down on your ground cloth.

"Next, your fingers on the bolt charging handle—that's that little thing sticking out to the right—pull the trigger and ride the bolt forward.

"Now, flip your guns over so the trigger and pistol grip are away from you. See that little lever right where wood meets metal? Put your left hand in a reversed grip on the pistol grip, then use your right to twist the wooden stock towards you . . . that's right; forty-five degrees and she's free. Remove the stock and put it down on the ground cloth next to the magazine.

"Now pull the trigger and pull backwards; you will find that the entire grip and trigger assembly slide off easily. You know the drill . . . put it on the ground cloth."

Daniil Kostyshakov was, himself, unfamiliar with the Lewis guns, though he'd read about them, and about light machine guns, in general, in various German military journals while incarcerated in Fort IX. These had mostly covered tactical employment, rather than the mechanics of the things.

Seeing Kostyshakov watching from the edge of the parade field, Nenonen turned matters over to a half-trained assistant and trotted over.

"I am beginning to doubt, Sergeant Major, that the Germans will come through with those machine pistols," Kostyshakov began. "That means we may be using these things to clear rooms, hallways, stairwells, and floors. Tell me about them."

Nenonen filled his cheeks and blew air out, in a fricative. "They're a really mixed blessing, sir."

"How so?"

"Well . . . in the first place, they're very complex. They're . . . mmm . . . best I show you."

Nenonen led the way to where one group of three men had just completed disassembly on their Lewis. "Go join one of the other gun teams," he told them. "Your gun will still be here when you get back."

Nenonen picked up one of the pan magazines lying on the ground cover. Turning it over, he said, "Problem one is this, sir. So are problems two and three.

"This holds forty-seven rounds. Captain Romeyko is sitting on some that hold ninety-seven rounds, but they've got their issues, too, so we don't know what to do with them. Note that it's open on the side that faces the gun and the ground. It has to be, given the way these things are loaded. It has the advantage of allowing dirt and mud to get out. It has the far worse disadvantage of allowing a lot more dirt and mud to get in in the first place."

Nosing around the ground sheet the sergeant major picked up a cylindrical tool, from a cubical leather case, which he affixed to a shorter cylinder that was part of the magazine. The tool had a hand-width diamond pattern engraved on the upper half to aid in gripping.

Nenonen explained, "You load these by inserting one round at a time and then"—here he twisted the tool by hand to demonstrate—"turning this to rotate the disk that holds the round in place. You have to do this forty-seven times to load the magazine fully. It is not easy and it is *not* quick.

"That's why we have twenty-two magazines for every Lewis gun: to keep up an adequate rate of fire for a long enough time, you need every one of those, fully loaded, to start.

"But the weight of twenty-two fully loaded magazines is about sixty pounds for the ammunition *and* thirty-eight or so pounds for the magazines. Add in the twenty-eight pounds for the gun, itself, and . . . well, a three-man crew is barely enough for the job. And they won't be exactly playing leapfrog with each other while they're moving across the battlefield, either.

"It's also a problem for marching fire. This magazine spins as it's feeding ammunition to the gun. If the gunner doesn't keep it well away from his body and cant it to the right, it's going to rub on, maybe even get caught on, his uniform. That means a stoppage.

"And then there's the overheating problem . . ."

"But I thought that shroud on the barrel kept it cool," Daniil interrupted.

"For a while—longer than you might expect—it does. That's not the problem."

Nenonen reached down again, this time picking up a smallish, flattish half cylinder. "It's this thing, the operating spring. Unlike most machine guns, instead of a long helical spring to drive the bolt and/or operating rod forward, it's got what amounts to a clock spring wound up inside this. But it's also near the chamber and it *does* get hot, hot enough to lock up the gun. And in a hard fight it will tend to do so long before those twenty-two magazines are used up.

"Oh, and speaking of heat"—here the sergeant major reached out and tapped the shroud around the barrel— "this thing gets hot within the first four magazines, too hot to hold without a glove, and that glove had better be thick.

"Also, sir, note that if you get to close quarters, there is no bayonet lug. It's also too heavy to manhandle quickly from one aiming point to another.

"Finally, there are fifteen distinct causes of stoppages, ranging from a freely rotating magazine that won't feed to a double feed. About half of those, eight, to be exact, can generally be dealt with by immediate action. The other seven? They require a good deal more effort, down to and including taking the thing apart, to one degree or another. This is a neat trick on a muddy battlefield.

"But, sir, all that said, what it does, which is to provide

mobile suppressive fire to the foot soldiers, it still does better than anything else in the world to date."

Kostyshakov nodded understanding. *And one problem you didn't mention, Sergeant Major: once we go into a building to clear it out and rescue the royal family, this thing is going to shoot right through all but the stoutest walls, at things we cannot even guess at, let alone see. Put the royal family in a clump, on the other side of one of those walls and, well, we shouldn't have even bothered to start.*

Interlude

Tatiana: The Changing of the Guard

My favorite days were the ones where the Fourth Regiment was on duty. There were still those who remained friendly to us and it made the day easier for everyone, especially Alexei.

Papa, Alexei, and I spent several hours with the men of the Fourth in the guardhouse. There was talk and discontentment, some of which they were reluctant to discuss. But finally they did, opening up to Papa about the grumblings in the Second Regiment.

Those grumblings came to fruition in the most unexpected way on February eighth. The soviet of soldiers of the Second had decided to replace Commissar Pankratov, the very man who worked so hard to "enlighten" them. They had decided that his ideology was not Bolshevik enough and called for a Bolshevik commissar to be sent from Moscow.

He was not their only casualty, however. That crass man, Nikolsky, must also resign. They "insisted." I confess, I looked forward to seeing *him* go.

I waited for Papa to ask what would happen to Commissar Pankratov, but he did not interrupt, letting the men of the Fourth lead the conversation now that they were so forthcoming.

They spoke of rumors that the new Soviet Russia was no longer at war and that the army was to be disbanded.

As they spoke their fears, he would pat their shoulders and say something encouraging, but his voice would break and sometimes he couldn't finish speaking.

The men continued to speculate, to hope, and he'd sit there, blinking like a man keeping tears at bay.

Finally, when there was no more to say, no more to hear, Papa nodded his understanding and shook hands with them. Something sad passed between him and the men huddled in the guard house.

That sadness descended onto my father's shoulders like a heavy cloak. Those shoulders that I once knew would hold up the world, remained weighed down even as he straightened, stood, and bid the men a good night. The cloak trailed behind him in the snow on the way back to the house, leaving invisible drag marks in the snow. He held onto my hand and Alexei's, our skin separated by gloves. Even through them, I could sense a different kind of cold than the one clawing at our faces.

A few days later I found out why that news had made them so sad. Several soldiers from the Fourth came in secret to say their goodbyes. The old soldiers, those most friendly to us, those we had called "our guard" instead of our guards, were to leave us.

March brought even worse news as I served lunch to Prince Dolgorukov and Papa in his study. Colonel Kobylinsky knocked on the door and came in. He had just received a telegram.

We were to be put on soldiers' rations and given a

stipend from which to maintain our household. Our expenses were no longer to be paid by the State. The same State that had taken everything from us, decided what little we could keep, and with the stroke of a pen, turned us into beggars as well as prisoners.

That cloak of grief and sadness that I was certain only I could see, that I tried and tried to blink away but couldn't, pulled at my father's soul. I could see the toll of it in his eyes.

Resolved to our new fate, to this new judgment, Papa and Prince Dolgorukov drew up the accounts.

I went to tell Mama, and she and I joined them as they went over the numbers again and again.

"We shall have to dismiss ten servants," Dolgorukov said.

Mama put her hand on Papa's shoulders, trying as if by magic, to draw away the weight of that wearying cloak. They spoke quietly, not of themselves, but of what would happen to the servants and their families, for their devotion to us had led them down this dark road that would start with beggary and end up worse. They would forever be tainted by their association with us.

Like Father Vasiliev, who had been sent off, like Commissar Pankratov who'd shown us kindness, they would be branded as traitors to the new Soviet Russia.

Was everyone who touched our lives to be condemned for doing so?

Chapter Eight

Bogdan Vraciu's Barquentine *Loredana*
("No man will be a sailor who has contrivance enough
to get himself into a jail." —Samuel Johnson)

Camp Budapest

The strategic reconnaissance section, under Lieutenant Turgenev, would be leaving camp in the morning. The Germans had come up with the money, though, as Hoffmann had said, mostly in paper, rather than coin. It had been increased substantially because of that. The pistols were in hand, each man in the section having put about three hundred rounds downrange. They also had eight of the much shorter Model 1907 carbines, and every man had requalified on them. The M1907s, moreover, had been disassembled, had their forestocks cut down, and now reposed in two cases that, from appearances, couldn't possibly contain rifles.

There was a portable telegraph set, with a small spool of wire, courtesy of the Germans. Indeed, it was a German set. The men wore civilian clothing, to include foot gear and hats. Uniforms were tucked into their bags.

There was a code set up. Indeed, the Germans, thorough as they tended to be, had had their Swedish Office send a message each to Tobolsk, Yekaterinburg, and Tyumen, addressed to Pan-Siberian Import-Export, to, in the first place, prove the lines were still up, and, in the second, give the team a reason to send a telegram, or a series of them, to Sweden.

The Germans had even found them a thoroughly unprincipled Romanian smuggler, a nasty old pirate named Bogdan Vraciu. He plied the Euxine, bribing who he had to or robbing, condemning, and killing whom he could. For a high fee he'd agreed to bring them approximately to Rostov-on-Don.

The budget hadn't gone up, even though there were now three extra men—Shukhov, a combat engineer, also called a "pioneer," Timashuk, a medic, and Sarnof, the signaler, added to the roster. Private Sarnof wasn't especially happy about the assignment. It would also be Sarnof's job to encode any messages. In his bag was also the portable telegraph and the copy of Chernychevsky's

What Is to Be Done?, just as Timashuk carried an aid bag, and Shukhov a limited quantity of demolitions, less the blasting caps, which were split between Turgenev and Mokrenko.

"If we get caught doing this," Sarnof insisted, "we'll all be shot!"

"Could be worse," answered Mokrenko; "they could hang us instead."

For some inexplicable reason, this thought failed to calm Sarnof down in the slightest.

"We're ready, sir," Turgenev told Kostyshakov, later, in the canvas walled officers' mess tent. "Materially, anyway, we're ready, except, maybe, for a potential shortage in cash. We can probably fix that with a bank robbery, if we absolutely must. But there's still a problem. What if others . . . well, I mean, of *course* there are going to be others; what if there's already a plot afoot to rescue the royal family? What if there are twenty such plots, as there may be?"

Daniil, who actually hadn't given that any thought yet, opined, "Probably more than twenty. We're Russian; plotting is what we *do*. What are your thoughts?"

"Yes, sir, probably more than twenty," Turgenev agreed. "However many, though, I think that, for the most part, we need to have as little to do with any of them as possible," answered Turgenev. "There may be someone who has useful information, I suppose, but what if they're really working for the Reds? I mean; the tsar has been deposed and under guard for almost a year, now, and no attempt at a rescue? That smells to me of someone trusted by someone else who is working for the other side and turning any rescuers over to the Bolsheviks.

"And—and here's the real problem, for us, anyway; for the entire mission, I mean—what if there is someone, or many someones, who are only exciting Bolshevik paranoia and causing the Reds to be more on guard? To have them calling in reinforcements? To have them putting the royal family under tighter control, maybe with guards present to shoot them on the slightest fear of a rescue attempt? What then?

"And what about the smugglers who are to transport us across the sea?"

Daniil thought upon that, silently, for a several long moments, before answering, "You probably need to kill them. Or to get the Bolsheviks to do so. Yes, it would be sad, especially if their hearts are in the right place, but the safety of the royal family and the future of the empire are more important than a few incompetents, even with good hearts. And as for the pirates who are supposed to transport you back home . . . dead men tell no tales, if you suspect these might tell some."

"Thank you, sir," Turgenev said. "I . . . we . . . had already come to those conclusions. We disliked it so much we needed, really needed, someone to give us the moral absolution of telling us so."

Daniil let his chin and eyes sink groundward. *That, I suppose, is what I get the lavish pay for.*

"Don't spare any tears for the smuggler the Germans found for you. They wouldn't use him if he were not both expendable and deserving of being expended. But how are you going to deal with him?"

"None of us can sail a boat," Turgenev said. "We need them for that. Moreover, we probably ought not do anything to them unless we have reason to become suspicious. If we have any hint they mean us ill, we figure to wait until he's a few hours out from Rostov-on-Don, kill him and his crew, dump the bodies, launch the lifeboat, set the boat on fire and row in."

"Sounds plausible," Daniil agreed. "The timing may not, however, work out so conveniently."

Burgas, Bulgaria

"I'm sorry," said *Feldwebel* Weber, indicating with his finger a sailing vessel moored to the group's front. As always, Weber stood slightly stooped. He added, "But this was all we could come up with. Be on your guard. Do not trust any of the crew."

Turgenev answered, "I understand. Needs must, and all. We'll be all right. Thank you, *Feldwebel*." Then he stomped up the gangway, more properly called the "brow," to meet the captain.

The ship, the *Loredana*, was considerably bigger than any of the Russians had expected. Rocking gently at anchor, tied to the wharf by Burgas's shipping district in the south of the city, she looked to Mokrenko to be about sixty *arshini* long, or maybe a trifle more. He knew the things sticking up from the deck were called "masts," that the cross pieces on the masts were "yardarms," and the white cloth hanging from them "sails," but there his nautical knowledge ended.

There was nothing wrong with his arithmetic, though; he counted five sails tied to the yardarms, plus two small triangular ones running from the top of the foremost mast to the wooden pole—he would soon learn it was called a "bowsprit," sticking out in front. There were also two large triangular sails behind each of the two rearward masts, as well as another being set between the first mast and the middle one.

While Turgenev spoke to the captain, Mokrenko watched the crew setting that between-the-masts sail, as well as the five on the yardarms. He noticed among them a small boy or, perhaps a girl or young woman, dark blond, peeking at the Russians from behind the rearmost mast. The confusion stemmed from the kid being in boy's clothes. On closer observation, though, Mokrenko decided it must be a girl.

I've never in my life been on any boat bigger than a little rowboat. And never on the ocean. Lord, please help me, help all of us, not to get seasick. I wonder who the girl is; captain's daughter, maybe?

There was a tone and tenor to the conversation between the lieutenant and the ship's captain that made it more of an argument. Mokrenko picked up bits and pieces of the conversation. "...balance the ship...not going to be separated...want to founder in a storm...still not...move cargo...so move it...you pay...how much? Segarceanu!"

When Turgenev joined Mokrenko, waiting on the wooden wharf, he said, "I trust that bastard even less than I expected to. We're going to stay two men to a cabin. Fifty percent alert. I'll pull my watch the same as anyone else."

"Suggestion, sir?"

"Sure, go ahead."

"We'd be better off with two armed men fully rested, awake, and alert, *outside* the cabins, watching all of them, than we would be with four, alone, struggling to stay awake against the darkness. And for meals we send two men together to bring them to us. One man eats; we wait an hour, to see if he gets sick, then the rest of us do."

The lieutenant considered that, then agreed. Pointing with his chin at one of the crewmen, he said, "That's apparently Segarceanu. He's to show us to our cabins. Which are all to be together."

"Put the rifles where, sir?" asked Mokrenko. The rifles were disassembled, with no bayonets since the M1907 couldn't mount them anyway. They sat on the wharf in two cases that looked to be, and ordinarily were, too small each to hold four or five rifles.

"Our cabin."

"Yes, sir."

The *Loredana*, the Russians were somewhat surprised to discover, had a powerful auxiliary engine down below. This served, using a small fraction of its available *oomph*, to move the ship out from the wharf and on its way to the channel that led to the sea.

"We don't look like we have the power," said the greasy, black-haired Captain Vraciu, standing on the bridge with Turgenev. There was a modicum of white mixed in with the black. "No one looks for a smuggler of this size unless they look like they can outrace the patrol vessels. We set the sails so most of the landlubbers don't notice the engine, which we keep as quiet as possible.

"Fuel's expensive, too, so we mostly use the sails

anyway. But if I see another ship approaching, one I don't know if I can take or bribe, then we call on the engines."

Turgenev regarded the skipper. *He stinks of old tobacco smoke, and not the good stuff, either. That, and he has liquor on his breath. That would tend to explain the bulbous veined nose and the perpetual five o'clock shadow: too lazy or drunk to shave. He should probably go to see a good dentist, especially given how many teeth are already missing. It would help, too, if he changed those baggy, dirty clothes. He also reeks faintly of shit.*

"How many days to Rostov?" Turgenev asked.

"Unless you want to pay extra for the fuel . . . ?"

Being already likely short of cash, what with the addition of the medic, pioneer, and signaler, with no chance to get more, Turgenev said, "No."

"Five days, then, *if* the winds stay with us."

Turgenev read that as, *Four days, then we shake you down for money, or it will take more than six, unless, of course, you've all gotten sick enough first that we can cut your throats and loot your baggage before then.*

The first to succumb was the Cossack Lavin. Three hours of travel and less than twenty miles out of port, he felt his gorge rising. A quick race to the rail and his five foot, eight inch frame shook as he projectile vomited into the sea.

Mokrenko and the signaler, Sarnof, each took a side to help Lavin below to his cabin. No sooner had they stood him up than the Cossack convulsed again, bending at the waist and painting Sarnof's trousers with bile. The signaler got one whiff of the stench, dropped Lavin, and threw himself half over the rail, his chest and abdomen heaving with the effort of expelling everything he'd eaten for what seemed the last month.

Mokrenko instantly stopped breathing, only exhaling slowly through his nose, to try to keep the infectious stench at bay, as he led Lavin back to the rail.

Standing between the two, fingers clenched into the material of their collars, Mokrenko looked out over the nearly glass smooth sea, wondering, *What the fuck happens if we hit bad weather?*

At that moment the air, which had been almost still, relative to the ship, suddenly picked up a breeze, cold and wet, bearing down from the north. A few minor capillaries appeared on the water, harbingers full of malevolent promise.

"Oh, fuck!"

The beating of rain and waves, the wind ripping through the rigging, and the groaning of the wood of the ship, all combined to create a cacophony that made thinking hard and speech nearly impossible.

Mokrenko held off the heaves by sheer willpower. All the rest, though, succumbed to a greater or lesser degree. The least affected, other than Mokrenko, was Shukhov, the pioneer. For the most part he was all right, with "all right" being occasionally interrupted by a bout of vomiting.

It fell to Mokrenko to fetch the meals, since Shukhov couldn't be counted on not to puke into the stew. Generally, he was able to load two double loaves of bread, or four pounds of hardtack, into a bag, carrying the stew in a clean bucket. Mostly the food went over the side, as the rest of the section was unable to eat even a bit.

It was when he was bringing food back to the cabins that one of the crewmen, a bearded, greasy sort in a short, black waxed jacket, pushed out a foot, tripping the Cossack and causing him to lose control of the bucket, spilling about half the stew.

There were seven crewmen present, not counting the cook. All laughed heartily. Also all had knives, including the cook. *Not a time to fight,* thought Mokrenko. *Not at these odds. But there will be a reckoning.*

"You'll clean up your mess," said black jacket.

"No," answered Mokrenko, fingering his sword, "I won't."

The worst was Corporal Koslov, "Goat." By the time Mokrenko got back with the food, Goat was begging all and sundry—*loudly*—to, "Please, for the love of God, *please* shoot me."

Passing the half bucket's worth of stew to Shukhov, Mokrenko proceeded to take away Koslov's pistol, his *shashka,* his *kindjal,* and his rope belt.

"Why the belt, Sergeant?" Shukhov asked.

"Lest the corporal try to hang himself."

"Oh."

Shukhov and Mokrenko did their best to estimate the size of the crew against the day of having to get rid of them. The best they'd been able to come up with, so far, was sixteen, including the captain and the cook, but not the roughly twelve- to fourteen-year-old girl who never said a word and seemed to be there for the captain's nocturnal entertainment.

The ship, meanwhile, adding insult to injury, was a continuous roller coaster, alternating deep, seemingly terminal dives into the troughs with shuddering efforts to rise onto the swells.

That cocksucker, Vraciu, is making it worse on purpose, thought Mokrenko, carrying a vomit-filled bucket up a madly swaying ladder, to dump the contents over the side. The puke was a disgusting mix of Turgenev's and Koslov's ejecta. Mokrenko couldn't quite bring himself even to look into the mess.

If either I or Shukhov succumb, the other is going to collapse from sheer fatigue. Then the crew will pile on us within the hour. I'd seriously consider attacking the bastards now, just myself and the engineer, but we can't man the ship. Don't know how and the two of us aren't enough even if we did. And Shukhov's not well enough even if we knew how and were enough. Maybe when the storm's over, we can, but in this gale we haven't a chance.

Hmmm . . . how about taking a hostage? No, Vraciu doesn't seem to care enough about any of his crew, not even that underage girl he likely buggers, for a threat to one or two of them to delay him in launching an attack for an instant. At least the way he slaps them around says they don't matter to him.

Mokrenko tied the vomit-filled bucket off to a line and dumped it over the side to wash it out. As he was hauling it back aboard, he noticed one of the crew—*Ah, yes, my friend, black jacket*—head covered with the jacket against the cold squall—moving unsteadily forward on the wet and swaying deck.

The bucket came back aboard just as the crewman passed close by, lost in his own thoughts, troubles, and miseries. Mokrenko took a quick glance toward the bow. *Nobody.* He looked even more quickly up into the rigging. *Nobody.* Then he dropped the bucket to the deck, bent down while lunging forward, grabbed the crewman about the thighs, then lifted and carried him to the gunwales, before launching the sailor over the side.

No one heard the splash, but Mokrenko took a deep personal satisfaction in watching the man treading water, far behind. The Cossack watched with glee as a three-meter wave crashed down upon the helpless crewman, momentarily sending him under. He popped up, struggling frantically, a few moments later. The next large wave likewise washed over him. By the time he should have popped up from that, the ship was far enough away that the mist, rain, and spray blocked any clear view.

Just doing Your work, Lord.

He probably won't drown, but the cold will kill him eventually. One down. Fifteen to go. Sixteen if we have to dispose of that little girl. That, I would much rather not have to do.

Barquentine *Loredana*, Black Sea, 28 Jan, 1918

The captain and crew were absolutely frantic, desperately searching for their missing crewman. Mokrenko was shocked, actually. *Who would have imagined that that old pirate would care about any of his crew?*

The mystery was cleared up when Vraciu himself came into the passenger area demanding to know, "Have any of you seen my son?"

Which would also tend to explain why the shit thought he could get away with tripping me.

"Why, no, Captain," Mokrenko lied. He felt zero obligation to be honest with known enemies. "What did he look like?"

Vraciu shot Mokrenko a look of sheer menace. He'd heard about his son's little game with the passenger and how the passenger refused to play his part in the game. *Maybe we'll hang you from the yardarm,* the captain thought, *before we toss your corpse overboard. If we don't find my son, alive and well, we'll hang you to unconsciousness a dozen times before we finally let you die.*

Barquentine *Loredana*, Black Sea, 29 Jan, 1918

Sarnof was the first of the stricken to show a recovery. Despite the continuing storm, he was well enough, indeed, that he could have stood a guard shift.

Mokrenko decided against that, very quietly telling the signaler, "No, they think there's just two of us able to fight. Be a big surprise to them to discover just that little bit too late that there's another pistol and sword in play. Stay in your cabin, Sarnof. Be quiet except for making the odd moan and gagging sound. You might even try doing vomiting imitations; you've had enough practice for that, I believe."

Now it was Shukhov's turn on guard. He had his pistol hidden under his tunic, his *kindjal* likewise, and his sword, his *shashka*, in one hand, across his lap, with the point of the scabbard resting on the floor.

It was hard, oh, so hard, to stay awake. It wasn't made any easier by the occasional waves of nausea that still swept over the young pioneer from time to time. Neither was it made any easier by the very limited moonlight that crept in through the few portholes.

Shukhov used the fingers of his left hand to hold one eye open for a bit, then switched to the other, then back to the first. Gradually, he became aware—or thought he did—of a small presence in the open area between the cabins.

Suddenly awake, the pioneer swept his sword from its scabbard, holding it pointed at where he thought the apparition stood.

"Quietly," the apparition said, in surprisingly good, albeit very soft, Russian. "Be quiet or they'll hear you."

"The . . . the girl?" Shukhov asked. "How . . ."

"How do I speak Russian? I *am* Russian," the girl replied. "I am Natalya, Natalya Vladimirovna Sorokina. The Bolsheviks murdered my parents, made use of me for a week or so, and then sold me to that swine of a captain for three cases of *rakia*. I'm sure you've figured out what the captain bought me for."

Shukhov didn't confirm that he could guess. *Why add to the girl's humiliation? Her accent says "very upper class." It will be harder on her, then.*

"They are coming tonight," Natalya said. "Even now the captain is giving half the crew, the half that will be used, their orders."

"What weapons?" Shukhov asked.

"Clubs, knives. The only pistol on board is the captain's.

He'd only ever entrust it to his son, who seems to have disappeared. If you are the one who killed him—*if* he was killed—you have my eternal thanks."

"Not me," the pioneer answered. "Someone else. When will they come?"

"Sometime after midnight. Now, I have to go. Be ready. And good luck."

Since the captain and crew had already made free with her, Natalya was free to go to her miserable bunk and lie down. She sent a prayer to a God she had come to have some doubts about, to take care of her countrymen about to fight for their lives. *Maybe He's there and maybe He'll listen. It was so easy to believe back when I was a . . . well . . . that doesn't matter anymore.*

The sense of being totally alone in the world, without even the presence of God to comfort her, was too much. As she did most nights, Natalya began to cry into the rough sack that served for a pillow. That actually helped, at least a little.

The terrible thing is there is nothing I can tell myself I should have done differently. I didn't act like a whore. I didn't talk like a whore. I was dressed normally, like a teenaged girl. I didn't do anything, so why should this have befallen me? Why? Can you answer that for me, God, if you're out there? WHY?

Of course I know the answer; my parents and I were in a nice carriage, with a nice couple of horses pulling it. That made us rich, made us "class enemies," the exact term the Bolsheviks used before beating me, or lining up for their fun. Or both.

Of course, the worst part wasn't even the violation, the being made to serve. It was making me pretend to enjoy it to avoid another beating. Funny how both the Bolsheviks and the ship's crew fixed on that. A certain kind of man? Are they all like that? No, I know they're not. My father was a good man. I think these countrymen taking passage on this ship are good men. At least none of them look at me like a slightly rotten piece of meat.

I think if they lose, I'm going to join them in the water. I can take at least that much satisfaction, depriving these swine of the use of me.

"After midnight," Mokrenko observed, in the forwardmost, portside cabin, "means not a lot of time. Okay, here's what we do. Shukhov and Sarnof, dig out four dynamo lights from our baggage. Then get a uniform . . . make it one of the . . ."

The sergeant stopped at sensing the unsteady presence of Lieutenant Turgenev standing in the door. "Keep doing what you're doing, Sergeant, but add me to the roster of those who can fight. At least somewhat, I can. I think."

"All right, sir," Mokrenko said, gently. "Can I ask you then to take one of your uniforms, cut open your cabin's mattresses, and use the stuffing to make us a dummy to sit out in the open area?"

"I can do this. It may smell a little of puke before I am done."

"That, sir, would be perfect. Now, Shukhov; get everyone's pistols but the lieutenant's, plus four boxes of ammunition, then meet me at the foremast. When you get there, pass out the pistols, at least two to each of us.

Sarnof, you get the dynamo lights and a piece of rope. Hmmm...on second thought, no, get pieces, two more than long enough for the width of this open area plus one about half that. And please bring something to secure the dummy.

"And, for God's sake, everybody, do so *quietly.*"

The ambush was laid out in accordance with the plan of the passenger area. This area was forward, in what might otherwise have been accommodation for the crew. In the middle was an open area, through which the foremast penetrated the top deck on its way down to the keel. It was flanked by six cabins, three to either side, plus a forward storage area kept under lock and key by the captain.

"Listen up," Mokrenko said, when everyone had assembled by the foremost portside cabin. "Everyone have their *shashka*?"

"Yes," answered each man in turn, just audibly, though Turgenev whispered, "I've got it. I'm *leaning* on it. But, while I can probably shoot, I have my doubts about using a sword very effectively at the moment."

"Not a problem, sir," Mokrenko said. "You shouldn't even have to shoot. First off, everyone gets two pistols except the lieutenant, who gets one. Everyone gets one of the dynamo lights. Shukhov, tie the lieutenant's dummy to the mast, facing the rear. Then you go over to the corner by the cabin we met in, also facing the rear of the ship. The 'stern,' they call it. If they attack before we're ready, light up and open fire. The rest of us will dive low."

"I understand, Sergeant," Shukhov whispered back.

"I'm putting my mess kit under the hat, so we get a louder sound if they try to brain it."

"Good thought."

Then Mokrenko, carrying both lengths of rope, led the lieutenant and Sarnof to the starboard side rearmost cabin. "Just wait here, sir. I'll be back."

From there, still carrying the rope, he crossed the deck to the opposite cabin. Opening the doorway—the "hatch," the sailors would have called it, he went inside and felt around for the fixed bunkbeds against the hull. He tied a rope each to the ends of these, one at the head and one at the foot, with the one at the head a half an *arshin* higher than the one at the foot. He then played out the rope behind him, on the deck, as he crossed back to Turgenev and Sarnof.

At the other cabin, he passed the rope around the bunks, handing the free end of one each to Turgenev and Sarnof. He worked as deliberately and carefully as his increasing sense of dread allowed. *I've never been in a fight on the water. What if it's different from on land?*

He thought it best to explain what he wanted and why.

"They've seen our swords," Mokrenko said. "But they probably don't have a clue about the pistols or the dynamo lights. If they had that clue, they probably wouldn't even try to take us.

"When Shukhov and I hear them enter this area, we're going to light them up and open fire. I think they'll run away ... but we don't want them to run away. That's why I want you two to haul on those ropes with everything you have as soon as we open fire. When they run, they trip, then Shukhov and I attack—and you, too, Sarnof, and chop them up good. No prisoners, no survivors."

Seeing there wasn't going to be any argument about that, not even from the lieutenant, who tended towards gentility, Mokrenko continued. "Once we've finished off this group, you two go up on the top deck and clear it of sailors. Any that want to surrender at that point can, but at the slightest sign of treachery or resistance, kill them. Meanwhile, Shukhov and I will clear this deck to the stern. Questions?"

"You don't want us to shoot from here?" Turgenev asked.

"No, sir; our pistols are enough for this part. Shoot only if one of them comes in here."

Mokrenko left those two and that cabin, working his way silently to the straw dummy—which did, indeed, reek of human vomit—then to Shukhov. He stiffened at the sound of rats scurrying across wood. *Them? Or rats fleeing them?*

"You awake?"

"Yes, Sergeant."

Mokrenko passed one end of the short rope to Shukhov. "Okay, loop the end of this rope around your arm. I'll do the same. If one of us is dumb enough to fall asleep, the other can wake him."

"I understand, Sergeant. Good idea."

"Also, you take the ones from the mast to the left. I'll take the ones from the mast to the right. We light them up, empty both pistols, draw our *shashka* and charge."

"I understand, Sergeant."

Mokrenko went then to the corner opposite Shukhov's.

There he sat carefully, laid his *shashka* across his lap, took one pistol in his right hand, and waited.

The remaining five men of the expedition were all, in considerable misery, collected into the portside foremost cabin, with the medic, Timashuk, armed with the last pistol, to guard them.

Well, thought Mokrenko, *if the ambush fails, it is unlikely, given Timashuk's continuing nausea, that any will survive. At least they'll be able to go down fighting.*

Unseen by any of the others, two little beady eyes watched out from a small out of the way cubbyhole. The eyes belonged to the ship's senior rat, thought of as Number One, keeping a wary watch out for the archnemesis of all maritime rats, the ship's cat.

With rather better than human vision, the rat watched the strangers' preparations with a keen interest, eager to see if any of them would prove detrimental to the continued health and prosperity of rat-kind.

The crew, when they came, did so with the quiet caution of rats scurrying softly across the wooden deck. Mokrenko had been shifting his eyes steadily, to try to keep his night vision going. It really wasn't enough. It also didn't help one stay awake all that well when there was nothing for the eye to see.

He caught himself nodding off a half a dozen times. Twice he'd jerked himself awake so violently that the back of his head smacked against the bulkhead of the storage room.

Indeed, it was only when he heard a human whisper,

slightly above the ratlike sound of dirty bare feet on the deck, that he came fully alert. He was about to pull on the rope leading to Shukhov when the pioneer began pulling on his own. He jerked it slightly anyway, to let Shukhov know he wasn't alone and the fight was about to start.

Mokrenko's right thumb reached for the safety, making doubly sure it was off. He left thumb went for the ring of the dynamo flashlight on his chest. His heart began to pound for the impending action. *Please, God, don't let that fuck up my aim.*

Mokrenko heard, *"Prostul doarme; bate în cap."* He spoke not a word of Romanian, but the meaning became clear as he heard the whoosh of something moving fast through air, followed by the sound of wood smashing into sheet metal.

Mokrenko pulled the ring furiously, creating both a whirring sound and the beginnings of a flash of light. It wasn't much, on its own, but given the previous total darkness it was just enough to make out eight rather surprised thugs with clubs and knives, standing on the other side of the foremast, between the two rows of cabins.

Shukhov's light joined Mokrenko's in a tenth of a second. Between the two, there was enough to fire by. The M1911s barked, once, twice, a half dozen times each. Mokrenko couldn't be certain of any given hit, but he saw two of the crew fall back like limp sacks overstuffed with shit.

He emptied the last two rounds, hitting, he thought, nothing, and then pulled the ring again. "Attack!" he shouted to Shukhov, drawing the full yard of his *shashka* as he leapt to his feet. Mokrenko realized he was shaking, not with fear but with rage. That smashed mess kit reinforced that they'd intended to kill him.

And now, you filth, I intend to kill you.

Mokrenko and Shukhov saw as many pirates go down to the twin tightened ropes running across the deck as had fallen to the pistols.

Two of the latter, felled by Shukhov, lay on the deck bleeding. Dead or not, Mokrenko wasn't taking any chances. The *shashka* swept down, guided by hand and by the marginal light of the dynamo lights, slashing one crewman across the throat so deeply that the head lolled back, unsupported by muscles or tendons. A fountain of blood shot out across the deck. The other rolled on his back, putting up defensive hands and pleading, *"Te rog nu mă ucide."*

Mokrenko lopped off one hand, raising a shriek, and, when the remaining hand went to staunch the flow of blood, pointed the *shashka* down and plunged it into an eye, then twisted it farther down into the brain.

He risked a glance to the side to see Shukhov fighting to get his sword free of the skull it was buried in.

He's not going to be any goddamned help!

At that point, Mokrenko resheathed the sword and drew his spare pistol. With his left hand still working the dynamo light, he proceeded to empty the thing into the backs of the crew still trying to escape in the throng across the deck. With each round fired he muttered a Russian curse: "Bitch"—*bang!*—"asshole"—*bang*—"cunt"—*bang*—"swine"—*bang . . . bang . . . bang . . . bang . . . bang.*

He put the pistol back into his pocket, immediately

regretting it as the muzzle was more than a little warm, then used the *shashka* to slash and stab. Shukhov joined him and likewise began to hack apart the crew to make sure.

"Never mind that," Mokrenko ordered. "Your pistol, one of them, is still loaded? Good, stand guard. Lieutenant Turgenev? Sarnof? Come on out and get topside, please, sir. Shukhov, cover me while I reload."

While the lieutenant and Sarnof took over the top deck, seizing and pistol whipping into unconsciousness the one sailor they found up there, Mokrenko and Shukhov reloaded, then worked their way down the ship, kicking open doors. There was nothing, though; the crew, if they were anywhere, had retreated to the stern.

"Come out, you swine," ordered Mokrenko, in Russian, standing by the galley's main hatch. "Come out, Captain, but throw your pistol out, first, or we'll cut you down where you stand."

Captain Vraciu's pistol was thrown to the deck almost instantly.

"Now *get* on deck."

One by one, under the irregular light from the dynamo lights, the just under half of the crew still remaining came out of the galley, to be followed by the captain.

"Lieutenant!?" called Mokrenko.

"Here," answered Turgenev, from the top deck.

"They're coming up, sir, what's left of them."

"We're ready. Send them up one at a time."

"You first, Captain," ordered Mokrenko.

"You cannot do this to—"

The captain never quite finished, as Shukhov smashed him across the face with the butt of his pistol, tearing open the captain's cheek and breaking his nose. The captain fell with the force of the blow, but only stayed down for a moment before Shukhov's well-placed boot took him in the midsection.

"Up, you crawling filth," the pioneer ordered. "Crawl up that ladder!"

The girl, Natalya, stepped forward from the crowd. "Am I to go with them?" she asked.

"No, Natalya," said Mokrenko. "You stay with us." Something about the girl—*Maybe her educated accent*— struck him as out of place as a kept slave on a Romanian ship. He tested his theory by asking her, in his own very limited French, "Do you want to stay with us?"

"I do," she answered in the same language, then thought, *Oh, that was probably a mistake. No one's supposed to know. Bad things happen to me when they know.*

"I need to get something," the girl said, disappearing briefly into the galley and emerging with a large cleaver.

At about that time the shaken, shocked, bleeding captain stuck his head above the hatchway. He found immediately a loop of rope was placed around his neck and pressure applied.

Oh, God, no; they're going to hang me. Not that, please, not that.

In fact, the captain was, at least for the nonce, wrong. The rope around his neck, though he could have been hanged with it, and though it did run over a yardarm, was only to maintain tight control. As soon as his feet were on

deck, the tension was released. Even so, he felt his hands
being roughly pulled behind him before being tightly tied
with a piece of rope. At that point, Sarnof moved to the
captain's side, put out one leg, and pushed the captain
forward, tripping him to fall face first onto the deck. Then
Sarnof knelt on the captain's back to remove the rope
from his neck.

"Next!" shouted Turgenev.

The sun was up now and the weather much abated as,
hands bound tightly behind them, the remaining crew and
the captain knelt upon the deck. One could read in the
eyes of each man a stark terror of what their future held.

The lieutenant, feeling much better now, took charge
again. He spoke no Romanian, and hardly trusted the
captain to translate to the crew.

"I've learned it well enough," said little Natalya, still in
defiance of what had been done to her. "You can learn a
lot about a language, even on your knees or all fours. I can
tell them what you want."

"Good, child. Translate exactly what I say to them."

"Yes, sir. I promise."

"You are all pirates," Turgenev began. "As such, we
need no higher authority than ourselves to hang you all."

Two of the crew, and Vraciu, himself, began to weep
openly at that, Vraciu first, because he didn't need to wait
for the translation.

"You all were party to an attempt to commit a high
crime on the high seas. Thus, you are all condemned."

"We will, however, give the remainder of the crew one
chance to possibly save their lives. This will be by faithfully

serving us to bring us to our destination, as close as possible to Rostov-on-Don.

"One man, however, we will not trust. That is the captain. He will die."

Immediately, Turgenev walked to the cringing Vraciu, and grabbed him by the hair. Using this, he dragged the captain to kneel beside the rope that had been used to control him earlier. Now snot ran down Vraciu's face, to match the freely flowing tears.

"Untie the crew," the lieutenant ordered. When this had been done he directed the crew, through Natalya, to get good grips on the running end of the rope.

"Noose the bastard, Natalya."

Happily the girl ran to place the loop around Vraciu's neck, and to tighten it just enough to ensure it would not slip off. After noosing him, she spat directly onto Vraciu's snotty, dirty face.

"Lieutenant?" Natalya asked. "I've seen these people hang innocent men before. It's too quick this way."

"What do you suggest, young lady?" Turgenev asked.

"Untie his hands, so he can struggle with the rope. They did that, sometimes, too."

Turgenev, apprised of the reason for the girl's hatred of the captain, thought that fair. "Do it."

Natalya used the cleaver. She chopped at the rope binding the captain's wrists but not neatly. Before she was done, two of Vraciu's fingers littered the deck, while a small pool of blood stained his trousers. Something else stained them, too, as the captain lost bladder control.

"His greatest crime was against you, Natalya. You can give the command to haul away to the remaining crew."

"Thank you, sir."

Natalya twisted the loop around the captain's neck to where it would tighten on one side. She'd seen them do this before, too. It kept the rope from cutting off blood to the brain, thus ensuring a slow strangle and an entertaining dance before unconsciousness took over.

Then the girl walked to a spot just in front of where the line of the crew clutched the rope. There, she tied a loop into the rope. From there, she walked to a point about ten feet farther astern, near where some rigging ran down to the gunwales and where a half dozen belaying pins sat upright in their frame.

"When I give the order," she told the crew, "walk, do not run, toward me. Stop just before running me over. Ready? NOW!"

Hesitatingly, the crew, still clutching the running end of the rope firmly, began to walk forward. Natalya paid them little mind. Instead, she watched as the rope first bit into the captain's neck, raising him to his feet.

The captain's bloodied hands, less those two fingers, grasped for the rope loop in an absolutely mindless panic. Before they could get a grip to try to keep Vraciu from strangling, the rope was taut everywhere but where it allowed blood still to flow. His fingers sought desperately to get between the strangling rope and his neck, even as his legs and feet began a mindless kicking dance for something to stand on, to relieve the murderous encircling pressure on his neck. Gurgling sounds came from the writhing form, a foot or so above the deck, as his lungs sought to draw in air through the tightly constricted airway. The captain continued rising as the crew continued their walk forward.

Soon enough, a matter of seconds, the crew were standing in front of Natalya, carefully keeping their eyes to the stern and away from the strangling, writhing, gurgling, dying *thing* at the other end of the rope.

At that point, Natalya took the loop and secured it to the ship with one of the belaying pins.

"Let him down *gently*," she said. There would be no merciful neck-breaking drop for this particular child rapist. "Now turn around and watch what waits for you if you do not obey the orders of these Russians *perfectly*."

Natalya then folded her arms and watched as the captain's struggles grew weaker and weaker. First his legs stopped churning, though his feet twitched for a good deal longer. Then one hand fell away from the rope, followed shortly by the other. His eyes began to bulge as a blackened tongue protruded from a gaping mouth. The lungs still tried to work for a while, until a heaving chest told of cardiac arrest.

Finally, with shit running down his leg and piss dripping onto the deck, Vraciu gave up the ghost and died.

"And now, you swine," said Mokrenko, "get below and start carrying up the bodies and dumping them over the side."

Interlude

Tatiana: Flirting

Mama was having one of those days when she was nearly a corpse. She'd woken tired and barely eaten any breakfast. We girls took turns attending her as she lounged on a couch with Joy curled up at her feet. She dozed off while reading. I pulled the blanket up over her shoulder and left Maria to keep an eye on her should she wake.

I glanced at the clock. Olga was supposed to come help out but she was almost half an hour late. I crept past Alexei's room. Anastasia was reading to him. Papa had closed the door to his study, but I heard another male voice as I passed. He was probably in another meeting and I didn't want to interrupt, just to check if Olga was in there without checking the other rooms first.

I entered the hallway leading to the room we girls shared. The door to our room was ajar, allowing light to fall onto one of the threadbare rugs covering the wood floor. A man of medium height and build was leaning into our room. The soldiers were not supposed to be up here and I couldn't imagine what had brought them.

As I approached, I realized that it was Sergei Chekov. Dirt and oil darkened his blond hair to an almost-brown where his cap usually sat. He had his hands shoved in his pockets as he mumbled something into the room.

I heard the scrape of a chair and the echo of lowered voices.

Chekov moved back into the hallway, allowing me to pass.

Inside, Olga was standing next to Anton Dostovalov. I recognized him, too, as one of the red soldiers. He had been raised on a farm. Just a few years older than Olga, he was a big man with a rumbling voice to match.

Olga's cheeks were bright red. She was standing against her bed, by the curtain that she'd hung at its foot in order to partition it from the rest of the room. The buttons down the front of her white shirt were lined up wrong as if she'd missed a hole. It hadn't been that way when I'd seen her earlier.

"Is everything all right?" I asked.

She cast me a quick glance, not quite meeting my eyes. "Yes, fine. Anton was just helping me look for something."

I knew it was lie from the way she said it, from the way neither of them would look at me, from the way Anton shuffled out of the room, and from the disapproving look on Chekov's face.

We stood in the awkward silence for a moment.

"You might want to re-button your blouse before you go down to see Mama," I said.

Her cheeks flared once again. Her hands shook as she fumbled with the buttons.

I should have been angry or disappointed, but I wasn't. These were normal things, things that young men and women our age did. We should have been going to dances and parties, meeting eligible young men, stealing kisses and looks, gossiping about them to compare notes on who made the best jokes, who was the best dancer, who was the most charming.

Papa would take such behavior with stoicism. Mama, I wasn't sure. The last thing she needed was another burden to bear.

Olga straightened her skirt as she turned for the door and stepped past me.

I grabbed her elbow, pulling her back gently.

She looked at me over her shoulder.

"Was it worth it?" I asked.

The look in her eyes said that it was. That she'd do it again.

And I couldn't blame her.

Chapter Nine

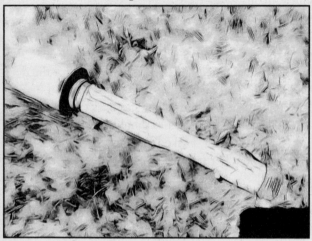

German Grenade (Stielhandgranate)

Range B (Machine Gun and Cannon), Camp Budapest

Progress is still too slow, thought Kostyshakov, *and it's really no one's fault.*

The ranges, so far, ran, from east to west, A, B, V, and G1. Range A was rifle and could handle a company in a day's firing. B was for machine guns and the light cannon. V was for grenades, and had sections for practicing with weighted wooden dummies, still being prepared, to throwing a live one to a target at a distance, and to, as the sergeant major said, "Grow some balls," by having a half dozen portions of trench system dug, for a soldier to count down the burning of the grenade fuse before tossing it around a corner.

Range G1, which would soon be followed by G2, G3, and G4, was a mock-up of a floor of a building, dug down into the ground to a depth of about twelve to fourteen feet. The log walls inside were still not quite complete.

A full *verst* from where the last G range was planned, there would be a demolitions range, D, for the engineers to practice and teach their trade. Past that, in three weeks or so, they would be finished building Course E, the bayonet assault course. Course Z, a confidence course comprised of obstacles that looked a good deal more dangerous than they were, would round out the training complex toward the end of the month.

Standing in a shaky range tower lashed together from tree trunks with the bark still on them, Kostyshakov watched as one of the two heavy machine gun crews frantically manipulated their gun's traversing and elevating mechanism to keep up with the unpredictable twists, turns, and speed of the sled downrange.

"Works after all," Daniil muttered. "I am surprised."

"What was that, sir?" asked Lieutenant Lesh, half shouting to be heard over the firing of the machine gun.

"Nothing . . ." Daniil twisted slightly to be able to speak more or less into the lieutenant's ear. "I was just thinking aloud about how well the moving target trick works."

"Pretty well, yes, sir. You might note how it speeds up

and slows down. We alternate the gun crews on the job of pulling the rope. They like to fuck with each other."

Kostyshakov nodded. "Good technique . . . do you have a grading . . ."

There was a explosion from Range V, off to the right. Daniil knew that Lieutenant Baluyev was experimenting with modifying the German stick grenades to serve as blinding and stun grenades. This explosion, however, was a good deal more powerful than one might have expected.

"Sir, I . . ."

"Never mind, Lieutenant," he told Lesh. "I'll go check it out."

Deeply worried, Daniil scampered down the crude ladder and then jogged for the first of the trenches dug on Range V. The closer he got, the more worried he became about what he might find there. By the time he reached the earthen ramp that descended into the zig-zag trench, he was practically frantic. Down he went, then zigged left before zagging right to find Baluyev and two men he'd apparently detailed to assist him. One of the men sat on the floor of the trench, blinking and rubbing his eyes while swaying from side to side. He managed to sway despite having his back up against the trench's wall.

The other of the enlisted men was still on his feet, but blinking even more than the first and only managing to keep to his feet by hanging on to an overhead beam supporting the trench's revetments.

The really interesting one, though, was Baluyev himself. Gone was the fierce moustache, now. Gone, too, was about an inch and a half of the officer's hairline. His eyes were closed, which closure did nothing to prevent a steady stream of tears exiting them to run down his face in a free cascade.

"Are you all right, Lieutenant?" asked Kostyshakov.

Baluyev used one hand to pry open a single eye. "I'm not blind, anyway, but we're going to have to tone down the packing of those hand grenades. Just replacing half the filler with photographer's flash powder is just too much, too much of both."

The lieutenant suddenly turned away to vomit on the floor of the trench. "And I suppose I've got a bit of a concussion. Sorry, sir."

"So what actually happened?" Kostyshakov asked.

"Replaced half the filler, like I said, sir. My two men and I were close up against the wall behind me. Unscrewed the cap. Pulled the big bead to start the fuse. Tossed the grenade around the corner. When it went off it was not only *still* powerful enough to knock us silly, but the flash powder followed the blast wave around the corner and just blinded us."

"Maybe you should start small and work your way up," Daniil suggested.

"Yes, sir. I think so, sir. I'll give it . . ." Again, Baluyev had to bend and retch. ". . . give it a try, sir." He wiped his fouled mouth on his sleeve.

"Are you able to carry on now or do I need I find another officer or senior noncom to handle the research?"

"I can start again in a couple of hours, I think, sir. The men . . ."

"Couple of hours, sir," answered the one on his feet, whose name was Poletov.

"Think so, too," agreed the other, sitting down. This one answered to Smirnov.

Kostyshakov looked more carefully as that latter soldier. He noticed, "You're bleeding, soldier."

"Yes, sir. I suppose so, sir. Must have been a bit of shrapnel, a part of the casing, that bounced off the wall and scored the top of my head."

"Baluyev, one of the people we're going to rescue, the tsarevich, is a bleeder. We can't risk even scratching him."

"Another reason to reduce the charge then, sir. Don't know how much, though."

"Yeah . . . once, again, restart, but start *small*."

Quartermaster's Office, Camp Budapest

Kaledin stood at ease in front of Romeyko's makeshift desk. "I think I've got three horses," the Cossack told the quartermaster, "and fifteen mules that should make it and even be in good enough shape in six weeks or so to get work out of them. The rest?" Kaledin's nostrils dilated as he shook his head, sadly.

"Have we found any turpentine yet, sir?"

Romeyko looked over at *Feldwebel* Weber, who answered, "Some, sir. How much do you need per animal, Kaledin?"

"Well . . . you give it to them—very diluted—over a period of several weeks. Some of them, too, need it applied externally for some of their skin problems. I think I need about two *vedro*. Call it, in metric, maybe twenty-five liters. I could use some tobacco, too."

"I found a dozen liters," the German replied, "and have

requests in for two dozen more. Tobacco? It's not going to be very *good* tobacco."

"Shitty tobacco would be fine. Also, maybe some diatomaceous earth, '*Kieselguhr*,' I think you call it. As for the turpentine, the dozen liters should do for now," Kaledin said, "provided the rest comes in."

"Provided," the German echoed, distantly and doubtfully.

"Problems, Weber?" Romeyko asked.

"Several," the German replied. The left side of his moustache went up in company with his curling lip.

Romeyko followed that up with a "give forth" motion.

"One problem is that we're on the ass end of nowhere and can't raise a huge stink lest the enemy start thinking we're more important than we seem to be. I mean, after all, he may not have many spies but he must have at least *some*. The other is that some things that should have been on the train never showed up, at least not in the quantities marked on the invoices.

"Example, we were supposed to receive one hundred and twenty kilograms of nails. Eighty showed up, with the remainder being taken up with rocks buried under the nails. There is no telling where the other forty went. Something similar happened with food, two days in a row. Taenzler fixed that by sending one of his men, armed, to the depot we're drawing from and escorting the food here. But he's *still* having to do that.

"Mine," the German continued, "is a very proper, correct, and honest people ... if ... well, frankly, a little pig-headed. When they start stealing things like this ... we ... we are in trouble.

"No," he hastened to add, his tone one of despair, "we will not lose the war for forty kilograms of nails, nor a couple of thousand daily rations. But those things are indicative of a deeper problem, a moral one, the rise of selfishness when total selflessness is needed."

The German's chin sank upon his chest. "I don't think we're going to win the war."

Neither Romeyko nor Kaledin nor any of the clerks present had anything immediately to say to that. Yes, they and the Germans had been at war until quite recently. But Weber had become an ally and perhaps even something of a friend.

"If it's any consolation," Romeyko said, finally, "in Russia it's worse."

"Not a lot of consolation, no, sir, but thanks for trying."

Range V (Grenades), Camp Budapest

An exceedingly rare pig, temporarily spared from Taenzler's butcher's knife, was tied to a log inside the trench. It, being a pig, didn't have much of an idea about what was to happen to it.

Nothing ventured, nothing gained, thought Lieutenant Baluyev as he unscrewed the safety cap at the base of the stick on the grenade he was currently holding.

Baluyev had, in total, a dozen modified grenades. The other eleven were lined up outside of the trench and far enough away that setting off one down inside would not set off the others.

The grenades were numbered, with one of his soldiers standing by to record the effects of each version. These ran from a half ounce to two ounces of TNT as the explosive filler, or a twelfth to a third of the normal grenade's filler. The flash powder ran from completely filling the remainder to roughly half filling it for most of the samples. The exceptions were the grenades with under an ounce of explosive. In these cases the remainder of the casing was only a quarter to a half filled with flash powder.

Baluyev and the men had already had quite enough of that much flash powder going off in an expanding cloud around them. This grenade, for example, "Number One," was the one with only half an ounce of TNT and perhaps a quarter filled with flash powder.

And it will be years, years, *before my moustache is presentable again! Years!*

The lieutenant let the screw cap fall to the floor of the trench. A small porcelain ball attached to a string dropped out.

"Grenade One," Baluyev announced to the recorder.

"One *lot*, two *dolya* TNT," the man answered, "two *lot*, four *dolya* flash powder." A Russian *lot* was equal to about twelve and four-fifths grams, a *dolya* to about a sixth of a gram.

Baluyev pulled the knob and immediately tossed the grenade around the corner of the trench. Four seconds later he was rewarded with a considerable bang, and a flash which lit up the opposite wall in a most satisfying manner.

Hmmm . . . could it be that easy?

Baluyev went to investigate and discovered that, sadly, even a half ounce of TNT, going off in the confined space of the grenade's head, was sufficient to shatter that head, sending fragments to scatter around the room. The pig, most satisfyingly, was staggering and seemed blinded enough that it ran itself, still pulling its log, head first into the wall.

Unfortunately, the pig was also bleeding into two places, small cuts from light metal fragments. This was no real danger to the pig, but what would have been almost harmless for the pig would likely have proven fatal to the *tsarevich*.

"No," Baluyev muttered, "it couldn't be that easy. Oh well, back to the drawing board."

Turning to his two assistants, he shouted—he had to shout; they were still half deaf from the previous extravaganza, "Pick up the remainder and let's give some thought to what we might be able to do to keep them from sending out any fragments. Oh, and give the pig some food."

Camp Budapest

Okay, thought Baluyev, later in his tent, *what do we know and what do we not know?*

We know that even a very small charge of TNT will shatter the casing and send out some fragments. We know, too, that it is sufficient to also set off the flash powder. We know that it is also sufficient, in an enclosed space, to stun an animal about the size and complexity of a man.

Do we know what's in the flash powder? Not exactly, but the drum says potassium perchlorate, magnesium, and lycopodium spores. I don't know how we'd isolate these, or even if they'd still work if we could. Yeah, we're stuck with what we have there.

How about if we strengthen the casing, make it stronger,

thicker and heavier? Hmmm…out of what? Cast iron? Steel? Outside of our own abilities and the Germans are already pressed. Not enough time, either. So no.

Make the casing softer? Cardboard maybe? No, never hold up to rough use, and the private soldier is the very embodiment of rough use.

Right; can't make it stronger, can't make it softer, can't reduce the charge. What's left? What's left? What the fuck is left?

Baluyev closed his eyes—he was still feeling the effects of the previous experiment—and lay back on his pallet. When the wave of nausea had passed, he opened his eyes to stare at the tent's off-white roof. The small stove's pipe ran up through a…

"That's IT! That's fucking IT! We can perforate the casing, then line it with cardboard. The casing will protect the cardboard from rough handling. The cardboard will disintegrate without fragments. Even the casing shouldn't fragment on that low a charge, if the blast can escape through the holes.

"Hmmm…we'll need to wax the cardboard to protect the whole thing from moisture, but that shouldn't be hard."

Baluyev stood, abruptly, bringing another wave of nausea. When that passed, he stepped from the tent, shouting at the top of his lungs, "Poletov? Smirnov? Get over here; we have work to do."

Not far away and not long after, Captain Romeyko annotated his list to add "cardboard" and "wax," as well as "hand drill" and "large bit."

Fortunately, thought the quartermaster, *all of that is obtainable no farther away than Sofia, which is not so far away*.

Range A (Rifle), Camp Budapest

Captain Cherimisov, commander of the Grenadier Company, spent the bulk of his work-day on two tasks; the first was evaluating potential snipers on Range A, the second was looking for Lewis gunners on Range B. Since Grenadier Company was slated to storm the compound and liberate the Romanovs, these selections were of much greater import than such personnel decisions usually warranted.

Today, it was Number One Company, the Headquarters and Support, refamiliarizing their troops on the Mosin-Nagant.

He didn't yet have a way to select for the kind of moral qualities, reactions, coordination, strength, and speed that he needed for his two assault platoons. Nobody did, to include Kostyshakov, and yet everyone knew, and Kostyshakov had pretty much said, that these kinds of qualities would be critical.

Kostyshakov left it largely up to Cherimisov to select his own company. For now, that meant technical skills, shooting, basically, which was all he could do.

For the nonce, this placed the captain directly behind one soldier, Guardsman Nomonkov, who seemed incapable of missing.

Part of that is probably vision, thought Cherimisov. *But there's something else going on, too. The target goes up and this man snaps off his five rounds, and when they're marked every one of them, even at seven hundred* arshini, *is within a circle of four inches or less. I've watched him go through forty rounds, now, and the center of the target is so far gone we can't really be sure he's even hitting anymore, though we don't really doubt he is.*

"Once he's done," Cherimisov told the range NCO for that firing point, "Send him to me, over by the control tower. Can you replace him?"

"Yes, sir, no problem."

"Sir, Guardsman Maxim Nomonkov reports!" The marksman subtly looked over Cherimisov, whose friendly grin completely failed to reach his cold, blue eyes.

As the soldier studied him, Cherimisov likewise studied Nomonkov's face and stature. *Short, stocky, little bit of an epicanthic fold to the eyes. Part Tatar or Mongol or something from the far east.*

He returned the soldier's salute, then ordered him to, "Relax. I just want to talk."

"Am I in trouble, sir? Because they couldn't figure out if I'd hit the target or not?"

The grin grew broader, and yet still failed to reach the eyes. "Not at all, Nomonkov, not at all. Tell me, where are you from?"

"Little village in Siberia, sir; place you never heard of, maybe sixty, sixty-five *versta* north of Tobolsk."

"Ever been to Tobolsk?"

"No, sir; they asked me that a while ago. My people stayed in their own place."

"Where did you learn to shoot?"

"My father. He's a hunter and trapper, a line of work I devoutly hope to follow him in."

"Have you ever used a scope with a rifle, Nomonkov?"

"Never even *seen* a scope on a rifle, sir, though I've heard about them. Probably don't need one, anyway."

"Why is that?"

Instead of answering, the rifleman just started scanning around the sky. Finally, he pointed and asked, "Sir, do you see that hawk up there?"

The captain looked, indeed, he concentrated, but finally, shaking his head, had to admit, "Nothing."

"I *do* see him, sir. As near as I can tell I can see about twice as far as any other man or maybe a touch more. Certainly I can see clearly twice as far as anyone I ever met . . . except for my mother, who is like me."

"Hmmm," mused the captain, "if you can see that well without a scope, I wonder—indeed, I marvel—at the thought of what you can see with one.

"Still, shooting's not about just eyesight. What's your best position to shoot from?"

The part-Tatar shrugged. "I'm compact. Pretty solid. Doesn't make all that much difference, though standing supported is best by a little."

"Is your rifle clear?"

"Yes, sir. Of course. They don't let us off the range with loaded rifles."

"Cock it then, please, and take up a kneeling unsupported firing position."

When Nomonkov had done so, the captain took a small coin from his pocket, an 1898 copper half kopek, and laid it on the barrel. The captain also took another one in his hand.

"Now squeeze off the trigger."

When the Guardsman had done so, the coin was still sitting, unmoving, atop the rifle's barrel.

"Do it again," Cherimisov ordered. He was sure this would cause Nomonkov to knock the coin off the barrel, but, no, it remained where it was throughout the manipulation of the bolt and stayed there again when the trigger was squeezed off.

"Well, I'll be damned. Never seen anyone who can recock a bolt action rifle and still keep it that steady."

"Sir, I learned that trick from my father, too."

That raised a laugh. "Indeed? Well, let's go find your commander or *Podpraporshchik* Mayevsky. You are now officially in the Grenadier Company.

"Oh, and how's your night vision?"

"Quite good really, compared to most, sir, but not up there with my day vision."

Baluyev being occupied with grenade development, and Mayevsky supervising the range, made the transfer simple, if not easy. The latter man glared at Cherimisov with his one remaining eye, and insisted there'd be hell to pay if the captain tried to "steal our best shot. I won't stand for it, sir. The company commander won't stand for it either. It's an outrage! It's just bloody theft! It's—"

"An order from Kostyshakov," interrupted the captain. "Mine, once formed, is the company that goes in to rescue the royal family. I get my pick of manpower because of that. But relax, Top; I'll go and steal my other sniper from Second or Third Company."

"Fuck!"

✛ ✛ ✛

Which really doesn't get me that far, Cherimisov thought. *I can do this with the snipers and my two future Lewis gunners, and their crews. But there's still no test for the rank and file. So how do I handle this?*

"All right, Cherimisov, all *right,* THINK, for God's sake."

We want toughness and determination; that seems obvious. All right, I go to Kostyshakov and request a weekly road march, the first one to be hard and the subsequent ones to be progressively harder still. That whittles the numbers down to what? Say sixty percent that never falter? Okay, so within a month or so, I'm down to maybe three or four hundred to choose from. "The people who are with thee are yet too many." But, don't forget that some who falter are not weak. Remember to look at their feet at the end; the man with eighty or ninety percent bleeding blisters on each foot but can keep up past the thirty versta *point has more toughness than the one who can but whose feet are fine.*

Soooo ... fine, when we've identified the tough ones, we select out from them the inept, the clumsy, the poor shots, the stupid. Maybe fifty more, then, that don't make the cut.

Past that, we look for courage, but how? A nasty obstacle course, when we finish building one, might do. Moving forward under low fire from the heavy machine guns might help. But it's got to be low *fire, just a few feet above the earth, to make it worthwhile. We may lose someone. And ... this is even riskier, maybe a count of three delay on using their grenades? No, not three ... no, yes, three, maybe even four, because they'll count faster than light.*

And then we ask—sure, why not just ask?—who wants

*to be in on the rescue. I can talk up the risks, both in
training and in the execution. So let's let them select for
who has what we've looking for.*

And then . . .

Officers' Mess Tent, Camp Budapest

The food was still nothing special . . . except that in
terms of the terrible hardships of the Great War it *was*
special. Kostyshakov's perforated buttocks were healed.
Better, the men had put on an average of fifteen pounds,
more or less evenly split between fat and muscle.

"Sir," Cherimisov told Kostyshakov, "at the end, if
we've got too many, we just put them in the ring and let
them fight over it."

"Now that's an interesting approach," Daniil said.
"Maybe. Let me add one more thing. Once we've got
everyone qualified, we're going to be having each of the
rifle companies undertake a long series of live fire
exercises. That should help find the witless and identify
the courageous.

"Also, at this point I'm beginning to doubt the
Germans are going to come through with their machine
pistols. In that case, the assault platoons will be going in
with flash and stun grenades and fixed bayonets, no
ammunition except in their pouches. So pay attention to
the ones who do well and poorly on the bayonet assault
course, once we're done with that.

"And one other thing; maybe, just maybe, we're doing
this wrong and we should think about some utterly
miserable, very hard, gut-testing selection course *before*
we do anything else."

Cherimisov spread some *ersatz* butter on a piece of toast while thinking that over. Looking at the butter killed any urge to smile he might have felt. "Well . . . yes, sir, it has some things to recommend it. I've given it some thought. But who runs it? Take a couple of weeks just to set it up and get the testers ready . . . if they can be gotten ready. After all, while we have some good noncoms and officers, they're all new to this, same as us."

"I think you can do it in less time," Daniil said. "I think you can set up a selection course in a week. We just need to identify, oh, your four lieutenants, your first sergeant, three *Feldfebels*, and maybe a couple of sergeants."

"I already know who I want for lieutenants and *Feldfebels*, sir. And for first sergeant I want Mayevsky out of First Company."

"Mayevsky? Jesus, won't Baluyev scream over that one?"

Range V (Grenades), Camp Budapest

As it turned out, it hadn't been as easy as all *that*. Certainly Romeyko had managed, with Weber's help, to produce cardboard, wax, and a drill, as well as a broad metal bit for the drill. So far, so good.

The first problem had been that drilling tended to deform the casing. Their first attempt at fixing this, carving and putting into each casing a wooden mandrel, had worked, well enough, anyway, but the process of drilling destroyed each mandrel produced, such that they'd need a fresh one for each grenade to be modified. Baluyev really didn't think there was time for that.

Smirnov had been the one to figure that problem out,

in the form of, "We're fucking idiots—begging your pardon, sir—but we don't need to be whittling on wood. Every grenade comes with its own mandrel, in the TNT that's been cast into it. We just need to drill them *before* we unscrew the heads."

That had, in fact, worked well. While the TNT was not especially hard, it was also not especially compressible and had nowhere to go.

The old grenades had just been emptied of flash powder and exploded, to prevent confusion.

After perforating the casings and then unscrewing them from the grenades' handles, the next step was cutting away the excess TNT. It was time consuming, but not that hard. What it was, though, was inherently sloppy and uneven, as the TNT was rather difficult to get out of the casing once it had been drilled.

What that had meant was that the top of the casing had to be completely cut away, to be replaced by more cardboard.

"Not a problem," Baluyev had pronounced. "The way they're carried remaining vertical will protect the top from rough handling . . . enough."

Still, it had taken an hour to cut away enough TNT from one grenade to add the flash powder.

"Too long," the lieutenant finally said. "Too long and too hard.

"Ideally," he continued, "we'd melt the explosive out, then recast it in smaller cylinders. But . . ."

"I've heard the fumes are stone killers, sir," said Poletov.

Nodding soberly, Baluyev replied, "I've heard the same

thing; munitions workers turning yellow as canaries and take all kinds of damage to some organs. No melting and recasting."

Smirnov offered a possible solution. "What if we take it all out, sir, then pulverize it and make a mix of TNT and flash powder? We can make a double wall of waxed cardboard, one right up against the holed metal casing, one inside to hold just the right quantity of TNT and flash powder. And we'll save time not having to cut the top off. We hold the top of the inner tube in place with poured wax, just a little. The detonator section holds the bottom in place."

"Let's give that a try, then," Baluyev agreed.

They'd nicknamed the pig Matilda, hence Baluyev's, "Stop complaining, Matilda, this may hurt a little but it's better than being turned into chops, ribs, and *salo*."

What Matilda thought about this was inscrutable. Besides, she was busy consuming the mush they'd given her.

"Grenade One," Baluyev announced to the recorder, Poletov.

"One *lot*, two *dolya* powdered TNT," the man answered, "two *lot*, four *dolya* flash powder."

Again, the lieutenant unscrewed the cap, letting the porcelain ball fall out. He gave the ball a sharp yank, moving the grenade's roughened steel rod through its friction-sensitive igniter, thus torching off the short fuse.

Baluyev wasn't, at this point, especially interested in letting the fuse burn down while the grenade was in his hand. He immediately tossed it around the corner to where Matilda stood, munching her mush.

It seemed longer, but it was only about four seconds before the party was rewarded with a satisfying, but not catastrophic, boom and bright flash.

Baluyev tore around the corner to see a very dazed pig, staggering aimlessly. The pig paid him no attention at all.

Good, at least temporarily blinded, but where's the grenade? It's gone. Shattered? Just because the pig isn't bleeding doesn't mean . . .

"Hey, sir," said Smirnov from the lip of the trench, above, "the grenade got knocked up here." He held it up to demonstrate that, "The casing is still entirely intact."

"Hmmm . . . must have been greater resistance to the blast underneath that overcame the otherwise equivalent blast above. Still, what works, works."

"Hey, sir, do you think we can get a reprieve for Matilda for her services to the army, the state, and the tsar?"

"Sadly not. It's a cruel world and Kostyshakov informs me he's planning a forced march for Saturday. The men will need what our girl here can offer. We can only remember her, with gratitude, in our prayers.

"And as long as we're on the subject, Smirnov, and since you brought it up, kindly leash her and walk her back to *Feldwebel* Taenzler, would you? Good lad."

Camp Budapest

Corporal Vasenkov took off his visored cap and ran his fingers through the sparse hair sprouting from his mostly bare scalp. He had never been a huge fan of hard marching, fast, and under heavy packs. He was even less enthusiastic given that he'd be marching in German boots, at this stage of the war footgear of even less than secondary quality, and not especially made for hard marching, given the stasis of the trenches to the west.

But, thought the corporal and secret communist, *this will have something to do with the selection of men for the grenadier company, while the grenadier company is where I need to be, where the revolution needs me to be.*

Sergeant Major Blagov walked the line, reminding the soldiery that, "This is going to be a stone bitch, people. Check your *portyanki* now, while you can."

At that, perhaps half the troops pulled off their boots and checked—and in a few cases rewrapped—their foot wrappings.

Each man also had the makings of a full pack currently laid out on their ground sheets. The squad leaders and platoon sergeants checked, but no one was allowed to repack until either one of the two sergeants major, their own company first sergeant, or one of the officers had inspected two men from each squad. The packs wouldn't have been unbearable except that, in addition, thirty-five pounds of rock were to be added to each pack. The rocks, too, sat on the ground sheet. They would be weighed for each man when the march was over.

"Vicious imperialist foolishness" is what I call it, thought Vasenkov, as he carefully repacked to put as much softness as possible between the rocks and what would otherwise have been the skin of his back. *It's the petty need for small men to show the world their authority.*

Worse, as if the rocks weren't enough, the men were also marching with their Lewis guns, and with the various support sections dragging, for example, the light infantry cannon and the heavy Maxim machine guns, while the poor bloody engineers had four flamethrowers—the newest portable German kind—"*Wechselapparat*," that had the donut-shaped fuel tanks with a sphere of compressed air in the middle, to port along.

And then came the dreaded cry, "On your feet, gentlemen; ruck up, and fall in."

Tsarist swine, thought Vasenkov, as he pushed his own slender frame upright.

The first four *versta* were easy. They were intended to be easy, more of a stretching exercise and chance for the *portyanki* to move than a test of character. When those were done, and the men feeling fairly good about it, Kostyshakov called a halt. Once again the sergeant major trooped the line with, "Boots off. Noncoms check your men's feet. No time to fuck around. Rewrap if they need it. Ten minutes only ... Boots off. Noncoms ..."

Twenty-four more *versta*, a full fifteen miles, and five hours later, with no more breaks, the men marched into camp, footsore—bleeding a bit in most cases, with aching backs, sweaty despite the winter cold, and utterly miserable.

Not that everyone made it, no. A full twenty percent, or perhaps a few more, had fallen behind, leaving the others to have to spend even more time porting and dragging the heavy equipment. Many of those who'd fallen out would find themselves with the replacement detachment.

But not Vasenkov. He marched into camp with the rest, mentally cursing the leadership every step of the way.

"Well done," Kostyshakov cheered the men who made it as they staggered in.

Swine, thought Vasenkov.

PART II

Chapter Ten

Loading Supplies on the Zeppelin

Jambol, Bulgaria

It was a huge building, one of the biggest Kostyshakov had ever seen. It was certainly the biggest he'd ever seen standing alone, with no other substantial buildings around it. Brinkmann waved with his cane for a German private to open the door, then ushered the Russian officer in.

"Well, he *did* say we'd be travelling in the highest style I could imagine, but this is way beyond my imaginings," said Daniil, craning his neck to take in the immense structure and the massive dirigible within.

Wilhelm, who'd just climbed out of the crew compartment after overseeing one of the maintenance electricians repairing the L59's wireless set, heard the harsh consonants of the Russian words echo through the cavernous space of the hangar. He didn't understand the words, but the wonder in the man's voice was clear as he stood with his neck craned back, staring up at the majesty of the *Afrika-Schiff*. Several other men in Russian uniform joined him and then—ah! Wilhelm felt his mounting anxiety lessen as a German major stepped through the doors behind them, followed by a *Feldwebel*. The Russians had dropped out of the war, of course, but until recently they *had* been enemies . . . and strangers were not permitted in the L59 hangar.

When none of the ground maintenance crew seemed inclined to approach the group, Wilhelm straightened his spine and stepped forward.

"Good afternoon, gentlemen," Wilhelm said as he clicked his heels together in perfect attention. "I am Signalman Mueller. May I help you?" He was careful to keep his bearing polite and professional—indeed, his pride demanded it!—but he did allow a clipped suspicion into his tone.

"Mueller, I am *Feldwebel* Weber," the tall, slender man said. He stood with his shoulders very slightly hunched and had a moustache so grand that Wilhelm couldn't help but stare. "I am escorting Imperial Guards Lieutenant Colonel Kostyshakov and his staff, along with Major

Brinkmann, to a meeting with *Kapitaenleutnant* Bockholt. On the orders of Major General Hoffman," he added after a slight, but significant, pause.

"I will be happy to show you the way, *Feldwebel*," Wilhelm said smoothly, inclining his head. He turned and gestured to the long, low row of buildings that lined the outer wall of the hangar, inviting them to walk with him.

"Our gratitude, Mueller," the Russian lieutenant colonel, Kostyshakov, said as they started moving. His uniform was different from the standard Russian army officer's uniform, Wilhelm noticed. Perhaps because of the guards designation? Regardless, Wilhelm schooled his face to impassivity, but he was impressed. The man's German was flawless.

"I see by your insignia that you're part of the L59's crew. Please elaborate on your duties for us."

"As a communications operator, sir, besides sending and receiving, I also encrypt and decrypt coded messages, as well as maintain the equipment." Wilhelm said, hoping that his formal reply would shut down any further questions. Perhaps the Russians were no longer enemy combatants, but they certainly could still be spies.

"A very important position."

"Yes, sir. Here we are," Wilhelm announced as they approached the captain's office door. He knocked twice, then waited for the command to enter before turning the knob and stepping in.

"Signalman Mueller reports that a Major Brinkmann, a *Feldwebel* Weber and a group of Russian officers are here to see you, sir," Wilhelm said, after coming to attention and rendering a razor-sharp salute. Captain

Bockholt looked up from his desk with raised eyebrows—he didn't normally require such strict formality—but he returned Wilhelm's salute and got to his feet.

"Very well, Mueller," the captain said. "Thank you for bringing them to me. That will be all."

"Yes, sir," Wilhelm said, dropping the salute. He turned on his heel and walked out, as Weber and the Russians filed in. He let them all pass, and then closed the captain's office door behind him. Then he waited.

He wasn't eavesdropping. He was just . . . there if the captain needed him. Just in case.

"Captain Bockholt, I am Major Brinkmann, and I bring you Major General Hoffmann's compliments," Brinkmann said as the young German airman left the room. He reached into his jacket and pulled out a folded packet of papers which he held out to Ludwig.

"Thank you," Ludwig said, taking the papers with a nod. "May I offer you some refreshment?" He waved a hand at the sideboard, which held a small but respectable collection of the local fruit brandy known as *rakia*.

"We can help ourselves, Captain," the Russian lieutenant colonel said in unaccented German. "This will be easiest if you take the time to read the missive that the major's just given you first."

"I see," Ludwig said, keeping the curiosity out of his voice. "In that case, please be my guests. The blue bottle is particularly good. Glasses are in the cabinet. I shall be with you in one moment."

The Russian officer nodded and took one of the two chairs that faced Ludwig's desk while Weber went to the sideboard and began to pour. Ludwig returned to his seat and opened the packet, his pulse accelerating as his eyes slid over the orders contained within. It didn't take long, as General Hoffmann was a succinct man. Ludwig read over the entire message twice before he looked up at his guest, now smiling at him over a glass of *rakia*.

"Lieutenant Colonel Kostyshakov, I presume," he said.

"I am pleased to make your acquaintance, Captain Bockholt. Your reputation precedes you."

"I wish I could say the same, sir."

Kostyshakov smiled, and Ludwig noted that it didn't, quite, reach his eyes.

"General Hoffmann will have told you the purpose of my visit here, and the object of my—now *our*—mission."

"Yes, sir," Ludwig said. "It is an audacious concept..." he paused, and studied the face of the Russian officer.

"And?" Kostyshakov urged him to go on.

"...And one of which, if it is not too bold of me to say, I heartily approve. Bolshevism is a cancer." Ludwig kept his voice quiet, but even so, he felt his emotions stir at the prospect.

"I am glad you agree, Captain. As to the audacity of the plan...well. The *Afrika-Schiff* rather specializes in audacity, do you not?"

Ludwig felt himself smile.

"It seems we do."

"Well, then." Kostyshakov returned his smile and lifted his glass of *rakia*. At some point whilst he'd been reading, someone had set another full glass down on Ludwig's desk. He lifted this in reply and the two men drank, as if in a silent toast to the success of their audacious and improbable mission.

"Now," Ludwig said. "If you'll forgive me, General Hoffmann's orders were a little sparse on the details. Perhaps I can give you a tour of my ship, and you can tell me exactly what men and equipment we will be carrying for this endeavor."

"Yes, of course. But first, Captain, you must forgive me. Do you think that your men all share your disdain for Bolshevism? I ask only because, as I'm sure you can see, our mission is such that a threat from within our ranks could undo us entirely."

Ludwig fought the urge to bristle and pursed his lips while he thought about it. He turned the glass of *rakia* in his hand, watching the light from his office window play through the pale gold liquor.

"I cannot say for certain," he said slowly. "But I would be very surprised if they did not. My men are elite, sir. They are the crème de la crème of the Imperial Navy. In my experience, men of that much talent, ability and drive do not gravitate towards the philosophies of Bolshevism."

"I see," Kostyshakov said.

"But," Ludwig went on. "We are no strangers to sensitive mission orders. Certainly they will expect to be told nothing until we are airborne . . . and even then, only what they need to know in order to perform their duties."

"That would probably be best," Kostyshakov said. "Well enough." He tossed back the rest of the *rakia* and put the glass down on Ludwig's desk. "Is now convenient?"

"I am at your service, sir," Ludwig said. He stood, took

his own last drink, and gestured for the Russians to precede him out into the yawning hangar bay.

Wilhelm snapped to attention as the captain's office door opened. One by one, the visitors filed out, with Captain Bockholt bringing up the rear. He met his crewman's eyes and a tiny smile played about his lips.

"Ah, Mueller. Just the man I was hoping to see. Find the *Obermaschinistenmaat*, please, and ask him to join us here. I will be giving Lieutenant Colonel Kostyshakov and Major Brinkmann a tour of the ship, and we will need his expertise . . . and yours."

"Aye, sir," Wilhelm said with a salute. "*Obermaschinistenmaat* Engelke is still in the cargo bay, sir, overseeing the new rack installation. Shall I lead you to him?"

"Yes, perfect," the captain said, and turned with a smile to the two other officers. "Wilhelm is one of our best enlisted airmen."

Wilhelm felt his face flush with pride and his chest puff slightly at the compliment from his commanding officer. He said nothing, however, merely turned and began walking toward the cargo bay entrance where he'd last seen his immediate supervisor.

"Hundreds, you say." Daniil thought on that a bit then asked, "How many men can you lift?"

"Depends on the weight per man. Total lift, fuel, equipment, men other than the crew, and water ballast, is a little over twenty-four tons. It's not all useable, plan on about twenty-one tons. We can trim the water ballast some, yes, but not all of it. And how much we can trim depends a lot on where we're going; the thing leaks lifting gas, hydrogen, like a sieve, but it leaks more when the gas expands in warm weather. Still, we need a good deal just to keep an even keel."

"I knew she was big," he heard the Russian lieutenant colonel say softly in German behind him as they walked. "But it is different seeing her up close. What is her range?"

"For a long distance flight? She traversed almost seven thousand kilometers nonstop during the Africa mission."

Kostyshakov was impressed. "Our mission will be shorter, but we will likely need multiple lifts."

"So I surmised. General Hoffmann's orders said four companies of men?"

"Five, as it turns out, but smaller companies. Plus equipment, ammo, and supplies for maybe two weeks . . . and the animals. Can you take animals on board?"

"Horses?"

"And mules."

"I am certain the captain will find a way," Major Brinkmann said smoothly.

"We can," Bockholt said, drawing his words out, as if he were considering them as he spoke. "But securing them during flight will require some thought. As well as on- and off-load procedures."

The group fell silent then, as they'd reached the loading ramp for the ship's cargo bay. The ramp was down, and the shadowed cavern of the bay yawned ahead of them. Had they been anywhere other than inside one of the largest aircraft hangars in the world, the bay would have seemed truly gargantuan. But as it was, tucked under the belly of the L59's magnificent bulk, it appeared only moderately large.

Still, Wilhelm thought. *Surely she has plenty of room for a few men and horses!*

"Gentlemen," he said as he started up the ramp. "Please follow me and stay to the foot traffic walkway. Some of the other areas are designed to hold cargo, but are not necessarily safe for walking."

The captain gave him a slight nod of approval, and Wilhelm allowed himself a small smile when he turned back and began leading them into the relative dimness of the bay.

"You call this a weld? *Herr* welder? Your time would clearly be better spent elsewhere. Go to the cafeteria *und fressen!*"

This furious tirade echoed through the metal struts and after a brief moment, a red-faced Bulgarian stomped past them, clearly upset at the dressing-down he'd just received. Wilhelm drew a deep breath and took a calculated risk.

"*Obermaschinistenmaat* Engelke!" he called out, "The captain and a delegation of officers are here to see you!"

Wilhelm thought he heard another muttered epithet, but his supervisor and the L59's senior NCO walked toward them with his spine straight and his working uniform looking sharp. No trace of the irritation he must have felt for the bumbling welder remained on his face.

"Captain," the senior noncom said, coming to attention and rendering a salute once he was within speaking distance of the group.

"*Obermaschinistenmaat*," Captain Bockholt replied, returning the salute with a tiny smile on his face. The captain then stepped forward, and dropped his voice to a whisper that Wilhelm could barely hear, "These Bulgarians are butter-fingered oafs, aren't they? Well done, but you must continue to keep a close watch on them."

"Aye, sir," the senior mate said, a tiny growl entering his tone. "The Bulgarian 'expert' was a ham-handed fool. Some are better. I will have one of our machinists break his weld and start over. It will not delay our progress."

"That is good to hear. This is Lieutenant Colonel Kostyshakov, of the Russian Guards, plus Major Brinkmann, of Ober Ost, and *Feldwebel* Weber. We have been given orders from General Hoffmann."

The senior machinist's spine got even straighter, which Wilhelm didn't think was possible.

The captain went on. "Perhaps you and *Feldwebel* Weber can go over the cargo requirements and begin to work on some loading solutions. This is to be a major movement, not quite like anything we have done before."

"Yes, sir," Engelke said. *Feldwebel* Weber stepped away from the group, and the two NCOs greeted each other and shook hands. Wilhelm took a step to follow them as they began walking back farther into the cargo bay.

"Wilhelm, wait a moment. Lieutenant Colonel Kostyshakov, Major Brinkmann, I think there is something else we must discuss," Bockholt said, beckoning to the two officers to come closer. Wilhelm, too, found himself being drawn into a circle of confidence, and he felt intensely uncomfortable at being in such company. *What could the captain want me for?*

"There is another matter we must consider," Bockholt

said. "The matter of getting past the Russian lines. Armistice or no armistice, I do not think the Bolshevik army is likely to simply let a warship of a recent enemy fly overhead with impunity. And they do have aircraft."

"What do you suggest?" Kostyshakov asked.

"In his orders, General Hoffmann said that we will have whatever we need. Major Brinkmann, what we *need* is a fighter escort. Two planes. Four would be better, but two will work, just to see us past the most dangerous part of the crossing, the front."

The two visiting officers looked at each other for a brief moment, and then Brinkmann nodded.

"I will send a message," he said. "The general gives this mission his top priority, so it is likely that he will respond quickly."

"Thank you," Bockholt said. "Now, Wilhelm here will be able to answer any questions you have about the ship and her capabilities. I must speak with my officers and begin the planning cycle. I will have a basic plan for you in twenty-four hours, pending any changes due to the general's answer about the escort."

"Yes, of course," Kostyshakov said. "Thank you very much, Captain. I am pleased to be working with you."

"And I, you, sir. We shall make history together, no?"

Again, thought Wilhelm, with more than a little bit of pride. *We shall make history together* again.

Ludwig looked down the length of the cargo bay and squinted his eyes, imagining it filled with men, equipment and—heaven help them all—even horses.

"It will be tight, sir, but we can make it work,"

Heinrich, his recently promoted XO said. After the Africa mission, Ludwig's previous XO had been given command of his own ship. The navy hadn't been able to provide a backfill, however, and so his young lieutenant navigator had been forced to step into the role. Overall, Ludwig was pleased with his performance and growth, but this coming mission would certainly put him to the test.

It would put them all to the test.

"Tell me how, Lieutenant," Ludwig said as he started walking aft. He beckoned to Heinrich to follow and then clasped his hands behind his back. "Tell me what you and the chief-machinist's mate figured out. I need to see it in my mind's eye."

"Very good, sir," Heinrich said as he stretched his long legs to catch up. "In the first place, the new aluminum cargo racks here in the forward area are significantly lighter than the previous versions. We will use those for standard sized cargo, food barrels, ammunition, et cetera."

"And how much weight?"

"Four and a half tons for food and water, and about eleven tons for the men and equipment for the first lift."

"The grenadier company?" Ludwig asked, knowing that they had been Kostyshakov's choice for the first lift.

"And about twenty-four men from headquarters company. Plus their heavy weapons."

"And where have you planned to put these men for the duration of the trip? We obviously can't have them moving around the cargo bay."

"No, sir. The plan is to cordon off this area where they will stay for the duration of the trip. As long as they don't leave that portion of the cargo bay, the loading balance should be stable. We'll have them hang hammocks from support struts to the ends of the racks starting at that stanchion there," Heinrich said, pointing. "To there. It's not a large area, but it will be enough that they can stretch their legs from time to time—and a few at a time—and keep their blood moving."

Ludwig nodded. It wasn't ideal—but then, what was? It would work, though he didn't envy those men the cold, miserable transport that awaited them.

"What else?" he asked, continuing down the length of the cargo bay. "How will we secure the heavy weapons?"

"The weight and balance calculations we ran suggest that they're best located dead center of the cargo bay, sir," Heinrich said, walking to that point. "The plan is to use horses to haul them in their rigs up onto the deck, and then immobilize the wheels in place and tie the entire apparatus down to our support struts, using our standard cargo eyelets. We'll use hempen rope, stiffened with tar for the tiedowns."

"With a lot of redundancy, one would hope," Ludwig said dryly.

"Of course, sir. I give you my word that the guns will remain immobile for the entirety of the trip."

"I hope so, otherwise we're going to deliver fewer men than we promised. Not to mention the godforsaken horses." He let out a sigh.

"Aye, sir, the horses are the trickiest part. The best plan we can figure is to construct half a dozen stalls in the aftmost portion of the bay."

"Stalls?" Ludwig felt his eyebrows go up. "You're going to turn my cargo hold into a stable?"

"Temporarily, yes, sir. We'll use the same support struts as anchors for lightweight wooden walls suspended from ceiling and deck using the same tarred ropes. Then we'll have a cradle of hay for each animal, to keep it docile and occupied during transit. We'll lay duckboards across the floor struts in between the stall walls to create a solid surface for the horses and mules to stand or lie upon."

Heinrich gestured enthusiastically as he pointed out where each of these things would go, and despite himself, Ludwig was amused. The idea of carrying horses and mules aboard his ship was a ghastly one, but then, this entire enterprise was equal parts ridiculous and incredibly ambitious. Perhaps diving in with enthusiasm and imagination was the only way to actually accomplish it.

"Fine," Ludwig said. "Though I will make it clear to Kostyshakov and Brinkmann that it will be their men, not mine, who are responsible for cleaning the horseshit out of my cargo hold. Now, let us discuss unloading."

After his walk-through with Heinrich, Ludwig was mostly satisfied with the load plan. As he'd suspected, however, the logistics of unloading were still murky at best. Chief among issues was that no one had briefed him on the specific destination—General Hoffmann's orders had just mentioned "somewhere east of the Volga, and probably east of the Urals"—and so neither Ludwig nor his crew knew exactly what type of situation they'd be flying into.

That was something he needed to rectify posthaste. So he headed to his office to pen a note to ask Brinkmann to come and see him.

"Ah! Captain Bockholt! I was hoping to find you. Do you have a moment?"

Lieutenant Colonel—or whatever the Russian Imperial Guards equivalent was—Kostyshakov stood outside his office door, a small smile on his face. Ludwig couldn't decide if he liked the man or not, but he couldn't deny that he was ambitious and aggressive . . . and he seemed fanatically dedicated to the success of his mission.

"What can I do for you?" Ludwig asked.

"How is your planning coming?" Kostyshakov asked, which surprised Ludwig and put him on his guard. Was the man doubting him and his crew?

"Rather well, actually," Ludwig said, trying to keep all hint of stiffness out of his tone. "Although I was headed to pen a note to Major Brinkmann. I'm afraid we can go no further with our plans until I have more concrete details about our exact destination."

"Ah, I don't have much more information on that, but I will tell you what I know," Kostyshakov said, his smile changing to a rueful grimace. "You have maps in your office?"

"I do," Ludwig said, and reached out to turn the handle of the door leading from the hangar. "But there are more and better in the planning room. First right past my office. After you, please."

Ludwig followed Kostyshakov into the large room that he and his officers used to plan their flights. Maps and charts hung on three of the four walls, with the fourth dedicated to large windows to let in sunlight. In the center of the room, a long table with an angled top held a large, detailed map of eastern Europe from the Mediterranean to the Baltic, and including most of Western Siberia. Kostyshakov made a beeline for this map.

"This is good quality," he said, admiration in his voice. "You Germans always did pay attention to the details."

"It is how we are taught, sir," Ludwig said. "The destination? Major General Hoffmann said east of the Volga?"

"Hmm, yes. So we don't actually know the exact location. Yekaterinburg, Tyumen, or Tobolsk, those are our best guesses right now. The latter is the last we've heard of, but they may have been moved to one of the others. The strategic recon team will find a place to land but it will depend on where the royal family is."

Ludwig leaned in to peer at the map where Kostyshakov pointed at the three cities in succession.

"Does your Strat Recon team know what to look for?" Ludwig asked. "What makes a good landing zone for a zeppelin?"

"I gave them some guidance. Describe the ideal to me."

Ludwig pointed at a spot on the map where the topographical contour lines curved away from each other with wide separation.

What he recited sounded much like what Kostyshakov had told Turgenev. "If we are to land, it must be a large area, flat with little to no vegetation. Some kind of water feature—a lake or wide river would be best—so that we can refill our ballast tanks. And most importantly, it must be secure. I am sure I don't need to remind you that our hydrogen lifting gasses are quite flammable. One enemy tracer round into our envelope and we are done. As a well-roasted beef haunch is done."

Kostyshakov snorted a soft laugh at Ludwig's dark humor. "There will be only a small force on the ground to receive the first shipment. However, we will do our best to ensure you have a secure landing area. Once the first lift is complete, of course, it will be simpler, for we will have the grenadier company on the ground. However, what other options do you have, if we cannot find this perfect meadow of yours?"

"We can land to a tower, like a steeple perhaps, though it will make unloading more difficult, at least for the horses. Supplies can be thrown out or lowered via rope slings, as can men. Or men could use a ladder. But the horses and mules will present a problem, as will the heavy weapons."

"How long will you need on the ground?"

"We will do a rehearsal in a day or so to practice onloading and offloading the cargo, so my men should be able to get it down to about thirty minutes. No longer than it will take to top up the ballast tanks. But I must tell you that approaching to land to the ground takes much more time than landing to a tower, and we will be quite vulnerable the whole time."

"Well, as I said," Kostyshakov shrugged, "we will do what we can. Let us hope your crew can keep from being spotted from the air while in transit."

"I do not like to risk my crew and my ship on the basis of *hope*, sir," Ludwig said tartly. Kostyshakov looked up at him with one raised eyebrow.

"Captain, is that not what we are all doing here?"

Ludwig said nothing, merely met the other man's eyes for a long moment, and then turned back to the map.

"On another topic, I do have a small request for you," Kostyshakov said, straightening and stepping back from the map table. "I appreciate that there are nuances to this business of mobility by air with which I am unfamiliar. I would like to have you appoint a liaison to my staff, if you wouldn't mind. Someone who can inform me and my staff of things we do not know."

"I am desperately short of officers, sir," Ludwig said with real regret. A liaison was a fantastic idea, and it spoke well of Kostyshakov that he would ask for one. "I am sorry that I have none to spare."

"I know, Brinkmann told me that you have only the one lieutenant as your XO. I thought perhaps an NCO might do the trick. What about that one young man . . . Wilhelm . . . ?"

"Signalman Mueller?" Ludwig pursed his lips and considered. "He is a good man and indispensable as our wireless operator . . . but as you know, this mission is so covert that we have literally no one with whom we can communicate. Your ground forces will be on the move too much to make a wireless practical . . . yes. That might do nicely, sir. I will speak with my senior noncom and have him release Wilhelm to your staff effective immediately."

"Thank you, Captain," Kostyshakov said with a slight inclination of his head. "I promise that we will take good care of the young man."

"Mueller, what are your thoughts?"

Wilhelm had been looking up at the underside of the L59 as his friends and crewmates lowered barrel after barrel out through the deck of the forward part of the cargo bay. The airship currently hovered ten meters above the ground, secured by her mooring lines as the crew practiced offloading cargo as they would do if they could not find a landing zone big enough to set down on the ground. Lieutenant Colonel Kostyshakov, to whom he'd been temporarily assigned for the duration of this mission, approached him, hands behind his back and that slight smile on his clean-shaven face.

"Sir?"

"How goes the rehearsal? If you're to be my liaison, you must be ready to explain the nuances that I might not immediately catch." Kostyshakov came to a stop beside Wilhelm and craned his neck upward to see what Wilhelm had been watching. "Is it going well?"

"This part is, sir. Our crew is very well trained with supply drops of this type. The hard part will be the animals." Wilhelm instinctively drew his spine up straight, then belatedly realized that the Russian officer was several inches shorter. Would he see that as an insult?

Not that Kostyshakov had time to notice. A deafening scream rent the air, causing both men to spin aft toward the stern of the zeppelin. There, a mule dangled, suspended in a canvas sling that wrapped under its belly and hung from chains that led to the zeppelin's winch. Wilhelm knew that the machinists, his friend Gustav among them, had been working all morning to move and reconfigure the winch to try to attempt this maneuver.

As Wilhelm and Kostyshakov—along with everyone else observing the unloading rehearsal—watched, the mule let out another scream of protest as the winch started to lower the sling. The animal kicked out with its hind legs, making its situation worse, as the sling began to lurch from side to side in response.

"Oh no," Wilhelm murmured. "This is bad."

"Bad? Why?" Kostyshakov asked.

"That oscillation is very hard on the winching gears. If the crew cannot get it under control, it could tear the winch right out of the support strut—or worse, cause it to grind itself up and start a fire. These ships are big, yes, but everything is very delicate." Wilhelm breathed in sharply as the animal kicked again and showed no sign of ceasing to struggle.

The swaying got worse, until Wilhelm found himself biting his lower lip in fear for his friends overhead. A loud *pop* echoed across the field, and the mule in the sling jerked, and then plummeted to the ground with another scream of terror.

A sickening *thud* echoed across the suddenly otherwise silent field. A tall figure that Wilhelm instantly recognized as Captain Bockholt stepped toward the crumpled animal and drew a Luger P08. The captain fired, and the mule finally fell silent, freed from its misery.

"They had to cut the load," Wilhelm said, hearing the sickness in his own voice. "Otherwise, it would have jeopardized the ship and everyone on her."

"Hmmm. Sergeant Kaledin is going to be very upset about the loss of his mule. But, yes, I can see that. What do you suggest?"

"Me, sir?"

"Yes, you. You're my liaison. Your captain wouldn't have assigned you to me if he didn't intend you to advise." Kostyshakov's tone was kind, but Wilhelm could hear the edge of impatience under the words. He took a deep breath, steeled his nerve, and opened his mouth.

"I suggest that your strategic recon team find a place where we can fully land, at least for the first lift, if not two. If panicking animals don't cause damage to the ship, they will almost certainly injure themselves and then they're no use to your forces, sir." Wilhelm kept his tone respectful, but he told the bald truth.

Kostyshakov turned to look up at Wilhelm, his tiny smile returning. "There," he said. "See? That wasn't so hard. As it happens, I agree with you, but we may not have a choice in the matter. And if the animals die, they can always be eaten."

"And so we will continue to rehearse," Wilhelm said. "Perhaps we can get the animals used to the procedure. Maybe if they try a blindfold?"

"That should be interesting," Kostyshakov said.

"Yes, sir," Wilhelm agreed. Privately, he had a bet with Gustav that at least three of the horses didn't make it to the actual day of the mission. But he wasn't about to tell the Russian that. Not after watching the horrible demise of one of the poor animals.

Perhaps later, after the mission was complete. *Still, poor "Lydia."*

Interlude

Tatiana: Alexei and His Bodyguard

Alexei's violent coughing had led to hemorrhaging in his groin. He lay in bed, in excruciating pain, and there was nothing anyone, including the doctors, could do.

As he moaned and cried, Mama sat with him, never leaving his bedside.

It had been almost six years since he'd had a bout this bad.

Deverenko was beside himself. The man who had been responsible for getting Alexei to wear all the various encasements he'd needed throughout his life wore a look of such utter despair that Papa gently suggested he leave. Most of the encasements, made of leather and canvas, to support Alexei's legs, arms, and body, were now too small for his growing body.

Alexei had always fought them, insisting that they didn't help, but we all knew that was just his stubbornness coming out. Like Anastasia, he had always had a mind of his own, and for days, I had expected that willfulness to surface.

But it hadn't.

Once Deverenko and Papa left, it was just Mama and I, sitting at his side. A basin of melted ice rested in my lap, long with strips of cloth, freshly torn from our most threadbare clothes.

Mama pulled one of the rags off Alexei's feverish face and set it aside. She rested her fingers atop his forehead, sweeping the strands of sweat-soaked hair aside.

I dipped a fresh strip of cloth into the chill water, gave it a squeeze, and handed it to Mama.

"I would like to die, Mama," Alexei said, his voice barely a whisper. "I'm not afraid of death."

Mama's hands froze mid-motion. Mama's hands, unfailingly steady through years of Alexei's illness, trembled now. She set the rag atop his forehead as she hushed him.

His eyes had become enormous in his head as his fever had thinned him and turned his skin yellow. He blinked his eyes open, holding her gaze with his own.

"Mama, I'm so afraid of what they may do to us."

Chapter Eleven

Grand Duchess Olga Nicholaevna Romanova
in Happier Times

Governor's House, Tobolsk

As winter settled over Tobolsk, Dostovalov and Cheko
were reassigned to day shift. Kobylinsky informed them

of the change himself in his office, across the street from Freedom House.

"Aside from the minor incident with that *samogon*," he said. "You lads have done excellent work, and the Romanovs seem comfortable with you, so I'm transferring you to day shift. No need to freeze your asses off."

This was, perhaps, optimistic of the colonel, as it was perfectly possible to freeze one's ass off, in Siberia, in the winter, in broad daylight.

As he spoke, Kobylinsky's eyes shifted to the window and his fingers drummed on the table. He was in a dark brown suit and coat. After an incident in which one of the men had torn off his epaulets, and the soldiers' committee had demanded the abolition of rank insignia, Kobylinsky had taken to wearing mufti, even during duty hours.

"Thank you, sir," Dostovalov said.

"Right," Kobylinsky said, his tone vacant. "Well, off to it, men."

The sun shone bright and clear on the morning of their first day. The air was still cold, but nowhere near as punishing as the Siberian night. The Romanov family, minus their mother and Tatiana, were out in force on the grounds. The children played while Nicholas and Prince Dolgorukov sawed firewood out back behind the mansion.

The change of duty was an agreeable turn of events, but Chekov noted with alarm that Dostovalov's mood was entirely *too* buoyant for a minor improvement in their situation. Moreover, he noticed that Olga Romanova seemed equally cheerful, and glanced every chance she could at *"Antosenka"* when she thought no one was looking. Dostovalov, for his part, simply smiled and smiled and smiled like a smitten jackass.

Of course Dostovalov would develop a crush on the tsar's daughter. Of fucking course he would.

Chekov forced himself not to glare at Dostovalov as they walked their paces around the Freedom House. Not that the moron would've noticed. While Maria and Anastasia made use of their swing set, kicking up snow with each forward swing, Olga ran around the yard, pulling her brother Alexei on a sledge through the snow. Dostovalov watched their antics with a beatific grin. Brother and sister were laughing uproariously as they careened to a halt in a snowbank on the edge of the lawn. Laughing along with them, Dostovalov walked over to the bank to help them extricate themselves.

"It's all fun and games until they kill the hemophiliac," Chekov muttered.

"Sergei, would you stop being such an ass?" Dostovalov hissed over his shoulder.

Dostovalov gently helped disentangle Alexei from his big sister, and then pulled Olga to her feet. Olga accepted his help to stand up. The pair smiled and held onto one another's hands for a long moment, close enough to kiss, before Olga broke away and began brushing snow off of Alexei's uniform. Dostovalov still looked on, grinning.

Idiot!

Something hard and cold hit Chekov in the back of his head, interrupting his fuming. He whirled about to find the youngest Romanov daughter, Anastasia, regarding him with a haughty up-turned nose and a second ball of ice and snow in her hand. Chekov regarded her with annoyance as he tried to scoop the snow out of his collar before it melted and trickled down to his shirt.

"And what was that for, you little assassin?" he demanded.

"Your ungentlemanly conduct, Comrade *Feldfebel*," Anastasia said. "Your big friend went to my sister's aid while you stood about doing nothing. What sort of guard *are* you?"

With that, the incorrigible teenager threw her next snowball, but Chekov stepped aside and the projectile whizzed past his head, thunking into the wooden fence behind him. A snort of genuine laughter escaped Chekov. He scooped up a handful of snow, and with practiced ease, packed it into a tight sphere, then pitched it expertly, hitting Anastasia right in her grinning mouth.

"Pah!" Anastasia ran a hand across her face and spit out a mouthful of snow; her now reddened face bore an immense grin. "This means war, good sir! Maria! To arms!"

Chekov sprinted around the corner of the mansion, boots sliding on the ice and snow, as the third and fourth Romanov sisters concentrated fire upon him. Snowballs splatted against Freedom House's façade while Chekov furiously crafted more ammunition.

"Maria, go around back!" Anastasia shouted. "We'll outflank him!"

Chekov ran and turned the corner around the back of the mansion himself before Maria could get there. He greeted her with a face full of snow. Maria laughed good naturedly as she shook her head to clear off the snow, and returned fire, but Chekov was already back around the front of the house, just in time to pelt Anastasia in the back of the head with another snowball.

Anastasia used a decidedly unladylike word and chased after him with another snowball. Chekov ducked away, laughing loudly. He laughed so much and so heartily that his abdomen ached from the unaccustomed exertion and, out of breath, he soon succumbed to a barrage of well-aimed and vengefully propelled snowballs.

"All right, all right, ladies!" He shouted, holding up his hands and tucking his chin into his shoulder to protect his face. "I surrender. Your victory is complete."

Maria joined Olga, Alexei, and Dostovalov who stood upon the front step laughing at the battle, but Anastasia let out a whoop and favored them with an impromptu war dance, circling around the defeated Chekov. Anastasia's rendition sent everyone, Chekov included, into peals of mirth.

Chekov posted himself by the window to the balcony while Dostovalov stayed with the family. He trusted even Dostovalov wouldn't be so stupid as to do something untoward in front of Olga's father so he didn't join them. Besides, Nicholas's children were one thing. Chekov had no desire to associate with the deposed tsar, no matter how refined the former autocrat's manners were.

His quiet vigil was interrupted only a few minutes in, however, by Nicholas's cultured voice.

"*Feldfebel* Chekov, would you come here, please?"

Chekov sighed, but came as called to the study. The five children were arrayed about the room. Olga and Tatiana sat on the sofa, each with a book in her hand,

Maria worked some brightly colored yarn with knitting needles, and Anastasia and the boy, Alexei, played on the floor with his cocker spaniel, Joy. Dostovalov stood in the near corner, well away from Olga, thank God. Nicholas himself sat at a lovely chess board with intricately carved ebony pieces for the black and sandalwood for the white.

"Yes, Citizen Romanov?" Chekov said.

"Your friend tells me you are an excellent chess player," Nicholas said.

Chekov glanced from Dostovalov's grinning face back to the ex-emperor.

"Well, I wouldn't know about excellent," Chekov said. "Since the war started I've only had rubes like Anton here to play, but I do enjoy the game."

Nicholas and Dostovalov chuckled good-naturedly, but Olga shot Chekov an annoyed glance.

Oh, climb down, Your Highness. Your boyfriend is terrible at chess.

"In that case, please, have a seat." Nicholas gestured to the leather upholstered chair in front of the ebony chessmen.

Chekov hesitated a moment longer but found no valid excuse not to play.

"Thank you, sir," Chekov said as he placed his rifle gently against a nearby bookshelf and settled into the comfortable chair on the black side of the board. Nicholas moved King's Pawn to King's Four, Chekov immediately responded by sliding Queen's Bishop Pawn two squares forward.

"The Sicilian Defense," Nicholas commented. "Very bold."

"Fortune favors us," Chekov said, evenly. "Or so I'm told."

Nicholas played well, making excellent use of pawn, rook, and bishop, but Chekov found him overly cautious with his queen, and his knights were an afterthought at best. After several minutes of forcing Nicholas to retreat from unfavorable exchanges into suboptimal positions, the former monarch smiled amiably at Chekov.

"Your friend was quite correct, *Feldfebel*," he said. "You are an excellent player. Who taught you the game?"

"I played at university quite a bit, but I learned most from my father," Chekov said. "He was a surgeon, but I think he would've loved to have been a chess grandmaster more than anything. He made it to the Moscow City tournament once and played Ossip Bernstein. He only lost as opposed to being massacred like most of Ossip's opponents that day."

"No small feat," Nicholas said, nodding appreciatively. He moved his bishop to threaten Chekov's knight. "Were you studying medicine at university? Following in your father's footsteps?"

"No, I was studying economics," Chekov said, responding to Nicholas's threat by positioning a rook to threaten the sandalwood queen. "At least until the war broke out."

Nicholas backed down from his attack as Chekov suspected he would, moving the knight directly in front of the queen to block Chekov's rook. The resignation of impending defeat clouded his eyes.

"Papa," Anastasia spoke up from the carpet. "Can we read more Sherlock Holmes tonight?"

"Oh, dearest, we only have a chapter left in *The Great Within the Small*," Nicholas said. "I know detective stories are more fun, but it's important to understand our situation and Nilus has the best read on all of this."

Chekov's pulse quickened and a hiss escaped his lips unbidden. Rather than complete the elegant trap he'd been setting to checkmate Nicholas he went on the offensive and began forcing exchanges of pieces.

"I take it you disapprove of Nilus?" Nicholas said as he removed Chekov's rook with his queen.

"I wouldn't dream of venturing opinions on such lofty matters," Chekov said, moving a bishop to check Nicholas's king. "I'm just a common soldier, after all."

Nicholas moved a pawn to obscure the bishop's line of attack unsupported. Chekov took the pawn with a knight.

"Clearly you've impressive faculties, *Feldfebel*," Nicholas said. "Speak your mind, good man."

Chekov clenched his teeth. Dostovalov, who stood behind Nicholas, shook his head emphatically.

"If you insist, Citizen Romanov," he said. "Nilus is a bigoted crackpot who scapegoats the relatively tiny population of Jews here in Russia for problems that have little to do with them, arguably that are even somewhat ameliorated by their presence."

Chekov threw his queen across the board into the midst of Nicholas's defenses.

"You know who did an actual scientific study on Jews in the Pale of Settlement?" Chekov continued, as Nicholas stared at the board, looking for some escape. "A fellow named Bloch. You're familiar with him? One of the reasons Russia has any railways to speak of?"

"Yes, I know Bloch," Nicholas muttered as he castled his king with his queen's rook. "I was the one who saw to it his *Future War and Its Economic Consequences* was distributed at the Hague Conference. If only my idiot cousin had read it, perhaps we would've avoided this whole catastrophe. I know that Bloch had Semitic sympathies, but I'm unfamiliar with any such study of the Jews."

"I'm glad you recognize the man's talent," Chekov said. "Bloch and a team of researchers compiled a five-volume study that comprehensively proved that not only do Jews do little harm; they enrich every single community of which they are a part, both culturally and economically. We were just praising Ossip Bernstein, for example, were we not? And he is, indeed, Jewish."

Chekov took Nicholas's rook with his own queen, cornering the sandalwood king behind a line of his own pawns and demanding the former tsar's queen as a sacrifice to remove the threat.

"Your father's ministers banned the study, of course," Chekov continued. "And I've only ever seen but one copy of the full study while I was at university in Yaroslavl. Bloch's research partner, Subotin, was able to publish a summary, titled, 'The Jewish Question in the Right Light.' It is somewhat easier to find, and infinitely superior to half-baked, self-serving mystical nonsense."

"Come now," Nicholas said, taking Chekov's queen with his own. "You mustn't think I hate all Jews, there are many who contribute to Russia, but clearly there are a larger proportion of malcontents amongst them than in the Christian, or Mohammedan populations. Surely, you've noticed the raw number of Jews among the Bolsheviks!"

"I think perhaps you're confusing cause and effect, Citizen Romanov," Chekov said as he removed Nicholas's queen from the board with his own rook. "For generations Jews have been brutalized and murdered and you and your ancestors have done little but scapegoat them, eat away at their rights and reduce the sentences of the bastards who prey upon them, then you have the audacity to wonder why revolution might appeal to some of them."

The room was absolutely silent until Anastasia stood and faced Chekov, hands balled into fists.

"You can't talk to my father that way," she said.

The remaining children were silent. Maria and Alexei looked uncomfortable, and Olga's features mirrored Anastasia's fury. Tatiana's expression was inscrutable, her gray eyes contemplative. Dostovalov's eyes were bulging, his eyebrows threatening to retreat into his hairline.

"I can, miss," Chekov said, quietly maintaining eye contact with Nicholas. "I can because he isn't the emperor anymore, and he isn't the emperor anymore *because* he refused to hear the things he didn't want to hear."

Chekov took the pawn in front of Nicholas's king with his rook, which was backed by one of his bishops.

"Checkmate," Chekov said, standing up and grabbing his rifle. "Dostovalov, you stay here. I'll post on the balcony. Good night, Citizen Romanov. Thank you for the game."

Dostovalov walked his paces in the main hall for several hours until a familiar silhouette detached itself from the staircase and hurried across the hall, out into the passageway. Olga poked her head back around the corner into the hall and grinned at him, beckoning with an ivory-skinned hand. She then tiptoed to the kitchen. No sooner had he stepped into the kitchen than she flowed into his arms, kissing him fiercely.

"Oh, *Antosenka*," she murmured, her voice low to avoid waking anyone else. "I'm sorry I've kept you waiting, it took forever for Tatiana to fall sleep tonight."

"It's all right," he said, leaning back a bit to look into her eyes. "I just thought perhaps you found better company."

"You're incorrigible," Olga said. "And that's my joke, plagiarizer."

"We're just lucky Sergei is still sulking out on the balcony," Dostovalov said. Olga leaned back, frowning. She withdrew from his arms, leaving Dostovalov with a confused expression.

"Why was your friend so rude tonight?" Olga said. "I know Papa is hard on the Jews, but why did he take it so personally? Is he Jewish?"

"Sergei isn't a Jew, but it *is* personal for him," Dostovalov said, his brow furrowing. "He has his reasons, but they are his to tell, not mine."

Olga stared at Dostovalov's unusually serious expression for a long moment.

"*Antosenka*, I'm not sure I trust him," she said. "He sounded so hateful."

"Sergei is a good man," Dostovalov said. "You can trust him as much as you trust me."

Olga frowned, but then her expression softened as she

visibly changed her priorities. She smiled impishly as she pulled loose the sash on her thick winter robe, letting it fall loose in the center to reveal the silken nightgown clinging to her body underneath. Dostovalov sucked in a large breath through his nose and stiffened instantly at the reveal.

"As much as I trust you," she said. "Really?"

"Well," Dostovalov said, then stopped, coughing lightly to clear his throat. "Perhaps not that much."

"*Antosenka*," Olga said, her voice low and serious. "I want you to do it to me."

"Do what?" Dostovalov said, then realizing his stupidity, shook his head. "Oh! Olga, we can't."

With a boldness that set Dostovalov on his heels, Olga stepped forward and grabbed his hardened cock through his pants.

"Oh, I think we can," she said quietly, her breath taking on the same rapid cadence as his.

It would be so easy. Olga was easily the most beautiful girl—woman—in face and form he'd ever seen much less laid hands on. So easy to pull aside their clothes and have each other. God, he'd never wanted anything more.

"No, Olga," he said, his deep voice tremorous. "God, what if your parents found out? What if you got pregnant?"

"I'm twenty-two and have never known a man, Anton," she said, her voice shaking with passion and fear. "I won't live long enough to marry; we both know that. I want a man, and I want it to be you."

"You will," Dostovalov whispered fiercely. "You will live to marry. I'll see to it. I will kill anyone who touches you."

"But you won't touch me yourself," Olga said, bitterly, turning away and putting her hands on the kitchen table. Her shoulders heaved as she took several deep breaths, keeping her back to him.

Dostovalov hesitated, then put his arms around her and pulled her back against himself. Olga resisted only briefly before leaning back into his embrace.

"I absolutely will touch you," Dostovalov said, and Olga gasped as he gently cupped her breasts with his hands. "And just because we can't consummate doesn't mean you have to go to bed in agony."

His left hand lifted the lacy hem of her nightgown and slid up the smooth skin of her thigh. Olga's words were lost in a low moan of pleasure.

Tatiana awoke in the middle of the night from a terrible dream, shadowy figures shouted accusations from behind gravestones, hurled litanies of sin against her with judgments of death and worse as her sentence. The black wraiths ripped her father and mother to shreds with flashing teeth, they cut little Alexei at the wrists and left him to spill his life onto the floor. They engulfed and consumed Olga, Maria, and Anastasia, leaving behind only contorted, broken corpses.

Worst of all, she was sure in her dream that the litanies were true, the crimes they laid before her real. She sat bolt upright, breathing fast, sweating despite the cold. Taking several shuddering breaths, Tatiana steadied herself.

Just the same room we were in last night, and the night before that and the night before that.

Tatiana swung her legs out from underneath the layers of heavy blankets and put her feet on the cold planks of the floor. A search of the room revealed two gently snoring mounds where Anastasia and Maria lay, but on Olga's bed . . .

Oh, damn it.

Tatiana rose hurriedly and draped herself in a heavy fur coat. She stepped out into the hallway, determined to catch her idiot sister in her ill-considered assignation with the big guard and force her to put a stop to it. A flicker of light, movement from beyond the glass door to the balcony caught her eye. The shorter guard, Chekov, the one who'd spoken kindly to her and brutally to her father stood on the balcony. Compelled by dreadful curiosity, the same kind of curiosity that leads one to poke at a sore tooth or pick at a scab, Tatiana diverted course and, on unsteady legs, walked down the hall to confront the guard who had dared snap at her father like an unruly recruit.

Chekov relished the bitterly cold night air out on the balcony. Anything was better than the company inside. The cold, unyielding stars were far superior in their silent regard to conversation with a delusional former autocrat, no matter how lovely his family.

How could he have been so stupid? Chekov shook his head at his own folly; letting himself get drawn into a conversation with *Nikolashka*. The man who'd ignored and avoided his duties as sovereign until the country was starving and on the brink of collapse. The idiot who'd played tennis even as the Imperial Fleet sank during the war with the Japanese. The simpleton who had the temerity to take personal command of armies engaged in the largest conflagration in human history when he wasn't fit to manage a mess tent.

But most of all, the bastard who spared my mother's murderers.

Chekov slammed a fist into the stone of the balcony railing.

I hope the Reds do *shoot the sonofabitch.*

Hours passed in silence. The Romanovs retired for the evening shortly after the chess match. The Red Guards across the street appeared to have bedded down. Chekov was left alone with his dark thoughts until well past midnight.

The balcony door creaked open behind him. Chekov turned expecting to find an angry Dostovalov coming through the door to confront him now that the Romanovs were asleep.

"Save the lecture, Anton—"

Instead of his tall, burly friend, Tatiana Romanova regarded him steadily from the doorway, starlight glinting in her sad, searching eyes.

"You hate us, yet you guard us," she said, without preamble. "Why?"

"I don't hate you, or your siblings," Chekov said, looking back out into the night. "You're children; children who should be in bed. It's very late and it is freezing out here."

"I don't think you're much older than me," Tatiana said. "And you didn't answer my question. If you hate my father so much why aren't you across the street with them?"

She nodded at the Kornilov House, which now held some of the Red Guards.

"I'm older than you'll ever be," Chekov said. "And I don't owe you an answer, miss."

"No, you don't," Tatiana agreed, but still she stood there, staring at him.

Chekov held her gaze for a long time, jaw clenched. In the end the words came, useless as they were, because he wanted this beautiful, good, brave girl to know the truth of the world she lived in, the one her parents had sheltered her from her whole life. Perhaps it was unnecessary cruelty, but he wanted her to *understand*.

"What do you know about the Kishinev Pogrom?" Chekov said.

Tatiana just shook her head and pulled her fur coat tighter about herself.

"Yes, that's what I thought," Chekov said, pulling a pack of cigarettes from his pocket. "I'm not Jewish, but my mother was. Or at least she grew up a Jew, she converted to marry my father."

"Oh," Tatiana said.

"Yes, 'oh,'" Chekov said around the cigarette as he flicked his lighter open. "When I was seven years old, she went to visit her parents in Kishinev. She had just convinced them to talk to her again after she left their faith."

Chekov took a long drag on his cigarette and his eyes lost their focus. Tatiana stood silently watching him, her expression grim. Chekov blew a cloud of tobacco smoke through his nostrils that mingled inextricably with the icy vapor of his breath.

"Father wouldn't tell me what really happened," Chekov said. "Just that mother had died and gone ahead of us to heaven. It wasn't until some years later I found out how she 'went to heaven.'"

Tatiana's face was deathly pale now, her eyes wide as she listened to him. Chekov hesitated, then, his features settling into something cold, bitter, almost alien, he continued.

"Seven men broke into my grandfather's home in Kishinev, slit his throat and stabbed my grandmother in the chest. My mother was still young enough to catch their eye, though. They held her down and took turns beating and raping her. She died of internal bleeding somewhere in the process," Chekov said, his voice utterly hollow. "But the bastards did a sloppy job on grandmother. She survived her stab wound and brought charges of rape and murder before a magistrate. Miracle of miracles, they were convicted and sentenced to life in prison."

Chekov took another deep drag off the cigarette.

"That is, they were *sentenced* to life in prison," Chekov said. "Until one of your father's ministers quietly commuted their sentences to five years each."

"I'm so sorry," Tatiana said in a small voice. Tears glistened in the corners of her gray eyes.

Chekov took in a lungful of the frigid night air and then another drag off his cigarette. He unclenched his fists.

"None of this is your fault, Tatiana Nicholaevna," he said. "And it is only natural for a girl to love her father, as he so clearly loves you all. But all this misery, this happened because your father is a weak, stupid, bigoted man. As emperor he led his people so poorly that millions now side with madmen and murderers against him. Whatever happens, you need to know that truth if you are to survive in this new world."

Tears spilled freely down Tatiana's cheeks now. She gulped once, then turned on her heel and retreated into house, leaving Chekov alone to contemplate the stars and the all-encompassing night.

Tatiana shut the door behind her and leaned against the wall, burying her face in her hands, trying not to sob.

Even in her sheltered palace life, Tatiana knew about the pogroms in the abstract the way one knows about an unfortunate historical event or bit of news. The young, plain-faced soldier with the vocabulary of a scholar had made it real for her, put the human cost right in her face in a way no one else ever had. And as she mulled over the dressing-down he'd given her father, a cold sliver of doubt pierced her soul.

What if he's right? What if Father failed us all? Heavenly Father, what if we deserve this?

Tatiana dried her tears and squared her shoulders, remembering what had drawn her out of bed.

Where the hell is Olga?

A search of the second floor revealed only her sleeping parents and siblings. Tatiana crept down the stairs, each creaking board setting her teeth on edge for fear it might wake Mama or Papa, or one of the other children. She slipped silently down the hall, past Gilliard's room.

Heavy breathing and hushed voices punctuated by a low cry from the dining room drew her onward.

"Olga, you have to quiet down," a deep male voice hissed.

"How can I?" It was Olga's voice in the whispered reply, but as Tatiana had never heard it before, low and throaty and dripping with something primitive. "I've never felt this way in my life, oh, *God, Antosenka ...*"

Tatiana rounded the corner into the dining room. Her sister stood, hands braced on the dining room table, her back to the big, handsome guard, Dostovalov. The tall, mustachioed man fondled her exposed breasts with one hand, while his other caressed steadily between her thighs. He lavished kisses on her neck as she rotated her hips and ground her rear back against him.

Tatiana's limbs seemed to be made of lead, her tongue too thick in her mouth to talk. She stood, mouth agape, until Olga's eyes met hers and her older sister screamed, snapping the surreal back to reality, albeit a reality in crisis. Dostovalov stumbled back against a cabinet, rattling the china and wine bottle inside.

"What in God's name are you doing?" Tatiana asked.

"What does it look like, Tatya?" Olga snapped as she jerked her clothes back into place. Her cheeks were bright red. Dostovalov stood in a corner next to a full wine rack, halfway across the room from Olga, his eyes firmly fixed anywhere but on Tatiana.

Chekov was the first to arrive, he took one look at his friend and strode right over to him and started laying into him in a low voice, Tatiana only caught, "you stupid ass." Dostovalov kept his eyes on the floor.

Pierre Gilliard followed close on Chekov's heels, black hair and thick handlebar mustache in disarray, a robe cinched over his pajamas. The sisters and soldiers fell silent instantly.

"Tatiana, Olga," he said in clear but Swiss-accented Russian. "What is going on here?"

"I'm sorry, Pierre," Olga spoke up immediately. "I . . . saw a rat."

"Indeed?" Gilliard said, looking to Tatiana for confirmation.

Tatiana took a deep breath, allowing the moment to rest on the knife's edge, waiting on her decisions.

Damn it, Olga.

"That's right, Pierre," she said. "Olga and I couldn't sleep, we came down here to chat so as not wake up Maria and Anastasia. Olga saw a rat and yelled, then Chekov and Dostovalov here ran into the room. I assume because they heard the scream?"

She made eye contact with Chekov and saw in his nearly black orbs profound gratitude.

"That's right," Chekov said, his tone level. "And since things seem to be under control here, we should really get back to our posts. Good night."

Without waiting for a reply, Chekov and Dostovalov beat a hasty retreat.

"Girls, you should head back to bed as well," Gilliard said. "What *is* going on here?"

Tatiana gasped a bit as her father rounded the corner behind Gilliard.

"I'm sorry, Papa," Olga said. "I'm afraid I woke up everyone up for nothing; it was just a rat."

Nicholas looked at his eldest, then stared at Tatiana for a long second.

"Why were you down here in the first place?" he demanded.

Tatiana's breath caught a little. Lying to Gilliard was one thing, but to her father...

Perhaps some of the truth ...

"It's my fault, Father," Tatiana said. "I had a nightmare and couldn't get back to sleep. Olga came downstairs too, she saw a rat when we walked into the dining room."

Nicholas held Tatiana's gaze for several heartbeats. Tatiana allowed her eyes to fall in contrition, thinking it appropriate to the story she revealed to her father. Apparently detecting no duplicity, Nicholas exhaled through his nose and his expression softened.

"I'm sorry you had a nightmare, dear," he said. "But you shouldn't wander the mansion at night."

"I'm sorry, Papa," Tatiana said.

"I apologize too," Olga said.

Nicholas's gaze shifted from Tatiana to Olga then back again.

"All right, girls," he said. "Back to bed with you."

Olga preceded Tatiana up the stairs. Tatiana stared at the back of her sister's head in mute rage as they made their way as silently as possible back to their beds. She wanted to yell at her for cavorting like a whore with a soldier she barely knew, but even a whisper might be audible to their father when he came back to his bedroom. Angry as she was, she wasn't ready to inform on her sister to their parents.

What the hell is the matter with you, Olga?

Certainly she and Olga had flirted with a number of charming young officers. They'd danced a little closer with their favorites than what was required by a proper waltz, and Tatiana herself had even allowed one of the boys to kiss her when her parents weren't looking. But what Olga and that soldier had been doing...

Tatiana's pulse quickened in arousal, just as it had sometimes during the innocent flirtations of her adolescence. This lust, though, made her feel perverse in a way previous thrills never had. She had seen her own sister in the grip of Eros and the only thing more disturbing than Olga's stupidity was how badly a part of Tatiana now wished she'd gone further with one of her favorites.

"Chekov, what the hell were you thinking?" Dostovalov said in a low voice, glaring at Chekov from across the table in the canteen sometime later. It was early morning yet and they were the first ones through the door. They had already shoveled their stew as fast as possible to avoid letting it go lukewarm. Now they sat, hunched against the cold in the drafty building, conferring in low tones so as to avoid being heard by the cooks.

"What was I thinking? What the hell were *you* thinking?" Chekov hissed. "Screwing the tsar's daughter in his own house? Are you out of what little mind you have left?"

"We weren't screwing. I know you have little experience in such things, but one generally has to pull out one's cock to screw a girl. My pants were up and buttoned," Dostovalov said.

"Okay, you got caught before you could finish the deed," Chekov said. "You want a medal for your restraint?"

"You think a little love-play is worse than calling the tsar a fool to his face?" Dostovalov said.

"Yes, you moron, it is," Chekov said. "And, again, you got *caught*. What happens if Tatiana decides to confess everything to her papa after all?"

"She won't," Dostovalov said, maddeningly confident. "The Big Pair are too close to drive a wedge between. Tatiana would never inform on Olga. Face it, it's not my pecker but your mouth that got you earmarked for every shit detail the First Rifles can find."

Chekov frowned. He knew Dostovalov had a point. He'd been stupid to let himself lose his temper with Nicholas; private citizen or autocrat, he was still a much more powerful man than Chekov. Kobylinsky, with Matveev standing behind him, had informed Chekov that he was off close guard duty and onto sanitary detail, VD inspection, and other such menial and degrading tasks until further notice. Despite that, Chekov knew that his friend getting entangled with Olga could only end in tragedy.

"It was still an inexcusably stupid idea to try to make love to Olga one floor down from where her entire family was sleeping," said Chekov.

"Oh, for God's sake, Sergei, what happens even if Nicholas does find out?" Dostovalov said. "He's not the tsar anymore, he doesn't rule a damn thing. For all that Kobylinsky kisses his ass, we all know the only real power in Tobolsk lies with that boy Matveev and that Latvian Jew and his Red Guards. Nicholas can do nothing to us without their say so."

"Assume you're right, assume the unit won't punish you because of Nicholas. How quick before the Bolsheviks label you an Imperialist for consorting with Olga?"

Chekov retorted. "How much quicker that I join you in a labor camp or in front of a firing squad for associating with counterrevolutionaries? They don't even need a court-martial anymore, for God's sake."

Dostovalov stared at Chekov for several seconds; the lines of frustration on his face eased and a resigned expression replaced them.

"You're right. I know it's dangerous," Dostovalov said, "And you didn't volunteer for more danger. But I love her, Sergei. I love her as I have never loved a woman before. I won't stop. If you need to distance yourself from me, I understand, and I don't hold it against you."

"Distance myself?" Chekov said. "You damn fool. I—"

Overcome, Chekov stopped speaking and glared at his friend for several seconds. Then he stood up from the wooden bench and stormed out of the canteen without another word, pulling his thick coat closer around himself.

Outside the mess hall, less than a block from the door, Yermilov took stock of Chekov's hunched shoulders and furious stride. When Dostovalov left and started walking the opposite direction from his short, ugly friend, his countenance clearly troubled, Yermilov smiled. He leaned closer to the two men standing close to him and jerked his head toward Dostovalov's broad, retreating back.

"Lover's spat, eh?" Yermilov said. His cronies laughed roughly. "Let's keep an eye on Dostovalov. He tries to meet the Romanov *peezda* for another little tryst and this will be the time we have a little fun ourselves."

✢ ✢ ✢

A long day of emptying outhouses and staring at other men's cocks looking for signs of chlamydia or syphilis left Chekov exhausted and despondent. He slept fitfully that night, waking several times at odd intervals. He hadn't spoken to Dostovalov since breakfast and he was still furious with his big friend.

I should. I should cut ties and look out for myself. That moron has been trying to get us in trouble ever since we got here. He couldn't just stick to whoring like a tomcat, he had to fall in love with the one girl likely to get us both killed.

Turning in his bunk, Chekov's eyes fell upon on Dostovalov's empty bunk.

Empty. He didn't have the duty tonight...

Chekov rolled back onto his back and glared at the timber ceiling.

Not my business. He said as much. I'm not his father, and a doomed affair with Olga is more important to him than survival. He won't listen to reason. If I try to stop him he'll just tell me to piss off. He's on his own.

Chekov took several deep breaths, willing himself back to sleep.

Son of a bitch.

Chekov swung his legs off the side of his bunk and slid quietly to the floor. He reached for his socks and pants and, swearing softly to himself the whole time, began to dress for the cold Siberian night.

Dostovalov peeled off a few bills and handed them to the guards on duty at Freedom House's back door, both of whom grinned and slapped Dostovalov on the back before trudging off through the snow. Yermilov shifted slightly, let his rifle rest on the ground, and put restraining hands on the men lying on either side of him under the hedge.

"Almost," Yermilov breathed. "Wait just a bit more."

Yermilov kept his companions still until the bribed guards were around the corner of the Freedom House and then for twenty breaths more.

"Now," Yermilov hissed.

The three men sprang from the snow-laden red bushes and charged. Dostovalov whirled to face them, but it was too late. Yermilov brought the buttstock of his rifle crashing down on the bridge of the man's nose, sending him crumpling to the snow, blood erupting from his broken nose and busted mouth. The big man lay still on the ground, knocked cold by the blow.

"Take him to the river," Yermilov said. "Break a hole in the ice and dump his body, then you can come back for your turns."

"Wait," the bigger of his cronies said in a thick voice. "No chance, we want to—"

"Do what the fuck you're told, Ilyin," Yermilov said. "We stay here arguing about it, someone will spot Dostovalov here and none of us will get a chance."

Ilyin looked mutinous, but he and Yermilov's other henchman grabbed Dostovalov by wrists and ankles and began to drag him through the snow, west toward the river.

Hopefully, the idiots don't get caught by some Red Guard assholes. Assuming any of them are awake and sober enough to care at three in the morning.

Yermilov turned away from the door. From behind his size and stature were very similar to Dostovalov's. He wanted to save Olga's surprise for the last possible moment. From a sheath on his belt he pulled a knife, not his issued bayonet, but a smaller blade for closer, more intimate work. The kind of work he'd plied in Petrograd's alleys since long before the revolution. Fortunately, the chaos of the Bolshevik coup had given him an opportunity to make an honest living out of his thuggery—at least it had until he'd been transferred to this outfit.

Kobylinsky and Matveev, those prigs, had kept him on a short leash since he'd been assigned to First Rifles. He'd been expected to stand his post and treat the reviled Romanovs with courtesy. Even after the men ripped off Kobylinsky's epaulettes and "abolished" rank, the First had kept too many vestiges of its dreadfully dull discipline and standards for a man like Yermilov.

Now, though, all that dreary waiting was going to pay off.

The door creaked open behind him. Olga, her blue eyes aglow with excitement, stepped onto the back porch. Yermilov relished the split-second transition of her lovely face from anticipation to confusion to terror as he turned to face her. Before she could scream Yermilov stepped into her, pulling her body to his with his left arm and pressing the knife to her ivory skinned throat with his right hand. He propelled her back into the house. Keeping the knife to her throat, he used his left hand to pull the door quietly shut behind him.

"Don't worry, *Your Highness*," Yermilov whispered, grinning. "You're going to get what you came for all the same, scream or struggle, though, and I'm afraid I'll have to *cut* it short; then maybe I'll go looking upstairs to finish. Nod if you understand."

Olga, lips quivering, tears streaming down her face, nodded jerkily.

"Good girl, now into that bathroom," he said. "And lock the door behind us, I'd hate to be interrupted."

Ignoring the threat of falling on his ass, Chekov sprinted up the icy steps to the front door of Freedom House and into the mansion. Inside, he heard nothing at first, then faint sobbing from down the hall. Treading as lightly as possible, Chekov strode down the hall to the dining room where once he'd caught Dostovalov with Olga.

Rounding the corner, he found not his friend and Olga *en flagrante delicto*, but Tatiana, standing with her arms around Olga. Olga sat in an upholstered chair, her face in her hands, shoulders shaking, the small, quiet noises of a wounded animal issuing from her throat at irregular intervals.

"What happened?" Chekov said, his eyes wide. "My God, Anton didn't—"

"No," Olga choked out. "Anton wasn't here. It was the ugly one, with the beard and the crooked teeth."

"Yermilov," Chekov said.

"He's still outside," Olga said. "He said his friends are coming back for theirs, and if I don't let them, he said they'll do the same to all of us and kill Papa, Alexei, and the rest."

Olga took a deep breath, and curled into herself, her teeth clenched, holding back a wail.

Tatiana let go of her sister, and with quick, decisive movements opened a drawer in a nearby cabinet and withdrew a large carving knife. Chekov stepped in front of her and grabbed her wrist.

"What do you think you're doing?"

Tatiana regarded him with eyes that might have been chips of gray ice for all the warmth they held.

"I'm going to kill him," she said. "Or he's going to kill me."

With a deft move, Chekov wrenched the knife from Tatiana's hand and put it on the table. She reached for it again, but he put a restraining hand on her shoulder and shook her once firmly.

"No, you're not going to kill anyone," Chekov said, drawing his bayonet. "I am. Listen carefully; all either of you know is that you heard a crash and someone yelling. Yermilov shouting drunkenly, and then I came in and fought him off. Unfortunately, I had to kill him because he wouldn't stop."

"What if he kills you?" Tatiana asked.

"Then do the best you can," Chekov said, already on his way to the door.

Chekov flung the door open and dove out into the frosty night, leaving the door swinging wildly behind him. Yermilov turned at the sound, his face twisted with contempt.

"Cunt, I told you to wait in—"

The rapist's eyes widened at the sight of Chekov, bayonet in hand, death in his eyes, charging him. He tried to bring his rifle to bear, but the small, wiry veteran was far too quick, the distance between them too short. The steel tip of Chekov's bayonet penetrated through uniform cloth, flesh, and sinew into Yermilov's very bowels.

Yermilov's hands clenched reflexively and the air rang with the *crack-thwit-shhing* report of his rifle as he fired, the bullet ricocheting uselessly off the stone steps of Freedom House. Chekov bore the bigger man to the ground, throwing all his weight behind the seventeen inches of steel lodged in Yermilov's belly.

"Drop your rifle, Yermilov!" Chekov shouted into the still night air as he dragged the bayonet around inside the wound, then pulled it out and stabbed again. Warm, dark, almost black blood coated his hand and spurted up onto his uniform, it instantly began to congeal into a gory slush.

"Don't make me do this, Yermilov!" Chekov said, and he withdrew and plunged the blade into Yermilov's guts a third time, angling up, under his rib cage. The man's eyes rolled back in his skull, he gave a gurgling gasp, jerked spasmodically three times, then lay still.

Chekov stood, his bayonet coming free of Yermilov's destroyed abdomen with a slurping noise. He looked around as he took several ragged breaths. In the doorway of Freedom House Tatiana stood, looking upon the scene, her eyes calm and clear, her back straight. Her face might have been carved from marble.

As his heart rate declined, something occurred to Chekov he hadn't thought about since finding out that Yermilov had raped Olga.

If Anton isn't here, where the hell is he?

As the question spiked his heart rate once again, he noted a splash of blood on the snow on the steps, too high up to have been Yermilov's. Scanning about rapidly it took mere seconds for him to recognize two sets of foot-prints and a large drag mark leading west, toward the waterfront.

Fuck, no, no, no.

Chekov wiped his bayonet clean on the skirt of his coat, sheathed it, slung his rifle and picked up Yermilov's. He worked the bolt of the Model 1891, ejected the spent case and chambered a live round, then handed it to Tatiana, who took it with a quizzical look.

"I think they dragged off Dostovalov when he came to see Olga," Chekov said, pointing to the wide trench in the snow flanked by two sets of boot prints. "I have to go after them. Wake everyone. The rifle is just in case Yermilov's cronies get back before Kobylinsky gets more guards here."

Tatiana nodded. Behind her light spilled into the hall, and Pierre Gilliard's disheveled form emerged from the bedroom closest the dining room, followed shortly thereafter by other forms, male and female in their dressing gowns.

"Thank you, Sergei Arkadyevich," Tatiana said, gravely.

Chekov shook his head, took his rifle in both hands and sprinted west as fast as his legs would carry him, praying he wasn't too late.

Chilk-chilk-chilk

A cloud of relentless pain filled Dostovalov's head as consciousness returned. The throbbing in his skull was quickly accompanied by sharper jets of agony radiating from his ruined nose and upper gums. His nerves inundated his foggy mind with further reports of

damage and discomfort; he was lying on his face in the
freezing snow and tightly bound with twine around his
wrists and ankles that had cut off circulation to his
hands and feet.

Chilk-chilk-chilk

"This ice is too fucking thick," a dull voice complained
from Dostovalov's left. "Yermilov will have bored the girl
out like a howitzer by the time we're done here."

Olga!

Dostovalov opened his eyes and rolled onto his side.
He was lying on the riverbank in thick snow turned red
and pink by his own blood and melted into slush by his
body heat. Yermilov's two cronies were poking away at the
river ice with their bayonets. Dostovalov struggled against
his bonds, pulling so mightily that the twine cut into his
wrists, and blood fell in rivulets over his clenched fists. He
coughed involuntarily, spewing out a sludge of his own
blood, snot, and snow that had invaded his mouth and
misshapen nostrils.

His captors turned at the sound.

"Shit, he's awake," the same dull voice said. The taller
of the two men stood, picked his rifle up off the ice and
walked toward Dostovalov.

Dostovalov tried to shout, but hacked up more blood
and phlegm instead, he strained harder against the bonds,
felt a hand start to slip out of position.

Pull harder, Anton.

"Fuck this," the shorter man said in a laconic voice.
"Shoot him in the head and let's get the fuck out of here.
We can say we were never here and didn't have anything
to do with Yermilov's crazy-ass plan."

"Why don't you do it?" The big man snapped back. "You want to keep your hands clean, tell them it was all me and Yermilov? Is that it?"

Dostovalov gritted his teeth and yanked his right hand free of its bonds, scraping a layer of skin off the back of his hand from wrist to knuckles. He screamed his pain and rage.

"Fuck," the little one shouted and leveled his rifle at Dostovalov's face. The big man felt every beat of his heart as he scrabbled frantically at the ground with his brutalized hands, trying to pull himself behind a tree stump for cover.

The *crack* of a rifle shot split the frigid night air.

No! Dostovalov shut his eyes reflexively. *Olga, forgive me...*

But Dostovalov felt no projectile pierce his body. Instead, when Dostovalov opened his eyes, his would-be murderer was lying flat on his back, the contents of his skull splayed behind him onto the ice. Another crack, followed by the sound of an overripe melon being sliced, and the tall one who'd been whining fell beside his comrade. Dostovalov craned his neck around to see a slight man, rifle leveled, emerge from behind a nearby cypress and march toward the dead men. Chekov worked the bolt on his rifle and examined each body in turn. Apparently satisfied that both men were dead, he turned back to Dostovalov.

Unsheathing a utility knife, Chekov started cutting the twine binding Dostovalov's legs.

"Thank you, Sergei," Dostovalov slurred through his missing teeth.

"Don't talk," Chekov said, his voice cold. "We need to get you to a doctor to see what can be done about your face."

"No time," Dostovalov insisted, dribbling on himself as he spoke. "Yermilov—"

"Dead," Chekov said, pulling his larger friend to his feet. "I killed him."

"Thank God," Dostovalov said, leaning gratefully on the shorter man. "Then Olga is all right?"

Chekov exhaled sharply and shook his head.

"She'll live. She'll recover, but no, Anton, she's not all right," he said. "I got there after Yermilov had finished."

"No, oh, Jesus, no," Dostovalov moaned. "This is my fault."

"Yes."

Dostovalov stepped away from Chekov and glared at his friend in shock, swaying as the pinpricks of nerves reawakening shot through his feet and legs.

"What, Anton? You expect me to comfort you?" Chekov said. "I told you fooling around with the tsar's daughter was dangerous and it was. You were nearly killed, you stupid bastard."

"Yermilov singled us out because you humiliated him our first week here," Dostovalov shot back. "And then, when I wanted to take care of him, you insisted we wait. So, yes, I nearly got killed and Olga—"

Dostovalov stopped, tears choking off his voice, he stood silently for a second, composing himself.

"Did it occur to you, Sergei, for one instant, that maybe you're not so fucking smart as you think you are?" He continued when he had a modicum of control. "That this time, if we'd done it *my* way, none of this would've happened?"

"Maybe," Chekov said. "And maybe we'd be standing trial for murder. The Bolsheviks have no problem shooting men for the encouragement of others."

"I'd rather that than have allowed the woman I love to be raped," Dostovalov grated.

The muscles in Chekov's neck and jaw worked for a moment as he returned Dostovalov's glare, but finally he looked away.

"What's done is done," Chekov said. "I'm sorry I didn't get there in time to stop Yermilov. I really am. But now, if you don't want Olga to suffer any more than she has to, we need to get our story straight. I'm assuming you paid the guards on duty to take the night off?"

Dostovalov, tired of talking, just nodded.

"Okay, can you stay on your feet awhile longer?" Chekov said. "Can you make it back to Freedom House on your own?"

"Yeah," Dostovalov said, despite the agony reigning in his skull and the lesser pains shooting through the rest of his body.

"Good, I'm going to find the boys you paid off, here's what we're all going to tell them—"

An hour later, in the deposed tsar's study, Chekov and the two guards, Blokhin and Virkhov, stood at attention while Kobylinsky, Matveev, and Nicholas all listened to Chekov's version of the night's events with intense interest. Tatiana sat in the corner wearing her customary inscrutable expression. Nicholas's own doctor, Botkin, was working on Dostovalov's face downstairs. When Chekov was done speaking, Kobylinsky turned to the two guards who were supposed to have been on duty.

"Is this accurate?" Kobylinsky said.

"Yes, Comrade," the younger of the two men, a boy named Virkhov said. His pal, Blokhin, nodded vigorously.

"Yermilov told you the guard roster had been changed mid-shift and you didn't think to check with me or the colonel?" Matveev said, his face screwed up in incredulity.

"We're sorry, Comrade Ensign," Blokhin said. "We didn't want to wake you, it being so late. Yermilov is one of the senior men, we didn't think he had a reason for lying."

"Get out of here," Kobylinsky said. "We'll figure out a proper punishment for you idiots later."

Blokhin and Virkhov needed no further encouragement; staggering just a little, for Dostovalov had found them at the bottle, they made their way hastily toward the stairs.

"It seems I owe you a great debt, *Feldfebel* Chekov," Nicholas spoke up. "I must ask, though, how you knew to come here so late at night?"

I was afraid you might ask that. Chekov had concocted an answer, of course, but it was the weakest part of their alibi.

"I'm afraid it was mostly a matter of providence," Chekov said. "I've had trouble sleeping lately, so I was out late myself. When I saw two lads who I knew were on the guard roster for the night, I knew something was amiss. Them already being in their cups, I grabbed Dostovalov and we got here as fast as we could."

Nicholas turned to his daughter.

"Tatiana, dear," he said. "Is all this reconciling with your memory of events?"

"As far as I could tell, Father," Tatiana said. "I awoke to hear the big ugly one screaming, then I heard a rifle shot and *Feldfebel* Chekov begging him to put his rifle down. Then *Feldfebel* Chekov gave me the man's rifle because he had to go after the others."

"Speaking of that rifle," Matveev interrupted. "While I applaud your initiative, Chekov, handing over a rifle to one of the Romanovs was a poor choice. While we will protect the former emperor and his family and will, of course, continue to extend them every courtesy," Matveev nodded at the ex-emperor, "they are still in our custody."

"Apologies, Comrade Ensign," he said. "But Yermilov's co-conspirators had assaulted and carried off Dostovalov by that point. I needed to act fast to save his life but did not want to leave the Romanovs defenseless until new guards could arrive."

"You obviously did the best you could with a terrible situation," Kobylinsky said, his voice much firmer than Chekov had ever heard it. The incident seemed to have put some fire back in the man. "You are to be commended."

Matveev glanced sideways at the colonel but said nothing.

"Indeed," Nicholas said, standing up. "*Feldfebel*, I have misjudged you. You are, indeed, every inch the hero your war record indicates you are. I am deeply in your debt. If there is anything within my diminished power that I can do to repay you, I will."

The former emperor thrust his right hand out at Chekov. Chekov looked at the hand, then into Nicholas's eyes for a long moment before he grasped his outstretched hand and shook once, firmly, before letting go.

A tall, thickset man with graying brown hair receding from a widow's peak, a beard just long enough to curl at the chin, and round spectacles walked into the study.

"Well, Yevgenny," Nicholas said to the newcomer. "How is our other hero?"

"I set his nose as best I could. He's likely to have noticeable scarring but he shan't be horribly disfigured," Dr. Botkin said. "I gave him something for the pain. I also gave Olga a mild sedative, she was very upset by the disturbance."

"Yes," Nicholas murmured. "My eldest has always been very sensitive."

Tatiana made eye contact with Chekov then for first time since entering the study. The sadness and terror in the girl's face pierced Chekov's heart, but he clamped down on the emotion.

I killed the bastard who did it. I'm not sure what else I could've done.

"Very well, gentlemen," Nicholas said. "If there is nothing else you need of us, Tatiana and I shall go speak with the rest of the family."

"Nothing else," Matveev said. "Thank you, Citizen Romanov. Chekov, I want to see you and Dostovalov downstairs in my office."

Once Dostovalov joined them, face covered by thick white bandages and his eyes hazy from narcotic effect,

Matveev shut the door to his office and regarded the two soldiers with a grave expression on his round face.

"Lads, you did the right thing," he said. "But I have to tell you I'm a little worried about your relationships with the Romanovs."

"How's that, Comrade?" Chekov said, frowning.

"Look, men, there are rumblings the Imperialists may try to take the Romanovs," Matveev said. "The Central Committee is sending a new commissar to take charge here, and if you are caught fraternizing with the Romanovs, they may assume you will be a liability in the event of a rescue attempt."

To Chekov's relief, Dostovalov said nothing in response, but his eyes, though hazy from morphine, narrowed.

"We understand, Comrade Ensign," Chekov said.

Matveev shook his head.

"I'm not sure you do, Chekov," he said. "The new commissar will have the authority to summarily execute men for counterrevolutionary activities—no trial. Get in his way and I will not be able to save you. If you cling to the Romanovs, you will likely be buried with them."

"This isn't *right*," Dostovalov said. Chekov glared at him, but Matveev nodded.

"It isn't right," he said. "But it *is* nonetheless."

Interlude

Tatiana: Olga Is Indisposed

Olga woke late into the next day, disoriented and confused. I had brought up her meals and helped her bathe and change while Maria helped Madame Hendrikova take care of Mama, and Anastasia helped Madame Schneider with Alexei.

My sister stared at the bruises on her wrists as if she didn't know how they got there. Her hands were shaking too badly when she tried, so I had to button up the sleeves for her. For a moment I thought she would break into tears but she didn't.

I mixed some of Mama's medicine into her tea, made her drink it, and tucked her back into bed. She nodded and closed her eyes.

And so it went for the next few days. I did her chores, giving her apologies to Mama and Papa who came to see her, but thankfully she was asleep both times.

Mama returned to painting little icons on paper to send as thank you notes to the people of Tobolsk who had sent us food, while my father received a guest. An old staff member, a monarchist from Petrograd arrived. He brought books and tea and also delivered clothes that Mama's best friend, Anna Vyrubova, had sent.

I wasn't supposed to know, but a gift of twenty-five thousand rubles also arrived. Papa used the money to pay the servants who had stayed on without pay. He meant for them to use it to pay for their way back home out of Tobolsk and gave the money to Prince Dolgorukov to distribute in secret. I overheard him say that it wouldn't be enough, but that he'd see it done.

After dinner while Papa read from a book that Madame Tolstay had sent us, I slipped out to find Chekov. He was standing outside the guard house smoking a cigarette. I gave him a look and he frowned back at me, but put out the cigarette and followed me into the kitchen.

He looked over his shoulder as he took his cap off. As always he kept as far away from me as possible.

I reached into the pocket of my apron and pulled out a strand of pearls. Mama had a matching set made for each of us girls.

"See what you can get for this, please."

I thrust my hand out at him but he didn't move. He just stared at me, at my hand, at the pearls.

Finally I set them down on the table between us.

He approached with enough caution to make me think he wasn't seeing a necklace at all, but perhaps a snake.

Chekov picked the pearls up and ran a dirty thumb across them. It was almost obscene, the way he caressed them, but when he looked up I didn't see greed.

"You'd trust me with these?" he asked.

Didn't he realize how much power he already had over our lives?

I gave him a nod. What else could I do?

"There's something I want to tell you," I said to him. "Something I need to tell you.

"You've always treated me as if I were very innocent. Oh, yes, surely, I am. But I think you have no idea just how innocent we all are.

"Once, when Olga and I were serving as nurses for the wounded—oh, yes, we did, and Mama, too—we decided to go into a store when our shift was over. We'd never been in a store in our lives, you see, not even once, either of us. So we went in and looked and, oh, it was *wonderful*. The *choices* people could make, choices neither of us had ever been able to.

"But then we realized it took money to make those choices and, not only didn't we have any with us, we'd never even used money in our lives. Neither of us had the first, tiniest clue of how money even worked.

"In that moment I realized that, wherever we lived, however we lived, in this one way, at least, we were poorer than the poorest citizens of the empire. We were simply so ignorant."

Chapter Twelve

Destroyer *Kerch*

Barquentine *Loredana*, Black Sea

Natalya was the de facto skipper of the ship now. A bright lass, she'd paid close attention to ship's handling and seamanship under Vraciu. Whatever his myriad other failings, Bogdan Vraciu had been a competent seaman. Now, the crew followed her orders, those orders backed up by the frightfully ruthless set of Russian demons striding the decks.

Progress wasn't appreciably slower under the reduced

crew than it had been with a full crew; at least it wasn't after Mokrenko clubbed one of them with a belaying pin and tossed his body to the deep. After that, little Natalya's commands were obeyed with stunning promptness. Notwithstanding this, though, the moon had set just after ten in the morning. It was, if calm, the most pitch-black night Mokrenko could even remember.

Because of the darkness, the *Loredana* had only three sails set on the top three yardarms of the foremast and was creeping ahead under sail power alone. It might as well have been a fish underwater for all the noise it made gliding across the now glasslike sea. Because it didn't make any noise, the passengers were able to hear everything around them quite well. What they heard...

The *Kerch* was no longer "His Imperial Russian Majesty's Ship," which prefix the Empire, in fact, didn't use. Neither had the Bolsheviks whose side the crew had taken yet gotten around to coining naval titles. Perhaps they never would. Nonetheless, though painted gray, the ship was redder than a party banner.

This was why the crew of the *Kerch* had taken some sixty-three officers, most from the Four-ninety-first (Varnavinsky) Regiment, though the Forty-first Artillery Battalion and the Twenty-first Caucasian Mountain Artillery Battalion had their representatives there, too, then tied them, attached iron weights to their legs and threw them overboard to drown.

Not a one of the officers so treated was in any sense nobility, either.

A few of the men were shot off the side by the crew,

and that was a series of sounds that was very plain. Most, however, were simply tied, weighted, and dumped. Generally speaking they sank quickly. At least one, however, either preternaturally strong or just lucky in partially slipping his bonds, still struggled, more than half panicked, calling for a help that, of course, the only ship he knew of in the vicinity, the *Kerch*, was most unlikely to give.

"Shit, they're murdering somebody," said Mokrenko, "a lot of somebodies."

Lieutenant Turgenev, standing with the Cossack on deck, nodded, unseen in the darkness. Turgenev was, while still a little weak from hunger and loss of fluids, otherwise completely recovered from his seasickness.

"Do you see their running lights?" the lieutenant asked.

Mokrenko strained for a bit before answering, "Ye . . . yes, sir. I see them."

"One's still struggling, at least one. Keep the crew and our men quiet. Have Natalya steer just to the left of the running lights; I think that man is to the left."

A fresh spurt of calls for help seemed to confirm this.

"Yes, sir, but . . ."

"I'm going in," Turgenev said. "I'll save him if I can."

"Sir, you're being an idiot. You don't have to do this."

The lieutenant sighed. "Sergeant, if I don't, I'm never going to be able to sleep at night again without hearing that in my head. Maybe I'll fail, yes, but I have to try."

"Well . . . shit!" Mokrenko exclaimed. "*Fine*, then, if you think you fucking *must*. But tie yourself off to a rope, before you go in. Be a better chance for you *and* for him.

Hell, if you're not attached to the ship you'll never catch up to us . . . and we can't afford the noise of furling the sails."

"Right."

Turgenev lowered himself over the side, with a length of rope looped around his waist, trailing by nine or ten *arshins* a life buoy from the running end. He started with a kick off from the hull, then assumed an Australian crawl stroke to eat up the distance.

The problem with that was twofold. In the first place it made noise and, while Turgenev didn't think the ship could hear, he didn't want to take a chance. The second problem was that the noise prevented *him* from hearing, where the sounds of the victim or victims were his only guide.

"Shit," he muttered, then took up a breaststroke, which was not only quieter, it better allowed him to keep his head above water.

"Heellllp! Heeeellllp meeee . . ."

Turgenev altered his direction slightly to aim more closely for the sound.

"Hellll . . ."

There he is, less than a dozen feet from me, I think, but I cannot see a thing.

There came some vigorous splashing then, uncoordinated, spastic, as if panic had taken over completely. Turgenev thought it would be enough sound cover for him to take up a more energetic stroke. He did, with furious, calorie burning reaches and even more powerful kicks . . .

Only to reach . . . nothing. He couldn't even tell if the water was disturbed by anything but his own swimming.

If he's not here then he's . . . Turgenev took a deep breath, then another, and dived down, then circled around, his feet propelling him as his hands reached for . . . nothing. *Shit.*

Oddly enough, it was the victim who found him, not he the victim. Just as the lieutenant reached the last of his oxygen, a single hand locked into a death grip on his left arm. There was nothing to do but go up, pulling himself with his one free arm while pushing with the kicking legs.

Turgenev broke the surface and only just managed to explosively exhale and draw in about a quarter of a breath before that dead weight on his arm pulled him under again.

Now it was Turgenev's turn to panic. He knew he didn't have much air left and he felt his body demanding it with a pounding heart and aching lungs. He struggled, he kicked, and just when he thought his fight was over that death grip on his arm loosened.

I'll be damned if you're going to die now, you son of a bitch, after all you've put me through.

Twisting once again, under water, with nearly the last of his strength and endurance, the lieutenant aimed back down again, once again feeling around for . . .

I've got him, he exulted. *Now how do I save him?*

Swimming is a miserably inefficient way of getting around, really. Pulling oneself along with a rope is much, much better. With one hand firmly on whoever the hell it was who'd nearly drowned him, he moved his other hand to the cord looped around his waist, and from there made his best guess of which cord ran to the life buoy. Once he'd made his determination, he looped the fingers of the other hand around the cord that ran to the life buoy, closed them, and began to pull, dragging himself and his charge upward, praying that he'd have enough oxygen and strength left to make it.

Ouch, the lieutenant thought, when he hit his head on the lifebuoy, which wasn't as soft as all that, really. In a half second, he was gratefully breathing fresh, salty air, even as he dragged the other man upward into the air, then threaded one of his arms through the buoy.

There came a series of wet, gagging coughs, accompanied by spasms as partially filled lungs forcefully emptied themselves.

"You've got to be quiet, friend," Turgenev advised. "I don't know if that ship can hear us."

Around more coughs, slightly suppressed, a weak voice said, "Thank you . . . whoever . . . you are. I'll . . . try to be . . . as quiet . . . as I can."

"Who are you?" Turgenev asked.

"Lieutenant . . . First Lieutenant . . . Sergei Babin . . . Four-ninety-first Infantry Regiment . . ."

"We'll talk later, Sergei, because I think . . . right about now . . ."

And with that, the cord from the *Loredana* to Turgenev snapped up through the water, then began to drag him, the life buoy, and Lieutenant Babin through the cold water with a startling speed.

Babin sat in the galley, nursing a cup of not very good tea with a healthy dollop of not very good *rakia* added to it. His uniform was drying, so for the nonce, he was wrapped in a couple of blankets. Despite this, he looked utterly miserable. Mokrenko and Turgenev sat with the rescued man, while the medical orderly, Timashuk, checked for temperature and pulse.

The rescued lieutenant spoke without emotion, deadpan, exhausted, and distantly, as if what he was describing had happened to someone else.

"There were forty-eight of us," said Babin. "Well, forty-eight from my regiment, the Four-ninety-first Infantry. I don't know how many were from the artillery units with us.

"We'd been sent on a transport to demobilize at Novorossiysk, together with the enlisted men. When we got there, the sailors of the fleet—the red fleet—demanded the men go and fight the anti-Bolshevik Cossacks on the Don. They refused but they were still on the transport ship. The *Kerch* then threatened to torpedo the transport, which would have killed a lot if not all of the men, unless they turned their officers over to the Reds. So they did.

"We weren't too worried at first. Some of the officers were even willing to go fight; after all, not a single one of us was even minor nobility. But the Reds weren't interested in that. They disarmed us, tied us, tied weights to our legs, and threw us over the side. Well, most of us; a few were shot over the side.

"I was lucky, just lucky, that they made a mistake when they tied my hands behind my back. I was able to get them free, and then one of my legs. If not"—here Babin showed just enough life to nod at Turgenev—"even your best and bravest efforts would have been too late."

"Not a one of us even from the minor nobility," Babin repeated, a tone of incredulity creeping in. "So . . . *why?* Why kill all those officers? What good did it do them?"

"Terror," answered Turgenev and Mokrenko simultaneously.

Babin shook his head, closed his eyes, and leaned forward to rest his head on his arms, above the table. Both Turgenev and Mokrenko had the good grace to look away, not wanting to see Babin's shoulders shaking.

They were nearing land. There wasn't a lot of time left to waffle over important matters. In this quiet time before sunrise, in their shared cabin, which was both guarded and sealed from eavesdropping ears, Turgenev and Mokrenko sat under the flickering light of a gimbaled lantern. The lantern was now fed by kerosene lifted from the late captain's cabin.

"Speaking of murdering people at sea, Sergeant, what are we going to do about the crew?"

"Kill them, of course," Mokrenko answered, "even though I don't like the idea. Still, what else can we do? We can't let them into port to raise a ruckus about the ones we killed or the captain's chest we took all their money from. We can't leave them here. It's not even a good idea to leave the ship still floating, really. Besides, they're all pirates."

"But kill them in cold blood?" Turgenev objected. "C'mon, Sergeant; there's got to be another way."

The sergeant shook his head doubtfully. "We can put them in a ship's boat with some food and water but no oars, sir. Then what happens when they get picked up by another ship? What happens if it's that Bolshevik ship that murdered all of Babin's comrades? The *Kerch*, was it? Think those cutthroats won't be able to put two and two together and come up with at least some questions about us? We're too military, too much a team even though we tried—not especially well, in my humble opinion—to hide it. And not under their authority, hence a threat to that authority.

"Or maybe," Mokrenko continued, "we try to put them ashore somewhere deserted. They can walk, still, so about the time we get to, say, Yekaterinburg, there's a battalion of Bolsheviks waiting for us with our descriptions.

"Or we leave them chained below, they get found and . . ."

A light and gentle knock on the door stopped Mokrenko mid-tirade. It could only have come from one person aboard ship. This was confirmed when she asked, "You sent for me, Lieutenant?"

"Come in, Natalya," Turgenev said, gently, then added, to Mokrenko, "There are some questions we need to ask her before we do anything rash."

The girl entered, then closed the door behind her. She'd dispensed with her dress and put on some clothing taken from the chest of one of the deceased sailors, killed in the attempt at murdering the Russians. She was tall for her age and sex and the sailor had been short, but she still had to cinch her belt tightly while rolling up the trousers and sleeves.

"Sit, girl," Mokrenko said. "The lieutenant has some questions for you."

"Natalya," began Turgenev, "first off let me say you're

doing a fine job of captaining the ship. Could you do it if we left it to you?"

The girl snorted with derision. "The crew would have me on all fours within the hour. They have before, after all. If you gave me a gun, they'd wait until I was asleep and do the same. Or they'd ambush me when I came out of my cabin."

Mokrenko scowled while Turgenev's face began to look mildly ill.

"Not just Vraciu, then?" the lieutenant asked.

"All of them but the two queers," she answered, "Zamfir and Vacarescu, and they didn't try to help me, either. Vacarescu was the one the sergeant had bludgeoned and dumped over the side.

"When the captain was done with me, any given night, he'd turn me over to his son. When the son was done, I was sent to the crew."

"There's your cold blood gone, Lieutenant," Mokrenko said. "I hate the bastards already. They're all fucking rapists and deserve to hang, except the one who is guilty by silent consent. But even *he* is *still* guilty."

"That's not the only question," Turgenev said. "Natalya, I'm not too sure about actually going to port, but can we get this ship into port without them? I mean the sails . . ."

"Sure, sir; the engine is fine and there's plenty of fuel for this short a trip. Let me know and we'll be in Rostov-on-Don before tomorrow morning. Or someplace else if you prefer."

"How about docking?"

She shook her head. "We'd need the deckhands if we were going to tie up at the pier, yes, but there's no need to dock. We drop the anchor in the harbor, then you can row ashore in the two ship's boats."

"Too many questions of an empty ship in port," said Turgenev. "I think we sink the ship well away from port, and find our way there on foot."

"Yes, sir," Mokrenko agreed. "And there goes the last argument for sparing any of them. Now how do you want them killed, sir?"

"Natalya?"

The girl thought about that a moment, then said, "Drowning's as good as hanging. Just throw them overboard." Natalya's face went blank then, and when she spoke again her voice was like something from beyond the grave, creaking and lifeless. "Once, early on, when I wouldn't cooperate, the captain had two of the men hold my head under water until I passed out, then revived me and did it again . . . and again . . . I don't know how many times. Eventually, I cooperated."

"Including . . ." Turgenev didn't want to think about that. Instead, he struggled for the unfamiliar name, "Zamfir, was it?"

The girl's voice returned to normal, though her face remained blank. "The sergeant said it, sir, he's guilty by silent consent."

Turgenev went silent for a bit, looking down at the deck. Finally, he said, "Sergeant, this court, having heard from sufficient witnesses to establish guilt for rape, conspiracy to commit rape, and conspiracy to commit piracy on the high seas, sentences the prisoners to death. No need for any ceremony; just take a large enough detail and drown them, please.

"Oh, and send Sapper Shukhov to me, if you would."

Mokrenko stood and saluted, pleased that his officer was not only doing the smart thing, he wasn't dillydallying about it anymore. "Natalya, you want to witness this?"

Life returned; the girl smiled grimly, answering, "Absolutely, Sergeant."

"Go up on deck, Natalya," Mokrenko said, "and order the sails furled and the men in the rigging to come down. Tell Visaitov to guard them carefully. Then meet me by the foremast below. When we bring out the crew stand back out of the way. They may get violent."

"Okay, Sergeant."

Once she was gone, the sergeant mustered everyone but Timashuk, the medic, now at the wheel, the lieutenant, Shukhov, Babin, and Visaitov, now guarding Timashuk and the few of the crew working the rigging.

He ordered Shukhov, the sapper, to report to Turgenev. The remainder he assembled—Corporal Koslov, Novarikasha, Lavin, and Sarnof—around the forward mast by the passenger cabins. "This has to be quick," he warned, "without any warning, forceful, decisive, and final. A cornered rat will fight, desperately. Koslov, Novarikasha; you're the seizure team. You bring them out one at a time. Club them if you must. Lavin, you're the binder. When the prisoners are brought out, you tie their hands fast and tight. Don't worry about discomfort; they won't feel it for long. Sarnof, you and I will be armed, watching over the other three. Got it?"

"Sure, Sergeant . . . yes . . . seems kind of cold-blooded to me . . . still . . . didn't like the bastards anyway."

"Back here in five minutes with everything you need. Go!"

"So, Shukhov," the lieutenant began, "we need a way to burn or explode the ship, with a longish delay, maybe two or three hours, to give us time to get away. It would be better if it looked spontaneous, an accident. Can you do this? How?"

"Well, I'm sure I can, sir, but without nosing around I'm not sure yet exactly how. Can you give me a little time, to see what I can come up with?"

"Sure. Once you figure it out, let me know what will work."

The crew, when not on duty, were kept in a cargo hold below, filthy, wet, and rat-infested. Mokrenko, in his most forcefully guttural Russian, gave the orders while the girl translated.

"All right, you filthy swine, we're going to scuttle the ship. With you, we're putting you into a boat to row to shore. Or, if you don't like that, you can try to swim or stay here and just drown. Don't like either of those ideas? Good. Come up one at a time."

The first one out, first by virtue of having the sheer bulk to force his way to the ladder, was the ship's cook. As soon as he had his feet on deck, standing under the unwavering pistols of Mokrenko and Sarnof, Lavin spun him about, pulled his hands together, and bound them firmly at the wrist. Then the cook was pushed to the nearest ladder leading upward.

"Do we need to put a rope around your neck to keep

you upright?" Natalya asked sweetly. The cook merely snarled and began climbing the steep ladder without any aid.

"Next!"

When all nine members of the crew who still remained were up on deck and bound, Natalya translated, "On your knees and pray to God. We're going to kill you now."

Naturally, this raised something of a ruckus among the condemned men. One man shouted, "You said we'd have a chance at life if we performed for you."

"A chance is only a chance," the girl replied, "not a certainty." She hadn't bothered to translate any of that.

"What did we do to deserve this?" that same sailor asked of Turgenev. "It was the others who attacked you!"

"It was not the others who attacked *me*," Natalya said. "That's actually what you're to be executed for, rape, over and over and over again. Don't you remember?"

"You said we'd be put in a boat and allowed to row to shore."

"We lied."

Zamfir stumbled over to kneel in front of the girl. "I never touched you, not so much as the lightest finger. Tell them, for the love of God tell them, to spare me."

"Silence is consent," she replied. "When you were on watch did that not free another man to rape me?"

"Please, Natalya?"

She shook her head, without showing the least sign of pity.

"Start tossing them," Mokrenko ordered. He'd considered cutting their throats first, but had his doubts the men would consent to be mere butchers. The four men of his detail, by twos, began lifting and tossing the captives overboard. Some struggled; some wept. Most begged. The cook stumbled to his feet and ran across the deck.

For the nonce, Mokrenko ignored the cook. Natalya concentrated on watching the doomed men splash overboard, then their short struggles before they sank beneath the waters.

"Okay, let's get fat boy," said the sergeant.

"Nooooo!" shrieked the cook as four men surrounded him.

Hmmmm . . . wonder what that big splash was, thought Shukhov, puttering through the galley for material he could use to blow up or burn the ship.

The engineer found a full-sized barrel loaded with sugar. Not caring much for the niceties, he found a hammer belonging to the cook and began to beat in the wooden top. *Well, that's a start. Now let's see . . .*

"I can do it, Lieutenant," the sapper said. "I'll be working a good deal of the night setting it up, but I can do it."

"How?"

"Well, sir, I'll set it up—except for a couple of key steps—before we drop anchor. Water drips into a bucket that tips a pot. The pot will contain lye; there's plenty aboard. The pot will tip into one of the big ceramic bowls in the galley. That will be surrounded by four bowls with gasoline from the fuel tank, and all of it will be by the fuel tank. Last minute, I pull the batteries from the engine and pour the acid into the central bowl, then pull out the stopper to get the water drip going.

"When enough water has dripped, the lye in the pot gets tipped into the battery acid. That starts a fire—big fire, really—hot enough to set off the other bowls containing gasoline. Those, between them, torch off the fuel tank—I'll puncture the tank to make sure there's plenty of gasoline for the purpose. That all causes a . . . hmmm . . . this is more complex to explain."

Accompanied by hand gestures, the engineer explained the mechanics of a boiling liquid-expanding vapor explosion. Two hands, spaced with the fingers and thumbs pointed toward each other provided the core of the diagram.

"When you've got a fire going outside of a fuel tank, fed by the fuel in the tank, the fuel inside gets heated." Here, the fingers writhed, indicating rising temperature and boiling liquid. "The more heated it gets, the more the pressure inside rises." Fingers and hands spread. "The more the pressure rises, the faster it pushes out fuel, which in turn causes a bigger, hotter fire." Hands almost joined as fingers interlaced. "At some point in time, the tank can't hold the pressure. It blows up"— hands and fingers spread widely—"releasing hot, misting fuel to the fire. Then . . . well, the blast is enormous." The engineer's hands fell to his sides, with finality.

"Enough to sink the ship?" the lieutenant asked.

"Sir, it's going to be like thirty or forty tons of high explosive going off; I'm not sure there'll be enough left of the ship to actually sink."

"Okay, get it set up."

"Yes, sir. And thus all but one of my demolition life's ambitions will be satisfied," said Shukhov.

"What's the other one?" the lieutenant asked.

"I want to blow up a safe, a real safe. Preferably in a bank but anywhere will do. I've blown down trees and blown up bunkers, houses, and bridges . . . and soon a ship . . . ah, but a good safe? That would be something to tell the grandchildren of."

"You are a criminal in the making, Engineer Shukhov."

"Yes, sir. I know, sir. Sad, is it not, sir?"

Southwest of Taganrog, Russia

With the ship stopped dead in the water, and while the lieutenant led everyone but Mokrenko, Babin, Natalya, and Shukhov through boat drills designed to get them as far from the ship as possible in the shortest possible time, Shukhov prepared the demolition but without either emptying the batteries of acid, filling the pot with lye, or puncturing the tank.

For their parts, Mokrenko and Babin moved everything the team had brought with them, plus the captain's little treasure chest, plus a few of the things they'd found on the ship that might be useful, up on deck. This formed a growing collection on the side away from the shore.

Watching from the deck, Mokrenko had been, at first, rather disgusted with the obvious cluster fuck that was the ship's boat. He saw oars being tangled, momentum being lost, and a good deal of instability in the boat as the lieutenant shifted people around.

Shaking his head and thinking, *We're so fucked*, he went back below to grab a couple of packs. When he came back, the boat seemed to have regained a degree of stability, but the oars were still a mess. Rather, the oarsmen were.

You would think that, having learned to march in step, they'd be able to pull an oar in cadence, too. Tsk.

Lieutenant Babin came on deck then, dragging one of the cases holding half the rifles and ammunition behind him. He, too, stopped to watch the boat's progress. He said it aloud, "We're fucked."

"Know anything about small boats, sir?" Mokrenko asked, hopefully.

"Not a thing. But you don't need to, to know that's not the way to do it."

"Yeah . . ."

I wish I had two drums and a couple of mallets to beat out the cadence, thought Turgenev.

"All right, people, let's give this one more try. We don't know the actual commands, none of us being sailors or yachtsmen, but we can figure out what has to be done and make commands up for ourselves.

"Once again, when I say 'Ready oars,' push the oars out until the handle part is right in front of you and all the oars are parallel to the water, with the blade—that's the thin part—pointed straight down to the water. Got it?"

"Okay . . . ready . . . .oars."

What actually happened then was that the men, the rowers, lifted their flaccid oars out of the water and held them, stiffly, more or less straight out.

So far, so good . . . . I think.

"Next, when I say 'Get ready to row,'[4] lean forward and push your arms straight out—yes, *still* holding the oar—so that the oars move up a little and toward the front . . . now . . . get ready to row.

"Yeah . . . no. Let's try that one again. First . . . ready oars . . . now . . . get ready to row . . . and once again . . ."

With the glass bowls arranged on the floor, and a convenient can of gasoline waiting to fill up the outer half ring, Shukhov contemplated the fuel tank.

Hmmm, he thought, *I'm not going to risk losing my kindjal to a quick retreat once I puncture the tank. Let's go see what the galley has available.*

With that, he left the engine room; a subset, but a slightly higher and much drier one, of the bilges where they'd kept the crew prisoner. Up one ladder and around the rearmost mast, or mizzen-mast, led the sapper back again to the galley. The crew had left most of the ship pretty filthy, but, to give the late cook his due, the galley was spotless, to include the pots, pans, bowls, dishes, and cutlery.

Puttering through one of the drawers, Shukhov thought, *I want a steady drip, or two or three of them, not a huge gusher. I think that leaves the cleaver and butcher knives out of consideration. Hmmm . . . wonder if I could arrange something burnable that would not even begin to leak much until the fire from the lye, the battery acid, and the gasoline in those bowls sets it on fire. But what?*

---

[4] The actual command is "Prepare to give way."

A-ha! I can make a good-size hole but plug it with a wad of cloth . . . yeah, that's it. Now, what kind of cloth shall I use? Something tight-woven and heavy, I think. Canvas would probably do nicely . . .

Mokrenko dropped the last rucksack on the deck, then walked a step to the gunwales, to watch the boat perform. *Better*, he thought. *Maybe the lieutenant used to be a yachtsman.*

Babin, after heaving down his load, went to watch. "They're getting better, you know, Sergeant."

"Yes, sir, but if the blast is going to be as impressive as Shukhov expects—thirty to forty *tons* of high explosive—I'm not sure there's anything quite good enough or fast enough to get away from it."

Babin's eyes grew wide, then narrowed. "I wish I had some way to detonate that inside the *Kerch*."

"The world would not be the poorer for a hundred or so fewer Bolsheviks, sir. Speaking of which, what do you intend to do once we reach landfall?"

"I don't know. No wife—she died, years ago, and I've never remarried. No children. Maybe I'll find an anti-Bolshevik faction and kill the Reds until they manage to kill me."

"We may have a better offer for you," the sergeant said. "I'll bring it up with my lieutenant."

Destroyer *Kerch*

The shout came up, "There's something or someone off the port bow!"

The ship's skipper—he'd been a petty officer not long

before but was Comrade Captain Razin now—gave the orders to investigate. What the object turned out to be, once recovered, was one very fat, white-clad Romanian with his hands, now quite blue, bound behind him and a bad case of hypothermia racing at a snail's pace to kill him.

Once the man was hoisted aboard, there being no way for him to climb, even though they untied him, the captain discovered that no one could understand a word he said. Indeed, with feeling—agonized feeling—rushing back into his tortured hands, the man could do little but scream and then moan for a long time. The crew had to pour hot, highly sugared tea into him, since he couldn't even hold a glass or cup for himself. This was not just because of the state of his hands, but also because of his uncontrollable shivering.

"Anybody understand what he's babbling?" asked the skipper.

Answered the mate, also a former petty officer, "Not a word, comrade, but it sounds...mmmm...Italian or Romanian, to me. I've heard that kind of language before. It's not French. Not Spanish; he isn't lisping despite the freezing. Italian or Romanian, most likely."

"Should we toss him back in, Comrade?" asked the mate.

"Let's see if we can get some use out of him, first. If he lives. Ask around and see if any of the crew speak either of those languages."

Barquentine *Loredana*

"Well," said Turgenev, as Mokrenko tossed him a rope to tie up the boat, "we're not very good but we're as good as we're going to be in the time we have."

"Yes, sir," agreed the sergeant. No one needed to
ention that they were already three precious days
hind schedule.

"Have Natalya start the engine and set course for
inity Taganrog."

Within minutes, with squeals and groans, a few coughs,
eral puffs of dense, black smoke, and some disquieting
attering, the engine sprang to life.

Interlude

Tatiana: The Staircase

I rushed towards the ruckus coming from the stairs

With our snow hill gone, boredom had gripped Ale
and he'd decided to make a toboggan out of a rug a
used it to slide down the stairs.

Something had gone wrong and he'd hit his knee. P₂
came into stairwell, terror hiding in his face. Re
flickered across it, but it was short lived. Alexei's har
squeezed tight around his right knee. He was hunch
over, his jaw clenched tight, a hiss of breath escaping
gasps.

I'd seen this before, when he'd fallen and h
something in his groin. He'd been in agony for days
what would have been a muscle pull or a bruise for any
the rest of us swelled up with pooling blood.

"I just want to be a real boy," Alexei said, his voice fil
with equal measure of pain and frustration.

"You are a real boy," Papa said, "not Pinocchio." It v
an attempt to lighten the mood, to make Alexei feel bett
the tone soothing and struggling so very hard to
humorous.

"No, I'm not." It was as if someone other than Ale
spoke. Someone older. Someone harder. Someo

342

wounded in a way that would never heal. "Even a wood puppet can slide down stairs without breaking."

The ache in my chest grew, swelling until I thought my heart would be crushed. But no. It kept beating, despite the look on Alexei's face, the one that said he'd be better off as a puppet, a lifeless thing that could feel no pain.

I took a step back as Papa drew Alexei into his arms. Tears pushed into my eyes. I blinked them back.

Blinked and held them in with a swallow. I knew then that I'd never forget the look on Papa's face. That gentle face now lined with worry unlike I'd ever seen before. It may have been Alexei who'd hurt himself, but the fall had wounded Papa as well.

His face was like a mask. I realized then and there that it was a mask of glass that he'd been wearing all along. It was cracked, spiderwebbed by tiny fissures that had been welded together again and again, sanded over, polished. But this crack, this fissure, had made all the previous ones stand out as if they had never been fixed.

Since Alexei was a baby, his illness had cast a shadow over Papa's reign. What was to be his joy, his heir, had been twisted into a weapon to be used against him. A weapon he loved so much he would allow it to destroy us all. This weapon—my beloved brother, for I loved him with all my heart—was why we had isolated ourselves from the world, wrapping our family in a cocoon of secrecy. If his illness were to become known then Russia had no heir. We had hidden Alexei from the world, and the world from ourselves. And it had all been for nothing. Papa was no longer tsar. Alexei was no longer his heir, no matter how much some of the men still thought of him as such.

It had all been in vain. If we'd only known then what was to come.

And then it hit me. What if Alexei was my child? Would I have done things differently? Could I bear a child knowing that this would be his life?

I shook my head.

No, I would not.

I loved children. I loved being around them, whether siblings, cousins, or strangers. But I wasn't Mama. I didn't have her strength.

Mama who had such a high sense of duty, who had been wholly devoted to her maternal obligations, who lived and breathed for her family. Who was often so preoccupied with her burdens that she seemed absentminded, who lost herself in a melancholy reverie, who became indifferent to the things about her.

It had cost her—us—because the sensitive, loving soul that was Mama was, to outsiders, nothing but a cold and haughty empress. Her enemies had used the mask she wore to cover her sensitivity and to project reserve against her. They had twisted everything that was good about Mama and used it to turn her into a weapon against Papa, against the empire, and there had been nothing anyone could do about it.

Even as the thought formed I knew it to be false. Mama and Papa had chosen not to do anything about it. They had chosen to believe that what others thought about them didn't matter. That was *not* a luxury a Romanov could indulge in. If only they had learned it sooner.

Dr. Botkin came into the stairwell. He examined

Alexei, who was rocking back and forth now, blinking back tears.

Papa moved around Alexei and grabbed him under the arms. Dr. Botkin grabbed his legs. Alexei's breath hitched.

I moved aside to let them pass and allow them to take him into his room.

I knew what awaited my sweet, charming brother. Blood would pool under his knee and spread down his leg. His skin would swell. The pressure from the blood and the swelling would press on the nerves. He would moan and cry as the pain grew worse with each hour.

Just like the last time when he'd fallen and hit his knee, there would be nothing to alleviate his suffering. Nothing anyone's tender love and care would cure. Papa no longer needed to steal moments out of his schedule to come in and distract him with stories. He could be with him the entire time, but that would likely make it worse for the both of them.

And worse for Mama as well. She too had no duties to tear her from her son's side. They would both don those glass masks as they tried to comfort and amuse him, dying inside a bit at a time.

Alexei would burn, hot to the touch, delirious with fever. He'd groan piteously, his face unrecognizable in its deathly whiteness. All of his suffering and distress would come out, balled up into one word: "Mummy."

And Mama would kiss his hair, his eyes, his forehead as if those loving touches could ease his pain or bring back the life that was always threatening to leave him.

How did Mama bear it? The impotence? The anguish of knowing that she herself was the cause?

Before, my sisters and I had lessons to distract us. But no more. We too would sit with Alexei and let the glass crystallize on our faces until the masks became who we were, until we could not pull it down for anyone. And inside would be the knowledge that any one of us girls could be in that bed had we been born boys. That any son of mine might inherit this terrible disease for which there was no cure—only tears and pain and death.

The cycle would repeat itself. Just as it had with Mama's uncle, her brother, her nephews. Death pursued all men, but it paid particular attention to the men of my family, taking up residence in their very blood.

Would Alexei come back from this fall as he had from all the others? As if he had forgotten his suffering? As if he was safe from death's pursuit? How long before his heart no longer filled with hope? How long before the gates of death finally closed behind him?

Chapter Thirteen

"Comrade" Sabanayev's Wagon, Taganrog

Barquentine *Loredana*

The ship's days were numbered now.

The *Loredana* had two of the sails of the foremast set. With the wind coming gently from the northwest, these would not only help to push it away from the fleeing boat, but might confuse people, if any were observing, as to the crew's course and destination. For that matter, it would reduce the chances of anyone spotting it until it was gone.

With the ship moving gently with the wind, the escape boat was being pulled along with it.

If what Shukhov said is true, thought Turgenev,

standing at the stern of the boat, *and I've no reason to doubt it, if we're not at least two or, better, three or four* versta *away from that thing when it goes off, it's likely as not to kill us.*

With the crew, all the personal and group baggage, as well as what was looted from the *Loredana*, the ship's boat was crowded. Indeed, when Shukhov came back from his mission of sabotage, there wasn't going to be a seat for him except atop a pile of bags.

Mokrenko sat up at the bow, with a shore spike clutched in one hand, the rope holding them to the ship in the other, and his cut-down rifle resting against one thigh. Behind him, the oar crew sat in pairs, port and starboard. From bow to stern, these were Koslov and Lavin, followed by Timashuk and Novarikasha, then Sarnof and Visaitov. The girl, Natalya, sat on the middle bench, squeezed between Timashuk and Novarikasha. Lieutenant Babin, likewise, was crammed in between Koslov and Lavin. Lieutenant Turgenev stood at the rear, both to manage the rudder and call the strokes to the oarsmen. The ship's cat, or the former ship's cat, sat atop Natalya's lap, reveling in an uncommon two-handed stroking.

Even as he reveled, though, the cat resented that there were rats left on the ship he'd likely never get to hunt down.

Each of the oarsmen had his rifle close to hand.

Turgenev's eyes shifted restlessly from the dimly seen lights of the town glowing off the clouds overhead to the ship, whence he expected to see Shukhov appear at any moment.

✛ ✛ ✛

The pot was ready, the water source likewise ready to unplug. The engine was running, at low speed, to draw in air to the engine room. The lye and battery acid were both in their appointed stations. All that remained was to puncture the large fuel tank, plug it with canvas, and start the water dripping.

Shukhov, working by the faint light of a ship's lamp, concentrated on the spot he'd chosen to plunge in the cook's icepick; that, he'd decided, being a better implement for the purpose than any knife on offer. The pick, itself, was for the most part round and thin, but jutting from a square portion, much thicker, near the handle. With a quick jab, he drove his stout arm forward and up, the icepick angled to take the fuel tank from the curved underside.

"Shit," the engineer said softly. "I should have known that any fuel tank on any ship owned by that Romanian reprobate would be weak, rusty, and defective."

In fact, the icepick had gone considerably farther into the tank than he'd expected or wanted. Indeed, it was gone far enough, creating a large enough hole once Shukhov withdrew it, if he did, that he had his doubts he could make a decent plug. Already fuel was, if not quite pouring out, leaking at a rate a lot greater than he felt comfortable with.

"Shit," he repeated, a little more loudly.

Briefly, the engineer thought about disassembling the entire apparatus and moving it to safety before pulling out the icepick and trying to plug the hole.

"But what if I can't plug it? What if the swine of a child-raping captain's fuel tank simply crumbles apart? It might."

As well as he could, given the need to keep the ship's lantern far from the leaking gasoline, Shukhov inspected the damage and the flow. *It could be worse*, he thought. *This is maybe twice the flow I wanted. We can still outrun it . . . I think. Better than the alternative? Maybe. I'm going to go with that, anyway.*

Mokrenko is never going to let me hear the end of this. On the other hand, if I don't hurry, I'll never get the chance to hear the beginning, either.

With a wild scramble, aided by ship's ropes and the waiting hands of his teammates, Shukhov clambered over the side and down into the boat.

"Sir, you've *got*—we've got—to hurry," said the engineer, rather more loudly and more excitedly than he'd intended.

Before Turgenev could say a word, Mokrenko asked, "Why? What did you fuck up?"

Breathlessly, Shukhov answered, "It was the fucking fuel tank . . . it was weak . . . rusted . . . made a bigger hole than I'd planned on. So we've got more gasoline flowing. That means a bigger fire once the water starts everything. It's going to go off sooner than I'd planned, a lot sooner. We've got to get the fuck out of here!"

"Idiot," Mokrenko muttered under his breath, as the lieutenant pushed the boat from the ship.

Calm yourself, Turgenev, the lieutenant thought. Taking in a breath, he let it loose, swallowed, and took another. *Must look and sound confident in front of the men.*

"Gentlemen," Turgenev said, "we can get out of this if

we maintain calm and pull our oars as one. You are all guardsmen on the oars, battle tested in some of the fiercest battles of the war, so calm you should be able to handle. The oars . . . well, we will ask God to help us there. So, gentlemen of the oars . . . get ready to row."

Destroyer *Kerch*

The ship rocked gently, silent and still. There was no place much to go and nothing much to do, at the moment, so why go there to do it.

"Has that fat tub of a foreign sailor said anything worthwhile yet?" asked Comrade Captain Razin, the former petty officer, coming to the former wardroom, now called, until they could come up with a more revolutionary term, the senior mess.

"Yes, comrade," answered the executive of the ship, nursing a glass of hot tea. "We found one of the sailors, a good communist, too, who spoke Italian. He said the other language was Romanian, which was about three quarters mutually intelligible."

"And?" asked Razin, drawing a glass of tea from the samovar bolted to a counter.

"He's a cook, a ship's cook off a smuggler, the *Loredana*. He says the Germans hired the captain to take some Russians home, nine of them. He says they killed the captain and all the rest of the crew. He says, too, that they intended to kill him, but his fat both kept him afloat and insulated him from the cold."

"Can he describe this *Loredana?*"

"It's a barquentine, like any other, Comrade."

Razin nodded, while thinking aloud. "Now *why* would

the Germans go to all that trouble to send nine Russians back? Did he describe them?"

"Yes, Comrade, but from ignorance. He didn't know what he was looking at or even looking for. Still... Cossacks, either entirely or mostly. Their swords and dagger gave them away."

Razin sipped at his tea while looking up at the seam of deck and bulkhead, above. "So the Germans sent back Cossacks via a smuggler. Counterrevolutionaries? Seems likely, the bastards. Troublemakers at a minimum, I am sure.

"This cook have any idea where the ship was going after they let them off?"

"He said Taganrog or the nearest shore to Rostov-on-Don, Comrade Captain."

Razin nodded. "Lay in a course for Mariupol. Stop about ten *versts* out. Then I want to parallel the coast—remember to watch out for the spit southwest of Sjedove—check out the harbor at Taganrog, then, if they're not there, continue to as close as we can come to Rostov-on-Don."

"Dump the cook overboard then, Comrade-Captain?"

"Don't be an idiot; we'll need him to identify this barquentine. We can toss him *afterwards* ... unless the mess section wants to keep him."

"They might," the exec agreed. "I'll ask. By the way, Comrade Captain, how are we even going to *see* this ship in this dark?"

"To stop the introduction of dangerous potential counterrevolutionaries into the country? Be serious; we'll use the searchlights. It's not, after all, like we have much in the way of threats here."

"There's one threat, maybe, Comrade Captain?" Without waiting for Razin even to raise an eyebrow, the exec continued, "Remember those counterrevolutionary officers we executed by drowning not long ago?"

"Sure," the captain shrugged.

"Well, the Romanian cook thought it likely that the Cossacks had rescued one of them."

"Shit."

Barquentine *Loredana*

The ship's rat was one of many. None of them had names but this one thought of himself, and was thought of by the others, as Number One Rat.

Chief rat or not, it was used to having to be a bit circumspect in its movements, as well as to having its way barred in many places. Thus, it was somewhat surprised to see the hatch open to what it thought of as "spacenoisystinky." It was even stinkier now, and the stink a little different, less toxic and almost alluring.

Number One hadn't gotten to be chief rat by virtue of taking too many chances. If something was alluring, it was also likely very dangerous. Standing on its rear legs by the hatchway's wooden frame, Number One looked around the spacenoisystinky. There were, he decided, a lot of weird things going on, all of which spelled "danger" in classical rodent. Or would have, if rats could spell . . . and if there'd been such a thing as classical rodent. He decided he wanted nothing to do with any of it. Even though he rather would have liked a drink of water, the enticing drip-drip-dripping wasn't enough to tempt him, given the strange smell. Instead, Number One turned away and, with faint scratching sounds from his claws on the deck, headed to a hidden passageway he knew of. That, in turn, led to the place he thought of as "foodfeedmeahgood."

Now *that* was a treasure trove. Someone had spilt sugar, sliced open bags of grain, left out some meat and beans.

I'll get the others for the feast after I've had my fill, thought Number One. *Yummyyummyyummy.*

Number One stopped his feasting when the galley porthole was suddenly lit up brightly by some external light source.

Ship's Boat, Barquentine *Loredana*

Natalya was the first to really notice. "Lieutenant Turgenev, sir," she said, "there's something behind us lighting up what is likely the *Loredana*."

The oars almost immediately fouled, nudging everyone lightly toward the bow.

Turgenev swiveled neck and body one hundred and eighty degrees to catch a glimpse. "Is that your little explosive device going, Shukhov?" the lieutenant asked.

"Too bright, I think, sir," Shukhov replied. "Mine should be a mostly dim glow, followed by the sudden rising of the sun. And it should have been over quick. We'd also have heard it by now."

"Searchlight, I think," offered Lieutenant Babin, "and a fairly powerful one. Could be . . ."

"Could be what?" asked Turgenev.

"Could be *Kerch*," said Babin. "I saw at least one large searchlight aboard before they tossed me overboard."

Fuck, thought Mokrenko.

"Reach into my pack," said Turgenev to Babin. "Inside there is a good pair of German binoculars. See if you can make out anything. As for the rest of you, Sergeant Mokrenko?"

"Calm the fuck down, people!" Mokrenko barked. He waited a few moments until he sensed, in the darkness, that he had their attention. "Sir?"

"Once again," said Turgenev, "get ready to row." When there was an absence of sound of wood on water or wood, Turgenev decided they were ready. "Now row . . . together. One . . . two . . . three . . . four . . . one . . . two . . ."

"It's hard to tell," said Babin, once he'd had a chance to look through the binoculars, "but if I had to guess . . . that's the *Kerch*, come to hunt us down. I can't make it all out, but I can see the searchlight and I can see part of the bridge, one . . . no, two, of the guns. There are other destroyers out here on the Black Sea, but she was closest. I think it's the *Kerch*."

"Probably not to hunt *us* down," said Mokrenko. "They've no reason to believe we even exist."

Destroyer *Kerch*

"Bring up the fat cook," Razin ordered, watching the portside searchlight playing back and forth along the hull of the anchored vessel. Bringing the cook took some time. When he arrived, it was without the Italian speaking sailor, which led to still more loss of time as that worthy was hunted down and brought to the bridge.

Meanwhile, the rest of the crew stood to battle stations, manning the four open 102mm deck guns, both of the

57mm antiaircraft guns, the four thirty-caliber machine guns, plus the four triple-torpedo tubes. There was even a small team, quite needlessly, on the racks toward the stern that held the ship's eighty naval mines, two of which they'd automatically prepared for laying.

Whatever else might be said of the *Kerch*, it couldn't be said she was under-armed for her size.

The searchlight swept the deck of the barquentine. "Nobody at the wheel, Comrade Captain," announced the exec. "I think she's been abandoned."

"Match course and speed. Get a boat over the side and a boarding party—a well-armed boarding party—ready. Also, bring us closer, no more than twenty-five *arshins* away."

"We could close to almost hull to hull, Comrade Captain, and save a little time, no?"

"We could," Razin agreed, "but getting the boarding party back might be difficult. Besides, we're a frightfully open ship and unarmored, to boot. I wouldn't want a dozen hand grenades going off on the deck."

Barquentine *Loredana*

Aboard the *Loredana,* Number One had finally summoned his followers to the feast with joyful squeaks and hisses. On the galley's deck and the counters, six score fat rats plus three gorged themselves on sugar, flour, and all manner of wonderful things. Like a lord, Number One sat atop a counter, enjoying the sight of his underlings feasting due to his own beneficence and boldness.

✦ ✦ ✦

The galley sat close to amidships. Farther to the stern, in the engine room, also known as spacenoisystinky, two drips ran continuously. One was of the water, slowly filling a pot that would tip over a good deal of lye into battery acid. This was getting near to full or, at least, full enough. The other was from the fuel tank, where gasoline ran in a small rivulet down to the lowest part of the curve of the tank, and then onto the floor, in a building and spreading puddle.

One thing Shukhov and Turgenev hadn't considered, since there'd been no obvious reason to consider it, was the action of the rocking of the ship on the entire Rube Goldbergesque self-destruct mechanism. This had been made a little worse with the setting of a few sails, thus allowing the ship to pass ahead of the wind. It hadn't made much of a difference to the water drip, and it would not make a difference to the lye pour.

But the icepick? To that, it made a difference.

With each roll of the ship, the more heavily weighted handle of the icepick moved, imperceptibly. The ship's bow rolls upward, going into a wave? The ship's stern rides over the same wave? With each roll, the pick's handle goes down. The stern then falls into a trough? With each fall, the handle moves a little up. Rinse and repeat, every minute or so, for some hours. Now add to that the pressure from inside the tank, so far not driven by heat, but still a force not to be discounted.

In short, eventually the ice pick fell out, allowing a much stronger stream of gasoline to leak onto the deck. This was not, so far, a huge problem.

Ah, but then the pot for water filled up enough to tip

the lye into the battery acid. A good deal of the lye missed, due to the same roll that had dislodged the icepick. Enough, however, hit the battery acid to start a fire, which spread very quickly to the four bowls filled with gasoline next to it.

The burning bowls did not, directly, torch off the puddle of gasoline on the floor. Rather, the flames from the bowls set the gasoline leaking from the icepick's hole and running down the tank's bottom on fire. This burning drip set the gasoline on the deck to burning. The sudden pressure of that had the effect of pushing the hatchway shut. This did not, it should be noted, cut off the supply of oxygen to the fire since the engine was still working to draw in air. What it did do, however, was increase the heat on the tank, quickly and sooner than anyone might have expected. It was not too much longer before the pressure building up inside the tank began forcing gasoline out the hole in a stream. This, too, increased the heat on the tank, hence of the fuel, and hence of the vapor from the fuel.

Even this might not have ruined the timing too badly, but for the worn out, rusty, crappy nature of the tank, itself. Another tank might have held on longer against the rising pressure from the heating fuel, but not this one. With about a third of the tank filled with fumes under high pressure, and the rest filled with fuel just held from boiling by that pressure, something had to give.

It did.

Destroyer *Kerch*

"That's her," said the cook, via the Italian-speaking interpreter.

"Send the boat and boarding party over now," Razin ordered. The captain had been scanning the ship, bow to stern and then stern to bow again, as the searchlight played across its length. With the launching of the boarding party, the searchlight crew put its focus on just sternward of amidships, at a spot the boarders would be able to climb up the hull. It was, in fact, the same spot where Turgenev, Mokrenko, and company had debarked.

Unlike the Cossacks escaping the *Loredana*, the *Kerch's* boat crew were thoroughly practiced and much, much faster. They reached the barquentine quickly, followed by two men clambering up the sides to tie the *Kerch's* boat off. Bearing slung rifles, the boarding party was soon all on deck. Moments later the rifles were in ready hands and the party was beginning to spread out.

The leader of the group was Comrade Pereversev, a clean-cut sort who was also a communist by conviction, and not merely one of convenience or envy. Pereversev sent two men to the bow, likewise two to the stern, and then, with the remainder, descended the ladder down into the darkened passenger and crew deck.

Looking to the bow, Pereversev saw nothing. Looking sternward, there was a faint glow leaking through a few imperfections and gaps in what he suspected was the engine room hatch.

"We'll start there," Pereversev ordered, adding, "One man, either side and just behind me. Now, who's got the lantern? Light it."

Someone struck a match, the sudden flash showing an open space, with no obvious threats. Within a few seconds, the glow of an oil lamp illuminated the deck.

"Come on."

Carefully, the boarding party followed their leader toward the stern, heads and eyes scanning left to right, then right to left.

"It's creepy, you know . . ."

"Shut up and watch," said Pereversev. Silently, he agreed, *It certainly is creepy. One hears stories . . . lost ships and crews . . . doomed men . . . The Flying Dutchman . . . and stop it, right now.*

It wasn't long before the boarding party was at the entrance to the engine room.

What gave was one end of the tank. It simply blew off, the super-heated gasoline suddenly flashing to vapor. The vapor immediately caught fire but so quickly that it was better defined as an explosion. *That* blew the hatch off the engine room, propelling it forward and carrying Comrade Pereversev forward with it.

Not so far away, Number One looked up from his feasting followers at the oncoming wave of flame. The rat had one unprintable thought before the blast took them all.

The passenger and crew deck instantly filled up with a mixture of air and gasoline vapor. This expanded forward into every cabin, nook, and cranny, as well as down below into the open cargo hold, and likewise into the galley. The fuel-air mix was beginning to escape up the open hatchways to the deck, but the wave of explosion spread outward before this pressure release could be of much use.

The explosive power was nothing like the theoretical

that Shukhov had claimed. Rather than being the equivalent of up to forty tons of high explosive, the actual yield was much less, perhaps eight or nine. But eight or nine tons of high explosive contained within the ship's hull was enough to shatter that hull.

Moreover, as more air was added to the mix, previously unspent fuel joined the conflagration. It spread uniformly in a large brightly lit demi-sphere. Indeed, the sphere was so large that most of *Kerch* was caught inside it.

The thirty-eight men manning and supervising the guns and mines were the first to go. First, the explosion concussed them, even as it caused inhalation burns in most. Most were then tossed right overboard into the cold water, where it was a race between drowning and being strangled by their own blistering throats.

Up on the bridge, the thick glass shattered, shredding the exec and blinding Captain Razin.

The fuel-air mix really should not have been enough to sink the *Kerch*. Kill the exposed crew, yes, certainly, but sink the ship? No.

What happened were several things, more or less simultaneously. In the first place, a piece of wreckage from the *Loredana* struck one or more of the Hertz horns of the mines in the racks to the stern. This released sulfuric acid, which ran down to the battery. After a slight delay, that battery, which had had no acid previously, was charged up enough to send an electrical charge to the detonator. Explosion followed, which then crushed a great many more Hertz horns, setting off all the rest of the mines, some ten tons worth of high explosive, in all.

That wasn't all the damage done, though. There were

102mm shells in ready racks at each of the four guns. The fuses still retained their safeties, but the propellant was vulnerable to both blast and heat. Somewhere, one or more of the shells had their brass casings torn off, and their propellant set aflame. Get enough propellant going, and the distinction between it and explosive becomes rather a fine one.

And then there were the very large warheads in the torpedo racks . . .

Ship's Boat, Barquentine *Loredana*

"Holy shit!" said Babin, still looking through the binoculars. "That was the *Kerch* going up with the *Loredana*."

This caused Turgenev to turn about, briefly, just in time to catch the sphere of flame and the towering inferno, punctuated by some very sharp blasts. The oarsmen, too, stopped rowing to watch the show.

Shukhov, still perched atop some bags, was about to congratulate himself when he remembered, "Cover your heads, everyone. Or, on second thought, maybe not. Anything with enough mass to reach us here isn't going to be stopped by crossed arms."

Something did come then, screeching across the sky. It didn't come close, though; if it had, the ship's boat would never have survived high speed contact with the rear tenth or so of the deck over the former engine room. Still, it made a splash loud enough to hear.

"Okay," said Mokrenko, "show's over. Back to your oars."

✤ ✤ ✤

The sun was a thin hint on the horizon to the east when the party reached the shore. Mokrenko was first out, leaping over the side and splashing through the water until he ran out of line between the boat and the shore spike. Aided by the oarsmen, he hauled on the rope until the boat was firmly against the sand. Then, raising the spike high overhead, he used both arms to drive it into the shore.

At that point, Turgenev gave the order to ship oars. The entire party then, less Natalya, took hold of the boat, pushing it still farther onto the shoreline.

"All right," said Mokrenko, "Koslov? Goat, get this son of a bitch unloaded. Sir, I'm going to need a few men and some money—maybe a lot of money—to go get us fifteen horses and a cart or wagon."

"Take what you think you need, Sergeant," Turgenev replied. "Don't forget rations, either." The lieutenant shook his head in disgust. "It would have been simpler for us if that swine, Vraciu, had kept his word and brought us all the way to Rostov-on-Don. What this will cost us in delay I can't even guess."

"A few days, anyway, sir," Mokrenko said. "Which is a few days more than we have to spare. Visaitov, Lavin and . . . yes, you, Sarnof; you're coming with me."

Taganrog, Russia

They found a stable a few blocks from the old Assumption Cathedral. Mokrenko'd had an urge to look inside. It was an urge that, given the sheer number of armed Red Guards around the church, he didn't find especially hard to overcome.

"I've no horses to spare, soldier," the stable master insisted. Long in the face, with a drooping mustache, he looked a bit like the horses he cared for...smelled a bit like them, too. Mokrenko instinctively trusted him, something that didn't come easy to the Cossack.

"No," the stable master insisted, "not at any price. What the Germans, Austrians, and Cossacks didn't take, the Reds did. Indeed, the Reds took everything but a bare minimum to move utter necessaries around."

"Of course they did," Mokrenko agreed. "And who says I'm a soldier?"

"Soldier," insisted the stable master. "I was once one, too. Takes one to know one." The stable master made a quick headcount, "Or to know four of them."

"We need horses and a wagon," Mokrenko insisted. "My party is encamped down the coast. We were, yes, soldiers, demobilized and put on a boat to come home. Boat sank, but we managed to save ourselves, our gear, and a couple of others. We've got, as mentioned, baggage. A couple of sick, too."

"Indeed?" the stable master asked in a voice replete with suspicion. "You boat was sinking and yet you managed to save your baggage as well as yourselves? Well, no matter. I've got a wagon, a good one, with four old nags to pull it. You interested in hiring me for the job?"

Mokrenko considered that. "How far will you take us?" he asked.

"How far do you want to go?" the stable master replied.

"Rostov-on-Don."

Shaking his head, the local said, "Now *that* far I can't take you. Not only would it take me away from here too long, but the odds are good some different group of Germans or Reds—or bandits, there's little to choose among them—than the ones hereabouts would just confiscate my wagon and mares.

"I can't take you," he repeated, "but, I have a friend of sorts—my first cousin, actually—down by the docks. I think he could. How big did you say your party was?"

"There are eleven of us," Mokrenko said, "including a refugee girl we've acquired—no, stop right there and curb your thoughts; she's just a young girl who needs help getting to her home—and an officer from a different regiment from ours who wants to get home, too."

"How much baggage?"

Mokrenko considered this. There were probably about eighty pounds per man, all told, some of which was disposable. He answered, "Maybe a thousand pounds."

"Tell you what; help me get my mares in harness and I'll take you to the docks. You can bargain with my cousin for passage up the Don. I won't take part, mind, because while he's my cousin, you are soldiers. This leaves me in a terrible ethical dilemma if I get between you. After you've worked out passage—pay him no more than half up front, I warn you; he's a thief—we'll go pick up the rest of your crew. Fortunately, with the cold, the roads are hard, so we'll make good time.

"My name is Sabanayev, by the way, Igor Sabanayev; and yours?"

Sabanayev's brown eyes twinkled as he said, "And so, Comrade Rostislav Alexandrovich—and, once you're past Germans lines, I advise you and your friends to say 'comrade' as often as possible and as publicly as possible; the Reds have eyes and ears everywhere—I see your sick have almost all recovered nicely."

"Quick healers, the lot, yes," agreed Mokrenko, dryly.

"A suspicious man, which of course, I am not, would wonder if sickness were claimed in a play for sympathy."

"One does not need to play for sympathy," answered Mokrenko, primly, "when dealing with a fellow soldier. One need merely ask."

In fact, thought the Cossack, *I trust you mostly because you spoke of the Reds as if they were "the other."*

"Indeed," Sabanayev agreed, "it is so."

The stable master looked over the contents of the wagon, made a quick judgment, and added, "Your young girl, Natalya; she should ride on the wagon. Also that Lieutenant Babin; mark my words, he looks to be coming down with pneumonia. At the very least, he's had a hard time of it recently."

"He has," Mokrenko replied. "Nearly drowned, actually."

"Put him in the wagon, too, then. As for the rest of you, you should walk. My horses—poor old ladies—are tired and worn, and haven't been as well fed of late as they'd like. We'll make better time with the rest of you on foot."

Interlude

Tatiana: Anger and Weakness

I was so happy to see Olga up and around doing normal things like helping with Mama and the younger children that I was expecting things to turn around. I blame it on my naïveté, on my need for something good to finally happen.

Why there was a part of me that thought that she'd simply get over being raped, I don't know. I'd never dealt with rape. I'd never been around women who'd been raped. It wasn't something one discussed in polite company, or at all.

Who would want the shame? Who would want the pity? Who would want the guilt? Who would want to know that she could not protect herself? Who would want to know that they could not protect their daughter, sister, or wife?

Papa was reading to us—I don't remember which book—and Mama sat under blankets with Ortipo in her lap, listening and rubbing at her temples only occasionally.

Mama leaned to whisper in my ear. "Tatiana, check on the tea, please."

I got up and crossed the yard to the kitchen. As I approached, I heard the whistling of a tea kettle through the door.

I stepped inside and found Olga standing by the stove, looking off into space. She might have been looking through the window, but I don't think she was seeing anything.

The kettle's whistle came to a stop. Still she stared, as if she wasn't even there.

"Olga," I said, coming up behind her slowly.

She must've not heard me.

The scent of heated metal rose from the kettle.

"Olga," I said again, louder.

Startled, she turned her head. We both reached for the kettle at the same time, bumping fingers. I wrapped my hand around the towel knotted over the kettle's handle and moved it off the heat.

"Are you all right?" I asked.

"Yes. No. I don't know." Her voice was hollow. So were her eyes.

I sat her down at the small kitchen table used to chop vegetables. Someone had left a stack of clean bowls set in the middle. Mismatched napkins had been neatly folded atop them.

Olga played her fingernails into the grooves left by knives and hatchets as I took a pot from the rack hanging above and filled it with water. I didn't want to wait for the kettle to cool down.

"Mama wants her tea," I said as I set a half-full pot atop the stove.

I sat down across from her, grabbing at her fidgeting hands and wrapping them inside of mine. She'd bitten her fingernails to the quick, something she had never done before.

She lifted her gaze to mine. It was no longer hollow.

"I don't care," she said without blinking.

I think a moment passed. I'm not sure. It must have been the shock of hearing her say that, of the time it took me to realize that she'd said it.

Olga pulled out of my grip, pushed the chair back, and stood. "I don't care." Louder, more forceful.

"Shh," I said rising. "Someone will hear."

"I don't care!" Olga pushed the chair over. Her hands were fists now, no longer uncertain, no longer seeking refuge in fidgeting.

Before I could stop her, she moved forward, swept the bowls off the table, sending them to the floor. The impact sent the shattered pieces across the floor.

The chair was next, thrust on its side and sliding to block the door. Her eyes were frantic, seeking. She knocked the pot with its water off the stove. It rolled away, trailing wetness in its wake.

"Olga! Stop! They'll hear."

The barrel in the corner got a kick. It was too heavy to move. She eyed the rolling pin perched on the bottom shelf of the wall behind me and moved toward it.

For a moment—a very brief one—I wanted to join her, help her smash every bowl and plate, every jar, every bottle. Instead, I grabbed her shoulders as she went past me, spun her around and pulled her to me.

At first, she resisted. Her whole body was tight with tension, but I was determined. Determined not to let her go. Determined to hold on to her. Determined to make sure that she didn't do something that could not be hidden.

I squeezed harder, anchoring my fingers in her clothing until my fingers hurt.

I don't know why she didn't cry out or shout. Her mouth was open like she was going to, but no sound came from it.

Her face was an ugly shade of purple, the kind that comes from not breathing.

For a terrifying instant I didn't know what to do. If she screamed, it would be over. It would bring someone and Papa would hear. He would want to know what happened. Why it had happened.

He would see. He would know. He would suspect.

So I squeezed harder. She spasmed in my grasp, gulping for air, swallowing it down. She must've been breathing because her lips weren't turning blue. She just seemed unable to speak.

And then, between one blink of an eye and the next, the stiffness in her body melted away and she collapsed in my arms, like a rag doll that had been torn open, the buckwheat inside it spilling out in a torrent.

It was like that with Olga.

We sank to the floor, her chin resting on my shoulder, the wetness from her tears hot and sudden. I could feel her jaw working beside my cheek.

"Breathe," I said, massaging her back. "Breathe."

Her chest swelled against mine. She was shaking. It was her fingers digging into my back, my shoulder now.

The words, "Help me," were the barest whisper, more felt than heard against my skin.

But I couldn't. Not really.

Oh, I did take her back to our room, made our excuses

to Mama and Papa, made up a story that someone had spilled water on the floor and she had slipped, knocking over the chair and the bowls.

I did all those things. I lied. Over and over again.

There was a part of me that watched Papa's eyes with the vain hope that he would, just once, be more aware. He watched with eyes that did not see, heard with ears that did not hear.

I wanted to think of him as a good and great man, a strong man.

But he wasn't. He wasn't any of those things. A seed of doubt was planted that day, the doubt that he had ever been any of those things.

Yes, he loved us. Loved Mama to the point where he could not see her for what she had become. Loved us children as well.

But his daughter had been raped right under his nose. He hadn't been able to protect her. He could not protect any of us. Not himself.

He was a good man but he was an ineffective man.

For a long time I don't know who I was angrier with—him or myself. I had contributed to that blindness, even prayed for it to hold because I didn't want him to know, because I cared more for him than for Olga.

God rarely intervenes to save us from our own folly . . . or our parents' folly.

Chapter Fourteen

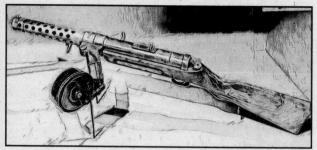

MP-18 Machine Pistol

Waffenbau Bergmann, Suhl, Germany

As it turned out—and it cost Brinkmann three days and a lot of difficult walking, aided by his cane, to find this out and fix it—the place to go was not Gaggenau, in Baden, but Suhl, in Thuringia. That was where Hugo Schmeisser worked, and that was where initial production of the MP18, the *Machinenpistole* of 1918, was being made.

In a side office, slightly insulated from the intense sounds of steel pounding or grinding steel, a tired and harried-looking, to say nothing of balding, Hugo Schmeisser faced an equally harried-looking and nearly exhausted Major Brinkmann. Between the two lay a table on which sat a shiny new submachinegun, with a brace of odd-looking magazines to either side, an inexplicable tool, plus one magazine that made a good deal more sense across the stock.

"Yes," said Schmeisser, "we've received an order for fifty thousand of the things from the army. It shouldn't be hard to divert sixty or even one hundred to General Hoffmann's request. But it's important you understand what you're getting, Major.

"There is, in the first place, no option for single fire; it is fully automatic and fully automatic *only*.

"Secondly, at almost four point two kilograms, it is by no means light. Note that that is *heavier* than our standard infantry rifle, the *Gewehr* 98. Empty. Loaded, it is worse.

"There is no option to attach a bayonet.

"On the plus side, though, at that weight, firing a nine-millimeter round, even on fully automatic, the recoil is negligible to a fighting man. It might be negligible to a not very large woman, for that matter. Indeed, I would say that the amount of recoil is perfect for getting a spray of bullets just broad enough to increase the probability of a hit, or multiple hits, at likely ranges. Moreover, the sheer bulk of metal, which is what's driven the weight, serves as a heat sink to help keep them from overheating.

"But then there's the magazine." Schmeisser reached out and picked up the box magazine, holding it out for Brinkmann to examine. His voice quivered with rage. "We gave the army *this* as a design: cheap, simple, reliable, compact." He dropped the box magazine with disgust, then picked up a drum magazine, normally found with the Artillery Luger. "This is what the army insists we use; complex, not especially reliable, quite expensive, overly large, and a true taste of hell to load in the dark in a muddy enemy trench. Never mind how much it unbalances the gun!"

"Why?" Brinkmann asked.

"Because we were already making these drum magazines, a fact not known to me back in 1915 when I undertook to design this piece. It would save time, they said. Never mind the time I spent redesigning the gun to take the drum magazine. Idiots!"

"I don't suppose . . ." Brinkmann began.

"Remaking them to take the box magazine? No, Major; that would be most impractical unless you have a few months to spare."

"No, no, we don't."

"I'd rather thought not."

"How many magazines can we have?" Brinkmann asked.

"Six or seven per; call it four hundred to six hundred," Schmeisser answered. "Production isn't quite what the General Staff anticipated. Loaded, they're not exactly light, either. And we'll have a loading tool—Oh, I can't *wait* to tell you about loading these things!—per weapon, too. We don't make the bags to carry the magazines in; there you're on your own.

"And so, would you care to fire the thing before you take delivery?"

Camp Budapest, Bulgaria

The messenger from the quartermaster's shop found Kostyshakov in the officers' shower. "Sir! Sir! The Germans have come through for us! Captain Romeyko says you should come immediately. We *have* the machine pistols we were promised. Oh, beautiful things they are, too."

Hiding his own excitement, Daniil said dryly, "Please tell the quartermaster that I will certainly take his request under advisement."

No sooner was the runner gone than Daniil was furiously working to remove the soap from his body, then dry himself on the thin and miserable *ersatz* towels that were all Germany could provide at this stage of the war. Still dangerously damp, he wrapped his feet, pulled on his uniform and then his boots, donned his overcoat and began to walk briskly the eighty or so meters to the quartermaster's shop.

"So show me this marvel of Teutonic weapons design," Kostyshakov's voice boomed as he strode through the cloth-hung door to the shack.

Daniil took one look, then pointed his finger at the same runner who'd come for him. "Get me all the officers in the battalion, plus the sergeant major—*both* sergeants major—and the first sergeant for the Grenadier Company. Have them meet me in the officers' mess."

As the runner scurried off, Daniil looked at Romeyko. "Can you show me how to use this thing?"

"No," the quartermaster answered, "but *Feldwebel* Weber has been shown how by Major Brinkmann, and he knows how."

"Please, then, *Feldwebel*, show me how this works."

There's no delaying it anymore, Daniil thought, as his senior leadership tramped into the officers' mess, lit by half a dozen flickering oil lamps. *Now we're going to have to do the sorting, and the commanders of First, Second, and Third companies are going to be crying fit to put them on stage as damsels in distress at what they're going to have to give up.*

"Gentlemen," Daniil began, "let's talk reorganization and assignments. Cherimisov, you first. What parts of the Grenadier Company are filled?"

"Just half the headquarters, the platoon leaders and platoon sergeants, the snipers, the Lewis gunners, and the flamethrower men from the engineers. Comes to sixteen men in total."

"Okay. You're going to be filled up to your full complement before we leave here. First Company; Baluyev?"

"I'm overstrength, sir, as you know."

"Yes, I know. Everyone is. Now nominate two medics, four pioneers, one of them a corporal or sergeant, and two signalers."

"'I expected this, but not so soon,'" Baluyev quoted a graveyard joke. He began listing names but stopped after Cherimisov began violently shaking his head "no."

"No, Lieutenant," the Fourth (Grenadier) Company commander said, "two *good* medics, not two castoffs."

Oh, well, it was worth a try. With a sigh and a grimace, Baluyev asked, "Corporal Kosyakin and Shulepov good enough for you?"

"They'll do," Cherimisov agreed. "Keep going."

Baluyev began calling off names, about two thirds of which were accepted. Finally, he gave up the last couple.

Cherimisov nodded his acceptance at Kostyshakov, who said, "Number Two Company, your fair share would be twenty-eight riflemen and noncoms, soon to be submachine gunners, for the most part. Give them up."

Captain Dratvin, commanding Second Company, said, "I asked for volunteers. There were seventy-two out of my current strength of two hundred and thirty. I am not nominating anyone who didn't volunteer. Seventeen of those I am not going to nominate because—as God is my witness—I don't think they're quite good enough."

"Right," Kostyshakov agreed.

"Cherimisov, I've also scrambled these names. I'll call a name, and you tell me if you want him. If you don't want him, he's out of consideration. If there are less than twenty-eight names you accept, you'll have to go to the battalion commander to somehow convince him that the men you rejected in the first place were somehow good enough."

"All right," agreed Cherimisov, "with reservations."

"Lebedev."

"No."

Dratvin crossed a name off the list with a pencil. "As you prefer. Vasenkov."

Cherimisov spared a look at his first sergeant, old one-eyed Mayevsky. "Fucker never falls out. He never complains. Sure, he'll do, sir."

"All right on Vasenkov."

"Ilyukhin," Dratvin said.

Cherimisov spared a glance at Mayevsky, who said, "The boy's a coal miner's son. Brave men, they are, those who go down into the mines, never knowing when they might be buried alive. And the fucking acorn never falls far from the oak."

"Ilyukhin's fine."

"He ought to be," Dratvin said. "Zamyatin."

Again, Cherimisov spared a glance at Mayevsky, who put out his hand, palm down, and wriggled it.

"No."

"What?" demanded Dratvin. "There's nothing wrong with Zamyatin!"

"Nonetheless, I don't want him."

It was at about that time that the arguments began.

Kostyshakov stepped out into the sun, exhausted, bleary-eyed, and desperate to never again endure another such meeting.

It was, indeed, morning before Cherimisov had his necessary eighty men, plus five more overstrength in case anyone got hurt or washed out. The officers shuffled back to their own companies to give the necessary orders, while the senior noncoms puzzled over how to move people around with the minimum disruption.

Those selected, when notified, felt a mix of satisfaction and fear. Cherimisov, after all, did have a reputation. And he never *really* smiled, almost inhuman, that way, he was.

Range Complex, Camp Budapest

Over on Range B, the machine gun range, *Feldwebel* Weber was putting the Grenadier Company, by platoons, through weapons familiarization on their new machine pistols. It was a waste of range, since the MP18s were close quarters weapons, while Range B was well over two thousand meters deep. On the other hand, they had to shoot the things somewhere; it might as well be some place where the sound of massed automatic weapons fire wouldn't be thought unusual for anyone listening from afar.

Every man got to load—with much cursing, especially at the loading apparatus—and fire six drum magazines, 192 rounds, before moving on.

Note to self, thought Weber, *This is going to take a thousand rounds per man, maybe two thousand, before they get good at it. Will the magazines take that much beating? I'd best ask Major Brinkmann about finding another six hundred or so.*

From there, they rotated to the Range V, the grenade range, where each man threw two live grenades at close range and then fired their American-made M1911s. This was done under Lieutenant Federov's and Sergeant Major Nenonen's tutelage.

The pistols were actually more of a challenge than the MP18s had been. While the machine pistols were, broadly speaking, close to a rifle in terms of feel, weight, and handling, hence all the men had a fair idea of how to go about it, almost none of the enlisted men had more than seen a pistol. Thus, what was intended to be a quick refresher turned out to be a half day course.

Worst were the ones who were simply terrified of firing a pistol, and there were three of those. Nenonen or Federov had to stand next to these, gently coaching them through every step and every shot.

And I don't think I will ever forget Dudnik, squeezing off the rounds with tears of abject terror coursing down his face. Though, on the plus side, terrified or not he didn't quit.

And it's not enough, mourned Nenonen. *They need another two days, and then more every week until we set off.*

It is beyond idiotic, Nenonen thought, watching First Platoon march off to the G ranges, *to issue each man two incompatible weapons, a nine millimeter machine pistol and an eleven-millimeter semi-automatic pistol. And I'd complain about it, I would, if I thought we had the slightest choice at this point. Still, I foresee problems.*

On the other hand, to be fair, that big American pistol's eleven-millimeter-plus bullet will put someone on his ass a lot more readily than a nine millimeter will, unless, as with the machine pistols, you hit him a couple of times. So maybe it makes some sense, if not logistic sense.

As Federov and Nenonen finished with one platoon of twenty-six men, including supernumeraries, they were sent over to the G Ranges and Captain Cherimisov, who would explain to them the drill he and Mayevsky had worked out for room clearance.

The G ranges—of which there were four of increasing size and complexity, plus non-firing, above ground buildings—were all for building clearing and noncombatant rescue. In the case of G1a1, what that meant was a one room shack with mostly open walls, one of four, above ground, in which squads could run through room clearing drills, in full light, without live ammunition, before descending into the underground room, G1, where they would practice with live ammunition.

Cherimisov waited until the entire platoon was seated, then began, "The first sergeant and I, with considerable input from the battalion commander, have spent a lot of time and expended a lot of thought on how to do this. By this point in time, everyone knows how to go into a building or bunker and clear it, leaving no one alive."

The captain scowled. "That's not our problem. It's not a tenth of our problem. Oh, no; *we* have to go into a strange building, and kill some of the people inside, while not harming a hair on the head of any of the others. Moreover, the people we're supposed to kill, once they realize what's going on, are going to stop trying to kill us, and put their efforts into killing the people we're trying to rescue. And if we fail to get the people we're supposed to rescue out, alive and to safety, we will have failed. Miserably."

Cherimisov gave the platoon a not quite smile. "It gets worse and harder. Because the enemy will try to move, or just go ahead and kill, the people we intend to rescue . . . hmmm . . . why don't I stop being indirect with my terminology here? The enemy are the Bolsheviks, and I'll call them that from now on. The people we're trying to save? You already know this; the 'people we're supposed to rescue' are the royal family, the Romanovs, tsar, tsarina, tsarevich, and the four grand duchesses, Olga, Tatiana, Maria, and Anastasia. We have no particular idea at this point what any of the Bolsheviks look like, but you will all be studying pictures of the Romanovs *diligently*. Why? Why because if we have a choice between saving some maid or footman, on the one hand, or one of the Romanovs, on the other, the maid or footman lose.

"Remember, that value judgment is implicit in our oaths.

"So, where was I? Oh, yes; the Bolsheviks, with any warning at all, will try to move the Romanovs, if they can, or kill them, if they feel they must.

"From there we can infer several principles we must follow. One is surprise, which comes in several forms. First is strategic or operational surprise; we cannot let them know we're coming. The second is tactical surprise; when and where we hit"—Cherimisov slapped the back of the fingers of his right hand into the palm of his left—"it must be as a bolt from the blue. The third is technical surprise; the detailed manner in which we assault must be something so new to the Bolsheviks that they are shocked as nearly into passivity as possible."

Cherimisov held up his left hand again, displaying his rather rare wristwatch. He tapped a finger against the crystal of the watch, saying as he did so, "Our second principle is speed. Every advantage we gain from surprise is fleeting. The longer we are in the area where the royal family is being held, the greater the chance we'll be spotted. The longer it takes us to clear a room, the greater the chance one of the Bolsheviks will recover his presence of mind sufficiently to shoot the tsarevich.

"Oh, and by the way, the tsarevich is a bleeder. He will probably not survive even a flesh wound. If it ever comes down to you or him—or me—we must stand in front of him and take the bullet. We'll have a chance, at least, of saving one of us.

"Our third principle is violence. We attack, attack, attack continuously, until the Romanovs are secure. We take no prisoners—no, not even if they try to surrender; every Bolshevik must be not only shot down without hesitation or compunction, but should be reshot once he's down, to make sure.

"And, finally, we must be able to discriminate. I mentioned you will study the Romanovs. That's not going to be all that helpful, for most circumstances. One thing we'll have going for us is clothing. *Probably* most or all of the Romanovs, when we go in, will be in their nightclothes. These will probably be white or, at least, light in color. Probably the most dangerous Bolsheviks will be the ones on guard duty; they can be expected to be wearing some kind of uniform, no different from the ones you lot are wearing. Five of the seven Romanovs—the women—should have long hair. We won't shoot people with long hair until we can examine them more closely.

"We'll have a couple of things going for us, with regards to discrimination. One will be the flash grenades, that will blind anyone in any room where they're used. Couple these to the dynamo lights you will be issued in a few moments. These you will wear on your chests, and activate just before entry. By their light, no great shakes but better than nothing, you will be able to see somewhat, while the Bolsheviks—oh, and the Romanovs, too—won't be seeing much of anything. Secondly, we're going to try to get the Romanovs to help us distinguish them.

"The entire family speaks English. So I want to you repeat after me, 'Romanovs get down!' Do it."

After a chorus of barely intelligible attempts at that, Cherimisov decided, "We're going to have to work on that one. A lot.

"All right now; everyone on your feet. Line up to draw

dynamo lights, then the first sergeant and I will talk you through the room entry and clearing drill."

Mayevsky lined up the First Squad of the First Platoon, six men, in three dyads, front to back. The rest of the platoon clustered round in a semicircle.

"This," he said, "is your standard formation for assaulting and clearing a room. Now listen carefully, shitheads; the way this is to be done is that the first pair have their machine pistols ready, the second pair are prepared to throw flash bombs, and the third pair stand by, but also have their machine pistols ready.

"Step one; kick the door open . . . Well, what the fuck are you waiting for; kick the door open!"

The front pair, consisting of the squad leader and one guardsman, looked at each other blankly.

"Oh, for fuck's sake," said Mayevsky. "This should be obvious even to you half-witted shitheels, the one who kicks is the one on the side of the door where the doorknob is. Now kick the door!"

The squad leader did kick it. The door opened violently.

"Step two, which should happen as soon as the door is open, is that the second pair pull the detonation cords on their grenades and throw them through the door. Man on the right throws gently, just hard enough to get it inside. Man on the left throws to hit a far wall. As soon as the grenades are thrown, they announce 'Flash!' and everybody closes their eyes and looks away, too.

"Okay, second pair, the door is open, do your part."

That was satisfyingly quicker; the grenades went sailing

immediately, even as every man closed his eyes and looked away.

"Idiots! You forgot to announce it. Try again.

"Fine. Now everyone waits until they see the dim outlines of two flashes getting just past their eyelids. This brings us to step three, use the thumbs of your firing hands to grab the ring from the dynamo lights on your chests and give them a sharp pull down. Do that, now.

"Will wonders never cease? You managed not to fuck that step up. Now you've got about five seconds of light to clear the room. If you're both quick and accurate that's all you need."

Mayevsky then went to the door and stepped inside. "This step, the fourth one, is more fluid. First pair, come to me and go through the door."

When they got to the door, a matter of half a step, the pair bounced off each other. "Problem one, two shitheads cannot normally get through one door at the same time. So who goes first? The door kicker! He shouts, as the captain said, 'Romanovs get down!' He then enters and takes to the wall on his side. He slides along this, with his back to the wall, shooting any man standing after the order for the Romanovs to duck. He continues sliding along the wall, shooting generally in the direction of the opposite wall."

Mayevsky physically pushed the first man to do what he wanted.

"The other man in that pair goes in after the first man, slides along the other wall, the one perpendicular to the one the first man has his back against. He also shoots anyone standing.

"Now note here; we think that if a blinded Bolshevik is going to be able to orient at anything it's going to be the door. Get out of the fucking door as quickly as possible, or you might well catch a random bullet.

"The next pair does the same thing, doorkicker side first—no, stop right there, numb nuts; your back is to the wall!—then the other man after. They look low for any threats—from the base of the opposite wall towards themselves—and take them out.

"Third pair follows the same pattern, doorkicker side goes in first. They look from the middle of the floor upward..."

Mayevsky took two of the open walled shacks, while Cherimisov took the other two, including the one with the platoon leader's squad, which still had to be ready to jump in and take the place of any other. With the sun going down, it was obvious that, "No fucking way, sir; these men are not ready to advance to the live fire room below ground yet."

Cherimisov reluctantly tended to agree. "Another day, do you think, or two?"

Mayevsky shook his head, doubtfully. "Could be three or fucking four, sir. They've got the basic idea down, but—if we're reading the problem rightly—this requires clockwork precision and *that* the shitheads do not have. Also..."

"Yes?"

"Sir, I think we need an obstacle course, something to restore their coordination for the kinds of obstacles we're likely to encounter."

The captain nodded, thoughtfully. "The obstacle course is a good idea, Top; I agree. The rest? This is going to fuck up the schedule pretty badly. Here's my thoughts; let's make arrangements to send them back to Weber, Federov, and Nenonen, tomorrow, for a day's more weapons work. We can pretend that was the plan all along. Then, later tomorrow we work on Second Platoon, here. First can practice tomorrow all the time they're not actually on the ranges. Then Second goes to the weapons ranges again, and we run First through this. If they've got the precision down, we can take them down to the simple live fire room."

"Yes, sir. Makes sense to me. I'll make the arrangements."

Range G1, Camp Budapest

There was an old Russian technique, going back at least as far as Victor Suvarov in the late eighteenth century, of having the troops chant their principles of operation, which is to say, their doctrine. Thus First Platoon double timed to the range chanting, "Surprise . . . speed . . . violence . . . discrimination . . . surprise . . . speed . . . violence . . . discrimination . . . surprise . . . "

Mayevsky met the platoon by the entrance to Range G1—a pair of uprights and a crosspiece with the name emblazoned—and then, in a flurry of pointing arms said, "First squad . . . Second . . . Third . . . headquarters! Medic; your ass stays with me. The rest; form up at the doors to your buildings and stand by to assault on my order or the captain's."

❖ ❖ ❖

The first squad to actually convince Cherimisov and Mayevsky that they were up to executing the simplest room clearing problem with live ammunition was Second Squad, under Sergeant Yumachev. They moved from the open walled shed down to the ramp leading to the underground room. This was an open excavation—whatever else might be said of the Russian soldier, he could *dig*—about twelve by fifteen feet, covered with logs and the logs then covered with dirt. The sides had also been revetted with split logs, or it would likely have collapsed before they were done with it. The door was hung on nailed canvas hinges, which allowed it to be turned around and upside down to change the position of the knob. For this run, however, the knob was on the left hand side, just as they were for the open shacks, above.

There was canvas laid over the top of the ramp leading down, to give the mens' eyes a chance to adjust to the darkness they could expect in the room and when they executed the actual mission, presumed to be at night.

Inside, three dark painted wooden targets waited, erect, along with two narrower white painted ones on the dirt floor. None of these were anything much, solid but thin wood held up by very thin sticks. A bullet strike should put them down.

One final word Cherimisov said, before giving the order to go, "You've heard this before but it can't hurt any if I repeat it; if I or anyone calls 'cease fire,' you are to immediately take your fingers off the triggers, pull and lock the bolt of your machine pistols to the rear, remove the magazine, then clear the chamber. Are we clear on this?"

"Yessir, yes, sir, yessirir, yes," came the answer.

He looked over the group. Sergeant Yumachev looked ready to kick the door. To his right, tensed like a wound spring and quivering with anticipation like a racehorse in the gate, stood Sobchak. Behind those two, Guardsmen Yurin and Ilyukhin gripped flash grenades and the pull cords. The grenades were the real article this time. Both had their machine pistols hanging from cords over their left shoulders. In the rear, Sotnikov on the left and Corporal Poda on the right held their MP18s muzzle-up by one hand, the thumbs of the others in the pull rings of their dynamo lights.

We need, thought the captain, *to tie cords from the weapons to the dynamo lights so they can pull them without ever giving up control. Discuss with Top, this evening.*

"Stand by," said Cherimisov, "make ready . . . two . . . three. . . . GO!"

Yumachev's foot lashed out, practically ripping the door from its hinges. As soon as it was out of the way, Yurin and Ilyukhin pulled the porcelain beads attached to the cords, and threw. Both threw to the far wall, which was not to plan.

"Flash! Flash!"

Every man closed his eyes and looked away. There was, however, only a single *boom.*

"Cease fire!" Cherimisov ordered. *Fuck! Defective grenade. It would have to be early on, wouldn't it? Couldn't be the last try of the day; oh, no, that would never do. Now we have to wait half an hour. Double fuck.*

✢ ✢ ✢

The defective grenade not being their fault, Yumachev's men didn't lose their place in the order of march. Instead, with the defective grenade dragged outside with a grappling iron on a rope, and new grenades issued, the six of them once again stood in three ranks of two, ready to clear the room.

Once again the captain said, "Stand by . . . make ready . . . two . . . three. . . . GO!"

The door flew open under the shock of Yumachev's boot. The first and second man in the stack each pulled the porcelain bead on their grenades, then flung them through the door.

"Flash! Flash!"

And there were two great flashes, following two smaller booms.

Yumachev opened his eyes and looked up. His right thumb pulled the lanyard of the dynamo light, then went back to gripping his machine pistol. The others followed suit. He stepped through the door and immediately opened fire on one of the dark targets. It went down.

As Yumachev stepped left while turning half right, keeping his back to the wall and scanning for more targets, Sobchak jumped through the door, firing. He, mirroring Yumachev, stepped right, put his back almost on the right wall, and fired again.

Unfortunately, Sobchak neglected to distinguish between a light painted target and a dark one. The target labeled "Grand Duchess Maria" fell over.

Next in was Yurin. He hadn't gotten very far before Cherimisov shouted, "Cease fire! You all forgot to shout, 'Romanovs get down!' Now clear your weapons if you already haven't, get out, and go practice that until you get it right. And tell the first sergeant to send down another squad."

Camp Budapest

"Did any members of the royal family survive?" asked Kostyshakov, that night in the officers' mess.

"Not a one, sir," Cherimisov answered, with misery in his voice.

"Is the problem with the drill we've worked out?"

The captain shook his head, slowly, answering, "I don't think so, sir. I think it's a case of needing more practice in making quick distinctions."

"You have any ideas?"

"Yes, sir, but it's going to require a lot of ammunition. We need another underground range, this one in the form of an obstacle course of a sort, but different from the above ground one we put in, with dozens of targets, some light, some dark. Maybe some we get painted with civilian features, girls' features. They have to be targets that appear very fleetingly, from odd places. It has to be confusing. And it has to make the men think quickly. And before we waste any more ammunition on something they're just not up to yet, we need to get them to perfection on distinguishing these things in an instant. And I don't want to use Range G4, the multistory complex one, because that's supposed to be a graduation exercise. Besides, the light sucks more than we'd want for this."

Kostyshakov thought about that for a few moments, chewing over the idea in silence. "No," he said, finally.

"'No?'"

"No, there's enough time to build what you want. There's not enough time to build it and run everybody through. So we'll do something different.

"I'm going to task both Second and Third Companies to build one maze each. Well . . . not really a maze; just think of a wide, deep, snaking trench. No cut and cover, we'll just dig down. The spoil we'll pile on either side as bullet stops.

"We'll put some platforms across so that the men running it can get from section to section. Then we'll have all kinds of wooden targets—some we'll paint as girls and boys—that can be moved, controlled, or released to gravity. We can move those around, too, so it remains unpredictable. Also, we can get or throw together some furniture and such to make it kind of an obstacle course.

"Let's suppose we make them four *arshins* by four, and about sixty *arshins* of trench. That's about eight cubic *arshins* per man in each of the two rifle companies. One day's digging; call it. Then another day to set up platforms and a target system.

"Then we can run every man in each of your assault platoons through three, maybe four, times a day, for three or four days, if we must."

Cherimisov thought about that. "I think that will work, as far as it goes. But I really wanted to be able to do it under limited light."

Kostyshakov tilted his head to one side, looking at Cherimisov as if the latter had suddenly grown an extra nose on his forehead. "Have you never, young captain, heard of these things called 'sunset' and 'night time'?"

Head straightening, Kostyshakov looked more closely. "When was the last time you *slept*, Cherimisov?"

No answer being forthcoming, he said, "That's about what I thought. Go to bed. I'll put the other companies to work on ranges G5 and G6."

"Yessir."

With a sketchy salute, Cherimisov stood, turned, and began to make his way from the mess to his own tent. On the way he heard several familiar voices—notably Mayevsky's and the two assault platoon sergeants— discussing the day's events. It was possible there was a slight trace of alcohol in the voices, but it could have been fatigue.

The troops will always bullshit, Cherimisov thought. *Wish we could put it to some good use. I'll just keep to myself and listen for a bit . . .*

Interlude

Tatiana: The Sewing Circle

It broke my heart, seeing Olga withdraw into herself. She had always been the most serious of us girls. How could she not be? For nine years, Mama and Papa thought she would be the future tsarina. Papa even had a decree drawn up stating that Olga would succeed him to the throne. He made her co-regent, along with Mama, should he die before Alexei reached the age of twenty-one.

Yet when Alexei had been born she'd been filled with joy. Some might say that as a child of nine she couldn't possibly understand, but they would be wrong. I remember the look on her face—the pride—when Papa made her Alexei's godmother.

She could have resented Alexei, but didn't, not even when he wouldn't listen to her, when he'd misbehave so badly that Mama would blame Olga.

As she stared out of our bedroom's window she seemed a very different person. It went beyond the melancholy woman she had grown into.

Once, she had spoken to me of the future of which she dreamed.

"I want to get married," she'd said. "To live always in the countryside, always with good people, and with no officialdom whatsoever."

I shared that dream. How it had soured.

Just the other day Olga had sat in the parlor with Mama, going through Mitya's letters. Her eyes filled with tears which she wiped away with trembling hands. I believed that she was getting better, or at least, forgetting. She still kept mostly to our room and avoided conversation. Fortunately, Anastasia was happy to fill the silence with her own chatter.

Mama seemed to be too much in her own pain—and Alexei's—to notice Olga's and for this I was grateful. There were times when I thought that Madame Hendrikova suspected, but if she did, she chose not to speak of it.

I could hear the chopping of wood and the barking of dogs down below in the courtyard as I shut the door behind me. Olga didn't seem to notice me coming in.

I knelt and reached under my bed.

"Here," I said, pulling out a small box. "Can you help me with these?"

She turned around, blinking as if she'd just realized that I was there.

I opened the box and pulled out the letters sitting within to reveal a false bottom. A good tap popped it free.

Olga looked inside and her eyes went wide. Several of Mama's brooches and earrings lay within, so tangled with each other they looked like cheap trinkets one might have thrown carelessly aside.

"Are you sure we should have these out?" she asked, glancing at the door.

"Mama wants us to sew them into our clothes. And a lot more besides these."

Chapter Fifteen

Pavel Khlynin, Red Guard, Tsaritsyn

Taganrog, Russia

The boat, while small, presented an image of order and cleanliness. It was gasoline powered, with a short stack, and lay about forty feet long by perhaps ten in beam at the waterline. A small, gray-bearded skipper stood just outside the tiny wheelhouse, arms folded and bearing a resentful and skeptical look.

"He told you I was a thief, didn't he?" queried the old man.

"What?" asked Turgenev, standing on the dock while the others unloaded the wagon. "Who?"

"My cousin, Igor," said the old skipper, pointing. "He told you I was a thief, right?"

"I don't know if he used quite those words," Turgenev answered. A quick glance at Mokrenko's nodding head affirmed that the stable master had, indeed.

"Well, I am *not* a thief. But times are hard, fuel is dear and hard to come by, both, and there are risks. That's why I charge what I do."

"Yes, you are a thief," said Igor, from the wagon, helping to hand bags down to waiting hands. His resolution not to get involved between the parties was apparently none too strong. "You charge too much."

"Do I, you horse-stinking bastard? Let's see you scrounge, beg, borrow, and steal enough gasoline to keep this boat moving, a boat, I remind you, that is about all that's keeping trade going between us and Rostov."

"Bah!" answered Igor. "You exaggerate, as always."

Mokrenko shrugged eloquently, *I have no idea what he's talking about; taking his boat to Rostov is the cheapest and most reliable way to get there. Probably also the fastest.*

"Relax, Comrade . . . ."

"Also Sabanayev, just like my asshole cousin, but Ivan in my case. But save that 'comrade' nonsense for when there are Reds around. I loathe the Reds."

For emphasis, Ivan Sabanayev spat over the side of his gently rocking boat. "Fucking godless communists bastards! Why, oh, *why*, did the Little Father abandon his people?"

"I suspect a few thousand Red bayonets pointed at the throats of his children had something to do with it," Lieutenant Babin commented.

Ivan's sad nod agreed. "It's still a terrible shame. Nor will any good come from this Bolshevik revolution. Well . . . never mind. Come; load your baggage and come aboard. You have my money, yes?"

"Yes," Turgenev, said. "Eighty rubles in gold, yes?"

"Yes, unless you want me to send my boy to go buy— well, *try* to buy—some fresh food in the market. But I can't use gold there; it's too tempting, too rare. Do you have silver or, maybe better, paper? I'll have to pay four times what it's worth in paper, mind you, but at least it doesn't attract attention."

"Can you get us a few days' worth of food?" Mokrenko asked. "Or maybe a week's worth."

Ivan thought about that. "Maybe," he answered. "The boy can try."

Turgenev tossed his own bag in, then jumped aboard and bent to dig out eight gold coins from his store. He then pulled about forty more rubles in low denomination paper from the same bag. These he handed over. On second thought, he added another two notes and requested, "See if the boy can get a *chetvert*"—a bit over a quart and a half, British—"of a decent vodka. I think everyone could use a drink at this point."

Got to love a thoughtful officer, mused Mokrenko.

"There are some newspapers, fairly recent, you can read while we wait," said Ivan.

Mouth of the Don

"I don't suppose you people are armed," queried Ivan.

"We might be," answered Turgenev. "Why?"

"Well . . . there are river pirates," said the old man. "Ordinarily, they're a lot like the Bolsheviks, just thieves, in other words. They stop my boat, take a small percentage as 'a toll,' as they phrase it. But ordinarily I don't carry passengers. Passengers mean money. And you have a girl and they're practically a medium of exchange, too."

"Sergeant Mokrenko!"

"Sir. All right you shitheads, break out the rifles and load up."

"Make a great show of the rifles," Ivan said. "Odds are good that will be enough to scare them off."

Mokrenko began posting the men of the strategic recon team around the boat, in such as businesslike way as to make it clear that trying to stop the boat would be a most bloody exercise. It must have worked, because at the points where Ivan tensed up, as if expecting trouble, no trouble materialized.

"You know," said Ivan, after passing the second place where he'd been expecting the river pirates to sortie out to take their "toll," "for another fifty *gold* rubles I'll take you almost all the way to Tsaritsyn."

"Define 'almost' and tell me how long it would take," said Lieutenant Turgenev.

"About forty *versta away*," Ivan replied, "and maybe three or four days. Nearest point is the town of Kalach, almost exactly west of Tsaritsyn."

"Probably more secure than taking the train, sir," Mokrenko said.

Turgenev nodded, but then said, "We don't have the time to spare anymore, though. We're five days behind where we should be, with no guarantees that we won't fall further behind. No thanks, old man, but no. We need to hop a train."

"It's none of my business," said Ivan, "but, if you don't mind my asking, what's your hurry?"

"We do mind, though," said Mokrenko.

Rostov-on-Don, Russia

The town was still occupied by German and Austrian soldiery, courtesy of Trotsky's silly notions about "neither war nor peace." The two armies, under the direction of Max Hoffmann, had demonstrated that the Bolsheviks didn't have the initiative Trotsky presumably thought. Still, they'd be going home, eventually.

The party had split up into four pairs and a trio, intending to stay away from each other until such time as they were past the chance of inviting close interest from the German and Austrian soldiery that seemed to be everywhere in the town, and nowhere so much as at the riverfront and the train station. The problem was security, not so much physical but in terms of safeguarding information about their mission.

People just talk too damned much, thought Turgenev. *Best to stay away from any of them.*

He did, of course, have a passport letter from Hoffmann himself, but that was for ultimate extremities, which this was not. And using it was bound to cause some ripples, unfortunate ones, somewhere down the line.

There are two decent ways to do this, thought Turgenev. *One is blending in with the other passengers and the other is not being seen at all.* He thought the other was the better of the two.

Thus, currently, Mokrenko and Shukhov, the engineer, were off at the marshalling yard, trying to bribe the group passage aboard one of the freight cars.

And the downside of that, thought Turgenev, *is that freight cars are generally unheated. Oh, well, we brought plenty of blankets . . .*

The Russian running the rail yard was accompanied by two Russian-speaking soldiers, one Austrian, one German. The Austrian was senior, which Mokrenko took for a good sign, since they were almost always easier to deal with than were the far more anal-retentive Huns.

"What I don't understand," said the Austrian, a Major Leitner, beefy and florid-faced, but friendly enough, "is why don't you just book a normal set of passenger seats and enjoy the ride. Do you know how *cold* those freight cars can be?"

"Once we get past your lines, Major," Mokrenko said, "we're getting into the beginnings of a civil war. Both sides may well be conscripting whoever they can get their hands on. Frankly, we've already all been conscripted for one war more than we cared to be in, in the first place. We just want to hide until we get close to home, and then disappear to our villages and towns."

Leitner looked at the Russian.

"I don't mind giving some discharged soldiers a hand getting home," the Russian said. "And they're right about the civil war that's coming, even though nobody's interfering with the movement of trains. But I'm going to have to bribe the passenger section to forget about their lost revenue."

"We got a decent discharge pay," Mokrenko lied. He was normally quite honest, but mission took priority when it was a mission of this importance. "We'll gladly pay the difference."

"All right," said the Russian. "How many did you say there were?"

"Eleven," Mokrenko replied, "but one's not a soldier, just a girl who lost her parents and who's got relatives in Tsaritsyn. She's had a pretty hard time of it, the last few months, and just sort of attached herself to us as a better—above all, safer—bet than any other she'd seen."

The Russian yard master pointed, asking, "See that car over there? Fourth one from the rear of that group?"

"The group with the locomotive backing up to it?" asked Mokrenko.

"That one, yes. Get your friends and meet me there. I'll smooth things over.

"By the way," said the yard master, "when you get to Tsaritsyn? Last we've heard here, the Reds own that. If you don't want to be drafted again, I'd stay under cover until nightfall."

The steady *clack-clack-clack*ing of the train over steel tracks whispered of progress, and, for a change, at some speed.

Turgenev and the others were somewhat surprised that there wasn't so much as a single stop and search between Rostov-on-Don and Tsaritsyn. The rail line, after all, was crossing what should have been the front line between hostile armies.

Lieutenant Babin, who had decided to join the group and commit himself to its mission, had the answer to that, when Turgenev brought it up. "Our army has collapsed completely. There are no security checks because there is no front line. Indeed, the most powerful non-Bolshevik Russian military organization within thirty or forty *versta* is probably us. It may be different once we get to Tsaritsyn.

"Until we do, though, and if we don't want to freeze to death, I strongly suggest we bundle up."

Railroad station, Tsaritsyn, Russia

"I have never," whispered Sarnof, the signaler, "not ever in my life, been so fucking cold."

Natalya Sorokina nodded vigorous agreement. At least it allowed her to quietly move a couple of muscles to generate a tiny bit of extra body heat.

"Okay," Lieutenant Turgenev said, "I'm going to go out and do a little bit of reconnaissance . . . Sergeant Mokrenko—"

"No, sir."

"What?"

"Sir, you're the worst possible candidate to send out alone—and it will be worse in company—to recon a Red-held area. Every move you make proclaims your aristocratic background. You couldn't act like a peasant if your *life* depended on it, which, in this case, it does. Ours do, too. Moreover, if you take someone with you, the habits of a lifetime will show. He'll defer and you'll act like you expect that deference.

"So, in short, if you have two brain cells to rub together, you'll stay right here. *I'll* go."

"Am I that obvious, really?" Turgenev asked, before admitting, "Oh, I suppose I am. Fine, Sergeant, you go and take two men with you. Let me dig you out some money; maybe you can get us some more clothes if it looks like they'll be useful. Hmmm . . . you might have to stay out overnight, so a bit for an inn, too."

"What if I can openly buy tickets?" Mokrenko asked.

"Good point, let me dig you out some gold rubles and more paper . . ."

The station was an early version of, perhaps even a predecessor of, Belle Epoch architecture, with onion domes compressed into octagons bedecking the roof and replete with pilasters on all sides.

The first thing Mokrenko discovered, on passing into the station, was, *We'll blend in better in our uniforms, provided we make them look scruffy, than we would in any civilian clothes. And we can be armed, as well, without inciting any curiosity. Now the question is, should we put on those red armbands some of the men are sporting or not?*

Leaving his two escorts, Shukhov and Timashuk, the medic, he walked up to one uniformed sort, a rather young and fierce looking man, and introduced himself, receiving, in reply, "Pavel Nadimovich Khlynin, at your service. You look to be a soldier, but from a worker's or peasant's background, yes?"

"Even so," Mokrenko agreed. "I'm just back from the front, such as it is, Pavel Nadimovich. I need to get back home to Yekaterinburg. I've got a few friends with me, too, from the same area. Once I've made sure my mother and father are alive and well, I hope to be joining the Red Guards."

A measure of the fierceness disappeared to be replaced by a warm smile. "A noble ambition that is, Rostislav Alexandrovich, and Yekaterinburg would be a good place to do it, since it is, by all accounts, firmly in the hand of the revolution."

"That is excellent news," Mokrenko replied, "most excellent." He made a show of looking around, then more closely at Khlynin's armband, and asked, "The armbands; are they just a show of support or a sign of enlistment in the revolution?"

"Good question, Comrade. Frankly, it's not entirely clear to me which is the case. I see my comrades in the Red Guards sporting them. I see filthy capitalist and aristocratic robbers sporting them. I see people I am pretty sure just want to be left alone sporting them. I see people who support the revolution sporting them. And I see people who do not support the revolution sporting them. At this point, all they really mean is, 'I am not an active enemy of the revolution, so don't shoot me.'"

"I see," said Mokrenko. "Well . . . is there a good place to buy some?"

Khlynin pointed in the direction across the street from the station, then let his fingers paint a simple map in the air. "Over there, take a left and around the corner; you can't miss it."

"Thank you, Pavel Nadimovich. For all your help,"— *and in the supposition that I can pump you for more information*—"can I buy you a drink or two?"

"Thanks for the offer, Rostislav Alexandrovich, but I am on duty . . . for . . . about another half hour."

"I thank you, my friend. We'll be back in half an hour, then. Now to go buy some markers of our show of support for the revolution, until we are placed to actively support it. Comrades, with me."

With which words Mokrenko led the way out of the station and across the street to purchase one short of a dozen red armbands.

The tavern wasn't much. The vodka wasn't anything special, either. A drink turned into two, two into three, and three into a somewhat sodden Red Guard named Khlynin explaining everything he understood about the situation to date.

"In the first place, Rosti"—with a sufficiency of drink went a good deal of formality—"while everyone is picking sides and recruiting furiously, the trains all run as if there were no conflict at all. It's almost completely inexplicable to an outsider but I think they'll continue to do so. Food and coal, after all, must still get to the cities, coal to the small villages, and food to the coalfields. It's in everyone's interest to let them keep flowing.

"The most I can safely predict is that recruits for the revolution will not be allowed to move by train from White areas and vice versa, while each side will have to make do with whatever arms and equipment they can make or import into their own areas."

"A strange thought," said Mokrenko. "It's as if we had kept up trade with the Germans even while fighting them."

"It could be so," Khlynin agreed. "I don't know. I worked the railways, myself—still do, after a fashion—so I was exempt from conscription. I confess, the guilt of this . . ."

"Don't feel guilty," Mokrenko said. "You didn't miss a thing. It was years of unending misery, failure, incompetence at the highest levels, bad food, clothing that, when it wore out, was always replaced by something cheaper and worse, and in the end, for nothing at all.

"I will say one thing, though; if you haven't married yet you should have. So many men killed that even the best-looking women will be there for the choosing."

Khlynin smiled a little drunkenly. "Now that much I can admit to. But with so many lovely blue- and dark-eyed girls, how can one choose between them?"

"For me," interjected Timashuk, "there's one girl. I haven't had a letter in a while, but the last letter I got she said she'd wait until the gates of hell itself froze, if that's how long it took."

"If true," said Khlynin, "she is a pearl of great worth. You must get home to her. Where is she from?"

"Tver," said Timashuk, "or, rather, a small village not too far from there . . ."

Instantly, Mokrenko's foot lashed out under the rough hewn table.

"But she moved to Yekaterinburg with her family,

about four years ago," Timashuk hastily corrected. "So that's where I'm going."

"Ah, Tver," mused Khlynin. "I have heard the women are of surpassing beauty there."

"It is so," said Timashuk. "And so many that even a small and none too well-favored boy like me can find a prize among them."

Mokrenko refilled Khlynin's glass from a bottle provided by the bartender. "So who, if we need help with the rails, should we talk to in Samara?"

Train to Samara, Russia

The sun was still up, lighting the broad fields of wheat and rye to the west and, past the train's own shadows, the mighty Volga to the east.

"And it was *that* easy?" said Turgenev, in wonder, for about the fifteenth time. The paper he'd been scanning for news of the tsar and his family he laid aside for a bit. "You just walk up, get the info, get the armbands, get the train tickets, and nobody says a cross word or suspects a thing?

"You were right, Sergeant Mokrenko; I'd have aroused suspicion, more likely than not, whether by my preparatory school accent or more subtle parts of my manner. Which makes me wonder..."

"Sir?" asked Mokrenko.

"It makes me wonder if I should even be here, if I'm that much of a liability."

"You'll earn your keep, sir, once we get where we're going and have to start figuring things out. Note, too, that I was only able to get us passage as far as Samara. We're going to have to change trains at Chelyabinsk and Yekaterinburg to get to Tyumen.

"Speaking, though, sir, of your inability to hide your roots, you need to get back to first class and pump the other passengers for information as well as make sure that none of them try to take advantage of your 'sister,' Natalya."

Train to Tyumen

As it turned out, Khlynin had spoken and predicted truly. There were no official impediments to travel from *anybody*. There was a day's wait at Samara, and another two days at Chelyabinsk, but these had to do with scheduling, not interference from Reds or Whites. Moreover, they were days both well fed and comfortable, in good but not lavish hostels and inns.

They'd also spent a little time in Yekaterinburg, just long enough to determine that the prisoners being kept in one guarded house were not the royal family, but a number of lesser members of the nobility, including the tsarina's sister, the nun, Elizabeth Feodorovna, also known as Elisabeth of Hesse and by Rhine. They'd also figured out, quite quickly, that Yekaterinburg was solidly red. Finally, a purview of the various mines, banks, and other repositories suggested that a good deal of mineral wealth was sitting there for whoever managed to grab it first.

The word on the street was that the royals were in Tobolsk.

Food was, it was true, a little dear, but then, as Lieutenant Turgenev observed, "We've been living mainly off Vraciu's gold and silver since we landed near Taganrog.

Well, that and some paper currency. We've hardly touched our own gold or silver."

The problem, when it arose, wasn't from any official source of power but from the *lack* of any official source. In short, bandits did not exist only at sea and along river banks.

Passengers boarded and got off at each of the first ten stops on the line. Some looked well fed and content, others a little lean and hungry. There were men, women, children, and the odd pet among them. None looked exceptionally suspicious, and none seemed to be in groups large enough to pose a threat. Some were armed, but with discharged and deserting soldiers taking their arms with them, as often as not, this was seen as routine.

What was not routine was something that could not be seen: in this case the common purpose of some seventeen of the embarking passengers, split up among the first ten stops, and in no case numbering more than three men at any stop. They boarded, took their seats sometimes near each other and other times not, and proceeded to read, or gamble, or simply look out the windows and at the other passengers.

Mokrenko looked over the two who'd boarded together at one of the stations along the route, then taken widely separate seats in the car. They had the collars of their coats turned up, quite understandably, against the fierce and biting cold. He dismissed them as harmless and unimportant.

The train consisted of a single locomotive, a coal

tender, one first class sleeper car, a first class dining and parlor car, a second class dining car, which held the kitchen for both, six second class cars, eleven freight cars, a caboose, and a second locomotive. The caboose looked less like a North American caboose and more like the boxcar from which it had been converted. Turgenev, Babin, and Natalya had gone to first class, while Mokrenko and the other seven men of Strategic Recon took up a good deal of the forwardmost of the second-class cars.

The central portion of their light wood-paneled car boasted a pair of wood-fired heaters, steel apparently, sitting on legs themselves atop tiled sections of the floor, with more tiles behind them, and with smokestacks running up through the roof of the car. They put out a rather pleasant smell but also tended to put people to sleep.

There was electric light in first class, but second had only kerosene-fired lanterns.

The car, which was right behind the dining car, had a dozen single seats, in six pairs, facing each other, on one side. On the other were a like number of benches, likewise in six facing pairs. The seats and benches were hard, but between the hour of the night, the heat, the steady *clack-clack-clack*ing of the train on the tracks, and the fact that the eight men in them were used to discomfort, everyone but Mokrenko and Novarikasha were dead asleep, some with their heads resting on the half-tables jutting from the walls.

For that matter, both Mokrenko and Novarikasha, who had watch, found themselves nodding off and pulling themselves awake only by sheer acts of will.

The sergeant grabbed the junior man's tunic and shook him awake by it. "Stay alert for a bit. Give me your cup; I'm going to go try to get us some hot tea from the dining car."

Passage between cars promised to be bitterly, even finger threateningly, cold, so Mokrenko was careful to put on both his overcoat and his gloves. He left his sword behind, along with his rifle. His pistol was tucked into his belt, in front of his stomach, but under his tunic. However, Mokrenko being a good Cossack, his *kindjal* remained with him, hanging from his belt, and was plainly visible if his coat was open. Buttoning the coat hid it so that, when he entered the dining car, he appeared unarmed.

Moreover, as long as his coat was buttoned, he *was* unarmed; he couldn't get to his dagger or pistol in a hurry if his life depended on it. As it turned out, what with a pistol pressed against his nose as soon as he entered the dining car, his life *did* depend on it.

Of course, he noticed the pistol first. The face that was covered below the eyes by a scarf and framed above by a large *kubanka*, he didn't notice until a moment later.

"I just wanted to get some tea," he said, helplessly. "I didn't want to start a fight over it."

"Get in and sit down," snarled a voice full of desperate purpose.

"Can I get some tea on my way?"

"Just hurry." Moving farther on, presumably covered by the gun, the Cossack saw two more seated passengers, by their dress from first class, cowering pressed against the side of the car while another robber, pistol held loosely in one hand, went through the contents of their bag and wallet with the other. These had been dumped out for inspection on a table.

It was then that Mokrenko realized that both were wearing standard Imperial Army overcoats, no different from his own, and both were open. *Probably so they could get at their pistols. They're likely soldiers, too, thrown on their own wits and having no more wit than needed to rob unarmed people.*

The dining car attendant, standing behind a counter with his hands high overhead, said, "Be careful, sir; the tea is *scalding* hot."

"Yes," agreed Mokrenko, trying to keep his voice calm. *He's trying to tell me....ohhh... scalding hot, is it? Damn, though; one would be hard; two is four times harder. So how do I...?*

The one robbing those two people has his concentration on them. I only have to deal with just one, at least initially. Can't make a lot of noise. No pistol. My kindjal, then. Can I get to it in time? That's a definite maybe. Is it worth the risk? Come on, be serious; they're robbers; they'll get the money we need to complete the mission. There's no choice but to fight.

As calmly as possible, Mokrenko filled first his own army-issue cup, and then Novarikasha's.

He started to go back to his own car, when the first robber he'd encountered motioned him to take a seat in this one. Mokrenko shrugged, as if indifferent, then began to turn away. He'd made a quarter turn, then lashed back around, launching two mugs of scalding hot tea at the face of the robber.

That one's face was protected by his scarf, true, but his eyes were not. Those took the full measure of scalding tea, causing the robber to shriek, drop his pistol, and begin to claw at his eyes.

In that brief moment of respite, Mokrenko ripped his coat open, sending no less than three buttons flying across the car, one pinging off a window on the other side. In a half a second the dagger was out, just as the other thief began to turn.

Mokrenko knew he was too slow; the pistol was lining up on him before he'd been able to get a good throwing grip.

One of the passengers, a fat man with dark gray hair and beard, propelled himself at the gunman, tackling him around the midsection and driving him to his knees. The bandit's pistol fired into the ceiling, punching a minute hole in the train car.

As the bandit clubbed the struggling old man with his pistol, Mokrenko lunged for him. Grabbing a hank of his greasy hair, Mokrenko yanked the bandit's head back and plunged his razor-sharp *kindjal* into the man's neck just below his ear, then he dragged it out and downward, severing the windpipe and the neck's sinews and blood vessels in a visceral spray that left the bandit nearly decapitated.

Mokrenko then launched himself at the other one, still occupied with his own agony and in scratching his own eyes out. Two quick jabs and the robber's heart, slashed through, gave out. Blood poured from chest and mouth. But didn't yet stain the overcoat.

Only then did the Cossack turn his attention to his

savior, the old man who'd launched himself at the second robber.

A woman, presumably his wife, was already on the floor, weeping and cradling her man's head on her lap. He bled from some scalp wounds, but not so freely as to appear life-threatening.

"Will you be all right, sir?"

"Yes . . . yes, I think. Little dizzy now . . . not too bad."

"Sir, how many people entered the first-class compartment that didn't really look like they belonged there?"

"Not sure . . ."

"There were three," said the woman, through her tears. "Only three. I think . . . maybe . . . one was the leader."

"Did any of them go into the sleeper car?"

"Don't think so, no."

"Did they say anything besides some version of 'your money or your lives'?"

"That they'd be getting off at the next stop," she answered. "But why would they get off there? I've ridden this route several times, there's nothing there to speak of."

Mokrenko answered, "Horses; they'll have their horses there."

Now the question is, do I try to take the parlor car, with its three, or go back to my own car which has only two, I think, and where I can get reinforcements? Right, back it is.

Running his eyes over the two bodies, he decided that the first robber, the second he'd killed was a closer match to him in size. He took from the corpse the *kubanka* and the scarf. Then he took that robber's pistol as well as the other one's.

"Sir," he asked of the old man, "Do you think you can still shoot?"

"Poor excuse for an old soldier if I can't."

"Old soldier . . . ?"

"Colonel, retired, artillery."

"I should have known. Sir, there are two pistols. Can I leave you here, with the dining car attendant, to guard my back and keep the other robbers from passing through this car?"

"Yes," said the old man, without doubt or hesitation.

Mokrenko cast a glance at the dining car attendant.

"I'll help, yes."

"Very good. Consider yourself under the command of . . ."

"Colonel Plestov," the old man supplied.

"Thank you, sir. You will be under the command of Colonel Plestov."

With that, the Cossack put the mask over his face, pulled the *kubanka* down on his head, drew his *Amerikanski* pistol, placing it in his pocket, which barely served to cover it, and started back the way he'd come.

Freeing his own car and the bulk of his men had proven almost laughably easy. The two robbers there had barely spared him a glance and a grunt before turning back to robbing the passengers. Rostislav's pistol spoke four times, twice for each robber, and then the section had their hands down, their knives out, and were carving throats.

Timashuk, the medic, was the odd one there. He sat atop one of the thieves, his dagger lunging again and again into the dead man's chest. "Bastard! Bastard! Bastard!" the medic repeated, mindlessly.

"Stop it!" commanded Mokrenko, changing the magazine of his pistol. "We have too much to do to leave messes behind. I need three men; Koslov, you cannot be one of them. So . . . Novarikasha . . . Lavin . . . Shukhov, get your pistols . . . forget the rifles and swords.

"Koslov? Goat, you take the rest and, when I start clearing forward you start clearing back. If you can't hear it, and you probably can't, start in ten minutes. A prisoner, if you can get one. I'd prefer two but no more than two. Kill the rest."

"Yes, Sergeant. Timashuk, Visaitov, Sarnof, with me. Same order of battle for arms except take your swords."

"Use whatever you can scrounge from the dead," Mokrenko advised, "to disguise yourselves to get close to them."

"Listen up," Mokrenko told his half of the recon section, in the dining car, just on the friendly side of the door to first class. "I'm going to pull the same trick I did in our car; just walk in like I belong there and open fire without warning. I want you three to climb to the roof of the first class car, then *crawl* across it—got it, *crawl*; no footsteps on the roof—and one of you, Novarikasha, I think, to get down between it and the sleeper car. The other two continue to the locomotive. The colonel's wife didn't notice any there, but I think there must be one or two.

"Novarikasha, your signal to burst in will be either"—here, the sergeant consulted his watch—"seven minutes from my mark, or when you hear shooting or screaming. When you come in, for God's sake remember that I am going to be dressed just like the robbers. But I'll be the one with the Amerikanski pistol. And don't hit either of the officers or the girl."

"Now who's got a watch? What? Oh, shit."

Help came from an unexpected source. The old colonel offered, "Here, give them mine, Sergeant."

"No, sir; keep yours. Here . . . Lavin . . . take mine. Sir, if you would tell me when seven minutes have passed?"

"Fifteen seconds, Sergeant," said the old colonel. "Ten . . . nine . . ."

Mokrenko was already out the door. He crossed the curved open platform, above the coupler, then opened the door to the vestibule leading to first class. He instantly saw Natalya on the floor, some ruffian trying to get her clothes off as she fought back fiercely. The other two laughed over it, even while keeping their pistols generally pointed at the two officers still seated.

Turgenev is ready to charge, even bare handed. Well . . . no need. Sorry, girl, but yours is distracted so you're lowest priority.

"You'll have to wait your turn, Sasha," said one of the robbers, "after we've had ours with the girl."

Mokrenko shrugged his indifference. He was about to pull his pistol and open fire when he heard a fusillade of shots from the direction of the locomotive. In an instant, he had his pistol out, and began blasting. One of the

obbers went down immediately, falling face forward. The
other, in confusion, turned to the louder and more recent
blast, but before he could get a shot at Mokrenko, Lavin
burst in, followed by Shukhov. He put several shots into
second robber. The third, just as he was about to get
Natalya's skirt up far enough, realized what was
happening, backed off and raised his hands.

"You can have the girl first, no problem."

Mokrenko looked at the weeping girl, looked at the
would-be rapist, and then looked at the heating stove. He
strode forward, then slapped the criminal upside the head
with his pistol.

"No, not good enough," he said to the bleeding thug.
Then he bent and grabbed the man's hair, dragging him
by it to the stove. In a moment, the air was filled with the
stench of melting and charring flesh, as well as a sizzling
sound and a very loud scream. The scream went on for a
long time, as the heat worked its way past the skin, past
the skull, and began to cook the brain underneath.

Interlude

Tatiana: An Ugly Reminder

I was helping Maria and Anastasia make use of a pa[ir] of Papa's long johns for their play without resorting [to] cutting them up and making them unusable again. As [I] contemplated the best way to keep Maria from trippin[g] while wearing them, I heard a scream.

I rushed out of the parlor and bolted upstairs as [I] prayed that no one else heard and then prayed that I b[e] the first to get back up to our room. But both Mama an[d] Papa had been upstairs and they reached Olga first.

Mama was holding on to her, rocking her back an[d] forth, barely holding up under her weight as she leane[d] into her. The look on Papa's face was full of concern, b[ut] it showed no rage. That mask of his hadn't cracked o[r] fallen apart. That's how I knew that I wasn't too late.

As soon as Olga saw me, she let go of Mama and fe[ll] into my arms.

Mama sank down into the bed, hand pressed to he[r] forehead. Coffee had become unobtainable and its lac[k] caused her horrible headaches atop the tally of ailment[s] she suffered day in and day out.

"I'm sorry," Olga whispered as she pressed her we[t] cheek into my mine. "I had a waking dream. A terribl[e] one."

"A dream?" Mama said as she continued to rub at her temples.

Papa moved to take Olga into his arms, but she flinched away. I turned, placing my body between them and pulled her head closer into mine. "It's all right. It was just a dream. You fell asleep, that's all."

I hated lying. I hated the deception. God forgive me, but it was necessary.

My own nightmares included Papa finding out that Olga had been raped. It would not only break him but I wasn't sure what he would do. He'd swallowed his pride again and again. He'd taken the "demotion" to Colonel Romanov and "Citizen" Romanov. He'd merely nodded when the soldiers had voted to get rid of epaulets in order to establish a more egalitarian, soviet system. He had considered it a great dishonor, but despite his anger, he'd done the only thing he could—wear his civilian coat over his uniform shirts so that the epaulets would remain hidden. It was a bit of defiance, but one that did not endanger us. I wasn't sure if his rage over Olga, if he'd known, could have been contained. So far, everything he'd done had been for Russia and to keep us safe.

Keeping us safe was the only thing he had left.

I'll never forget the relief that washed over me when he merely nodded, accepting the explanation of a dream. He kissed Olga and helped Mama stand.

Shock followed relief as I stood there. As soon as the door closed behind them, Olga's sobbing became a low, keening wail. Her pain washed over me and through me until I thought it would drown me. I shushed her, held her tight, told her it was going to be all right.

Eventually she let me lay her down and I found out why she remembered. Her courses had begun and the sight of blood had taken her back to that horrible night.

I wanted to do right by my dear sister and even then I had known that I could not. Such as it was, our family—and its safety—came first.

A tide of guilt washed over me as I exited the room and realized my relief at my parents' willful blindness. I was grateful that they did not see, could not, would not.

I was grateful and I hated myself.

Chapter Sixteen

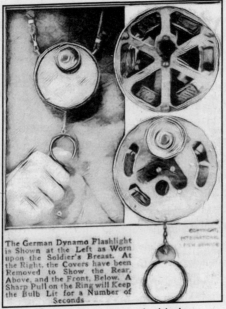

The German Dynamo Flashlight is Shown at the Left as Worn upon the Soldier's Breast. At the Right, the Covers have been Removed to Show the Rear, Above, and the Front, Below. A Sharp Pull on the Ring will Keep the Bulb Lit for a Number of Seconds

German Dynamo Flashlight

Range G5, Camp Budapest

The red range flag, warning people to watch out, flew from a stout pole raised over the range.

It had taken longer to build the new range than Kostyshakov had estimated. Indeed, the sun was already near to setting on this day before the range was ready to use.

But, then, it always takes longer than you expect it to, he thought, while standing and waiting to be the first man to go down this particular subterranean shoot-fest. *Sad, but true.*

Cherimisov had offered Daniil a guided tour, but he'd begged off. "No, I need to see it as every one of your soldiers executing it will see it; fresh and surprising. And I'll want to do it again after sunset."

Then Daniil had asked for a submachine gun and a magazine bag with six loaded magazines, holding one hundred and ninety-two rounds. He also had his pistol, his German flashlight on his chest, and his Adrian helmet on his head. Another bag with another six magazines was slung across Cherimisov, for the night rendition.

"Okay, sir," said the captain, "just stand by the window frame Second Company built. When I say 'Flash!' that will be your signal to go or to continue on to the next chamber. The rules of the game are, in the first place, shoot the ones in olive while sparing the ones in lighter colors, and in the second, get the ones in lighter colors behind you. Note that there are a couple of places where Second Company erected canvas barriers. I'll drop those at the right time. You may expect the unexpected on the other side.

"Ready, sir?"

Daniil noticed both his pulse and blood pressure rising as he took the bolt handle from the safety notch on his MP18. He replied, "Ready."

"Flash!"

Daniil hurdled the windowsill to stand on the floor of

the trench. Ahead, he saw a light painted target with what appeared to be golden curls—frayed rope—around the "head." Not a target, he knew. Overhead, walking behind and well above, Cherimisov used the toe of his right boot to lift the looped end of a rope off of a peg. Down below, instantly, a weighted target swung out from the side of the trench opposite the other target.

It took Daniil half a second to recognize another target, another half second to realize it was enemy, and then yet another half second to decide to engage. Above, Cherimisov counted aloud, "One . . . two . . ."

Daniil fired before "three," hitting the target with two of five rounds.

"Decent for a first run, sir, but you'll have to decide and engage faster—and so will the men—or you will be a very dead soldier. Mayevsky and I dry ran this thing several times, alternating playing Bolshevik. We figure you've got—maximum—a second and a half to decide and shoot. A bare second would be better and safer, though even then there's no guarantee. Also, your burst was too long. Shoot for three rounds, sir. Yes, it takes practice. Flash!"

Filled with anger—at himself, not Cherimisov or the range—Daniil moved forward and turned the sharp corner of the next section. There were two dark targets. Daniil fired at one, hitting it, then turned to the other. Once again, Cherimisov lifted a loop from a peg. This time a weighted target of an innocent swung out, half covering the remaining enemy target. Daniil couldn't just fire from the hip; he had to lift the machine pistol to his shoulder and aim.

Overhead, the captain counted, "One...two..." He got to "three..." before Daniil was able to fire at the target's head.

"We figure, sir, that pulling one of the Romanovs in front of himself, rather than shooting immediately, will take up a second or two. So, while you were slow, you weren't *that* slow. Flash!"

Breathing heavily, Daniil rounded the corner and came face to face with a blank piece of dark canvas. Above, unseen, Cherimisov toed-up another loop. The canvas fell. On the other side was a chamber full of furniture, couches, chairs, table, and a cabinet. Some pieces were real furniture, others had been tied and hammered together from thin logs. There were no targets immediately visible. Overhead a few logs crossed the trench.

Daniil saw a large rock begin to fall from the log. That distracted him enough that he missed the target half-appearing from behind a cabinet. Overhead, Cherimisov counted, "One...two...three. Sorry, you're dead, sir. You want to back up and try this again?"

"Yes, please."

Daniil went back around the sharp corner as the captain hoisted up the canvas again. "Ready...Flash!"

This time Daniil was ready. To his chagrin, however, a rock descended from near the half hidden target and, while he was engaging that, another—very small—target popped straight up from behind a chair. "One...two...three."

"Did anyone ever tell you that you are a dick, Captain Cherimisov?"

"Yes, sir. Many times. The second target would have gotten you. Ready... Flash!"

After perhaps ten minutes, an exhausted Daniil emerged from the final chamber into another but much narrower trench.

"That was... quite something," Kostyshakov said.

"Yes, sir," the captain agreed. "Can we start using it?"

"How many people can you run through in a day?"

"Maybe ten hours of adequate light, fifteen chambers, about fifteen seconds per, at full speed—but they won't make full speed right away, so call it thirty—and we can do both assault platoons, even reinforced, in maybe six hours. If the second rendition is faster than the first, as I think it will be, we can get both platoons through, twice, in one day."

"What about resetting targets behind them?"

"Mayevsky worked that out. A team follows the assaulter a couple of chambers behind, resetting the targets. Almost no delay. And we have a scheme to change the targets around so that they can't predict what will happen the second time through."

"Then start; there's no time to waste."

"Yes, sir. You feel ready to do the other one? It's not really for individuals, but for two-man teams."

"No, just show it to me. Can you start a platoon on Range G6 as soon as they finish here?"

"No, sir; in the first place, though the range is quick, it's also exhausting. In the second, I don't have enough people to run both at once. And I don't know that it would save time to stop and teach another group to run them, even if they built them. And besides, the rifle companies need their training time, too."

"Yeah . . . yeah," Daniil agreed. "That last point, in particular, is well taken. Now show me G6."

That evening, in the mess, Daniil observed to Cherimisov, "Those German dynamo lights, they really suck, don't they?"

"No, sir, not exactly," Cherimisov answered, wearing his normal serious face. "They're a lot better than nothing. But, yes, I wish they put out three times more light than they do, for three times longer. But . . . what can we do?"

"No idea. Then, too, it may be better with six lights going in a room."

"Yes, sir. Maybe, sir. Except I've tried it with six men and it's still less than ideal."

Range G6, Camp Budapest

The moon had set a little after eight-thirty in the evening. Even had it been up, as a new moon, or nearly new, it would have provided approximately zero illumination.

Everyone in both assault platoons, plus the supernumeraries, had been through Range G5 at least twice. Some had had to go through it a half dozen times before they could reliably be expected to identify and engage enemy targets, while sparing civilian ones, quickly enough to presume the enemy targets hadn't had enough time, had they been real, to kill either the soldiers of the assault platoons or the targets representing civilians.

They'd also gone, by buddy teams, through Range G6. But that was in daylight. Now they were going to do it again, as many as could be gotten through before dawn. Indeed, without tents, wrapped only in their overcoats and blankets, the men of the grenadier company lay in neat rows, sleeping until awakened by dyads to go through the range. It was darker than—as Platoon Sergeant Kostin said—"three feet up a well-digger's ass at midnight."

"Sotnikov," the platoon sergeant said, nudging the guardsman with his boot, "wake up your pal Sobchak and go report to the ready gate. Aim for the beacon fire."

"Yes, Sergeant."

Sotnikov rolled out from his blanket roll, then began to shake the man next to him. "Our turn, Sobchak. Get your gear on and let's go."

"Sure," said the other, as he likewise emerged from semi-warm bedroll into bitter, biting, icy cold. Aloud, Sobchak listed the items he donned. "Helmet . . . on head . . . magazine bag strap, over right shoulder . . . *nemetskiy* dynamo light . . . chain around neck, light in front . . . water bottle . . . over left shoulder . . . left boot . . . on . . . right boot . . . on . . . machine pistol . . . in hand . . . bolt handle in safety notch. Okay, let's go."

Wearily, the pair trudged up to the medium-sized bonfire by the ramped entrance to the range. There were two pairs ahead of them, which caused an inner groan, right up until the German mess chief handed them mugs of steaming soup.

"Keep warm," said *Feldwebel* Taenzler, in the broken Russian phrases he'd picked up since arriving in camp. "More—plenty more—if want."

"*Spasibo*," said Sobchak, echoed by Sotnikov.

"*Bitte schoen*," replied Taenzler, with a friendly smile.

He was fairly confident that all the Russians had picked up at least that much German during their time in the POW camps. *And, if not, the tone and smile surely cover it.*

As the pair nursed their soup, there were sounds of heavy but intermittent automatic fire, as well as shouted commands, coming from the other side of the fire. A couple of minutes after those ended, First Sergeant Mayevsky came back to bring another pair forward. Ten minutes later, and then it was the turn of another pair. Finally, with two more pairs waiting behind them, the first sergeant came to get them. His speech was unusually civil.

"Listen boys—Sotnikov and Sobchak, isn't it? Come over here to put your backs to the fire; you'll need all the night vision you can muster for this one.

"Now this is a lot harder than the ones you've done so far. The *nemetskiy* lights really aren't quite up to the job. So here's my advice: stay pretty close to each other. That way, neither of you will get in front enough to get shot down by your own partner. Talk; talk a *lot*. Watch out for furniture you might trip over. And here's a couple of pieces of string. Tie your machine pistols to the pull rings of the dynamo lights; it will allow you to start them up without losing any control of your weapon."

"Hey, that's clever, First Sergeant."

"It was Corporal Shabalin's idea; I can take no credit."

Mayevsky waited a couple of minutes, while the two tied the pieces of string. "Okay, are you ready?"

"Sure, Top," answered Sobchak.

"Sure," Sotnikov agreed.

"Move ahead to the first window frame and announce to the Captain who you are and that you are ready. Just

like the other ranges, he'll tell you 'Flash!' to indicate you
are to proceed. Remember to shout 'Romanovs down' in
both English and Russian before you enter any chamber.
Now, good luck."

"Thanks, First Sergeant."

Silently, then, the duo began their descent into the
earthen ramp that led down into the trench. The limited
light from the fire by the range gate ended there. There
were no sounds but those from their own footsteps. Even
that was limited by the ground, churned up by hundreds
of pairs of feet already today.

"I don't think they could have made this any creepier
if they'd tried," said Sobchak.

"What makes you think they didn't try?"

"Good point . . . Oh, shit . . ."

"What's the matter?" asked Sotnikov.

"Hit my fucking head on the . . ."

"Who's down there?" asked the voice of the captain,
unseen above.

"Sorry, sir, we misjudged how far in we were. It's
Sotnikov and Sobchak. We're ready, sir."

"All right," Cherimisov said. "Flash!"

Both men gave a tug downward on their machine
pistols, pulling the chains and causing the tiny generators
in their lights to whir to life. By the glow, limited though
it was, they could make out the window frame.

Sotnikov took up a position on the left bottom corner
of the frame, scanning ahead. He knew that the target
array for this rendition would be different from the ones
they'd engaged earlier, in daylight.

Sobchak leapt through the window frame, rolling once

on the other side before rising to one knee. His light went out before he could find a target, so he gave the MP18 another yank downward before returning the stock to his shoulder. His eyes swept left and right but saw nothing untoward. In a second or two, Sotnikov had taken a position to his left.

"Me, forward," said Sotnikov.

"Go," agreed Sobchak. Giving the light another pull with his MP18, Sotnikov walked forward warily. He heard movement ahead just as the light dimmed out. When he pulled the chain again, there was nothing there.

Was it in this section or the next one? I couldn't be sure.

Sobchak heard Sotnikov say, "Your turn." He gave the light another pull, even as Sotnikov's also sprang to life.

Overhead, the captain said, "You're awfully slow, gentlemen."

"Yes, sir. But we can't see much and I think there's something ahead of us."

Suddenly, a dark target dropped almost directly in front of Sobchak. He pulled the cord for his light and fired, hitting it several times, he thought. *Well, at this range it's hard to miss if you can see the target.*

The noise is somehow worse in the dark, thought Sotnikov. *Maybe it's the surprise.*

"Sobchak, where are you?"

"I'm set at the corner," said Sobchak. Below him, almost before he'd finished saying it, Sotnikov was peering around the same corner.

How the captain knew they were there they couldn't be sure, but he said, "Flash!" almost immediately.

"Romanovs *down*!" they both shouted, pulling the

cords to their lights and jumping out, ready to fire. In the light they saw two dark targets, to either side of the chamber, and a light-painted one in the center. Two bursts and the targets went down. They made it to just past the light-painted target before their lights died out again.

Neither Sobchak nor Sotnikov could recall how many chambers there were to the trench system of Range G6. They couldn't recall how many they'd passed through this evening. They knew they were confused. They knew they were tired. They weren't quite sure any more, each, where the other was.

The chamber was set up with three enemy targets and two friendly silhouettes. One of the enemy targets was hidden; the other two stood in the open. Likewise, both friendlies were in the open, with one farther away from the entrance to the chamber and one nearer.

Sobchak was on one knee, his MP18 sweeping left to right. He fired, once, twice, at the two enemy targets. From his position, he couldn't see the second friendly silhouette, this, quite despite pulling the cord on his dynamo light.

Sotnikov could see the second target. He also saw both enemy targets go down before there was a need for him to fire. He followed procedure—"get yourself between the Romanovs and any threat to them"—and so advanced to get on the other side of the second friendly target.

The floor was muddy here, a bit. Moreover, this was a chamber without any furniture to slow down movement.

Where the hell did Sotnikov go? wondered Sobchak. *There's no light, no shooting, nobody cursing from hitting his shins on furniture.* He was about to call out when Sotnikov lunged forward in the darkness.

There was a third target in the chamber, and it was on a trip wire. Sotnikov tripped it, causing a weight to raise it from the floor of the chamber.

Not knowing exactly where Sobchak was, at that precise moment, and trying to get on the other side of the friendly silhouette, Sotnikov lined himself up with the target and Sobchak. At that moment, when Sobchak pulled his light to life again, he only saw an enemy target. He fired.

"Sotnikov, go," said Sobchak. He received no answer. "Sotnikov!" Still nothing.

Maybe he's behind me or turned the corner into the next chamber, Sobchak thought. He called again, "Sotnikov!" and was rewarded with a low, pain-filled moan.

With a faint inkling of what had happened, Sobchak whispered, "Please, God, no," then sprinted forward, furiously pulling the cord of his light and frantically looking from side to side.

"God . . . no," he said, when he came upon Sotnikov's prone body.

"Medic!!!"

The medic, Antipov, had been following along and above with the captain, a stretcher on his shoulder. As soon as he heard the call he tossed the stretcher down into the chamber, them jumped down, following it. He was followed by the captain. The other two men, who had been following Sotnikov and Sobchak, resetting the range for the next pair, also bounded in, though from the same level.

"Put your lights on him!" Antipov exclaimed. "Let me see what I'm doing!"

Despite being in a state of shock and grief, Sobchak was the first to pull his light on. The captain and the other two followed suit.

There was blood everywhere, and a red froth coming from Sotnikov's back. When turned over, Antipov discovered he was also frothing red at the mouth.

"Oh . . . this is *so* not good," the medic muttered. "This is way past my level of skill. We need to get him to Dr. Botnikov." The medic put leather patches over the frothing exit wound and tied it off. He then flipped Sotnikov back over and did the same for the entrance wound in the back. He extended the stretcher, then asked for the others to help him get the wounded man onto it. When they had him placed, the four of them picked him up, somewhat roughly.

"This way!" Cherimisov ordered. "Shit, they were almost done. The quickest and safest way out is through the exit trench."

Almost done, Sobchak mentally echoed. *Almost done; God . . . why?*

Sotnikov died on the way out.

Camp Budapest

The mess tent was just big enough for the eighty-four remaining men of the Grenadier Company, plus Kostyshakov, Romeyko, and the sergeant major. The others could have their breakfast outside; for now, the grenadier company needed to talk.

But mostly they need to feel that this was a one-off,

thought Kostyshakov, *so they can continue to train properly*.

When asked what had happened, the most Sobchak could say was, "We lost track of each other, sir. Other than that, I have no idea of what happened."

"I think I do," said Cherimisov, who had talked extensively to Sobchak earlier in the morning. "Mostly. It was a combination of things. They lost track of each other, yes. But also the second Romanov silhouette 'called' Sotnikov to get it behind him, per our doctrine. No fault to Sotnikov. A target came up—it was automatic, on a tripwire—and blocked Sobchak's view of Sotnikov. He engaged; it was perfectly proper to have done so. Unfortunately..."

"Yes, unfortunate," echoed Kostyshakov. "Also unfortunately, we can't really change the training; not if we're to succeed in our mission. What we can do..."

He asked of the men stuffed into the mess like so many sardines, "Do you men know why we push the envelope in training, generally? Why we take risks?

"It's because unless we do things realistically, and realistically for the most dangerous environment in the universe, we cannot know if our doctrine and equipment are good enough. So what I hope to get out of this session, beyond assuring you we won't kill anyone deliberately, is fixing our doctrine and equipment. So, what can we do better?

"Sobchak, why couldn't you make out Sotnikov on the other side of the target?"

The stricken soldier answered dully, "The targets are the same color as our uniforms, sir. They're about man-sized. Their 'faces' are painted light about where our faces would be. And the light's not really good enough to make out fine distinctions."

"I think we all know about the lights. Nothing we can . . ."

"But, sir," interjected Ilyukhin, the coal miner's son, "there *are* better lights. Much better, if we can get them."

Kostyshakov made a give-forth gesture.

"Coal miners' lights, sir, carbide lamps. They're small, light, simple, reliable, cheap to operate, and put out a good deal of bright light. They're used on a lot of things, bicycles, some older automobiles."

"Well . . . *shit*," said Kostyshakov. "I never thought . . ."

From the muttering, some of it anguished, emanating from the crowd, nobody else had, either.

"Nobody did, sir. Even I didn't really think of it until this morning. But we need to be careful of which ones we try to get. The German ones tend to be bigger, heavier, overbuilt. I've never seen one you can wear on the helmet, though they may exist. The old man really liked the Amerikanski ones, especially Just-Rites and Autolites."

"I think our hosts might have trouble coming up with American lights, Ilyukhin," Cherimisov said.

"Maybe less than you might expect, sir; before the war these things were traded and sold all over the world."

"Maybe so," the captain admitted. "You said they're reliable. Are they so reliable we wouldn't need spares?"

"Not many moving parts, sir," replied Ilyukhin. "But there are things that can wear out. There's a ceramic nozzle for the gas that can wear out in cleaning it; they do put out a fair amount of soot. Also there's a felt filter inside, and a rubber gasket that keeps gas from leaking out of the chamber where the water and the carbide mix . . . well . . . mix isn't quite the right word but it will do. Sometimes the ball that controls the flow of water will wear out, and let too much water into the chamber. But on the whole, sir, if you look in an honest dictionary for the word 'reliable'? It should show a picture of a carbide miner's lamp."

"Military math, sir," said Romeyko. "Shit goes wrong. If you want one to work, you must start with more than one. If we want . . . what? Eighty-five . . . no, eighty-four, now, we need more than eighty-four to begin."

"Try for two hundred," said Kostyshakov. "And see if the Germans will get us a repair kit with a lot of spare parts of the kind that wear out."

"I'll try, sir."

"Sobchak? Sobchak? SOBCHAK!"

"What? Oh, sorry, sir, I was . . . thinking about Sotnikov. We were pretty close friends."

"I understand, but you're our only eyewitness. We need your attention here. We will have plenty of time to mourn later." *And I think maybe we need to ease you over to becoming a supernumerary and advancing one of the supernumeraries to your position.*

"Yes, sir. Sorry, sir."

"So would the light, these carbide lamps, have been enough that tonight's accident wouldn't have happened?"

"I don't think so, sir. Our uniforms still match the targets' and will match the Reds' when we go in."

"We can't do much about the enemies' uniforms. I don't know what we can do for ours."

A hand was tentatively raised.

"Yes, Fedin?"

A thin, wiry soldier stood up. "How about if we sew white cloth crucifixes on the backs of the uniforms, sir?"

"Problem there, is that when you boys are clearing a room you've mostly got your backs to walls. Don't see where a crucifix on the back . . . Sobchak?"

"It wouldn't have made any difference last night, sir. The target would have covered it up. No matter how big a cross it was, it would have been covered up."

"How about white smocks?" asked the platoon leader for Assault One, the Finn, short, pale, and blond Lieutenant Vilho Collan.

"Five hundred plus sheets," wondered Romeyko, aloud. "Or maybe six hundred. I don't know. Maybe. Oh, and a seamstress, I suppose."

"A sewing machine, Captain," said one of the junior noncoms, Corporal Shabalin. "*My* old man was a tailor. I picked up enough of it, as a boy, for this kind of thing."

"Sheets, white canvas, whatever our Teutonic hosts can come up with," said Kostyshakov. "And the important thing will be white color, not the material. And, as Shabalin says, a sewing machine."

Strelnikov, the spotter for sniper Maxim Nomonkov, said, "Sir, it's a long story but *two* sewing machines."

"Two it is," said Romeyko. "If possible."

First Sergeant Mayevsky stood up and announced himself. "Sir, how do we know a fucking room's been cleared? It hasn't happened yet, but it could happen when we go back to the G1 through G4 ranges, and it is *very* likely to happen in action, that someone infiltrates behind us through stairways we didn't know about, holes in walls the Bolshevik motherfuckers created themselves, holed ceilings and floors covered by rugs or furniture. And even if not, we'll waste time we don't have clearing rooms a second time. And what if the room being cleared a second time is occupied by some of our own people? Imagine a flash grenade going off in a room with one of the assault squads. I see a problem here, and it's not a small one."

Kostyshakov shrugged, not with indifference but with cluelessness. "I don't know, Top. Somehow I can't see us detailing one man per squad to carry around an open bucket of paint and a brush. Anyone?"

A very tall guardsman stood to his full six feet, four inches. "Lukin, sir. How about something simple, sir, like every man carries a piece of white chalk? No moving parts. It's pretty obvious and visible, or will be if Ilyukhin's lights are as good as he claims. Chalk, sir."

"Sir," asked one of the men, a Guardsman Poda, "what if there's no snow? Do we want to be wearing white smocks that will make us stand out like sore thumbs against the ground?"

Kostyshakov shot a look at Shabalin.

"Let me think over that one, sir," said the corporal.

"Not as much of a problem as all that," said Mayevsky. "If there's no snow on the ground on the approach, we take them off—they'll be thin, right?—and hide them under our uniforms. Then we put them on, a matter of a couple of seconds, before we begin the assault. Once inside, the Bolsheviks will be blinded, while we'll be able to see, so it won't matter if we're all in white."

"Shabalin," said Kostyshakov, "can you make these so they're easy and quick to get on and off, but aren't so loose they get in the way?"

"Would it be okay, sir, if they just cover down to, say, the crotch? For that matter, if we're worried about moving quickly without fouling our own legs, those overcoats could use a bit of shortening, like maybe an *arshin*'s worth. Or . . . Jesus, I'm a dummy. Take a bit but how about if I take every man's overcoat, cut it down, and then sew a white lining in it along with making some new button holes and adding some buttons?"

Kostyshakov looked up and to his left, chewing his upper lip and trying to picture it. Finally, he decided, "Romeyko?"

"Sir?"

"Add in about three thousand buttons to the request. But Shabalin?"

"Yes, sir."

"Don't remove the bottoms of the overcoats. Instead, trim them up so that they can be buttoned out of the way but let down for just standing, lying, or marching in the cold. Can we do that?"

Shabalin thought about it. "I'll need more people than just me and Strelnikov, sir. For this much work we probably could use a dozen good seamstresses."

"Romeyko?"

"I'll ask our hosts, sir."

"One other thing, sir?" asked Cherimisov.

"Yes?"

"If these miners' lamps Ilyukhin is talking about are that bright . . ."

"At night, in a place as dark as a mine, very bright, sir," said Ilyukhin.

"In that case, other than for a dress rehearsal we can probably do our live fire exercises in the day. Sir, we'd never have lost Sotnikov if I'd been able to see down into the chamber."

"Not all of them," Kostyshakov replied, "all these men still have to get used to a rescue under realistic conditions. But, yes, we can cut down the amount of nighttime work by a good bit.

"Anyone else?"

A junior noncom stood up. "Corporal Turbin, sir. We're probably going to Siberia, right? In the winter? Has anyone considered skis or snowshoes?"

Shit, thought Daniil. "Romeyko?"

"On the list, sir."

"Anyone else?"

"Poison gas . . . Big versions of those lights Ilyukhin talked about to blind those shooting at us . . . ladders that fold so we can carry them and can be fixed to climb . . . how do we get through windows in Siberia; they don't open . . . and how about an Orthodox chaplain? Men going into battle need a chaplain!"

Interlude

Tatiana: To Die or Not To Die?

Almost a year has passed since Papa abdicated the throne of Russia.

We sat in the Southeast room, sipping tea. They—the petty tyrants who run our lives—had declared that butter and coffee were luxuries we were no longer allowed to have. We accepted the restriction without complaint, yet I feared they saw it as defiance, because a few days later the soldiers' soviet decided to condemn our snow hill.

Its crime: being a source of amusement.

It was then that I realized that they were out to crush our very souls, to take away from us everything and anything that might bring us joy. Yet I knew that I could not convince my parents to act differently, to give in and show them what they wanted to see: suffering and begging.

That is what these people wanted. They wanted to see us suffer, openly and frequently. They wanted to feast on our pain and tears, to see us rip into each other, to fracture our family in every way imaginable. They wanted to take what was left of our dignity and devour it.

How empty they must be to find fulfillment in such things.

Mama passed one of the sweetmeats that the townspeople had brought us. I nibbled at it, not because I wanted to make it last, but because it left a bitter taste in my mouth.

If a hill was to be condemned for being a source of amusement, what would the empty men whose hate for us seemed to grow each week do to the kind people of Tobolsk who risked sending us eggs and other delicacies? I needed to find a way to ask Papa to turn away or discourage them, to let them know they were endangering themselves.

I got up to follow Papa and Monsieur Gilliard when they left the room, but Mama called me back to help clear the table.

A few moments later, I excused myself, pleading a need to use the bathroom and snuck to the door of Papa's study.

Whispers drifted through the door.

"There is no Bolshevik Government at Tobolsk, Your Majesty," Monsieur Gilliard said. "Kobylinsky is already on our side."

"The guards," my father objected.

"They are insolent, but careless. We should make our move before that changes."

I nodded silently. Even I had noticed this. I thought their carelessness was part of that arrogance that let them think they can run a regiment by vote, with each man deciding for himself what is and isn't acceptable. Seeing one man's sloppiness, the rest follow, for it takes effort to do one's job well, and if there's no penalty for a job poorly done, or reward for one well done, then most of them seemed to have chosen the easy way. Most, but not all.

The fanatics were motivated by their newfound ideology. They were the dangerous ones.

I held my breath in the silence, waiting, seeing in my mind's eye that heavy cloak on my father's shoulders.

"Who will help us?" my father asked. "I can't rely on good intentions."

"All we need are a few bold spirits, Your Majesty." Gilliard again, soft and uncertain.

Their voices dropped lower. I pressed my ear to the door in time to hear my father insist on two conditions. "My family must remain together. And we will not leave Russia."

I leaned my forehead against the door and closed my eyes. I waited for Monsieur Gilliard to argue against the second condition. I held my breath, and finally, in the silence, realized that he would say no more. The firmness of Papa's tone on the matter was not to be defied. Not even by someone like Monsieur Gilliard.

I pushed the door open. They turned to look at me. My cheeks and ears turned hot.

"Please, Papa. We have to leave. This is *Soviet* Russia now."

"No."

Just that. Nothing more. We stood across from each other in that room. It was a horrible breach in protocol. It was not my place, but I could not remain quiet. Not any longer.

I waited for him to rebuke me, to call me a child, to tell me to go back to helping my mother, to tell me that I had no say.

Monsieur Gilliard seemed as embarrassed as I and

perhaps it was his presence that spared me the dismissal that I deserved.

"Your mother will not leave Russia," Papa said. "Not even Soviet Russia."

I spent the next few days trying to get time alone with Mama, away from the guards, from my siblings, to beg and plead with her, but before I had a chance to say anything, fate intervened once again.

On the nineteenth of March I was cleaning up after lunch, still preoccupied with how I would get my mother alone, what I would say to her, when she said, "I would rather die in Russia than be saved by the Germans!"

She said it with such force, such power, that I dropped an empty teacup. It shattered. Apologizing, I rushed to clean it up, my heart pounding in my ears, the words, *I don't want to die*, catching unspoken in my throat.

Over the next few days I struggled, trying to understand what would make Mama want to die—want all of us to die—rather than be saved by the Germans. Wasn't it better to live, to get a chance to influence the world? Even if we did nothing but fade into obscurity, wasn't that obscure life, the one they'd always wanted, better than death?

Chapter Seventeen

The First-Class Parlor Car

Train to Tyumen, Russia

The cooked-brain corpse on the parlor car floor would serve as a reminder to the prisoners.

"I'll take care of the questioning, sir," Mokrenko assured Turgenev. "You may not care for what I'll have to do."

"After what they tried to do to Natalya," said the

lieutenant, "you can do what you like with the filthy swine. Including"—the lieutenant pointed with his chin at the brain-cooked corpse on the floor—"toasting them."

The rear door to the parlor car opened.

"Here's two of the bastards, Sergeant," announced Koslov, prodding, at bayonet point, two bound prisoners as he entered the parlor car. Goat wrinkled his nose at the stench of burnt flesh.

"The rest?"

Goat simply smiled, then drew his thumb across his throat.

"And the cost to us?"

With a deep sigh, Koslov answered, "Shukhov was shot, but Timashuk says it's not bad. He's patching him up now. But . . ."

"Yes?"

Goat gave a deep and regretful sigh. "I'm afraid to say that Visaitov didn't make it."

"I see." Mokrenko turned his attention to the two prisoners, neither of whom looked much hurt. "I've less than no reason to bear you two shits any good will. So here's what's going to happen. We're going to separate you. Can you smell that stink? That's the smell of someone's face pushed against a red hot steel stove until the face burns and then the heat cooks his brain. We're going to ask you some questions. If your answers match, then you don't get your face burnt. If they don't match, then you do. Note that there are two sides to your face, and when those are used up, you've still got arms, legs, chests, backs, feet, and genitals."

Without warning, Mokrenko kicked one of the

prisoners in the balls, causing him to give off an agonized moan before bending over and then sinking to the floor of the car.

"That's just so you know how much trouble you're in," he said, before telling Goat to, "Take the other one back to our car. We'll take care of this one. Novarikasha?"

"Yes, Sergeant?"

"You and Lavin get control of this one. I am going to ask the other one a question or two. Then I'm going to come here and ask the same question. If they don't match, faces to heaters; got it?"

"Got it, Sergeant."

With that, Mokrenko went to the second-class cabin and asked of the prisoner, "What is your name and patronymic and what is the name of the other one?"

The prisoner gulped, but answered unhesitatingly. "I am Vladimir Boroslavovich. My comrade is Stanislaus Fyodorovich."

"All right, for now." Mokrenko then went into first class and asked the same question, receiving the same answers, inverted. He then explained again, that if the answers didn't match perfectly, there would be pain.

"Now, how were you going to get away from the train after completing your robbery?"

"We have horses waiting about an hour farther up."

"How many horses? How many men?"

"Four men, twenty-four horses."

"Why the extra horses?"

"If we found a girl we wanted to keep, or if there was a substantial pay chest on the train. And for the food, of course."

He then went back to second class, asking the same series of questions. One answer was different: "Six men, twenty-seven horses."

"Cook his face for a count of five," Mokrenko commanded, then went forward again, giving the same order. When the screaming subsided, he explained, "One of you lied to me. You will both suffer for it. Face to the heater for a count of five," he ordered Novarikasha.

"Twenty-seven horses!" the prisoner blurted out. "Six men! Please don't burn me. *Please*."

"Count of five," Mokrenko repeated. The screams went on for a lot longer than five seconds.

"How will they hold the horses?" Mokrenko asked, once the screaming subsided.

"They won't," said the prisoners, through gasps and tears. "They'll be tied to a rope and that to two trees."

Mokrenko went back to second and got the exact same answer.

"Where is your camp?" he asked Vladimir.

"Not too far, maybe twelve *versta*; that's the truth."

"Do you have any captives there?"

"A dozen women, last I counted. No, wait, the chief had two for himself, so fourteen women. Well . . . some are more girls than women."

"Very good."

Back in first class the answer was substantially the same, except that Stanislaus had no trouble remembering the correct number of women and girls.

"How many men are back at the camp?" Mokrenko asked.

"Just two," Stanislaus answered. "The women and girls

et locked up when we go on foray, except to cook and . . .
vell . . . you know."

What a shitty fucking world, thought Mokrenko.

Once the robbers' rifles and pistols were passed around
to willing men who gave a reasonably convincing story of
previous shooting experience, and the Strategic Recon
section's were assembled, there were twenty-five rifles
and nine pistols manned and waiting for the word. Strat
Recon kept their pistols in their belts.

Mokrenko asked the old colonel if he'd be so kind as
to tell the locomotive's engineer and brakeman that, if
they didn't stop, he'd certainly shoot them.

"But why, Rostislav Alexandrovich?" the colonel asked.
"You can . . . ah, you don't want them to see your faces or
ask any questions?"

"Even so, sir. As a matter of fact, I'd appreciate it if you
would take complete credit for all of this, for having
tackled and shot the robbers yourself, plus organizing the
passengers."

"I don't really understand," said the colonel.

Mokrenko thought quickly, coming up with a suitable
tale. "Well, sir, the Reds have put a price on our heads. If
they have any inkling of where we are . . ."

"I see," said Plestov. "Well, I don't know how believable
it will be, but I'll try."

"I'm a much better liar than you are, dear," said the
colonel's wife. "You will be a little confused by a blow you
took to your head, so *I* will tell them in Tyumen of your
fierce courage and how you led the passengers of the train
to victory."

"Flatterer," said the colonel, a warm and loving smi[le] spreading across his face. "No wonder I've stayed with yo[u] for the last fifty-five years."

Wonderful woman, thought Mokrenko.

After Mokrenko briefed him on the situatio[n] Lieutenant Turgenev covered his face and walked th[e] length of the train, giving orders to his own men and th[e] newly armed passengers. "By order of Colonel Plesto[v,] acting commander of the train, put on as much of th[e] robbers' garb as you can. When we start to slow, open th[e] windows no matter how cold it is. As soon as we stop, rifle[s] out the side and kill anything human that looks arme[d.] Shoot the ones right in front of you, first, then look to th[e] sides. Try not to hit the horses. When the rifles go out, a[ll] unarmed civilians drop to the floor and cover your head[s.] By order of Colonel . . ."

Six men, wondered Mokrenko. *Odd that there should b[e] six men for twenty-seven horses. I'd have expected no le[ss] than seven, really. Because, after all, the robbers—th[e] mostly late robbers—didn't walk to the station where the[y] boarded from here. They must have ridden and then thes[e] six brought the horses to this stop. But there should hav[e] been seven or even eight men for this. Unless . . . .no[t,] damned, what was that breed of horse . . . the one's th[e] Tatars' cousins use? Short . . . furry . . . survive out in the ope[n] in the worst weather . . . find their own . . . ? Hmmm . . .*

Mokrenko went over to the bound robber with th[e] seared face. Kicking the man lightly, he asked, "What kin[d] of horses do you people use?"

"Yakuts," the thief answered. "Well . . . related to them anyway."

"Aha; that's the name I was trying to remember. Where did you acquire Yakuts?"

"Where else; we robbed a train that had them."

"I see."

"What's going to happen to us?"

"Probably nothing very bad, if you cooperate," Mokrenko replied. "You're going to lead us to your camp. Once we've freed your captives, I see no reason to kill you."

I also see no reason to keep you alive, either, but that's for another time.

Colonel Plestov got up and walked, slowly and carefully, to the locomotive. A few minutes later, Lieutenant Turgenev felt the train begin to slow, causing him to be pressed back into his plush seat.

Turgenev wore a mask taken from one of the thieves. His rifle, sans bayonet, had its muzzle resting on the seat opposite him. As soon as he felt the train start to slow, he reached up and unlatched the window, then opened it. After that, leaning forward, he took control of the rifle, while still being careful to keep it below the level of the windows. Up in first class only Colonel Plestov was armed, though each other car, plus the dining car and first-class sleeper car, had three or four armed men to it, each under one of the men of Strat Recon.

Turgenev didn't have much hope for accurate fire from the civilians, but at the very least, *They'll draw fire from my men. Shame about Visaitov. Can't afford to lose any more. And at least he wasn't a specialist. I don't know what we'd have done if Sarnof had been killed. Note to self, for the future any team dispatched like this must have redundancy.*

Mokrenko, standing on the small platform outside of his car, saw the horses all lashed to a single rope stretched between two trees. *Never ridden a Yakut before. Should be interesting.*

Natalya stood with him.

As soon as he caught a glimpse of the getaway party, he began to wave furiously. He also held up Natalya by one arm and shook her, to show the remaining thieves that the foray had been most fruitful. Her head hung down and her hair swished on her neck as if all the will had been beaten or raped out of her. He couldn't hear them cheering the prospect over the shrieking of the train's brakes, but he saw it well enough.

"Thanks for going along, Natalya," he said. "Good acting job. Now I'm going to pretend to throw you to the floor. As soon as I do, crawl to cover inside."

"Kill them all, Sergeant Mokrenko," she said, as soon as she was out of sight.

Mokrenko started counting and evaluating. *Only one man by the horses—his life is mine—and the other five . . . five? . . . yes, five . . . waiting roughly mid-way between the train and the horses.* He looked more carefully at the horses. *Hmmm . . . no, they're not all tied to the rope. There are two sleighs, two horses each, also.*

Before the train quite stopped he walked over to the prisoner in second class, kicking him hard enough to break ribs. The prisoner cried out, then bent over with clutched arms nursing cracked ribs.

"I told you to tell me everything. You should have mentioned the sleighs."

At that, Mokrenko went back to his window, bent, and, like Turgenev, got control of his rifle.

The train slowed . . . slowed . . . slowed . . . and finally stopped. As soon as it did, Mokrenko's rifle was the first to emerge from the open window. His shot, too, was the first. The robber nearest the horses threw up his arms and fell straight back.

As soon as that shot was heard, twenty-four more rifles opened up on the remaining five robbers. Most shots missed, of course, they always do. But few magazines were quite empty before the one hundred and fifty-odd rounds in the twenty-five magazines and chambers had felled the last of the robbers.

Immediately, all but four of the Strat Recon team charged out, followed by Babin and Natalya. The latter looked on without pity as a few shots finished off the wounded.

Moments after that, the remaining four men came out, or five, if one were to count the corpse of Visaitov, slung across the shoulders of Timashuk. They pushed ahead of them the two remaining thieves, one of whom was still bent, clutching his ribs.

The horses were a bit spooked. Instinctively, the Cossacks of the team went to calm the equines down and ensure they were all in good health.

"Fascinating beasts," said Novarikasha, gently stroking one of the Yakuts. "They've got fur at least three inches long and *thick*, and they're fat, *fat*, I say, despite this weather."

With the train still stopped, the men went back and began to unload their personal baggage, to include Visaitov's. This was carried to the two sleighs and deposited, more or less evenly. They left the rifles for the passengers who had joined the fight, but collected back the pistols and Visaitov's rifle, less the pistols previously given to the colonel and the dining car attendant.

After Mokrenko reported they were ready to move, Lieutenant Turgenev went to stand by the locomotive. He rendered Colonel Plestov a flawless salute, which was as flawlessly returned. Plestov then told the crew to continue on the journey, that he was sending the other men out to hunt down the robbers at their camp.

There wasn't a lot of discussion. "What the hell," the lieutenant said, "we're five days *ahead* of schedule now and there are fourteen women and girls enslaved and needing rescue."

And that's why I follow you, Lieutenant, thought Mokrenko. *I am probably ten times the soldier you are but you have the heart of a true and worthy gentleman.*

Natalya's thoughts, expressed rather differently, were, *I wish I could be a virgin for you. You deserve that.*

The two remaining robbers were mounted on horseback, hands bound behind them. Mokrenko was careful to tie a rope around the neck of each one, lest they decide to escape and warn the others. A few horses were tied in the string to the back of each of the sleighs. The remainder were not tied in a string, but led by five of the men of the team. Visaitov lay tied flat in the back of one of the sleighs.

"Now, you dickheads," said Mokrenko to the prisoners. "You will lead us to a covered and concealed position about half a *verst* short of your encampment. If you try any games, the ropes around your necks go over trees and your horses leave you behind, kicking and choking. Hanging's said to be a slow, hard way to die. Am I clear enough?"

When they'd reached a suitable position, Turgenev called a halt. The two prisoners were then removed from their horses and bent into C shapes, with the ropes leading from their necks being tied to their ankles. Turgenev and Mokrenko led four other men forward, leaving Natalya, Babin, Timashuk, and the wounded Shukhov to guard the horses and the prisoners.

There was a small snow-covered hill—or perhaps a snowdrift with delusions of grandeur—behind which the men with the lieutenant sheltered while he and the sergeant scoped out the encampment, perhaps one hundred *arshini* away. That consisted of half a dozen buildings, all of them made of logs, and two of them, at least, inhabitable and, based on heat shimmer above chimneys, apparently inhabited. In a fenced snowfield, a couple of dozen more of those marvelous horses hooved their way through the snow to eat the grass beneath.

"Fucking rabble," Mokrenko said.

"What was that, Sergeant?" the lieutenant asked.

"Was I speaking aloud? Shit, sir, I thought I was just

thinking it. But look, sir; there's smoke coming from two chimneys. There are people there, but no guards. Even if there are only two of them, as our prisoners said, one of them should be on guard. So, yes, fucking rabble."

"Yes, rabble," the lieutenant agreed. "Unfortunately, they're rabble with fourteen women and girls as hostage. What do you want to bet they've got two or three with them in one of those buildings, for obvious reasons, while the others are locked up in the other one? Do we want to risk the females?"

"Not if we can avoid it, sir, no."

"Then . . . we need to entice them outside. Who are the best two shots among us?"

"Myself and Lavin."

"Not counting you."

"Lavin and . . . oh, Koslov, I suppose."

"Okay, leave those two with me. Go back and mount up everyone else. Keep dressed like the train robbers. Come riding in—put Natalya on display like a great prize—and entice the two remaining out. Koslov, Lavin, and I will then shoot them, once they're away from the women."

"I kind of like that idea, sir. How much time for you to get ready?"

"We'll be ready in a couple of minutes. We'll be right here, so make sure that you and the rest are not in line between us and the remaining robbers."

"Do my best, sir."

"I know you will. Keep your pistols where you can get at them."

"Yes, sir." With that, keeping low, Mokrenko and the

rest returned to the covered and concealed position where waited the rest of the party.

The horses weren't loud and the snow and trees tended to muffle what sound there was. Mokrenko expected this, and so came in with Shukhov, disguised but otherwise prominently in front, bent but showing a bloody bandage around his midriff. Behind him rode Mokrenko himself, leading a horse on which was perched Natalya, with her hands behind her. She wasn't tied but, rather, had an unsecured coil of rope loose around them. Only one sleigh had been taken and the four remaining men of Strat Recon led only a few of the available horses.

On the way, Mokrenko passed them by where the lieutenant, Goat, and Lavin hid behind the snowdrift with delusions of grandeur. He'd already explained about leaving the three a clear field of fire.

Some things, thought the sergeant, *are just too easy. Fucking rabble.*

On cue, two men came out, only one of them armed and the other doing up his trousers with both hands. The armed one observed, "It went badly this time, eh? Well, I warned the chief, more than once . . ."

Three shots rang out in an instant, their bark preceded by the sharp snaps of near-passing thirty-caliber bullets. Two hit the armed man, one in the belly, one in the chest, laying him flat on the ground, lifeless and oozing bright blood onto the white snow. The other, *Mr. Just-Got-Finished-With-A-Girl*, as Mokrenko mentally dubbed him, was not so lucky. He took one in the throat, causing him to clutch it, hopelessly and helplessly, while blood gushed out. In mere moments, though, he, too, lay lifeless on the snow.

Mokrenko and the others dismounted, quickly. Two went for the other building from the chimney of which poured smoke, while two more, including the sergeant, drew pistols and stormed through the half open doorway.

Inside they found two women. One, an aetherially beautiful eastern Tatar or Yakut woman, or a close cousin to them, tended the fire in the masonry stove in the middle of the room. The other, young—*far too young*, thought the sergeant—clutched a fur blanket to cover her chest. He didn't think she was wearing anything underneath.

"Who are you?" asked the Tatar or Yakut girl, looking up warily.

"My name doesn't matter," the sergeant replied. "Think of me—of us—as your liberators. At least we were given to understand that you women and girls were held captive here."

"For about six months," the woman replied. "Some of us a little more, some a little less. And our captors?"

"Dead, all dead, except for two."

"And my horses?"

"Those we have. We don't need them all or, at least, not all the ones we have plus the ones in the field. We'll pay you for what we take. Why, by the way, horses? Why you?"

The lovely woman sighed sadly. "We were told the tsar was paying a good price for stout horses for the war. My father tallied up the extras we had, matched that to the price, and decided we could spare fifty. So he sent my husband and myself, with our children, west to Yekaterinburg to sell them. Our train was robbed. My husband and son killed. My daughter, like myself, was forced to become a whore for the scum who robbed us and murdered my man and boy."

"You're not a whore unless you both charge and do it willingly," Mokrenko corrected. "Even the fucking Moslems know that much. Neither you nor your daughter are whores. How much were you expecting to get from the tsar for your horses?"

"Eight hundred rubles, in gold, apiece," she said.

"I'm a little surprised the Imperial Army was willing to buy Yakut horses. They don't really meet the standards, even though I am sure they're fine animals."

"The representative who came to town said that the casualties among horses had been so high that the standard was being dropped for many of them, or there would be no new horses at all."

"That makes a certain sense," Mokrenko agreed. "It's a little high, but we can pay that for what we'll need. Up to the lieutenant, though."

"What's up to me?" asked Turgenev, coming through the door, rifle in hand.

"What we'll pay this woman for her horses. They belong to her."

"I see. Well, yes," agreed Turgenev, "of course we'll pay a fair price."

"Perhaps," said the woman, "you are our liberators, indeed." She thought for a moment, then said, "Come, there is something you must see."

"See to it, would you, Sergeant? I want to check out the other buildings."

"Sure, Sir. Lead on, Mrs. . . . ?"

"Saskulaana. That's my given name."

"Saskulaana," repeated Mokrenko, savoring the sound. *Truly, there is beauty to be found in every corner of the Earth.* "Very lovely, if you don't mind my saying so. Now what was it you wanted to show me?"

Leaving the large Russian stove, she led the sergeant over to a separate chamber, just off from the main room. It was something of a treasure trove, he noted, with stocks of fur, warm clothing, heavy cloth, tools like shovels and axes, and all manner of useful things stolen from the railroad.

"This was their chief's quarters. Mishenka was his name. I don't know his family name.

"There," she said, pointing. The object at which she pointed was a mid-sized iron safe. "No matter how hard he tried, he could never get it open."

"Where did it come from?"

"They took it from a train. I think it was heading east from Yekaterinburg."

"Indeed? Well, I have someone..."

There was something else in the room, a large pile of baggage and clothes.

"And this is?"

Saskulaana answered, "It's part of how they kept us here, when they were generally too lazy to post guards. We were allowed a single garment apiece, exchanged as needed. All of our warm clothes, though, were kept here so that it was death to escape, most of the year."

For the moment the prospect before him took Shukhov's mind off the pain of his still fresh and recently outraged bullet wound.

"If only I had some nitroglycerine," he muttered. "Well . . . make do or do without," he decided, heading to one of the sleighs to recover his mini demolitions kit.

Mokrenko accompanied the engineer because, after the miscalculation with blowing up the *Loredana,* only partially mitigated in the sergeant's mind by the fortuitous destruction of the *Kerch,* he didn't entirely trust Shukhov's abilities, demolitions-wise.

It had taken all of them, including the fourteen freed women, to both round up the horses and get them in shelter and to drag the thing on rollers out of the building, and then on sledge to a spot the engineer had picked for his first attempt at—*oh, be still, my heart*—safecracking. How much did it weigh?

I'd guess a bit over a ton, thought Turgenev, straining to move it with the rest.

"I need a pot and a good fire," Shukhov had explained. "'Why?' you ask. Because while I don't have nitroglycerin, I *do* have TNT, and it has a low melting point. Oh, and I need some fat or grease."

"Are the fumes toxic?" asked the sergeant.

"Yes, but they won't be bad outdoors if we don't go out of our way to breathe them."

Saskulaana brought one pot and a tripod in one hand and, in another, a pot with coals from the big Russian stove in the main room. Several of the other women brought armloads of wood, small enough gifts, they thought, for the men who had freed them from slavery. One girl, small and slight, brought a pot of fat, since the engineer hadn't specified how much he would need.

"Perfect, ladies, perfect," the engineer assured them. "Now go back to the building where it's warm and safe."

The safe lay on its back, door to Heaven. A close inspection told Shukhov that, *The door is tight enough to the frame to make sure the TNT stays in the crack, rather than going into the interior of the safe. This is good.*

It's also good—better than good, really—that the Germans gave me TNT rather than hexanite. I wouldn't dare try this with that toxic shit.

Carefully, using the sticks, logs, and kindling provided by the women, Shukhov nursed the coals into a fire. On this, he placed the pot, then tore the packaging from the TNT. He recognized that the letters and words on the paper packaging were in English, but whether they were American or British high explosive he couldn't say.

Free of its packaging, the two blocks of TNT were dumped into the pot.

"Sergeant," asked the engineer, "could you find us a longish twig about the width of the blasting caps?"

This wasn't especially hard to find. He broke the twig in two, dipped each in the fat, and then jammed each one at an angle into the crack between safe door and wall.

Humming, but making sure he stayed upwind of the pot, Shukhov stirred the explosive as it liquified.

Once it was a liquid, yellow and still fairly thick, he picked up the pot by the handle and, using a gloved hand, then carefully began pouring the contents to fill the crack. He could only do this on three sides, as the side by the hinges was quite tight and flush to the wall.

The liquid TNT filled the crack in a safe that was, by now, ice cold. One effect of this was that the TNT tended to freeze in the juncture of door and safe wall. This helped ensure that none of it, or so little as not to matter, would leak into the hollow of the safe even if there were a gap somewhere.

Pouring done, the engineer left things to cool while he went a distance away to prepare the blasting caps. These he held lightly in the fingers of one hand, then tapped, wrist against wrist, to ensure that there were no contaminants or debris inside. Then he laid them aside.

From his meager store of fuse, he selected a length of about two *arshins*. This he torched off with a match, counting slowly until the fuse burnt to the end. From that, he judged, *I need two—well, no, I'm slower than I would normally be, so double that—four minutes to make it to the cabin. Lots of protection in that stout log roof. So . . . I need about an* arshin *and a half per cap.*

Cutting these lengths off, and taking care to make them exactly the same length, even though they were not all that precise, one after the other the engineer fed the fuse into the caps as far as they would go. He then crimped the cap to the fuse with his fuse crimper.

Returning to the safe, Shukhov worked the twigs out, replacing them with fused blasting caps.

Picking up a burning stick from the fire, he took the fuses in hand at their very ends, then lit them.

"Time for us to go, Sergeant." After that, they began to run as quickly as the snow and his wound allowed for the shelter of the main cabin. He could feel it beginning to ooze blood again.

Interlude

Alexei: I Am a Pinocchio

Oh, no, not in the sense that my nose grows when I lie. I don't think I've told a lie, though I've kept my mouth shut, from time to time, since I was much littler than I am now. No, no; I am a Pinocchio in the sense that I cannot be a real boy, and I have no Fairy with Turquoise Hair to turn me into one. If I had one and she tapped me on the head with a magic wand, there's a decent chance I'd bleed to death.

I don't know how I'll ever become a real man, since I can't be a real boy. And if I can't be a real man, however could I have been a real tsar? So perhaps not much was lost from the revolution and my father's abdication on both our behalfs.

Certainly I'd have been more than happy—no, that's not strong enough, I'd have been so happy no one would believe it—to trade the throne for the chance to be a real boy and a real man. Unfortunately, no one ever did make, nor ever could have made, me that offer.

Though they suffer terrible anguish for it, Mama and Papa let me do more than they really want to. Indeed, I usually have to make myself refrain from doing everything I'm allowed to, since I know how much it worries them.

Still, I can do a little work, handle a sharp saw, play with my friends and my pets.

But the soldiers—the Red soldiers—shot my pets, back in our old place, and my friends have to keep from playing rough with me, in case I might get a cut or bruise. It's like people throwing chess games with my father, because he's the tsar . . . or, rather, was. Not much fun, not much of being a real boy, in that, is there?

I pray for a miracle, though I never prayed for, nor asked for help from, Rasputin. I never trusted him. And I wasn't sorry, except for Mama, when he was killed. He was no *starets*, no holy man. He was a fraud and a swindler and, though the rumors about him and Mama, or him and my sisters, were all false, it wasn't as if he didn't want them to be true. You could see it in his eyes and manners; he *definitely* wanted them to become true.

Though I believe in God, of course, I've never understood why he allowed me to be born like this. When I die, and it probably isn't all that far off, I intend to have some very cross words on the subject.

People wonder—I *know* some of Mama's friends did— how it happened that this old fraud was able, still, to create miracles where I was concerned. I have a theory; it wasn't his faith that did it; it was Mama's and Papa's faith.

Chapter Eighteen

Carbide Miner's Lamp

Parade Field, Camp Budapest

The chaplain, as it turned out, had been easy. When the Germans asked, Father Basil Seizmonov, from Burgas, had been directed by his bishop to see to their Russian co-religionists, even if they were, for the nonce, temporal enemies. Since Basil had attended seminary in Moscow and spoke excellent Russian, he'd been an obvious choice.

Now with the mass of the battalion on the parade field—less only a few Polish and Ukrainian Catholics and a couple of Finnish Lutherans, and even some of them had shown up—Father Basil began his homily.

"Today," he said, "is the Sunday of Zacchaeus, the tax collector. The questions presented by remembering this day are many. Why was Zacchaeus so determined to see our lord, Jesus Christ? Why did Christ, the pure one, not just associate with this vile person, this tax collector, but even invited Himself to the tax collector's house? What does this mean for us, we who are, all of us, sinners . . ."

Claptrap, thought Vasenkov, even as he joined the others in crossing himself, bowing, touching the Earth, and making prostrations. *One more dose of opium for the deluded masses. Fools, the lot of you.*

On the other hand, as even Vasenkov had to admit, the training regimen, so far, had been so time consuming and exhausting, both, that he hadn't had a lot of time to really think out what he was going to do.

Escape and try to warn the revolutionary government of what these Germans and their counterrevolutionary traitors are planning? How? It's a long way to Russia, and longer now—getting longer by the day—since the Germans have commenced a new offensive. I might manage to get away with one of those machine pistols, but the cadre and the Germans, both, are very damned touchy about ammunition. If I got caught with one or two rounds, maybe I could get away with it. A magazine's worth and they'd put me against a wall or chain me inside one of those room clearing chambers and use me for a live target. That bastard Cherimisov would and his lackey, Mayevsky, would be happy to put the chains around my neck.

No, I don't think I can get to the revolutionary authorities from here.

So, what do I do then? I cannot in good conscience allow them to start the counterrevolution. A bloody civil war is the last thing the Rodina *needs.*

All I can do, I suppose, is continue to play on and watch for an opportunity to sabotage them.

And as long as we're on the subject, could there be any better proof that this Christ was a charlatan than that he forgave a tax collector? I don't bloody think so . . .

As it turned out, Vasenkov wasn't the only one at services with concerns other than the divine.

Snow shoes or skis? thought Kostyshakov. *Snow shoes or skis? I've asked the senior Finns in the unit and they tell me snowshoes are a massive problem. They use different muscles and use them differently, so that someone just starting out might be laid up for a week or more with torn muscles. On the other hand, they are just as certain that they can have every man in the battalion skiing cross country, and a lot faster than they could march, in a day, two at the outside, given a little snow. And we've already got plenty of snow on the ground up in those hills to the north.*

The only thing I'm absolutely certain of is it has to be

one or the other. Booted feet would be the worst way for us to travel, once we're dropped off by the zeppelin.

I think it's in the hands of fate, really. If Romeyko can come up with skis, I'd prefer the skis. If all the Germans can find for us are snowshoes, snowshoes it will have to be.

And then there's that request for poison gas. I can certainly see the use of it. And Dr. Botnikov says we could make it ourselves with the right materials. Why bother with that, though; the Germans and Austrians have plenty and would likely lend us some.

But how would we use them? A cylinder? Oh, hell, no; the wind is far too unpredictable. There are no shells small enough for our infantry guns and, even if there were, there wouldn't be enough gas in one—or fifty—to do much good. Grenades? Similar problem with the added disadvantage that, if we did manage to get enough in one, my own people would be too close. I suppose we could take in a couple of dozen larger shells with us and put some explosive in where the fuse normally goes. But then what? We push them through a window into a basement full of Bolsheviks? What's the gas do that the high explosive wouldn't already? And if we're using high explosive alone, we can rely on the concussion in a closed space and don't need the weight of the shell.

So I think, screw it; no poison gas.

On the plus, we don't have to take two good men and put them to work making white smocks. The Germans asked the Austrians and they're providing us what we need, along with trousers. As for shortening the coats, the Germans suggest pinning them up. I think that works for me.

Meanwhile, apparently the Bulgarians mine a good deal of coal and have plenty of those carbide lamps Ilyukhin suggests. May even be here by now . . .

Quartermaster's Office, Camp Budapest

"I asked for two hundred," the rat-faced Captain Romeyko said, apologetically. "They sent me one hundred and forty. Of those, after he looked them over, Ilyukhin tells me sixty-five are good, and he might be able to fix up another forty or so from parts. To be fair, they did sent us a fair number of parts, flints, gaskets, even some reflectors and nozzles."

"How long before we have these one hundred and five, give or take?" asked Daniil.

"Three days to fix that many up, sir. I've gotten Ilyukhin a couple of helpers."

"So long? No!" Kostyshakov shook his head, emphatically. "We need those things in the hands of the assault platoons and their immediate attachments immediately. Yesterday, Sunday or not, would have been better."

Said Romeyko, "Takes a certain amount of training, the coal miner's son says, to use them safely and to get the best use out of them. And most of them still will need work."

"Okay, fine," Daniil agreed. "Today, late today, Ilyukhin trains the grenadier company to use them, as well as the officers and senior noncoms of the other three companies. Issue is to the grenadiers' assault platoons and engineers, plus the company headquarters. As he fixes more, they'll be issued to the other three."

"Why should Number One Company get any, sir? I'm not complaining, just asking."

"It's a good question, Romeyko. In the first place, because *I* want to have one. In the second, because being able to see your hands in front of you at night is useful to you, to the adjutant, to the heavy machine gun section, to the infantry gun section, and even to Kaledin, leading his horses and mules . . ."

"Okay, sir. Ummm . . . speaking of horses and mules, we have some problems."

"Oh?"

"Yes, sir. I've been working with the liaison noncom— I *think* he's a noncom—Captain Bockholt sent us, Mueller's his name, trying to figure out loads. It's tough. You want to see, sir?"

"Yeah, show me."

Romeyko pulled up a cloth to reveal a couple of chalkboards. "Sir, I started with the presumption that we've only got about nineteen tons per load. That's more than they took to Africa, and assumes we'll be able to load some heavy equipment and supplies low, to make up for ballast, plus that they'll be able to reduce fuel a good deal. It also means we'll have to land near a body of water and cut a hole in the ice for them to pump in more water for ballast. I think you knew that.

"It's also a five- or six-day round trip. That's got a couple of different implications. One is that the first troops on the ground will start eating carried rations on Landing Day minus three, and will not stop eating carried rations until maybe twenty-seven days later. That means that for every man we send in the first lift, we have to provide over eighty pounds of food. And, in this weather, that means probably one hundred pounds would be better. So our nineteen tons of lift means also that we can only carry a maximum of one hundred and thirty-nine men."

Kostyshakov looked over the calculations on the upper left hand corner of the chalkboard and said, "Okay, but . . . ?"

"But I don't think we should do it that way. Instead, we should go in as light as possible, in manpower, and carry extra food for later lifts. So, sir, I suggest that the first lift should be nothing but the Fourth Company and a small slice of your staff, no more than ten men, say. That means we can bring in an additional six tons, plus a little, of food and fodder."

"Speaking of fodder, the very last ones to come in should be Kaledin's mules and horses."

Kostyshakov held up one hand. "Stop right there. I need at least six horses to come in early, with the first lift, to mount some of the grenadier company for local security patrolling."

"Ugh," said the quartermaster. He began scribbling on the chalkboard. "That *seriously* screws up my calculations. But . . . okay, off the top of my head, six horses, about four tons, just in themselves, and then twenty-seven days of oats and hay . . . at twenty-six pounds a day, plus water for three days, at eighty pounds a day, minimum, for the three days of flight. Let me think . . . that's just under two tons for fodder, three quarters of a ton for water . . .

"Sorry, sir, but that's not doable. We need to leave behind maybe two horses, or maybe seven or eight men."

"No," said Kostyshakov. "Short the horses' fodder. We'll

bring in more with later lifts. Hmmm . . . I thought the captain said twenty-one tons of lift."

"He did, but once we figured out the modifications we would need to store the gear, the supplies, the equines, and the troops, we came up with about two tons of wood, chain, rope, buckets, and hay to spread under the horses and mules when they let go, which they will.

"Okay, sir, so we've got one lift and one company on the ground, with a half dozen horses. The next lift . . ."

The sun was still up, though it hung low in the west. The men of Fourth Company, plus another twenty from the other three companies, sat in a natural amphitheater between the camp and the ranges.

Ilyukhin had never spoken in front of a crowd before, let along one the bulk of whom outranked him. Still, he had the commander's backing, both commanders', as a matter of fact, and the courage of a coal miner to guide and guard him. If he was nervous, it was tolerably hard to see it.

"Gentlemen," he began, "oh, and you, too, Corporal Bernados, if I can have your attention."

The joke at Bernados' expense went over well, even if it was a tired joke in a dozen armies already. The engineer corporal shut up, since talking was what had made him the butt of the joke, then gave the coal miner's boy the *shish*, the Russian version—thumb between index and middle finger—of the universal, one fingered salute. This got more laughs, still.

"Now," continued Ilyukhin, "fun and games being over, if you would line up by twos and take one lamp for each two men, then return to your seat."

After each pair had taken a lamp, Ilyukhin held up one of the lamps for illustration's sake.

"There are at least four different models of lamps here. Most are Amerikanski. Some are British. Some are either locally or Russian made. A couple, even, are German. They all operate the same way and they all have similar risks. Oh, yes, there are some risks here.

"To begin with, the lamp works by combining water with calcium carbide to produce acetylene gas. The gas escapes out the nozzle of the lamp where it is set afire to produce light, which light is reflected in the shiny silver curved concave plate on front, around the nozzle."

At the word "gas," one of the senior noncoms from Second Company, Sergeant Dmitriev, began to look slightly nervous. Dmitriev was a late-caught POW, so had had the chance to be gassed by the Germans. Most of the cadre, having been caught earlier, had not had this experience, hence tended not to think about the fear of gas on the part of those who had, in fact, been gassed.

"Let's look at the parts of the lamps, shall we?

"In front, as I mentioned, is the reflector. In the middle of the reflector is the nozzle, the place where the acetylene comes out. If you look at the reflector, about halfway between its edge and the nozzle, you will see a rough, serrated wheel. That's the striker. You can't see it unless you look at the striker edge on, but there is a round flint under it that is being pushed against it by a spring.

"When the acetylene starts flowing, you can turn the striker to produce a spark to light it afire. In a bit, I'll show you an old timer's trick for that that the old man taught me.

"Look on top; you will see three things. One is the water chamber. The other is a cap that keeps the water from splashing out when it's filled. Go ahead and use your thumbs to open it.

"The last thing on top of the lamp is the control lever. This sets how much water is allowed into the calcium carbide chamber—the chamber below—to produce acetylene. All the way to the left, no water is flowing. All the way to the right, a fair stream is flowing. In between it provides less water than to the left and more than to the right. Make sure, for now, that your levers are all the way to the left."

As expected, the men didn't just make sure the levers were all the way left, nor that the water cap could be opened. Instead, they fiddled with both an average half a dozen times each. It was with difficulty that Ilyukhin controlled his exasperation at both the waste of time and the risk to the lamps.

Children; I'm in an army composed of children.

"Now hold the top piece firmly in your left hand and grasp the bottom firmly in your right. Turn the bottom piece to the right until it screws off."

Ilyukhin waited a bit, then walked around to help out those who were having trouble. To be fair, those having trouble were simply afraid to risk breaking these very unfamiliar lamps.

Returning to "center stage," the coal miner's son then said, "Go ahead and put the acetylene chamber down between you. Look now at the back of the lamp, by the water hole. Some of you have thick wire hooks there; others have flat and broad ones. Those, once we have enough to issue to everyone, are going to get forced into the slot of your helmets where the French insignia used to be. This wouldn't be enough to hold the lamps steady. Look below the hooks. See the thick wire projections coming out from the center?"

Here, Ilyukhin made a tripod from the index, middle, and ring fingers of his right hand. This he placed against the palm of his left. "It takes a tripod, you see, to get stability. Between the hook and the two prongs, a tripod will be formed, resting on and stuck in your helmets; that will keep them in place, and pointing wherever you aim your head.

"Big improvement over those pull toys we've been using, no?

"Now, a little warning; these things can leak gas from places where you don't want them to. If you look around the edge of the calcium carbide chamber you will see a rubber—or maybe in some cases thick leather— gasket. If that is defective, and you don't get a good seal of the chamber, the gas will escape and catch fire. You can burn the *shit* out of yourself, trust me, if this happens.

"Also, one nice point. When the water and calcium carbide meet, they create not just acetylene, but heat. When your hands are freezing cold, you can wrap them around the calcium carbide chamber and warm them."

Ilyukhin picked up a two-pound can of calcium carbide and opened it by prying the lid off. "I am going to pass this around. Each pair of men take about ten little pea-sized pieces and put them into the bottom chamber of your lamps. Do not screw the chambers on yet."

Ilyukhin waited while the can of calcium carbide made

its rounds. Shortly after the first row of students had taken their allocation and put it in the lower chambers, he said, "I'm now going to pass around a bucket of water and a cup. Open up and fill the water chamber of your lamps. Make sure that the control levers are all the way to the left before you do. Close the small round cover tightly as soon as you have filled it."

That took still more time. Nonetheless, the time came when the pitcher reached the last pair in the back row.

"Now here's the trick I told you about." Ilyukhin quickly screwed his chambers together. He then moved the control lever about halfway to full on. "I've now got water dripping down into the calcium carbide. Watch my hand."

He then covered the reflector with the fingers of his left hand, while holding the lamp with his right. "Note that my middle finger is resting on the striker. What is happening is that acetylene is building up in the area my fingers have sealed as it comes from the nozzle. My hand over the reflector is holding it in place. Now when I do this"—here, Ilyukhin pulled his left hand sharply away, dragging his middle finger over the striker, creating a spark that set the accumulated acetylene afire. It quickly devolved into a single bright flame, coming from the nozzle—"we have light.

"Go on and do it now," he finished.

The men screwed the lamps back together, then turned on the water flow. Sergeant Dmitriev took one sniff of the garlic aroma coming from his own plus the lamps all around him, and screamed, "GAS!!!"

Dropping the lamp before any of them but Ilyukhin's

had been set alight, Dmitriev covered his nose and mouth in the crook of his right arm, stood, and tried to run away. "GAS! GAS! GAS!"

This started a near riot as about half the others, knowing that some forms of blister agent did, indeed, give off a garlic aroma, likewise dropped their lamps and tried to run.

Kostyshakov drew his Amerikanski pistol and fired it into the air. "Freeze, Goddammit. It's NOT that kind of gas."

Fuck, thought Ilyukhin, *I should have realized.*

"It's harmless gas," the instructor said. "Yes, maybe it smells like some that are not, but *it* is. Just relax. Nobody's trying to poison or burn you. Now, gentlemen, if we may continue . . . ?"

Kostyshakov thought, *If the mere threat of being gassed can panic a fine old soldier like Dmitriev, maybe I should reconsider bringing some with us.*

Camp Budapest

There's an old army saying, common to many armies, actually, to the effect that uniforms come in two sizes, too large and too small. This was certainly true of the snow-white camouflage smocks and trousers the Austrians provided to the Germans, with no knowledge that they were to be used for Russians.

Fortunately, the Austrians produced skis—and those all fit, of course—along with the smocks. Also, fortunately, the overwhelming bulk of the smocks were too large, rather than too small.

Even with the lamps now issued and in use by the

Fourth Company and some of the leadership and specialty groups of the others, Kostyshakov had put in place and continued a moratorium on maneuvering live fire training until such time as distinctive white uniforms could be provided, to prevent another case of target misidentification.

"But time is getting short," he ordered. "Smocks and trousers that fit to the Fourth Company and the others going on the first lift. The others we'll alter as we can to make them fit."

"Skis must be fitted to the skier," said Sergeant Major Nenonen, the Finnish Operations sergeant major. "And so must the boots, as well as the boots to the skis, and each individual ski to a given foot, right or left."

The Finn found himself spending a lot more time doing things other than operations than he found strictly wise. Still, *if no one else knows how and I do, what's to be done but do it myself? And they don't, but within a couple of hours, Romeyko's clerks and the senior noncoms will have learned how to measure a man for skis and boots, and to fit the latter to the former.*

"Come right up, Top," said Nenonen to Mayevsky.

The one-eyed Fourth Company first sergeant was tall. Nenonen sized him up and said, "Put your hand straight over your head, would you, Top? . . . yes . . . call it 'three *arshin*, four inches.' " Nenonen hunted along a large number of skis, sorted by size, right to left. "Hmmm . . . these look about right. Put your hand up again, please."

Nenonen placed one ski's rear end on the ground and put the tip up to Mayevsky's hand. It just reached the first sergeant's palm. "Am I good or what? Okay, now what size boot do you wear?"

"I take a size forty-five," said Mayevsky.

"Size forty-five!" Nenonen called out to one of Romeyko's clerks, who promptly produced an Austrian ski boot.

"Looks a little goddamned big to me," said Mayevsky.

"They are. You'll end up wearing either two pair of wool socks or a double foot wrapping, because of the cold. No real need to try them on, since they *are* loose, but hold them to the bottoms of your feet to make sure they're a little big. Ah . . . yes, they'll do fine."

Nenonen drew a flathead screwdriver from his pocket. "Okay, Top, now let's fit these to your skis. Later on, I'll show you how to lacquer and wax the skis and how to attach climbing skins for uphill climbs. Also how to care for the metal edges. For now, watch closely because the next man *you* will fit yourself while I watch and critique. Oh, and, yes, let's get you a couple of pairs of real socks. They're not great socks, but they'll do for as long as we will need them . . ."

En route, Camp Budapest
to northwest of Sliven, Bulgaria

It did snow in Bulgaria but, being so far south in the Balkans, with so much moderation of climate by the nearness of sea, it didn't snow all that much. To find snow, one had to look for it. That was why Second Company, Fourth Company, and a slice of Headquarters and support were currently trekking, all in white, from their normal camp to the mountains north and west of Sliven. A fair sampling of their German guards, of course, came along too, while the best of Kaledin's patients, now fairly healthy animals, but in need of exercise, followed along, towing Taenzler's *Gulaschkanone* and wagons with tentage and rations.

As they marched, they sang:

"Soldatushki, bravyj rebjatushki,
A kto vashi otciy?
Nashi otciy—russki polkavodcyj,
Vot gde nashi otciy!

Soldatushki, bravyj rebjatushki,
A kto vashi matki?
Nashi matki—belye palatki,
Vot gde nashi matki!"[5]

It was an old song, "Soldiers, Brave Lads," of a century prior, written around the experiences, the lives, of Russian soldiers fighting Napoleon. It was also a simple song, suitable for simple soldiers. If simple, it was also buoyant and boisterous.

When the last verse of that one died out, echoing in the hills around Sliven, they broke into the "March of the Siberian Riflemen":

---

[5] Soldiers, brave lads,
  Who are your fathers?
  Our fathers are Russian commanders,
  That's who our fathers are!

  Soldiers, brave lads,
  And who are your queens?
  Our queens are white tents,
  That's who our queens are!

"From taiga, the dense taiga
From Amur, river Amur
As silent, fearsome thunder
Into battle march Siberians
As silent, fearsome thunder
Into battle march Siberians
Made them tough
Silent taiga,
Ruthless storms of Baikal
And Siberian snow.
Ruthless storms of Baikal
And Siberian snow."

Given where they were headed, the song made a certain sense. They left out the fourth verse, by common consent, since that one sang of invading Germany and Austria, reaching the Rhine and Danube. This the officers and men thought would be in very poor taste, all things considered.

They marched with their rifles and machine pistols slung, simple packs across their backs, bedrolls slung from their left shoulders to their right hips, and their newly issued skis and poles over their shoulders.

When they got close to a village, Kostyshakov called over *Feldwebel* Weber and asked if the German guards might sing something to avoid suspicion. Taenzler, overhearing, called out, *"Die Wacht am Rhein,"* since, after all, singing about defending against the French wasn't remotely anti-Russian, while singing about invading Russia would have also been in extremely poor taste.

Thus, a reborn regiment of the Russian Imperial Guards, of no name or number yet, marched through main street of the little Bulgarian village of Nicholaevo with the words ringing on the breeze and from the houses,

> "*Es braust ein Ruf wie Donnerhall*
> *Wie Schwertgeklirr und Wogenprall*
> *Zum Rhein, zum Rhein, zum deutschen Rhein . . .*"

Good-naturedly, the Russians, who had heard the song often enough in their prison camps, joined in with either words or by very loud humming or whistling. The effect was, on the whole, rather impressive.

Past the village, the Germans stopped their singing while the Russians started a new song, from another Guards regiment, one which began, "The Turks and the Swedes know us well . . ."

Setting up camp, despite the best efforts of both Russian and German noncoms, was slow and confused. The snowball fights that kept breaking out didn't speed matters up any, either.

Daniil was tempted to simply storm into the middle of it and start bellowing orders. Or at least have his sergeant major do so. But, *No, this is not a critical task and time, today, at least, isn't pressing. As long as they get it all set up sensibly that will be fine. And let them have their fun, anyway. They're good boys and have done well, so far. Hmmm. . . . maybe a little vodka?*

✠ ✠ ✠

Much to his chagrin and shame, Vasenkov found himself having a good time throwing snowballs, pitching tents, and even joking over dinner. The march had gone well, so the commander, that lackey of Tsarism, Kostyshakov, had ordered an issue of vodka for the troops. It was nothing too generous, of course, just a few ounces per man, doled out by the German, Taenzler, but it gave the entire enterprise a festive air, something free and fun.

I've never seen morale so high here, thought the hidden Bolshevik. *I suppose booze, freedom, and fresh air must be opiates of the people as much as religion is.*

Field Camp, west of Sliven, Bulgaria

"Hold the poles *loosely*, dammit," Nenonen bellowed, in a voice that threatened to cause an avalanche, to the hundreds of novice skiers struggling to move on their new skis. "Your hands will tire, gripping them like that, and then they, and *you*, will be useless. Let the loops take the force when you push off. Use your hands only for the lightest control."

Nenonen sought out Kostyshakov, who was having a smidgeon less trouble than most, and asked, "You think you're ready to take off, sir?"

"Well...lead from in front, and all that," the commander replied. "That said, let me see if I've got it straight, Sergeant Major; I push down with one ski, causing it to flatten out, and the way the hair on the climbing skins is facing, it causes it to grip the snow? The other one slides forward because the hair isn't facing that way? I use the poles a little for balance and a little to push forward, but not too much because my arms tire faster than my legs?"

"Yes, sir, and...No, goddamit!" Nenonen's voice returned to a bellow, addressing any number of the practicing troops. "I thought we had this down when you were doing one ski at a time, people; kick-glide-kick-glide!" Turning his attention back to Kostyshakov, he continued, much more sedately, "So, yes, sir. All that. Shall we see if you can make it to the base of that low hill and back?"

Back to the troops: "Angle your bodies a little forward, dumb asses! Opposite poles by your lead foot!"

With Kostyshakov seen off, to the west, Nenonen began skiing himself around the area, critiquing, giving tips, and selecting. "You, Sergeant Bogrov? You look like you're ready to head off. See the commander about halfway to the low hill? Go on and follow him there and back."

Father Basil wandered the area of the camp, talking to the troops and passing on the occasional benediction. Unlike them, he stood out by wearing his normal black cassocks and *skufia*. On two occasions he stopped to join in a snowball fight. By mid-morning, the shifting wind brought him the smell of a pretty nice stew, coming from the odd wagon with the smokestack on it. He wandered over to investigate.

"Hello, Father," said *Feldwebel* Taenzler, "Stew's almost ready; care to try some?"

"That's actually what I came to talk to you about," said the cleric. "Today is *Friday*. It's a fast day for us. So are all Wednesdays. It's not a strict fast day, insofar as the men can have oil used in preparing their meal, but no meat or fish."

Taenzler understood the problem immediately, if not in its full scope and depth. "Not even *fish*, Father? And I thought we *Catholics* were strict. But what am I to do? I've been begging, borrowing, and occasionally stealing food to put some meat on their bones. There is meat— horse meat, to be sure—in this stew. I can't just dump it; they need the nutrition, the fuel."

Father Basil considered this. With a whole continent on the verge of starvation, wasting food struck him as the greater sin, the thing more offensive in the sight of God.

"We fast more than half the year, *Feldwebel*, but... well...there *are* a lot of exemptions and exceptions. Let me think. We're are travelling, I suppose. Even if we're stopped for a couple of days. That allows some relaxation of the rules. Were you planning on feeding them before three in the afternoon? It is possible—according to Saint Isaac—to end the fast at three PM, by which time Christ's body had been taken down from the cross. And then, too, when receiving the hospitality of others, which—since you're a German, feeding Russians, this would be a case of— one doesn't turn up one's nose. You have a few Lutherans and even some Catholics among the battalion, yes? Well...a battalion is a kind of family, and when families are of mixed faiths that, too, allows some leeway. And, then, too, these men are still thin; I noticed it right off. To deprive them of food after their long captivity would be injurious to their health, and this is not permitted..."

"Father," said Taenzler, "I know some Jesuits that I would just love to listen to you talk with. I'll feed them this, as you say, today, and in the future . . . can you help me work out a menu?"

"Why, certainly, my son. I'd be happy to."

"You know, Father," said Taenzler, "the world would be a better place if more people were like you."

Basil shrugged. "The world would be a better place if more people tried to be like Christ."

"Amen, Father."

Field Camp, west of Sliven, Bulgaria

As with everything else, it took longer than it should have to get the men capable of skiing cross country on the flat. Now it was time for uphill . . . and down. Lieutenant Collan, the first platoon leader of Fourth Company and another Finn, stood in his skis on the top of the same low hill that had been the turn-around mark for the last two days. The lieutenant seemed almost unnaturally happy, standing taller, somehow, than his scant height suggested he even could.

Daniil stood at the base of the hill. Quietly, Nenonen coached him. "Remember, sir, tips wide apart and ankles folded a little towards each other and forward to ascend. The steeper the slope up, the wider apart. Tips close and ankles rolled together and back to slow yourself or, if there's a track in front of you, one ski in the track and one dragging on the outside."

"This, Sergeant Major, is not my idea of fun."

"Yes, sir, I know. But it's a lot like learning to dance with a girl. You look and feel stupid when you're first beginning, and spend every moment of the lessons embarrassed to tears ... ah, but once you learn how ...

"Now up you go, sir. And remember, poles behind you both up and down."

En route from Sliven south to Camp Budapest

There were a half dozen men, one of them, Fedin, from Fourth Company, who had to be carried in the now much-lightened wagons. These had broken legs and twisted ankles and, in one case, a fairly bad concussion from a collision with a tree. Three of those, at least three, would likely not recover in time to make even the last lift. There were enough extra men to more than cover the losses, though.

Even Vasenkov, the Bolshevik, marched with a song in his heart. *That was the most fun I've had since I was drafted, six years ago. Then again, that's a really low bar to meet.*

The Germans took over the singing again, as the battalion was passing through a Bulgarian village. This was the first chance since starting out that Vasenkov had actually had a chance to think. He didn't like what he was thinking.

I am a Bolshevik. I detest the tsar. I detest the entire aristocracy, to include the tsar's family. I was thrilled when I heard they were overthrown and more than a little pleased when I found out they'd been sent to Siberia, a fitting place given the numbers of revolutionaries the tsar and his minions sent to that cold and miserable place.

And yet these men with me, here, in this battalion ... they have become my friends and comrades. How do I turn on Levkin, who shared his private bottle of vodka with us? How do I stab Sergeant Bogrov in the back, when he's been such a kind teacher this whole time? I confess, I do not know if I can.

If I could stop the rescue from ever leaving Bulgaria, that would be fine. The wicked tsar and his rotten enemy-sympathizing wife will be shot, I am sure, and none of my friends and comrades will be hurt. But I have no idea how to do that.

Interlude

Sverdlov: The Indispensable Man

I'm actually not and I know it; Lenin is the indispensable man to the Party and the Revolution. What I am, though, is indispensable to Lenin. He knows it; I know it; and pretty much everyone else knows it, too.

I am indispensable for two reasons. One is because I know everyone who matters, and have a completely objective, unemotional, accurate guide to their abilities and weaknesses, their value and their limitations. The other is because I see things clearly, with no emotional chains to bind me from doing what must be done. Closely related to that, I also understand terror in a way that even Lenin does not.

Terror? There are three kinds. One targets nobody in particular. It's not very effective except as advertising, as an illustration of the weakness of the state, and insofar as it may cause the state to crack down in ways that make it even less popular. We Bolsheviks have engaged in this kind of terror, from bombings to bank robberies.

It's far more effective, though, to target specific individuals and, by doing so, to target the behavior of a great many more of those in sympathy with the ones you target. A *kulak*, lifted high into the air by his neck, dancing on that air, and choking out his life, sends a message to every other *kulak*, even those far, far from the gallows. That message is "cooperate or die."

And if killing one *kulak* isn't enough? Well, then, hang his entire family, down to the smallest babe nursing at his mother's breast. *That* message goes even further and faster, while it is received even more clearly.

The last and most effective kind of terror, however, is the kind that threatens to exterminate an entire people or class, to erase them from history, to bury their families, their friends, their values, their beliefs, their religion, their buildings and monuments, their entire culture. *That* is the terror men fear above all. Moreover, it has the distinct advantage that, once you are successful, there *are* no more enemies of the revolution.

And we intend to do it, too. The *kulaks*, the bourgeoisie, the aristocrats? Their foolish and wicked supporters? Their children and grandchildren? All will be swept away, killed in both body and spirit.

We Bolsheviks are not the weak and foolish tsars. What trivial numbers they did away with over the last century, to preserve their rotten system, we shall double and treble weekly, even daily if we must, to bring to life our better one.

Chapter Nineteen

The Ussarovskys

Late Robbers' Encampment,
south of the Trans-Siberian Railway

"Strangest snowstorm I've ever seen," said Shukhov, as a southerly breeze brought a flurry of currency into the encampment.

"Don't just stand there with your teeth in your mouth," the sergeant said, "start picking it up! Lieutenants? Girls! Come out!"

All of them, hale or not, stormed out and began collecting paper currency from the ground. The lieutenant, for the moment, didn't. Instead, he tramped to the source, the now very open safe, and looked into it.

It was only a minority of the currency, he decided, that had been blown into the air. Most of it was still in the safe, tied in bundles of what he presumed were one hundred bills, each. Turgenev pulled out a couple of bundles, seeing they all bore the portrait of Catherine the Great. Doing some quick counting followed by some equally quick math, he tallied, *three bundles deep, seven across, and thirty high . . . times ten thousand . . . over six million rubles in currency. Must have been somebody's pay chest. If they're all one hundred ruble notes. I doubt they are, though. Still, even if half . . . and then, too, there's been a lot of inflation, so maybe . . .*

Kneeling beside the safe and bending at the waist, the lieutenant brushed away some loose currency covering what turned out to be bags, some of them sundered by the blast.

"Oh, my," he said aloud. He reached in and picked up a single coin. Examining it, he thought, *I'd recognize that profile anywhere; a ten ruble gold piece.* Brushing aside loose coins, the lieutenant hefted one bag. It was shockingly heavy for its size.

"Mmmmm . . . maybe a *pood*. No, at *least* a *pood*." More kitchen math followed, resulting in, *Hmmm . . . roughly thirty thousand rubles to the bag, and . . . oh, maybe twenty five or thirty bags, I suppose. We need to have a little counsel with the ladies.*

"Who owns the money?" the lieutenant asked the assembly, fifteen women and girls, plus nine men, one of them wounded. The two living prisoners, tied and shivering outside, were *not* asked.

"Might be an army pay chest?" said Mokrenko.

"True," said Koslov, the goat. "But *whose* army was it going to? Might have been the Reds, you know."

"Good point," the sergeant agreed, nodding deeply.

"Might belong to the tsar," said Turgenev, "but somehow I don't think he's in a position to tell us what to do with it."

"It might," said Natalya, "belong to those who suffered rape, humiliation, and indignities galore right here."

"We never could have gotten it out ourselves," said Saskulaana, the lovely Yakut woman. "Split it?" she suggested.

"Frankly, sir," said Mokrenko, addressing the lieutenant, "that might be the fairest and best we can do, both, without risking the money going for a bad cause."

The lieutenant nodded, but only as if he'd heard, not as if he necessarily agreed. "Saskulaana?" he asked, "what do you women and girls want to do?"

"You're the first decent men any of us have seen in a while," said the Yakut. "Can we stay with you? We'd earn our keep."

Repeating the lie Mokrenko had told Colonel Plestov, Turgenev said, "We are men with prices on our heads. You cannot come with us. We *can*, though, escort you as far as the edge of Tyumen, where you can all catch trains for either east or west. You're probably"—here, the lieutenant permitted himself a smile—"very safe from train robbers at this point."

"We could take my horses and be completely safe from train robbers," said Saskulaana.

"About the horses . . ."

"I'm joking," the woman said. "We need fourteen and maybe as many for food and such. That leaves plenty for you and your men. Take them; with my blessings. We owe everything to you."

"If we take you as far as Tyumen, how many would then take a train either east or west?" Turgenev asked.

All the women seemed happy with that idea, each raising her hand.

"At that point, then, you wouldn't need horses, would you?"

"I'd still need maybe five," said the Yakut woman, "to get myself and my daughter back to our people. And a rifle, if one could be spared."

"We've got two . . . no, three . . . extras now. You can have your pick of those.

"As for the money," Turgenev continued, "You ladies can only carry so much weight. Those bags are remarkably heavy. Indeed, any three or maybe four of them would weigh more than any one of you. I'd suggest you should want the paper rubles, with just enough gold to see you through a hard time, maybe five thousand rubles' worth, each."

"That's giving us a lot more than an even split," said the Yakut.

"Yes and no," said the lieutenant. "Gold is gold; it always has value. But the four hundred thousand or so paper rubles you each get could turn into so much trash overnight. My recommendation would be to take the paper, and that five thousand in gold, each, and turn all the paper into gold and silver as soon as you get where you're going. If you can. As much of it as you can."

"Paper's pretty much useless among my people," said Saskulaana. "Might my daughter and I take, instead, a fair share of the gold and the rest can have paper? Or you can take my share of paper?"

"Sure," said Turgenev. "Let's say...mmm...five horses and two bags of gold between you, the rest to go with us?"

"Agreed."

"The rest of you ladies?"

The remaining women chorused their assent.

"Very well. Sergeant Mokrenko?"

"Sir?"

"A rest night for the men. We'll leave at first light, tomorrow."

"Sir, what about the two prisoners? They're still outside, freezing."

"Leave them to us," said Saskulaana. "We owe them something."

"They didn't tell us everything," Mokrenko observed, "so our offer of a chance to live is nullified."

"They're yours," said the lieutenant. "Oh, before I forget; we need to bury Visaitov. I don't want to leave him for the wolves and we can't really take him with us."

"Digging in the permafrost, sir?" said Mokrenko. "Do we have an extra two weeks?"

"Put him in one of the buildings," suggested Saskulaana, "and set it alight."

"Agreed," said the lieutenant, though his agreement was touched with sadness. "Sergeant?"

"Sir?"

"Loot the robbers' treasure trove, would you, for anything that might be of use to us?"

"These are good men," said Saskulaana, after the two prisoners had been castrated and their throats had been cut. "These are decent men. No girls are to go to them, but only women, fully grown. Are there nine of us for that?"

The Yakut was better dressed than she had been upon the arrival of their liberators. Indeed, they were all better dressed, as they'd been given back their own clothes. So, for that matter, was Natalya, who had been fussed over and dressed by the now free women and girls.

"Eight of you," said Natalya, as a female automatically brought into the women's conspiracy. "The lieutenant belongs to me."

"But you are so young," said the Yakut.

"*Eventually*, he belongs to me. But I claim him as mine now."

"Eight of us," agreed Saskulaana, with a knowing smile. "Come, ladies; let us go willingly to our men. And do not forget the one outside on guard. Evdokia, don't you have a specialty for a man standing in the cold?"

"I do, indeed," agreed one woman, a pure Russian by the look of her, blue-eyed, blonde, round-faced, and with a most impressive chest. "Let me just find something to keep my knees from freezing..."

The Yakut already knew who she wanted, and had marked his place on the floor by the great Russian stove when he'd first rolled out his bedroll.

"Shshshsh," she whispered to Mokrenko, as she pulled back the blankets covering him. "I mean you no harm. Oh, *quite* the opposite . . ."

Tyumen, Russia

Although it was not an idyll, nor without its risks, nor without the needs to maintain security, the ride to Tyumen had been as happy a time as any of the men had known since 1914, and happier than any of the women had known in the past half year.

All idylls, though, come to an end. This one came to an end at the outskirts of the town, where the men had to say goodbye to all the women except Natalya.

Whoever fell in love, Turgenev asked himself, watching the tear-filled goodbyes, *who didn't do so immediately or, at least, very quickly?*

Mokrenko was particularly smitten.

And no wonder, thought Turgenev, looking at the Yakut woman. She wore her own fine furs, with a light fur hood drawn up over her hair. A triangular beaded fabric diadem decorated her forehead. Her hair hung down straight from behind, to both sides of her slender neck, to cover the fur in front of her breasts. The lower portions of delicate ears peeked out between hair and hood. On her neck hung a necklace of flat, crescent shapes, a mix of wood, horn, and amber. Everything seemed well-calculated to adorn a heart-shaped, elfin face, with two large almond eyes, a delicate chin, perfect eyebrows, and a mouth that begged to be kissed.

"Where might I find you?" he asked Saskulaana, "If I live, I mean."

She smiled, having won the battle to bind a worthy man to her. "I'm a Sakha," she replied, "or, as your people say, a Yakut. Well, three fourths. The other quarter is Russian and, yes, I am an Orthodox Christian.

"Where else would you find me except near the town of Yakutsk? I'll be with my clan within a couple of hundred *versta* of the town, generally to the southeast of it."

"Can you wait? Will you wait?"

"I will wait two years," she said, decisively, "and will look for you in the town every six months. If you have not come for me by that time, I will assume you have forgotten me."

"I will never forget you, while I live," he said, "but I might not live." He considered the time, the hardship, and the risk, then agreed. "Two years is long enough for you to wait, one way or the other."

"Who knows," she said, eyes twinkling. "Perhaps when you come I may have a not quite two-year-old surprise for you . . ."

His eyes widened to a degree she would have thought impossible.

"If you are . . . if you do . . . will this make it hard for you among your people?"

"Are you joking?" she laughed. "With the amount of gold I'm bringing back, no one would *dare* criticize me for *anything*. We don't have queens, exactly, among my

people, but I'm going to be the nearest thing to one. Tha
also means I'll be easy enough to find."

Great Lake Shishkarym

The lake, or rather, lakes, since the area was dotted
with them, was about thirty *versta* east of Kutarbitskoye
Russia, and about fifty almost due south of Tobolsk. It was
an area barren, miserable, and cold, all three. If anyone
lived anywhere near here, they were keeping indoors.

"It's perfect," said the lieutenant. "No towns. No
witnesses. Water we can get at with a little cutting. Tree
for shelter and firewood. Perfect. And it fits the limited
guidance Kostyshakov had for us on a place to bring in a
zeppelin."

In other words, this place sucks, thought every man in
the section. *Dig in.*

Setting up a decent camp for the men and horses took
about a day. They had, by the time Turgenev and those
accompanying him left, a tent, double-walled on a stout
frame, enough firewood and food for a month. Left
behind were Lieutenant Babin, Koslov, Shukhov—still
healing and somewhat the worse for the long ride, and
Novarikasha. They also left both sleighs they'd taken at
the rail line, and another three they'd found in the
robbers' encampment, as well as any horse not needed for
the trip. All the treasure of the robbers' camp, less the
money, and certainly to include several cans of kerosene,
remained here, too.

The remaining six, including Natalya, rode north to
Tobolsk with eight of the horses, two of those packed with

necessities, to include enough cloth for a lean-to if they needed to erect one, plus a single sleigh.

Tolbolsk, Russia

It was overcast and windless in Tobolsk, something much to be desired given the sheer, terrifying Siberian cold. The town was a mix of the rough-hewn and the sophisticated. There'd long been a lot of wealth to be extracted here, which explained a good deal of the sophistication. And rough-hewn, specifically in the form of log cabins, some of them more in the line of log palaces, was explained by the sheer amount of wood available. The roads would probably have been mud, in warmer weather, a misery to all who might travel them, but for now, amidst the usual Siberian cold, they were hard and fine.

Ahead, the town's kremlin, or fortress, loomed steep and menacing. It was an old fort and, while its white-painted walls would not have stood a day against even the cannon of two centuries prior, none of the local threats had ever had even those.

We made it on time, thought Turgenev, with wonder. *Despite the distractions, diversions, troubles . . . all that, we still made it on time.*

Sarnof, the signaler, already had a message composed for when they found the telegraph office. It read, in the original, "Arrived Tobolsk Stop looking for market."

They passed by one rather large, two-story log structure. On the side facing *Great Friday Ulitsa*, it had eight windows per floor, each with a peaked pediment above it. There was a single gable on the roof facing the road. After they passed it, Turgenev turned around in his saddle to read a sign on the roof proclaiming "PHOTOGRAPHIA," as well as one very large window—he estimated it at perhaps four *arshini* by about six—composed of some forty panes.

Hmmm...I wonder if we can get them to...think carefully, first. Vast potential for compromising ourselves.

"Sergeant Mokrenko?"

"Sir?"

"What would you think about getting that photography shop to get pictures of the town for the main force to study and plan with?"

"Good idea, sir, if we could do it without compromising anything."

"Great minds, Sergeant, think alike."

Next, on the same side of the road, they passed a large church or perhaps a cathedral. A sign outside proclaimed it to be The Cathedral of the Annunciation. It was set back from the street, slightly, but had a bell tower with cupola that towered over the surrounding buildings.

It wasn't but a few minutes later that the horses brought them to a very large and quite ornate house, with guards posted on the doors.

"Sergeant? You do the talking if there's any to be done."

"Sir."

Mokrenko asked one of the guards, "Comrade, can you direct us to a hotel? We've been on the road looking to buy furs for too long now, and could use a hot bath and some decent food."

The guard addressed spat on the ground. "Decent food in Tobolsk is hard to come by. A hot bath? I seem to remember what those were, but it's been so long.

'Decent'? You want a *decent* place to sleep? We're all sleeping in the basement of this place, if that gives you any idea. For that matter, this place has rented rooms in the past; there's even one guest and her daughter here now. But we're full. Even so, there's a none-too-reputable place north of here and a bit to the east. This road doesn't go all the way; you'll have to take a left, a right, and then another right. If you find yourselves at the river turn around and go the other way."

"Thanks, comrade," Mokrenko replied.

On the left they passed a stockade in front of a smaller house, though it was still of respectable size. There were guards ringing it, not just posted on the doors.

I think, thought the lieutenant, *that we've found the royal family.*

From the vantage point of the horses, they could see a bit into the yard the stockade defined, and even to what looked, by the smoke coming from the chimney, to be a kitchen building to the west. There was a snow-covered hill—or just a hill of snow, it was impossible to be sure—standing in the yard.

Mokrenko glanced left from time to time, trying to see if there was any unambiguous sign of the royal family. He caught faint shadows and images, through the windows of the place, but these were not unambiguous. Two people, one of whom seemed vaguely feminine, cut wood in the yard, but that didn't prove anything. Another, by his dress a young boy, chased some turkeys about the yard.

"Move on! Move on, you lot!" commanded one of the men ringing the place. "The former royal family is no fucking business of yours."

Well, that answers that question, doesn't it? I wonder if we could see into the compound from that cathedral back there. Mokrenko turned as far as he could to the right and determined, *I think someone could. Have to check it out when I get the chance.*

"Sorry, Comrade," said Mokrenko. "We didn't know. Just seemed odd to have so many guards. We're in the fur-trading business, just in from the *taiga*, and, given the close guard, I wondered if maybe it was being used as a warehouse for especially valuable furs. Naturally, that would interest us."

"Oh, they're valuable, all right, but not for furs. Go look up around and behind the kremlin; there are a couple of traders there."

"Thanks, Comrade."

Heading farther north, and after taking those suggested turns, about as far from the royal family as the latter were from the photography studio, the half dozen passed by what the lieutenant said was the town's electric plant. *Not my call as to whether it's a proper target for the main force, but they need to know about it so they can decide.*

"There are a *lot* of churches here," observed Natalya, riding beside the lieutenant.

"About one for every thousand people in the town, or maybe more," said Turgenev, softly. "And none of them burnt and none of them, so far, appear to have any soldiers—presumably Reds—quartered in them. That might tell us something of the outlook of the townspeople. But then, too, I've heard that there are an enormous number of very rich people here, and that may be of use to us, as well."

"I think we turn right here, sir," said Mokrenko.

"The place feels unsettled to me," Natalya said. "The way the people walk ... the way they look over their shoulders. Something has changed here, and very recently. And I don't think anyone is really in charge yet."

"I think you're right," said Turgenev, adding, "*you*, my dear, are a very clever girl. We've passed a lot of what look like discharged soldiers so far. How many do you think there are?"

I'd have been a good deal happier if he'd said, "clever woman" or even "clever young woman." But then, by calling me a girl he also avoids having to think about the uses to which I was put, and maybe even helps me not to think about them.

"A couple of thousand, I suspect," said Natalya. "They may not all be disorganized rabble, though."

They came to a hotel soon, but it was anything but inviting. Said Turgenev, looking it over while hiding his disgust, "I'd like to set ourselves up a house where we can be secure from prying eyes and eager ears. But to do that without risk we'll need to nose around a good bit. And that takes time, while time demands shelter. So, in the interim, this ... hotel ... I suppose.

"And from here on out we're all on a first name and patronymic basis."

In Tobolsk, virtually everything was dear. This was unsurprising in a place mostly cut off from the rest of the world by snow and ice for eight months out of the year. That applied, too, to the accommodations. Indeed, given the quality of the appointments—the section was fortunate to have their own bedding—the price demanded was nothing less than insulting.

"We'll take the insult," whispered Turgenev to Mokrenko, who looked about ready to contest matters. "Rostislav Alexandrovich, we'll take it; for now there is no choice."

"One other thing," said the proprietor, "there is a shortage of firewood in the town, mostly because of a shortage of labor. Even the tsar—excuse me; the *former* tsar—and his family, I have heard, cut their own. A very modest amount, enough to keep water from freezing, comes with your room. Beyond that, if you want to be comfortable, you can either sit in the dining room or go cut your own. If you cut extra, I'll take the value of it off the price of your room."

"This seems very fair, sir," said Turgenev. "Perhaps we'll be able to cut some extra. Is there, perchance, a place to find uncut wood or should we trek to the forest? And, on the subject of trekking, is there a good stable nearby for our horses?"

The proprietor looked right and left, carefully, then leaned close and whispered, "Were I you, I'd take your horses out of town. There's a stable not too far east of the edge of town. But if the Bolsheviks see your horses, they're likely to commandeer them, 'for the revolution,' which you may take to mean for their own convenience and profit."

"Thank you, sir," the lieutenant said. "Rostislav Alexandrovich, would you . . ."

"Be happy to, s . . . err . . . l . . . err . . . Comrade."

Shit, I never told them my first name and patronymic.

"As my name is Maxim Sergeyevich Turgenev, I'll make

sure a dinner is saved for you. Hmmm, for the *two* of you; I think you should take someone else with you. Timashuk, you should be the one to go with Rostislav Alexandrovich."

Half an hour later, the horses had been taken away and all the gear, including the ridiculous amount of gold and currency, had been moved up to the party's rooms. These were three, plus a bath and a sort of living room. There was no proper Russian stove such as stood at the confluence of lobby and dining room. At about two tons, even the stout logs with which the hotel had been built would have given way under it. Instead, there were some smaller and less efficient heaters in the corners of the rooms.

"What do you want me to say to headquarters, s... err... Maxim Sergeyevich?" asked Sarnof. "I've already encoded one saying we're here and safe."

Turgenev dropped his voice to a whisper. "That won't do anymore, Abraham Davidovich. For now... let me think... Line One: We're here. Two: One man lost. Three: Royal family here. Four: We have over forty horses and five good sleighs. Five: Question: Should we try to buy rations? Six: Question: How much? Seven: There are about two hundred and two guards. Eight: Political leanings unknown. Nine: Cannot judge their competence yet. Ten: Target building is two stories and a basement. Eleven: Building area, per floor, about a fifteenth of a *deyatina*. Twelve: As many as two thousand and two disorganized rabble, under no command, in the town. Nothing but trouble. Encode that—don't use the line numbers at all—and then go find the telegraph and send it off to Sweden."

"That's going to require consulting the novels we

brought, s—comrade. We didn't think of all this with this much specificity before we left. I may not be able to get it encoded until too late. Moreover, I think we need to follow the telegraph lines out of town, to find a place where I can tap in and send messages unseen."

"Also, why two hundred and two guards, specifically, Maxim Sergeyevich? We don't know to that level of accuracy. Same for two thousand and two."

"The guards because no matter which way they read it, it will be *about* right. As for finding a place to tap the telegraph lines—also, come to think of it, a place to cut them—we'll do it in good time," agreed Turgenev. "Which is to say, we'll look tomorrow, first thing."

As it turned out, by the time Turgenev and Sarnof got to the telegraph station, it was closed. That meant a long, disappointed trudge back to their hotel, to an uninspired meal, which was at least hot, in a warm room, and then to cold rooms with cold beds. Mokrenko and Timashuk, the medic, made it back before dinner was over.

"Maxim Sergeyevich," said the sergeant, sitting down at the rough table, "we are in the wrong line of work."

"Oh?"

"Oh, yes, based on what that pirate of a stable master is charging us for the keeping of our horses. When the war is finally over, I propose we forget furs and form a company to import hay to Tobolsk. We'll need some stout wagons, mind, as well as strong teams of horses, since hay, between Tyumen and here, seems to acquire the weight of solid gold..."

"That expensive, was it?" Money was, honestly, the

least problem the team had. Even at Tobolsk prices, they were well set.

"Near enough to, yes," answered Mokrenko. "To be fair, though, the horses already there were well cared for and, one supposes, it probably is expensive to bring hay in or even to cut it locally. I told him that our horses could forage for themselves. 'Then let them go forage and stop wasting my time,' the bastard answered."

"That wouldn't have had them at our beck and call when we need them," Turgenev said.

"I know, which is why I agreed to the son of a bitch's price."

"Nothing to be done for it," Turgenev said. "Eat up, though, you and Timashuk. The food's . . . well . . . we're in Tobolsk. It will do."

"There was one bright spot," Mokrenko said. "Pirate or not, where his business is concerned, the stable master is pretty free with information."

Turgenev was about to kick the sergeant under the table when Mokrenko added, "Apparently, the best—well, at least the most convenient—fur wholesaler to deal with is the Stroganov concern."

As Mokrenko and Timashuk finished their meal, the proprietor came over to their table. "You can stay here as long as you like," he said, "but within the hour that great stove in the corner will start getting cold. As goes the stove, so goes the room. I advise buying a bottle and going to your rooms to drink yourself to sleep. Nothing else much helps with the cold."

"I shudder to ask," said Mokrenko, "but how much is a bottle of vodka in this place?"

"A *chetvert*, which is the minimum I would recommend, will cost you one hundred and thirty-five rubles."

"Dear God," said Timashuk.

"*Everything*," said the proprietor, "costs more in Tobolsk."

"We'll take it," said Turgenev. "Can we borrow half a dozen glasses, while we're at it?"

"Surely. Those are already paid for and, unless you break one, I won't have to pay more for them."

Once arrived at the central sitting room of their suite, and after a quick check for chinks in the walls through which they might be heard, the lieutenant said, "We've never worked out where we're going to sleep. There are only three beds, all doubles."

"The men can share beds," said Mokrenko. "The problem is with the girl."

"I am sure," she said, "that Maxim Sergeyevich is too much the gentleman to lay a finger on me. I'll dress warmly before bed, so I do not impose on his modesty nor he on mine, and he can share a bed with me."

Imagine my disappointment, she fumed, a few hours later, laying cold and shivering, despite her clothing, the blankets, and another body for heat, *when it turned out that he is, in fact, too much of a gentleman to lay a finger on me*.

Ulitsa Great Friday 19, Tobolsk, Russia

Once again, Mokrenko had had to explain to the lieutenant that he ought not be the one to speak to the photographers. "Your accent is still all wrong, Maxim

Sergeyevich. Maybe the photographers will be sympathetic to the royal family and closed-mouthed. But maybe they're flaming Reds, too. Better I should go and ask. Meanwhile, you and the rest can go scout out the town and start working on diagrams."

Thus it came to be that Rostislav Alexandrovich Mokrenko found himself passing by the mansion wherein the Romanovs were held prisoner. He passed it, waving to the same soldier who had hustled them on earlier. Then, taking a short left off of *Ulitsa* Bolshaya Pyatnitskaya, and then an immediate right, Mokrenko found himself in the photography studio of Maria Ussokovskaya, in the house she shared with her husband, also a photographer, Ivan Konstantinovich Ussakovsky.

It was the wife, Maria, who opened the door for Mokrenko, asked his business, and led him upstairs to the studio. On the way, the sergeant was surprised to see postcards of the town being offered for sale, as well as portraits of the entire royal family, as well as their servants, retainers, teachers, and friends. He was especially shocked to see one of the infamous Rasputin decorating a portion of one wall.

Mokrenko wasn't especially surprised that both were home. He'd assumed, not unreasonably, that the husband shared in the business. As it turned out, though, no, the husband, a government official, was home because the Bolsheviks had taken over the town and he didn't know if he even had a job.

"And you know, Rostislav Alexandrovich," said Ivan, a man of average height, hirsute, with his hair parted in the middle, "these people are lunatics. I mean, sure, a new government wants new people; I can understand that. But there are old services that still need to be performed and they haven't a clue even of their existence and value. You would think they might ask, but, no; these people are already certain they know everything of value. I have never encountered such arrogance. Compared to the average Red, the tsar himself is a model of humility. And his daughters? The most shy and self-effacing . . ."

"Beautiful girls, too," said Maria. She kept her hair rather short and had just missed being pretty. Even so, though, she was very well built and, on the whole, presented a pleasant aspect. "I'm a fairly good photographer, if I do say so myself, but I have never yet been able to capture even a small portion of how lovely those girls are."

"Are you constrained from selling the portraits you have taken?" Mokrenko asked.

"Only if I'd signed a contract to that effect. Generally, I do not sign such."

"Where did you manage to get portraits of the ex-tsar and his family?"

"At the governor's mansion, which they've re-named 'Freedom House,' of course. The poor creatures are only allowed out one day a week, Sunday, to go to church, and that only for a few hours . . . and not always. We had to take their pictures for the ID cards they're forced to carry—it's only for the humiliation; as if everyone doesn't know who they are—and I did a little extra."

"May I see?" asked Mokrenko.

"They're not secret or anything," answered Maria. "Of course, you can."

Mokrenko's eyes lit up when he saw the collection.

There were not only portraits of the royal family, but in the course of taking those the Ussakovskys had also taken pictures of between a third and a half of the interior of the house. *I shouldn't be surprised; this is the closest photographer, so of course this was always where the tsar or the Reds were most likely to go.*

The sergeant noticed the woman's eyes were misty, as she sorted out the photographs for him. "Are you all right?" he asked.

She sniffed, slightly, "It's just that those poor people have been put on soldiers' rations, and not generous soldiers' rations, at that, and have had their budget cut to the bone. And they're freezing in that drafty old house. I feel terrible for them. It's not fair, either; the girls and the little prince did nothing to deserve being mistreated."

"I wonder," asked Mokrenko, deciding that these people could probably be trusted either to support the royals or to not put two and two together, "if you would sell me copies of all the pictures you've taken of the royal family and their entourage. Also, if I may, I'd like to buy a selection of the postcards you have made of the town. There are some other pictures, too, I would like, if you have the time . . ."

"What a strange place," said Turgenev, after dinner, when back in their quarters. "We found the market today and saw the strangest things."

"Where's that, Maxim Sergeyevich?" Mokrenko asked. "And what was strange about it?"

"Center of town. Some booths. Some people just laying their wares on cloths on the ground. But it was the kind of things on offer that was strange. For example, I saw a general's full-dress uniform. Why would there be a general's full-dress uniform here? And milk? Do you know how they sell milk here? They cut it with an axe, then weigh it and sell it by the pound!

"There were fur dealers there, too. Lesser lights than the Strogonovs, these were men, oh, and a couple of women, eager to carve out their own share of the fur market for themselves. I think we can get some good prices there. And you, Rostislav Alexandrovich?"

In answer, the sergeant laid out a sheaf of photographs. "There are more coming," he explained and then, dropping his voice to a whisper, he said, "but with these we can truly brief the main force on the layout of the place, no?

"Oh, and Maxim Sergeyevich? I think you need to visit the cathedral we passed as we rode into town. Some very interesting things to be seen there."

Interlude

Tatiana: Dear Aunt Ella

Despair is a sin.

It was that thought that kept me company in the middle of the night as I lay there, exhausted, yet unable to sleep.

If I slept the nightmare would come back. I'd been snatching bits of something I could not call rest ever since the night that Olga was violated.

Raped. She was raped.

I sat up and threw the covers off, adrenaline coursing through my veins, heart racing. Clumsily, I shoved my feet into slippers and rooted through the blankets and coats atop my bed for my robe.

My fingers were still shaking as I cinched the robe tight. Given what had happened—*Raped. She was raped.*—I shouldn't have dared leave our room, shouldn't have dared leave my sisters, but I also couldn't spend another moment curled up like a child, hiding under the blankets, pretending sleep while I waited for Olga to start muttering and whimpering to herself.

I blundered my way past my sisters' beds, through the quiet halls to my father's study. There was something about its musty smell, the aroma of cigars, the lingering scent of uncleared glasses and ashtrays that soothed.

My fingers found the lamp and clicked it on.

One of Mama's blankets sat in a pile nearby. I picked it up to fold it, defaulting to habit, succumbing to the need to do something. Instead, I draped it around my shoulders, sat down, and pulled a few blank sheets of paper and a fountain pen from one of the drawers.

Dear Aunt Ella, I wrote. The tip of the pen paused at the start of the next line. A drop of ink pooled at the tip as I pressed it into the paper.

I eased it off before it could bleed more of its black blood.

I wanted to write about cheerful things, the kind of normal, frivolous things that make up happy times. Instead, my heart bled all over the letter.

I wrote about what happened, about Yermilov, the man who defiled my sister, who took all of his hatred of us and used it to hurt her, to tear her body and mind and soul apart.

My hand trembled as I wrote, distorting the script.

A tear dropped, hitting the fresh ink, spiderwebbing the black blood from the pen with its misery.

I could see Yermilov's hatchet face, his dark eyes, alive with hatred. Hatred for Russia, for us Romanovs, for royals and nobles.

God help me, but I could feel his hot breath in my ear, putrid and wet. It wasn't Olga he was hurting. It was me. And then Maria. And Anastasia. Alexei.

The ink on the paper no longer formed letters or words, or even lines. My chest was shaking like it did when it was too cold and I couldn't stop it.

The things I saw in Yermilov's eyes. The power. Power

over us, our lives, our bodies, our minds. I wouldn't understand it until years later that what he had done was for power. Finally, he was, at least in his own mind, equal. The Romanovs had been brought down. One of us, and in some ways, all of us including Mama and Papa, were under him, at his mercy, crying, begging.

All of us bled for him.

What a rush of power it must have given this small, angry, despicable creature that thought of itself as a man and what it could do as manhood. What a rush to put the mighty in their place, to fuck an uncommon girl, to hurt her, put her in *her* place, to give her what she and her kind deserved.

Finally, for once in his life, he had power over all the wrongs done to him, and somehow he thought that they could be remedied with raping an innocent who had no power, no say, in whatever injustices the world had dealt him.

And it would be many years before I could understand my own guilt because there was a part of me that was glad it hadn't been me, that all I had to complain about were my bad dreams. And I was glad that Yermilov was dead and that the little ones—my dear sisters and brother—would not have to fear him.

By the time the ink was dry, both my pen and my eyes were empty.

I felt wrung out, my limbs heavy, but I could finally take a breath without shaking. I thought that I could sleep again, at least for a little while, without nightmares. My eyelids drooped and I pushed away from the desk so that I would not doze off.

I gathered the sheets together, stacked them neatly, and took them to the hearth.

One by one, I ripped the sheets into small pieces, scattering them into the pile reserved for kindling. I dared not send the letter. Papa must not know. Not now, not ever. It would destroy him.

The last sheet shook in my hands, the last few legible words, *No one cares. The world has forgotten about us,* glaring back at me.

Chapter Twenty

Brest-Litovsk, Bolshevik Negotiators Arrive

Range G6, Camp Budapest

Down in the multistory underground building, otherwise known as Range G6, the boys of Fourth Company practiced what soon acquired the name of "ladder drill." This involved rapidly porting their self-created flexible ladders to a wall with an opening, setting them up without losing any fingers, and ascending them by squads, fast.

Every time, thought Daniil, *that I think we've got a*

handle on the problem, something new comes up. And half of it that I should have thought of myself was, in fact, thought of by the rank and file.

Take this, for example; if the people we want to free are on the first floor of a building, then we cannot go in on the ground floor, or we'll be, in the first place, late in securing them and, in the second, we'll drive anyone we don't kill in among them. So . . . what should have been obvious to me, and wasn't, was obvious to a private who was paying attention.

Note to self: Mark Guardsman Repin down for promotion and more advanced schooling, both for realizing we needed ladders and coming up with a design.

The design in question was, essentially, three six-foot ladders, with one in the middle tied to one on each of its ends, and iron pipes of the right dimension to hold them together and upright, once assembled. It was probably obvious enough a solution, but had taken a certain amount of trimming to make the upper portions of the downward two sections shorter so that the pipe would slide over them. It had the disadvantage of having two places with uneven rungs, and no really good way to shorten it if the target window or porch or door was low.

They'd experimented with one other design, an eighteen-foot ladder that was composed of two ladders, joined at the top and with a hooked chain to keep them upright. That had proven to be prohibitively heavy for rapid emplacement or carrying any distance in a hurry.

Still, at two poods per ladder, these aren't exactly light either. There's a difference though, between heavy and impossible.

There were only four ladders built, though given the rough usage, *I am pretty sure we ought to build another four. Yeah... another four.*

Down below, one of the squads—*Sergeant Bogrov's, I think it is*—seemed to have come up with an ideal drill for the ladders. This involved running forward to a wall, with four men, two on each side, carrying the ladders, and the other two watching out for threats. As soon at the top of the ladder reached the wall, Kostyshakov saw, all four let go. The back pair then bent, grabbed the section lying on top, and ran backwards with it. While that was going on the front pair pushed the iron cylinders into place. Then the four elevated the ladder and dropped it just under a window in the wall ahead of them. It took about eighteen seconds to erect one, from reaching the wall to the first man scrambling up, after a little practice.

"Sir?"

Kostyshakov turned to see one of the men from the intelligence office. *Guardsman Bernadelli, if I recall correctly.*

"Message, sir, from Strat Recon. There's a good bit in it, but the really important things, says Sergeant Major Nenonen, is that they've found the royal family; all are in Tobolsk. That, and Strat Recon has acquired fifty good horses."

Daniil suddenly felt his heart lift so far and so fast it threatened to emerge from his left shoulder. *Everything we've done, so far, was just a waste of time without this. Thank you, God, and thank you, too, Lieutenant Turgenev.*

"Wonderful!" he said to the messenger. "Best news I've had in months. Have the Germans been told?"

"No, sir. For different reasons, Sergeant Major Nenonen says you ought to tell them. He also says you had better come to headquarters before you do."

"I'll be on my way. Tell Strat Recon that we'd like hidden space for five hundred men and as much food as can be reasonably obtained."

"Yes, sir."

Daniil started to read down the twelve items in the message. The number in line twelve was a shocker. *I need to ask for more details about them. I'd be willing to take on two thousand rabble, but what if there's more a chain of command than Turgenev thinks?*

"The war's over," said Basanets, the ungainly-tall battalion executive officer, rarely seen but almost always operating behind the scenes. "As of yesterday, it's over. Well, not in the west but the Reds signed a treaty with the Germans. They've given up . . . God, I don't want to think about what they've—we've—given up to the *Nemetsy.*"

"It works out to a third of our population, half our industry, and almost ninety percent of our coal," said Nenonen. "And I don't know what to do. Finland is on its own; am I a Finn or a Russian soldier or what?"

"Did you agree to do this mission?" snapped Kostyshakov.

"Yes, sir. Of course, I did."

"Did you just say 'our' to describe what's been stolen from us?"

"Yes, sir, naturally."

"Then you're a Russian soldier, at least until we've

accomplished our mission, and for as long after as you adhere to the Empire."

"Yes, sir. Sir, I never meant I'd abandon the mission. It's just . . ."

"I understand."

"Do we tell the troops?" asked Basanets.

Kostyshakov went silent then, and stayed that way for some time, thinking. *If we tell them how do we control them and keep them from taking revenge on the Germans here? No, people are not rational. And an army is just a mob with a sense of teamwork. And how do we accomplish our mission without the Germans. We've no chance of getting anywhere without that airship. And we're not even quite ready to go even if we went now. I wonder . . .*

"Who knows?" he asked Basanets.

"Within the hour the whole camp will."

"I see. Assemble the battalion. I'll speak to them in two hours', no, three hours' time. Are Major Brinkmann or *Feldwebel* Weber available?"

"Brinkmann's already gone to consult with General Hoffmann, sir," said Nenonen. "Weber's here."

"Send someone for him."

"It's simple greed and paranoia," said Weber. "I wish I could put a better face on it than that, but I can't. Before leaving to see Hoffmann, Major Brinkmann told me that Hoffmann was dead set against this scale of theft, but he's already on thin ice with Hindenburg and Ludendorff, so couldn't do much."

"Is the mission still on?" asked Kostyshakov. "Will we have the zeppelin to take us where we're going?"

"As far as I know, sir. Certainly, I've seen no changed orders."

"Any suggestions on how I present this to my troops? We've all gotten along very well, so far, but this could turn your guards into real guards and my Imperial Guards into sullen mutineers."

"I'd say . . . be fairly up front and honest, but maybe not fully honest. For example, it wasn't the tsar who gave away all this, it was the Bolsheviks. That's still more evidence that they're enemies of Russia, isn't it, sir?

"As for us, what choice did we have? Did Germany have a moral choice? Should we, in fact, have condemned tens of millions of Russian citizens, as Christian as we are, ourselves, to Bolshevik slavery, to atheism, to the dictatorship of the Reds?

"Did Germany have a practical choice, either? We've got millions of men, here, ourselves and the Austrians, all of them desperately needed in the west. How do we move them where needed without a thick buffer it would take the Reds—or the tsar, for that matter—months or years to reoccupy?

"And then there's the future . . ."

"Break ranks," Daniil called out in his loudest shout. "Break ranks, gather round, and take seats."

"Anyone who hasn't heard yet, raise your hands." Perhaps fifty men, or a few less, hadn't gotten the news.

"Okay, for your sakes, here it is: The Reds have effectively surrendered to Germany, ceding about a third of our population, half our industry, and a huge portion of our coal, maybe as much as nine tenths."

Not unexpectedly, the battalion began a low grumbling, with the men casting angry glances the way of the German guards, though not, interestingly enough, at Taenzler.

"In the first place," said Daniil, "who can blame them? You think we would not have sliced away a good chunk of German and Austria-Hungary if we'd won? Be serious, boys; it's the way the game is played. We played; we lost; and now the Reds are paying up."

The grumbling reduced but did not go away.

"Now savor that, for a moment," said Daniil, "the Reds gave it away. Not the tsar, not the people, the Reds. You want to be angry at someone, don't turn on the Germans who've been helping us these last several months; think about the Reds who are holding our true ruler and his family as prisoners.

"Moreover, what should the Germans have done? Left all those people, our countrymen in the past and in the future, to the none too tender mercies of the Reds? To the terrorists? To the atheists? To the people who shout 'power to the people' but only mean 'power to the people who shout power to the people'? We should be happy that a third of our people have been kept out of the hands of the Bolshevik slave masters. For now, unless we succeed in our mission.

"Finally, I want you to think about the future. Specifically, I want you to think about how we get our patrimony back. The Germans aren't actually taking much for themselves, you know. So, if we do our job, and Russia acquires a legitimate ruler again, there's no particular reason not to expect our country to be made whole again, given a little time.

"Now, I have time for a few questions, but not many as we have to get back to training..."

Brest-Litovsk

"I have a question, sir," said Major Brinkmann, during one of the walks that had become quite infrequent since the beginning of what Hoffmann thought of as *The Budapest Project*.

"No need, Major; yes, of course I intend that the Russians should still go and save their royal family."

"Thank you, sir; I and they appreciate that, I am sure. But the question is really how do we do this legitimately, now that we're at peace with the Bolsheviks. Sending *enemy* armed forces on *our* airships to liberate *their* prisoners, you know, is not exactly a friendly act."

"Hmmm... good point, Brinkmann. Let's see. In the first place, I have carte blanche from the kaiser to do what it necessary to free his cousins and the Hesse and by Rhine women. Mind, he tends to fold when confronted by Hindenburg and Ludendorff, so I can't do any of that too openly. So... we have an airship..."

"An airship and two fighters, now, General."

"Oh, yes, I forgot about the two fighters. Where are they, by the way?"

"They're at Jambol, with the airship. Once a crossing point over the lines is picked they'll displace forward with their pilots and ground crew to act as escorts, to and from."

"Ah, good. Now where was I?"

"'We have an airship...'"

Hoffmann was not merely the best staff officer of the

war, he was great in a crisis, cool, calm, collected, and—above all—ruthless. "Ah, yes. We have an airship, but it's at loose ends. So we're going to report it as in serious need of maintenance after its flight to Africa, much more serious than originally thought—and didn't you say they're making substantial modifications to carry troops? Well, there you are. Then we're going to form a corporation, I think, in Sofia. Consult a lawyer there."

"A corporation?"

"Yes, an air transport corporation. Where there's a will there's a lawyer; find a competent one and let him figure it out. But let's call it something like 'Sofia-Moscow Air Transport.' Then we lease the airship to the corporation. Of course, the corporation will pay for the lease with money we'll give them from captured Russian pay chests, but let's not worry about trivia, eh? I think maybe the airship ought to have a double-headed eagle painted on it, too, to let anyone who sees it know it isn't German."

"All well and good, sir, I mean, except for the fraud and lies parts. Oh, and the theft and conversion and . . ."

"Cease, Brinkmann, your naysaying. It'll be fine. Now, as for the crew . . . arrange discharges into the reserves for the lot, then instant hiring, at much higher pay, by Sofia-Moscow Air Transport, Incorporated. Explain to them that they can go along with it, or they go into the camp that will soon enough be vacated by the Russians. I'm sure they'll see reason. Oh, and tell them they're back in the kaiser's service as soon as their mission is complete."

Brinkmann sighed, thinking, *This is so much harder and so much more dangerous—to us, personally—than he seems to . . .*

"And, yes, Brinkmann; I know the risks we're taking. Would you rather have the Bolsheviks on Germany's border eventually, or take a few risks now?"

Camp Budapest

Romeyko was ready to tear his hair out by the roots. After spending days, and nearly twenty-four hour days, at that, working with Weber and that aviator, Mueller, calculating how to get the battalion to western Siberia in five lifts, Kostyshakov had had the gall to come back and say, "Forget the animals, the fodder, and the wagons; they've all been taken care of for us."

And then the inconsiderate bastard had had the effrontery, as he left the quartermaster's office, to call over his shoulder, "Figure out, too, if we need to buy food there."

Okay, then; let's start by trying to work it as three lifts, with three days' travel, loading, and unloading travel each way. That means the Fourth Company will be in flight or on the ground, needing to eat, for ... mmm ... three days out ... six days until the next lift ... six days until the last lift ... then maybe one to get to the objective ...

No, wait; assume we leave to cross the front—which Weber informs me has moved east a good deal—at night. Okay, that means we leave ... mmm ... after lunch on departure days. Two hours to load, since the animals and their fodder aren't a factor anymore ... so only one meal required in flight. Zweiback, cheese, and what passes for sausage. So only one pound, for dinner only, in flight, lift-off day. That saves two and a half pounds per man ...

"Hey," he said to one of the clerks, "get me that new German, Mueller. Tell him to hurry."

"Yes, sir; you sent for me?"

"Ah, Herr Mueller, thank you for coming so quickly. There are some questions I cannot answer that I hope you can." *And he seems very young, but looks more than adequately intelligent.*

"If I can, sir, and if it isn't classified . . ."

"Well, only you can tell us what is and isn't a secret. Here, look at the map." Romeyko stretched their best large-scale map out over the chalkboards, brushing sticks of chalk away with one hand. "We're going from here to—so it appears now—Tobolsk, Russia, or a spot a bit south of it. We don't want to be seen crossing the lines, such as they are. So when are we going to have to take off, to make the crossing in the dark?"

"No matter what we do, sir," said the German airship sailor, "if we're leaving around the twenty-sixth of March, it's not going to be all that dark."

"No?"

"No, sir; it will be a nearly full moon up and it rises at about five-thirty PM. The sun sets half an hour after that and rises just after moonset the next day. In that time frame, there is no time we can count on complete darkness. What we'll do, though, is make sure that we never get between the moon and a major settlement. That should help."

"Ah . . . so when would we have to take off to cross over near say . . ." —Romeyko's hand searched the map—"this place, Yekaterinoslav, so that it's as dark as it can be when we cross?"

"Let me think, sir . . . distance looks to be about eleven hundred kilometers." Mueller turned his finger and thumb into a makeshift compass calipers and measured off the distance. "Yes, close enough to eleven hundred. We can travel at about one hundred and three kilometers per hour so . . . let's call it eleven hours of flight to get to Yekaterinoslav. To cross lines at nineteen-thirty, well after the end of evening nautical twilight, we'll need to leave at eight-thirty in the morning."

Romeyko did some more scribbling on his chalk boards. "That should work," he said. "We can feed an early breakfast and lunch, lunch out of Taenzler's *Gulaschkanone*, right at the airship's hangar.

"So let me see . . ." More chalky scribbling followed. "If we load for the first lift one hundred and thirty-seven men . . . at ninety of your kilograms each . . . and sixty-seven hundred kilograms of food . . . yes, that should work."

"What about the horses and mules, sir?"

"Did no one tell you? No animals; our forward reconnaissance team has found us enough and more. We needn't take wagons either."

"Praise God," muttered Mueller. "You can load more men or ammunition now."

"Well, yes," agreed the rat-faced Romeyko, "but then we're on God's work, no?"

Mueller only nodded, then said, "The skipper will be doing handstands of joy when he finds out he won't have horses and mules shitting all over his airship."

"Likely. Can't blame him. Okay, now for lift two . . ." Scribble-scribble-scribble-erase-curse-throw-a-piece-of-chalk. Then pick up another and scribble some more. "Okay, lift two . . . one hundred and fifty-three men, mostly from Second Company, two infantry guns with limbers, one hundred and sixty-one kilograms, plus another two hundred and ninety-one in 37mm ammunition, plus forty-eight hundred kilograms of food. That sound sensible to you?"

Mueller couldn't read Cyrillic, so had to go with Romeyko's words. "We might need to put in some ladders to get men up to hammocks in higher spaces but I think that's feasible, sir. Plenty of room for the guns and their limbers on the cargo deck."

"Good so far. Now let's think about third lift. It's got to contain Third Company and most of what's left of Headquarters and Support . . . one hundred and eighty-four men . . . two heavy machine guns with a ton of ammunition . . . just under two tons of food." Romeyko shot an inquisitive glance at Mueller.

Said the German, "I don't see a necessary problem, though sleeping space will have to be sorted out. I'm going to ask the skipper, when I see him in three days, if we can put in one hundred and eighty-four hammocks from the beginning, so we don't have to screw around with reconfiguring while loading, in a no-doubt panic-stricken hurry.

"Ummm," continued the German, slightly embarrassed, "sir, have you or any of your men flown before?"

"None of us, so far as I know," said Romeyko, "and *I* certainly have not."

"Then I'm going to ask the captain, too, if we can violate regulations and get everyone a little tipsy. I don't even want to think about dealing with a hundred tough Russian Imperial Guards in a panic and running amok . . . in an airship."

"Tell you what," said the quartermaster. "You ask your skipper and I'll talk my commander into it because, you are absolutely right, we do *not* want a panic."

"So," said Romeyko, "up to two and a half days in the air. Half a *chetvert* of vodka per man. There goes the food savings from feeding early breakfast and lunch. Oh, well."

"One other thing, sir?"

"Yes, Herr Mueller."

"I went up last night and watched your troops clearing one of the underground buildings you've set up. Those carbide lamps, sir? I asked one of your officers how they worked. Well, the skipper will *not* let them get aboard in anyone's hands. That won't be a negotiable point; they must all be collected and completely cleaned out of carbide. With the water chambers kept entirely separate from the carbide chambers."

Romeyko groaned as he immediately saw the pain in the ass of that. "We've got a dozen different sizes and makes. If we don't keep them together, it will be a pure bitch getting the right sections together again. We had one young idiot who set himself afire when he mismatched from two different types."

"Sir, I'm telling you what my captain is going to say. No fire hazard will be permitted aboard an airship. Umm... sir, are you flying with us?"

"Yes," said Romeyko, "though I'm planning on going on the third lift."

"Well, sir, all that space in the airship? It's almost all hydrogen gas. Very flammable, sir. Also tiny little molecules that leak out of the gas bags continuously. Sir, do you know what our aircrews do if they take a hit from a tracer and catch fire? They don't try to fight the fire; there's no chance of that. They just cross themselves and jump to their deaths, because *it's better than burning alive.* Not even any time to put on a parachute, assuming you're optimistic enough to trust something with a forty percent or more failure rate. Just jump and get it over with."

"I see," said Romeyko, with a sudden vision of doing the same himself. "When I talk to Kostyshakov about the vodka, I'll explain to him the problem with the carbide lights."

"And matches, sir. And cigarette lighters...any smoking material, actually. Ummm...sir, besides the vodka, you haven't accounted for drinking water. They're not going to be very active, of course, tied into their hammocks but they'll still need some."

"Can we drink from your ballast tanks? They're full of water, right?"

"Well...yes. It might not be very pleasant water. But the problem there is that, as you drink the ballast, and then piss over the side, the ship gets lighter and rises more."

"Yeah," Romeyko conceded. "Silly of me. I...hey, is there more than one ballast section?"

"Yes, sir, several."

"Can we drink from one and piss in another?"

Range G6, Camp Budapest

It was dress rehearsal, the final rehearsal, the proof of concept, the *sine qua non* of the whole enterprise. They'd been training in the day on the theory that the carbide lamps would provide almost as good light as daylight, but they knew this wasn't quite true. Even with six men, with six working lamps set on the highest setting, it wasn't quite equal to daylight still.

But it was decent, particularly with six of them flaring in a single room.

Pretty good, thought Daniil, standing on the lip of the great hole containing the two-story underground log building. Only the top floor of that was open to view. Control inside depended on the Fourth Company cadre.

Second Platoon had already gone through, and done well. Then, after a couple of hours' worth of setting up the building again, undoing the damage, and putting out some fires, it was First Platoon's turn.

Staggered up the ramp leading down to the ground level of the buildings, in a column of twos, waited, in darkness, the company cadre and the men of First Assault Platoon, Fourth Company (Grenadiers), plus their engineer, sniping, and medical attachments. The platoon was down to thirty men, including attachments, from the thirty-two they'd started with, as a result of one training fatality, Sotnikov, and one trooper, Sobchak, who simply lost self-confidence and asked to be moved to a position less taxing. Sobchak was a company runner now. There were also a couple of men with small injuries from training but, at this point, they'd rather die than miss the festivities.

If pretty good is enough.

"Annnndddd...GO!" ordered the First Platoon leader, Lieutenant Collan, the atypically short but still highly Nordic Finn.

Instantly, the platoon sprang into action. The scene lit up as twenty-eight lights—everyone's but the sniper team's—on twenty-eight helmets flashed to life, the men rolling the strikers with middle fingers. Then the lead squad, under Sergeant Tokarev, launched themselves forward, Tokarev and Guardsman Korchagin, each with a substantial section of log on his back, taking security while the other four carried the ladder forward.

Boom! and the ladder was on the ground. *Creak-squeak* and it was extended to its full eighteen feet. Groans and grunts from the four bearers as pipes were set and then, with another thud, it was hoisted against the wall, the top end just below a window. Up the ladder scrambled first Tokarev and then Korchagin. Dropping his MP18 to hang by its sling, Tokarev lifted the log overhead and smashed it through the light wood window frame in a move that would have smashed glass had it been there. Then pulling a flash grenade from his belt, Tokarev armed it, counted off three seconds, and tossed it into the room beyond the window. He closed his eyes and dropped his head below the level of the window until he sensed the flash through his eyelids.

Up, up, Tokarev scrambled. Shouting, "Romanovs down!" in Russian and heavily Russian-accented English, he scanned the room for visible targets. One he saw he serviced in an instant, with a short burst from his machine pistol, then he leapt through the window.

There were two hay-stuffed assemblies of female clothing on the floor. "Civilians get to the corner! Keep low! *Crawl* to the corner!" Tokarev ordered, in Russian this time, and done rather *pro forma*. Through the window came Korchagin, Corporal Shabalin, Jacobi, the shotgun-armed, demolition pack carrying engineer, and then, one by one, Guardsmen Fedin, Lukin, and Blasov.

Blasov kicked open the door to the next room, while the others made ready. Two more flash grenades sailed through the door, exploding with muffled booms.

"Romanovs down!" rang out, even as the platoon leader, Lieutenant Collan, entered the room through the window, one runner in attendance. Following Collan, Second Squad, under Sergeant Yumachev, began piling in, with the other engineer in tow.

Submachine gun fire rattled from further into the building.

"Shield your eyes," was followed by the thunderous *bang* as Jacobi blasted a lock apart with his shotgun.

"Romanovs to the floor! Romanovs down!"

"That way!" ordered Collan, pointing with an outstretched arm in a direction perpendicular from the way First Squad had gone.

"Follow meeeee!"

Boom-flash! "Romanovs down!" The MP18s resumed their chatter.

Sergeant Bogrov's troops were erecting a second ladder, Kostyshakov saw. He noted, too, that the snipers had taken a position just at and behind the building's corner. *Preventing reinforcements, I suppose, that being all they can do on this range.*

Between the flash grenades and the muzzle flashes, this place is like a movie theater with the projector rolling too slowly.

"Romanovs down! Get to the corner!" *Boom!*

Funny how it sounds like cloth ripping when three of the MP18s let go at once.

"Vasenkov! Bok! Guard that stairway down!"

"Sergeant Bogrov, Headquarters, assemble on me!"

That's Collan. Fine boy. We need to find a way to keep Finland in the Empire, whatever it takes. They're just too good to lose.

"Romanovs down!" *Boom. Chatterchatterchatterchatter.* "Follow meeee!" "Urrah!" "Down! Down! Down!"

From the initial entry point, Kostyshakov saw some of those bundles of clothing filled with hay being ejected. One of them fell on the sniper, Corporal Nomonkov.

They'll climb down in real life, the way sacks of hay cannot. But the escort part the boys seem to have down pretty . . . well, yes, pretty damned good.

"Romanovs down!"

Daniil stuck around for the after action review. He didn't have a lot to say, himself, beyond, "Well done. After everything I've seen, yes, we can do this. Oh, yes, we fucking *can.*"

"Captain Cherimisov?"

"Sir."

"Dismiss the men. Squad leaders on up, battalion mess for our movement orders."

"Sir!"

PART III

Chapter Twenty-One

Former Tsar Nicholas II and Crown Prince Alexei,
Sawing Wood

Tobolsk

The negotiations were for appearances' sake and
nothing but. With the amount of money on hand,
Turgenev—for once in a position where his aristocratic
accent and manners *weren't* a handicap—could have
bought considerably more than two warehouses and one
safe house.

As it turned out nothing worthwhile was for sale. There

were, however, places to lease. There were, in fact, two warehouses for lease, perhaps twenty-five *arshini* by thirty, in one case, and thirty by thirty-five, in the other. One was near the pretty much abandoned for the fall, winter, and spring river docks, the northernmost set, sitting inside a little apparently artificial bay. The other was at the southwestern edge of the town, perhaps a *versta* and a half from the Irtysh River.

The safe house, a decent sized log building with a good Russian stove in the center of the main room, was a bit to the south and several blocks to the east of the Cathedral of the Annunciation. It was two floors, with a basement, the basement having a kind of root cellar to it. The rent was appalling but, as the realtor explained, "It does at least have a winter's worth of firewood with it. That's something, this year."

"Can't you...?" began Turgenev, forcing a tone of exasperation into his voice that he really didn't feel.

"Sir," replied the realtor, who recognized "quality" when he saw it, "if I tried to drop the rent a *kopeck* the owner would skin me. And if I told him I was renting to a competitor—you gentleman are in the fur trade, yes?—he'd pour salt on the freshly exposed flesh as he cut."

"But I'm taking a lease for a whole year!"

"Even so. Sir, I can't."

With feigned disgust, Turgenev pulled out some of the oversized currency exchanged with Saskulaana and proceeded to peel off five hundred and one hundred ruble notes.

"Can you direct me," he asked, as he passed the wad over, "to where I can buy a large quantity of food? We're going to be bringing in a hundred hunters and trappers for two months and they'll need to eat."

"Oh, sir, this is the *worst* time to try to buy food in Tobolsk. We have no rail line so everything must come down the river or be pulled by animals. The river stays frozen for another two, maybe two and a half months. Yes, of course there will be some for sale, but you can expect the price to be outrageous."

"Even so, they must eat. I don't suppose . . . ?"

"I'll make some discreet inquiries."

Turgenev translated this as, "I will consider which of my relatives to favor and will jack up the price accordingly."

"You could, too," said the realtor, "do some hunting yourselves for meat. The animals, too, will be a little thin but still."

"Rostislav Alexandrovich?"

"Yes, Maxim Sergeyevich?"

"Since we have a couple of rifles, why don't you and one other of our party take a few horses, rent a sleigh, and do a little hunting."

"Define 'a little.'"

"A thousand *pood* would not be too much."

"I'll see what we can do. Do you mind if I range rather far? As we came north from our earlier scouting expedition I saw a lot of sign."

"Certainly."

While Mokrenko was making his arrangements, Turgenev took Natalya for a walk about the town. Whatever she imagined might be the purpose, there was not a shred of romance in his intent. She was, frankly, just cover. Who, after all, does combat reconnaissance with a young girl in tow?

Three blocks west from the safe house and a bit to the north led them to the Cathedral of the Annunciation, the very place, though Turgenev didn't know it, where the royal family was sometimes allowed to attend services.

They found the priest inside, standing at the altar and gazing intently at one in particular of the icons. Turgenev was loath to interrupt, but finally, *ahem*ed his way to the cleric's attention.

"Excuse me, Father," Turgenev said. "I represent a fur trading firm looking to expand our enterprise here in Tobolsk. We've taken a house a few blocks east of here. My sister and I were looking for a place we could attend mass."

"You don't want to come here," said the priest, who further introduced himself as "Father Vladimir Khlynov." "My predecessor, Father Alexei Vasiliev, is in terrible disfavor with the Reds guarding the tsar and his family, so Bishop Germogen exiled him to a monastery for his own safety. I cannot encourage anyone to attend this church; those men are fanatics and vindictive, both."

"A terrible combination," Turgenev agreed. "Are you, personally in disfavor?"

"No," answered the priest, "but while I am serving as in charge of this cathedral I might as well be."

"What happened?"

Father Vladimir gave a sad sigh, then stated, "The tsar was here for mass at Christmas and the chorus, at Father Alexei's direction, sang the '*Mnogoletie*,' the wish for a long life to the tsar. The Reds were not amused. But then we didn't do it to amuse them, did we, but to let our tsar and his family know that we support them still."

"Do you?"

"How can I not?" replied Vladimir. "They cannot come to mass here, anymore, so I go to them when it's allowed. And, when it isn't, I go up to the bell tower and bless them, from a distance."

"We saw the tower when we arrived," Turgenev said. "Can you see them from up there?"

"When they're in the right area, yes."

"Could I see?" Natalya asked.

"Surely, child," the priest replied. "Why don't you and your brother just go on up? While you're up there, say a prayer for our tsar and his family, why don't you?"

The lieutenant observed, "A single sniper up here, Natalya, could command *Ulitsa* Great Friday all the way to the Church of Zachary and Elizabeth."

"Does that matter?" she asked.

"It might. It might be a place for Kostyshakov to put in a sniper or machine gun team. It might be a place we need to make sure the Reds don't put in a sniper or machine gun team."

"I need to make a confession," she said.

Turgenev had been dreading this moment. The girl's crush had been obvious for some time, probably at least since the time he'd pulled a half-drowned Babin from the Black Sea. And he liked her, too, of course. Nor did he blame her for the abuse she'd suffered. But he was too old, or she too young, for anything romantic. *Maybe in five or seven years.*

"Go ahead," he said, dreading the expected revelation.

She leaned against the wall, back toward the governor's house. It was mostly to steady herself. Even then, though, she hung her head, ashamed.

"I should have told you when you first freed me but, you see, when the Bolsheviks murdered my parents, they knew who I was. Their abuse because of that was horrific, much worse than simple rape. So I didn't want anyone to know who I was anymore lest I be beaten or raped . . . well, raped differently . . . because of who my parents were. I suppose they didn't tell Vraciu because then he might have shown me some consideration before selling me back to one of my relatives."

"Tell him what?"

Again, she sighed. "Tell him the reason they abused me . . . sold me. Maxim Sergeivich, with the deaths of my parents, I inherited . . . well . . . their status. I am a baroness. No, no huge estates, but a 'proprietary' baroness all the same, since we do . . . did . . . have a decent sized farm. But . . . well . . . it's worse than that, really. The royal family . . . mmm . . . we've met. I was little then but they might still recognize me, because I look so much like my father."

"Does anyone else—anyone else in our party—know?"

"Sergeant Mokrenko guessed, I think. Then he caught me out, twice, at least twice, as having a better education than a simple peasant girl ought to have had, or to be expected to have had."

"Yes, if anyone would have guessed . . ." Turgenev laughed at himself. "You know, Baroness Sorokin, I can't tell if I'm disappointed or thrilled."

"Disappointed, why?" she asked.

"I was afraid you were about to utter a declaration of undying love."

"Why," she asked, dryly, "would I make a declaration of something that is *so* obvious? I've decided you think I'm too young and love you the more for that. I am; I *am* young, not stupid or blind. But in five years, or seven, at the outside, and maybe as few as three, Maxim Sergeyevich, you belong to me. Period. If, that is, you are not disgusted by what they made of me, the Reds and the crew."

"Don't be silly. You want to talk about peoples' bodies being used for obscene purposes? I'll tell you about the war sometime. *That* was an obscene purpose. And I had no more will in it than you did.

"All right," he said, "in five years we'll open this discussion again. In the interim, how do you actually feel about the royal family?"

"I don't know the tsarevich, Alexei," she replied, "but the four girls—OTMA, they call themselves, as a group— are wonderful. You would think they would be spoiled, right? Self-centered? Stuck up? Bitchy? They're *not*. They cleaned their own rooms, made their own beds, and took cold baths. Think about that; cold baths, in Saint Petersburg, in the middle of winter? They're regular people, at heart. They'd all *adore* being regular people, in fact."

Turgenev went silent for a moment, thinking hard. *I wonder if . . .*

"Hmmm . . . you know, it would help if we had someone who could act as a go-between. Do you think you could get in there as a maid to them? My little spy? But without telling them much of anything . . . or anything at all?"

"I will try. For you, I will try."

Governor's House, Tobolsk

It turned out, as such things will, to be harder than that; the former tsar wasn't hiring. Turned away at the gate by the main entrance to the Governor's House, Natalya wasn't sure what to do. She turned south again, heading to their safe house, and was met by Turgenev coming north on his continuing reconnaissance of the town.

"I don't know what to do, Maxim Sergeyevich," she said, when they turned east toward the center of town and the market. "How do I get in to work in a place that isn't hiring because they have no money to pay staff?"

Turgenev didn't reply immediately. Instead, he mentally counted the paces from the southwestern corner of the Kornilov House, to its northwestern corner, and then the same for two eastern corners of the Governor's House.

"Olga is looking out the window," Natalya said. "No, don't turn and stare. Just trust me, she's there with . . . mmm . . . someone I don't recognize . . . a man."

"Too busy counting to look," the lieutenant replied. "In any case, I believe you. Now, remember these figures, Natalya . . . thirty-four *arshini*, forty-one *arshini*."

"Thirty-four and forty-one," she echoed. "What are those, anyway?"

"The exterior dimensions of the Kornilov House and 'Freedom' House, on their long axes. I'll get the other dimensions later."

"Oh. Why do those matter?"

"I'll explain to you later, if you remind me. Indeed, you can help me with a certain project I have in mind.

"As to what to do, I don't know, Natalya," Turgenev replied. "If you offered them money to let you work there, it would raise suspicions. Maybe if we had a way to introduce money to the household, they could then hire staff. But would they hire a new girl or take back old staff they've had to let go? I confess, I don't know. While we think about this, let's go shopping for some rope and, after that, maybe get some lunch."

"What kind of rope?" she asked.

"Different kinds or, rather, different colors."

"What for? The horses?"

"No," he answered, with a shake of his head. "If we can yet find a way to introduce you into the house or houses, I want to use it to trace out floor plans for my boss, so he can plan how to liberate the family."

Natalya considered that for a bit, then her eyes widened. "With rope you can make a floor plan and then roll it up, so no one notices . . . is that it?"

"I've said it before; you're a clever girl."

She thought, *Five years, seven years, and maybe as few as three.*

As it turned out, the market was not a great place to buy rope, though the lieutenant did manage to acquire about two hundred *arshini* of a thin, plain hemp.

"You can find more and of different types," said the vendor, "either down by the river docks or at one of the logging firm's warehouses."

Natalya wasn't paying any attention to the rope

transaction, but simply looking around at the generally used wares on display and the people shopping for them. She saw a Tatar bargaining for a smoked fish with some old woman. The bargaining was in Russian. Near those two some fur-wrapped man wearing waders ran a complex net through his hands, examining it closely. Not far from there, a milk salesman chopped off chunks of frozen milk, weighing them for sale to someone dressed in a way Natalya had never seen, in furs of different kinds sewn together to form patterns. Their bargaining was completely silent but conducted with gestures. Two women chatted while watching the spectacle, much as Natalya was.

"What's that language?" she asked, pointing with her chin at the warmly and well-dressed women, talking between themselves.

Turgenev followed the direction and saw the same two women. He listened to their chatter for a bit, then said, "It's vaguely Germanic but not German. Some of the words even sound somewhat French. English, maybe?"

"I don't speak that," she said. "French, yes; Mokrenko caught me with that. German, too. No English."

Hoisting the coil of rope he'd purchased over one shoulder, he said, "They're here, so they likely speak Russian. Let's go ask."

"Sophie Karlovna Buxhoeveden," was the answer, in Russian, followed by, "And this is my friend, Miss Mather." Sophie then proceeded to translate some of that into English for her friend.

"Buxhoeveden...Buxhoeveden," Natalya rolled the name around her mouth a few times before coming up with, "Baroness Buxhoeveden; you were a lady-in-waiting to the tsarina."

"Shshsh, young lady," Sophie cautioned, "I have enough trouble already with the local authorities. And how would you know that, anyway?"

"That's a long story," Turgenev interrupted. "Oh, and please excuse my manners; Maxim Sergeyevich Turgenev, at your service. You seem very concerned about the local 'authorities.'"

"I've heard too much about what the prisons are like for a 'political' not to be. And since the Bolsheviks asserted their authority here in Tobolsk, not so long ago, I've felt the need to be careful. I mean, when it was just my dentist who was a Red, it wasn't so bad. And she, at least, was a competent dentist."

"Fair enough," he said. "I wouldn't want to see the inside of one and I have no political baggage whatsoever." This last, of course, was not remotely true. "Could I offer you ladies lunch? And, for languages; do you and your friend speak French?"

"We do."

"So do Natalya and I. Let French, then, be our language."

There was another hotel near the town center. It, too, offered meals for a price in a warm dining room. Turgenev, Natalya, and their two new acquaintances went in there and waited for someone to bring menus.

Looking around, the lieutenant said, "Place like this, I'd expect them to just post the menu on a chalkboard."

At the next table, a man, sitting alone, and already well on his way to drunkenness and slurring his words, said,

"Why botha? The men...men...menu this time of ye...ar is always the sa...me. Rye-ey bre...ad and soup. Sometimes the soup is bif...sometimes...sterlet....sometimes...well...sometimes you don' really wanna know. To be fairrr, when they have sterlet, it's actually ppppretty ggggood."

"Comrade," said Turgenev, "I know it's not my business, but isn't it a little early in the day for this?"

"Whennnn...you haf los' your jo...ob...that you hel' for t'irty year...zzz...wha' diff...er...ence...t'e time o' day."

"You have a point," the lieutenant conceded. "Who did you work for."

"T'e tsa...tsa...t'e tsar."

There is a God, thought the lieutenant. *Well...there is, but His hand may not be in this. Small town, after all, and what's a recently fired servant to do but get drunk?*

"I am Maxim Sergeyevich Turgenev," the lieutenant introduced himself. "To whom do I have the honor of addressing myself?"

The drunk leaned over and reached out a hand, only to collapse to the floor unconscious.

"Been expecting this to happen," said one of the waiters of the hotel. He called over a couple of men to pick the drunk up and toss him outside into the icy street.

Turgenev intervened. "Don't you have rooms here?"

"He isn't paying for a room. Out he goes."

The lieutenant reached into a pocket and pulled out some gold ten-ruble coins. "How many days in a decent room—with a fire—will this buy him?"

"With meals?" asked the waiter.

"Yes."

"Six days."

Certain he was being cheated, still Turgenev said, "Then take these and take him up to a room. And what *is* the soup for today?"

"Sterlet, served with bread and butter. Despite what the drunk just said, there is a little more pattern to the menu than that. Fridays and Wednesdays are always fish, yes, often sterlet, but sometimes other fish. Mondays tend to beef, Tuesdays to pork. Thursdays will be chicken or some other kind of fowl. Saturdays and Sundays are not that predictable, so it's best to ask.

"I can tell quality when I see it, too," said the waiter. "Today being sterlet, well, you gut a sterlet, you also get caviar. Would you and your . . ."

"My sister," Turgenev supplied, "and our friends."

"Of course. Your sister. And friends. Well, would you and your sister and your 'friends' care for some caviar with thin sliced toasted bread and sour cream?"

"Sour cream? In Tobolsk? In the dead of winter?"

"We have a deal with a nunnery that runs a dairy not too far from here. So will you have it?"

Turgenev stole a glance at Natalya, who seemed about ready to drool at the prospect.

"Yes, please."

"And the soup and bread?"

"Oh, by all means."

"Thank you, Maxim Sergeyevich," whispered Natalya across the table after the waiter had left. "Yes, thank you," added Sophie, a sentiment echoed in English by Miss Mather.

In the course of the meal, which was, as the drunk had claimed, "pretty good," Turgenev worked on extracting whatever information he could glean from Baroness Buxhoeveden.

"I was staying at the Kornilov House," she admitted, "right up until the Reds demanded I move out. Fortunately, Miss Mather was able to accommodate me in her rental."

Turgenev resisted the impulse to be polite and offer perhaps better accommodations. *That she knows things I want to know does not necessarily mean she should be trusted with things I do know.*

"As for the royal family; they're cold, hungry, miserable, and frequently unwell. But they persevere; it's an inspiration really."

"How are they doing for money?" Turgenev asked.

"That situation is not good. They've had to let many of their personal retainers go;" she replied, "that drunk was apparently one of them, though I couldn't put a name to his face."

"I'm not sure he could, either," muttered Turgenev, in Russian, rather than French, raising a titter from both the Russian-speaking females. Returning to French, he asked, "Is there a way to get money to them?"

"It's been done," Sophie answered. "I've been a conduit to pass things to the valet, Volkov. But I think a certain amount, whether of money or food, finds its way into someone's pocket or larder before it gets to the family."

"I confess," said Turgenev, "that the idea of the ex-royal family living in want disturbs me. Is it possible, then, do you think, to have someone else carry money in?"

Sophie thought about that for a moment. "Well, there are people who work inside but have quarters outside. So maybe."

"What is better to send, gold and silver coin or currency?"

"A ten ruble gold coin," she answered, "is worth as much as a one hundred ruble note, for some purposes. But, then, the notes are lighter and easier to pass."

"A mix, then, but I insist that what I send to the tsar gets to the tsar. Can you, Baroness Buxhoeveden, make arrangements for my sister, here, to bring money in. I'll be happy to give a ten percent premium to whichever person still working inside gets her in and out."

Sophie thought upon this, weighing the greed and corruption of both the Bolshevik guards and some of the tsar's remaining staff. "Kirpichnikov," she said. "He's a cook *cum* pigkeeper. It's very hard to tell where cooking ends and pigkeeping begins, too. But he's said to be extremely loyal and can come and go without much difficulty. He could, I think, bring an assistant with him."

"Perfect," said Turgenev.

Governor's House, Tobolsk

Since Natalya had been seen at the gate before, it seemed wise to disguise her a bit. This was done partly by lowering her standard of dress from the way the freed women had dressed her to something more approaching what would be expected of the local peasantry. The market had been most useful for this. Other changes included putting her hair up in twisted braids and adding a few smudges to her face. Perhaps most importantly, given that she'd be dealing with men, was that she now sported enormous breasts, monuments to both one of Sophie's own bras and one or more of the imperial mints.

"It will have to do," said Sophie, standing back and scrutinizing her handiwork.

There were, as usual, two guards on the gate. One held his rifle at port arms, more for show than for any other reason, while the other unlatched and pushed slightly open the broad wooden gate. Both had a hard time keeping their eyes off of Natalya's false chest.

"Thank you, my friends, thank you!" exclaimed Kirpichnikov. He had a small basket hanging from one arm. This, by way of a tip, he passed over to the man who'd opened the gate.

"And who's your little friend?" that guard asked. "She looks familiar, at least a bit."

"Oh, I'm going to put her to work as a scullery."

The guard shrugged. "But how are you paying her?" he asked. "You-know-who has no money."

"She doesn't cost much. She's an orphan. These days, such as her can be put to work for the price of a meal."

If there was a double entendre there, the guard chose to ignore it. He waved the pair through.

None of the royal family were out in the outer enclosure, though there was a big pile of unsawn wood standing near a saw and a couple of wooden sawhorses.

"This way, girl," Kirpichnikov ordered, leading her past a picket fence, through a rectangular opening in another wall, and to the kitchen, which was a separate building to the west of the main mansion, connected by an enclosed passageway.

Once they were safely inside, and no guards were seen hanging about, the cook and pigkeeper pointed east, toward the house. "Follow that passageway," he said. "There will be stairs to your left after you get to the house. The royal family will be either upstairs or in the dining room which will be to your left front. You have maybe twenty minutes to get back here and get to work on the pots and pans before it begins to look suspicious. If you see me with a guard when you return, thank me graciously for letting you use the toilet, clear?"

"Yes," Natalya answered, "clear enough."

"Now go."

Given that she weighed half a *pood*—about seventeen pounds—more than usual, with most of that being top heavy and front-centered, Natalya walked gracefully enough. That had required a bit of practice, too. Reaching the house and entering it, she stopped for a moment, to listen. There were no sounds coming from the room Kirpichnikov had told her was the dining room, so she turned and began to ascend the stairs.

At the top floor, she did hear voices. Most she didn't recognize but from her left front, over where the dining room stood, she thought she heard the Romanov girls. They were speaking Russian, but actually had non-Russian accents, a result of growing up in a household where the only language their parents had shared from the beginning, and still the lingua franca of the family, had been English.

She hurried across the floor and finding the door locked, knocked a few times to gain admittance.

The door was partly opened by a stout girl, stout,

though terribly pretty with enormous eyes. Those eyes could not be mistaken for anyone else's.

"Let me in, Maria," said Natalya, to the girl blocking the doorway. "For the love of God, let me in."

"Do we know you?"

"Yes, from happier times. Now get out of the way and let me in."

They all spoke in whispers, with Natalya making her re-introductions. "I'm that Natalya. My mother and father, sad to say, are dead, murdered by the Bolsheviks. A . . . a friend asked me to try to get some money in to you. Speaking of which, have any of you any idea how *cold* gold can be on one's tits? And it doesn't help when they're *small* tits."

With that, Natalya partially disrobed, then began taking out small packets of tightly cloth-wrapped gold coins from her sort-of-kind-of brassiere. The girls, Olga, Tatiana, Maria, and Anastasia stood open-mouthed at the sudden shower of wealth.

"That's about six thousand, five hundred rubles in gold," Natalya informed them. She then began to pull tightly tied bundles of cash from up under her skirt. "That's about forty thousand in currency. It's really only worth maybe as little as four thousand in coin. Now I need some clothing to fill up this enormous bra in its place."

The girls quickly began assembling a set of false breasts from whatever cloth could be spared.

As Turgenev had coached her, she continued, "And now, if you want the largesse to keep flowing, you need to take control of this money and show it to your parents. And then you have to get them to hire me. Can you do this?"

"We can't show it to Mother," the tallest one, Tatiana, said. "She not only talks too much but everything that happens that isn't a complete disaster is, in her view, a sign from God of our eventual release."

"Besides, she'll probably waste it," added Maria, the somewhat stout girl with the huge eyes. "Tati, you should take control of it and arrange to hire . . . by the way, tell me again, how do we know you?"

"We've met when my parents were guests of your family. I was little then; it was before the war. I am . . . well, since the murder of my parents I am now Baroness Sorokin. But you can't tell anyone that."

"Are you associated with Little Markov and a rescue attempt?" Tatiana asked.

"Who's Little Markov? And, no, I am sorry, but I don't know anything about a rescue attempt." *Well, one truth and one lie. Forgive me, please, God. Though, in fact, I don't know much about it. As Maxim said, "What I do not know cannot be tortured out of me."*

"Little Markov," Tatiana explained, "is a nice boy, a lieutenant of the Crimean cavalry, who writes to mother and would desperately like to rescue us from this place. I don't believe it will happen."

"Sorry, then," Natalya said, "but I've never heard of him. Anyway, time is short. If you can arrange to hire me in some capacity, pass the word to Kirpichnikov. He'll know where to find me."

"Why," asked Anastasia, the youngest of the lot, "would

you bring all this money then ask us to hire you for a fraction of it?"

"No time! I have to go now. Just arrange the hiring."

Camp, south of Tobolsk

Mokrenko arrived, after a day's hard ride, to find things well in order, the horses healthy, and a guard properly posted.

Lieutenant Babin rolled out from a lean-to shelter. Mokrenko saluted, then dismounted from his short Yakut horse. Corporal Koslov stood up from the fire he was attending and joined the trio. After an exchange of pleasantries, Mokrenko asked, "How's our man, Shukhov?"

"I'm fine, Sergeant," came from one of the other lean-tos. "Fine enough that, if you people need me to blow something up in Tobolsk, you had better bring me there. I've already prepared the lake, here, for blasting. If you need me to blow anything substantial up in Tobolsk, you had better get me some more explosive."

"Is he well enough to travel?" Mokrenko asked Babin, *sotto voce*.

"Probably. I'm not a doctor but I can, at least, say there's no more external bleeding and no sign of infection that I can see."

"All right, I'll be taking him with me, then. As for the rest of you, just wait. Cut wood for four big bonfires. And Lieutenant Turgenev says—well, a message from the rear says—that it would be a great help if you could hunt for a lot of meat. As much as we can get. Cold as it is, it will keep in this weather until needed. I'm going to be ranging to the east and northeast of here, looking for the same. I'll be taking four of the horses and two of the sleighs; Shukhov can drive the other one. We'll take my horse behind one of them."

"Define 'a lot,' Sergeant."

"As much as you can get. 'A thousand *pood* would not be too much,' Lieutenant Turgenev told me."

"I doubt we'll get that much," said Babin, "but tell him we'll do the best we can."

"No man can ask more," Mokrenko agreed, then bellowed, "Shukhov, you lazy excuse for an engineer, pack your bags! And set up two sleighs; we're taking them for the town."

Interlude

Sverdlov and Trotsky: Strange Happenings

Sverdlov could have figured it was someone coming to pay a call by the ringing bells from the carriage or sleigh. It had been, as was perhaps to be expected, Trotsky with some potentially dire news.

The Cyrillic type on the paper in his hand began to blur in his vision, but Yakov Sverdlov forced himself to focus on the report. Trotsky wouldn't have hand delivered this summary at midnight if it weren't important. Recently shuffled from Foreign Affairs to Military Affairs, the lateral demotion had done nothing to dim Trotsky's ambition, nor dissuade him from waking up Lenin's right-hand man for trifles.

On the heels of two major setbacks, Trotsky was still somewhat timid in council, and wanted Sverdlov's backing to bring up new business. Trotsky had initially opposed the dissolution of the Constituent Assembly *and* had failed to gain anything of note at the negotiations of Brest-Litovsk, but rather the opposite.

Reaching the end of the report, Sverdlov set the paper down, removed his spectacles and pinched the bridge of his nose.

"So, the Germans are sifting through our people," Sverdlov said. "Is that it?"

"Yes, Comrade Sverdlov," Trotsky said.

Sverdlov opened his eyes and examined the Commissar for Defense. A man of middling height with a shock of brown hair over a prominent forehead, beakish nose and goatee, Trotsky's eyes were bright and penetrating, even at this late hour.

"You don't think they're just sifting for manpower to use against the Western allies, do you?" Sverdlov said.

"No, I don't," Trotsky said, "though that's one of the stories they've apparently put out. From what we can tell, they're not asking anything about the Western Allies, but about ideology; how they feel about the tsar, about communism and such. Furthermore, it's not a broad enough effort for them to recruit significant manpower. The Germans have more than a million of our people imprisoned, but they're focusing their efforts on a few Guards regiments and maybe some Cossacks. Even if every man they've interviewed volunteered to fight for them, it wouldn't be enough to make a difference in France. They can burn up twenty thousand men a day there, some days.

"At this point, my best guess is that they intend to toss the men they've recruited into the scale, here, to start or exacerbate a civil war."

Sverdlov drummed the fingers of his right hand on the report.

"Right," he agreed. "We're the target. It's not many men, but perhaps enough to cause trouble for us. You're right, Leon, bring this to the committee at the next meeting. I will back you."

"There are some other oddities, too," Trotsky said. "Some very strange things going on."

Chapter Twenty-Two

L59 Being Launched

**Airship Hangar,
a mile and a half north of Jambol, Bulgaria**

Sergeant Kaledin was pleased, actually, that they'd nixed the plan to carry his horses and mules aboard the airship. Oh, they were healthy enough, those that had survived, but he really didn't know how they'd take to the changes in air pressure, the confinement, the noises and smells. *Just as well they're not going. And I'm glad that*

German had the presence of mind to put my poor mule,
Lydia, out of her pain. She was a good mule and should
not have been allowed to suffer.

Glad, too, I never had to make that case; I don't think
anyone would have supported me.

Kaledin led, rather than rode, a light wagon pulled by
one of the surviving horses. He'd made this trip already—
twice—to bring tentage for two hundred men along with
a good deal of food. More wagons stretched behind him.

Most of the battalion remained back at Camp
Budapest, but the first contingent to leave—Fourth
Company—marched ahead of the Cossack sergeant,
singing rather joyfully at being finally on their way to do
great things. Shortly before turning off the road and
heading straight for the hangar, they passed the ruins of
an almost completely erased monastery that had once
stood over a healing spring. The locals knew that a spring
was there, somewhere, but the Turks who had destroyed
the monastery had done such a fine job of the destruction
that the people of the neighborhood had long since lost
the memory of just where it had been.

Up ahead of Kaledin, the men marched with skis and
poles over their shoulders. Kostyshakov, marching at the
point, just ahead of Captain Cherimisov, turned about and
called out, "First Sergeant, can you and the men give us a
song?"

Mayevsky saluted and began:

Akh, vy, seni, moi seni,
Seni novyye moi,

At which point Fourth Company and that slice of Headquarters and Support with them began to belt out:

Seni novyye, klenovyye,
Reshetchatyye.[6]

The song continued with verses about leaving home, letting a falcon loose to fly, the falcon striking from the air, and an old man who was very strict indeed. Finally, it was also about going home at last.

"God," said Kaledin, the Cossack, "but I *do* love the Russian Army."

"They do sing rather well, don't they?" observed Captain Bockholt to his exec and navigator, Maas, from the gondola of the airship.

"Yes, sir. If they can keep it up, we'll have a more entertaining trip—or four or five—than usual."

"I'm going to go find their colonel, Kostyshakov. Station yourself in the cargo bay to support *Obermaschinisten-maat* Engelke, in case any of the Russians want to argue matters."

"Sir."

With that, Bockholt left the gondola via the ladder to the ground. From there he left the hangar by a side door and strode to the little tent village, no more than thirty tents, if that, set up west of the hangar.

---

[6] Very free and loose translation:
  Oh, you, my porch, my new porch
  My new latticed maple porch
  (Yes, Russian folk and army songs, to the extent these differ, often revolve around sentiments about the merest things of home.)

As soon as Kostyshakov spotted Bockholt, he told Cherimisov that he was going to see the German, and dashed away from the formation. He and Bockholt met in the middle ground, between airship and tents, and shook hands.

Said the skipper, "We'll be ready for an eight-thirty departure tomorrow to cross over the lines, just south of Yekatarenoslav, at half past nineteen hundred, tomorrow."

"Why just south?" asked Kostyshakov.

"Angle of the moon. We don't want to silhouette ourselves against it, but we equally don't want it lighting us up for the city to see."

"The two fighters?"

"They'll take off about an hour before we're supposed to get to Yekaterinoslav, with orders to down anything they see flying not positively identified as friendly. We're big, so more visible, but anything likely to see us will still— *probably*—be seen by them."

Bockholt continued, "For the rest of the trip we'll try to avoid major cities and bigger towns. It's not that we won't be spotted; we will. Rather, I want us, if we're going to be spotted, to be spotted as far from a telegraph station as possible."

"You heard no animals are going, right?"

"Yes. And you cannot imagine my joy at avoiding having my ship crapped on by a couple-score horses and mules. Or having them panic. Speaking of panic . . ."

"The vodka's in the wagons, Captain," said Kostyshakov. "Mind, I don't *know* that any of my men would panic, but I also don't know that they won't. I've never flown before, myself, and I don't mind saying I find the prospect a little frightening."

"So did I," said Bockholt, "before I tried it. Once I did, though, *well!* It's truly enjoyable . . . most of the time."

"And when it isn't?" asked Daniil.

"Hmmm . . . how many of your men speak German? No, I'm not changing the subject, but they need to be briefed on procedures and concerns."

"Well? Not many of them. Most of my officers do and a few of my noncoms. Is there a list of things the men should be told?"

Nodding, Bockholt answered, "There are a few. Number one is that it's going to be *cold* up there, so cold—especially at night—that you will imagine Siberia in the winter to be downright tropical. And the hammocks we've slung for the men will let body heat out in all directions. They need to put on anything and everything they have that will hold heat in."

"Right. We knew that."

"Did my man, Signaler Mueller, explain about the no fires rule?"

Kostyshakov nodded, "He did. We've collected up all the carbide lanterns and separated the chambers. It was a major pain in the ass, too, to mark them so we can get matching ones back together. I've also had all the matches and lighters collected, as well as the tobacco, so they'll have no motivation to try to create a fire."

Bockholt smiled, appreciatively. "They *will* have a motivation, of course, but there'll be nothing to burn they'll want to burn. Still, I cannot thank you enough for that. But speaking of cold and fires; we have a *very* limited ability to produce hot drinks. I need every bit of it to keep functional the men who must run the airship. There's none to spare—literally none—for anyone or anything else. I considered getting a thousand thermos bottles for hot drinks for your men, but the weight would have meant going over our limit."

"I understand."

"Ammunition?" Bockholt asked, though he was beginning to think his worries and doubts were silly.

"All stored with the cargo, to be issued, for the most part, only once we're on the ground. Some of it is ready-stored. We'll give that to the security men just as they debark."

"Acceptable," the skipper said.

"We've set up scales," he continued. "As each man arrives at the loading spot, fully equipped, we're going to weigh him. My crew will then lead him to a hammock that will give us the best balance for the airship. We'll try to pay attention to unit integrity, but I cannot promise it."

"Do what you must," agreed the Russian.

"We've cleaned and sterilized one ballast bladder for drinking water," the skipper continued. "Another is designated for urine. Since there's a delay between drinking and pissing, it is faintly possible we'll have to move someone around in flight. We won't unless we must.

"We're carrying fifteen chamber pots and have separated out and enclosed with cloth fifteen places your men can relieve themselves. They're marked, nine for crapping and six for pissing. Your quartermaster, Romeyko, has designated two men per lift to be the chamber pot ... mmm ... caretakers.

"I know my man, Mueller, suggested we'd be able to let the men stretch a bit and walk about. He was in error. We must have absolutely minimal moving about," said Bockholt. "Too many risks from people moving about in the ship."

"I understand that," said Kostyshakov. "Going to be hard on cold men."

"I know," agreed the skipper, "but not as hard as causing damage to the ship six hundred meters above the ground might be."

"Point. How long will it take to load?"

"Our best estimate is three hours but I'm holding out for five. We'll need to start putting men into their hammocks at five in the morning."

"Lord God, what is that heavenly aroma?" asked Mayevsky of Taenzler, the pair of them standing by the *Gulaschkanone*, itself in the center of the little tent village.

"Meat in the stew," the German chef replied. "Good meat. And good vegetables. And spices. Fresh bread with none of those less than desirable additives or undesirable subtractions. This is what I told your commander about; the kind of food that gives mixed feelings since we only feed this kind of food to our men when they're about to be ordered into the attack."

Taenzler shook his head a bit. "It's not just for morale, but also for strength, energy, and health. Which makes me wonder why we don't feed it to the men when they're about to *be* attacked. It's not like it's all that hard to predict, after all, what with bombardments lasting *weeks*."

"Above my pay grade," said Mayevsky, "but, for us, no,

you were never that predictable. This is tonight's meal, yes?"

"Yes. For tomorrow morning I've got *syrniki, draniki,* and *real* butter, jam, and honey. We'll issue the lunch and dinner—cold and dry, all of it, but the vodka and the *salo,* I'm afraid—with breakfast. After that you start loading. Though I've oversupplied tonight's meal and anyone who wants to take some tomorrow will be welcome to it."

"*Feldwebel* Taenzler," said Mayevsky, with complete seriousness, "you're a fucking treasure. Anyone's army would be lucky to have you. And if you ever want a job with a different army..."

"First Sergeant Mayevsky, thank you, but when this obscenity of a war is over I just want to go home to my wife."

"Ah, the wife," Mayevsky sighed. "I miss mine, too. I haven't seen her in almost four years."

"Same. She writes. Says times are hard at home, food even worse and more scarce than what we get. Not enough coal to heat the house. And the little ones...it's awful."

"Cheer up, old man," said Mayevsky. "At least you've had word. I've had nothing for over a year."

Taenzler nodded, chewed his lower lip for a bit, and then walked to the other end of the *Gulaschkanone.* He extracted a bottle and a couple of glasses, then opened the bottle and filled the glasses from it. The bottle went back to its hiding spot before he returned and passed one of the glasses over.

"*Ansatzkorn,*" Taenzler explained, though the word meant nothing to Mayevsky. "Here's to the success of your mission, the end of the fucking war, and getting home to wives and children we hope are still alive and well."

"May it please God," said the Russian before clinking glasses with the German and tossing off the glasses.

Half-choking and between gasps, the German explained, "It will serve...as a rather...strong... disinfectant, too."

Vasenkov couldn't help himself, he liked the old German cook who did so much to keep the men of the battalion well fed. As he passed by the *Gulaschkanone*, in the evening's fading light, he had half a loaf of bread under one arm and his mess kit held out by the other.

Using his ladle, the German scooped up and deposited a *most* healthy portion into the mess tin. Then he scooped up some more, about half a ladle, and deposited that, too.

"Eh, there's plenty," he informed the Russian. "No sense in letting any of it go to waste."

In fact, the *Gulaschkanone* was supposed to be able to serve two hundred and fifty men. The mere one hundred and thirty-seven of the first lift hardly overtasked it.

It's not impossible, either, that Taenzler was padding the head count a bit. ("Oh, it's *easy* as pie, *Podpolkovnik* Kostyshakov. Every man here is still officially here until the last of you has left and the camp is closed. Since there are no plans—at least, none *I've* been informed of—to close the camp, I drew a few days, okay, maybe a week, in advance...exigencies of war and all that.")

Vasenkov took his meal and went to sit. He'd always appeared something of a loner to the rest of the men, though competent enough, to be sure, that no one went out of their way to sit with him, leaving him alone with his troubles.

On the theory that whatever an imperialist or capitalist wants you to do, you should do the opposite, I have secreted on my person three wooden matches. I could, I imagine, under one pretext or other, get close to one of those leaky gas bags they warned us about, make a hole, and light one off. Bring the whole thing crashing down like a meteor streaking from the heavens, but moreso.

Of course, I, too, will be riding that flaming meteor down. I have always been willing to lay down my life for the revolution. Well, at least since having my eyes opened to the future by the works of Marx and Lenin, I have. But suicide? This is altogether a harder thing. I'm not sure I can.

And even if I could bring myself to do it, kill all these men who are my comrades and friends? No; I don't think I can do that either.

But I also cannot stand by and just let the royal family be rescued to serve as a rally point for the enemies of the revolution. If I believed in a God, I'd pray for guidance. What am I to do?

Vasenkov was one of the first to be loaded aboard. After a good—*no, it was a* remarkably *good*—breakfast, with his bedroll slung over one shoulder, his MP18 draped from his neck by his sling, pack on his back, breadbag and canteen properly slung, with his skis and poles over one shoulder, he presented himself.

"Skis, poles, and pack marked with your name?" asked his platoon sergeant, *Feldfebel* Kostin.

"Yes, Sergeant," Vasenkov answered.

Kostin took the skis and handed them to a platoon runner to place in a forming criss-crossing pile on the cargo deck.

"Anything in your pack you need?"

"Oh, shit!" said Vasenkov. "Yes, Sergeant. Thanks for reminding me! My mittens!"

"Dig 'em out, then. Then turn over your pack to Sobchak." This was the same Sobchak who had mistakenly shot his partner and friend, Sotnikov, and was now serving as a runner. The pack, too, went into a growing pile.

"This way, Vasenkov," shouted the first sergeant, glaring with his one good eye and gesturing with one hand. The first sergeant stood at the base of a flexible ladder, one of several, that led upward to and past a large number of hammocks. There was a scale by the first sergeant with one of the German crew in attendance. The German weighed the Russian—"Skinny fucker, aren't you?"—did some scribbling with a pencil on a notepad, then pointed to a hammock about eleven *arshini* above the deck.

Mayevsky asked, "See that fucking hammock the German pointed at, Vasenkov. The top one on that row? Empty?"

"Yes, First Sergeant."

"That one's for you. Up you go, boy. No dawdling. Get up there; make up your bed roll; and get in it. Once you're in you can have a belt of your vodka."

Vasenkov scrambled up the ladder leading to his bunk. With one hand on the ladder he used the other one to take his bedding from across his shoulder. Untying it proved to be difficult one-handed, so he ran an arm through the ladder up to the crook of his elbow and used both hands. Then he whip-snapped the bed roll lengthwise along the bunk. After spending a few moments opening it and spreading it out, he found that he had not the first clue as to how to actually get *into* the hammock.

There were reasons I avoided the navy.

Standing below and watching the mayhem, Mayevsky thought, *There's always something you miss. We should have had training in this, too.*

He pointed out the problem to the German sailor running the scales. The German muttered something that the first sergeant took to mean approximately, *There's always something that you miss.*

With a great Teutonic bellow, the German caught the attention of every man in the bay. Once he had that, with practiced skill, he, himself, scrambled up a ladder and demonstrated how it was done. This involved locking one's arms into the outside folds of the hammock, lifting one's lower body up to it, and then rolling over.

Well, shit, thought Vasenkov, as he retrieved his bedroll, draped it over his shoulder, and pulled himself in. Once settled in, it was still no easy matter to get the blankets and ground cloth under his body. He managed, eventually, as did all the others but one. That one, a cook from the First Company, fell to the deck screaming, arms and legs waving in panic. He hit with a thump that shook the ship, then had to be carried off with a possible back injury.

Some hundreds of German and Bulgarian ground crew stood around in clusters, each holding a strap that led to single, stouter straps that, in turn, led to the airship. Daniil couldn't tell how many of the lighter straps led from each heavier one, but it seemed to be about ten to a dozen, maybe more in a few spots.

"Notify Strategic Recon that we're on our way, Basanets," said Kostyshakov, just before boarding himself. "Our estimated time of arrival is between one and four AM, the day after tomorrow, winds depending. Fires to mark the landing spot, but not within one hundred and fifty *arshini*. Local security is their problem until we're half unloaded."

"Yes, sir," said the Exec, who then pointed with his chin at something or someone behind Kostyshakov.

Daniil turned to see Mueller, the signaler *cum* liaison, standing at ease. "The captain requests your presence in the forward gondola, sir. He says, 'This is something the Russian commander is going to want to see.' From experience, sir, the captain is right."

"I suspect so," agreed Kostyshakov, in German. Turning to Basanets, he continued, in Russian, "We'll be on radio listening silence unless something disastrous happens, something that scrubs the mission anyway. But you can get messages to us. Also, confirm that the two escort fighters at Yekaterinoslav are going to take off at the right time. Yes, not really our job, but maybe our lives if the Germans screw it up."

With that, Daniil followed Mueller back inside, then along the walkway that led to a ladder which, in turn, led down into the open and then into the command gondola.

"Ah, *Podpolkovnik* Kostyshakov; this is something you won't want to miss!" exclaimed Captain Bockholt. "The nly thing more exciting than takeoff is coming home in ne piece and unburnt."

In front of Daniil's eyes, the great hangar doors were lowly swung open wide. One of the command crew said omething in aeronauticalese to the captain, who gave an qually incomprehensible answer. No matter, the import of he message was made clear as the ground crew began valking forward, dragging L59 forward with them by the traps.

It is grand, thought Kostyshakov. *But it's not the view r, rather, not the view alone. Rather, it's knowing how big his bastard is* combined *with the view, the knowledge hat men can not only build something this big but move t by hand and foot power.*

It took just over two minutes from the moment its ose reached the opening for the airship to fully merge. Presumably on command, all the men holding traps let go. The ascent was fairly gentle, but there was o doubt, even without being able to see, that the ship vas going up.

"There are problems with ascending," Bockholt xplained. "If we go too high, the air pressure differential auses us to lose hydrogen. Lose enough and we lose lift. And, too, the lower temperature up there causes the ydrogen to lose volume hence to lose lift, too. Unless ve're bombing England, when we have to go as high as oossible to stay out of the reach of the defenses, the smart ourse for an airship is rather low, a couple of hundred neters. That's another reason for us to traverse /ekaterinoslav at night. Of course, too, we're going to have o go a bit higher to get over the Urals."

"How will we know where we are?" Kostyshakov asked

"A mixture of dead reckoning—landmarks, compass and speed—but we also use celestial navigation, chronometer and sextant, just as if we were on a ship at sea. Don fear, we'll put you down where your forward team said they'd be waiting."

Daniil took a last look out a side window. The groun was fast slipping behind. *About two hundred and fift arshini up, I should think.*

"I think I should be getting back to my men, Captain.

"Of course, sir. Sleep well. You're as safe as in you mother's own arms."

My mother's arms were never this fucking cold, though Kostyshakov, shivering miserably, like everyone else, i the unheated compartment. Some of the men apparentl had no trouble falling asleep, indeed, seemed to go t sleep as a way to avoid the misery.

Note to self: If I survive, and am ever in a position t do something about it, a way to heat airships, th designing of. Other note to self: After the troubles are over back to school for engineering.

Nice to hear no one is panicking. Rather, it's nice to no hear it. This whole flying thing? I'm not sure it's got future for anything but lunatics who actually like bein someplace they can fall to their deaths from. For me, swear, I will never take this mode of transportation agai if I can avoid it. What was it that old Englishman said something about being on a ship is being in prison, bu with the added chance of being drowned? Well, at leas on a ship you can walk around freely. Being on an airshi is being in an insane asylum, with a straitjacket on, and the chance of being burnt alive.

Daniil took out his signed picture of Tatiana Nicholaevna Romanova. He never let any of the officers or men of the battalion see that he had it, lest they think this was all a personal crusade. But he'd look at it, sometimes, in the dead of night, by the light of a candle.

The fact is, I don't even know if you still want me. There were only those couple of letters before I was captured, and those I had to destroy lest the Germans use them against you and Russia. Only this picture did both I and the Huns miss. Well ... I can hope your heart has not grown cold toward me. And, if it has ... well ... this is still my sworn duty to you and your family.

Yekaterinoslav, Russia

It was about an hour before sunset, the weather clear and fine. Two German fighter pilots stood by their machines on an unimproved grass strip. The planes were both fueled, with a ground crewman standing by each to twist the engines to life.

Sergeant Karl Thom was an experienced pilot, first flying a reconnaissance plane and then, with twelve victories, to date, as a fighter pilot. He deeply resented being pulled from his slot in *Jagdstaffel* 21 for this nothing mission at the ass end of nowhere.

Adding insult to injury, he hadn't been sent off with a new Fokker D. VII, oh, *no*. Instead, when tasked, his commander had decided that an old Albatros D. V would be plenty good enough.

To be fair, thought Thom, *at least he let me take my*

pick of the D. Vs. And, given there's nobody here to fight, a D. VII would have been a waste. I'm just angry at being pulled from the action. Well, that and that the D. V is a simply rotten aircraft, from its tendency to fall to pieces in a dive to its miserably placed instrumentation suite.

Thom's mate, from a different squadron entirely, was also a Carl, with a C, Sergeant Carl Graeper. Graeper didn't seem nearly as annoyed as Thom felt.

Maybe it's because his squadron, Jasta 50, wasn't getting D. VIIs when he was pulled out.

Thom consulted his watch. "About that time," he announced to Graeper.

Both men climbed up their aircraft and into the cockpits. Two of the ground crewmen stood in front of the planes, their hands grasping the propellers. Another pair stood on tires, helping the pilots to settle in.

At a signal from their pilots, the former jerked the propellers counterclockwise, causing the motors to shudder into life. They sprang back, instantly, to avoid losing hands to the spinning blades. Then each pair bent down to drag away the chock blocks that held the planes in place.

Thom fed a little more gas to the engine and was rewarded with a steady drone and a propeller that disappeared into the thin blur in front of him. He began to taxi to the runway, then swung into a wide right turn. The grass stretched out before him. Using his left thumb, Thom applied throttle, increasing his speed rapidly. In no time he was airborne and making a slow spiral upward.

Glancing over his left shoulder—*God bless whoever decided to get rid of that miserable, sight-blocking headrest*—to see Graeper rising behind him on the same basic upward spiraling pattern.

The spiral gave way to a long, slow set of turns, scanning three hundred and sixty degrees around for any threat to the airship he was tasked with protecting. There was nothing there, though.

For all the need for me here, I could have done as much by flying in France.

Making another left-hand turn, it was the shadow of the airship that Thom first saw, a huge, darkened, and regular shape on the ground. Until he realized it was too regular, the pilot initially thought it was a cloud casting that shadow. Adjusting his gaze then, he saw it, the L59, lower than he really expected, gracefully and effortlessly moving toward Yekaterinoslav from the west.

Again Thom consulted his watch. *A bit early but the sun will still be down before they cross by the town.*

He began to descend to a lower level, largely with the fixed intention of getting on the ground before it became necessary for the ground crew to light beacon fires.

L59

High in his hammock, Vasenkov thought, *I do not think I have ever been this cold in my life. Forget the calming effect; if it weren't for the vodka making the blood flow faster, I think my hands and feet would be nothing but blocks of ice. And it's worse for me than most because I am so thin.*

But vodka won't keep me from freezing solid on its own.

From his bread bag he took a sausage, squared off, hard, and dry, as well as a chunk of bread. *"Landjaeger,"*

Taenzler called these. We don't have sausage like this back home. Oh, well, how bad can it . . . At his first bite, Vasenkov realized he had fallen in love. *These are perfect, wonderful. The perfect blend of lean and fat, perfectly cured, dry on the outside but, oh, so juicy on the inside.* "Two with some cheese and a half a pound of bread makes a meal," he said. *I can see where they would.*

Now if only those religion-addled fools in the other hammocks would stop praying so loudly . . .

From Yekaterinoslav, the L59 didn't make a straight course for the landing point south of Tobolsk. Instead, it went generally east-northeast to a spot about thirty kilometers north of Severodonetsk, then turned due east, passing over the Volga River well north of Tsaritsyn. From that crossing, another five hundred kilometers saw it turn on a course of forty-five degrees, heading straight for the Urals' southern foothills in the vicinity of Krasnoshchekovo. All of these legs were lengthened by the fact that the ship took a zig-zag course, partly to avoid towns likely to have telegraph service and partly to cast doubt about their ultimate objective.

It wasn't until they passed a point just north-northwest of Petropavel that Bockholt ordered a turn, due north, toward the landing zone south of Tobolsk.

And then . . .

Landing Zone A, south of Tobolsk

Daniil was back in the control gondola, having been awakened by Mueller, who looked completely worn out, a sunken-faced, slack jawed zombie.

One suspects, thought Kostyshakov, *that it's a tougher job than it looks from the outside.*

This part they hadn't really been able to rehearse. Kostyshakov hadn't had any real choice but to kick the strategic reconnaissance team forward as soon as possible, with only limited guidance on how to prepare to receive an airship. The airship's crew had had limited time to both figure out and then show the men of Fourth Company how to secure an airship.

Going to be a total clusterfuck, thought Daniil, *especially in the dark . . . even with moonlight.*

The moon, for that matter, was pretty low in the sky. *We're so fucked.*

A sudden light from above, from the skin of the airship, caused Daniil to jerk his head up. *But where is the light . . .*

He looked out of one of the open windows and down. There, hanging below him, was a very bright flare, rocking from side to side as it descended under a parachute. *I did not know they could do that.*

Within a couple of minutes, Daniil saw a bright flash from below and forward, followed by a tremendous bang and a rumbling sound. A couple of minutes later four large fires sprang up, two by two, forming a rectangular box around a narrow inlet in what appeared to be an icebound lake, below.

"Very good," Bockholt said, with something approaching a tone of wonder in his voice. Turning to Kostyshakov, he added, "I don't think my own men could have set it up any better. They even got the wind angle as right as they could, given the terrain."

"What now?" asked Daniil.

"Now we vent hydrogen to reduce buoyancy and descend. It's a little tricky. It's also incredibly wasteful of hydrogen; that's why we wanted your troops to blow a hole in the ice so we can pump up water as ballast to make up for the loss of load when you all unload. I wish there were some other way to do this, but there isn't. Maybe someday."

Back in cargo, First Sergeant Mayevsky was kicking hammocks, some of them, and prodding others from below with a stick he seemed to have acquired from somewhere. "Up, you turds! Up! It's time to earn our pay again. And if any of you lowlifes have somehow been so negligent as to have let yourself freeze to death, so signify by staying in your hammocks. We'll just throw you overboard from a thousand feet. Don't worry; you won't feel a thing..."

Interlude

Sovnarkcom, the Council of Peoples' Commissars: Beware the Hun

The fire roaring in the hearth combined with the body heat of the men assembled in the meeting chamber of the Central Committee managed to bring the temperature in the room up to stifling—no mean feat in early spring in Petrograd. All the Party Commissars, from State to Railway Affairs, were gathered around the long wooden table that dominated the center of the room. Sitting at the head of the table, sweat glistening on the dome of his massive bald forehead, Vladimir Ilyich Lenin listened intently to the newly elected minister of agricultural affairs, Semyon Sereda. Sereda was the fourth man in as many months to occupy the Agricultural Commissariat since the October Revolution.

Lenin's eyes were red-rimmed with lack of sleep and darted nervously about the room, from the faces of the Commissars to the doors and back again as he listened to Sereda's litany of bad news. Seated at Lenin's right hand, Yakov Sverdlov regarded his friend and leader with frank concern. It was only two months since the last assassination attempt on the man, less than that since they'd forcibly disbanded the democratically elected Constituent Assembly.

The strain is visibly aging Ilyich before us.

Still, worn ragged or not, no other man had the same vision, the same will. The Revolution *needed* Vladimir Ilyich Lenin at its helm. Sverdlov had long since renounced the God of Abraham, so he eschewed prayer, contenting himself with a fervent hope that Lenin would remain cogent and healthy enough to continue the work for a while longer.

Semyon finished his doom-laden report.

"...in summary, comrades, we have shortfalls in every crop imaginable. Worse than that, our ability to move produce from the farms to the cities before those crops spoil is diminishing daily due to sabotage by monarchists and other undesirables. Furthermore, the *kulaks* often hide the grain we so desperately need—or if we don't send sufficient force, will often fight our troops to keep their grain."

"Bloodsucking rich bastards," Lenin said. "We know the problems, Semyon, what solutions might we enact?"

"Comrades, I wish your permission to commit a larger body of troops to redistribution activities and to incur summary punishment for *kulaks* who do not cooperate," Sereda said. "The *kulaks* will be less likely to resist once they see a few of their neighbors hanging from a scaffold. Also, if we can focus the peasants' and workers' anger and anxiety on the rich landowners, that binds them all the more tightly to the Revolution."

Lenin leaned back and stroked his goatee for several seconds.

"Yes," Lenin said. "An excellent thought, Semyon, work with Trotsky to allocate the troops. Is there anything else?"

In the silence that followed, Trotsky looked at Sverdlov for permission to bring up the reports from Hungary. Sverdlov nodded slightly.

"Comrades, I have a matter that may be of some import," Trotsky said.

"What is it, Leon?" Lenin asked.

"The first item is that the Germans have been recruiting former Imperial Guardsmen, in numbers that wouldn't matter to their war in the west, but that could matter to us. In relation to this, comrades in Hungary offered us, as a show of good faith, a potentially troubling bit of intelligence. Reports of strange activities on the part of the German Army there," Trotsky said.

"Where in Hungary?" asked Lenin.

"Somewhere around Budapest, but our friends have not been able to pinpoint a site."

"That is hardly our concern," Sereda said. "We are now neutral in their war. Besides, no location? It could be all fanciful."

"Agreed," Trotsky said. "It could be. But what if it's not and the Germans want them for further operations against us? Perhaps something covert?"

"That seems a little fanciful, too," Sereda said.

"Is it?" Sverdlov interrupted. "The Germans saw to it Comrade Lenin made his way back to Russia when it suited them. If our Revolutionary activities are worrying them now, it's not inconceivable they might use the same tactics twice."

"An excellent point," Lenin said. "Ensure we keep funds flowing to our friends in Germany and the Austro-Hungarian Empire. If the Germans intend to use our own people against us, we must know about it."

"What else, Leon?"

"Someone massacred a group of bandits who were attempting to rob the Trans-Siberian near Yekaterinburg. A retired colonel named Plestov claimed to have organized the resistance there, but our man on the ground didn't believe it was possible. This Plestov is practically senescent, and the train's other passengers were no soldiers. We didn't have any Red Guards in the area at the time, nor were any of the White Army formations, as far as we can tell. So who would have done it?

"And then there was a ship that blew up, taking one of our destroyers with it. The timing is too good, too precise. I think the Germans have already introduced some people to thwart the revolution by raising a counterrevolution. Ten men here, twenty men there, and pretty soon the *kulaks* are in arms against us, with competent leadership and maybe weapons."

"That could be troublesome," Lenin agreed. "A series of sparks that ignite a forest fire."

Chapter Twenty-Three

L59, Just Touched Down by the Ice-Covered Lake

Great Lake Shishkarym

It's very hard, thought Lieutenant Babin, *to just wait for something, in the bitter cold, in the open, with no real expectation of the thing you're waiting for ever showing up. Turgenev said they'd be here by between three and five, but...*

The lieutenant's thoughts came to a sudden halt, as a bright star burst in the heavens, illuminating the underside of what could only be a gargantuan airship.

Germans, thought Babin, *they overbuild everything.*

"Corporal Koslov," the lieutenant cried out.

"Here, sir."

"Blow the charge in the ice."

"Sir!"

"Novarikasha?"

"Here, sir."

"Start lighting the northern signal fires. I'll get the southern ones."

"Sir!"

Babin trotted over to the southernmost of the beacons and picked up a can of kerosene waiting there. Taking the top off, he poured half the contents onto the wood piled four feet high, a mix of tinder, small sticks, and more substantial logs. Then he pulled from a container in his pocket a wooden match, one of perhaps a score. Bending his leg to lift a boot, Babin struck the match on the sole. Instead of tossing it, he knelt and gently moved the flaming lucifer to the kerosene-soaked tinder. He was quickly rewarded with a fireball, rushing upwards into the night, and then, shortly after, a good deal of tinder alight and moving to light fire to the small sticks.

There was a great *boom* roughly centered between the pyres. Shortly after the explosion, bits and pieces of ice, smaller and larger, began pelting down.

Immediately, Babin set off for the second southern bonfire. As he ran to it, he saw one of the northern pair spring to life. Within no more than five minutes, they had all four lit.

Looking up, he saw that the airship had lined itself up in the open space between the fires and was gracefully descending.

I will tell my children about this sight. Assuming we live, of course.

Along the sides of the airship, the crew let down the leads that had been used to guide the ship out of its hangar at Jambol. Inside the passenger and cargo compartment, the ship's exec issued a coil of rope each time as he let out one man at a time to meet with Mueller or Machinist Proll. These then led each debarked passenger to one of the leads used by the handlers on the ground, tied one end of the rope coil to the lead and, in broken, recently learned Russian, directed the former passenger to find a tree to tie the rope off to, "Tightly!"

They alternated the tying off, forward-rear-center-center-rear-forward.

It took a good deal of stumbling and no little amount of cursing before Mueller could go and stand under the control gondola to tell the skipper, "She's tied off, sir."

"Very good. Lieutenant Colonel Kostyshakov seems to be on the ground somewhere. Please find him and advise him that his men can unload the materiel."

"Yes, sir."

"Oh, and Mueller?"

"Yes, sir?"

"After you find Kostyshakov, pack your bag in a hurry; you'll be staying here with them. Next time we show up, I want them trained to tie us down in mere minutes. Work out useful signals with the exec. Also, make sure Kostyshakov understands we'll need all his people to set us free once unloading is completed. And *you* are to make it happen."

Mueller's heart sank a bit. He tried to think of an objection but, *No, he's right that we need a more rapid and efficient tie-down. And I've got everything I need, probably better than the Russians have, to be honest, to keep from freezing to death here. But . . . shit.*

"Yes, sir."

Tobolsk, Russia

Natalya walked along a section of rope laid out in the southeastern rented warehouse. She counted off, ". . . fourteen, fifteen, sixteen . . . window here . . . seventeen, eighteen, nineteen . . . stairs down to the basement here," she stopped to point, "door leading to the kitchen over there."

As she recited the latest findings from her spying in both the Governor's House and the Kornilov House, Turgenev, Mokrenko, and Sarnof tied colored pieces of rope and cloth to the sections of rope already laid out, marking the windows in white, stairs in red, and other features in other colors. Furniture was outlined in black, but, since it tended to get moved around, was less precisely located than the walls, windows, stairs, and doors.

"Wonderful," congratulated Lieutenant Turgenev, meaning it. The girl preened and then flushed pink. The others affected not to notice.

"There's something else going on," said Natalya, "but I'm not sure what to make of it."

"Go on," said Turgenev.

She hesitated, then began, "Two of the guards, Chekov and Dostovalov—Chekov's the senior of the two—are involved with two of the Romanov girls, Tatiana and Olga, respectively. Anyone with eyes to see could see it. But that seems to rule out men, generally." *Because yours is a dumb sex, my very dearest.* "The tsar does not see it. The tsarina is usually bed-bound, so has never had a chance to see it. But the other two girls, Maria and Anastasia, most definitely *do* see it. If they rolled their eyes any harder they could see the backs of their own skulls from the inside.

"It's not a romantic connection with Tatiana, but it's something complicated—and powerful. But for the other two . . . well . . . they're in love. Obvious as the nose on my face. No, that's not good enough; it's as obvious as the hill leading to the Kremlin of Tobolsk. But . . ."

Again, Turgenev prodded, "Go on."

"Something terrible happened to Olga, I think. Something like . . . what happened to me. And if guilt were heat, Dostavalov could heat the whole building on his own."

Turgenev inclined his head to one side. "You don't think that he . . . ?"

"No, I don't. It was someone else. I overheard a couple of the guards talking about Chekov killing someone who, and I quote, 'was in desperate need of a good dose of killing.' But somehow it was Dostovalov's fault, or he believes it was, even if he didn't do it. I can't tell you how I know, but I *do* know. It's part of being a woman." *And stew on that "woman" word for a while, Maxim Sergeyevich.*

Natalya glanced at Turgenev, eyebrow raised, but he didn't challenge her self-designation.

"That's going to complicate things, I suspect," said Mokrenko.

"How's that?" Turgenev asked.

"I'd be really surprised if Kostyshakov hasn't given the word and been training the rest of the battalion to take no prisoners. It's what I'd do in his place."

"Sure, makes sense," agreed the lieutenant.

"Now picture what happens when one of the rescue force is about to eliminate, say, this Chekov person, and Grand Duchess Tatiana tries to save him."

It wasn't hard to imagine. "Shit. Ugly."

"She might or might not," Natalya said. "The relationship between those two is complicated. But I have no doubt at all that Olga would stand between Dostavalov and a charging tiger, unless he overpowered her to stand between the tiger and her."

Turgenev nodded slowly, then said, "And even if the rescue force can kill those two guards without harming the girls, what do the girls do at seeing their loves shot down? This is going to be tough enough for the rescue force without having to carry two of the Romanov girls..."

"They're big girls, too," Natalya interjected.

"...two of those *big* Romanov girls," Mokrenko continued, without a pause, "while those girls are crying and screaming and kicking and biting, doing everything, in fact, except cooperating."

"Where do these men sleep?" asked Turgenev.

"In the basement with the other guards," she answered. "Of whom, by the way, there are about a hundred in each building. I couldn't be more accurate than that, sorry."

"Would they be missed?" Turgenev asked, adding, "No

need to apologize; we haven't been able to be any more accurate than you."

"You're not going to kill them, are you?" Natalya asked. "They're really very nice men. War heroes, too, in fact. Also, there are two sailors there who care for and guard Tsarevich Alexei. They've done so since well before the revolution. Devoted to him, actually. Klementi Nagorny is one, Ivan Sednev the other. If you opened up a dictionary to the word 'loyal'? There would be a little picture of Klementi Nagorny and right next to it one of Sednev. What about them?"

"Worse and worse," Mokrenko muttered, then quickly added, "and no blame to you, Natalya. Without the information you've gotten . . . well . . . this thing would be a lot closer to impossible."

Turgenev asked, "Is there anything else you can add to our rope and cloth diagram, Natalya?"

"I don't think so," she replied. "Not without getting out a tape measure and acting very suspiciously."

"Fine. We're kicking this up to higher. Rostislav Alexandrovich, let's roll up our diagrams, put them on a sleigh, and go see the big boss."

"There's another problem, though," Natalya said. "The tsarina. I don't know if she's actually that unwell or just playing for sympathy, but you've got to account for the possibility she'll need to be carried."

"Oh, great," said the lieutenant, letting his forehead fall onto the fingers of his left hand. "I don't think any of us considered that. And I suppose the tsar and their children would never leave without their mother?"

"Not a chance," she replied.

Great Lake Shishkarym

When Turgenev and Mokrenko arrived on their sleigh at the forward assembly area, they were unsurprised to see a zeppelin there, disgorging men, equipment, and supplies, but shocked almost speechless at the size of the thing.

"You know, sir," Mokrenko said to the lieutenant, as he pulled the reins to bring their pair of Yakut horses to a stop, "as much as anything I've ever seen, that airship tells me the Germans are just too dangerous to leave free. We've both seen how good they are, tactically, in the field, but that thing shouts that they think too big, *dangerously* too big."

"First name and patronymic, Rostislav Alexandrovich, first name and patronymic."

"Sir, we're among our own. I won't forget when we're in Tobolsk, but it would be too hard to explain here."

"All right, then, Sergeant Mokrenko. But we can't, either of us, forget once we leave here."

"Yes, sir."

Mokrenko stood up in the sleigh. He looked around and saw Panfil and the rest of the 37mm cannon section working with a couple of the stouter looking Yakut horses to move around their guns and limbers. *Couple of days practice still needed, I think*.

He was pleasantly surprised to see every man clad in white from head to foot. *That makes fine sense*.

Elsewhere, his own friend Kaledin seemed to be doing much the same with sleighs and pairs of the Yakuts. Not far from the lake's edge, a very informal looking encampment was surrounded by a dozen burly guards. No one inside looked familiar. Indeed, they looked like a collection of random citizens, and none of them looked too happy about being there. *I wonder...*

Turgenev caught sight of the commander, Kostyshakov, walking to their sleigh. "Bring the sleigh," he said to Mokrenko.

With a shake of the reins and a pull to one lead, the Yakuts padded off, turning themselves and the sleigh in the direction of Kostyshakov. When they were about ten or so *arshini* from the commander, Mokrenko pulled back, making the horses stop. Then the two of them stood and saluted, while Turgenev reported that he and Mokrenko wished "to speak to the commander."

Kostyshakov made a *come here* motion with his fingertips, saying, too, "Come on, Maxim, I'm not all that formal."

"Well, yes, sir; I know, sir," replied the lieutenant. "But I've got a problem and I'm not sure how to deal with it."

"Right, come on, let's go to the tent. There's hot tea there and..."

"Sir," said Mokrenko, "if I may ask, who or what are those people over there being guarded?"

"Local civilians, hunters, that kind of thing, Sergeant. As soon as we landed the first group and got organized, I mounted up as many as knew how to ride and sent them out on a long sweep to drag in anyone who might have seen us or the zeppelin. Some of them are still out hunting, too, especially in the area between us and Tobolsk. But for about ten miles around here, there shouldn't be anyone free but maybe for the odd ghost."

"I see, sir. Thank you."

"Sergeant Mokrenko," said Turgenev, "I think you should come with us. You've got insights the commander should have."

"Yes, sir," agreed the sergeant, once again flicking the reins and causing the horses to walk sedately in the direction of the tent.

On the way, Turgenev related the problem with the four men, Chekov, Dostavalov, Sednev, and Nagorny. He thought he saw Kostyshakov's face tighten a bit at the mention of the possibility Tatiana Nicholaevna might be emotionally involved with one of them. It was only a momentary dropping of the curtain, though, so the lieutenant couldn't be sure.

Still interesting, if I really did see that.

In the tent, Daniil drew tea for the three of them. Lumps of sugar sat on a small tin plate. "So what are you suggesting?" he asked of Turgenev.

"Sir, the possibilities seem to me to be three: One, ignore the problem. This I cannot recommend. Two: Kill the four of them. Especially in the cases of Nagorny and Sednev, this I also cannot recommend. Three: We kidnap the lot and hold them."

"Well, no," Kostyshakov agreed, "we can't ignore it. I'm inclined to say kidnap them if you can; kill them if you must."

"Yes, sir, we'll try that, then. The other thing is the *Nemka*."

"What about the tsarina?" he asked. Few Russians really liked "the German woman." "I've met her, you know. She's not so bad, really, just very shy and fully aware she's not much liked, without the first clue of what to do about it."

"She's going to have to be carried out of the house," said Turgenev. "She's alleged to be weak, sickly, and is generally bedridden. She is usually in a wheelchair when she's not in bed."

"Crap," said Daniil. "That means we can't take her out one of the upper story windows, so we're going to have to secure the main floor, as well. How many guards did you say were in the building?"

"We think about a hundred in each of the basements of the two buildings, sir. You would think we could be more accurate than that but we can't. They're not disciplined enough to be able to count those on duty and multiply for the number off duty. The town is full of discharged soldiers, half of them or more armed and still wearing uniforms and we can't be sure which is which. They're as poor on insignia as on discipline. We can't count the number of squatting holes and multiply by eight because they have a little problem of shitting anywhere. Same with urinals. They tend to eat down in their basements, too, so we can't count them at meals."

"I'm beginning to think I should have listened to that soldier about poison gas," Daniil muttered.

"What was that, sir?" asked Turgenev.

"Nothing important; never mind."

"We did bring something that might be useful, sir," Mokrenko said.

"What's that?"

Turgenev smiled. "With the information from our little spy we were able to assemble floor plans, very accurate for the Governor's House, maybe a little less so for the Kornilov House, for all the above ground floors. She was willing to go to the basements but I told her not to, too dangerous for a young lady and ours has already had problems enough."

"Good," said Daniil, "very good. We can use them to lay out a rehearsal . . ."

"No need, sir," Turgenev said. "In the sleigh? All that rope and cord? Roll it out. Wherever there's a loop, drive in a stake and make it a ninety degree angle. That's the layout of both floors of both houses. There is one important exception, accuracy-wise. The walls are about two *arshini* thick, to include the interior walls, except where there are windows and doors. Nobody will be shooting through those with anything smaller than a cannon."

The lieutenant reached into his coat and extracted a small sheaf of papers and photographs. Handing them over, he said, "These are the codes for the cord diagrams, plus a layout of the town, and pictures of everything important in it. Also a scale of how long to get to what seemed to me the obvious target areas from the safe house and warehouses we've rented."

Daniil immediately started thumbing through them. "You know, Maxim, I'd had my doubts about sending you, a mainly military intelligence type, to lead this mission. I was wrong."

"Thank you, sir. The sergeant deserves as much or more credit. One other thing, sir?"

"Yes?"

"I think you and the company commanders, as well as

the Fourth Company platoon leaders, ought look at the town, personally."

"I don't disagree. But we'd probably stand out a bit."

"No, you won't, sir," said Mokrenko. "Wear army uniforms without insignia. Dirty them. Don't bathe for a while or go roll in pig shit. Put some dirt on your faces. Address each other as comrade or first name and patronymic and no one will look twice. Like the lieutenant said, we have a safe house you can use, though I think the warehouse by the river docks would be better."

"I can take Fourth Company's officers with me now plus the commander of Second Company. Will the sleigh take us all?"

"Sure, sir," Mokrenko replied. "These little Yakut horses are plenty strong enough for that."

"Then let me round them up. We'll leave within the hour."

Tobolsk

It was brightly moonlit when Turgenev and Mokrenko returned to the safe house, with their five passengers, Kostyshakov, Dratvin, short, dark, and stocky, plus Cherimisov, Collan, and Molchalin, the latter of whom rarely spoke much. Back at the landing zone for the zeppelin, the rest of the force went through clearing drills under their senior noncoms.

For the five of them, Kostyshakov had decided, the safe house would invite less commentary from the neighbors than the five of them alone would, in an otherwise empty warehouse. With the passengers covered by a tarp, just before they entered the city proper, Mokrenko drove up

Ulitsa Slesarnaya, then turned left on Yershova, and left again to enter the frozen way leading to the back yard of the safe house.

They found Natalya waiting for them. After bowing and curtseying for the presumptively august personage of their commander, she launched into what amounted to a panic-driven tirade, though the object of the tirade were the Bolsheviks.

"Since you've been gone," she exclaimed, "another two hundred and fifty Bolsheviks have shown up from Omsk!" She pointed, frantically. "Right over there; across the intersection! Another group of fifty red fanatics has come from Tyumen! Supposedly another four hundred and fifty are coming from Yekaterinburg! And there's rumor that another group is coming all the way from Moscow or, at least, at Moscow's direction, to take the royal family elsewhere!"

Kostyshakov spoke, first taking the girl's hand, "That's fine. Natalya, isn't it? The lieutenant and the sergeant have told me of your good work. We can deal with these, though it may be a little harder and bloodier than we hoped. Do you know where these new troops are staying? Do you know when the other four hundred and fifty are coming?"

"I don't know about that four hundred and fifty," she said. "As for the Omsk men, they're at the Girls' School." Again, she pointed, "Right. Over. There. I don't know about the other two groups. I do know that the Omsk men and the royal family's guards are talking about cooperating to get rid of the Tyumen lot."

"Where do rumors come from," Kostyshakov asked, "in a place cut off by snow and ice?"

"Telegraph office," was Turgenev's immediate reply.

"Right. Now can we bribe or threaten them into revealing who is coming, when?"

"Bribe, I think," said Sarnof. "Maybe a couple of hundred gold rubles to the head of the office to get the information. Although, it might, you know, be less suspicious if I took him to lunch again, one telegrapher to another."

"Right," agreed Daniil, again. "We'll go with Option B. But bring enough gold with you if that doesn't work."

"Yes, sir. First thing in the morning . . . well, I'll make the offer first thing in the morning. I trust the chief of the station, to a degree, but am far less sure of his underlings."

"Now, the objectives. Tentatively, I want to send one company to take care of the Omsk detachment, less than one to secure a perimeter around both houses, one platoon to take care of the Tyumen lot, and one platoon from Fourth Company for each of the two houses."

Turning to Turgenev, he asked, "Anything sound inherently unworkable to that?"

"No, sir, on the face of it it sounds workable."

"Sir," asked Shukhov, the engineer, "if there's a small target I could conceivably rig a bomb to take the whole building out. Assuming, of course, you brought enough explosive in the zeppelin. For myself, all I've got left is enough to do a thorough job on the telegraph line."

Mokrenko interjected, "Sir, while we've maybe enough to take on Omsk and Tyumen, plus rescue the family, we don't have enough to take on the Yekaterinburg mob, too. What if they're here tomorrow? What if they're here tomorrow along with those sods sent by Moscow?"

"The short version, Sergeant, is we can't dawdle much anymore, can we? We recon...get back...wait for the zeppelin...move here...let's call it a week from tomorrow night. The last combat company won't be here until just before then. And even then, we'll have left a good deal of the reserve ammunition and the replacements detachment behind."

"And if they get here sooner?" Mokrenko asked.

"Then we'll have to figure something else out. Maybe hit them on the way to Tyumen as they cart off the royal family. We have to hope, too, that their orders aren't to murder the royal family immediately."

"Maybe..." Turgenev began.

"Yes, Lieutenant?"

"Maybe if we move now we could get in position to ambush the newcomers."

Kostyshakov shook his head. "I like our odds of hitting them at night when they're mostly asleep better than I like our odds of finding them as they approach and fighting them in broad daylight."

"Finding them won't be such a problem," said Turgenev. "They'll follow the telegraph line. Defeating them...while being sure that none get away to warn the guards? That's a lot tougher."

"Oh," Natalya interjected. "Finding them; that reminds me. Nagorny never leaves the tsarevich's side, and Sednev rarely does. But whenever Chekov and Dostovalov are off duty and not asleep they're usually in a little dive called 'The Gilded Lark.' I walked by it, earlier, to see. It's a pretty pretentious name for what is not much more than a hole in the wall."

"We'll need you to take us by that, too," said Turgenev. "In fact, while the commander and the others rest, why don't you take myself and Rostislav Alexandrovich by it now?"

The tavern was only a few blocks to the north of the safe house, nestled in among some shacks no better than itself, with a crude, handpainted sign on the road indicating what it was. The noise coming from the tavern sounded like nothing so much as a brawl. Natalya was reasonably sure she heard the words "Menshevik swine" and "Bolshevik filth" being bandied about, interspersed with the sounds of breaking bottles and chairs ... and possibly heads.

"At those prices," observed Turgenev, looking at the lettering under the sign, "even here in Tobolsk, one expects that the vodka will be of the very worst."

"Maxim Sergeyevich," said Mokrenko, "I think perhaps you should escort the young lady to the general vicinity of the Governor's house before she is missed. Meanwhile, purely in the interests of reconnaissance, I am going in there. If we decide to kidnap the two who have grown close to the Romanovs, it would probably be a good thing if I didn't seem a stranger to the waitstaff."

"Don't shoot anyone, Rostislav Alexandrovich; it would raise too many questions."

"Speaking as a good Menshevik or Bolshevik, myself, of course," said the sergeant, as he ground his right fist into his left palm expectantly, "whichever may prove most convenient in the near future, I would not dream of it."

Telegraph Station, Tobolsk

The telegraph itself was silent. The chief telegrapher

of the place, clad in a suit of old-fashioned cut, with a thin bow tie on, leaned back in his chair, reading a two months out of date newspaper. He immediately looked up, then, wearing a broad smile, stood up. The paper he left on the table.

Sarnof was a frequent caller at the station, enough to be on a first name and patronymic basis with the staff there. So far his cover for sending obviously coded messages had held, "We are a highly competitive business, Arkady Yevgenovich; furs, and our markets fluctuate daily. Any advantage that can be gained for our employer, any business secret we can keep to ourselves, pays large dividends."

How long this would continue to work was the subject of difficulty sleeping compounded with not infrequent nightmares.

"Good morning!" exclaimed the chief of the station. "Good morning, Abraham Davidovich! What brings you here today?"

The best lies contain a good deal of truth, Sarnof reminded himself, before answering, "A deep curiosity about just how bad the situation in the town is about to become, and whether we can expect a full scale civil war between the guards on you-know-who and his family, and the newcomers from Omsk and Tyumen. My boss, Maxim Sergeyavich, says we may have to cut our losses and leave with what we've already gotten if it gets much worse."

"Well, just between you and me," said the civilian telegrapher, "I think it's going to get a lot worse."

"How could it?" asked Sarnof. "Fights in the streets? Fights in the taverns? Armed men being stood off from other armed men at the old governor's mansion?"

"Four hundred and fifty more Bolsheviks coming," answered the telegrapher.

"Oh, Jesus," said Sarnof, "as if we need more of them. How long?"

"Not sooner than ten days from now, I think. I asked my counterpart in Yekaterinburg and he says they're a disorganized rabble, still trying to commandeer enough food and drayage for the trip. But . . ."

"Yes?"

The telegrapher pointed with his chin. Turning around, through the paned window, Sarnof saw a cavalcade trotting down the frozen street toward the telegraph station. The leader wore a combination beard and mustache that reminded Sarnof of nothing so much as the hairy space between a woman's legs, though it remained a matter of some doubt whether any human female had ever been so thickly matted. The signaler wondered if a smile had ever crossed that face. *Could you even see it, one wonders, past that thick bush of a goatee.*

"That lot have come to take the tsar and his family away."

The cavalcade stopped at the telegraph office, with the leader dismounting, handing his reins to an underling, and striding confidently into the office. He made a look at Sarnof that as much as said, "Get out."

I wonder if that block of ice has ever had a human feeling in his life?

"So, lunch at the hotel by the central square at one, Arkady? My treat, today, of course."

"I'll be there, Abraham Davidovich."

And with that, Sarnof took his leave and, stopping only

to get a quick count of the numbers of the newcomers, hurried back to the safe house, to report.

Safe House, Yershova Street, Tobolsk

When Sarnof arrived back, he saw Mokrenko sitting at the kitchen table, sporting an impressive shiner and individually checking each tooth in his upper jaw for firmness of fit.

"Where's the lieutenant?" Sarnof asked. "Better, where's Kostyshakov?"

Moving a front tooth that seemed a little looser than one might prefer, Mokrenko sighed, said, "Helluva fight, that was," then answered, "They're with Natalya, the captain and platoon leaders of Fourth Company, looking over the Governor's and Kornilov's houses. Kostyshakov and Dratkin are with the lieutenant, scouting out the Girls' School."

"Well, we've got a new target and problem. The Reds who are supposed to take the royal family away have arrived, on horseback, about one hundred and fifty of them and *they* look like they know what they're about."

"Shit," said Mokrenko, standing and reaching for his coat, loose tooth forgotten. "Tell you what, you go by the Governor's house and tell them what's up and to come back. I'll go find the lieutenant and bring that group back."

PART IV

Chapter Twenty-Four

Some Members of Number Four Company,
Preparing to Set Forth

Safe House, Yershova Street, Tobolsk

It took until noon to find and bring back the reconnaissance parties. By that time, Sarnof had gone to the hotel where they'd first stayed to pump the telegrapher for information over lunch.

"Time and tide wait for no man," said Kostyshakov. "We strike tomorrow night. The third zeppelin load should be down by the time I get back to the lake camp.

We won't need the fourth load for this, but only for after this."

Cherimisov nodded, then said, "We can do this. The men will have been practicing the assaults on both buildings for some time now on that rope schematic Lieutenant Turgenev so thoughtfully produced. All the rest need to do is contain the Reds. If you send one company less one platoon after the Omsk men, to hold them in place, one platoon after the Tyumen men, and one company less one platoon after these newcomers, then use one platoon to seal off the area of the two houses, we can clear the buildings, guard the people we've rescued with one platoon, then reinforce the group keeping the weakest group of Bolsheviks pinned, eliminate them, then all of us go after the next weakest, and so on."

"So think I. But we'll need a couple of things. Lieutenant Turgenev?"

"Sir?"

"We're going to be coming in a column, mostly on skis, with those stout little Yakut horses pulling the infantry cannon, the machine guns, and the sleighs. Might have to put the heavy weapons on the sleighs, actually. We'll be very quiet. We'll need an easily identifiable release point from our column of march to lead us to assembly areas, just after dusk. That means you need to meet us with…well, probably four men, two to lead us to each warehouse."

Turgenev shook his head, doubtfully. "Don't think we can, sir. We've still got to kidnap the two guards and Shukhov has to blow the telegraph lines. That's everybody I've got."

"I can lead one party," said Natalya.

"Give me Shukhov," Mokrenko added, "before he sets off to blow the lines down. He and I and . . . let me see . . . Timashuk, I'll need him to make sure the prisoners don't die on us. But it would be better to present them with really bad odds, so they don't try to resist."

"Two more men, Sergeant Mokrenko," said Daniil, "because you're right that more numbers will help with a kidnapping."

Turgenev thought furiously, then said, "Mokrenko, Timashuk, Sarnof, and Shukhov for the kidnapping. Myself, Natalya, and Lavin to lead the companies to the warehouses. That leaves us one spare for that."

"That works for me," said Kostyshakov. "Best of the bad hand we've been dealt. Now, I hope I remember how to drive a sleigh."

"Doesn't take much skill, sir," said Mokrenko. "The Yakuts are surprisingly gentle horses."

"Do we know," asked Turgenev of Natalya, "if those two *special* guards will be going to the Gilded Lark tonight?"

"They've the night off," she answered. "I know that much. I also know that's where they usually go. I think Chekov, who isn't much of a drinker, takes Dostovalov there to keep him away from Olga."

"All right, then," finished Kostyshakov. "Gentlemen . . . if we've neglected or forgotten anything, we're just going to have to pull something out of our asses. If someone would set up one of the sleighs for me . . . ?"

"I'll take care of it," said Mokrenko.

"Now where," asked Kostyshakov, "should our link-up point be?"

"You wouldn't have seen it," said Turgenev, "covered as you all were on the sleigh, but there's an island south of the town, formed by the Tobol and Irtysh Rivers. Nobody lives that way. The trees of the island block any view of the lower town and vice versa, while the upper town is too far away to see much. We'll build a small fire and put up something to keep it from being seen in the upper town, either from the walls or the towers of the Kremlin of Tobolsk. We can meet there and then split, with one group going for the warehouse by the docks, and near the royal family, while the other goes for the warehouse south of town. We could, if you want to try it and think the men of Fourth Company could be as quiet as mice, billet the company here, in the safe house. There's a basement the size of the first floor, and half the rooms above are unoccupied. It won't be comfy and it will be tight, but it puts you within a few minutes of the Romanovs."

"Let me mull that over," said Kostyshakov. "But I think that with that reinforced company of Reds across the intersection it's too risky. I like the advantage of proximity but dread being seen before we launch our attack."

"From our point of view, sir, it wouldn't make any difference. You can tell us where you want people when we link up. Just remember that the warehouses can fit hundreds, easily, while we will be a little pressed to squeeze under a hundred into this place.

"What's our sign and countersign?"

Kostyshakov considered this briefly, then decided, "We only need a running password. Make it Liberty or Death. One other thing."

"Sir?" asked Turgenev.

"People get lost in strange terrain, especially at night. You, young Lieutenant, will come with us to guide us back."

The Gilded Lark, Tobolsk

Although it was just a hole in the wall, and somewhat sparsely furnished after the fights that had taken place, the tavern was warm and had sufficient rough wooden boxes and crates for tables and seating. Also, despite the generally poorly washed clientele, the smell of food was as thick and hearty as the food itself, and went a good way, if not all the way, toward covering up the stench of people.

Those people were almost entirely soldiers, though whether they were ex- or current was a hard call, since clothing shortages had an amazing number of men wearing their old uniforms, sans insignia, or, perhaps in some cases, someone else's cast-offs.

Mokrenko really hadn't had a good look at the surroundings, the previous night, since he'd plunged immediately into a riot. Most especially had he not noticed, since they'd likely fled at the first sign of trouble, the waitresses hauling glasses of vodka, mugs of beer, and trays replete with bread and soup, plus the occasional plate of *pelmeni*.

There were no photos of the pair but Natalya had described them well. "One is short and stocky, but very graceful and quick. You will be surprised at how much so. That's Chekov and he looks—and is—far more intelligent than his comrade. The other one, Dostovalov, is tall, strong, and has his head currently bandaged against a rather bad blow he took. You won't have a hard time getting the latter to drink himself insensible, but with the former you might."

Looking around upon closing the tavern's leather-hinged door behind him, Mokrenko didn't see either man, and certainly not such an oddly matched pair together. He let a waitress—blonde, almost pretty, and remarkably large-breasted—lead him to a bench. She introduced herself as "Xenia."

"Bottle of vodka and a glass," he replied, when she asked him what he'd be having. Then he looked at the menu over the bar and asked, "What's in the *pelmeni?*"

"Oh, today is special," she replied. "Then owner came back with a nice deer, so it's venison *pelmeni*. They're wonderful. I can say that because I snatched a couple when the cook wasn't looking."

"I predict you'll go far," Mokrenko said to the girl, inciting a saucy answer, accompanied by a knowing wink, "I'll go further than any of the other girls here; faster, too."

That got her the laugh she expected.

"Let's try the *pelmeni*, then."

After the previous night's festivities, it seemed no one was willing to talk politics and risk another fight breaking out. Indeed, it seemed no one was willing to get so close to anyone else they didn't already know. This left Mokrenko alone with four empty chairs while the other chairs filled. Two of those chairs, after polite inquiries, found their way to other tables. When someone asked for a third Mokrenko answered, "Ah, no, sorry; I have a couple of friends coming to join me."

Fortunately, no fight broke out over the matter.

Or at least no one is fighting yet, thought Mokrenko. *But, needs must when the devil drives, and I've got to get them somewhat inebriated and outside.*

The vodka and *pelmeni* arrived before the two guards did. So intent was Mokrenko on the food that he almost missed them when they came through the door. He found Natalya's description spot on, except for one thing. *She never said what an air of sadness and doom surrounds the bigger of the two.*

Chekov and Dostovalov walked silently, side by side, down the street leading to their current favorite hole in the wall, after the Reds taught the old butcher a nasty lesson. Dostovalov himself was the very picture of misery. He wouldn't even be here, but would have been with his beloved Olga, except that the newcomers had relieved the guards of their duties and forbidden them from coming into the main or second floor of the house. At the same time they'd locked down on the Romanovs, hard, even as they were stuffing several dozen more aristocrats and staff into the house.

"Don't worry, don't complain," the chief of the new men had ordered, "you won't be here for long!"

No, not long . . . not here . . . not anywhere, thought the short noncom.

Chekov had his own issues. Tatiana was his friend, one of only two in the midst of this terrible world. And despite his best efforts not to, he cared for her sisters and brother as well.

What will we do? What can we do? I don't give a shit about Nicholas or his hypochondriac loon of a wife, but his children deserve to live. I've spent years trying to isolate and harden my soul, and now if Tatiana and her siblings die, a part of me will die with them. And Anton is likely to kill himself in a futile attempt to save them if I don't sit on him. Tatiana will still die, Olga, Maria, and Anastasia and the boy, Alexei, will all still die.

And then I will be alone with only the coldest, blackest pieces of myself for company.

Chekov stopped at the tavern door and listened. *Ah, good, no riot tonight. Helps, I suppose, that the Tyumen mob have been run out of town.*

How will I even earn my bread, after this? Fighting for the Reds? Murderous bastards, and when they're not murdering innocent children, they're starving the commoner in the name of progress. I could join the White Army—but they prey upon my mother's people as readily as they do the communists. If the God of my forebears does order the universe, He must be little more than a sadistic puzzle-maker.

He turned the latch and pushed the door half open, just enough for him and Dostovalov to get through while letting as little heat out as possible. *Now to find a seat in this mess.*

The tavern had filled up quite a bit since the sergeant's arrival. Both Chekov and Dostovalov searched left and right, near and far, for an open couple of seats. Since no one else invited them over, Mokrenko waved and made an expansive "come on down" gesture.

Seeing his friend hesitate, Dostovalov said, "Oh, for Christ's sake, cut it out. We've got no secrets to spill. We're about to be unemployed. I cannot see my one true love before she leaves and you are about to lose your arguing partner, student . . . and friend. We're about as important as the horse turds we passed getting here. Nobody is a threat to us, my friend, because we just do not matter."

Ordinarily, thought Chekov, *I'd sit outside rather than share a table with a gregarious stranger, but he's right. What difference does it make now? No future, no job . . . no Tatiana. So what difference?*

Gratefully, the two made their way over and took rough, uncushioned boxes for their seats.

Introductions proceeded apace, "Rostislav Alexandrovich Mokrenko . . . Sergei Arkadyevich Chekov . . . Anton Ivanovich Dostovalov."

"Gentlemen," said Mokrenko, pointing to the vodka, "please, help yourselves. I just got paid by my company and am pretty flush at the moment. Oh, my manners; Xenia? Couple more glasses."

"What company is that?" asked Chekov, innately suspicious at any show of generosity from a stranger.

"Pan-Siberian Import-Export Company. Originally started in Vladivostok, I understand, but branching out to the west now."

"You haven't been with them long . . ." At that point, Xenia arrived with a couple of apparently clean glasses, which she set down on the table.

"Oh, hi, Anton Ivanovich," she said to Dostovalov. "Haven't seen you in a week or two."

"Old friend?" asked Mokrenko, after the girl had left to see to another table.

"Something like that," Dostovalov replied.

Mokrenko nodded, then answered Chekov's question. "No, not long. They were recruiting good shots who could ride and didn't mind living rough when I was discharged from the army. I had nothing better to do and the pay promised to be a lot better than the army had ever given me."

"I knew you were a soldier," Chekov said. "Don't ask me how."

Mokrenko reached for the bottle of vodka and poured a couple of mid-depth drinks. "Probably the same way I recognized you two as soldiers. It wasn't the uniforms without any insignia; half the men of the town are wearing old uniforms. It's in the walk, in the voice, in the mannerisms, and in the way you look around suspiciously. It's me sitting here with my back to the wall and you two taking turns looking to see who comes in the door. If you're one of us and halfway observant you just *know*. Though I suppose you could have been sailors, too."

"There are, in fact, a couple of sailors who work around us," said Dostovalov. "Good men, devoted to the . . . ouch! What the fuck was that for?"

"I'm sure Comrade Mokrenko isn't interested in our work or who we work for," said Chekov. "I kicked you so you wouldn't wear out our welcome."

"Not especially interested, no," Mokrenko agreed. "Though if you ever get discharged, look me up; the company always has openings, as far as I've been able to see. And they pay in gold and silver, none of this paper crap."

The sergeant noticed that Dostovalov had tossed off his vodka rather quickly after being kicked under the table. He refilled the glass without being asked.

"I hate eating alone," said Mokrenko. "You guys hungry?"

"We can't impose . . ." began Chekov, before Mokrenko cut him off with, "I told you; we get paid in gold, and good wages at that. I can afford it. Hey, Xenia!"

Three and a half hours later, the first bottle of vodka was gone and the second was more than half finished. Both Mokrenko and Chekov were pretty sober or, at worst, mildly tipsy. Dostovalov, on the other hand, despite the food he'd eaten, was utterly drunk, slovenly drunk, crying in his arms drunk.

"He acts—he drinks—like a man who knows his soul is damned," said Mokrenko. "What could he have done . . ."

"It's not what he did," said Chekov, "it's what he failed to do. Long story, and ugly. And I don't have the right to pass it on."

"I understand. Well . . . can you carry him on your own? He's a big boy, after all."

"Oh, I can get him home eventually," was Chekov's reply, repeating, "eventually."

"Tell you what," said Mokrenko, "you take one arm, I'll take the other, and we'll *both* port him home . . . .ummm . . . where is home, by the way?" He reached into a pocket and then put some small coins on the table.

"For the nonce, it's the basement of the Governor's house. A basement suddenly a lot more crowded than it used to be."

Mokrenko forced his eyes to widen. "You're guarding . . . mmm . . . you-know-who?"

Chekov nodded, then said, "For another day or so, maybe two. Well, not guarding, exactly, since we've been relieved. They're being taken away by some Bolshevik fanatics soon."

"You don't sound happy," Mokrenko said, standing, pulling first one, then the other, of Dostovalov's arms through his army-issue coat. Then, he pulled the drunken Dostovalov up well enough to get control of an arm.

Chekov, walking around the table to take the other answered, "I'm not quite happy about it, no. *He*, on the other hand, is devastated."

"You sound rather less happy than 'not quite happy.' "

"Honestly, I don't know how I feel. I am . . . fond . . . yes, fond . . . of one of them, and like most of them . . . even the tsar is more ignorant than evil . . . okay, all together now . . ."

With a pair of grunts, they pulled Dostovalov up and away from the table, the triple discrepancy in height making the exercise a lot more difficult than one might have expected. To get him through the door would have been impossible without either dropping and dragging him or, as was offered, the assistance of Xenia.

With Xenia's help, in any case, they got through the door and into the street. Down it whipped a bitter wind from above the Arctic Circle. Its force, fury, and frigid bitterness brought Dostovalov to a limited degree of consciousness. He began to weep and muttered the name "Olga," more than once.

They reached a point at which the sergeant could see the two men and sleigh he'd posted by an intersection. They began to walk toward the trio.

"Oh, *that's* his problem," said Mokrenko.

"The center of his problems," Chekov said, "but he has still others."

"Well, one is that he's going to catch pneumonia with his coat opened up." Without a word, Mokrenko slipped out from under Dostovalov's arm, leaving the entire weight of the man to stagger Chekov. As he did so, he pulled his M1911 from under his own coat.

"Friend," he said to Chekov, once the latter could see the pistol under the streetlights, "while it would pain me to shoot you, still I *will* shoot you at the first peep above a whisper or act of resistance."

"Bastard," spat Chekov, albeit quietly. He was still struggling to hold Dostovalov up. "And stupid bastard at that; I haven't enough money to even pay for the vodka and meal."

"This isn't a robbery," Mokrenko said. "Moreover, I am doing you a number of favors at the moment, even if you can't see them. Now let the drunk down and you lie down on your belly as well.

"This would have been easier if you'd drunk your fill. I should have listened to Natalya."

"You know the new servant girl?" Chekov asked, as he lay Dostovalov on the ground.

"She works for us, for my . . . mmm . . . organization, yes. Now get on the ground."

About that time, Timashuk, the medic, left Shukhov and the sleigh behind, and trotted up the frozen street.

"Tie their hands and feet," Mokrenko ordered, "starting with the short one. Don't be any rougher than necessary. Search them for matches or anything that might be used to start a fire."

"The short one has a pistol," Timashuk said, tucking the pistol into his own pocket.

"Who *are* you people?" Chekov asked, as he felt his wrists being bound behind him.

Mokrenko leaned down and whispered, "We're the people who are going to save your girlfriend and her family." Turning to Shukhov, he said, "Bring the sleigh here. We'll load them on, cover them up, and take them to the safe house."

The safe house had never been designed to be a prison. Even so, there was a kind of storage area in the basement, unheated but at least dry, with a strong door with a lock on it. Chekov, feet untied, was marched down to it by Timashuk, pistol at the ready. Meanwhile, Mokrenko and Shukhov carried Dostovalov down. Down below, two pallets had been made up as beds, with hay for bedding and several blankets each. Between the pallets stood a wooden box with an assortment of food and a couple of jugs of water. A chamber pot, courtesy of the owner of the place, stood to the right of the stout door.

"I wish I could take your parole," said Mokrenko to Chekov, "but, under the circumstances, I really can't. You could try to make noise to attract attention but—and I've already tested this—from down here nobody can hear you outside." Here Mokrenko decided that a brazen lie was in order. "Indeed, I tested it also by shooting into the floor there; if you dig you can find a couple of Amerikanski bullets. Nobody heard *those*, either. You might contemplate the implications of *that*, before you decide to make trouble. I regret the lack of light but you might just be dumb enough to start a fire. We'd leave the house and let you burn alive, of course, so no skin off my dick, but I'd really rather you stay alive."

Chekov scowled. "You said you were going to 'save my girlfriend' and that the new serving girl, Natalya, was in on this. In the first place, while Tatiana isn't 'my girlfriend,' we are friends. I'd help save her if I could while Dostovalov would gladly die for his Olga. Let us help!"

Mokrenko shook his head. "Don't be silly. The teams that are going in to rescue the royal family have been training for months. Even *we* are not fit to go in with them. They've rehearsed the assault dozens—no, scores of times—on an outline of the actual houses..."

"Not houses," said Chekov.

"Of course, houses, plural; the Governor's House and the Korni—"

Chekov cut his words off. "No, the newcomers under that Bolshevik fanatic, Yurovsky, have taken over the Kornilov House. All the aristocrats, the staff, and the guards have been booted over to the Governor's house and the wooden one just to the north. They're stacked in like cordwood, and it would be worse if about twenty-five of the guards hadn't elected to follow their proletarian sensibilities and to just walk off the job. And why not, since the Romanovs aren't going to be there to be guarded for much longer?"

"I didn't see—"

Again, Chekov cut him off fiercely. "Of course you didn't. I was paying attention to the turns; you completely avoided Great Friday Street and went down Slesarnaya, didn't you?"

"Correct," said Mokrenko, impressed.

"How many men are coming?" Chekov asked.

"About five hundred."

"It's not enough."

At that point, Sarnof came down from upstairs. "Has anyone seen Rostislav Alexandrovich? Has anyone . . . oh, there you are, Sergeant. We have a problem."

Like we need more problems. "What's the nature of it this time, Sarnof?"

"Took me a while to decode the message, but the airship has a problem with one of its engines and will be delayed for a couple of days. Third lift is delayed."

Oh, shit. Not five hundred men. Not even three hundred. Not even three hundred including us. Oh, shit. Oh, fuck.

Camp and Landing Zone, South of Tobolsk

Kostyshakov nearly screamed, "They *what!?!?*"

"The zeppelin carrying Lieutenant Lesh's Third Company," said Captain Basanets, from on high, "it never came. We've got no way to contact them from here, either."

"So what have we got, then?"

"One rifle company, Second, the heavy machine guns and the light infantry cannon, the antitank rifles, most of the engineer platoon, plus the Fourth Company. In all, there are two hundred and eighty-seven men on the ground, or two hundred and ninety-five if we count strategic recon."

Mentally Daniil recited what he knew was waiting for them in Tobolsk. *Two hundred original guards, two hundred and fifty thugs from Omsk, fifty worse thugs*

*from Tyumen, and soon another hundred and fifty
fanatical cavalry from Yekaterinburg. I've got to take on
six hundred and fifty men, with less than half that many?
God, I know You like to test men, but I don't think . . .*

"We can still do it, sir," said Cherimisov, from the back
of the sleigh. At Daniil's doubtful glance the captain said,
"Well, we still have to try. We'll never get another chance.
They may be cold and rotting corpses in the ground
before we find them again. Sir, it doesn't matter what the
odds are; we *have* to go anyway."

*And that much, at least, I know is the merest truth. We
don't have a choice.*

"Get me Romeyko," Kostyshakov said to Basanets.
"No, wait; he's still in Camp Budapest, isn't he? Instead
get me the senior man from the quartermaster's shop. In
fact, get me the senior man present from each staff
section, and supporting platoon . . . and get me that coal
miner's son . . . mmm . . . Ilyukhin."

"Well, sir," said the coal miner's son, "while, yes, you
can make acetylene explode—indeed, it will on its own
under some circumstances—you really don't get much
rumble for your ruble. A full pound of the calcium carbide
only makes about a half a cubic *arshin* of gas or maybe
somewhat less. Now that, of course, spreads out and
mixes, but it's still not all that much. And we only have . . ."
Ilyukhin shot a glance at the representative from the
quartermaster's office.

"We've got a hundred pounds, sir, plus every man with
a lamp is carrying a bit under a pound of his own. It's not
much."

"All right, then," Daniil agreed, "we'll skip that idea. You may return to your unit," he told Ilyukhin. "How are we fixed for regular high explosive?"

"That's in the engineers' bailiwick," said the logistics NCO.

"About eight *pood* TNT, sir," said the engineer platoon leader.

Kostyshakov just nodded, then said, "Let me mull that one, then," said Daniil. "Now, one hour, every man ready, the sleighs packed, the lanterns charged with their fuel. Meet me here, everyone; I want to address the men.

"Oh, and Dratvin, Cherimisov, before you go, we need to have a little talk."

The hour passed not so much swiftly as furiously, as the men raced to pack themselves, fit their skis, and get the heavy weapons ready for movement. For now, the few tents would be left behind.

As the men assembled in the now familiar semicircle, Kostyshakov thought, *I need to put on a performance that would credit an actor at the Mikhailovsky. The important thing, here, is to let them know—well, think—that I'm not worried. They won't fret over how literal my words are, but will take the grand jest to heart.*

"Very well, gentlemen—at ease!—it seems that God has said we're just too good, and the enemy too weak and contemptible, for us to need every man to take them on. It's on us, one short company of grenadiers, one rifle company, heavy on the light machine guns, plus two heavies, two antitank rifles, and two infantry guns. Plus engineers with flamethrowers.

"Moreover, since they *are* stinking Bolshevik rabble, they needed to be reinforced. At about six hundred and fifty of them, and a bit under three hundred of us, I still think God is being generous to us. Why, as it is, we'll have to hang our heads in shame for the rest of our lives that it took three hundred men of the Guards to destroy twice as many Bolshevik rabble. We will have to console ourselves, when telling our families and friends, in the future, that, if the job was too easy . . . well . . . it was a mark of God's favor on us, and nothing else.

"But . . . you know . . . then again . . . Second Company? Captain Dratvin—Ivan Mikhailovich—would your men be too upset if I left them behind, to even up the odds with the Reds? I mean, seriously; they're fellow Russians, however misguided they may be. They deserve at least a chance, don't you think? What say you, Captain Dratvin?"

Dratvin folded his arms across a compact torso, and scowled, "I say, sir, and I speak for every man in the company, that if you try to leave us behind you will have a mutiny on your hands. Now, if you'll take me alone . . . yes, sir, yes, I know; that would too thoroughly disadvantage the Reds. But, you know . . . if my men can't go, well, I am still going."

Daniil scowled and said, "Mutiny, do you say? Mutiny? There is no more serious crime in the military! What say you, men of Second Company? If I leave you behind what will you do?"

The chorus was most impressive. "MUTINY!"

Daniil sighed. "So you really all insist, do you?"

"YES, SIR!"

Daniil theatrically put his forehead into the crook of

his right arm, while exclaiming, "Tsk...all these long months and I find myself in command of nothing but lowly mutineers, practically Bolsheviks themselves. Oh, the *shame* of it."

The laugh that followed told him the men understood the little play he was engaged in.

"Fourth Company, since those mutineers of Second Company insist on going, surely you will voluntarily stay behind, so that at least some of us will have bragging rights in the future. Captain Cherimisov?"

"Not a chance, sir. As little glory as there is to be had on this trivial excursion, we're not letting Second Company have all of it!"

"Grenadiers? What say you?"

"NO, SIR. We're going!"

Act over, Daniil smiled and said, "By the three hundred, then, shall we save them. Follow me." With that, Daniil pivoted left, skied to the right flank, and began the long trek to the north.

When the sun fell, about halfway to Tobolsk, it could be seen that they were ghosts, phantoms, sliding across the often bleak and snow-clad Siberian landscape without a sound. Of course they were phantoms, the more obviously so from the few eerily bright lights that led the way. Eyes, they must have been, eyes from some hell-spawned demons.

No, no, might some have insisted; they were a monster, a millipede but composed only of snow and ice and demon-frost, as their legs flashed, driving their skis onward. Of course the assemblage was a monster, nothing ever seen in historic memory in frozen Siberia resembled this, though some of the old legends may have spoken of it.

But, no, they were neither ghosts, nor phantoms, not even an icy millipede. Rather the glowing eyes told of the biblical monster, Leviathan. They were, thus, a snake, a landbound leviathan almost straight out of Psalms.

They are my men, thought Daniil, feet sliding as fast as any of his men, *following me into danger and death . . . and I don't think I've ever been so happy or proud in my life.*

The ground fell behind quickly as they slid at a steady five miles—eight *versta*—an hour, heading to the north. The moon rose on their right, within twenty *versta* of setting out. It was a waning gibbous moon, bright enough to cast ghostly shadows across the land and across the sleigh- and ski-borne column. Given their white smocks and trousers, they remained approximately as invisible as if they had been in complete darkness. The lights were soon put out as unnecessary, Leviathan sleepwalking to take a nap.

The column pushed on, unheard, unseen. Oh, occasionally a voice might be heard by those very close: "Pick it up, Blagov; you're falling a little behind" or "Next break, Isayev, check your bindings. Looks like they're getting loose to me."

Breaks were simple and infrequent. Indeed, there were only three. One was after going about half an hour, precisely to let the men check and adjust their bindings and their packs. The other was not quite midway in the trek. The third came at about midnight. And then, finally . . .

✣ ✣ ✣

"Liberty or Death," said a small, female voice.

"Natalya?" asked Turgenev, up front with Kostyshakov.

"Yes, it's me, Maxim," the girl replied. "Lavin kept nodding off, so I told him I'd take the watch. Get up, Lavin; they're here.

"But things have changed a bit," the girl said, more to Kostyshakov than to Turgenev. "In the first place, your third load for the zeppelin is delayed. I supposed you must know that they didn't show up. But at least they're not crashed and dead."

"That *is* welcome news," said Kostyshakov. "Go on."

"Yes, sir." The girl continued, "The layout of the enemy and our…mmm…friends is different too. All the prisoners and their staffs are now stuffed into the Governor's House. The guarding has been taken over by the newcomers from Yekaterinburg, and they are mostly alert, mean, and tough. They've also taken over the Kornilov House for their own barracks. The old guard company is still stuffed into the basement of the Governor's House and the wooden building just north of it but now they're overstuffed. They're not allowed into the upper story, nor even the ground floor. Colonel Kobylinsky made his objections and only shut up when the leader of the Yekaterinburg men said he would be shot if he uttered another word.

"On the plus side, the Tyumen men left in a huff. And Sergeant Mokrenko has the two guards locked up in the basement."

Kostyshakov digested that, then sent word back, "Orders group, up to the point."

Interlude

Lenin, Sverdlov, and Trotsky: The Troika

"Ilyich, look at the facts," Sverdlov recapitulated. "We know Tobolsk is full of counterrevolutionaries and their sympathizers. Our friends are reporting a training camp in Hungary where the Germans have been training Russian traitors, and two days ago someone massacred a large and well-armed group of bandits in Siberia. Shortly before that a sailing ship blew up in the Black Sea, taking one of our loyal destroyers with it. We didn't do either of these and our scouts cannot find any White element in position to do so either."

Lenin leaned back in his chair. Trotsky sat silently.

"Move the royals as soon as possible," Lenin said. "And reiterate to Yurovsky that at the first sign of trouble, he is to execute the Romanovs."

"That may be too late," Sverdlov insisted. "We should liquidate them now."

"Yakov, Britain, France, America, all the Imperialist powers only leave us be because they are busy elsewhere and because they cannot sell the idea of all out war against us to their people," Lenin said. "Would you so easily hand them a propaganda coup? I can see it in their newspapers now, 'Communists Murder Innocent Romanov Children.'"

"Comrade Lenin has a point," Trotsky said. "I lived in America for some time. They are not without their virtues, but as a people they are highly prone to emotional decision making. They can be quite easily stirred to outrage, and their capitalist masters would love any excuse to direct that outrage at us."

Sverdlov frowned at the shorter man. He would have a word with the defense commissar about the ill-considered act of contradicting him in front of Lenin.

"I still think leaving the Romanovs alive is dangerous," Sverdlov said. "But I will not bring it up to the full committee now."

I hope you're both right. But I am still going to tell Yurovsky, in your name, that he is also to frame the lot for counterrevolutionary activities, so we can get rid of them at an opportune time.

Chapter Twenty-Five

Maria and Anastasia Nicholaievna Romanova

South of Tobolsk

Briefly, Daniil laid out the changed enemy situation to the orders group.

"Turgenev," asked Kostyshakov, "are either of the warehouses big enough to hold us all?"

"Both of them, really, sir, though it might be a little cramped."

"We can live with cramped." Kostyshakov pulled up a mental map of the town. "The west one, then, by the river docks. We're all going there. Now, Ivan Mikhailovich?"

"Sir?" asked Dratvin.

"Can you hold the Omsk people in place—might be for several hours—with two platoons?"

"I'll need both heavy machine guns," Dratvin replied. "Plus one of the antitank rifles."

"Why?"

"I can plug them on the north and south, but that's not enough to hold them north, south, east, and west. The two heavies, firing up the avenues to east and west, maybe supplemented by a Lewis gun, each, can hold them, and, while there might be a few leakers, they won't be many and they won't be organized. The antitank rifle is to panic them into trying prematurely, by showing there's no cover in the building."

"All right," Kostyshakov agreed, "both heavies to you, plus one 13.2mm. Now figure out a time you have to leave to get from the western warehouse to the target. I'll take your Third Platoon."

"Yes, sir." Dratvin then coralled the section leader for the heavies and took him off to one side.

"Cherimisov?"

"Sir?"

"You've still got two targets, the Governor's House and the Kornilov House. I don't think I want to send thirty or so of your men into a building occupied by five times that in Bolsheviks. So what I want to do is surround the place with one of your platoons and, I think, the two infantry guns. Get flamethrowers up and start fires in the basement and maybe the upper floors, too. Shoot them as they try to escape. Use the infantry cannon and snipers to break up organized concentrations in the fenced yard behind, plus any firefighters that may arise, insofar as they can be seen . . . also to panic the horses they've probably got there."

"Can we add some explosives to the mix?" Cherimisov asked.

"Engineer?"

"Yes, sir?"

"How much of your platoon is here?"

"Just two squads, sir."

"Fine. One of them is to be attached to Fourth Company, to reinforce the engineers already there. You are attached, with the other squad, to Lieutenant Turgenev and Strat Recon, to take down the power plant and shut off the town's lights. Turgenev, can you do this?"

"Yes, sir, though I'm glad to have engineers along to keep me from fucking up the plant. Can the engineers come to the safe house? Less chance of being noticed that way."

"Yes, they can. And good. Now back to you, Cherimisov."

"Sir."

"So one of your platoons, a squad of the engineers, and the infantry cannon section are to surround the Kornilov House, set it afire, and destroy the Bolsheviks inside it. Let none of them escape."

"Prisoners, sir?"

"None. Accept no surrenders."

"Yes, sir."

"The other platoon is to assault the Governor's House to free the prisoners there. Lastly, the platoon I stripped from Dratvin is to be used to neutralize the original guards in the log building north of the Governor's House, some of whom have likely had to move from the Kornilov.

"Now, coordinating measures. We're mostly worried about timing. Everything needs to kick off at the same time. There is only one signal we can use that will reach everyone at once. This is the killing of the town's electrical power with the dousing of the lights.

"Turgenev?"

"Sir?"

"I want the lights down and the attack to commence at zero-four-thirty. Plot when you must leave the safe house, navigate to the power plant, take down any guard, and prepare to kill the power based on that."

"Sir. That's also when we'll want Shukhov to take down the telegraph lines, yes?"

"Correct. I don't know that they have their own power source, for a back up, but they might."

"Dratvin?"

"Yes, sir?"

"You have a longer distance to go than Cherimisov. Calculate how long to get to the Girls' School and set up in the buildings around it."

"Sir."

"Also Cherimisov; I'll be with you along with the command group. We'll be the last to leave the warehouse. At the warehouse, Second Company, minus, plus the heavy machine guns have the left side. Fourth Company reinforced, with headquarters, has the right.

"Finally, each company grouping can send up to one squad, early, to neutralize exterior guards, if they can be *absolutely sure* of doing so *silently* but, even if they cannot, to cover their occupation of assault positions.

"Now prepare to synchronize watches . . . at the mark

it will be zero-two-zero-seven ... five ... four ... three ...
two ... one ... mark.

"Now, Natalya, since you were awake to greet us, lead
off. Turgenev, take your engineers and lead them to your
safe house as you think best. Everyone else; pass the word;
drop skis and packs here ... complete silence from here
to the attack."

Fortunately, because the Tobol and Irtysh rivers were
prone to flooding, nobody had built any houses within
about two to three hundred meters of the rivers' banks,
much farther south than the promontory on which stood
the Kremlin of Tobolsk.

Moreover, the moon was now at an angle that cast a
shadow down onto the rivers' ice, but didn't illuminate the
men from one side. The men, having changed to more
familiar boots taken from their packs, leaving their Austrian
ski boots behind, made barely a sound on the thick pad of
ice. Only the sleighs made any noise, and that not much.

In short, the passage to the warehouse was as secret
and quiet as anyone might have hoped for.

Recognizing a landmark, Natalya whispered to
Kostyshakov, "We turn right here, sir." The column duly
cut right, crossing just south of the little river port. From
there, the column filed by twos into the warehouse
standing just west of Zavodskaya. Lavin was there first,
and opened the wide double doors facing the river.

Kostyshakov stopped, listening carefully, once he
reached the door. There was no sound from the town
other than the distant hum of the power station and the
occasional barking of a dog.

Inside, in the relative darkness, the senior noncoms manhandled the men into something resembling an orderly arrangement for sleeping.

Will anyone sleep? wondered Kostyshakov. *I certainly won't. Which reminds me . . .*

"Natalya?" he whispered.

"Here, sir," came the reply from the darkness.

"You and Lavin need to get back to the safe house. Can you lead me and a couple of guards there, along some route that won't be hard to retrace our steps with?"

"No problem," she replied. "Though . . . now that I think about it, the best way lies through a park with no road, with *Ulitsa* Yershova dead-ending on either side."

"That will be fine. Sergeant Major Blagov?"

"Here, sir."

"Couple of pistol armed guards, no white smocks, as soon as you can drum them up."

"Five minutes, then, sir. Maybe a little less."

Cherimisov then asked Daniil, "Sir, I've got three platoons that are going to be stretched out a good distance. Do you mind if I send three three-man teams to secure up to the last position with concealment? And my first sergeant to run herd on them?"

"Mayevsky plus nine? Sure, go ahead."

"Also, sir, I was thinking."

"Go on."

"We've got those ladders, but are they the right tool? The rope diagram Strat Recon brought us shows two sets of perfectly useful stairs, and from the side we're coming from. I think we can get more combat power to the second floor quicker using those than we could with wenty ladders. Sir, we're presuming we've got surprise, anyway; let's *use* it. Besides, we'll need the ladders for the tockade."

"Do it." *Note to self, we need a way to inculcate more individual initiative, at least among our leaders. Cherimisov should not have had to ask me a question like that, but just should have gone ahead and done it.*

The sergeant major returned, saying, "Your guards are ready and standing by, sir."

The only dangerous spot on the route was in the relatively open area south of the Governor's House. There, Daniil elected to take a right, and then a left, before turning north again at *Ulitsa* Volodarskogo. A knock on the back door and they were face to face with Turgenev and Mokrenko.

"I want to see the two prisoners," Daniil said.

"Take him to them, Sergeant," the lieutenant said.

The lights still worked, so there was no problem getting down to the storage room. When the door was opened, both Chekov and Dostovalov sat up, squinting against the sudden light. The latter had a worse problem than light sensitivity, though, and held his head against a cosmic scale headache.

"I need to ask you two a few questions," said Daniil, without identifying himself. "It would be better for you to answer, if not . . ."

"If not, we separate them and apply duress," said Mokrenko, "until the answers are forthcoming and match." He then added the lie, "I have the iron pokers in the fire, all ready for that eventuality."

"Why not just shoot me and put me out of my misery?" Dostovalov groaned.

"I'm not especially interested in putting anyone out of their misery," Daniil said. "What I am interested in are your feelings toward the Romanovs. And the Bolsheviks."

Chekov answered, "Fuck the Bolshviks. We don't care all that much for the tsar, and the *Nemka* can go to hell as far as we're concerned, but the children . . ."

". . . are wonderful," Dostovalov finished. "I would die for Olga, and he, though he is loath to admit it, would fight for Tatiana."

Daniil raised an eyebrow. *Would he, indeed?*

"Yes," said Chekov, "I suppose I would."

"Why should I trust you?" Daniil asked.

"In your shoes, I would not," Chekov replied.

"That's an honest answer, at least."

"I'm an honest man," said Chekov.

"Could I trust your parole?"

"You couldn't trust mine," said Dostovalov, "but, then you don't need to. If you're trying to save my Olga that is all the trust you need. *His* word, on the other hand, you can trust. And I generally do what he tells me."

Daniil nodded, "I'll trust you this far, if you accept. You can come with my headquarters group, under guard, with your hands bound and your ankles tied a single *arshin* apart. Any false move whatsoever and your throats will be cut on the spot. I only needed you two out of the house so that when we go in, you don't get killed and set the girl to hysterics. But whether you are alive or dead when we've brought them out safe doesn't really matter, we can chivy them along at that point. Accept or refuse, now."

"I accept," said Chekov. "So does he."

"Sergeant Mokrenko, bind them please."

As his hands were being bound, Chekov's eyes adjusted enough to take in the submachine gun in the hands of one of the guards. "What is *that?*" he asked.

"Think of it as a short range machine gun that can carried and operated by one man," Kostyshkov replied.

"My," said Chekov, "isn't *that* a very nice idea?"

Warehouse, Tobolsk

One of the squads, rather, a squad sized composite, from Fourth Company, left the warehouse early, as Daniil had allowed. One of the squads from the remainder of Dratvin's Second Company had left ten minutes before. Already, Dratvin's men were lining up at the warehouse door nearest the river to begin their slightly longer trek to the Girls' School and the communists from Omsk. As they left, Daniil thought, *Maybe we should have left the heavy machine guns covered on the sleighs . . . nah, if a hundred and eight armed men aren't enough to excite suspicion, a couple of Maxims aren't very likely to, either.*

The little Yakut horses seemed as excited as the men, but no more fearful. *I suspect they pick their cues for fear up from us. If they're not skittish, it's probably because they can't smell fear off the men. I can only consider that a good sign.*

In a column of twos, Dratvin leading and with the T-Gewehr and the Maxims in between his first and second platoon, that company left out the rear door and began their movement to action. They had bayonets fixed and orders to try to kill anyone potentially hostile that they encountered with cold steel, rather than hot—and noisy—fire.

Daniil consulted his watch just as the last member of Second company disappeared through the door.

Twenty-five minutes and we start to move.

Safe House, Tobolsk

If we don't leave now, thought Turgenev, *there's a small chance we'll run into Dratvin's crew somewhere. This would be what we call a "bad thing," at least potentially.*

"Are we ready, Sergeant Mokrenko?"

"No, sir," the sergeant replied. "We're *eager.*"

"Engineers?"

"No less than Strat Recon," the young officer replied. He and his men had a single large log perched on alternating shoulders.

Natalya ran out and threw her arms around Turgenev. "I won't try to stop you," she said, "but even if I am too young, if you don't give me a kiss for your own good luck, you're a fool."

"You're not too young for a good luck kiss," he said, and then delivered on the statement. "Now stay here and keep down in the basement, even if it's miserably cold. There's going to be a good deal of firing from many points and in all direction, especially from that nest of communist vipers across the corner. Will you promise me?"

"I promise." She stood back, freeing him to leave. "But you should have let me go to the house to get everything ready."

"With those fanatics on guard? With all that lead flying around? Oh, no; you, my girl, stay here."

Well, at least he called me his girl.

Turgenev raised a hand, with his middle and index fingers projecting, and the rest forming an O with the thumb. As he said, "Then at the double, let's . . . *go!*" he brought them down, pointing north, then led the way out the side gate of the safe house yard.

If there was a guard on the back of the Girls' School he hadn't been paying much attention.

The men quickly took up a trotting pace. Once on the street, Turgenev turned left and led them almost two blocks to Christmas Street. From there the group went right, travelling two more, but double, blocks to where a little footbridge crossed a corner of the sharp-turning River Kurdyumka. At Epiphany, the street that on a different timeline might have been named for Rosa Luxemburg, they turned left again. With a one hundred and thirty or so meter dash, they reached the main door to the power plant. The engineers took their log off their shoulders and prepared to beat the door in.

"Just one second," said Mokrenko, who reached out, turned the knob, and found the door completely open.

"Well, fuck," said the engineer officer.

In through the open door they poured. They found one guard, asleep, and butt-stroked him off his chair and onto the floor. Lavin dropped out to tie the man's hands and feet. Moving inward, they came to a very hot open area, glowing with fires from the coal that ran the steam turbine. There were two sweating men there, shoveling coal into the open maw of the furnace. As soon as those men sensed the presence of Turgenev's little task force, they turned. When they saw the red glow reflecting from ten bayonets and almost a score of rifle barrels they dropped their shovels and raised their hands.

"Who else is in the plant?" asked the lieutenant. "Your lives depend on the honesty of your answers."

"Just one, the night shift manager," the fire stokers answered. "Well, two, if you count the woman with him."

"Where are they?"

Both of the men pointed at a room on the upper level, at the head of a flight of steps.

"Sergeant, see to them."

"Sir." He came back shortly with a man and a woman, both trying to get dressed in a hurry. At the same time, Lavin dragged the now well-trussed guard in by his heels.

"Did my wife send you?" the man demanded, while being trussed up.

"Ummm...no," said Turgenev. The lieutenant consulted his watch. "And now we wait a bit." Addressing the night shift manager, he added, "But in the interim, you are going to explain to us how to shut off all power to the town, or we'll try to put out the fire by stuffing you into it."

"Well, if you will promise not to tell my wife? Yes? Then the first step..."

Daniil consulted his watch again. *Three minutes.* He felt his heart rate begin to pick up as it had not on the strenuous ski trek to the town. *Under three hundred against over six hundred. Bad, yes, it's bad...but I've got better men, better armed and trained, and total tactical surprise. They don't know we're here or there would be firing by now.*

Was it smart to let Cherimisov use the ladders for the stockade? Yes, I think it was. It made sense to be ready for a second floor ascent without stairs but with the stairs and surprise? Yes, I think it made sense.

Should I have told Turgenev to put the power back on after a period of time, maybe ten or fifteen minutes? I don't know. But I do know that with the headlamps and the flash grenades we've got an advantage in the dark the enemy can't deal with. I think . . . yes, it was better to leave the power and lights off. And Dratvin and Cherimisov have flare pistols if they need a little short-term light.

What have I missed or screwed up? Dear God, I know I haven't thought of everything.

Two minutes now. The three platoons under Cherimisov are already forming in three columns. Too dark to make out faces. I wonder if any of them are reconsidering their claim they'd mutiny. Maybe one or two, but they're good men and not afraid of much.

I know I've screwed up something. What is it? Can I fix it in the . . . ninety seconds left to me? No, not a chance, even if I knew what.

One minute. Blagov and Mayevsky are opening the front doors, the ones facing the town. It's still lit . . . AHA! That was something I missed. While the town is lit, the guards' eyes will be used to light and less likely to see us. No lights between here and our assault positions.

And another thing; why the hell didn't I arrange to get

some vodka smuggled to the old regiment of guards to put them at ease or asleep? Am I going to lose men and Romanovs because I didn't?

Ten seconds...nine...eight...seven...good luck, boys...five...four...God go with you...two...this is a holy cause!

The three columns left at the same time, with Dratvin's detached Third Platoon peeling off half to the left and Cherimisov's first peeling off to the right. They had the longest way to go, since they had to get at least one squad and the platoon's Lewis gun all the way around the Kornilov House without alerting the guards.

In the center, behind Second Platoon, following Lieutenant Collan, the short Finn, Daniil and his command group trotted along, to the east-northeast. Behind Daniil, under a couple of guards, Chekov and Dostovalov simply could not keep up, given how their legs were bound. Even so, they crouched as low as possible while shuffling forward, an approach that set the guards to wondering if perhaps they could be trusted.

Daniil and his party passed across barren fields, over a thirty-foot wide patch of ice, then more fields before entering some woods. They they veered slightly to the right, following the woods to an open field.

Looking east, illuminated by street lights, he saw an open field and Cherimisov's men past it, hard up against a building that stood perhaps ninety or so *arshini* west of the target. Daniil held up one hand and whispered, "We wait here."

Still looking, Daniil was able to discern single guards, none too alert, at the corners of the stockade around the

Governor's House, plus two men at the gate. He'd seen earlier that this pattern was repeated to the east.

Well, we've got the ladders to get men over the stockade quickly.

After some minutes, Chekov and Dostovalov joined them.

"Now keep quiet," Kostyshakov reminded them.

"Yes, sir," they both said, almost as if they considered themselves part of the rescue effort.

Well, thought Chekov, *maybe I do.*

"Take their bindings off them," Kostyshakov told their guards, "but watch them even so."

South of the Kornilov House

Lieutenant Molchalin had never been the overly talkative type anyway. Tonight, this was an advantage. He led his reinforced platoon due west, across the same barren fields and frozen streams Kostyshakov had crossed. Before reaching Great Friday Street he detailed off the infantry cannon west of Little Pyatnitskaya Street.

"Federov, your two guns and the antitank rifle here. Is there any problem with firing on the Kornilov House?"

"Not the ground and upper floors; they're easy. I can displace forward as the enemy gets suppressed to engage the basement windows if I need to."

"Right. Shouldn't. You'll know they're suppressed by the amount of screaming you hear as the fire reaches them."

"Now wait a minute," Federov said. "Did you just tell a joke? The ever so silent and serious Lieutenant Molchalin told a joke? I can't wait to write my parents ..."

He stopped his quiet little tirade only because he

realized that, without a word, Molchalin had simply left him behind.

At Great Friday Street, by the opposite corner from the Cathedral of the Annunciation, Molchalin halted them, gathering the lot into a very tight lump of humanity.

"Nomonkov?"

"Yes, sir?"

"Anyone looking our way from the Kornilov House?"

The sniper, with his remarkable vision, looked northward, scanning carefully left to right and then right to left again. "No, sir."

Taking the sniper's word, Molchalin led his platoon pell-mell, charging across the street and into the cover provided by the church.

"Nomonkov?"

"Here, sir."

"You and your spotter, up into the bell tower. The church is open. Don't ring any bells. Your orientation is generally to the north."

"Yes, sir. Come on, Strelnikov." Without another word, his spotter and guard in tow, the sniper went to the main church door to find that it was, indeed, open.

From there, Molchalin led the rest of his platoon north. Just shy of Tuljatskaya Street he dropped off two squads and two of the flamethrowers with his platoon sergeant. He then, with his headquarters, one squad, the Lewis gun, the other sniper team, and the other two flamethrowers, skirted wide around the Kornilov House before taking up a position to its northeast.

They found a single guard, armed but passed out apparently drunk, in the lee of one of the buildings.

Without another word, Molchalin cut the man's throat. *No sense taking needless chances*.

"Ladder, here," Molchalin ordered, then stood by as the squad with him erected one ladder on the far side of a building from both the Governor's and Kornilov houses. That squad, with the Lewis gun team, scrambled up then took station behind the peak of the roof.

Sergeant Oblonsky and Corporal Panfil went through the routine of unlimbering their guns, maneuvering the limber, and getting the ammunition chests opened. Though they'd done it for speed, and silently, many times before, this time was different.

This time, thought Panfil, *we might just get our fucking heads blown off*.

"Gunner," Panfil whispered, "take aim at the northernmost window on the upper floor. Once this circus starts, we'll put a round in every window, then start again at the northern one. Unless of course, someone shoots back when he gets his own little donation of shells."

Meanwhile, Sergeant Oblonsky was giving slightly opposite instructions to his gunner: "Main floor, southern window."

"And now we wait for a bit," said Federov.

Girls' School, Tobolsk

Billeting troops in a place that doesn't have barracks and where it's too cold for tents, even if available, is a problem. Occupy the government buildings? This brings government to a screeching halt. Occupy factories? The economic costs of this can be devastating. Occupy hospitals? Not a great idea, actually. Put them in peoples' homes? Ask the British how badly that can turn out.

So . . . schools. Education may be delayed, but that can be made up by shortening vacations. They've got offices. They're almost always well heated. Commonly they've a kitchen suitable for feeding large numbers. There will be gymnasiums and nearby open fields for physical training.

It was never entirely clear if the commander of the men from Omsk, A. D. Demyanov, really understood any of this. Expelled from a seminary, his military credentials were vanishingly tiny. But he had seen the Girls' School as a place out of the cold. This was enough.

Of course, his men ran riot in the town, creating one incident after another. He not only lacked any clue as to how to control them, Demyanov also had no interest in controlling them.

His assistant, Degtyarev, was a former cavalry ensign. Thus, while he did have some military training, he—the current Bolshevik—had formerly, some years before, in university, been a member in good standing in the Union of Archangel Michael, one of Russia's more reactionary groups. Having held membership in both tended to indicate a certain fecklessness and lack of principle in former Ensign Degtyarev.

The Girls' School, itself, sometimes knows as the Girls' Gymnasium, lay just east of the Slesarka River, on the opposite corner from the safe house. It had buildings, houses, mostly, east and west, in lines parallel to Great Archangel Street, on the east of the school, and Slesarka Street, to the west. Additionally, to the west, and for which the double street was named, was the River Slesarka, now a ditch with a narrow line of ice in the bottom, plus a number of low fences of dubious obstacle value.

North of the school was the Church of the Archangel Michael, with a hundred-foot gap separating it from the school. South were a few houses and a couple of wooded areas, with a considerably narrower gap.

Dratvin winced as a woman's scream emerged from one of the houses east of school. The scream was over quickly, and hopefully without bloodshed.

But what is it that can cause a woman to scream, yet create not the slightest curiosity among the Reds from Omsk. Maybe... maybe, they became used to the sound of women screaming from frequent violations of all those around.

To hold the Omsk men inside the school until reinforcements could arrive sufficient to exterminate them, Dratvin had the two heavy machine guns, water cooled hence capable of firing for literally hours, half a dozen Lewis guns, and about seventy riflemen not otherwise needed to serve the Lewis guns. He was badly outnumbered, but probably had an advantage in firepower... up to a point.

If it were an open field, mused Dratvin, *or even some woods with cleared fields of fire, it wouldn't be a problem; we'd just eat them alive. But this close? We might get to bayonet fighting before we're done, and for that, I really don't have the numbers.*

Bell Tower, Cathedral of the Annunciation

Nomonkov, the short, stocky sniper with the better

than perfect vision, kept his back almost to the bell. He might have been able to see the ground and what was going on there without any artificial illumination, but between the streetlights and the moon, he could see extraordinarily well.

He took stock of the areas he could see well enough to engage, once the fight started. *East side of the Governor's House and the log house beyond it . . . south side of the Governor's House . . . a little dead space behind the stockade . . . south side of the Kornilov House . . . some of the enclosed yard behind the Kornilov House . . . the whole street and the open area—I suppose it must be some kind of park—to my west. Roof of both houses. Past the dead space behind the Kornilov House, I can see all the way up Great Friday Street until it turns off to the right.*

Kornilov House, Tebolsk

For the fortieth time, Yakov Yurovsky reread his orders. They contained no leeway and no doubt; the Romanovs and any who might have aided and abetted them were to be taken to Yekaterinburg. Then an excuse was to be manufactured, implicating them all in counterrevolutionary activities. And then, finally, *I am to shoot them all, even the girls and the little boy. Even the servants. Even the teachers and doctors.*

The signature on his orders said "Sverdlov," but he knew where they'd originated. *Ilyich himself has decreed that the royal family must die. Sverdlov I might have argued with, but Lenin? No, he is the father of the revolution, which makes him the savior of the world. If Ilyich says that the little boy must die, then die he must.*

Still, it's a hard duty. And I suppose I'll have to do most of the dirty work myself; the louts I brought with me won't be worth much.

In a notebook, Yurovsky began to sketch out his plan. *Here to Tyumen, open sleigh or vozok....rail to Yekaterinburg...complete isolation there...except...mmmm...let me think. No, not complete. I'll use one of my own to bring messages to the former tsar, saying there will be a rescue attempt...and...mmm...requesting Nicholashka's cooperation as well as intelligence on the security arrangements. The message or messages...it or they should have a full menu of slurs against the revolution, to get Nicholas to do the same.*

But what about the Nemka, the children, and the others. Can I get away with shooting them over the "crime" we will entice Nicholas into committing? No...no, that won't quite do. So I'll have to get him to comment on the readiness and morale of each of them, family and staff, so let him condemn them by his words. Yes, I think that works. Or, better, the "rescuers" can demand that every member of the family sign to prove they want to be rescued.

And, yet, it is still hard. It's hard not to like them, yes, even the former tsar. They're so simple and uncomplaining, so thoroughly pleasant, barring only the Nemka. And even she has her moments, I am told.

And, still, the Revolution demands they die, so they must...and shall.

Governor's House, Tobolsk

There were four guards on each floor, plus a senior Bolshevik, a Latvian, Adolf Lepa, to run herd on them, plus one supernumerary to act as messenger and to relieve any man who had to relieve himself. In addition, another twenty-one men men slept on the floor of the dining room, the other two shifts for the twenty-four hours of guard duty.

One of the guards, one of those on the first floor, stood watching the stairs that led down to the basement. The previous set of guards were down there and were, under no circumstances, to be allowed up to mingle with the Romanovs.

Power Plant, Tobolsk

The engineers manned the switches to kill the power. The night shift manager had been most helpful in explaining how to do so quickly and without damaging anything. There were different switches sending power to different parts of the town. Turgenev could have cut power only to the areas about to be attacked but had no orders to limit it that much.

And besides, who knows how many guards may be out getting laid, hence could return and interfere if they had light to see by? No, the whole town goes into darkness.

West of the Governor's House, Tobolsk

Daniil was a little surprised that the streetlights and the lights inside the houses didn't go out immediately. First he sensed more than heard the power plant's hum dropping, four hundred and fifty or so *arshini* to the north. Then the lights began to dim out. And then it was all blackness, except for what light came from the moon, now well down in the west.

And here we go.

Interlude

The Tobolsk Soviet:
"We've Got to Get out of This Place."

Amidst what sounded like a war come to their doorsteps, three members of the Tobolsk Soviet met in the house of the leader of the three, Khokhryakov. The other two were Semyon Zaslavski and Alexander Avdeev.

"What the hell can it mean?" asked Zaslavski.

"It could be anything," said Khokhryakov. "The old guards on Citizen Romanov resisting the new men under Yurovsky? The Omsk men trying to take control themselves? A bloody free for all? Or...you know... maybe even something else."

Avdeev, who would miss his opportunities to steal from the townsfolk's largesse toward their former ruler and his family, observed, "Whatever it is, it bodes no good for us. I think it's time to leave."

"Not just yet," said Pavel. "Wherever we might go there are going to be questions, and we had better be prepared to answer them. Here's what we'll do: Alexander, your face is too well known to all the parties, and not well enough liked. You go beg, borrow, or steal us a good sleigh with horses. Bring them here."

"Yes, comrade," the former keeper of the Romanovs agreed.

"Semyon, you are not as well known. Get as close as you safely can to the sound of the fighting and collect whatever information is safe to collect. Even rumors will be better than nothing."

"Agreed," said Zaslavski. "And what will you be doing?"

"I'm going to empty my house of food, drink, and blankets. Then all of us together are going to trek to Tyumen and get the word to Moscow and Saint Petersburg."

Chapter Twenty-Six

17874

Lewis Gun

Log House, North of the Governor's House, Tobolsk

Lazarev, the platoon leader for Dratvin's Third Platoon, attached to Fourth Company, was unsure of what to do. His men had spread out as they ran toward the log house. Only one guard had been encountered, and he'd been half asleep, leaning against the stockade with his eyes fluttering closed.

The bayonets of three men had pinned that guard to the stockade. He'd only awakened for a tiny moment before a rifle butt knocked him into next week. Half a second later, the first of three bayonets passed through his heart, cutting off even the chance to scream.

And now what? wondered Lazarev. *Nobody's awake in the log house. They're going to wake up though, as soon as the shooting starts.*

Hmmm...lights still on...maybe I have time to set something up.

"First Squad?"

"Here, sir."

"You and your squad, take all three Lewis guns. Set up northwest of the house, facing generally east. Don't let anyone escape."

"Okay, sir."

"Second and Third?"

"Here, sir."

"Here."

"We're going to go through that door," the lieutenant pointed. "Fixed bayonets, regular grenades, minimal shooting, maximum shouting and screaming. I want to panic the men in there into running...and there go the lights.

"Follow me!"

Kornilov House, Tobolsk

It was weapons free as soon as the lights went off. As such, the reinforced squad above Molchalin, on the roof of the one story building northeast of Kornilov's, opened fire on whatever they could see of the guards, on the north and east sides of the Kornilov House. As the firing began, the lieutenant slapped one of the flamethrower men on the back, shouting, "Follow me!" He and his assistant did. Another man, who hadn't gone up on the roof, followed as a guard. All but the lieutenant bore extra donut-shaped fuel and spherical air tanks on their backs.

The four of them ran forward, as quickly as the heavy burden of the German flamethrower allowed. They came to the wall surrounding the yard where the newly arrived Reds had secured their horses. There was one guard there who called out a challenge before Molchalin fired a burst at him. The lieutenant was rewarded with a scream, a groan, and a thud.

"Over the wall with the flamethrower, quickly," the lieutenant ordered. He and the guard boosted the flamethrower operator to the top of the the the wall. From there, the man swivelled himself around on his belly before gingerly letting himself down on the other side. The assistant quickly followed. In half a second, Molchalin dropped beside him.

"Let the horses escape!" were the lieutenant's last words to his guard before dropping to the ground.

To their front, horses, panicked by the shooting, reared and stomped, ran the short distance available, then turned to run back the other way.

"We'll keep close to the wall," Molchalin said. "Horses may be dumb but they don't run themselves into walls. Come on!"

As fast as humanly possible, skirting as close to the wall as possible, the two dashed for the building. No guards barred their way, though Molchalin thought that he heard sounds coming from inside the building. *Probably guards alerting from the firing.*

When they reached the building the lieutenant kicked one booted toe through a basement window, knocking out a single pane that would leave a space for the flamethrower's nozzle.

Ordinarily, a flamethrower is used to suffocate an enemy by burning up all the oxygen in an enclosed space. In this case, however, the objective was to burn down the entire building, preferably with the enemy inside. That meant they *wanted* oxygen to get inside. To this end Molchalin pulled a regular concussion grenade from his belt. He quickly unscrewed the cap, letting the porcelain knob fall out. Grasping both knob and the stick handle of the grenade firmly, he pulled the knob down and the grenade up. Then he threw the grenade into whatever room in the basement was on the other side of the broken window. He and the flamethrower team pressed their backs against the wall as the grenade blew the remains of the window across the yard.

Shouts came from above. To Molchalin they sounded very panicky. Behind them, the horses screamed. Some of them had probably been hit by pieces of flying glass.

"Burn them!"

In half a second, the nozzle was inside the window, pouring out a couple of seconds' worth of intense flame. They didn't wait to see what had caught fire; something almost certainly would.

Somewhat distantly, Molchalin heard the twin booms of the infantry cannon, punishing the entire western face of the Kornilov House.

They've got to be shitting themselves in there, and hardly even imagining yet that we're setting them afire.

From there, the two raced to the east to almost the halfway point on that side of the building. Once again, a grenade followed a booted toe and was, in turn, followed by flame. This time, screams came from the basement even as the panic-stricken shouts above grew.

"Now the next story corner!"

Kick-Boom-Fwooosh!

"All right," said Molchalin. "Now the second floor."

"Got to change tanks, sir."

"Well, do it, but hurry!"

Once the tank was changed, with both machine pistol and flamethrower nozzle raised, the pair backed out and away from the building. This was risking being trampled by the horses, now outright mad with fear, but there was no help for it. Molchalin turned for a moment, ready to shoot any that came too close. He discovered that, dumb as they might have been, the horses were still not so dumb as not to recognize the source of the explosions and fire that had them panicked. They did their screaming and shrieking while doing their best to stay far away. Some were also escaping out the gate opened by the guard of the small flame party.

"Good enough," said Molchalin. He took a not especially careful aim at the second window in from the eastern corner, then blasted it out with his MP18.

"Flame!"

Instantly, the flamethrower shot a jet of hot burning fuel through the shattered window. It bounced off the ceiling inside, then splashed down onto the rest of the room. This time there was no doubt; Molchalin heard intense screaming coming from inside. He changed magazines while the flame was ongoing.

"One more. Will that thing reach the top floor?"

"Yes, sir, no problem."

"Good."

Another window was shot out. Molchalin saw, illuminated in the glow of the rising flames, a man leaning out a window with a rifle. The Lewis gun firing from the roof to the north drove that Red back inside.

With a window open there was no particular need to shoot out another one. The flamethrower operator fired through the open window, once again splashing flame down. The scream that came from that was *truly* horrifying.

"Any fuel left?" Molchalin shouted.

"Maybe two seconds' worth, in this tank, sir."

"Good. Expend what's left on this one." Again, the machine pistol chattered, shattering wood and glass overhead.

Whoooooshshshsh.

"Now let's get the hell out of here!"

"We've got one more fuel tank, sir."

"Save it."

Girls' School, Tobolsk

Dratvin had only his second platoon, south of the school, open fire initially, as the lights dimmed out, and that with rifles only, and those with a deliberate effort to do no harm. The Lewis and Maxim guns he wanted to be the first of several surprises he had in store for the Bolsheviks from Omsk.

Given the trouble and bad blood between them, the Omsk Reds are most likely going to think we're the original guards, come to settle some scores. They won't take us too seriously, and may just come charging out. And for that . . .

For that, Dratvin had two Lewis guns, cross firing along the streets to the south and north, and a Maxim and a Lewis gun, each, sighted to fire up the avenues, east and west. He also had the two remaining flamethrowers from the engineer platoon, but was holding them in reserve as he absolutely did *not* want to cause a rush from the building greater than he thought he could handle.

He also had a flare gun, ready to illuminate the scene when they tried.

And, sure as hell, they're going to do it.

In the muzzle flashes from the rifles Dratvin caught the image of a mass of men, maybe as many as a hundred, pouring out of the school's main entrance and then charging down Great Archangel Street with wild shouts and cries.

He raised the flare gun and fired. The starshell arced up, then exploded into light approximately over the school's eastern side. Instantly, the heavy machine gun on that side, plus the Lewis in support, plus the other Lewis that was intended to cross fire from east to west, all opened up.

The two Lewis gunners shifted their upper bodies, left and right and then right to left again, each emptying a forty-seven round magazine onto a street and open area less than seventy feet wide. In a couple of seconds the magazines were changed and the guns firing again, right to left and then left to right.

The Lewis guns were firing low. Few were killed by them until the bullets shattering ankles and femurs brought their owners' torsos to street level. Then shoulders and skulls shattered, too. Likewise were hearts exploded and lungs perforated. The worst were the kidney hits, that silenced the receivers for a moment, with the sheer agony of the thing, but then set them to screaming like lost souls as they bled out there, into the street.

While the Lewis guns fired low, the heavy, water-cooled Maxim was sighted to fire at about crotch level. The gunner depressed the trigger, sending out a steady spray of bullets at a rate of something between nine and ten per second. With the trigger depressed, he began slapping the gun, also left to right and then, once it had swept all the way to that side of the street, after switching firing thumbs, right to left.

At the same time, the one squad stationed east in the houses along the north-south avenue added their little bit to the carnage.

By the time the overhead flare had burnt itself out, forty or fifty Omsk Bolsheviks lay dead and dying in the street, while the rest, among them a number of wounded, some badly so, had scampered back into the school in abject terror.

So now, wondered Dratvin, *do they try to fight out to the west or to the north? I don't think they'll risk the east side street again. But what I don't want is to give them much time to think.*

"Antitank rifle?"

"Here, sir."

"Start putting rounds into the center of the building. I want to try to panic them into trying another attack."

"Yes, sir. Sir, have you any idea how much this is going to *hurt*? Not complaining, sir; just asking."

"Just do it."

"Yes, sir."

Infantry gun section, Southwest of the Kornilov House

Both ends of the building were blazing merrily, now, with flames pouring out of the windows, north and south, and scorching the exterior walls. Even over the firing and the roar of the flames, it was possible to hear wounded men screaming as the fire reached them.

While the 37mm projectiles were blasting out windows and exploding against walls opposite the windows inside the rooms of the place, the antitank gunner, with his Mauser T-Gewehr, began putting rounds into the building more or less at random. The objective wasn't actually to kill anyone, since the fire would take care of that part, but to frighten the occupants and disorganize or break up any firefighting parties that might arise.

It's a damned good thing no one is expecting me to aim carefully, thought the gunner, *because it's all I can do to force myself to pull the trigger, knowing how much it's going to hurt.*

Trying to protect a thumb he suspected had been broken by the slamming of the pistol grip against it, the gunner slapped the bolt handle up with an open palm, then pulled it back with the four so far undamaged fingers of his right hand.

"Put another round in," he told his assistant gunner, "I can't hold it."

With the round in place, he used his palm, again, to close the bolt and then rotate it down.

He was still praying for a blessed misfire when the gun section's chief noncom, Yahonov, knelt beside the Mauser and said, "Put a couple into the area behind the door; the lieutenant thinks they're getting ready to make a charge out."

The first explosion was muffled enough to make Yurovsky think of a faulty heating system. The second one, however, left no doubt. *That's enemy action.*

Instantly he'd tucked his orders into a jacket pocket and was on his feet. Bounding from his quarters, he began to shout for his men to take up their rifles and to defend themselves. It was good for him, at least for the moment, to have left his room when he did, because the place was lashed by machine gun fire coming from somewhere outside a bare moment later.

There were more explosions coming from inside the building, he heard. *But they're smaller, I think. Maybe not much more powerful than the muzzle blast from a rifle . . . okay, maybe two or three times more, but what could that be? Some kind of small hand grenade?*

And then Yurovsky smelled smoke. He turned around and looked back through the door he'd just passed through. Through the now broken windows, he saw fire reflected from the buildings on the other side of the street.

Oh, shit. Those Omsk bastards!

Governor's House, Tobolsk

Lepa was one of the first to realize an attack was in progress. He, however, also assumed it was coming from the Omsk louts. This was, in fact, a not unreasonable supposition, as the distance away of the platoon designated to seize the Governor's House and free the Romanovs meant that, for the time being, there was nothing much— and nothing noisy—doing about the Governor's House.

As de facto sergeant of the guard, Lepa was stationed at the southeast corner of the house, in a room previously designated "for officers." Just to the north of that was the small room that normally contained Lili Dehn, now much overstuffed with Lili, plus Catherine "Trina" Schneider, and Countess Anastasia "Nastenka" Hendrikova.

Shouting the alarm, Lepa filled the officers' room with the four guards on the main floor. They began firing at the large muzzle flashes coming from across the town park, to the due south.

"One of you," shouted Lepa, "go rouse up the ones asleep in the dining room. I'm going to direct the men up above."

With that, Lepa bounded north up the corridor, cut left, and then practically flew up the main set of stairs to the upper floor. He found there the four guards for that floor, looking through the windows at the fire in the Kornilov House.

"What are you idiots doing?" Lepa demanded. "Shoot back, for fuck's sake."

"Shoot at what?" asked one of the men.

"Muzzle flashes, you idiot."

Lepa turned and retraced his steps down to the main floor, then turned left again, heading for the dining room. There he found men half asleep, but fast awakening, pulling on bits of uniform and boots.

"Forget the boots and shirts, you idiots! All you need are your rifles and ammunition. The house with the commander and our comrades is under attack. Half of you . . . no, that's wrong . . . the second shift, upstairs to the large hallway and return fire. The third shift, come with me."

Meanwhile, Ortipo, Tatiana's little French Bulldog, ran back and forth, barking excitedly at all the noise and confusion. Lepa thought briefly of shooting the animal, but, *All things considered, he's not as annoying as those three women shrieking behind the officers' room.*

South of the town park, Tobolsk

It's the odd crack of a passing shot that tells one someone has become annoyed with him. Those shots started coming in, filling the air with a malevolent sound, like a nest of hornets on the rampage but smacking head-on into a glass wall.

Federov shouted, "Panfil and Oblonsky, get those guns on the . . ."

Crack. Down went Federov, with blood gurgling in his lungs and pouring from his lips to the ground.

The section sergeant, Yahonov, ran to his downed officer. He flipped him over, only to see a seeping hole in the lieutenant's chest by the flash of a firing cannon. There was no pulse, no sign of breathing.

A bullet cracked by, far too close for comfort, especially given the dead young officer on the ground.

Yahonov heard Panfil ordering his gunner to shift fire left. Even as he did so, another shot bounced off the steel gunner's shield, setting it to ringing, long and loud.

"Goddammit," Panfil cried, "that's too close. Target: Main floor windows, right. Fire! Continuous fire!"

The infantry gun began pouring forth high explosive shells at a rapid rate, twenty shells a minute. True, they weren't bunker busters, but twenty of them a minute made them nearly as good, especially exploding in a not very large room. On the other hand, the Governor's House was very thick-walled indeed; if a shell didn't go through a window or explode on the inside of a window opening, it was pretty much useless.

A couple of seconds after Panfil's gun switched, Oblonsky's joined in, blasting at the upper floor windows on the southeastern corner.

It didn't stop the firing from that corner of the Governor's House, but it reduced it in both volume and accuracy by a good deal.

The problem of the Kornilov House, however, remained, and one antitank rifle could hardly be sufficient to solve it if the men from Yekaterinburg tried a breakout.

Still, thought the gunner, squeezing the trigger as his sights lay on the right side of the main door, *I've got to try . . . no matter how much it hurts.*

Governor's House, Tobolsk

With the dousing of the street and house lights, the group with Cherimisov—his company Headquarters, battalion Headquarters, and his Second Platoon under Collan—lit their head lamps and leapt forward. One squad threw itself against the door leading to the kitchen, sending it crashing, while two more erected ladders against the stockade and crossed over by a mix of those and men boosting each other over. Collan's Headquarters followed through the broken kitchen door.

Only one guard was present on that section of the wall, and he was distracted by the initial firing coming from the Kornilov House. He hardly noticed the clubbed machine pistol that split his skull and laid him out from behind. Slammed forward into the stockade, the guard crumpled at its base, alive but bleeding and insensate.

"Repin," said Sergeant Bogrov, "kill him quietly." Repin promptly drew his knife, knelt down beside the prostrate guard, lifted his head back by his hair, and then slashed his throat from ear to ear. The gushing blood made little sound in comparison to the hellstorm arising across the street.

From both sides of the kitchen, and through the door, Second Platoon converged on the passageway to the Governor's House. Briefly, confusion reigned until Collan said, "Second Squad, take point," physically pointing Sergeant Yumachev in the right direction.

Second Squad, under their sergeant, followed by First, under Tokarev, bounded through the door and up the stairs. The glow from their carbide lamps flickered and flashed in the cut crystal of the overhead dome light just inside of the doorway. Ahead, they could hear firing to the right and the sound of men trying to organize and equip themselves to the left.

We have to go into the hall to go upstairs, thought Yumachev. *But that means instant fighting.*

"Flash," Yumachev said to the man following him. Then the sergeant pulled a flash grenade from his belt, unscrewed the cap, armed it, and tossed it down the hall in the direction of the dining room. The man following, Ilyukhin, the coal miner's son, did the same thing in the other direction. They waited a few seconds until they heard two *booms*, in rapid succession. Then Yumachev shouted, "Romanovs down! Romanovs down!" while charging down the corridor toward the dining room.

It wasn't entirely clear that the men in the dining room could see anything at all. But Yumachev and Ilyukhin beside him could see well enough by the light of their carbide lamps. They began firing, spraying bullets as if water from a hose, cutting down the Yekaterinburg Bolsheviks with neither hesitation nor mercy. As the other four men of the squad showed up they came on line and likewise began firing into the mass of writhing, screaming, begging, bleeding, and—most importantly—dying communists.

"All right," said Yumachev, "back to the stairs and up."

Meanwhile, covered by the fire and bodies of Second Squad, Tokarev and First Squad entered the corridor, rounded it into the staircase, and continued on up.

First Squad, third in order of march, came out of the stairwell and, recognizing that there were two kinds of fire at play, and only their side's was going to be full automatic entirely, turned right in the direction of the other. The Bolsheviks there were not so stunned. Yes, Ilyukhin's grenade had stunned and half deafened them, but because they'd been facing out, it hadn't done nearly as good a job of blinding them.

Thus, when First Squad came south down the hallway, five Bolsheviks were waiting and almost ready. They fired first, taking down the squad leader, Bogrov, one of the men, Levkin, both dead or soon to be, and wounding a third man, Bok, before the automatic fire of the remaining three cut them down while they were trying to reload.

Lieutenant Collan, meanwhile, guarded by his runner, Lopukhov, stood in the main floor corridor shouting, "Romanovs here after freed! Romanovs here after freed!"

His platoon sergeant, *Feldfebel* Kostin began searching the rooms. This was done by a process they hadn't rehearsed, but hit upon by Kostin once he realized the rooms were too small down here, most of them, for the flash grenades. Instead, he kicked open a door, then had his assistant place a flash grenade at the opening.

In this way, Kostin was able to evacuate first about nine maids, all still sound of health but deafened, blinded, screaming, and utterly terrified, back to the lieutenant, who pushed and prodded them towards the kitchen. For the next two rooms, a set of toilets and a bath, the platoon sergeant did throw flash grenades inside, before entering with the intent to kill anything moving. There was nothing, however, in either place.

In all three cases, Kostin chalked a large X on each door.

"Make sure they're all dead," he ordered the other two men, pointing at the corpse-littered dining room. Short bursts of machine pistol fire, methodically moving from body to body, rapidly followed.

At the other end of the hallway, the three remaining men of Bogrov's First Squad stood heaving over the communist corpses in the front room and the officers' room. From inside the room behind the officers' room came a woman's voice. "This is Countess Hendrikova, a friend of the empress. For the love of God don't shoot!"

"Come out," said Corporal Turbin.

"There are three of us!" Hendrikova warned.

"Then come the fuck out, all three of you. We don't have a lot of time to waste."

Immediately three women, one older, two more or less of marriageable age, came out. All were in nightgowns but in the process of pulling on coats.

"Go to the lieutenant," Turbin ordered. "He'll direct you to safety."

"Hey, Corporal?" asked one of the men.

"What is it, Repin?"

"You ought to see this."

Turbin went to the window from which Repin could see out and said, "Shit."

From the 37mm position, the platoon sergeant saw the flash of a grenade, saw the firing, very distinct from single shot rifle fire, of the MP18s, and made the proper call to the two guns. "Cease fire! Cease fire!"

"Romanovs down! Romanovs down!" shouted both Sergeants Tokarev and Yumachev, along with all their men, as their squads fanned out, north and south, from the head of the stairs.

Yumachev wasn't taking any chances with this group of Bolsheviks, He had thrown six flash grenades into the open hall into which the stairs opened. In that sudden storm of thunder and lightning, all five Bolsheviks, including Lepa, were stunned silly and blinded. The six men of the squad, per the usual drill, split along the walls, firing, firing, firing, until not a Red remained standing.

They then fired some more, to make sure. Yumachev then kicked open the door of the ex-tsar's study and, with only three men, cleared it as well, all the while shouting, "Romanovs down!" From that room came two assistant cooks and a scullery maid.

In the other direction, Tokarev and his crew started clearing northward, room by room, always half expecting a female scream. The first room clearance, however, caused no screams. It was the drawing room, normally abandoned for the evening, but now containing, mostly asleep on the floor and on the couch, a half dozen of the male prisoners previously held in the Kornilov House. A door kick, a flash grenade, a quick entrance by two men, identified that none of them were armed, and at least one was recognizable, Prince Vasily Alexandrovich Dolgorukov, the Marshall of the Imperial Court. It was probably the presence of the prince that kept the rooms's occupants from simply being massacred on the spot, as being altogether too male to be trusted.

"Come out," ordered Tokarev. "Hands up so you don't get shot. Feel your way to and down the stairs. Our lieutenant will tell you where to go, downstairs. Go! Go! Go!"

"God bless you," said Dolgorukov, as he led the way onward.

The next room on the hit parade was known to be Tsarevich Alexei's. It was a no grenade room by previous orders, too. Thus the door was kicked open and a man in a sailor's uniform was seen standing between the door and Alexei's bed.

"You'll take him over my body," said the sailor, Nagorny.

"That could be arranged easily enough," Tokarev replied, "but it really isn't necessary. This is a rescue, not a kidnapping."

"Oh."

"Now, if he can walk, get him to walk. If he can't, carry him. Where? Downstairs to the lieutenant. He'll direct you to safety."

Nagorny, stunned despite the lack of a grenade, slowly turned, bent, and picked up Alexei in his stout arms. Before he'd turned back, Tokarev was gone and there was a sound of shouts—"Romanovs down!"—and explosions from both the boudoir, next door, and the royal sleeping chamber, across the hall.

"Wait, Klementi Grigorievich," said the crown prince. "I'll leave when my sisters and parents do. Stay here until we see them."

Once in my life, thought Alexei, *oh, please, God, just once in my life to be able to do something as brave and grand. Is that too much for someone cursed with my disease to ask for?*

Kornilov House, Tobolsk

With shouts just barely able to overcome the sounds of roaring flame, screaming and burning wounded, shots, and explosions, Yurovsky managed to get all but a handful of unwounded men, with arms in their hands, plus some with grenades, assembled at the main door, fronting Great Friday Street.

"This," he shouted, to the mass of men standing and crouching ready to charge across the street, "is an attempt by the Omsk mob to seize control of the Romanovs, hence of the revolution. We must prevent them from doing so; the future demands it. Now are you . . ."

Before Yurovsky could say, "ready," a single shot smashed through the door, sending wood splinters everywhere. It then butchered half a dozen crowded men, tearing off limbs, disemboweling some of them, exposing one set of lungs, and removing one head completely, before ricocheting off the far stone wall to take out four more.

Oddly, between the fire and the shooting coming from the other three sides, the single, devastating bullet didn't panic the men and drive them back. Instead, it panicked them into opening the door and charging across the street for the stockade around the yard in front of the Governor's House.

Everyone in the infantry gun section not actively involved in manning the guns turned their own rifles on the Yekaterinburg men. One squad among those left with Molchalin's platoon sergeant, to the south of the Kornilov House, were likewise able to bring fire onto them. It was not enough. Roughly one hundred and twenty men had been in the Kornilov House. Perhaps ninety or even one hundred of them massed at the door. Eighty or ninety burst through the door to charge for the stockade. At least forty-seven managed to get over the stockade. Meanwhile, the bodies of the remainder littered the street and formed a mass at the foot of the stockade.

That left forty plus inside the compound, terrified, exhausted, and unsure for the moment of what to do. Yurovsky, himself, lay unconscious in the street, his life only spared by the effect of cold in helping to clot the stump of a missing leg.

Then one of the Reds had the presence of mind to shout, "Secure the Romanovs!"

Bell Tower, Cathedral of the Annunciation, Tobolsk

Nomonkov watched the scene playing out below, rifle at the ready but having little to shoot at. He tried to take out one guard on the stockade as soon as he heard the firing erupt from Molchalin's platoon. Whether he'd hit anything, though, was a matter of conjecture; the lights died before the first shots rang out while the Kornilov House itself hadn't yet truly caught fire enough for any useful degree of illumination.

Once it had caught, though, the sniper had a bit of a field day. Down went the guard of the stockade's eastern gate. Down went another one, on the southern side. Inside the Kornilov House's upper floor, yet another was thrown back as the sniper's bullet tore out his throat in a misty red spray.

And then there weren't any targets for a while, not until Nomonkov saw a human wave of Bolsheviks—charging or fleeing; it was impossible to say and it may not even have made any difference—moving across the street to the stockade.

He was as surprised as anyone by the charge, so didn't have a chance for a fourth kill until the mass was at the stockade. Then, with ease, the sniper dropped two men at the base of the stockade, mere seconds apart.

It wasn't until the mass turned on the main entrance to the Governor's House that Nomonkov could really reap large. Into the backs of the mob—*hell, one hardly needs to aim*—he fired again and again. What he didn't quite realize, however, was that this was actually driving them forward into the house.

Basement, Governor's House, Tobolsk

With more than thirty men shouting "Romanovs down" in both Russian and English, and none of them shouting it together, it was probably inevitable that some of the guards in the basement should have heard it as "down with the Romanovs." It was no more surprising that, having heard this, some of them would have inferred that, rather than being a rescue, or even a kidnapping, what they were hearing overhead was most likely an attempt at mass assassination.

A few of the men in the basement, loyal to their previous mission if not to the Romanovs, themselves, insisted they should intervene and save the family. The rest, almost a hundred of them, said "To hell with that," and sat on those few, literally, while the storm raged overhead.

Interlude

The Tobolsk Soviet: Dashing Through the Snow...

Alexander Avdeev came back first, leading a two-horse team, themselves pulling a sleigh.

"Hide it in back," Pavel Khokhryakov ordered. "Quickly, now, before we're seen with it. I've assembled enough food for two weeks and enough blankets for bitter cold. Plus two pistols and three rifles. Start loading the sleigh, but keep the pistols and rifles where we can get at them."

"Where's Zaslavski?" Avdeev asked.

"Semyon's not back yet and, yes, that has me worried."

"No need to worry, or, at least, not about me," said Zaslavski, suddenly appearing at the corner of the house. "Not that my little foray didn't have its moments."

"What the hell went on this morning?" demanded Khokhryakov. "Did the Omsk crowd try to take control of Citizen Romanov and his family?"

"Much worse than that," replied Zaslavski. "Apparently a group of Imperial Guards has rescued them, or some of them. The details are fuzzy, though. I don't know how many survived the experience."

"We'll need to stick around then," said Avdeev. "At least until we find out more."

Chapter Twenty-Seven

Tsarevich Alexei Romanov

Log house, North of the Governor's House

Surprise, when achieved, can be a considerable force multiplier. The men of the old guard force, tired, out of sorts, humiliated by their treatment from the Yekaterinburg Bolsheviks, were just barely coming awake from the firing to the southeast when some of their windows were smashed in, followed by a flurry of concussion grenades exploding in the air, on the floor and, in one case, on someone's belly. He didn't scream, but the two men who saw him coming apart in the center certainly did.

This was followed by a chorus of banshee howls as two dozen men burst through the door, hacking, stabbing, shooting, and bludgeoning everyone they came in contact with. The limited light that came in with those men, from the couple of carbide lamps issued to the lieutenant and platoon sergeant, added to the terror.

Not that there were many casualties from this; there were not. As almost a single being, the men on the first floor ran outside through the northern door and windows, in their underwear, without even any boots on, where they were swept by the fire of three Lewis guns and ten rifles. The rifles hit nothing; one has to see to aim and, with the moon so low, there wasn't much to see. Conversely, the Lewis guns, just maintaining a steady fire and not shifting in the slightest, let the fugitives run into their bullets. Perhaps a few escaped through that storm of lead, but they'd have been very few, and disarmed and quickly freezing rabble at that.

That still left the men on the second floor, of whom it could be well presumed that they would be armed and ready. The Third Platoon leader didn't relish the prospect of charging up a tall flight of steps to try to winkle them out.

The orders are no prisoners, but, what the hell, it's not like I'm a professional or anything. What do I know about orders? And we can always shoot them later, if necessary.

The lieutenant found his way to the stairs and shouted up, "You've got two choices. You can drop your rifles, bayonets, or any other weapons you have, and come down, one by one, to become our prisoners. Or you can stay here while we set the building on fire. If we set the building on fire, you will also have two choices. You can stay inside here and burn alive—and that's going to *really* hurt—or you can try to escape, in which case you will be shot down without mercy. You've got five seconds to decide!"

"Don't shoot," came the reply. "We'll come down. Don't shoot and for the love of God don't burn us. But let us get some boots and coats on."

"Best be quick, then, we're standing here with kindling and matches..."

Governor's House, Tobolsk

The very last room to be cleared, on the upper floor, was the one on the northeastern corner containing the four grand duchesses, Olga, Tatiana, Maria, and Anastasia, along with a few of the others forced out of the Kornilov House. Telling Olga to get the younger two, the "little pair," as they were called, into the clothing with the jewels sewn in, Tatiana donned her own and then opened the door, shouting, "Romanovs here; we're coming out! With friends!"

She emerged into a corridor lit by the strangest light she'd ever seen, a bright, sunny yellow glow that seemed to come from a dozen spots in the corridor and to drown out all shadows. Even without the benefit of the flash grenades, Tatiana was almost blinded.

"How many friends?" asked Sergeant Tokarev.

"There are seven of us, total," answered Tatiana, still blinking against the light. This wasn't exactly the answer to the question asked, but it was close enough.

From farther south, the tsar shouted out, "Tatiana, is everyone all right? Alexei?"

"I'm fine . . . we're fine . . . scared but fine."

"Thank God!"

"No time for chit chat, Your Majesty," said Tokarev. "You and your family need to get downstairs. Lieutenant Collan will direct you from there."

"Yes, yes, of course," agreed Nicholas.

"First Squad," shouted Tokarev, "positions around the royals!"

"Second Squad," echoed Yumachev, "fall back and cover the evacuation of the royals."

Daniil noticed the buildup of some kind of group, just to his north, west of the log house. Leaving Chekov and Dostavalov with their guards, he went to investigate.

"Sir," said the lieutenant, "I had a choice. I could fight my way upstairs—maybe—and win over superior numbers and—maybe—come out alive with as many as two men, or I could tell them to surrender. I chose the latter."

"It's all right, son," said Kostyshakov. "The no prisoners order was based on a set of circumstances that changed on us. You did exactly right. How many of them are there?"

The lieutenant gave an unseen shrug. "Dunno, sir. Haven't had a chance to count them yet. Maybe about fifty."

"Okay do you know where your company is?"

"Yes, sir; I've studied the diagrams and maps. They're over by the girls' gymnasium, northeast of the corner of Yershova and Slesarnaya."

"Good, very good. Leave one squad to guard your prisoners and you take the rest of the platoon to reinforce your company commander. I suspect he's having all he can handle."

Girls' School, Tobolsk

Three times the Omsk men had tried to break out, and three times Dratvin had been able to hold them. The last one, though, had ended up in hand to hand and at bayonet point to the south of the school. That had only been driven back with the aid of the cross-firing Lewis guns.

And, at that, thought Dratvin, *half of the platoon here is down. We can't hold another one, if they really try. Maybe time for the flamethrowers.*

A shout came from the building. At first, half deaf from the shooting, Dratvin couldn't make out the words. Eventually, he was able to hear, "We want a parley."

Hmmm . . . I wonder if they can see where we are? Maybe time for . . .

"Engineer?"

"Here, sir."

"Have one of your flamethrowers give a short spurt of fire, almost straight up. Just enough for them to know you're here."

That side of the school was suddenly lit up, almost as bright as day, by a long tongue of flame.

"No terms are offered," Dratvin shouted back, "but

immediate and unconditional surrender." He decided to try a tactical lie or, rather, two of them in one. The lie was made credible, first by the sheer number of machine guns Dratvin's company had in play, and second by the rather large battles and the amount of fire to be heard coming from the west. It was enough to make credible his tacit claim of having a battalion *and* that another one would be arriving shortly. "I am about to be reinforced by a second battalion. Once they arrive, there will be no mercy."

"We've got a lot of wounded."

Dratvin answered, "We've got limited medical capability ourselves, but the town has its share of doctors. Bring your wounded out with you. Bring everyone out with you because when we go in to search the building we will give no second chances."

Governor's House, Tobolsk

It didn't help any, when the Yekaterinburg Bolsheviks forced the front door open, that Sergeant Bogrov was dead and Third Squad had lost half its strength. One of them was shot down more or less instantly, and while a second one emptied a magazine into the horde pouring through the sundered doors, it was not enough. The third, Vasenkov, inside the officers' room, threw his back against the thick wall between the room and the corridor, waiting for an opportunity to . . . *I'm not sure just what.*

The Bolsheviks shot those two down, bayoneted the prone bodies, then knocked off their Adrian helmets and smashed their skulls for good measure.

Farther in, Lieutenant Collan, trying to direct the rescued prisoners, took one look and simply forced them bodily back through the door and into the staircase area. That cost him his life as his headlamp became a beacon for the fires of over a score of men who had not previously been blinded by flash grenades. Collan's immediate guard, Lopukhov, dropped to one knee, firing into the mass charging down the hallway. He, too, was felled, just as his lieutenant had been, given away by both his muzzle's flash and the light on his head.

The little French Bulldog, Ortipo, meanwhile, continued his running back and forth, accompanied by furious barking. He had no idea what was going on, but knew for a fact that he didn't like any of it.

Farther up the main floor hallway, Sergeant Kostin, the Second Platoon sergeant, and the few men with him, took cover in the doorways of previously cleared rooms. Shots then slashed back and forth, between Kostin's men and the Yekaterinburgers.

Then two grenades—and not relatively harmless flash grenades—sailed out from the Bolsheviks. One landed in the hallway, not far from the dog. The other bounced off the doorframe leading to the stairwell, then fell to the stairwell's floor.

His sisters, of course, made a great fuss over Alexei, borne in Nagorny's sturdy arms, petting him and covering his face with kisses. He bore it with as much dignity as any hemophiliac crown prince could be expected to.

"I'm FINE, I told you," he insisted, to absolutely no effect on his sisters.

The boy's eyes darted around the little area. There was a press, he saw, by the door opening to the passageway that led to the kitchen. It created, in effect, a kind of traffic jam.

I've got to get one of those lights, he thought, as well.

In the light of the carbide lamps he saw something fly against the doorframe, then bounce off to land on the floor under his sisters' feet. Not every adolescent boy would have recognized it, but Alexei did. *Grenade*, he thought. *Grenade! My sisters!*

I've lived as a mere shadow of a boy, a Pinocchio that bleeds...

The boy didn't think about it, any further. Instead, he simply pushed and rolled himself out of Nagorny's arms. The fall might have killed him to internal bleeding anyway.

...but I die like a man.

Falling to the floor he pushed himself over the grenade and then lay on top of it. Just before the explosion came, with his body between it and his beloved family, Alexei's last thought was, *Thank You for my deliverance, Lord.*

The pooch didn't really need the light from the headlamps to see the stick thrown at his feet. His night vision was naturally better than any mere human's.

Finally! The dog thought, *something I can understand. Someone wants to play* fetch.

The dog picked up the slightly more than one pound grenade with his teeth, then bounded in the direction from whence it had come. Unseen, he dropped it as the feet of the crowd of soldiers there, then ran back up the hall, expecting it to be thrown again. He was almost as far as Kostin when the grenade went off. After stunning the

Bolshviks silly, the blast and shock wave roared down the hall. The dog was picked up bodily and tossed a dozen feet.

That, it thought, *is the last time this little puppy plays fetch with* anyone . . . *ever.*

The four girls and their mother let out a collective scream sufficient even to drown out the sound of firing. "Alexei!"

Nagorny, being closest, was the first one to get to the boy. On his knees, weeping, "My boy, my boy, my little prince," the sailor rolled Alexei's body over. "Oh, my God . . ."

The sight of that was sufficient to set the women to screaming again but, to be fair, even the normally placid former tsar joined them at seeing what the grenade had done to his only son.

As Nagorny lifted the corpse back up into his arms, blood simply gushed and splashed on the floor from the boy's virtually disemboweled midsection. His skin was ghastly pale, even in the yellow light of the carbide lamps. One arm, his right, hung free, fingers lightly curled. His face was unmarked and smiling. In a way, that made it harder on his family, as, despite being so pale, he looked otherwise like he might have been merely sleeping. At least, he looked that way until one's eyes glanced down at his abdomen.

Daniil finally found something to make himself feel useful during the rescue. Arriving at the door from the kitchen passageway to the main house, he began physically dragging some through and pushing—and punching—others back to make room for people to leave.

"Behind me to the kitchen!" he shouted. "My sergeant major is waiting with a security detail to escort you away! Behind me to the kitchen! No dawdling, now; run!"

He hardly noticed when Olga passed, one arm around Tsarina Alexandra, supporting her. Behind Olga came a flood of maids and other servants. After that came the tsar—or, technically, ex-tsar. Then came Maria and Anastasia, weeping profusely.

Oh, Lord, please no, don't let Tatiana have been . . .

Kostyshakov was so relieved to see Tatiana pass by that he almost wept, himself. With the light shining above his head and in her face, she didn't recognize him.

Or it could be that she was crying, too.

Then came the sailor, with the pale, torn form of the tsarevich cradled in his arms.

Daniil took a single look and thought, with sinking heart, *And that's why. I have failed, failed miserably.*

Out in the hallway, he heard someone shouting commands.

With the explosion among the Bolsheviks—*Where it came from I haven't a clue*—Sergeant Kostin saw his chance. Shouting, "Guards! Follow me! Urrah! Urrah!" he leapt from his position in a doorway and charged down the corridor, his men following and, likewise, shouting the old Russian battle cry, "Urrah! Urrah!"

They fired from the hip as they came on, ghost-clad and having an even more terrible effect on the Reds than actual ghosts might have. The twenty or so Bolsheviks still living and inside the hallway fled south, back out of the Governor's House and into the open area.

By this time Molchalin had one squad, one Lewis gun, and the flamethrower in position along the stockade and at the eastern gate to it.

"Is that thing reloaded?" he demanded, when the Bolshviks began to run out.

"Yes, sir."

"Then send them to hell."

Almost at the same instant as the order, a long tongue of flame lanced out in an arc from the gate. The operator played it around, long and short and left to right, until every man among the Bolshviks trying to escape had been burnt. In some cases, the burning was so thorough that that they ran off, living roman candles, toward the opposite side of the stockaded compound, waving their arms and shrieking.

"Don't shoot them," said Molchalin. "Let the communist bastards *burn!*"

The lieutenant was to be deeply disappointed when some Second Platoon men appeared at the doorway and began putting the burning Reds out of their misery.

"Well, hell," muttered Molchalin, "go on and ruin everyone's fun, why don't you?"

His platoon sergeant then came running up, two squads in tow. "Sir, no chance anyone's still alive in the Kornilov House now."

Molchalin turned to see that, indeed, the entire building was a mass of flames and the roof shuddering as if it, too, was about to collapse.

"Right. Have all the bodies out here searched. If any

of them are still alive, I suppose we can let them live for any intelligence we might squeeze out of them. But collect the living somewhere they can be watched and post a guard. Medic for their wounded; they might as well be healthy before we shoot them for treason. I'm going to go report to the company commander."

Thought the platoon sergeant, *That's the most he's ever said to me at one time in the last four months.*

Vasenkov took a little, but only a little, satisfaction at not having killed any political co-religionists except in point self defense. *That was something*, he thought, *but not much.*

What am I to do now? I have helped to free the . . . .the ex-tsar? No, I suppose he's the real tsar again. And I helped free him and restore him to power. Great is my sin, vast beyond all accounting. The revolution is probably doomed now, and I'll have helped kill it. What am I to do? What is to become of me?

"Vasenkov, you idiot," shouted Sergeant Kostin. "Come join us, son; we still have a job to do."

Church bells were ringing now all over the town. Whether they were ringing in alarm or in joy remained to be seen. Certainly few, if any, of the clergy could have any intimation of what had just transpired or who was in command of the town, now. Tobolsk being a hotbed of traditional monarchism, if the bell ringers had known, the bells would have been ringing in sheer joy.

The plan was to collect and organize all the royals, aristocrats, and other rescued people in the kitchen, surround them with security, and then move the lot to the warehouse before moving the force on to help out Dratvin at the Girls' School.

That latter part seemed unnecessary; Kostyshakov could see and hear that the fight at the Girls' School was over. *But did Dratvin win or lose? If he lost we've still got to get the royals out of here.*

Chekov and Dostovalov were let in, with their guards behind and keeping close watch. The kitchen was lit almost brightly as day, what with thirty or more carbide lamps spreading their golden light.

All six of the remaining Romanovs, as well as a half dozen of their friends and retainers—the distinction often blurred with them—were clustered on their knees around Alexei's body. They wept; they prayed; they crossed themselves in Orthodox fashion, right to left. The tsarina leaned heavily against her husband, head bowed and body trembling with what had to have been nearly the ultimate in psychic anguish.

Others stood around that small knot of grieving humanity, alternately looking at and turning their eyes away from the ghastly damage done to the boy's midsection.

Kostyshakov, ashamed at the partial failure, stood back, leaving them to grieve for a moment in peace.

Over toward one corner, some of the men of Fourth Company were preparing stretchers, not only for Alexei's body, but also for the tsarina and the few other wounded—all lightly so—in attendance.

Dostovalov exchanged glances with the guards, then inclined his head toward Olga. The senior of the guards, a corporal, shrugged his indifference. He walked over and took one knee down behind her. Leaning forward, he said, "I am *so* sorry, so *terribly* sorry, Olga. He was a fine boy."

Spinning in place, she threw her arms around him, pressed her face into his chest, and redoubled her sobbing. He held her in one arm, stroked her hair with the other hand, and whispered whatever words of condolence came to mind, certain that none of them could possibly be adequate.

Chekov, on the other hand, just stood behind Tatiana, as a friend might, then reached down and patted her shoulder. "I'm sorry."

For her part, Tatiana dried her eyes on her sleeve and then stood up. Crossing herself again, she then turned, took a single step forward, and leaned her head forward, into him . . . also as a friend might.

She then lifted her head and said, "We wondered where you two had gone to. We were worried."

With a sigh, Chekov told her the very short version of his story. "We went to a place we know to think about how to rescue you. We were kidnapped from there by . . . the people who actually could rescue you—most of you—and did. They were afraid you and Olga would become uncooperative if we'd been shot down before your eyes."

"How would they know that?" she asked.

"The new servant girl, Natalya, was working for them."

"Ah."

Chekov's eyes widened. Shouting, "No, dammit, no!" he reached out and grabbed Tatiana by both shoulders. Shocked, she instinctively tried to draw back but was foiled by the strength of his grip.

✣ ✣ ✣

Suddenly, when he arrived in the kitchen and saw the Romanovs under the yellow light, Vasenkov knew exactly what he had to do, the only way he could make up to the revolution the disservice he had done it. Arc of vision narrowing, he raised his machine pistol to his shoulder and took aim at Nicholas, the former tsar. He fired a short burst, two rounds of which entered Nicholas's torso and one of which basically exploded his head. The former ruler of Russia fell in a heap.

Vasenkov didn't even have to adjust his aim; as Nicholas fell, Alexandra, now unsupported, fell on top of him. Another burst ended her medical complaints forever.

Sweeping left, he fired a long continuous burst at the two youngest Romanov girls, both of whom fell over at the force of the blows. Next he took aim at the older one. A large man in uniform tried to interpose himself between them, but he was too late. Olga fell over.

Exultantly, Vasenkov took aim at where the last of the Romanovs stood . . .

Chekov saw the white-clad, machine pistol-bearing soldier open fire. It was preternatural, how quickly he fired and then took up a new aim. He couldn't stop the shooting; all he could do was grab Tatiana and spin them both around, so that he stood between her and the shooter. He was also able to push her down a bit—she was a tall girl— so that her head was below the level of his shoulders.

A half dozen submachine guns fired just as Vasenkov squeezed the trigger on the last of the royal enemies of the people. Though he felt bullets tearing into him, none of that mattered. He kept the trigger depressed and his point of aim on the back of the traitor shielding the Romanov girl. Finally, though, with half his organs ruptured or simply gone, he fell backwards. Even as he did, the last few bullets in his magazine sprayed the high ceiling of the kitchen, knocking out chunks of wood and plaster to rain down on the scene of slaughter.

It was only sheer force of will that had kept Chekov on his feet as long as he'd managed to stay on them. The hits had come close together, but not so close that he couldn't feel them as individual blows. He continued to stand, for just a few seconds after the murderer had been taken out. It was actually the absence of more penetrating body blows that told him he could let go now, and fall.

Letting go of Tatiana, he did fall, like a sack of wet noodles, sinking to the floor and then flowing outward in the direction of Alexei. For a moment, Tatiana tried to hold him up. Failing that, she did her best to ease him to the floor.

"The bells," he said. "Mother, I can hear the bells. Mother! No! Don't leave me again!"

"I won't leave you," Tatiana answered. "I'm here, Sergei."

"You waited for me, Mother, all these years. I doubted . . . but the bells . . . the ang . . ."

Chekov's breath rattled in his throat. His body spasmed, twice. And then he was no more.

Tatiana sat back on her haunches. It was just too much. Her parents were dead. All her sisters had been gunned down. Even her little brother was a bloody ruin. And now,

Chekov had died for her. Chekov, who owed her nothing, but had defended her and avenged Olga. Chekov, whose family had been treated like vermin under her father's rule, but treated her with kindness. Chekov, whose loyalty she had done nothing to earn and whose forgiveness she would never be sure of now.

She couldn't scream anymore. What she could do, and did, was let her head fall onto her chest and the tears to flow freely.

"I am so alone now," she whispered, but not so lowly as she couldn't be heard by her surprisingly still living sister, Maria, who knelt down beside her.

"No, you're not, Tatiana. Ana and I are still here."

"Was I hit then, too?" she asked. "Am I dead and talking to spirits?"

"No," said Anastasia, kneeling on her other side. The youngest of the Romanovs had something shiny in her hand. "It was this . . . or these," she said. "The jewelry Mama had us sew into our clothes. That stopped the bullets that hit me. This sapphire, in particular; it was over my heart and stopped the bullet cold. And, yes, I'm sore, but I'll live."

"Same with me," added Maria. "Olga's didn't save her because she was too busy getting us into ours to put on her own."

None of the girls wanted to look at their dear dead. Maria, on one side, Anastasia, on the other, they closed in from the flanks, creating a troika, of sorts. And then all three, their arms about each other, buried their heads in each others' shoulders, and then broke down into sobs and howls of pure grief.

✣ ✣ ✣

The sun was rising as Dratvin deposited the more than one hundred and fifty hale and wounded prisoners he'd taken in the open area south of the Governor's House. He put his men in a ring around them, sending a runner to inform the guards on the prisoners taken by his Third Platoon to bring their charges to join the larger group.

While this was going on, Cherimisov, just north of there, in the Governor's House, shouted down the stairwell leading to the basement, "My orders are to kill you all, but I'm willing to take a chance on saving your lives. Come up with your hands in the air, your mittens or gloves, hats, coats and bedding, your mess kits and canteens, and nothing else. You will be searched. If we find a weapon on you, you will be shot on the spot. You have two minutes to get your gear and start coming up. After that, we burn you alive."

With the example of the Kornilov House, across the intersection, plainly visible from the east side basement windows, none of the men in the basement of the Governor's House doubted but that these men could and would do as they threatened.

Led by Ensign Matveev, they began filing up. On the main floor, Molchalin's platoon took charge of searching them. The fourth man up was found with a sap in his pocket.

"You were told 'no weapons,'" said Molchalin.

"Yes, but..." the former guard on the Romanovs began. He never got the chance to finish as Molchalin's runner shot him through the midsection.

"'No weapons,' I told you," shouted Cherimisov. "That one didn't listen. He's dead now."

From the main floor, the company commander could hear the sound of what he guessed were between twenty and thirty metal implements, hitting the stone floor of the basement.

"What the hell are we going to do with all of these?" Cherimisov wondered aloud.

"The other warehouse," said Malinsky, "since the former prisoners are being housed in the one we used as an assembly area until we're done securing the town. It doesn't have any heat, mind, but at least it's out of the wind. There aren't any windows and only the two doors, so it won't be hard to watch from the outside. And the ground is way too frozen for them to dig out."

"Makes sense," Cherimisov agreed. "See to it, would you, Top?"

"Yes, sir."

Molchalin's platoon sergeant reported to him that the prisoners and bodies had been searched. He also passed over a sheaf of papers, saying, "And sir, you need to read the one on top. Why don't you do that while I take over here?"

Molchalin read by the rising sun. His face remained cold and expressionless until he got to a particular passage. At that, his eyes widened and his lips curled into a rictus grin. He walked immediately to Cherimisov and pointed to that particular passage.

"Bring them to Kostyshakov," Cherimisov said. "He's at the warehouse to the west."

The bodies of the Romanov dead, plus Chekov, cooled rapidly in the freezing Siberian air inside the warehouse.

It was the warehouse previously used as an assembly area *cum* assault position for the rescue. Fully conscious of the great weight of guilt now resting on his shoulders, Kostyshakov sought out Tatiana. He began to say, "I'm sorry..." but then she cut him off brutally.

"You beast!" Tatiana exclaimed, standing in the crowd of rescued people in the western warehouse. "You murdering monstrosity on two legs! You incarnate *idiot*! Yesterday I had a full family and a good friend. Now, thanks to you, I've lost two parents, my closest sister, my little brother, *and* my friend. Great job, Daniil Edvardovich Kostyshakov. Great job. You could have left things alone, but noooo, not you..."

Daniil simply stood there and took it. Nothing she said could possibly make him feel worse than he already did. Shoulders slumped, he turned away and walked off.

Lieutenant Molchalin, standing in the warehouse's small personnel door, heard it all. He shook his head. *Talk about ingratitude.* He walked directly over to where Tatiana stood and, as was his wont, wordlessly passed her the pertinent document, the one taken from the now one-legged Yurovsky.

As Tatiana read, her normally pale skin turned even whiter. "They were going to ... oh, my God ..."

"God had abandoned you all," said Molchalin, speaking loud enough for everyone in the warehouse to hear. "Only one man had the guts and vision to try to save some of you. And you just insulted him. Well done, Your Highness! Oh, that was *so* well done." As loudly as he'd spoken, Molchalin began to applaud and sardonically to bow.

Maria and Anastasia came up. "What's ... ?"

Wordlessly, Tatiana showed them Yurovsky's orders. They both read through quickly.

"They intended to murder us all?" wondered Anastasia. "Even the children of the staff? What kind of monsters . . . ?"

"I think maybe you owe him an apology," said Maria.

"A private apology for the public wrong I did him?" asked Tatiana. "No." She looked around and, in the light filtering through open doors and cracks in walls, she spotted a dozen hay bales, piled against one wall. She went to them and climbed.

"People . . . oh, God, do you have any idea how much I *hate* speaking in public? People, listen to me. Come here, gather round, and listen."

When they had, all of them. She began to read from Yurovsky's orders, with particular emphasis on framing the tsar and his family members, as well as on the open statement that any and all witnesses, must die.

"So the only reason any of us will be alive in two weeks' time is that some brave Guards, under a brave commander, risked their lives to save us. And I, I, Tatiana Nicholaevna Romanova, am a total and complete and unforgiveable bitch for insulting him.

"That is my *public* apology. Now I am going to seek him out for a private one."

Tatiana found Daniil, sitting alone on a pile of logs, facing the Irtysh River, with his back to the warehouse and the town.

"I can't tell you how sorry I am," she began. "I can only ask you to . . ."

"I screwed it all up," answered Daniil, before she could finish. "A million things I should have done differently and . . ."

Tatiana went and sat down beside him. "You got the important thing right." She handed over the orders to Yurovsky given her by Molchalin. "Read. We'd all have been dead within a couple of weeks, anyway. If I have any family left at all it's because of you and your men."

He did read, muttering and cursing as he did. "Communist bastards!"

"I'm not just sorry," Tatiana said. "I also owe you an explanation. Yes, of course I was—am . . . always will be—hurt by the loss of my parents, sister, and little brother. But there was something else going on, too. You see, I was—and, again, am—absolutely terrified of what it meant that I was now the senior Romanov.

"My father had, before Alexei was born, made up a new rule, countermanding the old rule against a woman succeeding to the throne. It was supposed to be Olga if there was no male heir. She never let on to anyone but me—we were extremely close, you know—but she did *not* want to be tsarina.

"Well, she's gone; Alexei is gone; and the new-old rule remains. I am going to have to be tsarina if anyone is. And that scares me to death, Daniil. I am so frightened of it that I can hardly think straight. And half of the fear is knowing that my father's huge mistake, worse than all the others, was in signing too many pardons and not enough death warrants."

She placed a hand on his shoulder. "I think I was more angry at that than I was about the loss of my family."

"I think you can do it," Daniil assured her. "Moreover though it pains me to speak ill of the dead . . . well . . . yo can hardly fail to do a better job than your father."

"I know," Tatiana agreed. "He was a fine father but don't have any illusions about what a disaster of a rulin couple he and my mother were. But . . ."

"Yes?"

"Not all of my mother's family were such complete . . I'm not sure what the word would be. Idiots doesn't cove it; my mother was intelligent enough. Is there a word t describe those completely lacking in wisdom? I confess; don't know it."

He shook his head, not sure where the conversatior was going.

"My Aunt Ella. She is the best candidate for sainthooc I know. And she is terribly intelligent. She is also, quite despite having become a nun, ruthless enough when the situation demands ruthlessness. She may have begged the tsar for the life of her husband's murderer, and prayed fo him, too. That's because the deed was already done, nc one would be deterred by the execution, and so it woulc do no good.

"But she knew they were going to murder Rasputin knew it and let it happen because he *did* have to go."

Daniil shrugged, not understanding.

"If I am going to be stuck with this job," she explained "I need my Aunt Ella's shoulder to lean on, her advice t rely on. I need you to take your men and go save her Quickly, because, if the Reds ordered us murdered, orders to get rid of her cannot be far off."

"I'll try," he said. "We know she's in Yekaterinburg, o

was, a few weeks back. Now? Now it's anybody's guess. I'll kick Strategic Recon out this afternoon. Third Company should be showing up here soon. But . . . no, there's not a chance of catching the zeppelin before it goes back for the next lift. It's supposed to come into Tobolsk with that final lift. We'll stop it then and use it to get near Yekaterinburg. That's the best chance we have."

Interlude

Lenin and Trotsky: "What Is To Be Done?"

Trotsky, Lenin, and Sverdlov stood around Lenin's desk in his flat. Trotsky had woken Sverdlov in the middle of the night with the catastrophic news. Sverdlov had dressed quickly and crossed the hallway to awaken Ilyich.

"Reports are confused," Trotsky said. "But we are certain that Yurovsky and the bulk of our men at Freedom House are dead or captured. At least some of the Romanovs escaped . . . rather, to be honest, were rescued."

Lenin slammed his fist into his desk, Sverdlov smoothed his mustache and glared out the window. They were arguably the most powerful men in Russia; they had sacrificed everything for the power to cast down the autocrats. Now that was all in danger, thanks to their leader's indecision.

"How did they get there?" Lenin demanded.

"We don't actually know," Trotsky replied, "but I have a sneaking suspicion."

"What's that?"

"An airship, one of the big lighter than air jobs the Germans use, was spotted in a couple of places over the previous two weeks. It's impossible to tell its direction from the spottings because literally nobody who saw it had a watch or a compass. But, for my money, it carried the Guards to Tobolsk."

"Comrades," Lenin said. "The Revolution has never faced more danger. We must do everything, *everything* to stop them. Right now as our enemies squabble among themselves, they give us time to prepare. A Romanov figurehead could unite them. This *cannot* happen."

If only you had listened to us earlier, Ilyich.

"What are your orders?" Sverdlov said.

"Convene the Central Committee, meet me there," Lenin said, reaching for his coat. "We will bring the full might of the Revolution against these imperialist traitors."

Later, Lenin looked at Trotsky's proposed deployments in and around Tobolsk for only a few seconds before handing the map and papers back to the Commissar for Military Affairs.

"I trust your judgment, Leon," Lenin finally said. "But give your commanders one order directly from me—if they do not return with the Romanovs, they are not to return at all."

"My judgment," said Trotsky, "may be sound . . . at least when not dealing with rapacious Germans. The problem is that it takes information to have judgment and I don't have much information. One small party of the town's ruling soviet escaped, with a tale of monstrous airships, enemy battalions, incredible firepower, and a lot of killing. They had no idea how many of the Romanovs survived, only that some did and some didn't. Oh, and that among those who didn't was the small boy and one of the girls."

Lenin felt an immediate tightening in his gut. Dead,

sick boys and dead, beautiful girls were extremely bad propaganda for the cause.

Trotsky continued, "I've halted the battalion from Yekaterinburg before they could leave for Tobolsk and ordered the expansion to a regiment before they move. But will a regiment be enough? I don't know. Nobody knows but the commander of the enemy at Tobolsk. . . . whoever *he* may be."

"How soon will that regiment leave?" asked Ilyich.

"If there were any competence there," Trotsky answered, "they'd have moved out long before my halt order reached them. Obviously there isn't much. So . . . a week? Ten days? Two weeks? Even a *month?* It's impossible to say. I can say I've sent three trains with roughly two thousand tons of food, arms, ammunition, sleighs, and horses to try to speed them on their way."

As the rest of the Central Committee carried out the business of the Party, Lenin stood alone in a corner of the room, eyes fixed on the embers of the slowly dying fire on the hearth.

It's too late. I should've listened to Sverdlov. Now the Whites have their figurehead and the bourgeois abroad have their propaganda coup. We're not merely murderers, but bungling murderers, which is far, far worse. What future for the Revolution now? What future for Russia?

Chapter Twenty-Eight

Her Imperial Highness Tatiana I Nicholaevna,
Empress of all the Russias

Tobolsk: The Coronation

A Russian coronation was a blend of the religious and the political. The ruler was believed to have been chosen by God, anointed by God, thus to be the link between the divine and the secular. It was also something of a marriage between the ruler and the Russian people.

Accordingly, the bells of all the roughly two dozen churches in the town rang out, but this time with joy, not with alarm. Tobolsk had never been a pro-Bolshevik city and could now, once again, revel in the fact.

From the Governor's House, now well-heated, cleaned out, and guarded by Dratvin's company—soon to be renamed as First Company, Semenovsky Regiment—Tatiana stepped out followed by her sisters and her makeshift retinue. On the frozen street east of the building, Fourth Company stood in ranks, still wearing their white camouflage smocks and helmets, and bearing their arms. Between the late Lieutenant Collan's platoon and Molchalin's a space had been left. In this stood one of the sleighs and a brace of Yakut horses, all done up for the occasion, with ribbons and gilding, fragrant pine branches and a golden cloth canopy held on a frame lashed to the sleigh. A single seat in front held Sergeant Kaledin. Behind him, a somewhat grander seat was tied in for Tatiana. Behind her, a bench for the two sisters completed the arrangements. Natalya, as a newly minted lady in waiting, would walk immediately behind the sleigh.

One of the icons was of the Blessed Virgin. Ordinarily, a coronation would be held in Moscow and the first stop of the tsar's party would be the Chapel of Our Lady of Iveron, home of the Icon of the Blessed Virgin of Iveron. Instead, in these constrained circumstances, a priest held forth the icon, as Sergeant Major Blagov placed a kneeler on the ground for Tatiana to use to avoid soiling her white dress.

Solemnly, Tatiana crossed herself, knelt, and crossed herself again. The icon was moved forward close enough for her to kiss it, then removed. She stood, crossed herself a third time, then proceeded into the sleigh.

The rest of the entourage fell in behind the sleigh, except for Kostyshakov, who stood to the left of it, Sergeant Major Blagov, to the right, and, just ahead of them, a color guard of three men, bearing and guarding a hastily done "Banner of State," in this case mere painted cloth, as there had not been time for embroidery.

Ahead of the color guard and Banner of State, Father Khlynov stood, censer hanging by a chain from his right hand, with the slack of the chain taken up by his left. Behind the priest stood several other religious personnel, one bearing a cross on a staff, a "ferula" it would have been called by Roman Catholics. Still others bore icons of saints and relics in cases.

As far as I can tell, thought Daniil, *nobody in this town has ever been to a coronation. What that means is we're probably not doing it quite right, even accounting for not being in Moscow, but, on the plus side, who knows enough to criticize?*

Cherimisov faced to the rear, watching for the signal from Kostyshakov. When it came, in the form of a deep nod of the head, he turned about and ordered First Sergeant Mayevsky to "March the men to the Cathedral."

That Mayevsky could do this with a complete lack of invective surprised no one as much as himself. "Fourth Company of the Guards, Forward at the slow step . . . march!"

The procession began to move south to the intersection of Great Friday and Tuljatskaya. The slow march had the soldiers swaying left to right and back with each pair of steps. As they moved, the bells of the town were silenced, one by one.

Daniil mused, *I wonder how the church arranged that*.

At the intersection they turned left, following Tuljatskaya all the way to Archangel Michael Street. With another left-hand turn at Archangel Michael, they moved toward, and then stopped at the beginning of the long, long staircase leading into the town's kremlin, which also held the place of the coronation, the Cathedral of Saint Sophia.

From before the first step the people of the town, in unprecedented numbers, had lined the way. They crossed themselves and knelt as Tatiana's sleigh passed, bringing tears to her eyes. *I am unworthy. I know I am unworthy. All I can do is try to become worthy. Even so, Tatiana, keep your head up and try, at least, to project confidence.*

Soldiers from Third Company, arrived early the day before, were interspersed amongst the crowd, armed and ready to stop any assassination attempt by a hidden Bolshevik. Tatiana and her sisters, with the example of how well jewels sewn into clothing could serve as body armor, wore their own. Natalya wore Olga's, tied in places to provide a snug fit on a thinner girl.

I thought it would be harder, thought Tatiana, rocking in her seat, with the pulling of the Yakuts, *to get Hermogenes, the Archbishop, to override the Pauline laws on succession. But he had that argument down better than we did: "Your father overruled those the moment he designated Olga as his heir. And his was the unreviewable power to do so." We didn't even need to mention Peter the Great's rule on the subject, nor the admirable record of Catherine.*

But I think the real reason he decided to support us was, in the first place, sheer fear of the Bolsheviks. Then, maybe, too, he was tickled by the idea of presiding over a coronation. It's never been done here, before, after all. And, unless we win and beat back the Reds, it will never be done anywhere, ever again.

Another horse was waiting, all saddled up with a side saddle, for Tatiana, at the base of the staircase leading to the kremlin. The sergeant major gave her his hands, fingers interlinked, to boost her up. Once seated, with her right leg hooked in the leaping horn, Tatiana automatically stroked the horse to calm it. With the mildest nudge, and a very light touch of the whip to the horse's right flank, the Yakut began to follow Cherimisov's first platoon up the way to the fortress gate.

Passing under the gatehouse and into the open area of the kremlin, Tatiana saw two preposterously small cannon, crewed and standing by. *Needs must*, she thought.

Just before the cathedral, Cherimisov took the reins of her horse with a strained smile, while Mayevsky helped her dismount. Bishop Germogen of Tobolsk stood in front of the church in all his finery, a beatific smile adorning his bearded face. *Be of stout heart*, the smile seemed to say to Tatiana. *This will be long, but you and Russia deserve no less than the best I can offer.*

Would he smile so benignly, wondered Tatiana, *if he knew how many death warrants are going to be presented to me tomorrow? Not only many of the prisoners from the rescue battle, but every Bolshevik apparatchik in the town?*

Germogen held out the crucifix for Tatiana to kiss. As

she did, followed by her sisters, another priest sprinkled the lot with holy water. Turning, then, Germogen led the way into the cathedral. As he did, the chorus sang the one hundred and first Psalm—"I will sing of your love and justice; to You, O Lord, I will sing praise..."

Hundreds filed in after her: her soldiers, the town's leading citizens, the pre-Bolshevik political leadership, and a youngish couple bearing a camera on a tripod and an old style flash. They would have one chance, as Tatiana was leaving, to make a record for posterity.

As the chorus sang, Tatiana advanced to stand in the front center of the cathedral. There, she was invited by Germogen to recite the Nicene Creed: "I believe in one God, the Father, Almighty, maker of Heaven and Earth, and of all things, visible and invisible...."

From there, Germogen went to the Ambon and read three pieces of scripture, drawn from Isaiah 49, Romans 13, and Matthew 22. From the rear of the church, two underpriests brought out a purple robe, the best they could do in the circumstances, and draped it over Tatiana's shoulders and around her body.

"Bow your head," commanded Germogen. He then laid hands upon her, and prayed, "O, Lord, our God, King of kings, who through Samuel, the prophet, chose thy servant, David, and anointed him to be king..."

With the end of that prayer, Germogen called out, "Peace be with you," after which the deacon commanded the entire populace present in the church to bow their heads.

Another prayer followed, shorter than the first.

"I am sorry," said Germogen, then, "that we lack a

crown, scepter, and orb. But those things are merely material..."

Thereupon a young private of Second Platoon, Fourth Company, stepped forth, hesitantly and shyly.

"I know...I mean...Your Majesty...well...ifyou havenoother crown...well...take this and use it. It's not much but it's mine and you're welcome to it."

Tatiana smiled gently at the boy. Then she reached out, touching his arm and saying, "Thank you. Thank you *so* much. I will wear your helmet with pride."

"Give it here, then, son," said Germogen.

The young guardsman passed his helmet over to the priest. To Tatiana he said, apologetically, "For what is ahead of you, Your Majesty, this may be more suitable than any crown." The boy returned to his spot in the throng.

Kostyshakov, too, then came forward. He took off his machine pistol, saying, "This will likely serve you better than any mace." The priest took this too.

Molchalin came forth next. He passed the priest a grenade, saying, "I took this from the body of a lieutenant who died defending the royal family. Lieutenant Collan, a Finn, would be pleased if she could use this in lieu of the orb. It's live, so don't unscrew the cap or pull the little bead unless you need to."

Germogen accepted it, whispering to Tatiana, "The boy speaks absolute truth. And you can always have an orb fashioned around it."

Finally Mokrenko then came forward, *sua sponte*, handing over his own *shashka*, or Cossack sword. "And she will need one of these, too."

With the helmet, Germogen crowned Tatiana Empress, reciting with it her titles: "By the grace of God, I crown thee Empress and Autocrat of All the Russias, of Moscow, Kiev, Vladimir, Novgorod; Tsarina of Kazan, Tsarina of Astrakhan, Tsarina of Poland, Tsarina of Siberia, Tsarina of Chersonese Taurian, Tsarina of Georgia; Ruler of Pskov and Grand Princess of Smolensk, Lithuania, Volhynia, Podolia, Finland; Princess of Estland, Livland, Courland, Semigalia, Samogitia, Belostok, Karelia, Tver, Yugra, Perm, Vyatka, Bolgar and others; Ruler and Grand Princess of Nizhny Novgorod, Chernigov, Ryazan, Polotsk, Rostov, Yaroslavl, Beloozero, Udoria, Obdoria, Kondia, Vitebsk, Mstislav, and all of the northern countries; Master and ruler of Iberia, Kartli, and Kabardia lands and Armenian provinces; hereditary Sovereign and ruler of the Circassian and Mountainous Princes and of others; Ruler of Turkestan; Heir of Norway; Duke of Schleswig-Holstein, Stormarn, Dithmarschen, and Oldenburg, and many, many others."

Then the archbishop slung over her shoulder the MP18—that it would, in time, become a holy relic, all who saw it knew—slung the sword over the other, and placed the grenade through her belt.

Shortly after this is where Tatiana, by her own will, violated protocol. Called upon to swear an oath that she would preserve the autocracy intact, she swore, instead, that she would preserve the monarchy and the Russian empire. These were subtly but importantly different things, and not lost upon either the priest, the soldiers, nor the witnesses filling the back of the temple.

Communion followed, after Tatiana passed through the

Royal Doors, which she, as tsarina, was the only lay person allowed through. There she received communion, bread separately from wine. Following communion, with the repeated words, "the seal of the gift of the Holy Spirit," she was well anointed with the Holy Chrism, on her forehead, eyes, nostrils, mouth, ears, breast, and both sides of each hand.

The "many summers" still rang in Tatiana's ears as she emerged from the cathedral. Instantly the bells of the cathedral rang, to be picked up by every other church in the town, to include the Catholic one at the foot of the hill. At her first appearance in the doorway, the two small cannon began a slow fire, one round each per five seconds. This salute went on for over four minutes, while the crowd outside cheered, the soldiery shouted "Urrah! Urrah! Urrah!" and the town's small band struck up *God Save the Tsarina*, the voices of the townsfolk and soldiers joining in until the lyrics echoed from every wall and building of the Tobolsk Kremlin.

And now I am truly stuck with it, thought the new tsarina. *God save us all.*

L59, The Catastrophe

A few days later came the last lift of men and supplies from Bulgaria. They'd be on their own now, with the airship returning to German service.

The men aboard would more than replace the numbers lost in the rescue. More importantly, though, the ammunition would be badly needed in the fight to restore the throne to Tatiana and the Romanov line. Still more importantly, Daniil Edvardovich Kostyshakov intended to use it to get Fourth Company and some reinforcements close enough to that city to rescue Tatiana's Aunt Ella, even while the rest of the battalion, plus as many trained townsfolk could be trusted, engaged and destroyed the battalion alleged to be coming from Yekaterinburg.

Mueller stood by Kostyshakov's side, with most of the staff and the commanders clustered about. He, however, had been the critical one in turning the deep cut into the southern face of the hill of the kremlin into a suitable temporary shelter and docking station for the airship.

Tatiana was there, too, though she was not wearing the helmet given her as a crown. The MP18, on the other hand, hung by her side.

"There it is!" shouted Nomonkov, the sniper, and the man with the best eyesight in the battalion. "Almost due east and isn't she just *grand*?"

It was at least another ten minutes before anyone else could seriously claim to see the airship. It was another twenty before it began its graceful turn to port to line itself up on the cut.

"What the..." Nomonkov asked of nobody, in particular. He'd seen them first, two small jets of fire coming from the airship's flank.

Wilhelm Mueller only barely refrained from screaming at the sight of the flames that rushed to envelop the ship. It was full, after all, of nearly every friend he had in the world.

So rapid and complete was the destruction that no one was seen to have jumped from the ship before it nosed down, smashing into and crumpling against the ground, just east of the eastern Irtysh riverbank. The flames expanded into a fireball as the gas cells and fuel tanks were ruptured, feeding their contents to stoke the flames.

"My God," said Kostyshakov, in horror.

How the hell do we get to Yekaterinburg now? wondered Molchalin, still not much given to talk.

Tobolsk, The Court

"I want to save what—rather, who, they're not merely dry goods—we can," insisted Tatiana, to Daniil.

It wasn't much of a court, but it was more than most thought the Bolsheviks deserved, especially as word of Yurovsky's orders began to circulate. The stack of death warrants had begun almost a foot high.

"No," insisted Tatiana, again, shaking her head forcefully, while seated at her father's old desk in the Governor's House. "I want separated out from these the irredeemables, whom I presume to include all Bolshevik commissars except Pankratov, if he's still in town. I think I can work with him. Also, the leadership of the Omsk and Yekaterinburg mobs, to the extent we haven't already . . . hmmm, what was that word Lenin or Sverdlov used in the order to execute my family? Ah, I remember, 'liquidated.' To the extent we haven't already liquidated them.

"The world will not miss them and neither will I. Then I want to see our old guards assembled so my sisters and I can sort out those who made our family's lives pure misery. After that, I'll sign all of that crew's death warrants, without further ado.

"But, no, *no*, NO! The rest I will not have shot. They can provide labor here of greater value than the cost of guarding and feeding them. Also I want to talk to them. I *know* there were good men among our guards, men who wanted only the best for Russia. I intend to give them the chance to see that, even if I'm young, I am still a better bet than the Red fanatics."

"I'll see to it, Your Majesty," said Daniil.

"And another thing," she said, shaking her finger at him, "that 'Your Majesty' stuff? Maybe it's important in public. But when we're alone, Daniil Edvardovich? Or in closed cabinet? *Please* make it simply 'Tatiana' or, if you're trying to make me see reason on something, 'Tatiana Nicholaevna.'"

"As you wish . . . Tatiana," he answered. He said it in a soft voice, one suggesting that there was more meaning behind the simple phrase.

"Daniil Edvardovich?"

"Yes . . . Tatiana."

"I have to have at least *one* friend in the world. Have to."

"Yes, Tatiana." As he said it, he dropped his eyes slightly. As he did, it made her feel as if a little of the light had left the world.

Daniil was gone, off to deal with how they were to rescue Aunt Ella, he'd said, leaving her alone.

I'm going to be alone, to some extent, for the rest of my life. I can't even have a boyfriend, not even Daniil . . . or not yet, anyway, because my power as "The Virgin Tsarina" is greater than my power as the wife or anything else of so and so. Mama? Papa? Did you realize that, because you put your marriage before everything else, that

your successor may never be allowed to marry in her life?
I'm going to have . . .

There was a light knock on the door. It was her sister,
Maria, serving as Tatiana's secretary for the time being.

"There's an 'Anton Dostovalov' here to see you, Tati.
Was he Olga's . . ."

"Yes"— *Now* there *is someone who's lost as much as I*
have—"please send him in."

Dostovalov walked in and, as Maria closed the door
behind him, immediately went to his knees and burst into
tears, hands clasped in front of him in supplication.
Between sobs and choking it was hard for him to say an
intelligible word, but eventually she realized he was
begging for forgiveness.

And he thinks, as the one nearest to Olga, that I am the
only one who can give forgiveness in her place. He really
did love her, didn't he?

"Rise, Anton Ivanovich," she commanded, in her best
imitation of an imperious voice. "Do you believe in our
faith?" she asked, once he'd risen to his feet.

"Yes, Your Highness," he managed to get out, between
sniffles.

"Then you know my sister is not dead. She is with God
now and *knows* that you tried to save her."

"I did . . . I really did . . . but I was too slow. Sergei wasn't
too slow."

"Big men usually can't move as quickly as smaller ones,
and Sergei Arkadyevich was in a better position to see that
madman before you could. You don't believe me," she
said, seeing that he really didn't.

"I . . . don't know what . . . to believe," he replied.

And he got those words out quickly enough, with less sobbing. Maybe . . .

"Would you like to take a little sabbatical?" she asked.

"Highness, I don't even know what that word means."

"It's a kind of a vacation," she explained. "it's a period when someone goes somewhere where he or she won't be harassed, and thinks, and studies."

"Studies? Me?" The thought was almost enough to make him laugh. Almost.

"Maybe you've just never had the right teacher," she said. "Let me make some inquiries."

Dostovalov wiped his arm across his eyes to clear off the tears. "Olga always said you were the smart one. If you think . . ."

"I do." She reached up to place one hand on his shoulder, saying, "And I think Olga would like for you to have the chance. She loved you too, you know; she really did."

Daniil was still gone, pursuing his duties. Anastasia and Dr. Botkin were in the hospital, helping with the wounded. Natalya and all her retainers and ladies in waiting were away on various tasks at her behest. Tatiana sat alone at her desk in a moment of unexpected quiet, a stack of papers, and on a side table, her father's chessboard.

Tatiana reached out and picked up the sandalwood queen, the queen with which *Feldfebel* Sergei Chekov had defeated her father all those weeks and lifetimes ago. Rolling the chess piece between her palms she allowed herself to slip into a reverie.

*I never wanted this, and I don't know what strength—
or if enough strength—resides within me; but I will give
every measure of what I have to serve all Russians. We
will, God allowing it, save the empire from these madmen,
and then, then I will make a country that venerates men
like you, Sergei Chekov, regardless of birth or creed. I will
earn your faith, and the faith of all the others who have
and surely will have died for me. I will redeem my father
and mother. I will avenge my brother and sister, or I will
die in the effort.*

"This I swear in the name of Almighty God," Tatiana
whispered. "May His divine will so bind me, now and
forever."

Epilogue

Volleys of rifle fire, often with codas of single, duller pistol shots, resounded in the prisoner's warehouse from dawn unto the fading half light of dusk. Georgy Lesh's Third Company was chosen for the executions. This was partly because they'd already been set to guarding all the prisoners, anyway, and partly to give them, too, a chance to bloody their hands in preparation for what would surely be a long and bloody civil war.

Yurovsky, now missing a leg, was not the first, indeed, he was not even among the forty-first, of the Reds to be shot. The doctors had argued that he was too ill to be put to death, a plea that moved nobody, though it did get a few laughs from the rank and file. Still, it wasn't important when he would be shot, only that he *was* shot.

A party of four showed up at that portion of the prisoners' warehouse serving as an aid station, bearing two stout poles. They laid four pieces of rope on the floor, then put the poles across the ropes. Tearing the blanket off of the Bolshevik's bed, they folded it around the poles to form a stretcher. Then they lifted him bodily and laid him on the now folded blanket. A few quick and simple knots and the Bolshevik was secured to the stretcher.

Once the makeshift stretcher was lifted, it was a short walk to the execution site, nearer to the river. There were a few trees there, being used to hold the condemned prisoners upright for "processing." A not particularly small pile of bodies was assembled to the west, atop a fairly large assembly of logs. They'd all be incinerated and their bones scattered and dumped in the river once the executions were finished.

Yurovsky seemed only dimly aware of his surroundings as he was carried out of the building and toward the execution site. He muttered odd phrases on the way: "But why . . . kill the boy's playmate? . . . Citizen Romanov . . . corruption . . . the bodies . . . frame them . . ."

He became more aware when the stretcher was leaned against one of the trees. Perhaps it was the cold reviving him, perhaps something else. He knew, for example, when a rope was used to secure the head of the stretcher to that tree. He said, "Tie it tight, boys. If I fall over I might hurt myself."

One of the stretcher bearers caught the humor of that. "That's right, old man, take it well. Want to make a statement? Care for a cigarette? There's a priest standing by, too."

"I'll take the cigarette," said the condemned Bolshevik. "People who fail aren't entitled to last statements. Besides, would anyone present even want to hear it? And I wouldn't have any use for a priest. Nor even a rabbi."

"Likely not," said the soldier. He took out a pre-rolled cigarette, lit and puffed it to life, then placed it between Yurovsky's lips. The Red drew deeply, then coughed so hard the cigarette flew away. The friendly stretcher bearer picked it up and replaced it. Then he patted the Bolshevik's shoulder and, with the others, backed away.

"No need to hurry," said Yurovsky, around the cigarette. "Stick around and chat for a while, why don't you?"

He and the stretcher party both laughed.

Yurovsky's eyes swam in and out of focus, several times. He thought maybe his stump had started to bleed again. At some point he became aware of nine men marching up to stand in front of him, plus one who followed behind. He searched his mind for an old, old memory, something from his boyhood, drilled into him by an overbearing father. It came to him in spurts.

"I acknowledge before the source of All that life and death are not in my hands."

"Left . . . face," sounded from the commander of the ranks of armed men before him.

"Something . . . something . . . something   I   don't remember. Ah . . . I remember this: To all I may have hurt, I ask forgiveness . . . to all who hurt me . . . I grant it."

"Ready!"

"Hear, O Israel . . ."

"Aim!"

". . . is one."

"Fire!"

The shots rang out so close together as to form a sound of a single, larger and more powerful shot. Five of them stuck Yurovsky's chest, more or less exploding it. The force of the blows caused the stretcher to twist around the tree. The Bolshevik's head flopped loosely to one side and downward.

Even so, the commander of the firing squad, a Sergeant Rogov, marched briskly to the body, removing his Amerikanski pistol from its holster as he did. Once there, he thought Yurovsky was about as dead as dead could be. Even so, in case there were some residual consciousness still in pain, he aimed the pistol at the head of the condemned. The shot that followed ended the possibility of any remaining consciousness, as it blew a fair chunk of Yurovsky's brain out the other side of his skull and onto the snow.

Appendix A
Table of Organization
(Minus the group of replacements)

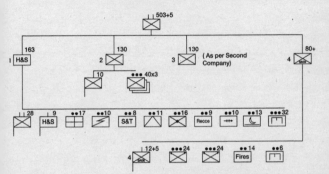

Major End Items:

    20 x Lewis Guns in 7.62 x 54R

    2 x 37mm Infantry Guns, with limbers

    4 x Bell Mare (Pack)

    24 x Mule (Pack or Cart)

    2 x Water-cooled Heavy MG

    4 x Flamethrower

    2 x Shotgun

    60 x MP18 Machine Pistols

    2 x Sniper Rifles, scoped

    12 x Panje Cart

    100 M1911, including spares

    600 Rifles, M1891, including spares

1 x Field Telegraph Set (German version)
1 x Extended Zeppelin (OPCON)
115 x Carbide Lamps, various makes
1 *Gulaschkanone* (OPCON)

Appendix B
Songs Touched On in the Story
(As of this writing, all can be found on YouTube):

"Farewell of Slavianka"

"Mnogoletie" (Many years, many, many, many summers)

"Preobazhensky Regimental March"

"Semenovsky Regimental March"

"Soldiers, Brave Lads" ("Солдатушки—бравы
   ребятушки")

"March of the Siberian Riflemen"

Die Wacht am Rhein

"Oh, You Porch, My Porch" ("Ah Vy, Seni, Moi Seni")

"God Save the Tsar(ina)"

Appendix C
Historical Notes

1. In fact, L59, the *Afrika-Schiff* and the zeppelin in our story, blew up over the Mediterranean, on the evening of 7 April, 1918. The loss was observed by the German submarine, UB53. There were no survivors. The cause of the accident has never been explained.

2. We encourage the reader, especially the reader who retains some sympathies for socialism, to look over the Nexmuse pictures of the Romanov children, and then to realize how they were killed. In our time line, in the first place, they were tricked into the basement of the Ipatiev House, the "House for Special Purposes," on the night of 16–17 July, 1918. There, a firing squad entered, opened fire, and shot them: father, mother, five children, doctor, footman, maid, and cook. In the words of chief murderer Yakov Yurovsky, "The firing went on for a very long time." Because their mother had had them sew jewels into their clothing against a possible escape, the children did not die quickly. Rather, they were finished off with bayonets, rifle butts, and close-ranged head shots. That took about twenty frightful minutes. Even *after* all that, one of the girls was found to be still alive while being carried out.

She was shot yet again in the head. Remember, too, they were three innocent young women and a girl, plus an equally innocent boy, aged thirteen. The Reds also killed two of the three pet dogs, one immediately and one sometime after. Perhaps they were worried that the dogs would testify in court someday.

You know, this is the sort of thing that makes one hope there is a Hell.

Glossary

Arshin: AKA "Russian Cubit." An obsolete Russian linear measure, set by Tsar Peter the Great at exactly twenty-eight English inches.

Chetvert: An obsolete Russian liquid measure of a bit over a liter and a half. There was also a dry measure called the same thing, but differing vastly in value.

Desyantina: Obsolete Russian unit of measurement for area. Roughly one hundred and seventeen thousand square feet. A bit over an hectare

Dolya: Obsolete unit of Russian measure, roughly a sixth of a gram

Draniki: A savory potato pancake

Ersatz: A German word meaning substitute or replacement, but with strong connotations of being an inferior product

Euxine: Old name for the Black Sea

First floor/Ground floor: Americans are unusual in considering the ground floor of a building to be the first floor. In most of the world, the first floor is the first *rise* above the ground floor.

Funt: Obsolete Russian measure, a bit under a pound

Furazhka: Visored, peaked caps

Gulaschkanone: A mobile field kitchen, generally pulled by horse, capable of making both stew and hot drinks. It's called a "Kanone" because of the stovepipe.

Gymnasium: In European terms, a gymnasium is a school for those of higher intelligence and greater scholastic achievement, to prepare them for university. Boston Latin, in the United States, is a Gymnasium.

Hauptmann: German for Captain

Jagdstaffel: Fighter Squadron

Kapitaenleutnant: A German naval rank roughly equivalent to naval Lieutenant or Lieutenant Commander. If in command of a ship, he is still *the* captain.

Kasha: One or another variant on porridge

Kolbasa: Russian for Sausage

Kontrabandisty: Russian for smugglers

Kremlin: Russian word for fortress or fortress inside a city

Kubanka: Also Papakha. A usually rather large, usually cylindrical, but sometimes hemispherical fur hat, with one open end.

Kulak: Russian, a prosperous peasant farmer. A kulak owns more than eight acres.

Lewis gun: An American-designed, British- or American-built light machine gun.

Lot: Obsolete unit of Russian measure, twelve and four-fifths grams

Mikhailovsy: A large theater in Saint Petersburg

MP18: A German submachine gun or, in their parlance, machine pistol

Mudak: Russian for shithead

Nemetskiy: Russian word for German

Nemka: The German woman, a none-too-flattering term for Alexandra, the tsarina

Obermaschinistenmaat: Senior Machinist's Mate

Oberst: German, Colonel

Oberstleutnant: German, Lieutenant Colonel, though called "Oberst" out of politeness

Peezda: Russian for cunt

Pelmeni: Russian dumplings, much like Polish pierogi but with a thinner shell and never sweet

Pevach: First run of Samogon, q.v.

Pood: Russian measure of weight, 16.38 kilograms

Portyanki: Foot wrappings. They serve in lieu of socks and are not without their advantages, though using them is something of an art.

Prostul doarme; bate în cap: Romanian for "beat his head in."

Rodina: Russian, Motherland or Homeland

Salo: Unrendered pork fat, usually salt or brine cured, sometimes smoked or spiced, eaten cooked or uncooked.

Samogon: Self-distillate, hooch, rotgut, moonshine. It might be pretty good or pretty awful or downright dangerous.

Sapogi: Russian for boots

Skufia: A soft-sided cap worn by Orthodox clergy

Solyanka: A thick, spicy and sour Russian soup

Soviet: Russian for council

Sterlet: A smallish sturgeon

Syrniki: A kind of dumpling made with cottage cheese

Taiga: Sometimes swampy coniferous forest of the northern latitudes

Te rog nu mă ucide: Romanian for "please don't kill me."

TNT: Trinitrotoluene, a high explosive (Yeah, yeah, we know, but *somebody* isn't going to know that.)

Tsar: Emperor

Tsarevich: Crown Prince

Tsarina: Empress

Tsaritsyn: Volgograd, AKA Stalingrad

Ulitsa: Russian for street

Ushanka: A Russian fur cap with folding flaps for ears and neck.

Vedro: Obsolete Russian unit of measure, about three and a quarter U.S. gallons

Vozok: A kind of enclosed sleigh with very small windows and sometimes some means of heating it

Yekaterinoslav: Dnipr, AKA Dnepropetrovsk

Acknowledgments
in no particular order:

Lee van Arsdale, for how to actually think about
and do this sort of thing

Rostislav Alexandrovich Mokrenko, who figures
prominently in the book

MCX, whoever that may be,
for their video on cross country skiing for beginners

Tim Mulina, for railroad expertise